The Twins of Narvik

Part II

A Historical Novel by

David Trawinski

Drawn from the Case Files of

Sterling Investigations International

The Twins of Narvik, Part II

Second Edition, 2022

Published by DAMTE Associates.

Cover painted image by Kellen Churchill
Cover Layout by David Trawinski
Edited by Elizabeth Marie Trawinski
Proofed by Paul Catterton, Jim Sprouse and Jack Coffman
Photographs by Elizabeth Marie Trawinski,
unless attributed otherwise on page 494

With Great Thanks to the following sources:
The International Churchill Society
The Polish Institute and Sikorski Museum of London
The World War II Museum of Narvik, Norway
The Ofoten Railway of Norway
The Witchery at Castle Gate Restaurant, Castle Hill, Edinburgh
McNaughtan's Bookshop, Edinburgh
Excerpts from Sir Winston Churchill's "The Second World War"
(pp. 6 & 323) used with permission
And Special Thanks to Allan Foster, Author of Book Lover's Edinburgh

Historical Novels
by David Trawinski

The Chopin Trilogy

The Willow's Bend (2016)

Chasing the Winter's Wind (2017)

War of the Nocturne's Widow (2018)

Ever Blooms the Rose (2019)

(Co-authored with Marie Trawinski)

The Life of Marek Zaczek Volume 1:

Under the Wings of Eagles (2020)

The Twins of Narvik (2021)

This Volume is Dedicated to All Those

Brave Men and Women Who Selflessly Risked

Their Lives During World War II.

Many Were Taken Forever from Their Families,

But Thankfully Many More Returned Home to

The Lands and Loved Ones for Which They Fought.

The Latter Included My Own Father,

Leon Trawinski,

Who Played Only a Small Role in the War at its End,

But Such a Commanding Role

In My Life at its Beginning.

Figure 22: View of Narvik Harbor and the Ofotfjord

The Passage Which Inspired This Novel

Winton Churchill recalls his return flight from France as the Germans close in on Paris

"Lack of suitable petrol made it impossible for the twelve Spitfires to escort us. We had to choose between waiting till it cleared up or taking a chance in the Flamingo. We were assured it would be cloudy all the way. It was urgently necessary to get back home. Accordingly, we started for home alone, calling for an escort to join us over the Channel. As we approached the coast the skies cleared and presently became boundless. Eight thousand feet below us on our right hand was Havre, burning. The smoke drifted away to the eastward. No new escort was to be seen. Presently I noticed some consultations going on with the captain, and immediately after we dived to a hundred feet or so above the calm sea, where airplanes are often invisible. What had happened? I learned later that they had seen two German aircraft below us firing at fishing-boats. We were lucky that their pilots did not look upwards. The new escort met us as we approached the English shore, and the faithful Flamingo alighted safely at Herndon."

The Second World War
by Winston S. Churchill
Revised Edition

WWII Historical Chronology of Events in this Volume

September 1, 1939	**Nazi Germany Invades Poland**
September 17, 1939	**Soviet Union Invades Poland**
April 8/9, 1940	**Nazi Germany invades Norway and Denmark**
April 10, 1940	**First Naval Battle of Narvik**
	Sikorski visits Polish Podhale Rifle Brigade (Malestroit)
April 13, 1940	**Second Naval Battle of Narvik**
April 21, 1940	**Sikorski Visits Polish Podhale Rifle Brigade (St. Renan)**
April 23 - 24, 1940	**Polish Podhale Rifle Brigade departs Brest, France**
May 7-8, 1940	**Polish Podhale Rifle Brigade arrives Harstad, Norway**
May 10, 1940	**Nazis Germany invade France and Low Countries**
	Churchill Appointed Prime Minister by King George VI
May 27 - 28, 1940	**Allied Land Invasion drives Germans from Port of Narvik**
May 26 - June 4, 1940	***Operation Dynamo,* The Evacuation of Dunkirk**
June 7-8, 1940	**All Allied Forces Withdraw from Norway**
	Scharnhorst* and *Gneisenau* attack *HMS Glorious
June 18, 1940	**Last of Allied Troops Evacuate France in Brittany**
March - June 1940	**Soviets Massacre 22,000 Polish Officers at *Katyń***
July10, 1940	***Battle of Britain* begins**
July 22, 1940	**Churchill creates *Special Operations Executive (SOE)***
August 31, 1940	**First Flight of *303 Kościuszko Squadron***
September 7, 1940	***Luftwaffe* begins Bombing London (*The Blitz*)**
October 31, 1940	***Battle of Britain* Ends (Official Date)**
February 25, 1941	**German Battleship *Tirpitz* Commissioned**
May 11, 1941	***Luftwaffe* Ends Bombing of London *(The Blitz)***
June 21, 1941	***Operation Barbarossa* commences; Nazi Invasion of Russia**
December 5, 1941	**General Sikorski received by Stalin/Molotov in Moscow**
October 18, 1942	**SOE *Operation Grouse***
November 19, 1942	**SOE *Operation Freshman***
February 18, 1943	**SOE *Operation Gunnerside Drop***
February 27/28, 1943	**SOE Operational Raid on Norsk Hydro Vemork Facility**
April 13, 1943	**Germany announces *Katyń Commission***
April 16, 1943	**Soviets break relations with Poland over *Katyń***
July 4th, 1943	**Sikorski and staff die in tragic aircraft accident at Gibraltar**
February 20, 1944	**SOE Attack Ferry *Hydro* on Lake Tinn**
November 12 1944	**Battleship *Tirpitz* sunk**

Author's Note:

This volume is a continuation of the story which is developed in "The Twins of Narvik, Part I" throughout Chapters 1 - 37.

In Part I, some chapters are marked Historical Reference and contain only historical elements which complement but may not directly impact the story narrative. This afforded some readers a choice to skim or even skip these chapters to continue more quickly with the story.

In Part II, the story narrative is deeply embedded even within such historical chapters. Thus, readers will not have such an option as in Part I.

I mention it here as a courtesy to my readers.

David Trawinski

38 Diane's Texas Outbrief

"He has all of the virtues I dislike and none of the vices I admire."

Winston Spencer Churchill

"Can you believe that people actually live like this?" stated, more than asked, Flake Ferris. His voice was a whisper, as he looked around the library of Jake Conley's Texas mansion.

"Not many," responded Diane, her own voice as low as his had been.

"Well, Emory would have gone crazy over this collection of books," said Ferris, remembering his trip with Hauptmann to MacNaughton's book shop in Edinburgh. "It's ironic, because it was his love of books that first triggered the idea of the switch in me."

"Emory is on another pressing engagement for me in London just now," Diane replied, "where there are many, many fine bookshops. I'm sure he'll get his fill."

"I bet not a one of them is like this," Flake said, craning his neck to the volumes that lined the beautifully hand-carved shelves hovering overhead.

"Diane," Jake Conley called out, "the floor is all yours. Time has come to undo what the other investigators concluded, so do some damage!"

Diane had just finished connecting her laptop to the 75 inch display that had been wheeled into the library. The stand had been custom made to match the cabinetry of the shelves. Jake had refused to have anything electronic in this, his sanctuary from modernity, but for tonight he agreed to violate its purity. Diane assumed this had not been the first time Jake had ever violated the purity of the unspoiled over his many years.

"We could have our little soiree in the boardroom," Jake had said over dinner, "but somehow the library feels so much more appropriate."

At eight o'clock that evening, Diane stood aside the monitor whose screen bore her title slide. She pulled a last sip from her drink, which for this occasion was nothing more than ginger ale. Diane stood next to the monitor, and around her were four matching leather wing chairs in a shallow arc. Jake (carefully transferred from his wheelchair), Wade, Flake and her own, which, of course, was empty.

"Before you begin, Diane," Wade said, "does anyone need anything beyond this?" He gestured to the drink cart, which sat behind them at the top of the arc of wing chairs for easy access throughout the night. "We have asked the staff not to interrupt us once we begin."

"No, thank you, Wade. We are all set to proceed," Diane answered, looking over to Flake, who was imbibing on a 43-year old Scotch Whisky, one of which she had never heard.

"I have to try this," Flake had said as they were setting up. "I have never had a forty-three year old. Well, not a forty-three year old Scotch, anyway."

"We're all set, Wade," Diane repeated, not sure that he heard her initially.

"OK, then, *little missy*," Jake said, using the salutation intentionally to lash out at his more politically correct son, "go ahead and tell me who it is that I really am. I can't wait to find out."

Diane smiled, remembering "little missy" was what Jake had called her when they had first met. That moment had seemed like an eternity, but was actually only a few months before.

"Thanks, Jake. Let me say first that I am about to tell you a most interesting tale. For the sake of time, I will not get into details as to how we have come to know the information we are presenting unless you stop us and ask. To protect yourselves legally, our collection methods are not included in our outbrief either. However, whatever you may decide to ask, we will, of course, answer."

"In other words," Jake chuckled, "there are some things we are better off not knowing. We get it. Go on."

Diane explicitly thought of the listening device that had been implanted in the Polish-British commemorative sculpture that they had given Miss Anna Barrett in her London flat. It was no longer an issue, as it had been removed and replaced with a duplicate non-functional sculpture while the elderly woman was enjoying her trip to Edinburgh.

Nonetheless, the listening device had been an illegal intrusion of Miss Anna's privacy that her client needed not to know in detail. After all, plausible deniability was as much a service to her client as the information she was about to present.

Diane pressed the small remote in her hand and the oversized display filled with an image of the Trojan horse being dragged into the gates of Troy. No words, just the foreboding image.

"Cassandra was the daughter of the Trojan King Priam," began Diane, repeating the story that Quindon Sprouse had shared with them in what seemed an eternity ago. "She spoke the truth, but no one listened. They all believed she was mad. Likewise, Jake, your mother Cassandra spoke the truth."

"BLUF!" said Jake Conley crisply. The response unsettled Diane, until her client clarified his comment. "Bottom Line Up Front, always the best way to start a presentation. I am intrigued, Diane, please go on."

Diane drew in a deep breath, and said, "Your mother was not born Cassandra Barrett as you have thought all your life. She was born in a small Norwegian fishing village as Tulla Jacobsen. That is where your Nordic DNA comes from. I will walk you through how she became Cassandra Barrett over the next hour."

"Jacobsen, you say," interrupted her client, "it would seem mother gave me more than just her Nordic DNA. She named me Jacob after her original family name?"

"It would appear so," said Diane. "We confirmed this by comparing your DNA to that of members of the Jacobsen family still living on the island of Skrova today. They were a match, right down to the *Sámi* markers."

The discussion quickly devolved into an explanation of the *Sámi* indigenous nomads of Scandinavia. Diane used this as a springboard to brief Jake on the manner in which his mother had met her first husband, Birger Alvorsen, and came to live in the UK. After about an hour, Jake Conley called for a break, with the serving staff entering the library to refresh their drinks as well as the extensive selection of exotic olives and nuts that had been laid before them.

"So Tulla, is it?" Jake said to Diane. "She sounds as if she was a real hellion."

"So much so that she turned her children over to a nanny," answered Diane, "and then took off for Liverpool and later New York City alone."

"Funny thing," replied her client, "I was raised, for the most part, by a nanny. Well, an *Au Pair*, to be precise. Bridgette was a Godsend. I always felt guilty for feeling closer to her than I ever did to my own mother. As a child, I felt as if Cassandra didn't really love me. Then, I got older and convinced myself that this was just how the rich raised their children. Funny how a fella can fool himself into believing anything that takes away from his unwanted first impression."

"I understand this must all be very hard for you to digest, Jake," Diane said.

"Actually, everything you are saying is ringing true," Jake said. "Mom was always a very moody person, always up and down. When she got so low that she did nothing but rail on my daddy, he would send her off on some excursion. Spain, Greece, Rhodes, and Egypt. If they had a tongue you couldn't understand, she was off there for several months at a clip. Never to England or Scotland, or for that matter to Scandinavia, that I can recall. She'd come home exhausted and Daddy would be just refreshed enough to put up with her moods again."

"Well, that's certainly consistent with what we have unearthed about Tulla," Diane said. "We pulled her passport info. Your mother did travel extensively, as you say, but never to either the UK or to Norway. Closest she got was a Baltic cruise that ended up in Copenhagen. Oh, and Paris. She seemed to love to go to Paris."

"The only thing still gnawing at me is why on earth our other two investigators never uncovered any of his? I used to think Wade had pre-programmed them not to." Jake salted a sour eye at his adult son who was speaking with Flake about the intricacies of single malt Scotches. Wade had studied these heavily despite being more of a Bourbon drinker himself. Of course, he loved his Texas Balconies, which while being a single malt, could not legally be called Scotch any more than those single malts brewed in Japan, France or elsewhere.

"If you're ready to start again," Diane suggested, "I can pick the story up at exactly why your previous investigators never would have found all this out."

The staff departed and Diane resumed the presentation, and went straight to the one chart that Flake had contributed. It was his famous X chart, updated to show *'Madame X'* as Tulla Jacobsen. Diane wanted to use it to illustrate just how valuable her Intelligence connections were in unearthing the truth.

"There are two reasons why your previous investigators never found out that your mother was actually Norwegian," Diane started. "The first reason is that they either never considered the possibility of a switch in identity, or never found proof of it if they suspected. That would have been extremely difficult to unravel, because they would likely have never known that Tulla's husband, Birger, like his father before him, was on the staff of the British Secret Service."

"What?" exclaimed Wade, "This is all getting a little too far fetched."

"If you run that mouth any further," Jake blasted, "You may be fetching it from the next room, I'll slap you so damn hard! Now, let Diane continue, damn it."

Diane pulled a sip from her refreshed ginger ale, and then went on.

"Birger's father had sailed in the Royal Navy with the SIS's founder, Captain Mansfield Cumming."

"You keep saying SIS, or British Secret Service," Wade said, "do you mean MI6?"

Jake shot his son another glare.

"At that point in time, they went by the designation MI-1(c)," Diane said, demonstrating her much deeper understanding of the subject matter. "But yes, Wade, they did become MI6, eventually."

"Then why not just call them that?" he said.

"They really don't call themselves that any more. The official name is now Secret Intelligence Service, or SIS. The building at Vauxhall Cross that they show in all the newer Bond movies is officially the SIS Headquarters. Reporters and fiction writers still call them MI6, but that officially ended years ago."

"Wade, can you please let Diane get on with this story?" Jake retorted. "So, Diane, I get it, you've got deep contacts in this world, but wouldn't other skilled investigators be expected to find this out as well?"

"Not necessarily, Jake," she answered. "The SIS not only provided Tulla the passport that allowed her to become Cassandra Barrett, but at the same time changed the real Cassandra and Birger's names as well. Birger Alvorsen became Brigand MacAlvor, and the woman born as Cassandra, instead of taking his wife's name, Tulla, took up the identity of Matilda "Tilly" MacAlvor. With the stroke of a green pen and the Norwegian Birger became a Scotsman, and the British-borne girl became his Scottish bride Tilly. This would have been extremely hard to have worked our way through had we not had the help of very recently unclassified files of the SIS."

"Tilly went on to raise my twin brothers?" Jake asked.

"Half-brothers!" Wade could not resist interjecting.

"So, I have two half-brothers and a half-wit son," responded Jake. "Any more interruptions from you and I'll have a half-share son."

Wade went silent after that. He understood the inheritance reference.

"Yes, Tilly raised the boys," Diane stated. "She had suffered a stillbirth in the year before she came to the Alvorsens, and found that raising the twins was therapeutic for her. It fed the mothering, that is, the nurturing needs of her personality. But your half-brothers were so young that they likely never remembered their true mother, Tulla, the same woman who later gave birth to you, Jake."

"This is amazing," said Jake, trying to take it all in. "I hope you both can stay on beyond tomorrow so I can come to understand and internalize all this."

"We've both cleared our calendars for the rest of the week," said Flake, who had felt he needed to contribute something.

"Good, good," said Jake. "We'll make you more than comfortable, I assure you. Now, Diane, what did you say these brothers of mine were named."

"Einar and Gunnar MacAlvor," she answered.

"Identical twins, huh. Einar was older?"

"No, actually, Jake, Gunnar was a few minutes older," Diane said.

"What were they like?" asked the old man. Diane imagined just then he was feeling like a child again himself.

"How could she possibly know?" Wade asked.

"To the contrary, Wade, we have a ton of SIS documentation on these two, including their psych profiles. This is what we know. Einar was strong and decisive, whereas Gunnar was more analytical and bookish. Sometimes Gunnar's understanding all the risks would keep him from acting, but not so for Einar, who was inherently a man of action."

Diane looked at Wade, to see if she had satisfied his doubts. She felt sorry for the man, who wore a defeated look. He feared only losing his inheritance, and that, in itself, was sad.

"You said earlier that both Birger and his sons, these twin brothers of mine, were also drafted into the British Secret Service?" asked Jake.

"That brings us to the next chapter in our story," Diane answered and clicked ahead to a slide which contained only an image of the mountains and fjords of Norway.

Diane took another long drink from her ginger ale. They were finishing their break after about two hours. Diane was surprised that Jake had the strength and will to keep going. He had been energized to discover that he actually had two half-brothers. In the past hour, they had just gone through Diane's reiteration of Jake's mother's tale, who even Jake, himself, was by then calling Tulla.

The story had been told by Diane of how Tulla had married Birger Alvorsen and relocated from Skrova to Dundee. How she had abandoned Birger and her own twin sons before she made her way to the States. Even when Diane discreetly told Jake of his mother's dance hall days along the Liverpool Albert Docks, the client was not in the least way surprised.

"My mother always loved a good time," Jake had said, "and this business of disappearing is totally consistent with what she did to my father. She would disappear for weeks, not days, mind you, on end. Would leave without so much as a word. Wore my father's nerves to down to a frazzled stub. His wife likely took thirty years off his life. She was just too spirited a filly for him to try to ever rein in."

Diane next explained the switch between Tulla and Cassandra, and the subsequent name changes demanded by the British Secret Service for Brigand and Tilly.

"That certainly would have been a dead end for the other detectives that Wade hired to look into this, Diane. Without your connections, they would never have been able to track Tulla back to her roots as you have. Damn, I knew I had to trust that great feeling I had about you about you ever since that first dinner we had together. Looks like those intuitions are paying dividends tonight."

"Third time's the *charmer*..." said Wade sarcastically. Diane knew he must be aghast at just where her findings might lead. Especially if it had any negative impact on the inheritance of Jake's fortune he must be so tired of waiting upon.

"Go to hell, Wade," snapped his father, "you tried your best to talk me out of hiring Diane, and it doesn't take a genius to figure out why. Now you sit and listen or I will throw your ass out of here altogether. Better yet, I'll have Kellen do it."

Diane remembered Kellen from her previous visit as the security specialist whom she had pegged as former special ops military.

Wade said nothing. He just threw open his hands as if to say, *What did I say?*

"Jake, to tell you the truth," Diane confessed, "we had some real good luck in being able to ever track this all back to the truth. Flake Ferris over here was crucial in our coming to understand all the genetics, and I was fortunate that a very good friend of mine at SIS had access to all the files I needed. But even that wasn't enough - had it not been for those diaries saved by Tilly's granddaughter, we might never have come to know what happened to those twins."

"You knew I'd want to buy that diary," Jake said.

"And now you have it, Jake, complete in digital form," Diane answered, "including her letters from Brigand and Einar."

"To hell with the digital form," exploded her client. "I want to be able to hold those journals in my hands, the story of the life of my mother's twins. What the hell good is having all these volumes," Jake raised his arms to the vast library surrounding them, "if I can't possess the one set of books that really matters?"

Diane waited for a second or two to allow Jake's outburst to echo and fade from their minds.

"That will be a job for your representatives to negotiate with Miss Mattie MacAlvor directly, then, isn't it, Jake?" Diane said. She told her client she would make the introductions, but that was all. She kept to herself that she did not wish to be in the middle of Jake Conley bidding against his own fear of dying first.

Diane intentionally did not tell Jake, nor any member of her team, about the second pair of items he would most certainly wish to procure from Miss Tilly MacAlvor. That she would save for much, much later. Just as she and Flake had discussed.

"Yes, yes," said Jake Conley, "my lawyers will handle that." His eyes sparkled like a child's on Christmas Eve, who wanted only to unwrap one more present this night before he gave in to a much needed sleep. "Diane, go on and tell me what became of Einar and Gunnar after this Wells fella pulled the quickie to get them both deployed…"

So Diane began once more, wondering as she did how long it would be before her client ran out of his renewed boyish energy. It was nearing ten o'clock, and she herself was fighting some residual jet lag, although coming west was always easier for her than going east. Yet, still she wondered would her client even make it to midnight? She thought not.

"Certainly, Jake." Everyone took their places, and she soon began again. "Commander Graham Earnest 'Wincer' Wells did indeed get his way, and the twins were deployed back to Norway in the last days of July 1939. The same fisherman's cover this time. Their base of operations was Skrova, where their grandfather's family still lived. The same island where they had stayed for their enhanced language skills deployment with Brigand and Tilly the summer before."

"Looks like this Wells fella had this in the works all along," interrupted Jake. "But why on this island out in the middle of the open fjord? Why not in the town of Narvik itself?"

"Well, Jake, for three reasons," explained Diane. "Operationally, in Skrova it would be much easier to explain them as visiting family if anyone questioned why they were there. Secondly, they could see anyone coming from off in a distance. The twins were likely trained to keep a burn bag. If they thought adversaries were on their way to Skrova, it gave the boys an easy thirty to forty-five minutes to destroy any incriminating materials. All they would have to do was pitch the burn bag into a fire they kept lit continuously in the fireplace of his mother's home."

"And the third reason?" asked Jake.

"Recovery. If they needed to be extracted, it would be easy for the Brits to get a submarine into the wide expanse of the *Vestfjorden* under the cover of darkness and pick up the twins from a small craft of some sort. Same for getting any urgent supplies to them, if needed."

"Imagine that, my own brothers, spies for Her Majesty's Secret Service," said Jake, delighted in these findings.

"Half-brothers," Wade once more chirped in.

"Oh, just shut your trap, Son," said Jake, "they are your uncles after all."

"Half-uncles," Wade said, knowing it would irk the old man, "and half-wits, if you ask me. They could have been shot for what they did."

Diane was amused by the running friction between Jake and his son, but in consideration of the late hour decided to press on. "Yes, they were indeed British spies, but their mission was never intended to be that dangerous. After all, Norway was never expected to be at war with England. The twins were only sent to do some spying on the infrastructure and capacity of the Ofoten Railway connecting Narvik to the iron ore mines just over the mountains in Sweden. Sure, they were also expected to reconnoiter potential sabotage locations, but if the Brits wanted to put that railway out of business, they would have sent in a commando team. All in all, a very safe mission profile. I doubt that Brigand would have ever agreed to expose his sons to anything even remotely dangerous."

Jake looked confused. "You said the boys were trained in Scotland on weapons and explosives, as well as the mountain training. If the mission was that safe, why bother with all this?"

Diane could see that Jake had fallen into an infatuation with his half-brothers having been men of action. She knew he was not to be disappointed, but like any good storyteller, she wanted to maintain a sense of suspense.

"They were hardly boys any more, Jake," Diane said. "They were twenty-six years old by this point. As far as your question, there is one thing I am free to tell you about my operational days with the agency. It is that whenever you send someone into the field, you best have them trained up for all contingencies. Mission planning is like insurance, you hate to be caught without it. You don't think you'll ever need all these skills, but you can never fully anticipate the exact situations that may arise. Now, let me go on with what we know about the twins' deployment to Skrova."

And so Diane began a long discourse on the client's half-brothers being deployed to Norway in the months leading up to World War II.

Einar and Gunnar were inserted at Skrova by a Royal Navy vessel disguised as a fishing trawler on its way to Oslo. The trawler crept into the *Vestfjorden* under the cover of darkness, after having had declared an emergency just outside the great open fjord. The ship navigated past the lighthouse at Skrova. It rounded the island and came close to the fishing village, where it dropped anchor. That night the twins and their gear were stealthily offloaded ashore. The Norwegian coastal patrol vessel boarded the trawler at first light, but found her explanation to be in order. The next day the ship was "repaired" and late in the afternoon left the Norwegian territorial waters before anyone could become too suspicious. The Coastal Patrol escorted her out into the open waters of the Norwegian Sea.

Ashore in Skrova, Einar and Gunnar were secretly hosted by their Aunt for three weeks. The intent was that the townsfolk should not associate their appearance with the trawler's unexpected incident. After three weeks, they were covertly taken to Narvik by their father's cousins, Hakron and Erik. These men were both some twenty-five years the twins' seniors. They dropped the two young brothers at the dock in the early hours of the morning with their rucksacks full of traveling clothes and necessities. Even though the Arctic summer's light had long been up, the townspeople of Narvik, with rare exception, still slept.

Once in Narvik, the twins walked from the dockside across town to the passenger terminus, where they waited for the first daily run of the Ofoten Railway. They would that day ride the rail line from Narvik to Kiruna, where they would disembark and later that afternoon return. This would be the first of many such round trips.

Einar and Gunnar each carried with them a counterfeit Norwegian passport that had been issued to them by MI6, and which marked each man as a proud citizen of the isle of Skrova. Stitched into the lining of each man's parka were their UK passports, just in case a need should arise for an unexpected escape into Sweden or beyond.

Their first train ride of that mission along the twenty-seven miles of ascending mountain track was strictly for pleasure. They boarded and sat alongside the left hand window for a dramatic view of the *Rombaksfjord* below as the train climbed. The intent of this first mission was familiarization and visual recognition of the stations that they had, up until then, only studied on maps and rail schedules.

The railway had been electrified some sixteen years earlier and the ride up the mountain was smooth and the scenery absolutely stunning. As the twins looked down the slopes below them, they could clearly view the frothing white waters of streams dropping from the mountains above them, fed by melting summit snows. Even in August, these crystal waters fell violently over rocky stream beds as they raced to join the blue depths of the placid fjord below. They could not have hoped for any easier or more peaceful assignment than this. Nor could they begin to imagine war in a setting this sedate and God given.

The train on which they rode was for passengers only, having only three cars, each outfitted with wooden seats and benches. The much longer iron ore trains ran upon the same single line of track. Periodically, on its ascent, their train would pull along a side track to stop as a long procession of massive hopper cars, loaded to their grimy brims, passed the twins in the downhill direction. On their return trip, they had pulled aside to allow a train of empty hoppers to ascend, which to the lads looked like the dancing vertebrae of a twisting skeletal creature.

The last time the twins were detained on these side tracks, it was at the final station in Norway, called Bjørnfjell. The station was named after the peak upon which it lied. The name is Norwegian for “Bear Mountain”. The classic red station house, trimmed in white, was located on a relatively flat span between two tunnels undercutting the surrounding mountains, above and below. At Bjørnfjell there stood that red station house and very little else, save a few ski huts belonging to the locals of Narvik.

The twins had studied this twenty-seven mile line between Narvik and the Swedish border extensively while in the Highlands of Scotland. They knew that not only had the railway opened in 1902, when Hundalen was the last stop before the border, but by 1913, there was demand for another stop, and the Old Bjørnfjell station was opened further east. In 1923 the line had been electrified, increasing its ability to carry both iron ore and passengers. By 1925 another stop even further east was required, just before the border, and the “new” Bjørnfjell Station was opened. That station was only 1.5 kilometers from the border, less than a mile, although that border lay in the middle of the train tunnel between it and Riksgränsen, the first station inside of Sweden. Of course, that border in the tunnel was actually a calculated extension of the tradition border that was marked off on the peaks overhead between the two countries.

That day the twins rode the line all the way to Riksgränsen. There, they had to physically change lines to continue on the Swedish lines to Kiruna in Sweden. Kiruna was the source of the iron ore, a great mining town. The twins familiarized themselves with it, and then began their return journey to Narvik.

After eventually returning to Narvik Station, Einar and Gunnar found Hakron and Erik "waiting" for them. The two great uncles heartily welcomed the twins, creating a masterful fiction in case anyone had been watching. The twin's cover story was that they had just arrived by rail from Stockholm. The false passports bore stamps that verified this alternate truth. Hakron and Erik, for effect, even carried the rucksacks for the travel weary twins. The four men first stopped to eat a hearty meal, and afterward walked through the streets of the town to Hakron's sailing vessel, which had been moored in the small harbor marina opposite the great working iron ore loading docks. It was easy to distinguish between the two harbors, as one was full of massive freighters covered in black iron ore dust; the other was full of small, wooden craft covered only with the endless white mass deposited by retiring sea birds.

The four of them sailed back to Skrova, arriving in time to assure the entire village would note the "arrival" of the two men who had spent the summer amongst them the year before. As it was summer in the Arctic, there was light well into the late evening. Nothing could be more natural. The twins had arrived by train from the Baltic coast. No one would associate the boys arrival with the overnight stay of the crippled trawler some three weeks earlier. This was critical should the villagers ever be questioned about the twins' "arrival" in Skrova.

The brothers then worked out a schedule for their reconnoitering of the Ofoten Line. No longer would Hakron and Erik assist them. The boys were more than capable of taking their great uncle's sailboat to Narvik, and return after their business was over. Even so, in their provisions secretly offloaded from the British trawler, was an inflatable rubber raft and outboard motor they could use, if necessary. However, this would be hard to explain to the locals, and as such was kept only for emergency usage.

The twins had no responsibilities to meet any agents in Narvik, such as *"Skaoli"*, the agent with whom their father had once rendezvoused. That agent had long since retired.

There was, in fact, no longer a need for MI6 to even have an inside man on the rail commission after the tracks had been electrified in 1923. The ore volumes going to the Germans were fairly constant at about 3 million tons a year.

The purpose for having the twins on-site in the Lofoten area was three-fold by August 1939. First, to become familiar with the railway and identify opportunities for sabotaging the line should war break out. The navy would send in commando teams to actually conduct the demolition. Second, the twins were expected to map escape routes into Sweden for Britain's military should they eventually be deployed, and as unlikely as it was, to have a vessel sunk from under them. The third was to scout the waters of the *Vestfjorden* for German naval vessels.

Einar and Gunnar soon commenced their scheduled runs on the Ofoten line. The twins would get off at varying stops on each rail trip. They would go on long hikes, which allowed Gunnar to sketch and photograph various landscapes and to make detailed notes on the infrastructure. They had been trained in the Scottish Highlands for what to seek out: bridges with supporting columns that could be readily blown out and tunnels with potential structural weaknesses. It was too dangerous for them to be inside the tunnels themselves given all the train traffic, so the twins instead focused on the columns upholding the railway spans. For the Ofoten Line, the best opportunity for sabotage was the *Norddal Bridge,* the longest bridge in the Norwegian mountains. In Norwegian, its name was the *Norddalsbron.*

The twins would also learn all the vertical mountain trails and service roads that had once been used by the railway workers. These generally rose from the shores of the fjords up to where the line was being constructed. The twins were to assess these for use as escape routes, in case a warship was to become stranded in the fjords below, which neither twin thought would ever occur.

Finally, the twins were to monitor the *Vestfjorden* for any signs of advancing German Naval military vessels. For the latter, the boys would spend hours atop the Hogskrova hill, from which any warship entering the fjord could easily be spotted with the assistance of simple field glasses. For days when they were away upon the Ofoten Railway, they would confer with the Skrova villagers. Any unexpected vessels in the *Vestfjorden* was tremendous news among these fishermen, and warships would certainly not pass by unnoticed.

So, on the days that Einar and Gunnar did not sail the fjords or ride the rails, they climbed the Hogskrova and watched the *Vestfjorden*. They would stay atop the Hogskrova for the entire cycle of the sun, from early in the morning until just before the onset of dusk, usually well after the start of the eleventh hour past noon.

Their days could be extremely boring at times. Gunnar brought along his collection of Shakespeare's works that his mother had given him. He would read aloud atop the Hogskrova, while his brother Einar kept watch over the seas.

The sky was often blue and cloudless. The sun seemed like a brilliant marble that would barely seem to drop beyond the horizon. On the few overnights that they stayed on that hill during the summer days of the *Midnight Sun*, they watched as that disk seemed to only skip and roll left to right before it began to rise again in the east.

"I know I should hate being up here for so many hours atop this windswept nest of rocks," said Einar, "but instead I find the beauty and dramatic landscapes most peaceful and reassuring. For some strange reason this place comforts me. Do you know what I mean brother?"

"I am happy wherever I am as long as I am aside you, my brother," answered Gunnar. "As the bard once said, *We came into the world like brother and brother, and now let's go hand in hand, not one before another*."

"A Midsummer's Nights Dream" guessed Einar.

"A Comedy of Errors," Gunnar corrected him.

Neither Einar nor Gunnar would ever know that it was upon that very hill that they were conceived, before fate opted for that single embryo to split into two within young Tulla's womb.

Figure 23: Poland 1939
(Austria and Czechoslovakia Shown Pre-Anschluss and Pre-Sudetenland Annexation)

39 *Zosia's* London Outbrief

"We are asking the nations of Europe between whom rivers of blood have flowed to forget the feuds of a thousand years."

Winston Spencer Churchill

Sophie Czystowska sat in the dormant, after-hours restaurant with her client, Henia and her husband, Mierek. Before her sat a complimentary *"Zywiec"* beer, imported from Warsaw. Also in front of them was a small tray of *Krusciki* traditional Polish pastries.

"These are usually reserved for Christmas," Henia said softly, "but I like to have them also for special events. Every so often we have a Brit or American ask if we have the '*Polish Bowties*'. I always correct them, in a very respectful way, that they are not bowties but Angel's Wings. Here, try one, *Zosia*, I made them just for you."

Sophie took one of the delicately light, fried confections that were covered with powdered sugar. As she bit in to it, she felt the telltale snap, and saw the light cloud of a white puff of the confectioner's sugar. She finished the treat, before taking a drink of her *Zywiec* beer, a coupling she herself would not have made. Yet, it worked well in one respect, for it somewhat calmed the young woman's nerves. After all Sophie had been through with Diane, this was her first solo briefing to a client, even though this client could not afford to pay. Even given the calming tastes of her homeland, *Zosia* was still, nonetheless, very nervous indeed.

"Where shall we begin, *Zosia*?" asked the shop owner Henia. "What have you discovered about my great uncle Bogdan? Have you found evidence exonerating him from the false claims of his being complicit in General Sikorski's death?"

"Well," Sophie said, "since we last met, I have spent much time at the Polish Air Force Academy in the town of Dęblin, where your great uncle Bogdan was training just before the war began. Let me start there. Your great uncle, (Sophie nervously repeated herself), Bogdan Bratajewski, was training to become a fighter pilot for the Polish Air Force. His brother, your great uncle Albin, was training to become an alpine soldier. Perhaps Bogdan would have been better off taking that route, because he was not to be successful in his quest to become a fighter pilot."

Sophie went on to tell the story of Bogdan Bratajewski. It was late August 1939, and on the 25th of that month, Bogdan was called into his superior officer's quarters and informed that he would no longer be flying the attack aircraft on which he had been training. His reflexes were deemed to be too slow, and there were far too few of the Polish built PZL P-11 fighters not to have them in the hands of the more capable pilots. Bogdan was crushed, as this had been his dream since childhood. He was told he could fly the transport aircraft, and possibly the PZL P-24 bomber aircraft. Overall he was a good pilot, he was told, just not necessarily good enough to deserve to command one of the most precious of Poland's aircraft, the PZL fighters.

PZL was a state-owned aircraft factory located in Warsaw and had upgraded the fighters and bombers of the Polish Air Force following the Polish Soviet War of 1920. The bi-planes of that era were replaced by more aerodynamically designed aircraft with single overhead "gull" wings. This wing design had a secondary benefit of improved pilot visibility. The planes still employed open cockpits, but even these by then had Plexiglass windshields to protect the pilots. The fighters employed British-built Bristol Mercury radial-piston engines, increasing their airspeed, but that airspeed was still limited by the fixed (non-retractable) landing gear common to the time. They were good planes for the early thirties.

Yet, these Polish planes were no match for the Messerschmidt aircraft of the Third Reich. The 1920s and 30s were years of rapid development in aircraft design as the science of aeronautics became more clearly understood. Germany, as well as Britain, had some of the finest aircraft designers in the world at that time. Poland did have one man who was, if not their equal, certainly within their peer group. His name was Zygmunt Puławski, and his designs released in the 1920s were perhaps some of the most progressive of the era.

The "gull" wing Puławski introduced on the PZL P-1 in 1929, soon became known throughout the industry as the "Puławski Wing". However, Poland's predominant aircraft designer would die in 1931 in an aircraft accident while flying an amphibious flying boat of his own design. He was caught in an unexpected heavy gust of wind upon takeoff. With this loss, the Polish designs became frozen in time, and were over the next eight years extensively surpassed by those of the British and, unfortunately, the German aircraft.

Not only were the Polish aircraft inferior in design quality to their German adversaries' single wing Messerschmidt fighters, but there were far fewer of them as well. There was one area of operation, however, where the Polish fighters equalled or surpassed the *Luftwaffe* pilots (if the results of the Battle of Britain are to be used as a measure), and that was in training. The fact that Hitler was not able to come to Warsaw until the fifth day of October despite his army's technological superiority speaks volumes of the ability of these valiant Polish airmen to squeeze every last bit of performance out of their overmatched and outdated aircraft. The Polish pilots learned through experience that the only hope of bringing down one of the German fighters was to bear in close upon them before opening fire. Otherwise, at greater distances, the German planes would simply outmaneuver the less agile Polish aircraft.

Hitler's invasion plans were initially planned to be executed in the overnight hours of August 25/26. He delayed that plan upon learning that the British had entered into a defensive treaty with the Poles the day before. After assessing the situation, and determining correctly that neither the French nor the British would have the moral fortitude to come to the immediate military assistance of the Poles, the new date was rescheduled for the first day of September. Some aspects of Case White had already been pre-positioned, as we will see.

Like the *Anschluss* invasion plan of 1938 and the invasion plan of Czechoslovakia named *"Case Green"*, the plan to invade Poland, *"Case White"* would be deferred. But unlike the other plans, *"Case White"* would eventually be executed in all of its unmatched fury and brutality.

This postponement would lead to a commando skirmish on the overnight of the 25th/26th along the Polish-Slovak border. A group of *Abwehr* (German Military Intelligence) commandos, dressed in civilian clothing, attacked a critical train station at the Polish border village of Mosty, as was called for by *Case White,* or as the invasion plan was known in German, *Fall Weiss.* Their objective was to secure the Mosty train station and secure intact the nearby train tunnel that was critical to the Nazi military thrust. Somehow, these *Abwehr* commandos had not been made aware that the invasion had been postponed.

At just after four in the morning on the 26th, the commandos fired upon Mosty station. They were also not aware that the station house had a military communication link in the basement. A brave Polish female telephonist set off the alarm, and soon the German commandos, who had by then captured the station, were surrounded and outmanned by Polish troops from nearby locations. The insurgents came under very heavy fire and soon scattered into the woods. These *Abwehr* commandos had never reached their real objective - the train tunnel itself.

The commandos' objective had been to remove the demolition charges that the Poles had earlier set and armed within that critical border tunnel. The Nazis had deemed this infrastructure as essential to the execution of their plan.

Poland protested to Germany vehemently over the incident. The next day, incredibly, the German Major General Ott apologized to the Polish Command for this incursion by "rogue" activists, supposedly outside his direct control. However, the German hand had been played in plain sight, and it foretold that war was most certainly coming.

The war had started in the early morning hours of the first of September 1939, in the most insidious of ways. After World War One, the German City of Danzig (today the Polish port of Gdansk) was declared a Free City (meaning neither German or Polish) under the protection of the League of Nations. Despite this, its population remained approximately ninety per cent German, with most of the rest of the minority of its citizens being Polish.

By the treaty's provisions, the Poles were allowed to operate two institutions within the free city. The first was the military garrison of the *Westerplatte*, located on the small peninsula where the Vistula River emptied into the Baltic Sea. The second Polish institution was the Polish Post Office, which like an embassy, was considered sovereign soil of Poland itself.

Both of these extensions of the Polish State would be ferociously defended by their defenders during the invasion, despite being massively outmanned and outgunned.

Hitler had since March of 1939 threatened military action unless the Poles agreed to the return of Danzig to the Reich, as well as the strip of Polish lands that connected Poland to the sea (and separated Germany from Danzig). This Polish land would become known as the Danzig Corridor and Hitler was determined to have it, unifying Germany with not only Danzig, but also East Prussia beyond. Poland refused, and kept the garrison manned within the *Westerplatte,* but only with less than 200 military personnel.

At that time, it was not uncommon for Germany to send her training ship, the aged battleship *Schleswig-Holstein* to Danzig on goodwill missions. Poland had no authority to prevent its visit to the Free City. On this docking, unlike previous visits, no civilians were allowed to board the training vessel, which was, by definition, a fully functional battleship. Below deck were secreted over two hundred commandos awaiting the opening salvos from the *Schleswig-Holstein's* deck guns that would mark the beginning of the invasion of Poland.

Hitler had used Danzig as a pretext, but made his generals aware that his real objective was to crush the nation of Poland. E*very tongue that spoke the Polish language,* Hitler was to have said, *be it man, woman or child, was to be crushed.*

Ever since March of that year, when the Nazis had overrun the remainder of the Czech lands, the Poles had been preparing for the Nazi invasion. In May an invasion had been closely averted. Even with the continued heightened threats from Hitler over Danzig, by August many Poles were hopeful of a last minute settlement. Instead, those dreaming these last thoughts of hope were to become the first to fight, as Poland became the first nation to go into conflict against the Nazi war machine. And despite the horrible consequences of their initial fight against the invasion, Poland would remain the single country which battled the Nazis from the first day of the war to its last.

On paper, it appeared to be a battle of approximate equals, at least relative to the size of their armies. Germany had one and a half million soldiers, and Poland one and a quarter million. However, there the comparisons ended, as Germany's *Wehrmacht* and *Luftwaffe* were much better equipped in not only the quantity but also the devastating qualities of their fearsome weapons of war. Nowhere were the differences more stark than in the planes that would do battle in the skies over the invaded Polish countryside.

The *Luftwaffe* had the updated ME-109 fighters and Stuka dive bombers while the Poles fought aloft in the outdated PZL fixed-gear open cockpit aircraft, whose design had frozen with Puławski's death in 1931.

On the ground, Poland had antiquated tanks, but even those were in small numbers compared to their opponents. The *Wehrmacht* were about to unleash their feared Panzer tanks for the first time on the Poles. Perhaps the most distinct difference was not in the weaponry itself, but in the strategies and tactics of their use. The Poles fought conventionally, with static entrenchments and lines of defense, while the Nazis employed the coordinated lightning-paced *Blitzkrieg* attacks utilizing the astounding speed of the their tanks and fighters in unison with the abject terror evoked by the screaming Stuka dive bombers.

There remained one last mismatch, one that truly separated the two forces along the border, as it soon would divide the world. The Poles fought employing the accepted rules of warfare at the time. Those rules were based on a code of morality, if such a thing can ever be applied to war, which was not only discarded by the Nazis, but was actively reversed by the Germans to drive terror into the enemy's populace. No sooner had the first shots been fired than Stuka dive bombers would lay waste to purely civilian towns in nothing more than a demonstration of Hitler's willingness to take the innocent lives of the women and children of his opponents.

The Nazi concept of total war was based openly upon the writings of Friedrich Nietzsche. That German writer and philosopher, who coined the phrases *"God is Dead"* and *"The Will to Power"*, exalted the concept that the strong are not only free to prey upon the weak, but are duty-bound to do so by nature. How ironic it was that at the end of his life in 1900, when his brain was racked by mental illness, that he renounced his Germanic roots and claimed to be of Polish ancestry.

What the Nazis were about to do in 1939 to the Poles, the Jews, and eventually the world would have sickened even Nietzsche's own heart of darkness.

That last phrase, *Heart of Darkness*, was the title of the classic novel published by the Polish born author Joseph Conrad in 1899. The story described man's increasing loss of morality and social norms as he travelled up the Congo River in Africa. How aptly, if not prophetic was that plot as a metaphor for the tenets of the National Socialist Party. The more deeply the German leadership became immersed in the depths of National Socialism, the more they shed the conventions of societal norms and morality itself. Simply put, they became monsters.

In the early hours of that dreadful morning of the first of September 1939, the battleship *SMS Schleswig-Holstein* slipped its moorings and headed out of the harbor of Danzig, ending its goodwill visit. At 4:47 AM, it trained its massive 15 inch guns on the *Westerplatte* garrison and fired from point blank range. Thus, on the end of a *"goodwill"* visit, World War II had begun.

Coordinated with this, a squadron of Stuka dive bombers decimated the small Polish town of Wieluń. This sleeping provincial town had no military significance other than to provide target practice to the *Luftwaffe*. After all, they must have been out of practice dive bombing on unarmed civilians since the Spanish Civil War ended earlier that year in April. In fact, the attack on Wieluń was almost exactly two years after the eerily reminiscent Nazi *Luftwaffe's* leveling of the Spanish village of Guernica.

The Polish town of Wieluń would not be remembered by the world in the same way, but just as in Guernica, men, women and children would perish during the undeserving barrage of the screaming Stuka dive bombers. Innocents all, they slept not knowing that war, with no formal declaration, had been initiated. There was no resistance from the Poles. The town had absolutely zero military value. Wieluń was obliterated. The *Luftwaffe's* 380 bombs dropped produced at least 127 confirmed dead, but most believe the real number of deaths numbered in the vicinity of five hundred innocents.

Back at the Polish town of Mosty, the border tunnel was still intact. Yet it still was bearing the demolition charges set by the Poles. At about six o'clock in the morning, just under two hours since the attack on the *Westerplatte* in Danzig, German forces approached the Mosty Tunnel from the Slovak side. Having seen the Germans' true intentions days earlier, the Poles dynamited the tunnel and put that critical element of *Case White* out of operation for the next five months.

Figure 24: Luftwaffe Bombed Town of Wieluń

In Danzig, SS regiments moved quickly against the Polish Post Office. The Poles had decided they would not yield this facility without a fight. Knowing that Hitler was planning to attack, just not knowing exactly when, they had fortified the post office with small arms and machine guns. The Poles valiantly held off the attacking SS assault for fifteen hours. When the bulk of Polish defenders took refuge from the shelling in the building's basement, the Nazis brought in a tanker truck (bearing the name *Sudetenland*) and pumped gasoline in through shot out windows.

The Germans then threw in grenades, setting the facade and the basement interior aflame. When the siege of the Polish Post Office was over, the SS shot the first two Poles coming out of the building under a white flag of surrender. That was apparently justified by the SS as warped retribution for the Poles not having surrendered quickly enough.

In fact, the Nazis had tried to justify their overall use of overbearing military force by the pretext of a secretly conducted false flag operation in the pre-invasion hours. A group of SS commandos, dressed in stolen Polish military uniforms, shot up a radio station just inside the German border.

The SS had even brought Polish corpses taken from their concentration camps to leave behind as fallen raiders. They overpowered the German radio attendants and then "attempted" to broadcast false insurrection messages to the Polish countryside. But by then, the world had become accustomed to the *Führer*'s methods of operation and the pretext was entirely ignored.

At the garrison of *Westerplatte*, 184 Polish soldiers held off wave after wave of Nazi assault. The fortification had been stocked with enough munitions to hold out for only twelve hours, after which time help was expected to have arrived. That help never came. The Polish soldiers at *Westerplatte* held firm, despite having only one cannon, a few anti-tank guns and several machine guns. They held on long enough to learn that on September 3, Britain and France had declared war on Germany. Then the *Westerplatte* troops held even longer, perhaps hoping that some relief might come from the mighty British Navy upon the waves of the Baltic Sea.

That was not to happen. Amazingly, the Polish garrison at *Westerplatte* held out until the seventh of September when they ran out of munitions and were forced to surrender. These men had set the standard for the entire Polish population throughout the war by resisting the Nazis to the very end. Indeed, the Polish Resistance would arise and become the most formidable underground rebellion that the Nazis would face until the very end of the war.

In early September, 1939, war raged across Poland, well beyond Danzig and the Polish Corridor that Hitler had used as his prevarication for hostilities. From the west, *Wehrmacht* troops poured in from Germany and from the south they came from Slovakia. From the north, Warsaw was attacked by the German military forces concentrated in East Prussia.

The country and its beautiful cosmopolitan metropolis of Warsaw never had a chance. The capital was laid waste, becoming nothing more than shelled out frames of crumbling brick and mortar. Wave after wave of Stuka bombers dived repeatedly upon the city with the horrifying screams of their engines that announced far too late the attacks from the skies. Yet, like the *Westerplatte* before it, Warsaw would hold out as long as it possibly could. The capital city would not fall until September 27, ten days after the Soviets had so sinisterly begun invading Poland from the east.

It was clear after the first few days that Poland could not hope to match the German military forces. While the Poles fought with magnificent bravery, their leaders knew the cause was lost. Thankfully they had sent their small navy of three destroyers and a few submarines to Scotland only a few days before the war started. It had become apparent to Polish leaders that by the time the Soviets attacked on September 17, they had to consider the delicate balance of which troops to commit to continue the fight, and which to extract from the battle-zone for future resistance from outside the country.

With Germany and Russia surrounding Poland on all sides, there was only one way out of the country. It was a funnel shaped strip of land that today lies mostly within the borders of Ukraine. That strip of land was then the only route connecting Poland to Romania. Through it poured the escaping military and Polish civilian refugees alike. That escape route became known as the *Romanian Bridge*. And after the invasion of the Soviet Union from the east on September 17, the *Romanian Bridge* would not remain open for long.

As the fighting had progressed, the Polish pilots fought against the *Luftwaffe* with an unmatched fury. It was their antiquated aircraft, not their skills, that hindered them. As the *Luftwaffe* overtook the Polish airspace, Poland began grounding its skillfully trained fighter pilots and then sending them across the "*Romanian Bridge*". They would live to fight on in other days, in other theaters.

As for Bogdan Bratajewski, he was never allowed to take to the skies in defense of his homeland during those first few days of the war. It was not until the eighth of September that he was called into his commander's office.

"Bratajewski, I have a very important mission for you," the commander said. "Please keep in mind this is a volunteer mission, and I will respect your wishes should you refuse."

"Yes, sir," Bogdan replied, at rigid attention. His mind turned to wonder what type of aircraft he would fly for his country.

"Here are photographs of three men. They are stranded in the town of Siedlce, near its train station. You are to take an unmarked truck to that town and find them. Then you are to drive them out of the country into Romania. I have false documents for yourself and these three men. Also, I have gold coins for your use in bribing the border guards, as I am sure this will become necessary. There is enough to also get the four of you to the West and to safety. Do you understand this assignment?"

"Yes, sir," Bogdan replied. Then he waited.

"You have a question, Bratajewski?"

"Yes, sir," Bogdan replied. "Why not allow me to fly them over the border in a transport aircraft?"

His commander looked perturbed to be questioned so.

"It is far too dangerous," the commander finally said. "The *Luftwaffe* would clean you from the skies before you ever would make it to the border. Even if you evaded them somehow, there is no telling if the Romanians would not shoot you down as you entered their airspace."

"Sir," snapped Bogdan, "but it is common knowledge we have begun sending our PZL fighters there. After they land, the Romanians keep the jets and our pilots are allowed to leave of their own accord. Word is those pilots are heading west to General Sikorski in France."

Again the commander seemed agitated by the young pilot that questioned him.

"Listen to me, Bratajewski," the commander said, "these three civilians are more valuable than all the PZL fighters we have combined, do you understand?"

"Yes, sir!"

"We are not to risk these men in the air under any circumstances. Understood?"

"Yes, sir!"

"You are correct in that your mission is to see that these men are delivered unharmed to General Sikorski in France, even if your life depends upon it. Understood?"

"Yes, sir!" Bogdan said a fifth time.

"*Dobrze,*" the commander said with a certain level of relief. He reached for the documents laying on his desk.

"Here are their profile sheets, with photographs for your recognition. These three men are mathematicians. They are likely on the list of the Nazi death squads that have been reported to have been coming in behind their army. All intelligentsia appear to have been marked for arrest or execution. You are to get these men to France, or any other safe non-combatant state if that is not possible. Under no conditions are these men to fall into German hands. This is of the utmost importance. You are being entrusted with a most vital mission, Airman Bratajewski. Deliver *Pan* Rejewski, *Pan* Różycki, and *Pan* Zygalski to Paris and to freedom."

"Yes, sir," said Bogdan. His face remained stoic, as he awaited to be dismissed. It was in this heavy second that his mind wandered: *How could these three men be so important? What if I fail and they are captured? Surely I will be successful if I travel under the grace of Our Lord and the Holy Mother.*

"Bratajewski," said the officer, "I have many men to which I could have entrusted this mission. I chose you because you are the most reliable I have to draw upon. Do you understand?"

"Yes, sir." He did not, in actuality. This same commander had only days before told him he was not good enough to fly to face the German threat, but now he was to be entrusted with a critical mission?

"When you get these men to General Sikorski, your mission is over, but I told the general that you are a skilled pilot. He will be able to use you. Serve him well. He is a good man."

"*Dziękuję*, sir," said Bogdan.

"And for God's sake, Bogdan," said his commander, "get out of that uniform and wear civilian clothes. Blend in. Your country is counting on you to get these men to Paris."

40 Brigand's Dark Day

September 1939

"It must be understood that an adequate supply of Swedish iron ore is vital to Germany…"

Winston Spencer Churchill

The advent of war in Europe sank Brigand MacAlvor into the deepest depression he had faced since his father's death over a quarter century before. Even the loss of his leg had not dropped him to depths as dangerously dark with his very existence threatened by the despair that saturated throughout him. It was as Hitler's *Luftwaffe* rained its vengeance upon Poland, and as the Hun's *Wehrmacht* rolled over that meager country's defenses, that Brigand became aware of the true threat of the atrocities spreading throughout Europe.

Brigand feared for his own mortality. Not from the German war machine, but from his own hand. For it was then that he realized that he had gambled with the most precious thing he had ever possessed - the lives of his twin boys.

On hearing the news of a State of War being declared between Britain and Germany, Brigand had gone directly from his London Blackfriars flat to Wincer Wells' office at the St. Ermin's Hotel. He demanded that the boys be brought back from Skrova immediately. *I should never have fallen for your greedy manipulations*, he thought as he pleaded with Wells. *I should have paid heed to Tilly's instincts all along. My God! What she must think of me!*

"Out of the question, old boy," Wells replied to Brigand's pleadings. "Your sons are perfectly safe, and are precisely where the King and Realm need them most. They are no longer mere boys, but are what now, twenty-six? Pull yourself together, my friend. I will never let any harm come to them."

"You are not my friend!" Brigand hissed. "You cannot be as long as my Einar and Gunnar are at risk!"

"They are two thousand miles away from any fighting, for God's sake, Brigand," snapped Wells. "They are sending us very valuable information, indeed."

"At least let us extract Gunnar," pleaded Brigand. "He will not be able to take the strain of war. Einar is stronger, and will thrive, but I fear for Gunnar."

"You," replied Wells, as he paused accusingly and pointed his finger at Brigand's chest, "were the very person who argued against this. *'They cannot live separated lives,'* you said, *'or they will both cease to exist.'* It was you who refused to give me Einar alone, and now the stage is set. We will let it play out. The lads will be fine, this you will soon enough come to see."

Their argument, as it was too emotional to be termed merely a conversation, went on for another hour. At one point Brigand screamed at Wells, "I have a bloody good mind to take the *Nordlys* and retrieve them to safety myself."

Even Brigand knew that in his own crippled state this would be nearly impossible for him to do. Yet that did not stop Wincer from responding forcefully, "Damn it, MacAlvor. If you should dare to do so, I will have you shot for treason and your boys imprisoned for as long a sentence as I can get a magistrate to confer upon them. We are at war, man! Where is your patriotism?"

"To hell with patriotism," Brigand seethed. "My sons are in the way of the Nazi war machine. Not today, but soon enough…"

"Yours and those of every other father in Britain, confound it!" Wells raged in an exasperated anger, as his face dynamically contorted into that of a gargoyle's. He recovered, only to explode once more upon Brigand, "Leave me this instant, MacAlvor, or I should have you detained. I mean this literally, for this is not an idle warning, I assure you!"

The rage in Wincer Wells' eyes convinced Brigand that any further engagement between them would be futile. Brigand huffed out of the St. Ermin's, and thought briefly of taking his case two streets over to the SIS headquarters at 52 Broadway. There he could plea his case before the second iteration of "C", Admiral Hugh "Quex" Sinclair. He did not, however, after thinking it would only inflame the situation with Wells to an irreparable state.

Instead Brigand headed for the parks. There he hobbled his way through the paths of St. James, Green and Hyde Parks in a fusion of frustrated energy and self-blame. With every crippled step he took, Brigand would conjure previously unimagined scenarios in which the lads were ultimately captured by the Nazi forces.

Brigand could find no solace in his train of thought, as his reasoning had given way only to the most somber of emotions which consumed him. There seemed to be no way out of this situation, except one, which he pushed back into the darkest recesses of his mind. He refused to consider escaping his leaden yoke of responsibility by his own hand, as had his own father.

As Brigand plowed Hyde Park's labyrinth of walking paths, each step taken radiated in sharp pain upon his stump. Mercifully, he came to exit at Speaker's Corner. A man was railing against the encumbrances of capitalism and the need for socialism in England. He argued that only through an uprising of the workers to take control of the government could England effectively resist the fascists. Even in the depths of his despondency, Brigand thought this communist banter to be rubbish and was glad Tilly was not there to hear such dross.

It was at that second when he realized exactly how much he needed Tilly to rescue him from the raging thrusts of his own distressed mind. *Would she reject him because she had for so long warned of Wincer Wells' increasingly devious interest in their beloved twins?*

Tilly was not the twins' natural mother, he knew, but her protective love of these boys was as strong as that of any mother whose own breasts had once been swelled with childbirth.

Will her love for the twins manifest itself as a sword of anger against me for my sins? His dark thoughts tried to convince him so, *but could she really reject me in his hour of my desperate need for her mercy?*

Brigand thought not, especially when she came to understand the all-threatening demons with which he wrestled. He feared what insidious actions they might lure him to undertake in his weakness as the shadows around him became all the more dense.

Why should I stay here in the darkness away from the penetrating light of her healing smile? He was already so lonely and outcast in this city of millions.

He decided on catching the last train to Edinburgh, and after crossing Park Lane caught a cab to Euston Station. He needed Tilly to steady him, as she had done after he had lost his leg. *Damn this throbbing stump and the wooden prosthetic I am forever to hobble about on!*

Brigand hoped that if he could just make it back to her tonight, he would soon again be safe back in Dundee with his loving tender wife. Her soothing touch he had not felt in over a week, since before the news of war had broken.

He made the train, just so, and burrowed himself into a corner seat looking out over the darkening countryside. His emotions teetered on the edge of a complex physical breakdown. He held himself together, just barely, as the specter of his feelings raced menacingly like a devil's breeze through his increasingly irrational array of thoughts.

In Edinburgh, he would catch another train to Dundee, having just enough time to make the connection. He departed the train at Broughty Ferry Station and soon after entered the house on the Tay. Within seconds Brigand was in Tilly's arms, and once there, he fought the swell of emotions he had been holding back. His eyes bloated with the thick heaviness of tears that initially refused to be shed. Slowly, they thickened until they could no longer cling to the emptiness of his mournful gaze. Tilly squeezed him tighter, and patted him consolingly upon his back. His chest then heaved, and he failed in one last attempt at not expelling his sorrow. His eyes streamed as his heart bled. His frame collapsed down upon her fully as Brigand could no longer support the weight of his despair. His chest contorted spastically as wave after wave of sorrow was drawn from his being. He was not completely absolved of his wretchedness in Tilly's arms, but the depths of his despair seemed to shallow somewhat.

Tilly held and caressed him until she no longer could. She then drew a warm bath for him as she undressed him. She removed the prosthetic from his swollen, lightly bleeding stump, as she had done a thousand times over the last two dozen years. She steadied him as he cleared the rim of the tub, his stubbed leg swinging over. She then held him upright under his shoulders as he used his arms to lower himself into the bath's soothing waters. She washed him, humming gently as she did so, because she had found long ago it calmed his spirits. When she stopped, she spoke in soft phrases, convincing him that the twins were safe, and would stay so, even though she did not believe it herself.

Tilly consoled her husband, with the only objective being that he would survive this night. She told him that the boys were safe amidst the early autumn beauty of his homeland, unthreatened in any sense. She then convinced him that the only threat to anyone was that which they both allowed to creep between them.

Tilly finished bathing him. She helped Brigand to stand balanced with her aid on his good leg, before she slipped under his opposite arm as a human crutch. She braced him even more mentally than physically that night, as she led him to the bed that they had for so many years shared.

She had faced these moments of crisis with her husband many times, and increasingly over recent years. Tilly had long ago learned how to deal with her husband's dark days, those he would call his "days of the black dogs." She had learned that what seemed to calm him most was the tender caress of her skin upon his. It was no different from how an infant responds to a mother's touch, she thought. It cannot be explained via logic, but only through tactile response. But the very thought of an infant's needs made her think of her twins. *Were they really as safe as she was making them out to be?*

Tilly lay Brigand down in the bed upon his back, tenderly, and stood over him, stroking his face in a most intimate sharing of spirit. She then leaned over him and repeatedly kissed his brow. Tilly then straightened and slowly removed her clothing. She climbed upon Brigand, as she had done many times since his injury. All uneasiness with his injury had surrendered to reposition many years ago. Her tender palms then stroked his strong muscular chest as she straddled him. They did so until she could feel the tension ease from his body, but not the expectation of what came next. She stopped stroking his muscular torso and pressed down upon his chest as she positioned herself over him. Soon they were rhythmically entwined in each other's amorous passion. She continued to soothe Brigand through the act of love-making. At the height of his fervency, he pulled her as close as he physically could. He whispered in halting breaths in her ear, "You are the salve to my restless soul, Cassie."

Brigand had not called her by that most affectionate form of her birth name in many years. In fact, it had been a dearth of decades. The falling of its sweetness upon her ears at such a poignant moment reduced her to the sweetness of joyful tears. Tilly made no attempt to wipe the tears away as she pulled her straddled self upright over him once more. The teardrops fell unabated upon his chest, like those drops released from a priest's censor upon the throngs assembled at a holiday mass from her youth.

"I am so sorry I forced you to take up this charade of a life, my love," Brigand whispered to her, his body easing muscle by muscle into the sheets beneath him.

She smiled, still crying. "Heaven knows you can be such a dolt. When will you learn that it was you who saved me? You who have given me the very life that I have been denied for no reason other than fate. The very life I had always yearned for, but never thought possible."

"I am only sorry I could not give you a child of your own," Brigand mumbled as his body readied itself for sleep.

"Perhaps you just did..." Tilly smiled softly at him. In any case, it is my body's own doing. The doctor's opinion was that I would never have another child after my stillbirth ..."

Having said those last few words triggered something from the deepest recesses of her being, and a terrible bitterness crept into her tears.

"Doctors have been known to be wrong, love," Brigand consoled her as he began to drift off into a much needed and relaxed slumber.

"Then perhaps you indeed just gave me what I always wanted," she said. "If it's a boy, I shall name him after the man I fell in love with - Birger."

"No, love," her husband replied with a fading breath, "I demand you should name any son we might have after yourself."

"Matilda? Tilly? How very foul," she said, playfully slapping her palms in a mild rebuke upon the rise of his chest.

"Mattie ... Matthew," Brigand softly feathered through his easing breath, "It means 'Gift of God' ... for you have been my own gift from God..."

She rubbed his chest until he gave in to the sleep and escaped from the fears that had tormented him for so long. As a deep slumber overtook him, she dismounted from atop him to lay aside him, her shoulder eased into the nook of his arm. Her head rested gently upon his chest. Soon enough she joined him in a temporary escape from the worries of their world.

41 Escape from Poland

September 1939

"Poland has again been overrun by two of the great powers which held her in bondage for a hundred and fifty years, but were unable to quench the spirit of the Polish nation."

Winston Spencer Churchill

Sophie looked compassionately into Henia's eyes, as she had forced the woman to think of her mother's uncle being denied from taking to the air to fight the Germans during his country's invasion, only to be assigned to locate and caretake a gaggle of mathematicians. To be a babysitter of academics as his country was being destroyed, as his countrymen were being needlessly killed in acts of savage brutality, was an insult to the man, no matter how important his commander made the task sound.

"Perhaps, I should stop for a bit," said Sophie, speaking, as she had been in the tongue of her homeland.

"*Nie*, *Zosia*" said Henia, as she fought back tears, dabbing at those that continued to escape and roll down her sloping cheeks. "Please continue. Was Great-Uncle Bogdan able to find these men in Siedlce?"

Zosia looked at Henia's husband, Marcin, who only said the Polish word "*Proszę*," as he rolled his wrist, meaning, *please, go on*.

Sophie took a deep breathe. "Rest assured, Henia, your Great Uncle Bogdan was indeed able to find them."

Bogdan Bratajewski had arrived immediately after the Siedlce train station had been dive bombed by Nazi Stuka's. As he approached in his truck, he could hear the sickening scream of the dive bombers, and see the crowd scattering in terror. No one knew where to run, so they imploded into each other. Every man, woman and child could only move in reaction to the horrifying screech of the diving aircraft, knowing the destruction that in seconds would follow.

Bogdan arrived to find lifeless piles scattered randomly like discarded clumps of clothing. He became violently ill as he realized that each of these garments were nothing more than bloody shrouds covering the remains of his butchered countrymen. There were no soldiers here. He looked to the sky, as if expecting another wave of hatred to rain down upon these civilian survivors and himself. He was fair game, even out of uniform, but they were not.

From the airbase in Dęblin, Bogdan had already been made aware that the Germans had, by that point, gained nearly total air superiority over all of Poland. The skies overhead were blue with clarity, which in this case meant red with deadly intent. There was no weather to hamper the plans of the *Luftwaffe*. He knew he must act quickly and locate these three men.

Bogdan scanned the crowds as he walked along the bomb cratered platform. It seemed to shudder as it lay above the twisted metallic ribbons of steel that had been torn away from the railroad ties and were mangled into tortured relics of the last attack. The smell of cordite and sulfur choked at him, as did the moans and screams of the wounded. He knew he had to focus on his task at hand, but even this duty was not enough to keep him from retching. He jumped down into the rail bed and began to heave. He leaned forward as he emptied the bile that had collected so acidicly within him. As he vomited, lurch after lurch, he reached out to steady himself on an upright segment of twisted smoking rail.

The heat from the metal rail seared into his palm causing him to reactively release it. The bones in his hand seemed to carry the radiating effect of the burn throughout his body. His arm shook in quivers of pain. He dropped to his knees, unaware that he was kneeling in his own vomit.

Bogdan turned his throbbing palm upright, and already could see a distorted red image across it. He could smell the burnt skin. The pain was unbearable. His first thought was that he would surely lose this hand, and then realized that meant he would never fly again. Certainly not a fighter, perhaps not even a transport. A great pity cascaded over him, and mixed with the unbearable pain into an instant despondency.

It was then that he remembered his duty. He must find these three mathematicians. As he thought this he heard the moans of the wounded around him. He looked about him, and realized those poor souls were suffering far beyond the pain to which he, himself, was subjected. Bogdan wrapped his hand in a handkerchief that he drew from his pocket, and he knew he must press on to do that for which he had been sent. Despite his swelling hand, he must search for the three men who's images he had burned into his memory, even though their photographs remained safely enclosed in his shirt's pocket.

After searching for perhaps another twenty throbbing minutes, he found them. It was Marian Rejewski's glasses that first caught Bogdan's glance. Those round wire rimmed spectacles sitting atop those passive, pensive, angelic eyes identified the man. Bogdan reached into his pocket with his left hand and awkwardly pulled out the three photographs. He needed not to reference them, as Bogdan had recognized from memory *Pan* Rejewski, and then *Pan* Zygalski who was standing next to him. However, there was no sign of the third man, *Pan* Różycki. Bogdan walked toward the two men briskly, once again glancing upward into the clear sky for any movement. He saw none, but knew this could change at any second.

"Why do the Nazis bomb a civilian railroad station?" He could hear Zygalski ask as he neared them.

"You gentlemen are to come with me immediately," Bogdan said as he thrust forward the photographs with his left hand. His right hand was throbbing, and each pulse seemed to be shot from a crossbow's frame. "I have been sent to collect you both and escort you safely to Romania."

What happened next he did not expect. Both Rejewski and Zygalski looked strangely at the three photographs. Then in unison they began rotating their heads, as if attempting to curl them into their shoulders.

Bogdan only then realized that the prints were in his hand upside down.

"Who would send you here for us?" Rejewski asked, his voice gentle, but with an underlying firmness that demanded a rational answer.

"I am from the Air Escadrille in Dęblin," Bogdan answered, "but I am instructed to tell you that I am sent on behalf of Polish Intelligence. Come with me."

"I am not getting into any damned airplane," said Henryk Zygalski. "We will be like a lonely sparrow among a sky full of hawks."

Marian Rejewski looked at Bogdan, as if saying, *How do you answer?*

"I do not have a plane, only a truck," Bogdan replied, "now, where is *Pan* Różycki?"

"Why is your arm shaking so, young man?" asked Rejewski. Bogdan looked down at his right side. He raised his elbow, bringing his quivering handkerchief-enwrapped palm up to his waist.

"I grabbed something I should not have," he said. "Where is *Pan* Różycki?"

"So we are to go with an airmen who is to drive a truck with a hand that does not work?" sneered Zygalski.

"You presume we have better options to explore, my friend?" countered Rejewski. He then turned to the young man before him. "Jerzy is over there, looking after his young wife and infant child. I will get them both. Stay here."

Soon the five of them, along with the infant, were driving out of the town of Siedlce, heading east to the town of Brześć to join a column of regrouping military which also intended to head south to the Polish city of Tarnopol and then beyond to the town of Kuty on the border with Romania.

In Brześć, Bogdan was able to find a medic to look after his hand. He had found the man treating others, far more seriously injured than himself. The medic was brash, almost rude to the wounded. Bogdan assumed it was the man's personality defense mechanism protecting his mind from all the suffering he was treating. Bogdan patiently waited to present his wound. Then, his turn came. He presented the blistered mass.

"Is it serious?" Bogdan asked.

"Yes, it is very serious," said the wisecracking medic, who surely this day alone had seen tragedies in need of far greater care. "I think I will send you back to Warsaw for treatment."

"That's funny," Bogdan said. The medic treated the hand with a heavy greasy ointment, then wrapped it carefully. "Not too bulky, my friend, I have a truck full of passengers to drive."

"They might be more comfortable walking," the medic quipped. Then he nonchalantly said, "It will scar over, blister like you have never before seen, and then the skin of your hand will slough off like that of a snake's. That, my friend, is no joke. Keep it as clean as you can and reapply this thrice daily. " He handed Bogdan the tube.

"Keep this for others who will need it," Bogdan said.

"It is for you," the medic sneered, "when you no longer need it, look for someone who is badly burned, and pass it to them. I doubt you will have too far to look."

Thank you, lieutenant," said Bogdan.

"The best way you can thank me is by living," the medic said with a serious look upon his exhausted face. "Take care of those civilians."

"We are all civilians," Bogdan said to him, trying to sell his cover.

"Young man, at the Romanian border," the medic said, "and God bless us that we should make it that far, they will separate we military from the civilians and detain us, or at least try to. Of course, we will fight, because if we do not, they will turn us over to the Gestapo. The civilians will be allowed to go free under the banner of Romania's purported neutrality. You wear a civilian's clothes, but you carry yourself like a soldier, like a recruit. My best advice to you, my friend, steal a peasant's cap and cover that haircut. You just may survive long enough to become an emigre."

Bogdan then walked back to the truck and those he was to protect. Soon the military column would begin its lethargic crawl towards the south.

"Isn't it dangerous for us to be joining this military convoy?" asked Marian Rejewski. "Isn't it more probable that we will be attacked?"

"Yes, of course," replied Bogdan, "and should we be attacked we are amongst a large column of heavily armed soldiers. It is our only chance of surviving. The Nazis are west of here, but who knows how far? If one of their scouting detachments comes across this column, they won't dare to attack for this is far too large an armed group. They'll report it, and we can only hope the Germans don't have the resources to come after us before we reach the border."

Rejewski looked at the young man, as if he had made the mathematician's point.

"But," Bogdan continued, "if we were traveling alone, although we'd move faster, but even the smallest Nazi detachments would shoot us with their machine guns until no one moved, not even that pretty woman and her infant in the back. Do you understand, *Pan* Rejewski?"

Rejewski looked at him with a mock expression of surprise.

"Yes, of course I understand," the mathematician said, "it is a simple case of probabilities. Here we move slower, but have a higher probability to survive attacks, unless, of course, we are found by a large column of the Nazi army."

"And according to what the military officers have told me," Bogdan replied, "they seem to be holding off to the west of here. No one seems to know why they are not pressing east further. I am only thankful they are not."

After another hour, the truck, and all of its precious human cargo, pulled out along with the column of military vehicles. It soon headed south to the "*Romanian Bridge*", that long thin strip of land that connected the rest of Poland to the neutral country.

Despite his injured hand, Bogdan drove the flatbed truck. With every heavy shift of the gears, bolts of fire stabbed through his palm and into his arm. Rejewski sat in the front of the cab with him, while Zygalski rode in the back with Różycki and his young wife and infant child.

The days ahead were filled with monotonous plodding. When his passengers suggested going out on their own and advancing ahead of the column, Bogdan responded viscerally.

"Have you not seen those shot up vehicles alongside the road? Those are not the work of the Germans. Those are holes from Polish rifles, Polish bullets, retribution for those who think themselves more important than others. We stay here. We stay in the queue."

On the 15th of September, the column was strafed by a lone Messerschmitt fighter. His machine guns tore up the trucks and cars directly in front of Bogdan's truck. Rifle fire exploded from the soldiers of the column, but it made no real threat to the fighter. The plane made a second strafing pass just further ahead, before it peeled off and headed west.

"Why is he leaving?" Rejewski asked, "He knows where we are. He will bring back more planes. We are trapped."

"Relax. He has a radio to call in our position. He must be low on fuel," said Bogdan, with his pilot's mind imaging exactly what the German pilot must be thinking. "Some patrol must have called us in."

"Yes, yes," said Rejewski, "others planes will be back. Soon."

"Perhaps not," reasoned Bogdan, "or they would have sent more than this lone aircraft. More likely we are too far east, just at the edge of their range. Maybe a lone pilot was halfway here and decided to fly out for some easy prey. Must have been further than he thought to only get off two strafing runs and head back. He knows that if he doesn't get that plane back in operational order, even if he survives, the Nazis will shoot him dead for this folly."

"I hope you are correct, my friend," Rejewski said.

"You won't be when you hear what I say next," Bogdan said. "I feel that the trap is tightening on this *'Romanian Bridge'*. I simply do not understand why the Germans are staying so far west of here. There must be a reason."

As the wounded ahead of them were cared for, Bogdan exited the vehicle and made sure all in the flat bed were uninjured. His passengers only wore the wounds of fear that had scarred their faces. It was the first time that they had come under live fire of someone intent on killing them. Except for the train yard bombing at Siedlce. Certainly, a bombing can be horrific although somewhat indiscriminate. But to look up and see a plane making its way directly to you, knowing that you are its selected prey, that is truly capable of freezing anyone in terror.

My first real time, too, thought Bogdan Bratajewski. He then moved forward to assist the other drivers in administering to their wounded, but due to his hand he could not help in the throwing of the dead along the roadside. There was no time to bury them, so the corpses strewn along the road formed a wake, like that of a boat upon the water, as the column crawled ahead once more at a snail's pace.

The green countryside passed slowly before them, but as they reached the border the density of the column grew thicker along their sides.

The river of refugees widened around them. War had not yet touched this remote corner of Poland, but surely it was coming even here. For now, the scourge of its refugees was to be its first infliction.

By this point, *Pan* Rejewski had switched places with *Pani* Różycki and her child, to get the infant out of the wrath of the sun's rays. The infant boy cried incessantly. Bogdan just wanted it to stop. The drone of his wail plucked the fiber of his last throbbing nerve.

"I am so sorry, *Pan* Bratajewski," she said, "Janusz is hungry."

"We are all hungry," Bogdan replied, "but if you can feed him do so."

The young mother blushed red in her face.

"Of course you can always go back among the others if you prefer," Bogdan said. "Do you even have food within you to feed this child?"

"I think so," she said, slowly unbuttoning her blouse as the driver looked away. She nursed the child to her bosom and it drank of her motherhood.

On September 17, they reached the refugee swollen border town of Kuty. The poor village could not accommodate the wave after wave of military vehicles and their burdens of humanity. They pressed upon the town, until it was drowned in their exasperation. Now it was only a question of how many hours would it take to get across that relatively short stretch of border into the freedom of Romania.

It was then that Bogdan went off in search of food. A man with a megaphone was attempting to control the crowds, who were becoming more and more restless. A voice behind him sounded familiar as it said, "So, my friend, how is your hand?"

It was the same medic who had treated him in Brześć.

"I am standing and walking, looking for food," said Bogdan, smiling, "so it is good."

"*Dobrze, dobrze*," said the lieutenant, "this makes me happy. You have heard the news, no?"

The medic's face had soured as he asked this.

"What news?"

"As of today, the Russians attack from the east," he said.

"Those Soviet bastards," Bogdan thought aloud. "So that is why the Germans held back west of here, kept their planes from over our heads."

"It will not be long before that Red Army reaches us," the soldier said. "They still seek revenge for these lands they lost to us in the 1920 war. You need to get your party across that border as quickly as you can."

"We have a child," he said, "his mother needs food, any food."

"Down this road," the medic answered, "no more than half a mile, is a small farm. I saw soldiers slaughtering a dairy cow for its meat. They surely must have some milk stored there. The meat the soldiers will kill you for, but the milk, perhaps not so much."

"Thank you, my friend," said Bogdan. "thank you for your kindness."

The medic looked over his shoulder, and then whispered to him.

"Here is another kindness for you. I have seen that young mother you are transporting. She is very beautiful, too beautiful among all these men. If anyone wishes to take her, tell them you are a doctor. That it is essential she gets to Bucharest for she has the plague. They will laugh, but if they have a brain, they will leave her alone."

Bogdan thanked him again. The thought of the Red Army pressing in from the east consumed his thoughts. He soon found the farm, where a peasant woman cried over the slaughtered corpse of her cow. It lay stripped of its meat, its ribs slicing through the fatty film that was all that was left of its hide. The soldiers roasted its meat over a large fire they had ignited.

"*Pani, Pani,*" Bogdan said to the crying woman. Her hands covered her eyes just as her head was covered by a kerchief, so that only a mass of wrinkles and gray hair was exposed. "*Pani*, I am sorry for what these barbarian's have done to your farm. I have a mother and infant child nearby. You must have some milk for them."

"How will I live?" she sobbed. "That cow has fed me, her milk has allowed me to trade for food. She was such a peaceful animal. Look at her, butchered!"

"*Pani*, the milk. *Proszę*," With this Bogdan reached into his pocket, and removed a single gold piece. He hesitated, knowing he would likely need this for getting across the border. Then he thought of the infant, and cupped his hand over the coin so that the nearby soldiers could not see. He showed the gold piece to her.

"I have only one bottle of milk," she said, slowly catching her breath as her sobbing subdued.

"Two bottles," demanded Bogdan, "or I walk away".

"It is all I have," she cried.

"You lie, woman," Bogdan rebuked her, "and for disrespecting me so, I leave!" Bogdan began to walk away.

"No, no," she ran to him, and pulled him towards her barn. She disappeared within it and emerged with two bottles of fresh milk, uncapped, each with a layer of thick cream already having risen to its top. He pressed the single gold coin into the woman's hand and told her to be quiet, or the soldiers would take it from her.

Bogdan walked a bit down the road, until he was alone. The smell of the roasted animal flesh reminded him of how hungry he was. He set the bottles carefully on the dirt farm road, and removed the jacket he had been wearing. He pulled it over his shoulders like a cape. He then picked up the bottles and very carefully pressed them both between his left forearm and his side under the jacket. Next, his heavily bandaged right hand drew, also under his jacket, the military standard issue Walther P-38 semi-automatic pistol he carried in the waistband of his pants. The gun fit awkwardly as he loosely gripped it aside the wad of bandages.

Bogdan feared the gun would not be respected in his left, uninjured hand. He also felt his good arm was more importantly reserved for gripping the milk bottles. Bogdan prayed he would not be forced to fire the pistol to defend his bounty, for the recoil would likely sear through his arm, and most likely even the bottles in his other arms would be lost in the process. He only hoped to scare off anyone brazen enough to try and take the milk from him.

Bogdan returned to the truck and found Różycki's wife, Basia, and the infant resting in the front seat. He set his gun on the floorboard, and from under the shroud of his jacket he produced a bottle of milk.

"Here," he said, as he secured the second bottle that had begun slipping from his arm's grip.

"It is very kind of you," she said, "but my child cannot stomach this."

"It is for you, *Pani*," he said. "Drink until you are filled, then I will share what is left with the men. It will help you make food for your child. Drink. Drink for you both."

Bogdan pushed the bottle into her hands.

Moved by his compassion, she cried, then hungrily raised the bottle to her lips. When she was finished, slightly more than two-thirds of the bottle was drained.

"Bless you," she said, "my child has drained me."

Bogdan then raised what was left of the first bottle to his lips. The milk was beginning to warm and was thick like honey. It tasted just as sweet to his parched palate as he drank it down.

He then held up the second bottle to her, but she waved it off. "I can drink no more."

"Then the last bottle is for the three men in back. What could be more fair, we all get a third of a bottle, even your child!" Bogdan smiled at her. Then, he left to rejoin the men.

"I am sorry, gentlemen," he said as he approached them, "all the vodka was already gone. We have only fresh cow's milk."

"Basia, first we give it to Basia," Różycki said.

"*Pan* Jerzy," said Bogdan, "your wife has already had her fill from the first bottle. As have I. Now you men will need strength. We are not even out of Poland yet."

"And the filthy Russians are closing in from the east," said Zygalski.

"So you already know..." said Bogdan. "I think we will be all right. We are so very close, my friends."

He was indeed right, a few hours later they crossed into Romania. The truck was impounded and the border guard threatened to turn them back. It was then that Bogdan bought him off with another of the gold coins he had retained.

They walked to the nearest train station, where Bogdan used another coin to buy food, enough to fill all their stomachs. They took this with them on the train, on which Bogdan used the last coin to secure a compartment for the six of them to Bucharest. They had escaped war torn Poland, but were then penniless, like all the other refugees around them.

In Bucharest, they went to the Embassy of the British, seeking refuge. So, too, did hundreds of others. Their hearts sank. They were lost in a sea of desperate faces, and not a one of them spoke English. Their cries for help went unheard.

The voices that were heard were those that spoke English. The mathematicians from Poznan all spoke fluent German, but that was of no use. Their cries in Polish and

German bounced off the English guards at the gates like rays of the sun off of Embassy's mirrored glass.

Then Rejewski suggested they try the French Embassy, as he spoke that language in a limited capacity. There, they found another swarm of refugees, although somewhat smaller, that besieged the gates. Bogdan and Rejewski worked their way to the fence, pushing through the mass of wailing, desperate bodies.

In French, the mathematician told the French guards through the fence that they had something very special for "*Bolek*". The message was passed inside, and within the hour the gates were opened to allow the six of them, including Jerzy Różycki's wife, Basia and infant child inside.

"Who is this *Bolek*?" Bogdan asked Marian Rejewski as they were escorted through the embassy. "You mention his name and the gates of the embassy magically open."

"Just a friend from Paris," Rejewski replied, "who is knowledgable of what we can do."

"And what is that?" asked the airman turned escort.

"We solve puzzles," Rejewski said. "Very complex puzzles."

As it turned out, "*Bolek*" was the code name for Gustave Bertrand, the French Intelligence officer with whom Polish Intelligence had a long relationship. Gustave Bertrand had been at the conference below the Kabaty Woods just over a month ago. In a few days, the six of them were on another train that would take them through safe passage across the south of Europe, and eventually to Paris.

In the capital, after an exhausting ride, the three mathematicians were received by none other than "*Bolek*" himself at the *Gare de l'Est*. Gustave Bertrand was a very prominent figure in French Intelligence's "*Deuxième Bureau*", and for him to personally greet these men bore testimony to their collective importance. After the greetings were concluded upon the platform, Bertrand began ushering the men through the station with haste.

Bogdan spoke no French, so Rejewski acted as his interpreter. He matched the brisk pace so unusual of this man, or any Frenchman, for that matter.

"Monsieur *Bolek*," said Rejewski, "my friend Bogdan says his orders are to deliver us to General Sikorski. He demands we go there immediately."

"Tell your friend," said Bertrand, "that he has done a magnificent job protecting you all. However, he is now in France, and his orders are meaningless. The Deuxième Bureau has some magnificent accommodations for you all, and out of respect for your protector, I will have my associate take your Monsieur Bogdan to General Sikorski's headquarters in a separate car. Once there, he can get that hand some proper attention." Bertrand raised his nose as a way of pointing to the soiled wrappings of Bratajewski's right hand.

Thus they parted ways, Rejewski, Zygalski and the three Różyckis climbed into a massive *Citroën Traction Avant* sedan, while another man led Bogdan to *Peugeot 202* convertible. He had never before seen such elegant automobiles, and certainly this Peugeot was the finest vehicle in which he had ever ridden.

At General Sikorski's headquarters, Bogdan was welcomed in his mother tongue. Everyone spoke in Polish, and the complex was abuzz with activity. Bogdan was forced to wait two hours before the general received him in his office.

"Where are my mathematicians?" The general demanded, as he returned Bogdan's salute.

"The man they call '*Bolek*' took them from me," said Bogdan. "I am sorry, but…"

"I know, I know," General Sikorski smiled slyly, "we have an agreement with Monsieur Bertrand. They are safe in his care. In some ways it is better that you are not aware of their location. Better for you. Most certainly better for them.'

"Yes, sir," replied Bogdan.

"At ease," said Sikorski. "You have completed your mission with distinction. You kept those men out of the hands of the Gestapo. Well done."

"Thank you, sir."

"I am told you are an excellent pilot," the general said. "As it turns out I am in need of a pilot. Can you fly a transport?"

"Most certainly, sir," said Bogdan, "but I would prefer to be in a fighter."

"I already have more Polish fighter pilots than the French have available aircraft. You'll find that we are second class citizens here in France. They look down their noses at us, so prepare yourself."

"Yes, sir."

"Tomorrow you will report for familiarization with my transport aircraft, understood?"

"Yes, sir."

"You will be my primary transport pilot starting next week. Can you manage that? "Of course, sir."

"How badly is your hand injured?" Sikorski then asked.

"A minor burn, sir." Bogdan lied.

"Show me," Sikorski demanded Bogdan slowly removed his soiled wrappings, and the dead skin delicately peeled away along with the gauze atop it. This exposed an angry cross-shape welt where the skin had sloughed off.

"Is it still painful?"

"Somewhat, sir," Bogdan lied, as it throbbed tremendously.

"I see," said General Sikorski, as he moved his head side to side inspecting the injury. "We shall have to have that attended to further. Wanda, *proszę…*" With the last two words the general's secretary stepped into the room.

"Take Airman Bratajewski to the medical ward to care for his burned hand," said the general.

"Most certainly sir," she began to lead Bogdan away. The pilot-to-be grabbed at his wrappings from the floor.

"No, leave those," said the general, "no sense rewrapping what will just be removed again. Tell me, Airman Bratajewski, how did you come to have such an unusual burn?"

Bogdan looked down at the seared cross image in his palm. It looked as if it had been intentionally scalded upon his hand, as if some entity had branded him for life.

"In Siedlce, sir, I grabbed at the end of a train-yard rail that had just been bombed. I grabbed at the top of the "I", which was distorted by the blast and my hand folded over to created the imprint of the cross."

"How appropriate," said the general. "It is a good omen."

"I am afraid I do not understand, sir" he replied.

"Your name is Bogdan, is it not?"

"Yes, sir," the airman replied.

"Well, the devil be damned," Sikorski said, "you don't know, do you?"

"Know what, sir?"

"That your name Bogdan means '*Light of God*'!"

42 The "*Sitzkrieg*" & The Winter War

October 1939 - April 1940

"I sympathized ardently with the Finns and supported all proposals for their aid..."

Winston Spencer Churchill

Poland was bisected after the Russians advanced from the east to join up at secretly predetermined positions with the German forces. The *"Romanian Bridge"* soon closed after the Soviet's advanced on the 17th of September. Those Polish military forces and civilians who had not crossed the border and taken refuge in Romania were trapped. The Polish officers were rounded up by the thousands and transported east to imprisonment camps by the Soviets. Stalin, in a sinister foresight fueled by his own paranoia, had the most devilish of plans for these men, and in a very singular case, a woman. Janina Lewandowska was the unfortunate pilot of reconnaissance aircraft captured by the Soviets.

Hitler's Nazi advance was very much concluded when Warsaw finally fell on September 27. The Polish army had fought valiantly, but the advanced weaponry and lightning attack tactics of the *Wehrmacht* were too much for them to forestall. The Polish people, by then under Nazi occupation, soon were to taste of its tyrannical control. After the brutal initial onslaught of the predators that made up the German army crept in the Nazi SS *Einsatzgruppen* death squads, like a shadowy pack of ravenous, bloodthirsty jackals snarling their vicious teeth at the defenseless, conquered civilians.

These paramilitary forces arrested many suspected leaders of resistance, current or potential, and assassinated them in their homes, or in the town's squares. Others were shipped to concentration camps where they would endure forced labor until their deaths. Political figures such as mayors, alderman and administrators on prepared lists were taken or killed. Intelligentsia such as university professors, journalists, literary personnel, newspapermen, and even student leaders were brutally murdered, or boarded on trucks or trains to the camps.

Police, firemen, priests and uniformed personnel of all types were rounded up and either shot or shipped out. Basically, any element of authority and respect in the Polish lands were carted off, or were openly executed. Certainly the three Polish mathematicians rescued by Bogdan Bratajewski would have been on those deadly lists.

Many healthy Polish young men were rounded up from the streets to provide labor for the conversion of former Polish military barracks into concentration camps. Students had been taken off the streets around Krakow's renowned Jagiellonian University, which had immediately been closed by the Nazis after the invasion. The students had been taken from Krakow to the camp that had been the Polish army barracks at the town of Oświęcim. That camp would soon be known by its German name: Auschwitz. The Poles and Jews interred there soon were forced to labor in its expansion, and ultimately, after the experiments of gassing its captives proved effective, the slave labor was forced to build the horrific scaled-up gas chambers and crematoriums of Auschwitz II - the dreaded death camp known as Birkenau.

As ghastly as all this was for the Poles, Jews trapped in Poland were given especially horrendous treatment by the Nazis in the early months following the invasion. Those who were not shot in the streets or town squares were driven into areas which would soon become walled in as ghettos. The densities of these ghettos were increased to the point where ten to fifteen families were forced to jam into the living quarters intended for a single family. With such concentrated quarters and the hunger that followed from restrictions on food, disease was soon rampant. The deaths of many of the elderly and the weak resulted. Once the ranks of the Jewish population was thinned out in this way, the ghettos would be cleared out and its surviving inhabitants shipped by rail to the Nazi death camps.

Finally, in those early months, many young men and women would flee into the country's vast forests and form what would become the most active Resistance against the Nazis throughout the war. Poland never willingly collaborated with their invaders, as would the Vichy French and the Norwegian traitors under Quisling's government. Poland formed not only a network of resistance, but even a government of defiance. Under General Władysław Sikorski, first in France and later in London, the Polish Government-in-Exile would control not only its regrouping army in France and its courageous airmen who would later fight heroically in the Battle of Britain, but it also developed a network of agents throughout its occupied homeland.

After the invasion of Poland, Germany and Soviet Russia settled the final boundaries of their dual regions of hostile domination over her people. Poland was failed by her allies. While Britain and France did declare war on Germany on September 3, they quickly decided to not immediately come to the aid of the Polish people militarily. Having voluntarily disarmed themselves after World War I, they felt they needed time to reconstitute their own war fighting forces.

The months that followed the attack on Poland, from October 1939 through March 1940, would come to be known as the "*Phoney War*" in Britain and as the "*Drôle de Guerre*" by the French, so called for the lack of engagement by the Allies against Hitler's *Wehrmacht and Luftwaffe*. The Germans would come to know it as the "*Sitzkrieg*". Hitler strategically used this time to his benefit, to reallocate the mass of troops he had in the east to the west and prepare for the invasion of the northern lands of Scandinavia in early April, as a predecessor operation before his campaign on Western Europe was to begin in May.

Stalin, by comparison, refused to wait that long. On November 30, his Soviet Red Army invaded neutral Finland on the basis of needing to protect itself from the Finns' supposed aggression. Like Hitler, it was an excuse for a land grab, and also like Hitler, the justification was rejected by the West.

The Soviet-Finnish "Winter War" took place during December 1939 through the middle of March 1940. Stalin soon found that both he and his generals had underestimated the level of fight in the Finns. Their troops fought with extreme dexterity on skis in the nearly imperceptible camouflage of all-white winter wear.

The Finnish fighters readily navigated the thick forests of their homeland which seemed impenetrable to their invaders. The Finns ambushed the Soviet forces by trapping their tanks with fallen trees. They decimated the surrounded Russian forces with the deadly accurate firing from the agile Finnish ski forces, whose mobility the heavily laden Soviet troops could not match.

On the day that Britain and France declared war on Germany, Winston Churchill was once again pulled from near obscurity to be reinstated as the First Lord of the Admiralty. Winston, exuberant to have regained this previous pinnacle of his career, threw himself into his work. He immediately issued two proposals, both of which affected neutral Norway. The first was to mine the Leads of Norway, its intracoastal waterways, to prevent the shipment of iron ore to Germany.

The second initiative, a few months later, was to use the Arctic port of Narvik to support the Finns via the Ofoten and Swedish railroads.

By early September 1939, Einar and Gunnar had become very knowledgable regarding the Ofoten Railway. They had communicated coded radio messages from atop the Hogskrova hill on Skrova. Gunnar took great pride in recording and encrypting the messages. Einar detailed their findings of traffic patterns of German-bound ships, as well as ore volumes and potential sabotage locations taken from their trips along the *Ofotbahnen,* Norway's Ofoten Railway, and Sweden's *Malmbanan,* the trans-Swedish Railway to which it is connected. The twins had been acknowledged in reply messages from London as having delivered very vital information.

On the first of December 1939, in a frenzy of encoded radio traffic, they received new instructions from Wells to survey deeper into Sweden along its *Malmbanan* Railway for potential supply routes of British aide to the Finnish troops engaged in battle with the Soviets.

They spent all of December, January and February doing exactly that, traveling far into Sweden, well past the mines at Kiruna. Each week, Wincer Wells' team communicated new queries and locations in Sweden for the twins to scout. They used the Ofoten Railway, which connected to the *Malmbanan* Rail Line at the border station of Riksgränsen, Sweden. The *Malmbanan Line* would then transverse the expanses of Sweden all the way to the Baltic port of Luleå.

Wells' instructions at various stations were to explore the possible options of using each stop as a potential armory from which to arm the Finns. Acting on Churchill's concept, they would assume that arms smuggled through the port of Narvik could use the railways to ensure they got into the hands of Finnish insurgents. The twins merely had to reconnoiter various Swedish train stations, and assess the potential logistics of their use in arming the Finns. The flurry of orders coming from Wells' team reached its crescendo in February, and Gunnar assessed the plan was readying to go into implementation.

However, in late February of 1940, there came an abrupt end to the requests for the twins to reconnoiter the Swedish line any longer. Instead, during the first week of March, Wells had the Twins ride the Swedish trains to its terminus in the frozen Baltic port of Luleå.

In Luleå they were to report on the ice conditions in the harbor and the Gulf of Bothnia beyond, and communicate back if any shipping was being conducted. The twins visited the port, and reported back that no shipping was ongoing because the ice of the gulf waters was "thicker than a London fog."

Shortly after their return to Skrova, the radio transmissions received above the Hogskrova went suddenly silent. After a week, the twins received a transmission which instructed them to stand down and go to ground. This meant they were to blend in with the villagers on Skrova. They had no idea why such a radical turn of activity had taken place.

In the forests of Finland, the Soviets were now making headway. They had brought in their own winter troops from Siberia, who quickly proved effective in countering the Finns' forest tactics. By mid-March, the war was settled with the Soviets having gained the minor concessions of those Finnish lands closest to Leningrad, along the Kirelian Isthmus, and also around the valuable Arctic town of Petsamo in the far north.

While Einar and Gunnar were scouting the railways of Norway and Sweden, Bogdan Bratajewski was settling in as the chief pilot for General Sikorski in Paris. In mid-January, he flew Sikorski to London for a conference of the extended Allied War

Figure 25: Narvik circa 1928

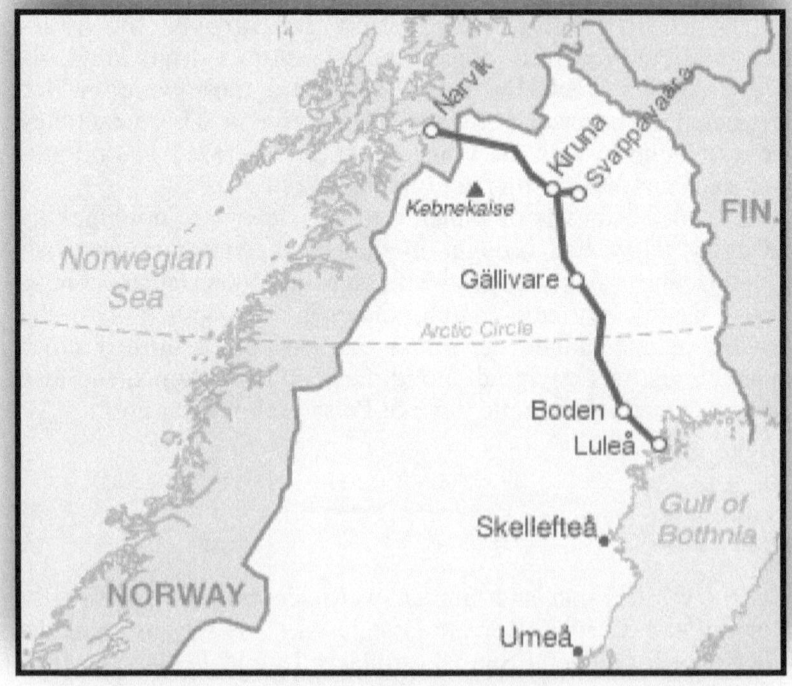

Figure 26: The Trans-Scandinavian Iron Ore Railroad

Council. The general was accompanied among others by his daughter, Zofia Wanda Leśniowska and his staff.

Bogdan knew that Zofia had just that month arrived from Warsaw, and came to serve her father as his secretary and personal aid. What Bogdan did not know was that during the outbreak of war, her father had charged her with establishing the Polish Resistance Movement, which she faithfully did out of her apartment in Warsaw. Bogdan also was not aware that she had smuggled critical resistance documents with her out of Poland on her trip to Paris.

Bogdan thought Zofia to be a lovely brunette woman. She was only twenty-six years old, but had already been married for three years to a military engineer in the Polish Army. Zofia was vibrant and in the prime of her life.

Bogdan was impressed that the general's daughter had also found time to serve in the Polish Red Cross, and was herself a lieutenant in the Polish Army.

Upon landing in London, Bogdan stayed with the transport aircraft as the others attended the conference. He methodically checked it over for the return flight. When the general did not arrive for the return flight with his daughter and the others, a concern came over him.

"Where is the general?" Bogdan asked Zofia.

"He was requested to have a private meeting with Mister Menzies," she replied. "Father said to wait for him, of course, as he did not expect to be long."

"Who is this Menzies?"

"I am not quite certain," she said, "and I found it quite odd. The Brits are very proud of their titles, and every gentleman introduced to father had his full title read aloud. Except for Mr. Menzies, they appeared to be very tight-lipped about exactly what his role was."

Major General Stewart Menzies, was, in fact, the third Chief of British Intelligence, MI6. He had been deputy to Chief Hugh "Quex" Sinclair who unfortunately had a prolonged battle with cancer. On October 29, 1939, just less than two months after the outbreak of the war, Sinclair underwent an emergency operation, and perished only six days later.

Menzies over took the leadership of the Secret Intelligence Service. As Sinclair's aid, Stewart Menzies had been very active in the establishment of Bletchley Park as the secret wartime home of the GC&CS, the British Government Code and Cypher School.

The delay gave Bogdan and Zofia a chance to become better acquainted. "So, where are you from, Pilot Bratajewski?" Zofia asked him.

"*Proszę*, call me Bogdan," he replied. "I am from a small village near Zakopane, in the Tatras."

"Yes, yes," Zofia smiled, "very beautiful. I myself was born not too far away in the town of Lwów, but it was called Lemberg back then when I was raised there. It was ruled by the Austrians at the time."

"Of course, and now the Russians have their filthy clutches on that beautiful city," said Bogdan. "It is why I wish for nothing more than to fight against these devils - the Russians or the Nazis. One is no less vile than the other."

"Patience, my countryman," Zofia said, "I am sure that with my father representing us among the Allies that they will lead us to regaining our homeland."

"Is it true that the English will not consider declaring war on Russia as your father seeks?" asked Bogdan. "Do they not see that they invaded our country as well as the Germans?"

Zofia said that a great rift had developed between her father and the British. "My father knows how evil Stalin is, every bit as much as Hitler. Yet, the English wish to not fight them as well."

"It appears the English wish not to fight anyone at all," said Bogdan. "It has been five months, with no real engagement whatsoever. What do they wait for? The *Luftwaffe* to come screaming out of the sky at them?"

"Let's talk of other things, Bogdan," Zofia said, "I understand that your brother was in the war as a member of the infantry."

"Yes, my brother Albin," he said, "but I do not know if he survived the Nazi onslaught. He was stationed at the citadel in Poznan, and I fear that he may have died there."

"Oh, my, I am very sorry you have to wrestle with not knowing," she said. "So, perhaps there is still a chance that he did indeed survive. You must cling to that thought, and not let the darkness of his possible death enter your thoughts."

"So I am trying," Bogdan said, "but I have to admit it is difficult. Do you not worry about your husband?"

"I am fortunate, for I have the luxury of knowing that he is safe," she said.

They chatted further, and the conversation eventually turned to Zofia's love of horses. She was an accomplished rider, and her face lit beautifully as she spoke of it.

After about an hour, a car pulled up from which General Sikorski emerged with another young man.

"This is your Menzies?" Bogdan asked Zofia.

"No, not at all," she replied. "I have never seen this man before."

He was a gawkish man, young and dressed out in a heavy tweed suit with no overcoat. His hair was covered in a heavy barber's cream, and combed to one side in almost perfectly diagonal straight lines. He looked about almost vacantly, taking everything in, as if the sight of the aircraft held unanalyzed secrets.

"Zofia, this is Professor Alan Turing," the general said in English to his daughter. "Professor, this is my daughter and personal secretary Zofia Leśniowska."

"Hello," said Turing awkwardly. "I am not actually a professor, people just seem intent on calling me that."

"It must be because it suits you, sir," said Zofia. "I am charmed to meet you."

"Should I add the professor to our manifest, General Sikorski?" asked Bogdan.

"Do no such thing," the general replied, "just prepare for us all to leave immediately."

"Including the professor?"

"Yes, Airman Bratajewski," General Sikorski said in frustration, "including the professor."

Soon they were off over the Channel on their way to Paris. Zofia tried to engage "Professor" Turing in smalltalk, which did not seem to come naturally to him. Finally, she drew from him that he was a scientist.

"Ah," she said, as if she had just struck gold, "my husband is an engineer. He is a man of science also, a scientist."

"An engineer is not a scientist," Turing corrected her.

"He considers himself a scientist," Zofia said.

"An orange may consider itself an apple," the *Professor* said, "but it still does not make for a good pie."

"So, then, Professor," Zofia said, "explain to me the difference between a scientist and an engineer, please."

"Well, it is actually quite obvious," Turing replied, "as a scientist discovers the laws of nature, and the engineer harnesses those laws into functions serving mankind."

"For the greater good," she replied, "does that not make the engineer of greater use to the world?"

"Not always," Turing said. "The scientist, in this case a chemist, discovers a certain compound is unstable, and the engineer produces bombs from it. Is that for the greater good?"

"So, precisely what sciences do you excel in examining, Professor," she inquired. "Chemistry?"

"Heavens, no," he replied with a laugh, "although I do find chemical processes fascinating. Extremely so. My favorite disciplines are mathematics and biology."

"How interesting a combination," Zofia said, "I never would think the two would have much in common."

The odds seemed to turn a switch on in Turing. He was no longer awkward, but quite natural as he expounded on his thoughts as to how the two disciplines were highly interrelated. Turing went on to give an expansive oral treatise on how biological functions are deeply rooted in numerical processes. He argued that the proper application of mathematical theories to biology could produce tremendous increases in the yield of crops and allow for dramatic advance in treating diseases.

General Sikorski took the opportunity to avoid this discussion and slipped into the cockpit with Bogdan. He buckled himself into the copilot's seat, and then watched as the shores of France crawled forward slowly under their view.

"When we get to Paris," the general began, "there will be an escort from our friends in the *Dieuxieme Bureau*. You see, Monsieur Gustave Bertrand asked for me to bring Professor Turing back to Paris with me. It appears he is greatly interested in the work of the three men you escorted from Poland, you remember, those mathematicians from Poznan."

"Of course, my General," Bogdan replied, "you mean Rejewski, Różycki and Zygalski. They are still in Paris?"

"Only Bertrand himself knows for sure," Sikorski said, "but they must not be far, as he will have only a car waiting, or so I am told."

"Well, these are three very good men," Bogdan said. "Must I plan on flying this man back to England?"

"No, that will not be necessary," said the general. "Mr. Menzies has assured me he will return commercially. He carries with him a gift for our Polish friends that is very valuable, I am told, so they wished to have him safely in our own hands in this direction. I also believe this man to be valuable to Britain's war effort, from the way they value him."

"I see," Bogdan said as he began his approach into Paris.

After they touched down and taxied to the hangar, none other than *"Bolek"* himself, Gustave Bertrand, was waiting.

Bertrand took the "Professor" away from the airstrip and to an elegant country manor house just outside Paris known as Chateau de Vignolles. Here, Bertrand had established his Polish guests with a codebreaking station, although they were without their reverse-engineered enigma devices, or the "*Bombas*" that had been used in Poland to crack the daily codes. Therefore, the process was laboriously slow, done by hand using Zygalski sheets punched from cardboard.

Professor Turing hand carried a briefcase which appeared to be quite heavy. The gift that Alan Turing brought for the Polish mathematicians was a complete set of Zygalski sheets that he had punched in metal according to the Polish plans shared months before with Dilly Knox under the Kabaty Woods. It was here at the Chateau de Vignolles, it has been reported, using those sheets, that the first Enigma messages of the Second World War were decoded.

Over the next two days, there was great discussion between Turing and the trio of exactly how the Poles mathematically discerned the wiring of the Enigma and the internal wiring of its rotors. Turing spoke no Polish, and they no English, but with some assistance from translators, they immersed themselves in the international language of mathematics.

Turing had not been at the Kabaty Woods conference. But Dilly Knox had shared with him all he had learned from the Poles in those two days. Now, Turing had several days to himself to more deeply understand all that these men had accomplished. Especially of interest to Turing was the design and fabrication of the Polish *Bomba* mechanical decrypting device. These details would aid him greatly when he returned to Bletchley Park, where he would put them to use to not only repeat the success of the Poles, but with the knowledge of their methods he and his team would greatly surpass their achievements.

It is said that the work ultimately conducted at Bletchley Park shaved at least two years off of World War II. This surely saved millions of lives. But one must think that, if given an additional two years, what other weapons might the scientists and engineers of Germany have devised? At the end of the war, they already had the V-2 flying rocket bombs, and the first operational jet fighters. It is known that the Nobel Prize winning physicist Werner Heisenberg had been working on producing a Nazi atomic bomb at the war's end, but without great success.

One might suppose given an additional two years or more, if the Germans had managed to perfect the atomic bomb, even if only after America had already done so, how this could have changed the length and possibly the outcome of the war. Only in thinking so, can one really understand just how valuable the work of these Polish codebreaker volunteers really was. It has also been assessed that their early breakthroughs may have saved Turing's team a full year in cracking the Enigma.

While Winston Churchill had lost his chance at interceding in the Winter War between the Soviets and the Finns, he was still the strongest advocate among the War Cabinet for mining the Leads of Norway. He was all the more enthusiastic after reading reports originating from the twins that the other route of shipping ore was not feasible because of the extensive icing at the port of Luleå, Sweden. Churchill's plan was approved by the War Cabinet and April 8, 1940, was set as the date for the Royal Navy to execute *Operation Wilfred* to mine the Norwegian coastal waters.

Beginning in early April, Einar and Gunnar began receiving new tasking to support *Operation Wilfred.* The twins were assigned on April 6, two days before the start of the operation, to assure that the Ofoten Railway was functional and the border with Sweden was open. While the Royal Navy expected no resistance from the Norwegians, they knew that they were taking pre-emptive measures in the waters of a neutral country. The *Ofotbahnen's* rail lines just might have to be used as an escape path to Sweden should any British forces come under attack and find themselves stranded.

The two brothers had ridden the rails to the border town of Riksgränsen, Sweden, carrying only one rucksack each. In these packs they carried typical mountain gear - ropes, crampons, pitons, and such. They also carried the contraband of a pistol, a radio set, and the set of five faux Enigma rotors. They confirmed that the rail border was open. They then hiked with the assistance of snowshoes across the overland path through the mountains to assure it could be used if the rail and road borders were sealed.

The twins trekked from Riksgränsen, Sweden to the Norwegian town of Bjørnfjell. This was a distance of just over two kilometers, just under a mile and a quarter, although along some very treacherous terrain. They avoided the border road crossings on the relatively flat high plateau, which were heavily manned by Swedish and Norwegian troops. Instead they traveled the mountain pass, which the twins determined to be navigable by foot, although its deep bed of snow definitely required the use of snowshoes.

Einar was still in good physical shape after the mountain crossing, but Gunnar was exhausted. They found shelter that night just uphill from the Bjørnfjell train station house, in a vacant mountain ski hut. It stood along the rise of Bjørnfjell mountain, in the clearing just along a deep patch of evergreens that lined a deep ravine.

It was the tradition in these mountains to leave the ski huts unlocked, and well stocked with dry wood, so that in case of any emergency, such as a blizzard, that they could be used for shelter by anyone who might become stranded there. This particular hut had no store of food, which they had hoped for, because the provisions they carried had already run low.

The ski hut was built in the traditional Nordic manner. The exterior was painted in the high visibility red with white trim that the Nordic peoples had long ago favored. After all, what value was shelter if you couldn't find it in the life threatening winds and blinding snows of this country's blizzards? Even in near whiteout conditions, the red ski hut could be readily seen.

This shelter, once entered, was not much more than a single room cabin lined with wood planking on the walls, ceiling and floor. It was amazingly insulated, despite each wall having large windows to allow in whatever winter light was available. It featured a cast iron wood burning stove, but no fireplace hearth, as the latter would allow too much loss of heat when not in use. The stove was used for both heating the hut and cooking. It rested on an L-shaped stone pad built into the walls and floor to protect their wood surfaces from its tremendous output of radiant heat. Catercorner from the stove across the room were two rows of bunks, four beds in all, built into the walls for the weary to rest upon. Each wooden perch was covered with what appeared to be hand made goose down cushions and blankets made from the furs of mountain animals. The most abundant of these skins were those of reindeer.

Einar built a fire in the wood stove to drive off the winter's chill while Gunnar emptied his rucksack to take inventory of what little food they carried. Tomorrow, they agreed, after tonight's meal and a full night's rest, they would survey the *Rallarveien,* an old railway workers' dirt road that descended down from the Bjørnfjell mountainside to the shoreline of the *Rombaksfjord* below.

This *Rallarveien* was a steeply inclined dirt work road that might just become the Royal Navy personnel's only route to freedom, should they become grounded while laying mines and were forced to climb it's rise to escape from being interred by the Norwegian home guard. The next morning the twins planned to descend it down to the fjord, then climb back up as grounded sailors might have to. They would return to this same ski hut tomorrow night.

The next morning came, and Einar and Gunnar awoke to snow. A bounty of beautifully refreshing flakes had fallen all night, blanketing the slopes in several more feet of powder and making that day's mission impossible to carry out. They called in their position via the wireless set that Gunnar had long ago mastered. They were told to stay in place until the weather cleared. The rest of the day was a winter holiday of sorts for them, as the twins. Their only duties were to forage for food and firewood. They decided to check the Bjørnfjell station house to see if any emergency food stores were provisioned there.

The mountain air was fresh and crisp. The snow continued to fall as they had never before seen. Heavy drifts of snow were blown across everything, up to six feet in some locations. At the station house, they indeed found a meager stash of provisions, enough food for perhaps two days, left for any poor souls caught unprepared in this upcountry in a blizzard. Einar deemed themselves to have met those requirements, and the twins absconded with the canned foods. It was then that they noticed in an unlocked side shed an old fashioned handcar. They made note of it and thought it might, at some point, carry them across the relatively high, flat plateau and through the border tunnel to the safety of Riksgränsen, Sweden, should it be needed.

Upon their hike back to the ski hut, Gunnar carried the food to the cabin while Einar scavenged the woods behind the cabin for fallen limbs they could burn for heat. His brother soon rejoined him with a bowsaw that had been hung on the wall next to the stove. Gunnar then searched for usable low, dead limbs that could be sawn. He found several and soon filled the small trough of space above Einar's arms not already filled with freely fallen limbs and boughs. His brother had already collected much, certainly enough to warm them through the night. This did not stop Gunnar from loading his arms further, to the point that Einar could not even see where he was walking.

In that way, they played like two boys who had never experienced this much pure powder. They joked and laughed, as the large flakes of the spring snow showed no signs of letting up. Then Einar said to his brother it was time to return to the ski hut for the night.

"Stay behind me, brother," Einar said to Gunnar as they began their walk back. His arms still overloaded, Einar said, "Walk where I do, step in the tracks of my snowshoes. In this heavy of snow, it will be much easier for you."

"Yes, Einar," Gunnar laughed, "one never knows what evil dangers lurk below this pristine powder."

Their walk was short, but at one point, Einar stepped upon snow that had drifted over ice which had frozen level across a small rocky ravine. The layer of thin ice had bridged the ravine and the snow heaped upon it hid its drop. As Einar stepped with his snowshoe onto its white powdery surface, the ice gave way. He sank hard into the virgin powder, and the rocky ravine below, causing his snowshoed leg to twist in a distorted manner.The impact had imparted enough force to twist Einar's snowshoe in a rotated fashion, and forcefully turn his ankle within it. He felt something in his lower leg give way. His pain was instant and such that his arms immediately scattered all the wood they had so painstakingly collected into the deep snow. The injury pained Einar to the point that it caused him to limp noticeably the rest of the way back to the hut. Night fell on that second day, and the heavy snows continued to fall.

Gunnar attended to his brother's injury, after which he returned to collect as much of the scattered firewood as possible. After he returned to the hut, Gunnar nursed Einar's ankle further. He applied alternating hot and cold compresses to alleviate his brother's pain and swelling. It was nothing too serious, either of them thought, just enough to hamper Einar's movements over the next few days. Certainly, they would not be negotiating their way down the steeply inclined *Rallarveien's* dirt trail the next day with his foot in this condition, even if the skies should suddenly clear.

As they laid their heads down to rest that night, the fire that Gunnar had stoked in the wood stove gave off a warmth that was comforting at times, and at others became overwhelming. Gunnar had just finished attending to his brother's ankle one last time, when he looked upon Einar's restive face. There, the radiance of the flickering tongues of flame glistened. "Einar, my brother," he said, "I am glad you were not more seriously injured."

"As am I, Gunnar," his brother replied.

"Thank you, Einar."

"For what, my brother?"

"I noticed how you always lead the way for me when we are out upon the mountain," Gunnar said. "You knew there were perils about, only to have me so stupidly mock you.Yet, despite this you went first."

Einar smiled, as the light from the stove's fire danced upon his dimpled face.

"You give me entirely too much credit Gunnar," he said. "I only went first so that my tracks would ease your travel. Besides, I should be thanking you for caring for my injured leg. All is good, my brother. Now, good night to you."

Gunnar looked lovingly at his twin. They had been through so much together in life, and they always had the comfort of knowing that whatever new challenges might arise, they would face them together.

"To attend to your suffering is no different than caring for my own, my brother," Gunnar said, "for we are like a mistakenly stamped coin, with both faces that appear to be the same, and in that way are struck from the same mettle. Good night, Einar."

43 Operation Weserübung

April 9, 1939

"If Britain must choose between Europe and the open sea, she must always choose the open sea."

Winston Spencer Churchill

The date for *Operation Wilfred*, Churchill's initiative to mine the Leads of Norway, had been set for April 8, 1940. Germany had not yet attacked Western Europe, and Churchill was intent on disrupting the delivery of his enemy's ore supply. He also thought it a good strategy to open a northern front against Germany. This would draw away resources from the Nazis' expected impending attacks on the low countries and France.

Whether by the chance of coincidence, or more covertly contrived, Hitler would disrupt Churchill's *Operation Wilfred* with his own. Germany's *Operation Weserübung* was to be initiated on the very same day. Hitler had become consumed with Churchill, the Nazi dictator's greatest critic throughout the thirties, especially with Winston's having re-taken the office of First Lord of the Admiralty on September 3, the same day Britain and France had declared war on the Nazi regime. Hitler knew just how impactful one man's determination could be, and that Churchill was the only real force standing between Germany's military might and England's capitulation to it.

Hitler was also concerned that Churchill would co-opt Britain's government into violating the neutrality of both Norway and Sweden. *Der Führer* had warned both countries that any intrusion by the Allied forces would be a reason for Germany to send forces to "protect" their sovereignty.

One such event had already taken place. In February of 1940, a British Navy destroyer had pursued the German tanker *Altamark* through the neutral waters of Norway. The British Navy had cause to believe the *Altamark* was transporting British sailors taken as prisoners from British ships lost in an earlier battle encounter with the German pocket battleship *Admiral Graf Spree*.

The *Altamark was* traveling through the Norwegian Sea on its return voyage to Germany. Its captain knew they were being pursued by the British, and intentionally entered Norway's neutral coastal waters. The Brits continued to pursue her, neutrality be damned. A British destroyer trapped the *Altamark* in a southern coastal fjord, boarded her, and rescued three hundred British sailors destined for German POW camps.

All this took place while nearby Norwegian Coastal Defense ships stood by, but did not interfere. This incident had infuriated Hitler. It very well may have been the impetus for his decision to expedite *Operation Weserübung,* for even then its planning was well underway. These coordinated invasions of Denmark and Norway would launch on April 8.

Perhaps there is another explanation for the curious timing of Hitler's Scandinavian invasions. The Nazis were, at this time, allied with Stalin's Soviet Union. The Soviets had earlier recruited multiple agents from British Universities in Cambridge, including "Kim" Philby, with the intent of installing them within the British Government. Philby himself would go on to the highest echelons of British Intelligence, all the while spying for the Soviets. Was there the possibility that Churchill's intention to mine the Leads, and *Operation Wilfred's* timing was obtained by Philby for Stalin, who then shared it with Hitler?

In any case, Hitler launched *Operation Weserübung,* on April 8, the same day that Britain's *Operation Wilfred* went into effect. Nearly the entire German Navy, the *Kriegsmarine*, took part in this massive attack, leaving their home ports in Germany that day.

The next morning, April 9, the attacks on Denmark and Norway would commence in the early morning hours. Hitler had offered "to protect the neutrality" of both countries. Denmark would be conquered within hours, as the country's King Christian X refused to fight against the invading Nazi forces. Denmark had ordered its troops to stand down as the *Wehrmacht* rolled across its borders.

However, in Norway, the Germans were in for something of a nasty surprise. Denmark's King Christian X's brother was King Haakon of Norway, who had become ruler of Norway with its independence in 1905. Unlike his brother, he was not willing to passively accept the invading Nazis.

Hitler had been in talks since the previous December with the former Norwegian Defense Minister, Vidkun Quisling. Quisling had been an ardent follower of Hitler's dogma, and equally detested the communist threat to his home country of Norway. He met in Berlin with Hitler on December 14, 1939, telling *Der Führer* that he would support a "peaceful" invasion of Norway.

Quisling went so far as to assure Hitler that his country's monarch, King Haakon, could be pressured into accepting the Nazi troops. However, over the next four months, King Haakon refused steadfastly to give in to increasingly direct pressure from Berlin.

To his great credit, King Haakon continued to stand strong through the invasion, and rejected all German demands that Norway accept the Nazi troops as "protectors against an Allied incursion of their neutrality."

Churchill's plan to mine the Leads seemed to be the exact incursion of Norway's neutral sovereignty that Hitler had predicted. On the eighth of April, as the *Vestfjorden* and other Norwegian coastal waters were beginning to be mined by British ships, and as the *Kriegsmarine* was *en route* from German ports, the Polish submarine *Orzel* sank the German troop transport ship *Rio de Janeiro* off the Norwegian southern coast. It was destined for Bergen. The transport ship had three hundred thirty invasion troops aboard, as well as a crew of fifty. Only one hundred eighty survived after their ship was sunk. The German survivors were rescued from the chilling waters by Norwegian Coastal Defense vessels.

The next morning, April 9, at approximately four o'clock, German warships sailed up the *Oslofjord* en route to the capital. There had been no declaration of war by Germany against Norway. As they came upon the Norwegian fortress *Oscarsborg*, they were illuminated with searchlights. The ships were greeted with defiant shore fire from the fortress' batteries. The lead invasion ship, the German cruiser *Blücher* was sunk, with as many as one thousand souls lost. Quisling's "peaceful" invasion had turned very hostile indeed.

The *Blücher's* sinking delayed the taking of Oslo just long enough for the royal family and the government of Norway to escape the capital along with all the gold in its treasury. After their departure, Vidkun Quisling effected a coup d'état just in time to welcome the delayed Nazi invaders when they arrived belatedly in the capital.

The *Kriegsmarine* invasions were coordinated along a stretch of the Norwegian coastline over a thousand miles long, and occurred in unison that morning. This massive naval group, broken down into five task forces for each of the major ports, was spotted leaving the Baltic by British planes. Incredibly, the British thought the armada was making a move to reach the open Atlantic, and the Royal Navy repositioned all her assets away from Norway's coast to the sea lanes in hope of intercepting the German vessels.

The actual effect was to leave open to the Nazi invaders the coastal waters of Oslo, Stavanger, Bergen, Trondheim, and Narvik. Near the *Lofoten* Peninsula, despite the British mines laid the day before, a group of ten German destroyers sailed through the *Vestfjorden* and into the smaller and tighter *Ofotfjord* surrounding Narvik.

These destroyers were met by two much smaller Norwegian Coastal Defense ships, who refused to surrender. The fighting that ensued was a monstrous mismatch of firepower, and the two Norwegian ships were soon sunk. However, the bravery of their captains and crew demonstrated her country's willingness to fight on.

In the early morning hours, atop the mountains, on the plateau leading to Sweden, Einar and Gunnar were awakened by the sounds of warfare in the fjords below. The sun had not yet risen. Gunnar volunteered to become a human crutch for Einar's tender ankle, but they were not able to move to any point overlooking the waters. For in addition to Einar's ankle, the sky had been filled once more with a heavy white wall of snow that would surely have obscured their vision. It was the shuddering sounds of the naval engagement that were enough to fill them both with horror at the thought of the lives surely dying in the depths of the fjords below them.

Occasional flashes of light would reflect in blazing ripples across the low, heavily laden gray clouds. Amidst the falling snow's veil of purity followed the echoed booming of shells through the mountains.

Then the mournful explosions of the projectiles impact, mixed with the screech of wrestled metal was heard. Gunnar would later contend that he could hear the screams of the sailors themselves amongst the cacophony of sounds reaching their ears.

"O war! Thou son of hell, Whom angry heavens do make their minister..." Gunnar solemnly quoted Shakespeare aloud.

Einar did not fashion a guess, nor did Gunnar offer the answer as *"Henry VI Part 2"* as the mirth of the game of their previously peaceful life had been painfully stripped of them.

Brigand MacAlvor was at his home along the Tay in Dundee when he first heard the news of Germany invading Norway over the wireless. His heart, which had already been heavy with the knowledge that he, himself, had hand delivered his own twin boys to Wincer Wells, was then lit aflame with a raging panic. He called to London, to Wells' office at the Saint Ermin's Hotel, and was surprised when his call was patched through. Wells answered with a singular word, "Yes?"

"Where are my boys, Wincer?" Brigand pounced.

The silence of Wells assessing the unexpected voice and its question followed, but only for a half measure.

"They are perfectly safe, Brigand, relax," Wells answered.

"Where are they?" asked Brigand again.

"In the mountains," Wincer said, with Brigand knowing he would not offer much more over the telephone.

"I am coming to London," Brigand stated.

"Stay where you are, my friend," cautioned Wells, a fresh tension coiling in his voice, "we have been in touch with them. There is nothing for you to do here, now."

"If ever you needed my knowledge of those waters," Brigand stated, "it must be now."

"Sorry, Brigand," answered Wells, his voice tight and tinny in the handset's earpiece, "but the Royal Navy has that all quite under control at this point. Lord knows that I don't need a feverish father roaming about the halls down here just now. The boys are in the safest location in which they possibly could be. They are as safe as the Crown Jewels in the Tower."

"Tell me exactly where they are, Wincer," responded Brigand, "or I will come there and thrash it out of you, damn you."

The voice in the handset became absolutely taut, like the overstretched wire of a musical instrument.

"If I shall so much as see your face, then I will have you arrested and thrown in the brig," Wells threatened. Then a tense silence followed, which Wells, himself, finally pierced, feeling he had pushed back entirely too firmly against his long-time asset. "The twins are in hiding outside of the mountain town of Bjørnfjell, one station away from the border with Sweden. They are safe, and less than a mile away from freedom."

Then Brigand heard a click as the phone disconnected. He realized that Wells had just given him vital information over the open phone line for which Wincer could be brought up on charges. He suspected that Wells only did so because he knew Brigand would not rest his mind until he had some concrete information on which to sustain himself.

That information, passed to him by Wells, was intended to quell the dark thoughts of his mind. Instead, it only became the seed of a thousand scenarios in which his sons were maimed or killed by the German invaders.

After the attack in the fjords below had raged, and the sounds were that of the Nazi ships unloading in the harbor, only then did Gunnar and Einar discuss what they should do. One option was to take the train across the border into Sweden, but the trains had stopped running. The other option was to take the workers' road down to the fjord below, but Einar's leg nixed that. Even if they could in the heavy snow, they would likely be spotted from the sea along the shoreline. Besides, there was no hope of getting back to Skrova with the German destroyers in the *Ofotfjord.* Even under the cover of darkness, the odds of surviving that were minuscule. It was also entirely possible that the Nazis had already landed at Skrova, in order to secure the *Vestfjorden,* thought the boys. In reality, the Nazis had not.

Another option was to travel by foot to the Swedish border at Riksgränsen, but Einar's injury also nixed that play.

In the end the twins decided to take a risk and radio London using encrypted morse code, as they had been trained. They waited until the cover of darkness, and engaged the emergency radio frequency and began typing out their extraction request code, with their emergency codeword *"Gemini"*.

Gunnar stopped and listened to the hollow hobbling pitch of the unresponsive radio ether. Then an immediate acknowledgement code came back and was decoded by him as HOLD FAST, STOP.

The twins waited, as the static whined with a spiraling signal that seemed to last forever. After that eternity another coded message followed, STILL IN LAST PEW STOP.

Gunnar recognized Wells' codeword pew for position. "Still in last reported position?" was being asked.

Gunnar tapped out the answer in the affirmative. Soon a message was transmitted, which Gunnar then decrypted.

STAY IN PEW, AND BLESS ALL SOULS ATTENDING MASS STOP was received. A few minutes later the last message followed, FORGIVE ALL HERETICS IN THE CHOIR LOFT STOP TAKE CONFESSION STOP KEEP OFF THE ALTAR STOP TAKE PENANCE OF SAINT SIMON IF NEEDED FULL STOP.

After decoding the message, the boys recognized Wincer Wells elaborate codewords that had been drilled into them over and over in the Highlands of Scotland. Each phrase had meaning, if one knew the keywords.

They had previously confirmed to London that they were still near the Ofoten train station atop Bjørnfjell Mountain.

STAY IN PEW meant maintain your current position.

BLESS ALL SOULS ATTENDING MASS meant report the quantity (mass) of all those enemy troops arriving at your position.

KEEP OFF THE ALTAR meant don't use the rails. *"Think Altar Rails"* they remembered Wells telling them.

FORGIVE ALL HERETICS IN THE CHOIR LOFT meant the enemy are taking to the mountains, do not engage.

TAKE CONFESSION meant help is on the way.

Finally, TAKE THE PENANCE OF SAINT SIMON IF NEEDED meant for them to extract through Stockholm (Saint Simon Stock) as required. Since that was coupled with KEEP OFF THE ALTAR that would require a climb through the overland pass into Sweden.

That journey was out of the question given the overnight heavy snowfall, which would make the climb quite treacherous. Still there was the injury to Einar's leg that kept them from making that climb even had conditions been favorable.

"What are we going to do?" Gunnar asked his brother.

"Shut down the wireless set, Gunnar," said Einar. "We are going to do just what we were instructed to do. We will sit tight and monitor the railway station. I can watch it from here with our field glasses."

"Do we keep the fire in the hut going?" Gunnar asked.

"Do you want us to freeze?" responded Einar.

"Won't they spot our smoke?"

"Not in the dark, and not until they get here," said Einar glibly. "We will get our things together and pre-position our rucksacks in the woods along the ridge. If someone comes and spots our smoke we will have enough time to get there, gather our things and move out."

"I am scared," admitted Gunnar. "We could die up here. Especially if we are forced to stay exposed to the elements."

"Be not afraid, my brother," Einar consoled Gunnar. "We are well trained. We know the Brits have assets here in the *Vestfjorden*, or at least nearby. Were they not mining the fjords' waters only yesterday? The message said help is on the way. We stay here until that help arrives. I am sure it will be soon."

"What happens should we be captured?" asked Gunnar.

"We are just a pair of Norwegians from Skrova doing a climb for recreation when we became stranded by the weather in the mountains, yes? Not very unusual at all, for here."

"The radio? How will we explain that"

"I will stash it in one of the rucksacks. We can easily get it should we need to report anything at all to London."

"What about your ankle, Einar?"

"It is already getting better," Einar lied.

"And yet you limp so terribly," said Gunnar.

"By tomorrow it will be much, much better."

"We are again running low on food. We have already consumed those provisions stored in the Bjørnfjell station house."

"Stop worrying, my brother," said an exasperated Einar. "Tomorrow is a new day. The snow is already easing. In the morning we will find something else to hold us over. We have my pistol, if necessary we can always hunt a reindeer."

"Yes, that would feed us for quite some time," chuckled Gunnar, "although the *Sámi* would be very upset with you."

Einar laughed, and both men tried to suppress what they were actually thinking.

After several seconds, Gunnar finally said to his brother, "Don't you find it odd about Wincer Wells' code?"

"Odd? How so?" asked Einar.

"Well, we are Lutheran, Wincer is Church of England, and yet his codes for this trip all are based in Catholicism, aren't they?"

"I never would have even thought about that." Einar said. "You think about things too deeply, Gunnar."

"Well, I mean taking confession," Gunnar said, "that is surely a Catholic sacrament. Also, of all things, referencing Saint Simon Stock? I had never heard of Saint Simon Stock. I had to look him up. He was an Englishman and leader of the Carmelite Order that the Blessed Virgin Mary was reported to have bestowed a visitation upon during the Middle Ages."

"Yes, those Papists surely are devoted to the Mother of Christ," Einar said, as if somehow appeasing his own brother's insatiable curiosity. "By the bye, where does one even go to look up unknown Catholic Saints?"

"You remember that day just before we left that you and father went for one last sail without me on the *Nordlys*?"

"Yes, I remember it well," Einar said. "you said you had something terribly urgent to do that day."

"Well, that day," Gunnar said, "Mother took me to Saint Margaret's Church in Barnhill."

"They are not even Catholic, are they?"

"No, actually they are not," said Gunnar, "Church of Scotland, but the minister there was very knowledgable in the Catholic saints and knew many of the details of Saint Simon Stock's life."

"This was more important to you than spending one last lovely afternoon upon the North Sea Coast with father and me?"

The words of his brother clawed at him, but Gunnar did his best to ignore the hurt hidden amongst them.

"Of course," said Gunnar. "Suppose that these messages were intercepted by the enemy. Assume they would question us, if captured, on the Penance of Saint Simon? What would we say?"

"Ok, so who is this Saint Simon Stock?" inquired Einar.

"He was an Englishman in the thirteenth century, a Prior of the Carmelites who the Blessed Mother is said to have appeared to."

"And who are the Carmelites?"

"A group of Catholic monks in the Holy Lands that lived on Mount Carmel. When the Holy Lands fell back to the Muslims again during the Crusades, these monks moved to Europe. Saint Simon was among their number."

"So, what was this Saint's penance from Our Lord's Mother?" Einar inquired.

"He and the Carmelites were told to wear scapulars," said Gunnar.

Einar's face was riddled with confusion. He had never heard the term."What, exactly, my brother is a scapular?"

"It used to be a garment, part of the Monk's habit, their mode of dress," explained Gunnar. "It was made up of a heavy woolen piece of brown cloth covering the chest, another covering the back, and two strips connecting them together over the shoulders, hence the name scapulars. The wool was heavy and irritating, and for some reason was always died brown."

"Hardly much of a penance," quipped Einar. "So when we are sweating out a Nazi interrogation, and they ask us where, exactly, are our scapulas, what do you intend to tell them then?"

"Simple," answered Gunnar, "they are in my rucksack?"

"Really?" asked the incredulous Einar, adding, "They?"

"Yes," Gunnar replied, matter-of-factly. "I purchased two. One for me and the other for you, dear brother."

"You were keeping these a secret from me?" Einar asked.

"I did not know how you would take this, after all we are not Catholic," Gunnar explained.

"I will take all the help I can, at this point," Einar admitted. "Let us wear them, if not as tribute to the Mother of Our Lord, than as a remembrance of our own mother."

Gunnar then ruffled through his rucksack until finding the two scapulars, and handed one to his brother.

"Are they both the same?" Einar asked.

"Exactly, my brother."

"But they are not large garments," Einar said, "they are only two little pieces of brown woolen cloth connected by entwined cloth strips which are no more than string. What are these designs?"

"These are modern day scapulars," Gunnar answered. "They have shrunk over time. The designs are the Sacred Heart of Jesus, with the Crown of Thorns wrapped around it, to be worn over the chest. The cloth to go over the back has the Immaculate Heart of Mary pierced with a dagger."

"The dagger represents what, exactly?"

"Mary's sorrows," Gunnar explained, "for how Her Son was rejected by men and put to death on the cross. And for how even today mankind rejects the complete acceptance of Jesus and his teachings."

"To wear these scapulars has what benefit?" Einar asked. "Did they tell you that?"

"Yes. The Blessed Mother told Saint Simon that the soul of anyone who died wearing one would be saved."

"Then, by all means, there is no question we must both wear one," Einar reaffirmed, "as we both can use all the blessings we can get. And as you have gone to such great trouble to procure them for us, we will each wear them. After all, we should each have the same blessings, as we are both cut from the same bolt of cloth, are we not?"

"In some ways not," Gunnar grudgingly admitted.

The answer surprised Einar at first, but then he had to admit that his brother had a valid point.

"Well, thank God for that, my brother," Einar said as he softly smiled, "for nothing could be more boring that living each day with an exact copy of myself."

"I like to think," said Gunnar, "that we each live with the other halves of ourselves. We each have strengths and weaknesses. I know that I never feel whole when I am away from you, Einar."

"Nor do I, Gunnar," his brother concurred.

It was a subject they had discussed often. They felt closer than mere brothers could ever begin to comprehend. They were split from a single egg of their mother's, forever bonded in that way, destined to be together until their deaths, of that they were each certain.

It was only then, as they chatted so casually, that each brother came to realize the depths of the dilemma in which they were trapped. Together alone on an Arctic mountainside upon which Nazi *Gebirgsjäger* elite mountaineering troops were ascending. Of all the possible outcomes that awaited them, they both knew this to be a very serious situation, indeed.

If they were to stay in the sheltered hut which they had found, they surely would be captured by the Germans. If they took to the most remote parts of the mountain to evade the enemy mountaineers, they could possibly freeze to death.

They each placed the scapulars under their garments, so that the rough wool patches pressed up directly against their tender young skin.

That night Gunnar and Einar took turns watching the Bjørnfjell railroad station house, but noted no train traffic whatsoever. When Einar slept, Gunnar watched. When Einar watched, Gunnar worried, for he could not possibly relax enough to begin to sleep.

In Paris, on the evening of April 9, Bogdan Bratajewski, the personal pilot of General Władysław Sikorski, the Commander-in-Chief of the Polish Army-in-Exile, was called to his general's office. There, the pilot took an assignment from the leader. They spoke in Polish, as Bogdan's French was slow in developing.

"Tomorrow morning," said the general, "we will fly to the town of Malestroit, near Vannes. Prepare accordingly."

"Yes, sir," Bogdan replied. They had a respectful relationship, but he had learned to be at ease in the general's presence.

"You know of the Polish Independent Podhale Rifle Brigade?" Sikorski asked.

The Brigade had formed in France in late 1939. It consisted of approximately five thousand Polish troops that escaped the country during the Nazi onslaught, as well as numerous patriotic emigres who had volunteered to fight for their homeland. In Polish, the group's name was the *Samodzielna Brygada Strzelców Podhalańskich.*

"Yes, of course, my General," replied Bogdan, "as you know, they are named after the elite Podhale Rifles of the Polish Army. This area of Podhale includes my own hometown in Southern Poland. Many of these men escaped, just as I did through Romania. Like me, they headed here towards France. Why is it that you ask?"

General Sikorski twitched his fine mustache, as if it trembled with indecision, which was something that Bogdan had never before seen in the man.

"Tomorrow, my hand will have the honor of presenting the Brigade's colors and deployment orders for General Zygmunt Bohusz-Szyszko. However, I plan to leave you there and have another pilot fly me back to Paris," General Sikorski replied.

"Sir," Bogdan responded, "I am honored you would leave me with my countrymen. Do you desire that I fight alongside them?"

"No, no, you are far too valuable to me, Airman Bratajewski," Sikorski said, drawing out his words with deliberate suspense, "but I am expecting you to thoroughly inspect the newest of the Brigade's acquisition on my behalf."

"And that is what, my General," asked Bogdan, "a new piece of artillery? Perhaps an aircraft, that would make sense for me to stay behind…"

"More vital," General Sikorski replied. "It is a very important soldier."

"What single soldier could be so important to you, General Sikorski?"

Upon Bogdan offering up these words, the general said nothing, as if objecting to this airman's questioning him in any manner. General Sikorski raised his head slightly, his mustached nose angled to the ceiling, as his eyes slid in their slits to examine his pilot.

"Perhaps not so much to me, but very important to you, I would think. I have come to learn that in the last few days that your brother, Albin, has joined the Highland Brigade."

"Albin is alive? Praise be to our Lord!" exclaimed Bogdan.

"Yes, Private Albin Bratajewski had, along with a few of his brigade members, crossed the *Carpathians* to freedom. They took a long time in making their way to France, but as soon as they did they reported to General Bohusz-Szyszko. Tomorrow, you will attend while I present the colors and these important orders to their camp outside the town of Malestroit in Brittany. After which, I will return to Paris and you will stay behind for a short reunion with your brother."

Bogdan beamed at having the heaviness and uncertainty of his brother's status lifted. He had long imagined Albin's body lying riddled with bullets, killed defending the homeland.

"Thank you, General Sikorski, but what is so urgent that I must stay behind and see him tomorrow? I know it is my personal duty is to pilot you back here safely. I can always take a train later to see my brother."

General Sikorski raised his arm as if to indicate he would hear no more of this nonsense. He cleared his throat softly.

"As I have said, tomorrow you will fly me and these orders to Malestroit," Sikorski repeated, this time more sternly. "Since you question me, I must remind you that I will be communicating the brigade's deployment orders, as well. Airman Bratajewski, please answer a simple question for me. When you are at leisure here in France, where do you choose to spend your time? You speak almost no French, so you must spend your time with other Poles, yes?"

Bogdan was surprised by this line of questioning.

"I believe you are aware that I enjoy spending time with the other Polish pilots," he said.

"You mean the Polish *fighter* squadrons, Airman Bratajewski?"

"Yes, my General," Bogdan admitted.

Bogdan had been seeking out his countrymen and fellow pilots. He sought nothing more than to one day fly alongside them and engage the *Luftwaffe* with them, although these men looked down on him as a lowly transport pilot. They thought of him as race car drivers would consider one who drove a bus. Their anger was always at the surface because in France there was no outlook for any of these pilots to join the battle against the enemy. So instead, they mocked Bogdan.

General Sikorski said nothing, instead his eyes scoured over Bogdan with disappointment as a father's would over a wayward son.

"These are brave and highly skilled pilots," said General Sikorski, "but they have become rancorous hooligans here in France. Their behavior is not desirable, it speaks ill of we Poles. Now, their reprehensible ways appear to be rubbing off on you, as well."

Sikorski was sternly reprimanding his pilot. Bogdan felt perhaps he had become a bit too familiar with the general, and feared that Sikorski might sack him permanently as his pilot. Yet this was not to be. General Sikorski had merely intended to get the attention of Bogdan.

"My General," said Bogdan, "forgive me, I do not mean to question your orders. As for these fighter pilots, they are only greatly bored. The French will not allow them to fly. They want only to take to the air and prepare to engage the Nazi *Luftwaffe*, but no one will allow them to do so. This frustration is at the root of their behavior."

"Yes, you may be correct," said the general, "but even so, when I give you an order, I expect you not to question it. Not even in private, let alone soil it by your public exploits. You are to no longer fraternize with these pilots, do you understand? Tomorrow you will deliver me and these orders that I will be carrying to General Bohusz-Szyszko, and then stay behind with your brother, as I have ordered."

"Yes, sir, my General!"

General Sikorski had intentionally been excessively stern to keep his young pilot respectful of the chain-of-command.

"Since at least you were not so bold as to question me on the nature of these deployment orders," the general continued, "I will share with you their essence. The Polish Highland Brigade are to prepare to deploy along with French infantry brigades and elements of the French Foreign Legion to the area around the port of Narvik in the Arctic Circle. They will fight the Nazis in Norway."

A look of shock overcame Bogdan as he absorbed the moment. Albin was being rewarded with what he himself desired. His younger brother was returning to war against the Nazis.

"Narvik! You mean the same port that the *Kriegsmarine* captured only this morning? Albin will be going to fight the Nazis at Narvik!" Bogdan echoed with amazement. "He is so fortunate. I envy him so."

"Well, Airman Bratajewski," said General Sikorski, "only this morning you moped about fearing your brother was dead. Now you celebrate his going into battle against the Nazis where he very well could be killed. Perhaps you are envious? Or perhaps a little mad, eh? In either case, you should get no ideas of joining him. You are needed, very much, by my side. However, not for the next two days. I have arranged for your brother to be granted leave. I am also advancing you two weeks pay, which you can pick up with this memorandum from the paymaster. Enjoy your time with your brother."

General Sikorski handed Bogdan a hand-written memorandum torn from the top of a thick printed pad.

"I am stunned by your generosity, my General," replied Bogdan.

"*Nie ma za co! (It is nothing!)* It is settled. You will take your brother to town and enjoy his companionship over dinner. I only hope his French is better than your own. If not, you both may starve."

Both men laughed at Sikorski's joke. The general then reached out to pat Bogdan on the arm, almost as a father would a son.

"*Dziękuję*, my General," said Bogdan, thanking him. "You are truly too kind to me."

Here, the general allowed the moment to linger for a second, so not to be perceived as brushing away his pilot's gratitude.

"Well," General Sikorski then added, "you know what the proverb from our homeland says, *'Wait too long and the opportunity will vanish.'* One never knows just what the future may bring. Enjoy your time with your brother, Albin. Just return to me after you have spent your time with him. We have much to do together."

"I am very indebted to you, sir," said Bogdan. "And I respect you so much that I would fly you straight into Berlin itself and land in your plane in the Tiergarten, if you should request that of me. Yet, I hope before the war is over you might release me so that I also might fight the Nazis, myself, at some point. Just as my brother will soon be doing."

"I promise you, my young airman, that I will do that," at this point General Sikorski smiled warmly, his pencil-thin mustache, bowing gently upon his smile, much more warmly than its usual rigid formality. "When the time is right, Bogdan, when the time is right."

44 The First Naval Battle of Narvik

April 10, 1940

"If Hitler invaded hell I would at least make a favourable reference to the devil in the House of Commons"

Winston Spencer Churchill

Overnight Gunnar and Einar had, between them, spotted about two hundred Norwegian troops passing through Bjørnfjell Station. They came from the fallen garrison in Narvik, no doubt, and were working their way north to join up with Norwegian units known to be in that vicinity. They were all on foot, as no trains had run, a sign that the Germans had not yet secured the railway. Einar and Gunnar had to decide if they were going to evacuate to Sweden or stay put as Wincer Wells' message had directed. They decided to follow the instructions from London.

The twins then decided to take a chance early the next morning, while it was still very dark, to see if more provisions could be found at the next station house down the tracks at Old Bjørnfjell. They had decided to take only one of the two rucksacks, the one which contained the wireless set and the pistol and their mountaineering gear. The other rucksack Einar left well hidden in the ravine behind the cabin. In it were the five faux rotors given to them by Wincer Wells and the British passports. The twins determined they could not afford to be caught with these highly incriminating items of contraband should they become captured by the German troops working their way up along the Ofoten Railway from Narvik.

The wireless set in the rucksack that they carried clearly implicated them as spies, but the twins could not bring themselves to abandon their only link to London. This would become a necessity should they need to be evacuated by British naval forces. Besides, it could always be hidden or discarded.

Since there were no Germans in Bjørnfjell yet, the twins felt safe leaving that one remaining rucksack hidden in the overgrowth in the side of the ravine. After he had re-stashed the stay-behind rucksack in its hiding place, Einar slipped the other rucksack containing the wireless set and the pistol over his shoulder and led his brother through the deep snow over to the station house in Bjørnfjell.

This short snowshoed trek nearly convinced the twins to give up entirely on the idea of following the tracks down to Old Bjørnfjell, as Einar's leg caused him incredible pain with every step. This was despite Gunnar crutching him at times. Even after his brother took the weight of the rucksack from him, Einar's pain did not cease.

Then, Einar recalled the handcar that they had found the day before in that shed on a side track. Nothing more than a wooden platform no larger than the size of a raft, the handcar was mounted upon steel wheels powered with a hand operated pump mechanism that looked much like a children's teeter-totter. The car also had a leg activated manual brake.

The boys were at first unable to free its frozen brake mechanism in the darkened shed. After several tries, Einar searched the shed and found a box of long burning flares. At first they used one within the shed for light. Then Gunnar thought of thawing the brake with it, and they both hoped this would allow the cart to move. It did not.

Einar rested his aching leg by sitting on the forward half of the flat bed of the handcar as his brother toiled with the flare. After thawing the brake, Gunnar pushed the other side with all of his might without any effect at all. He finally thought that the steel wheels of the car had frozen solid. He used the concentrated heat of the burning, smoking flare to thaw them. Its use was risky, as it could have been easily spotted in the darkness as the shed doors were open, but they were not concerned with being spotted by any Norwegian troops, although they had not seen any more of these soldiers in the hours after sunrise.

Half an hour and three more flares later, the handcar was moving. Gunnar had one flare lit under each of the cart's four rail wheels, and after some time was able to roll it out of the shed. He ditched three of the burning flares outside in a deep drift of snow, where they would continue to burn until they consumed themselves. The fourth flare Gunnar would take with him to the handcar.

The downward incline was slight, but enough that once the car began moving, Gunnar was able to hop on, stand upright, and pump the teeter-totter handrails that powered the car. Einar lay reclined on the front side next to the rucksack. His injury kept him from assisting his brother in propelling the vehicle. Gunnar's foot trapped the burning flare beneath it as he pumped the car.

They began picking up a slight momentum, running along the side track, until it came to the point where it joined onto the main track. There, the handcar slammed violently into something neither twin could see nor had expected. Gunnar at the handcar's rear was thrown forward onto the slowly undulating handrails, bruising his side, but only mildly.

Einar, who had been in the front, was thrown clear from the car onto the rails below. He howled in a fresh onset of pain to his leg and ankle, but quickly composed himself.

"Are you all right, my brother?" Gunnar asked after recovering from his own unexpected lunge forward. He rubbed his own ribs which had struck the still icy steel handrails.

"I am fine, brother," said Einar. "This damned handcar must have run up against a closed rail. There must be a manual way to allow this car to transit onto the main rail line. If you can find the rail switch under all this snow, look nearby it. There should be a long metal bar to stick into it and manually throw it open."

"Maybe this is God's way of telling us this is not a good idea!" Having said this, Gunnar assisted his brother back onto the front of the handcar. He then searched the snow covered ground, first using the light of the flare, and then using his removed snowshoe as an ineffective shovel. After several minutes, he did finally find the switch, and several more minutes later located the steel bar needed to throw it.

While his brother worked to open the track switch, Einar hobbled to collect the rucksack from the snow. It had been jarred clear of the handcar, but had luckily landed in a deep drift of powder. Einar returned it to his side of the cart, where he would tend to it as they soon travelled down the mountain.

After the track switch was thrown open, Gunnar asked Einar again, "Do you really think this is a good idea, brother? What if a locomotive should come upon us while we are on the main line? Who knows what dangers we may not be anticipating."

Einar appeared eager to get moving again. He was massaging his leg, and was unaccustomed to allowing his brother to perform the manual labor that he would otherwise be doing.

"I heard you before, brother," Einar said. "Now is not the time to second guess our plan, Gunnar, as we finally appear ready to roll again. My leg is throbbing, and sitting here in the cold only makes things worse. We have seen not a single train since yesterday's attack in the fjord. It is very likely the Germans have disabled the rail lines altogether to keep the Norwegians from using it to their own advantage. Once the Nazis gain its full control, they will begin the trains running again. But they are not even here in Bjørnfjell yet. It is time for us to go, my brother."

Gunnar felt embarrassed by his brother's gentle reprimand. He climbed aboard the car bed, stood upright and began pumping the handrails.

The handcar transitioned smoothly onto the main tracks. With each of Gunnar's downward strokes, the handrails dived deeper and required less of his energy. Soon the brothers were moving near effortlessly through the early morning alpine darkness.

The ride down the mountain tracks to the Old Bjørnfjell station was just under four kilometers, or roughly two and a half miles. However, there were two short tunnels separated only by a brief interlude of open air track between the two stations.

As he continued to pump the handrails, Gunnar's sweat collected under his insulated clothing. There it slowly began to chill. Soon, he was drenched in an icy bath from his effort beneath his outerwear.

Gunnar's labors continued and they soon came to the opening of the first tunnel leading to Old Bjørnfjell. Within it, the flare trapped beneath his feet glowed an eerily reflected orange off the chiseled granite walls. At the same time Gunnar's labors increased slightly.

Halfway through the tunnel the burden of his efforts lightened, and soon Gunnar seemed to be barely pushing on the handrails. The handcar had cleared the highest point of their transit, and soon after would exit the tunnel in descent.

The frigid air that washed over them when they re-emerged was alive with the freshness of the countryside. The solvated scent of the pines seemed to burn as Gunnar drew it in deep breaths into his still panting lungs.

Before long they were re-immersed in the second tunnel's darkness. The pace of the handcar was picking up as the tracks began a slow descent.

The handcar re-emerged from the second tunnel and soon Old Bjørnfjell Station would be upon them.

"Slow the cart, brother," Einar yelled.

Gunnar heard him and found the footbrake in the glow of the flare whipping about in the darkness of the pre-dawn Arctic night. The dawn would be upon them soon, but as of yet offered no light for assistance to the twins.

The handcar hurtled past the Old Bjørnfjell Station.

"Gunnar," Einar yelled, "you've missed the station. Stop the cart."

"I cannot," responded Gunnar. "I am standing with all my weight on the brake and it is barely slowing."

In fact, the cart would continue to pick up speed as it descended the slope of the mountainside.

"It's all right brother," yelled Einar, "we will stop at Hundalen Station next."

After a short period, the handcar then came upon the *Norddalsbron,* or the *Norddal Bridge,* that spanned a deep ravine. This had been the very bridge they had reconnoitered for potential sabotage by the Allied commando force that was never sent. Amidst the span, Gunnar realized that the first glimmering haze of the Arctic dawn light was filtering into their surrounding darkness. Gunnar could for the first time see the rolling but rocky landscape that surrounded them. He could make out the steep ravine over which the bridge spanned.

"That flare has done us well," yelled Einar at his brother, "time to rid ourselves of it, Gunnar."

Gunnar agreed and used his foot to kick it from the car's bed. He watched as it hit the decking of the bridge, bounced free and fell spiraling like a wounded aircraft into the stream below.

In the mountains of the Arctic Circle, April was not yet spring, but an echoed remnant of winter's fury. When the weather warmed and the snowpacks melted, the stream under the *Norddal Bridge* would rage with a fury of its own. Its waters raced downhill as rapidly as possible to join the fjord below.

Both brothers knew this part of the Ofoten Rail line with utmost precision. Every upcoming landmark that they had scouted was clear in their minds, although still obscured somewhat in their vision by the slowly lifting darkness.

"We will be coming upon another tunnel in a short bit," yelled Einar, and true to his words the handcar became enveloped in a stiller form of darkness, which closed more tightly around them without the reflected light of the flare. Its air lacked the scent so noticeable upon the open breeze, for there was none, and there was no breeze. Only the stale smell of frozen water that clung to the barren rock greeted them as they progressed.

"We will be coming upon Hundalen Station quickly once we come out of this tunnel," said Einar. His words echoed around them both like muffled explosions. Gunnar, who neared exhaustion from continuously working his arms, found the pumping much easier. Then the handcar picked up momentum, and the handrails required no pressure on the downstroke. After that, they seemed to pull Gunnar's arm violently on the uptake.

"Stop pumping Gunnar," said Einar as the car picked up speed from the descent along the incline. "Use the foot brake to control our speed."

Gunnar could not find the brake with his foot in the tunnel's darkness. He wished now that they had not jettisoned the still burning flare over the side of the *Norddal Bridge*. The handcar continued to pick up speed. Just then they saw a hazy spot of light that drew larger as they approached it. For a second Gunnar feared it was an approaching train, but soon realized it to be only the gray square of ambient morning light at the tunnels opening.

"The brake, Gunnar! Apply the brake now!" screamed Einar as they exited the tunnel.

In the morning's light, Gunnar found and re-applied his leg to the brake. It was nothing more than a wooden arm covered in leather. As Gunnar put the weight of his body on the wood, the arm pressed the leather pad onto the wheels, slowing the handcar somewhat, but not enough for their having any hope of stopping it completely in time to make the Hundalen Station.

The morning haze of light as they emerged the tunnel had also revealed a drastically different landscape. The track ran along a ledge bevelled into a dramatically plunging mountainside slope. They were no longer in the high plateau, but careening along the mountainside which dropped down precipitously from the Bjørnfjell peak overlooking the *Rombaksfjord*. Their speed was increasing, despite the depressed foot brake. The icy wind howled over them. The evergreen trees that had grown on the slopes below the track sped past them. The cart began to rack side to side as its wheels shifted upon the curved track.

Gunnar's leg had become strained, and as he lifted his weight off of it to rest its muscles, the handcar picked up even more speed. The double handrails pitched up and down in a greater frequency in a sort of devil's dance with the increasing grade of the mountain descent.

"Gunnar, we are going too fast!" yelled Einar. "You must slow us with the brake!"

Gunnar then stomped with the already exhausted muscles of his leg onto the brake. The handcar again slowed somewhat, but still travelled downhill at a dangerous rate.

"Slower, Gunnar, slower still," yelled out his brother.

"I cannot hold it," answered Gunnar, a near panic in his voice, as his leg seemed locked in a perpetual cramp.

"We are coming fast upon Hundalen station," yelled Einar, "we will have to jump."

To the car's inner side a wall of chiseled, rocky mountain sped by; to its outer side was a snow laden slope that dropped away in a deadly fall.

"I can't do that, brother," cried out Gunnar. "Help me stop this car."

"I cannot with my throbbing leg. And there is no way past these handrails. I just cannot possibly get to you to help," Einar repeated. He then grabbed the rucksack they had brought and prepared to jump. "Let go of the handcar and jump, brother."

"No, I cannot," cried Gunnar, "I am too afraid. We are going too fast."

The fear in his voice was the same that Einar had heard upon the mountainside in Scotland, where Gunnar had frozen from fright in the middle of his rappelling test.

"Don't be afraid," responded his brother, "I will be with you. If I can do it, you can do it also, brother."

The Hundalen Station house then flew by them, and before Einar could again coax his brother to take action, they were enveloped by another tunnel. In its darkness, Einar could hear the echo of the panicked terror in the voice of his brother.

"Einar," Gunnar screamed, "don't leave me Einar!"

"I am here, my brother," said Einar in the echo of the tunnel's darkness, "I will never leave you. Apply the brake, now. You must apply the break."

The fearful voice from the darkness responded, "I cannot find it again, brother."

They then broke back into the diffused morning light. Gunnar found the brake, but even his greatest exertions could not slow the vehicle even slightly. Einar could now clearly see the fear in the taut lines of his brother's face, just beyond the wildly articulating teeter-totter of the handrails. Both brothers felt a jolt as the speeding car slammed sideways from rail to rail.

Einar realized the danger of staying any longer on this handcar. He knew he had to somehow force his brother to jump. He rose, carefully lest a sudden sway throw him clear of the pitching handcar. Einar stood, braced himself upon his aching forward leg to throw the rucksack. He lifted it slowly, then timed his effort with the rhythm of the undulating handrails. Einar then heaved the rucksack as hard as he could at his brother.

The rucksack cleared the pair of handrails closest him, but clipped the wildly swinging pair nearer to Gunnar, and gave off an audible crack. The rucksack was deflected to Gunnar's one side, and threatened to miss the brother altogether, but Gunnar's reactions took over. He stretched to catch the bag, which he did, but in doing so Gunnar seemed to wobble in a precarious balance along the edge of the car.

"Fall, damn you," Einar cursed, but his brother did not. However, Gunnar's foot did come off the brake, and the quickening jolt of the handcar's momentum was enough to force Gunnar's weight to shift enough that his fall was inevitable. Gunnar then slowly tumbled from the handcar's platform, as if pulled gently by invisible hands.

Einar watched his brother fall into the heavy drifts of snow alongside the tracks. His momentum rolled him over and he saw his brother slide down the steep snowy slope, out of sight. The image immediately drove fear into Einar, and that fear precipitated action. All throughout his life, fear had always driven Einar to act, whereas his brother was always frozen by it.

The handcar truly began to barrel down the tracks without Gunnar's weight on the brake. Einar knew he must jump before the car picked up even more speed and ultimately flipped.

Einar threw himself from the handcar. As he did so, a fresh screaming bolt of pain seared through his leg. He had to push off violently, for if he did not the handcar likely would have impacted him and possibly have dragged him down the mountainside. Einar landed on his broad back, as he had hoped, but the momentum of his trajectory also rolled him until his aching leg slammed into the soft snow, which did little to cushion the frozen earth beneath it. Einar screamed aloud as the pain in his leg reached a new level altogether. He lay on his side, his momentum halted by the rise of his pain. He looked up to see the handcar careening down the rails.

The abandoned car picked up speed as it barreled down the track, and the handrails bobbed frenetically, each offset by the other. It was, by then, completely unimpeded, and Einar could no longer distinguish which handrail moved up or down. Each was nothing more than a swirl of motion. The handcar began to rock, slamming hard from one rail onto the other. Einar watched in horror as it jumped the tracks at the next turn, and rolled end over end down the mountainside.

Einar then rolled onto his back and thought only of the throbbing in his leg. For an instant he thought he had to suppress it as best he could, so as not to worry his brother.

My God! What has become of my brother? Einar thought. “Gunnar,” he yelled out. “Gunnar, where are you?”

There was no answer. Einar rolled onto his stomach, and looked up the tracks, where he saw the rucksack marking where his brother had gone over the side. Einar dragged himself by his elbows up the snow and ice laden embankment of the tracks. After a great period of time, he reached the rucksack, then called again for his brother. He peered over the mountainside, where below him he saw a lifeless pile of clothing about ten meters below him on the slope. It was trapped by an outgrowth of trees, which had kept his brother from falling further down the steep slope of the mountainside.

Einar called down to Gunnar his brother’s name, but there was no response. The louder he yelled, the more Einar feared that his brother was dead.

Then Einar thought he saw his brother shiver, and then once more. It was an involuntary, automatic bodily function. Einar, who still lay upon the snowy trackside, realized that his brother was shaking not from the cold, but from the terror of the death that he had just narrowly escaped. Gunnar couldn’t return Einar’s call, because he still had not wrestled his breath back from his fear of injury along with a very real chance of dying.

At that instance, the hillside around them shook. Its reverberations rolled up the mountainside. It was interrupted by the echoing thunder of another blast, and then a third time.

"Einar," screamed his brother, his terror replaced by a fresh fear in his voice, "what is that noise?"

From their vantage point high above the fjord, Einar could see warships in the *Ofotfjord.* Very large warships. Firing their deck guns. Even at this distance, he could clearly see belches of yellow-white flames from the ships' guns soon followed by gray-black plumes of smoke.

"Are you all right, brother?" Einar called to Gunnar.

Another massive boom shook them.

"Yes, I think so," answered Gunnar. "I am not ashamed to tell you my nerves are shattered. What is that awful noise?"

Another crack, this time of a more immediate explosion. If the guns' sounds had been painted in their ears in the resonant hues of deep booming browns and the drizzled gray that hung over the fjords, the explosion's sound had the timbre of brilliant yellow flashes tinged with curling flares of magenta.

From Einar's vantage point, the mountainside precluded a direct line of sight to Narvik harbor, but he could see the warships in the *Ofotfjord.* One was now aflame. Then, only faintly at first, the smell of smoke crept so foul upon the fresh alpine air that had surrounded them.

"I believe that awful noise is actually the sweet sound of the guns of the British Royal Navy, my brother," said Einar, smiling broadly. "I believe that they are attacking the Germans at Narvik."

The previous day the ten German destroyers had faced only light resistance from two Norwegian coastal defense vessels as they approached Narvik's harbor. These small craft were no match for the destroyers and were quickly sunk. The only disappointment for the *Kriegsmarine* that day was that only one of three tanker/supply ships had made it alongside the destroyers. Two others had been delayed and rerouted by the British mining operations. Ultimately, both would be sunk, denying the German destroyers fuel much needed for their intended immediate return that same day to the Fatherland.

Instead of departing that night back to Germany, as they had been ordered to do, they spent the night in the confines of the *Ofotfjord.* In order to conserve fuel after offloading their troops, several of these ships took up positions in the smaller fjords surrounding Narvik where they were more protected from the winds. None of these fjords had any other outlet to the sea except through the *Ofotfjord.*

That first day in the port of Narvik, April 9, the Nazi task force had efficiently unloaded its fifteen-hundred elite mountain troops from aboard the ten *Kriegsmarine* destroyers. These soldiers quickly secured Narvik, and then were deployed up into the mountains surrounding the port. These were three battalions of the crack 3rd *Gebirgsjäger* Mountain Infantry Brigade. They were filled with elite troops taken mostly from the Bavarian and Austrian Alps. The mountains of Norway, as dramatic as they appeared, were of no significant challenge to them. They were led by none other than Hitler's favorite leader of the entire *Wehrmacht*, General Eduard Dietl.

General Dietl had actually joined the Nazi Party before *Der Führer* in the early 1920s. With Hitler's rise to power, Dietl had continually demonstrated extreme loyalty to the charismatic leader.

One of Dietl's first objectives in Narvik was to capture the Ofoten Railway intact, and once done, assure that they and not the Allies would control its usage. It was to become the provisioning link to supplies already prepositioned in railcars on the Swedish side of the border, just beyond Bjørnfjell Mountain. Therefore, after the invasion, the rails went silent until the Nazis controlled line all the way to the Swedish Station of Riksgränsen, but Dietl would assure that the Ofoten Railway stayed intact. He sent one battalion up along its route with the objective to capture the line up to its last station at Bjørnfjell, around which a Nazi camp would be established.

The following dawn, the 10th of April, was the morning of the twins' adventures on the runaway handcar. That morning, the British had sent five destroyers through the *Vestfjorden* and deep into the *Ofotfjord*, whose waters cupped the port, with its five smaller fjords radiating out like misshapen arthritic fingers. These were the *Herjangsfjord,* the *Rombaksfjord,* the *Beisfjord*, the *Skjomenfjord*, and *Ballagen Bay.*

The Royal Navy had limited intelligence as to the number of German vessels in these fjords. They did not think themselves to be significantly outnumbered. They had gone ashore at the mouth of the *Ofotfjord,* but their inability to communicate with the locals left them to believe there were only five or possibly six enemy warships in its waters. They were soon to find they were off by nearly a factor of two.

When the commander of the battle group, Captain Bernard Warburton-Lee, reported the lower number back to the Admiralty, he was told to use his judgement. Captain Warburton-Lee then gave the order "follow me" from his flagship, the *HMS Hardy*. The other four destroyers were the *HMS Hunter, Havock, Hotspur* and *Hostile*. They entered the *Ofotfjord* at dawn during high tide.

They initially spotted two of the ten German destroyers as they entered the western end of the massive fjord, with the rest being hidden from view, many in the smaller adjoining fjords. The *HMS Hardy* neared Narvik harbor and encountered the two destroyers. Hardy fired three torpedos at the vessels, but all missed. This was not unusual in these waters.

These Arctic waters, so close to the magnetic North Pole, were to wreak mischief with the guidance controls of the torpedoes of the Royal Navy, but even more so those of the *Kriegsmarine*. In most cases, the German torpedos were nearly unusable, and only in rare cases, did they hit their targets.

The British destroyer *HMS Hunter* followed *Hardy* and fired upon the two German destroyers. Then the *HMS Havock* engaged the ships as well. The first German destroyer, the flagship *Anton Schmitt*, took artillery hits until a British torpedo strike from close range broke her in two. The flagship then rolled over and her mast became entangled with a second German warship. A third German destroyer by then had joined the fight.

At dawn, Narvik harbor was ablaze. The brazen British attack had left three German destroyers either sunk or incapacitated. The British destroyers then left Narvik harbor and returned deep into the *Ofotfjord*. They regrouped and all five British destroyers then raced back toward Narvik's harbor to finish off the German warships. They were not aware of the seven German destroyers still hidden in the smaller fjords.

As the British warships resumed their attack, three German destroyers sprinted in from the adjoining *Herjangsfjord.* They surprised the attacking British warships. A naval barrage between the opposing destroyer forces took place within the relatively tight confines of the east end of the *Ofotfjord* just outside Narvik harbor. The destroyer battle continued, and black smoke rose above the waters of the *Ofotfjord*. Soon, one of the British destroyers was hit, and the order was given for all to retreat back to the open waters of the *Vestfjorden*. The British commander had radioed for help and anticipated the arrival of additional British warships.

Unfortunately, two of the remaining German destroyers had been hidden in the waters of *Ballagen Bay*, at the western end of the *Ofotfjord*, and past where the British destroyers would be forced to travel to escape. As the destroyers of the Royal Navy raced westward across the *Ofotfjord*, the two German destroyers cut off the escape path of the British flotilla. The British flagship *HMS Hardy* initially mistook these enemy destroyers for British cruisers sent to aide his destroyer group. He was, of course, mistaken, and the *Hardy* was soon sunk as a consequence. Only due to the exceptional navigation of the *Hardy's* crew under fire were many of her seaman able to make shore and survive the warship's loss.

On that day, April 10, a total of 15 destroyers (ten German, five British) battled in the dawning hours in the waters of the *Ofotfjord*. The British had two of its five destroyers sunk (*HMS Hardy* and *Hunter*) and another (*HMS Hotspur*) heavily damaged. The Germans lost two of its ten destroyers to the sea, but had another four heavily damaged. Also, a vital ammunition ship was sunk, as well as six other smaller support vessels.

Worst of all for the *Kriegsmarine*, due to the severity of the fuel shortage after these battles, all remaining German warships were stranded in the *Ofotfjord*, where they could only await another British attack. They could not make for the open sea, for by the end of that day they could observe additional British warships collecting in the waters of the *Vestfjorden*. How exasperating it must have been for those captains to be incapable of reaching the other Norwegian coastal harbors to the south (Trondheim, Bergen and Stavanger) that were already controlled by the *Kriegsmarine*. How disheartening it must have been for the German sailors to await their fate from the increasing number of Royal Navy vessels gathering in the *Vestfjorden*.

Both nations' naval commanders were killed in action during this first engagement. The British commander Captain Bernard Warburton-Lee was posthumously awarded the Victory

Cross, the war's first. The *Kriegsmarine Kommodore,* Friedrich Bonte, was awarded Germany's Iron Cross, also posthumously. Both sides had fought valiantly. The *Kriegsmarine* licked its wounds while the Royal Navy waited patiently to re-engage.

There was one saving attribute for the Nazi forces. By the time this battle had been fought, all of Dietl's 3rd *Gebirgsjäger* Mountain Infantry Brigade, numbering approximately fifteen hundred highly trained mountaineers, had not only been offloaded ashore, but were well into the mountain's lofty heights surrounding Narvik. They secured the highest positions, all except for Bjørnfjell. In this way they adhered to one of warfare's first tenets: *the high ground always secures the advantage*. Once that was done, they began to work their way up the Ofoten Railway, and the long climb to Bjørnfjell Station.

The same day, in a field outside of Malestroit near the Atlantic coast of France, General Władysław Sikorski reviewed the Independent Podhale Rifle Brigade and would formally present the unit's Colors and Standard to its commander, General Zygmunt Bohusz-Szyszko. Sikorski conducted himself in the most disciplined manner, with the composure and aplomb befitting the occasion. Both generals knew that soon these Poles would be among the first to engage the Nazis outside of their homeland. Many of them might not return from their first real taste of battle. They wanted to assure that those who did would remember this day with dignity and reverence.

General Sikorski, who served as Prime Minister of the Republic-in-Exile (in addition to his function as Commander-in-Chief of it's armed forces) was joined by the President-in-Exile, Władysław Raczkiewicz. This was the man to whom Sikorski reported, and reportedly often had very different thoughts with regard as how to proceed. Also attending the day's ceremony was the Polish Bishop Józef Gawlina to bless the Brigade. The Standard was his personal gift to the Rifle Brigade.

The ceremony drew many ambassadors and dignitaries, including several generals from their host nation. The French generals also knew that these Polish soldiers would soon fight alongside their own troops, both the *Chasseurs Alpins* mountaineers and those of the Foreign Legion. In an eerily prophetic moment, one of the British representatives turned out to be a Scottish Highlander, attending in full military dress regalia, including kilts and tam o'shanter headwear.

After the dignitaries were received and welcomed, a Mass was held in the open air by Bishop Gawlina. This was followed by General Sikorski's addressing the troops.

"It will be your honor to lead the way," said the general in his speech to the assembled troops which numbered more than five thousand. There was an air of excitement that rippled through the soldiers. They realized that the rumors were assuredly true - they soon would be deploying to battle the Nazis.

Sikorski concluded his speech, at which time he was joined by the Bishop and the President of the Polish Republic-in-Exile to present the Highland Brigade's Colors, as well as the Standard which was a gift from the Bishop. These were presented to its commanding officer, General Bohusz-Szyszko, who knelt in the dirt while receiving them from this highest remaining tribunal of his country's leadership.

The highlight of the ceremony was when the honor guard presented the Colors and the Standard to the troops, marching them past each of the five thousand soldiers. Then these men were paraded past a grandstand improvised from branches and boughs, and decorated in a field garland of flowers. Sikorski took each and every soldier's salute. Afterward, the General departed in the same transport aircraft in which Bogdan had flown him in that morning.

Bogdan watched the plane climb into the late afternoon sky. A twinge of dread raced through him, knowing that the general was in the air, but not under the skills of his own talented hands. As the plane shrank into nothing more than a small dot on the cloudy horizon, Bogdan turned away, knowing he was literally not in control of Sikorski's fate that day nor the next.

That same night, in the center of the nearby French town of Rennes, two brothers shared a delightful meal. Neither man spoke French, but both spoke very capable German from their years on the Schenning farm in Silesia. It was a language that did not serve them well here in Brittany, for even if their waitress did happen to speak the tongue, she certainly would not have admitted to it. So, instead, the brothers pointed to dishes they

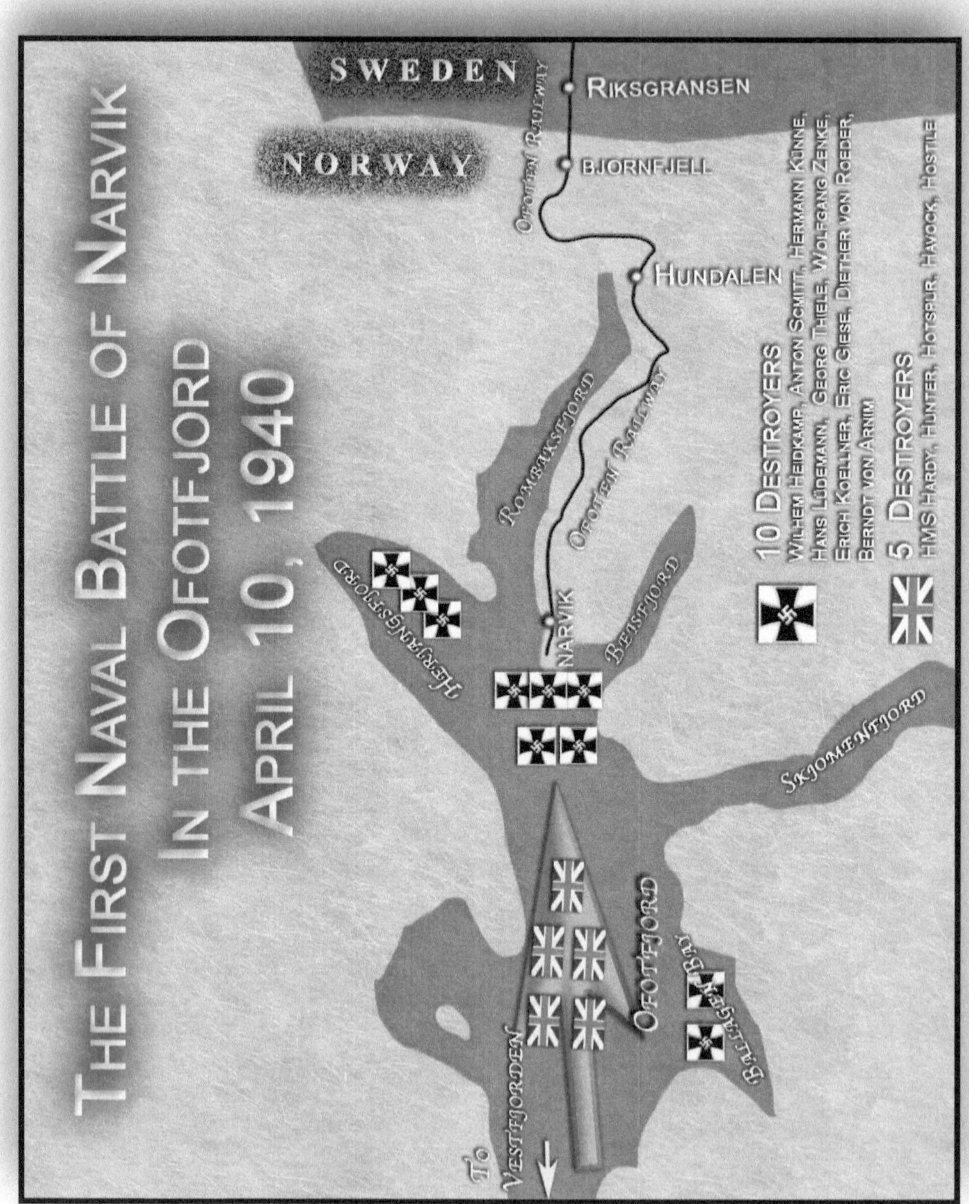

Figure 27: The First Naval Battle of Narvik

recognized by name from the menu, and in that way, they were served. As they awaited their meals, they spoke to each other in their native Polish tongue.

"I so feared that you were lost in the German invasion," Bogdan said to his brother.

"We fought with every ounce of strength that God had given us," said Albin, his blonde locks nearly radiating as brilliantly as the light of his smile. "We made for our escape over the Tatras Mountains only when it was clear the Soviets were invading from the east. To stay at that point would have been to sacrifice for nothing. To leave was to live to fight the Nazis on another day, on other soil. I am overjoyed that we will be going to fight them along with the French."

"I am tremendously proud of you, Albin," said his older brother. "I only wish I could be joining you." Albin looked surprised at his brother's last comment.

"Remember the many nights when we rested after a hard day's labors upon that Schenning farm," asked Albin, "of how you always spoke of flying?"

"It is all I ever wanted," said Bogdan, "and all I ever dreamed of."

"Well, now, you are doing it," replied Albin with a proud smile, "and for none other than General Sikorski. You would trade that to carry a rifle?"

"I would trade that to fight the Nazis," Bogdan replied.

"Tell me, Brother, what is the General like?"

"He is a good man, Albin," said Bogdan, "and very strict. But in the same way that the farmer Schenning was. Stern initially, but he warms up to you as he gets to know you. Yes, I am flying in the war, chauffeuring the General to England and back, but my heart's real desire is to become a fighter, like yourself."

"What kept you from becoming one in the air?" Albin asked him.

"Reflexes," Bogdan answered. "At Dęblin, they said my reflexes were too slow, so they assigned me to transports. There is nothing wrong with my reflexes, my brother."

"You always were a step slow. I have always said so," joked Albin. "But how do you fly if you speak no French or English? How do you communicate with the airstrips?"

"I have learned enough to be functional with them, mostly from the General," Bogdan replied. "He is quite a brilliant man, so he teaches me phrases in both French and English. 'Requesting permission to approach,' and 'Am I cleared to land?' and of course '*M'aidez*!' When we fly, the General often sits in the co-pilot's seat as we prepare to land, in case his linguist's skills are needed."

"Well, my brother," said Albin, "it appears you have just enough vocabulary to get lucky with either the French or English ladies," Albin said as he laughed aloud. They finished their meal, and then the discussion became more serious as they lingered over their second bottle of the house wine.

"Our sister Justyna," said Albin, "you have heard of her predicament?"

"No, what has happened?" asked Bogdan.

"After we both left to sign up for the military, she ran off. She apparently signed up to go to work in Germany several months before the invasion. She had received a postcard from her friend, Aniela, to join her. Aniela had gone to work in a factory there several years before."

"Do you mean Aniela who was pregnant but unmarried?" asked Bogdan. "That was only her way of escaping her father's wrath and her mother's shame. Why would Justyna sink to this?"

"Did you ever think," Albin answered, "that she was thinking that she wanted to be like her two older brothers? Go to German soil to work and earn enough to keep the family alive? Even if, in our case, it was once Polish soil that the Germans long ago stole."

"You don't think she was …?" Bogdan used his hands to make an expanding motion over his stomach.

"Pregnant? Our little Justyna? She is only seventeen," replied Albin. "No, it is impossible!"

"I guarantee you that it is entirely possible, my brother," Bogdan replied, "but I agree it is most improbable. Has mother or father heard from her since she left?"

"I am told they have, brother," Albin said, "but you know since the invasion the Nazis censor the mail terribly. Even simple postcards."

"It saddens me that there is so little we can do," said Bogdan. "The day will come when I will go to Germany and search every town until I find her."

"As God is my witness, I will be at your side, my brother," answered Albin.

Two other brothers lie side by side in the snow alongside the tracks of the Ofoten Railway. Einar had lowered a rope from the rucksack, and Gunnar had been able to climb the ten or so meters back up to his brother. Both were constantly looking up at the billowing plumes of black smoke that rose from behind the mountain that separated them from a clear view of Narvik harbor.

"Who do you suppose won that battle?" asked Gunnar.

"I don't have any idea," answered Einar, "why don't you get the wireless set and perhaps we can pick up some chatter."

Gunnar reached into the rucksack and very gingerly lifted out the remains of the radio hardware. It was broken in two, as it had hit the wildly undulating handrails when Einar threw the sack at his brother.

"Now we are in deep trouble, Einar," said Gunnar. "You should never thrown this rucksack at me."

"Had I not, brother, we both would be in much worse trouble, lying somewhere below in the wreckage of that handcar."

"Surely, you would have jumped," said Gunnar.

"As I told you," said Einar, "I will always be with you. To the bitter end, if necessary. If I was unable to get you off that car, then I would have ridden it over the side with you. Thank God you took your foot of that brake and fell."

"You know why I did, don't you?" Gunnar asked. "Because you cursed me. *'Damn you, fall, Gunnar'* you said. I was shocked to hear you damn your own brother so. It wounds me still."

Einar was incredulous that having just barely survived physical calamity, that Gunnar was wounded by the words that slipped from his tongue during the moment.

"I am sorry, Gunnar," he said, "to have hurt you so. But as to the result, I am not sorry at all. I am so happy that you are unhurt."

"I wish I could say the same for you and the wireless," replied his brother. "What shall we do now?"

Einar looked around them on the tracks. "Sooner or later the Germans will be coming up these tracks, either onboard a train or on foot. We must get back to the Bjørnfjell station house and regroup. Our other rucksack is still up there. We need to gather it before it is spotted and gives us away. I just am unsure how much more I can do on this leg today. We shall rest this day in the station house at Hundalen, the one we flew past on the other side of this tunnel. Help, me, Gunnar."

"This leg is much worse than the mere sprain you claimed it to be," said Gunnar.

"I am afraid that it surely is, brother."

They rested for a bit more, before Gunnar once again crutched his brother and began the climb up the tracks and through the mountain tunnel. When they emerged on the other side, Einar had to rest. Gunnar took him inside the station house, set him down to rest and evaluated its layout. Then he returned to his brother's side.

"It is empty, Einar," his brother said. "There is food, but very little. Perhaps enough for us to stretch to two days if we are careful. There is a stove that we can light and a little dry firewood."

"No, we cannot risk the smoke being sighted, not now," Einar said. "However, let us remain sheltered here inside."

The two brothers then waited inside, sheltered from the wind, but not the penetrating cold. They huddled together under a single wool blanket that they had taken from the rucksack. It was during this time that both young men began to question how they had come into this situation.

Night fell and they felt safe to light the stove. There was dry wood stored inside the Hundalen station, but they only used enough of the starter kindling to get the fire going. Then they fed it with whatever wood Gunnar could find along the mountainside. That night they slept in a luxurious bath of warmth, but deep in their bones they knew that they would revisit the penetrating cold the next morning.

The next morning returned along with the frigid bite of dawn. "We urgently need to move today, Einar," Gunnar said. His brother gingerly tried to place weight upon his swollen leg, but could not. They decided to wait out one more day in the station house at Hundalen.

The third day, the 12th of April, the brothers became aware of activity on the tracks far below them. They could see a German patrol manning an artillery gun secured to the platform of a flat bed railcar, which they practiced rolling in and out of a tunnel on the tracks. Once inside the tunnel, after the railcar had been chocked, the weapon was safe from bombardment by the naval guns of any British ships in the fjords.

"They are working their way up the Ofoten line," said Gunnar, as a frantic look overtook his face once more. "What will we do?"

Einar again rose to test the leg. He grimaced in severe pain as he placed his weight upon it.

"I still cannot walk, brother," said Einar. "I fear that the time has come for you to leave me behind. If you can make your way up to the ski hut at Bjørnfjell, recall that I buried Wincer Wells' faux Enigma rotors in that canvas rucksack in the woods behind the cabin, in the location marked by three stacked rocks."

"Don't be foolish, Einar," said to his brother, "Whatever fate awaits us, it will await the both of us together. It was smart of you to not bring those things along to this station. If only you had done so with the wireless set and the pistol as well."

Einar's face dropped as it became heavy with frustration. He looked at his brother and knew they could not afford to be found with these working tools of British spies. He also knew his leg was in no position to allow him to hide them.

"Oh my, I had forgotten about them both. If we are captured, then we are nothing more than Norwegian citizens fleeing the city along the tracks. But if we are caught with the wireless or the pistol, we will be marked as spies and will be shot. You have to get rid of them today, before the Germans reach us."

"Yes, you are right Einar, but where should I stash them?"

"Not on the hills overlooking the tracks," said Einar, "for when the Germans deploy their troops, they will take the high grounds to protect the station house and the tunnels. Drop down below the station house on the hillside and bury them both, and cover them with snow. Here, wrap them in this blanket, so we can grab them quickly later."

Einar handed his brother the large wool blanket in which to enwrap the radio and pistol.

"It is our only blanket, brother," Gunnar protested.

"Do you wish to explain to the Germans why two Norwegian fishermen carry a Scottish wool covering?" responded Einar. "It is as incriminating as the wireless or the pistol. We should not have brought it."

"I thank God that we had it over the last several days,"

responded Gunnar, "but you are right, as always. We must hide it also."

Gunnar was able to hide the bundle on that day, taking great care not to be seen, and even greater care when he lowered himself by rope below the tracks. He was careful not to lose his footing and tumble down the heavily inclined slope beneath the station house.

He found a small recess, one might call a grotto had it been somewhat larger. Nonetheless, it was just large enough to cram the blanket wrapped pistol and the broken wireless into. He packed it with snow until it was no longer visible. He then carefully climbed the slope back up to the tracks, and joined his brother inside the station house.

"It is done," Gunnar said. "We are safe now."

"You did well on the rope," said his brother, "you have mastered your fear!"

"Hardly brother," Gunnar said. "This slope is steep, but not like hanging over a cliff. Besides, I picked a line with a tree below to catch me again if I fell. At least the contraband is well hidden now."

"Yes, thanks to you. Let's hope the Nazis do not find the British passports and the faux rotors stashed in Bjørnfjell," said Einar.

"The Germans are not there, yet," said Gunnar. "We would have seen them pass."

"Unless they came across the border from Sweden. Should those things be found, then we just left our signature," said Einar, "the Germans will cry out, *These are the tools of spies!* The passports will give them our names and photos. It will not take them long to figure out the purpose of the faux rotors."

"Do not be so hard on yourself, brother," said Gunnar. "Wells was foolish to ask us to carry them."

He then cleared his throat, announcing another round of the Shakespeare game was to follow.

"When sorrows come, they come not single spies, but in battalions," Gunnar quoted Shakespeare.

"That's easy," said Einar, "*Hamlet*".

"For once, my brother," said Gunnar, "you have guessed correctly."

45 The Second Naval Battle of Narvik

April 13, 1940

"The Hun is always either at your throat or at your feet."

Winston Spencer Churchill

The next morning was once again shattered by the blaring echoes of explosions in the fjords. Both twins exited the Hundalen station house, with Gunnar once more crutching his brother. They carefully navigated the length of the tunnel, then carefully climbed out onto a rocky outcropping. They risked this because here they had a clear view of the *Rombaksfjord* and points beyond, while they themselves were concealed. Einar's mobility was greatly challenged by this excursion, but he had to see what was ongoing in the fjord below.

From their mountainside perch, they could see a biplane circling in the distance. They could not see what it attacked directly, as their line of sight was obscured by the *Rombaksfjord's* distant shore, but there arose a great plume of oily black smoke from behind it. Einar possessed knowledge of the terrain, even more than Gunnar, and he assessed the aircraft was attacking some vessel in the *Herjangsfjord*, the fjord just beyond the *Rombaksfjord* which they looked directly down upon.

What the twins saw that morning, but could not comprehend, was that the plane was a Fairey Swordfish biplane which had been catapult-launched from the British battleship *HMS Warspite*. It was sent to scout the fjords for an attack later that day. As it did so, it engaged and sank a German U-Boat that had been spotted on the surface of the *Herjangsfjord*.

Figure 28: The Second Naval Battle of Narvik

The U-Boat's crew was for the most part able to make landfall, which added to the growing number of *Kriegsmarine* sailors safely deposited on the shores of the fjords surrounding Narvik. This would remain the only U-boat sunk by a plane launched from a battleship throughout all of World War II. Little did Einar and Gunnar know that they were in for an even more incredible show of British naval might later that day.

After the sinking of the U-Boat on that morning of the 13th of April, the *Kriegsmarine* naval forces trapped in the *Ofotfjord* prepared for another British attack. The Germans had eight remaining destroyers, several of which had been badly damaged in the first battle, accompanied by other smaller supporting surface ships. All were precariously low on fuel and ammunition. The German sailors knew their position to be precarious at best. It was akin to being beaten ferociously in a blind alley, but even though you got your licks in, your assaulters merely waited for reinforcements as they guarded the only exit.

The Royal Navy no longer expected to be afforded the element of surprise. It attacked with a flotilla led by the *HMS Warspite*, an iconic battleship that had participated in the First World War's Battle of Jutland. It was accompanied by nine additional British destroyers. Their mission was to eliminate the remaining German warships in the fjords surrounding the port of Narvik. In doing so, Narvik would then be prepared for a later landing of Allied infantry.

The twins waited all morning for the attack. They watched the fjord patiently into the early afternoon. As the first hour after noon approached, the British flotilla entered the *Ofotfjord* and the battle commenced.

The twins' vision was obscured, but they found that they could see some of the action directly. What they could not see, they could certainly hear and feel as the sound and shockwaves of the naval guns echoed through the mountains overlooking the fjords. In fact, the high, sheer granite walls just across the *Rombaksfjord* from them reflected the sounds so clearly that neither Einar nor Gunnar could be sure from which original direction the blasts had come. Their nostrils filled with air tainted with a distant burnt scent, as the German destroyers began laying massive defensive smoke screens in the *Ofotfjord*. To this would soon enough be added the pungent fumes of the destruction of the captive German destroyers themselves.

Two of the these Nazi warships ranged out to attack the oncoming British flotilla. One of these German destroyers was quickly sunk in the western end of the *Ofotfjord,* and the British warships advanced on Narvik. Two other German destroyers remained moored in Narvik harbor due to engine damage, yet their crews continued to fire upon the approaching British vessels. The German crews fought valiantly, but without the tactic of mobility, their ships became ready targets for the guns of the British flotilla. No sooner than had the two *Kriegsmarine* vessels expended the last of their ammunition, they were quickly sunk. The British Royal Navy enjoyed a commanding advantage in both fuel and munitions, as well as the sheer number of warships within the waters of the *Ofotfjord*. With the escape path to the *Vestfjorden* sealed, it was only a matter of time until the rest of the German destroyers were to be sunk.

The naval battle turned out to be frustrating to Einar and Gunnar because from their position, they could hear but not see the action. Flashes of the man-made lightning bounced off the overcast clouds, but the twins' view was mostly obstructed.

Perhaps the most interesting story of any German destroyer was that of the *Hermann Künne*. It fought valiantly, and for some unknown reason did not receive the order to retreat. Its crew, out of munitions, attempted to scuttle the ship in the shallowest waters of the *Herjangsfjord*. The British destroyer *HMS Eskimo* came upon the *Hermann Künne* and fired at least one torpedo, and soon after the ship was ablaze. It is unclear whether it was the torpedo that caused the fire, or the scuttling charge set by the Germans. In either case, the *Hermann Künne* was also sunk. The *HMS Eskimo* was set upon by other German warships and was rammed. She ended up having her bow sheared off cleanly. Amazingly, she survived the incident and later, after repairs, was returned to the war.

Einar and Gunnar then saw the most incredible sight. The last four surviving German destroyers retreated into the inescapable waters of the *Rombaksfjord* immediately below them. The warships sailed the long fingerlike fjord, from which there was no recourse. The British battleship *Warspite* had blocked the *Rombaksfjord's* only entrance. It was clear that the German destroyers had no intention of taking on the much larger and better munition-supplied battleship.

At the other and of the fjord, the last four destroyers were scuttled. Just below the twins, the four German warships began off-loading her sailors, as demolition crews prepared their ships to be scuttled. Whatever guns could be scavenged were taken ashore. Then, the four massive destroyers, entrapped in the narrow fjord below them, began to be detonated by their own crews and sank one after the other, to prevent them from falling into the hands of the British.

Even with the loss of the last of these German destroyers, the battle raged on. The guns of the *Warspite* shelled the German shore batteries, causing heavy damage. Narvik was once again burning, and her harbor was a maze of sunken hulls.

As the *HMS Warspite* returned to the open waters of the *Vestfjorden*, two U-Boats got off torpedo shots at her. As was common in this Arctic waters, both weapons missed.

Of the ten German destroyers sent to Narvik under *Operation Weserübung*, all were now lost in the waters of the surrounding fjords. It is astounding to think that this made up one-half of all the destroyers in the *Kriegsmarine*. While the British had also lost destroyers (2 sunk, 3 heavily damaged), her count was not as heavy, and the Royal Navy had a much larger fleet to draw upon. This created a marine war-fighting inequity that would never be resolved by Hitler. In the end, the assets of the *Kriegsmarine* that were lost in Norway would frustrate his future plans. In the end, the dead weight of those lost weapons became the anchor that ultimately would drag the Third Reich into the abyss of history.

Einar and Gunnar ended the day in a state of shock. While they were watching the battle unfold, the German gun that had been hidden below them in the Ofoten Railway tunnel had been fired several times. After each shot was fired, it was pulled back into the protective enclosure of tunnel. This drew fire from the guns of the *HMS Warspite*. The shells were incapable of taking out the enshrouded German gun, but the British volleys seemingly shook the entire mountainside. The twins had never experienced anything like it in their lives.

Both brothers could only pray that the shells would not find them, and thankfully they did not. Nearly all the rounds slammed into the granite outcroppings above the railway, causing masses of debris to slide down onto the tracks. Yet, this meant trouble, for the Germans would surely send crews to re-open the rail lines, which would also bring them into close proximity to Einar and Gunnar's position at Hundalen Station.

Figure 29: Hundalen Station House built in 1902…

…and View of Rombaksfjord From The Rails Near Hundalen Station

46 Survival in the Mountains

April 14, 1940

"Mountaintops inspire leaders but valleys mature them."

Winston Spencer Churchill

Einar and Gunnar spent the night of April 13 in the Hundalen Railway station house. Einar's leg precluded him from any significant transit. Most of all, his injury kept him from hiking upward along the railway bed in an attempt to return to Bjørnfjell Station and the ski hut where they had deposited the other rucksack in the ravine.

The twins built a fire in the wood burning stove within the station house. They had waited until night had finally fallen, for with each passing day its sunlight grew longer by nearly another quarter hour. It would continue to do so until the summer solstice occurred in late June, on which day the midnight sun would only dance along the horizon, and never set. That day would have no night.

Einar and Gunnar had been holding out on the last of their food stores. This night they could stretch what little food they had left no longer. They consumed the last morsels hungrily that night. Einar comforted his brother, "Eat, Gunnar. Tomorrow we will find more food."

To this, Gunnar merely quoted Shakespeare. He cleared his throat as he always did to announce he was playing their game.

"Give them great meals of beef and iron and steel, they will eat like wolves and fight like devils."

Einar reactively thought of the German mountaineers working their way up the railway. He did not feel like playing along, but it might take his brother's mind off of their situation.

"Julius Caesar," Einar guessed.

"Henry V," answered Gunnar.

"That's not fair," objected Einar. "You've already recently quoted from *Henry V*!"

"Actually," answered Gunnar, "that quote was from *Henry VI Part 2*, which is another play, and king, altogether."

"Well, Gunnar, I am going to stop playing this silly game if you insist on cheating with these *damn Henries...*"

At that moment came a thunderous rapping upon the front door of the station house. Both twins instantly froze in terror. They had been speaking in the Norwegian tongue, as they did whenever they went off the islands of Skrova.

The thunderous rapping repeated, with the same militaristic precision as the first cadence. It persisted in an aggressive manner, and was soon interspersed with the German phrase, "*Öffne die Tür!*".

The twins had been given a crash course in the German language during their training in the Scottish Highlands. They recognized the instruction, and slowly Einar opened the door.

No sooner had the door been cracked when a boot crashed into it from outside, knocking Einar back and aside. Two soldiers entered wearing belted field-gray military greatcoats bearing the *Wehrmacht* insignia, as well as combat helmets, and rushed in as they drew their rifles on the twins. Then, stabbing the weapons in the air at them, one of the soldiers screamed, *"Heben Sie Ihre Hände hoch, wo sie sichtbar sind."*

Gunnar was quick to recognize the command, "Raise your hands where they can be seen." He raised his hands slowly, and his brother immediately followed.

It was then that one of the soldiers looked to his partner and softly uttered the phrase, "*Sie sind Zwillinge*!"

Gunnar recognized the word *Zwillinge*, which meant twins. They had been warned in their training to split up if they were likely to be captured, as the Nazis even then were known to have an infatuation with twins. Of course, both Gunnar and Einar knew that they would never separate from each other, especially if their freedom or their lives were endangered.

Then the first soldier said to the other, *"Holen Sie sich den Oberstleutnant."* The soldier who spoke these words kept his weapon trained on the brothers as the second trooper excitedly departed the station house.

Gunnar worked through what he remembered of his German. At first he thought the soldier had said to the other, "Get the *Oberleutnant* (or First Lieutenant)," but then he realized that the soldier had actually said "*Oberst*" not "*Ober*". He remembered that an "*Oberstleutnant*" was a lieutenant colonel.

"Gibst du auf?" said the soldier, moving his rifle barrel in a motion toward the ground. *"Gibst du auf? Kapitulation?"*

Neither Einar nor Gunnar understood him. The soldier became more and more frustrated, repeating the phrases with an increased volume and urgency.

"He is asking if you surrender," said a calm, resonant voice from behind the soldier. "He will allow you to lower your hands if you simply tell him you surrender." The voice was speaking a German-accented dialect of Norwegian.

It was then when an older man in a snug winter white mountaineer's uniform, sans greatcoat, came forth from the doorway. The shoulder straps he bore identified him as a lieutenant colonel, and the Edelweiss flower patch on his arm identified him as a member of the elite *Gebirgsjäger* Brigade.

"Forgive him, he is one of the sailors we have dragged up into the mountains with us. His destroyer was sunk by the British. He is literally a fish out of water."

The officer then flashed a smile, warm and disarming. His bright teeth seemed to complement the gray tinges along the temples of his otherwise sandy colored hair. His face was strong, and ruggedly handsome.

"I am Lieutenant Colonel Alois Becker," he said without a trace of any threat. "As it is evident that you do not speak German, please forgive my weak hold of your Norwegian tongue. Now, if I might enquire, who are you gentlemen and why do you hide in this train station. And, please, lower your arms."

Colonel Becker was exactly the opposite of what the twins had been told to expect of the Germans. They do not smile. They do not engage in small talk. They are precise, but not courteous. Colonel Becker did not seem to fit the mold. His smile was pleasant and polite manners rang true in his words. He spoke to them almost in flourishes, not the curt direct orders they would have expected.

"Tell me friends," he said, "who are you?"

"We are fisherman from Skrova," Einar answered.

"Where is this place, Skrova?" asked the lieutenant colonel.

"An island in the *Vestfjorden*," Einar added.

"So, two more fish out of water, eh?" Becker laughed, "What brings two twin fishermen up here to the mountains? Why do the Gemini seek Pisces among the Aries?"

Gunnar could not help but chuckle, then interjected, "My brother was teaching me to climb. We were taking a short holiday."

"In a train station?"

"No, of course not," said Gunnar. "We were atop the Bjørnfjell, the next mountain up the slope. We stayed in a vacant ski hut there and got snowed in. We ran out of food. So we came down here in hope of finding some provisions. Then the fighting started in the fjords and we did not know what to do but stay put."

"And you have identification of some sort?" asked Becker politely.

"Yes, of course," said Einar, and they each passed their false Norwegian passports to the lieutenant colonel. He inspected them carefully, then passed them back to the brothers.

"So, Einar and Gunnar Alvorsen of Skrova," let me see your rucksack. They handed it over to the officer, who went through it in detail. Having found mountaineering equipment including ropes, crampons, harnesses, and ice picks among other essentials such as clothing and empty food wrappers, the lieutenant colonel appeared to be satisfied with their story.

"Well, my misplaced fishermen," Becker said, "I am sorry to tell you that you may not stay here. We are commandeering this railway. We need this station house forthwith. I am going to have to throw you out in the snow. Besides this, a bright red hut on the snowy white mountainside will only become a target for the British naval guns. Neither of you are very safe here. You will have to leave at once."

"But we cannot leave. My brother has badly injured his leg," said Gunnar.

"I have noticed him favoring his leg," Becker said, as he turned and ordered instructions to his soldier. The soldier then turned and exited, leaving the two brothers alone with Becker, who had drawn his Walther P-38 pistol from its holster.

"Forgive me, gentlemen," Becker said as both brothers stared at the weapon, "but war is war, after all."

"You are going to shoot us right here, in the station house?"

Becker looked upon the two men, and slowly began to snicker. The brothers looked nervously upon him, waiting for his response. He seemed to be enjoying their unsettled discomfort.

"If I were going to have you shot, it would be done outside," he laughed, "and not by myself. I meant to say 'excuse me' for the precaution of drawing my pistol. With war being as it is, I have to assure for my safety in being alone with you both."

In a few minutes another mountaineer carrying a leather bag joined them.

"This is my medic," said Becker to them. Then to Einar he added, "You will allow him to examine your leg." It was not a question.

"Yes, of course," said Einar, and the medic soon asked him through hand gestures to lie down. He probed Einar's lower leg for several minutes before rendering a diagnosis to the lieutenant colonel in German that neither brother could understand. Then, the lieutenant colonel interpreted for the twins.

"My medic seems to think that you have torn your Achilles Tendon. This is very painful, of course, and will not heal on its own. At some point you will require surgery, or else you will hobble for the rest of your days. He says if it should completely tear in half, you will be in instant and unbearable pain. Then you will beg for me to shoot you. That last line was from me, not the medic."

Colonel Becker again chortled, taking any tension completely out of the situation.

"Wonderful news," said Einar with a heavy dose of false enthusiasm.

"I suggest your brother find himself another climbing instructor," said Colonel Becker. "My medic said this did not occur in the last day or so, so how did you both get down here from Bjørnfjell?"

"We rode on a handcar," said Gunnar.

The colonel began to laugh heartily. The medic looked at him with an inquiring gaze, although he dared not question his commanding officer. Becker noticed this, and shared something in German with the medic, who then began to laugh heartily aloud along with the lieutenant colonel.

"So you two are the *dumkopfs* who came down the mountain on that handcar, eh? That settles it, you truly must be fishermen. It was likely meant only for use on the plateau between Bjørnfjell and the Swedish Station. But as you both found out, those carts are quite dangerous on any slope of more than two or three degrees. We saw it thrown over the side below and thought it must have been some sort of sabotage plan gone awry. Now we know, just a couple of idiot fishermen playing in the mountains, not realizing just how dangerous their toys were."

He laughed until the idiocy of the situation no longer amused him. He gave direction to and then dismissed the medic, after which his tenor changed to a very serious tone.

"So, Einar and Gunnar, tell me about Bjørnfjell station. I am told there are the remains of a Norwegian garrison there. How many men?"

"You would have us spy for your invading army against our country?" asked Einar.

"Invaders? Us?" scoffed Becker. "No, my friends, you are our Nordic brothers. We are all from the same shared heritage. We are not here to invade your lands. No, we are here to protect your neutrality from the English who have demonstrated time and time again a willingness to dishonor it. It is because the English have given in to that war-monger, Churchill, who leads their navy."

Both Einar and Gunnar knew better than to take the bait. This could simply be an opportunity for the two to entrap themselves. It was then that another mountaineer entered to offer cold rations to the two brothers, apparently upon the colonel's command. Einar and Gunnar took the food and ate eagerly.

"See, would I treat an enemy so?" asked Becker. "You both are our Nordic brothers, therefore I will treat you as such. So, how many soldiers escaping from the garrison in Narvik are now at Bjørnfjell?"

They both hesitated, before finally Gunnar answered. He decided to give a number lower than what they observed, so that the Germans might not be adequately prepared for any forthcoming engagement. "Between fifty and one hundred men, but I cannot be more precise."

"Goodt, Goodt," said the colonel. "Tomorrow we will press on to Bjørnfjell. You will join us. Once we drive out the remnants of the Norwegian Army, and then you both may return to your ski hut."

"But my brother's leg…" protested Gunnar.

"He will ride along with our equipment on a rail-sled. But you, my friend," Becker said as he pointed at Gunnar, "you will have to walk alongside. Now, I need you both to clear this building, for we have need for it. My men have built a warm fire in the mouth of the tunnel. There you will be comfortable, and protected from any naval shells or strafing from British aircraft when the sun comes up. And remember, in the morning, we are on to Bjørnfjell."

Gunnar and Einar collected their rucksack and went outside. As they departed the station house, a soldier carried in a wooden box about the size of a typewriter case that bore an oval insignia. Within the oval, the word *Enigma* was clearly imprinted.

Figure 30: Bjørnfjell, January 2020

47 Back to Bjørnfjell

April 14-15, 1940

"The English never draw a line without blurring it."

Winston Spencer Churchill

The next morning came slowly for the twins. They sat alongside the fire in the tunnel for warmth, not captives precisely, but neither were they free to roam. At one point, Gunnar needed to relieve himself, and as he began to exit the tunnel to access the nearby trees, he was stopped by a German guard. Unable to communicate verbally, Gunnar grabbed at his crotch with both hands. The guard understood, but followed him outside the tunnel to the edge of the railway bed, where he watched as Gunnar projected an unending arc into the darkness enshrouding the slope below him.

Neither twin slept. Their minds were racing. Gunnar feared for their safety. Einar thought only of how they might get their hands on the Enigma device that was set up alongside the field radio in the Hundalen Station house from which they had just been ejected.

At four AM precisely, the men of the German Alpine Regiment began appearing in large numbers along the tracks of the railway. Lieutenant Colonel Becker then came out of the warmth of the station house, and began giving orders to his regiment's commanders. Soon after, a force that Einar estimated to be of about five hundred men began their march upward along the Ofoten Railway Line towards Bjørnfjell.

As the mass of men began moving out, Lieutenant Colonel Becker came over to talk to his two "guests."

"Gentlemen," he said in his German accented Norwegian, "we move on to Bjørnfjell. You will stay here with these men who will guard you along with the equipment to be moved. I have instructed them to treat you as our guests, meaning no harm will come to you."

"Good, Colonel," said Gunnar, " but why not release us to return to Skrova?"

"*Nein, Nein*," Becker said in German, before continuing in Norwegian, "It is entirely too difficult. The British will be coming ashore soon. Very soon. You will come with us to Bjørnfjell. There we can protect you. You would never make it to Skrova. You likely would not even get out of Narvik. You cannot trust the English. They are not Norway's friends."

Gunnar thought he detected a hint of concern in the *Oberst's* tone. Was he actually unsure of these two men? Did he suspect them for what they really were - British spies? They had not spoken to each other all night, even though Einar was itching to discuss the Enigma device they had both seen being carried into the station house the night before. They knew it was a common ploy to have one of the guards among them, unknown to them, who was literate in their tongue, in this case Norwegian. So they opted not to speak to each other at all for the duration of that night as they warmed in the tunnel by the fire's side.

"We will clear out any Norwegian troops at Bjørnfjell," Becker said to them, and then you and the equipment will follow. "I wish very much for there not to be any accidents, so please obey these men. If there are any misunderstandings, I will clear them up once we are together in Bjørnfjell. You know what I am saying to you, yes?"

"Yes," said Einar, "we are your prisoners. You will not allow us to go free."

The lieutenant colonel frowned in an overly expressive way. "I was afraid we would have some error in understanding given my limited knowledge of your language. We could never hold a fellow Nordic soul captive. No, gentlemen, you both are our guests. It is entirely to insure your safety. We can protect you from the English. Besides, with your leg, my friend," he said to Einar, "you are in no condition to descend this mountain to Narvik. No, you will stay with us up at Bjørnfjell. We will look after your leg there."

With this Lieutenant Colonel Becker barked some orders out to the three armed guards, at which one went into the station house only to return with cold rations for the twins.

"Eat, my friends," said Lieutenant Colonel Becker, "this cold will rob you of your energy faster than you think. You must maintain your strength."

With this, Lieutenant Colonel Becker turned to climb the railway by foot in the rear of his men, surrounded by other officers. He did not look back. It was then that Gunnar had thought perhaps they were being left behind to be executed.

That same day, Brigand MacAlvor was again successful in raising Wincer Wells on the phone.

"What do we know of the boys whereabouts, Wincer?" asked their father in the voice of a desperate man. Wells was taken aback by his directness over the open line.

"We haven't heard from them in the past two days," he finally replied. "They were directed to proceed to Stockholm, and it is likely they are en route there as we speak. Consider them safe."

"Safe?" Brigand said incredulously. "How could you possibly think so?"

"They were only a few kilometers from neutral Sweden, damn it," replied Wells. "Why on earth wouldn't I think them to be so, Brigand?"

"They would have contacted you," said Brigand.

A stealth of silence befell the line.

"It is highly unlikely that even in Sweden they would be able to pull out a wireless and tap out an update. Relax, Brigand, they are surely fine."

"They are not fine," Brigand replied. "They are atop a mountain that the German forces are fleeing up into."

"Mind your grammar, my friend," teased Wells, "they are atop a mountain into which the German forces are fleeing."

"Sod both you and your blasted grammar," replied Brigand. An ice cold silence which followed told Wells his jest was untimely.

"Damn you, Wells," said Brigand, "allow me to come to London, I can be of great use to you, now, for certain."

"Out of the question, old boy," said Wincer Wells. "Sit tight and stop calling. Should I hear anything regarding your lads, I will contact you straightaway."

The conversation ended with nothing more than a click. Brigand MacAlvor was left with only the dread of not knowing the fate of his two twin sons. Despite Wells' surety of their safety, Brigand feared this not to be the case at all. Yet, it was the uncertainty that drove him once more into the darkness of his own thoughts.

How could I have turned my own flesh and blood over to this man? he thought. *Tilly was right, I have done this to them just as my own father had so done to me.*

Within him, a sinking feeling rendered a visual thought of his father lying face down in the sea, his body bloated beyond recognition.

I shall not give in to the darkness as he had, thought Brigand, only to realize his vow was more of an aspiration than a surety.

Later that day, a motorized device was brought out from the shadows of the tunnel. It had in fact been a small gasoline powered flatbed, no larger than the handcar that Einar and Gunnar had so wildly ridden down the mountain upon. The three guards were soon joined by the radiomen and the Enigma operator who had taken up residence the night before in the Hundalen station house.

Soon, Einar was being helped by the guards onto the flatbed, where he found himself lying next to the radio equipment and the Enigma encoding machine. He lay on his back, as the guards removed the stone circle in which the fire had burned within the tunnel. They carefully inspected the rails afterward, Einar noted, to insure they could again be brought into operational use.

Soon they ascended the mountain along the rail line. Einar and the equipment were upon the flat bed of the motorized device, which had been fitted with steel wheels to fit the gauge of the railway. Einar guessed that the railcar had been brought aboard the destroyers from Germany just for this purpose.

Einar also noted there were few provisions on the bed of this device along with the communication equipment. Surely each of the five hundred or so soldiers he had seen that morning carried some rations with them, but it became apparent to Einar that these troops were radically short of the necessities required to survive for very long in these mountains. He did not know of the supply ships that had been sunk in the harbor before they could be unloaded, but Einar MacAlvor was quick to recognize the supply shortage that resulted from it.

Gunnar walked behind the motorized rail car. The pace was slow and even, and always inclined upwards, until they came into the tunnel just before arriving to Old Bjørnfjell station. In its darkness, the slope leveled out, and both twins realized they had reached the mostly flat plateau that lay between Old Bjørnfjell Station and the Swedish border. They continued on past Old Bjørnfjell and on to the last station before Sweden - Bjørnfjell.

As the twins returned to Bjørnfjell station, the air they breathed was laced with the smell of gunpowder and cordite. The small garrison of escaping Norwegian soldiers had been overrun. Now the *Gebirgsjäger* Mountain Infantry of the *Wehrmacht* held the last of the high ground over Narvik. Now, the *Wehrmacht* controlled the gateway to neutral Sweden.

Figure 31: Bjørnfjell Station
2020 and 1940

48 Survival in Bjørnfjell

April 16 to May 10, 1940

"In war, as in life, it is often necessary, when some cherished scheme has failed, to take up the best alternative open, and if so, it is folly not to work for it with all your might."

Winston Spencer Churchill

On the morning of April 16, Einar and Gunnar awoke once again in the ski hut that was on the hill overlooking the Bjørnfjell train station. Lieutenant Colonel Becker had kept his word. The twins were allowed to stay there without any presence of guards, although they were warned against attempting to leave the immediate area. "It is for your own safety," Colonel Becker had assured them.

"After all," Becker had said, "we do find ourselves in the middle of a war zone." This truth was said glibly, as if it had not been so only because of *Der Führer*'s own machinations.

As the brothers looked down upon the railway and its station house, Einar and Gunnar could perceive that the hive-like buzz of activity was in preparation for some significant undertaking. That event, they were soon to learn, was the arrival of the leader of all the *Gebirgsjäger* Mountain troops, General Eduard Dietl. He was to command of all the Nazi land forces scattered across northern Norway from this site. This included the thousands of sailors stranded ashore when their warships had been sunk or scuttled.

It was later, as the day was winding down towards dusk, that Becker again showed up at the door of the twin's hut. Einar asked him what he wanted, but it was Gunnar who pushed past his brother to allow the Lieutenant Colonel and three soldiers to enter. He knew the *Oberst* could easily have them ejected from this life sustaining shelter, and wished not to allow his brother, in a rash moment of emotion to give him any reason whatsoever to do so.

"I am afraid I must call upon you to assist me locally as an interpreter," he said. "You will go with these three men on my behalf."

"What can we possibly do?" Gunnar asked.

"Not the both of you," Becker replied, "only you, Gunnar. Your brother Einar will stay here and rest."

It was the first time the German officer had used either of their names in conversation, save for his reading their false passports aloud.

"I need you, Gunnar, to accompany my men in a truck and explain to the local *Sámi* herder that we are taking three of their reindeer for meat. Explain to them that we would not do so were it not required. I am afraid I cannot leave my station here to assist them myself, so you will be my Nordic messenger."

"But Colonel, I do not speak the *Sámi* language," Gunnar said, "and if they do not speak Norwegian we will not be able to communicate your message."

A broad smile came across Becker's face, as if he had just visualized such a scene. "Should that situation come to pass, the herders will understand what is happening, but I would prefer you to explain it, if at all possible."

"You do not need me if you only intend to take it by force anyway," Gunnar said.

"There is another message," Becker said, ignoring Gunnar's reasoning, as his smile withered upon a stern face. "Should these herders be caught harboring any enemy forces, including those of the Norwegian Army, you are to tell them that they will be shot. You are to say nothing more, but make sure they understand my meaning."

"I cannot say that, *Oberst,*" protested Gunnar, after sharing startled glances with his brother.

"You can," replied Becker, "and you will. If you refuse to, I will stop treating you and your brother as the Nordic brethren that I believe you to be. If you continue to refuse to understand that we are here only to protect you and your country from the British, then you will find yourselves treated very differently. Let not my Austrian civilities fool you, my friend. I can be very insensitive when the situation demands it. Now, Gunnar, you will go with these troops."

The last statement spoke volumes. These troops were from Austria and Bavaria in the southern alpine regions of the Reich.

"I will go," said Einar, knowing his brother did not possess the strength to utter such threats to the passive *Sámi* herders.

"No!" shouted Becker. "He will go, and you will rest. There is to be no further discussion on this. I must return to continue the preparations for General Dietl's arrival. Be quick. We still will have to butcher and roast these beasts. Go now."

Gunnar went over to his brother, and in Norwegian said to him, "It is fine, it is fine. I will handle this. Rest, Einar. I will return shortly."

"*Goodt*, now go," said Becker, before adding, "*Schnell! Schnell!*"

They walked back to the station where a truck awaited with its motor running. It was fitted out with spiked tires for traction in the snow. Gunnar was helped up into its bed, which was open to the environment. Upon this flat surface the cargo of the three reindeer carcasses would be placed. Soon they were on their way. It was not very far at all before they came upon a tremendous herd of grazing reindeer. Gunnar knew the *Sámi* herders were surely nearby and would come once the Germans made their intentions known through their actions.

The truck pulled in by the drifted snow along the road. It had been a short distance, and thanks to the open truck bed, Gunnar was able to identify landmarks should he ever need this route for escape.

Off in a distance, Gunnar could see the lights of the flames of a pair of fires, one each within two *Sámi* tents, or *lávvu*, which illuminated both structures.

The German soldiers began to draw rifles. Gunnar knew that if a single shot rang out and dropped a reindeer, that the rest of the herd would quickly be driven drive off and scatter away from the threat. He said to the German who began to take aim upon the first animal, *"Nein! Nein! Zusammen! Alle drei müssen zusammen sein!" or Together! All three must be done together!*

Figure 32: Sámi Herders (above) and Lávvu Tent Encampment (below)

Gunnar surprised himself that he had recalled the German word for together, but the message had gotten through. Two other soldiers raised their rifles as well.

It was then that they first heard the yipping of the dogs. Off in the distance, they all could see a small sled, plowing through the pure, newly fallen snow. Gunnar raised his arm in a motion to wait. The soldiers, much to Gunnar's surprise, waited and watched. The only explanation for them doing so must have been Lieutenant Colonel Becker having told them to do what this man said.

The dogsled pulled up aside the four men. The faces of the eight Huskies that pulled it were painted with permanent smiles adorning their bobbing heads. After ceasing their pulling of the sled, the dogs began to bark and howl at the soldiers. The sled to which this team was tied carried two figures: an old man in the standing position of the driver, and sitting forward of him a young girl.

The old man stepped off the sled and began raising his voice in a dialect unknown to all. Gunnar attempted to intercede in Norwegian, but it was apparent that the old man did not understand him.

One of the soldiers then leveled his rifle at the man and the girl Gunnar thought to be his daughter. Again, Gunnar motioned to the soldiers, and their weapons were lowered. The girl spoke in the same *Sámi* dialect to the old man and then turned to Gunnar and spoke in Norwegian.

"Father says you have no right to harass our herd," she said. "We have nothing to do with your people's battles between your countries."

"These are invading German soldiers," said Gunnar, "and they are here to take three of your reindeer that they need for food. I strongly suggest you give them these three animals and move the rest of your herd away from here, or they will simply come back again and again for more and more of your herd."

She spoke again to her father, after which he replied to her, all in a language as foreign to Gunnar as his Norwegian was to these soldiers.

"Father refuses to sell any of his herd," she said, "and these are our herd's seasonal feeding grounds, from which we will not be driven."

"You do not understand," Gunnar replied, "these German soldiers will take what they want and pay you nothing, so long as you are here nearby. If you satisfy them this night and move your herd into the Swedish lands, they cannot harass you there."

She again translated for her father. Gunnar could tell by tone and facial expression that he again refused.

"Father says he will not be driven from these lands," she relayed to Gunnar, "as it is our birthright to graze our herds here at this time of the year. You will not intimidate us from our way of life."

Gunnar could sense the soldiers behind them had become agitated, as if they kept a running clock in their heads. One kept repeating the colonel's word, "*Schnell!*"

"I am not German. I am Norwegian," Gunnar explained in a half lie to her. "These soldiers have been ordered to take three reindeer, and they will, one way or another. These German soldiers have no respect for your way of life. What they do have in the truck are machine guns. They can kill every animal on this feeding ground in only minutes. And I can assure you, they will do so if only for sheer spite should you give them the slightest reason."

She turned to speak to her father once more. As they spoke, the soldiers had become completely restless and raised their weapons to slay the three beasts as they had been commanded to do. Gunnar said to them the only words he could draw in his very limited German vocabulary, *"Nein! Nein!"*

As Gunnar spoke these words, the girl walked calmly to the spot between the soldier and the herd. The dogs yipped and barked. The father became greatly animated, screaming at her in their native tongue. Finally, he said something to her, and she slowly reached inside the fur jacket she wore to slowly produce three lengths of rope. She turned her back upon the soldiers, their carbines still pointed at her. She then slowly walked into the darkness, and came back with a single reindeer, a lead around its neck.

The first soldier began to point his rifle at the animal. The others had by then lowered their weapons.

"Tell him not to shoot the beast," she said to Gunnar. "It is not far to their camp. Tie its lead to the truck. If he shoots it, even the four of you will never lift its dead body. You will also only excite the other animals."

Gunnar once more said, *"Nein! Nein!"*. He then walked up to the peaceful animal and took the lead and tied it to the stationary truck. As he did this, the girl walked into the herd and culled out two more creatures. The soldiers now realized what they were to do and tied the animals to the truck.

"So long as they drive slowly," she said, "the animals will follow the truck. Do not drag them, for it will only panic the animals and their meat will bruise. Do not come back, for in the morning we will move the herd."

"Into Sweden," Gunnar said, "it is neutral. The Germans will not follow."

"Was Norway not neutral also?" she asked.

Gunnar had no reply for her.

Then he remembered, "I have another message from the Germans for you."

"You are their faithful servant?"

"I tell you for your own safety," he said, "should they catch you giving shelter to any soldiers, even Norwegian troops, they will return to shoot you and your family."

"You tell me this for our safety?" she said bitterly. "You threaten me violently with safety. It is no wonder that your people destroy each other in the name of safety."

She made no attempt to communicate the message to her father. She only continued to scowl at him.

"It is not my message," Gunnar said, "I am only the messenger for the leader of these troops."

"*It is not my mouth that kills*," she said mocking him, "*but my body's hands that choke the life from others.* You are all one and the same. You have your three animals. Be gone from us, traitor."

The last word cut him deeply in a way he did not think it possibly could. He merely had done what he was forced to do. Yet, somewhere in his soul, Gunnar knew she was right. He had refused to resist the assignment given to him, because to do so would have brought pain and possibly death to himself and his brother.

He had placed their needs above that of the pain done to others. He knew at some point, he would be forced to resist in a more active manner, no matter what the cost to he and Einar.

The three soldiers huddled inside the truck's cab, and Gunnar, denied access to the truck bed by the three animals, stood on the vehicles running board and clung to its side. He yelled into the cab, "*Langsam! Langsam!*" meaning "*Slowly! Slowly!*" The vehicle was soon underway with the reindeer obediently in tow, being led away to the slaughter. Gunnar could only wonder if he and his brother were not in the same circumstance as these reindeer.

The next day, April 17, brought great commotion. At midday, a train arrived from the Swedish Riksgränsen station, just on the other side of a long mountain tunnel from Bjørnfjell. The train was massive and loaded with supplies that the Nazis had prepositioned in Sweden for their troops invading Norway, those that had by then been cut off from the sea by the British. The train was partially unloaded and then what was left slowly descended down the mountain line on its way to Narvik.

During the previous days, the Ofoten Rail line had been cleared of all debris and repaired in spots where necessary. It was clear to the twins that the rail line was always intended to become the logistical lifeline of the stranded German troops in the town of Narvik. Those troops waited anxiously in the port town for their enemy's onslaught and expected the British to attempt a landing on that small Norwegian peninsula.

That evening, Lieutenant Colonel Becker and two guards arrived again at the ski hut. One carried a package of some sort. After they had entered into the hut, the colonel gave a hand gesture and the guard placed upon the small table a woven basket filled with German goods, including jams, jellies and bread. Spread amongst them was a chain of sausage links, freshly roasted. The sausages filled the small hut with an aroma that immediately evoked the saliva response of both twins.

"I wanted to personally let you know that General Dietl very much enjoyed the venison roast that you made available to us, Gunnar." Becker's smile broadened, while his eyes seemed to search the room as he spoke. "Had it not been for your abilities, these sausages would likely not have been as fresh as they are. *Danke*, my friend, *danke schoen*. These gifts are to show our appreciation."

Becker opened his arms in a gesture of sincere thanks.

Gunnar initially said nothing. He walked over to the basket, but instead of examining the food, he ran his hand over the craftwork of its weaving. He wrestled with accepting these goods, but the hunger in his gut outvoted his conscience.

"Ah, yes," Becker said aloud, "you are wondering how do we get such beautiful baskets in the middle of a war zone, yes? I will tell you, my friend. These are woven in all the towns of the Reich, by women whose husbands and sons are away at war, protecting our Aryan way of life. The provisioning train was full of such baskets, as well as the jams and mustards sent along as well. It is too bad we took so long to clear out the railway. I will warn you that the bread is already somewhat stale, but it is still very much edible."

"An entire train filled with care packages from home?" teased Einar.

"Not entirely, Einar," responded Becker. "It was more than enough room to fill it also with guns, ammunition and other weapons. Is that what you are enquiring about? There is enough food and munitions to supply all of our troops for the next four months. Does that satisfy your curiosity?"

It was as if the colonel was accusing them of being spies. Perhaps Becker's superior did not agree with his decision to keep these two stranded fishermen alive.

"Thank you," interjected Gunnar, slicing through the tension that had stretched between the colonel and his brother. "Thank you for this bountiful gift. We are very appreciative of your generosity."

"You are welcome, Gunnar," Becker said. "It might be of interest that our patrols have reported that those *Sámi* herders have taken their animals back into Sweden early this morning. Why would they do that?"

"Perhaps they knew you would be back for more and they did not wish to have their herd slowly stolen from them."

"Foraging," said Becker, crisply. "It is not stealing, it is foraging. If I wished to steal, I would have had the whole herd slaughtered."

"Was it not this very action that they might have feared? Their precious animals turned to carrion rotting in the fields?" asked Gunnar. "Perhaps this was the sight that they could never have brought themselves to witness. These people love these animals, and to needlessly see them slaughtered would have broken their hearts."

"And this you told them?" Becker asked of Gunnar. "You warned them to move their herd?"

"No, Colonel," Gunnar lied. "They are nomads, but they are not fools. They are quick to learn a lesson, and I am sure that they merely wished not to have their herd thinned any further. They are a people who live and learn from their experiences."

Becker stared at Gunnar, as if to say he did not believe him. Then he released the lock of his gaze and turned to Einar.

"How is your leg today, brother Einar?" he asked.

"It feels better," Einar responded, "almost as if it were back to normal."

"Yes, that is what my medic predicted you might say," replied Becker, "but once you put your weight upon it regularly, the pain will return."

"I certainly hope he is wrong, Colonel," said Einar.

"Tell me, why do you think it is that the English do not attack? For days now, our ships lay on the bottom of the fjords. Their ships only sporadically fire upon the port, but do not mount a serious threat to invade it. Nor do they attempt to sabotage this rail line. There are those amongst us who believe they have not attacked our rail line because the scouts for their sabotage team have been taken prisoner. Our people think, perhaps, that the saboteurs know not the lay of the land, nor the trails to the base of the bridges and tunnels that they should destroy."

"You will have to ask those questions to the English," Einar responded tersely. "Why would we ever be able to answer such questions?"

"Yes, indeed, why would you?" The colonel said coyly. "Be aware that your hut is being watched and monitored for any radio transmissions which might emanate from it. I, myself, don't believe you two to be spies, but I must be able to prove it to those that do. And if you are making a fool of me, I will personally squeeze the trigger that ends both of your lives."

A razor-edged tension had ripped the air from the room. Lieutenant Colonel Becker then smiled tightly, and added, "Enjoy your basket." He then spun on his heels and marched out of the hut and the two guards followed.

Gunnar raced to the window to watch them walk away.

"Why would he accuse us so openly, only to walk away like that?" asked Gunnar.

Einar limped to the window to stand beside his brother, as if he needed one last look to answer the question.

"Perhaps, he, himself is unsure," said Einar, as he patted his brother on the back. Then he hobbled over to the basket on the table. "Or perhaps others on General Dietl's staff are accusing us. Perhaps he wishes very hard for it not to be true. Remember, he is Austrian, not German."

"It is the same now," argued Gunnar. "Austria is part of the Reich, ever since the *Anschluss*."

Einar almost seemed not to hear him as his hands took inventory of the basket's provisions. Then he finally responded.

"That does not mean they do not have different cultures, Gunnar. He is a Catholic, certainly. These are mountain troops from Austria and Bavaria - both heavily Catholic regions."

"So they are Catholic, are they not still Nazis?"

"Not really," Einar replied. "The Nazis are a political party - the only political party - but many of these officers in the German Armed forces aren't political at all, just career soldiers and officers."

"Why does their being Catholic matter?"

"Because when the medic examined me for my leg," Einar explained, "he not only noticed this scapular that you gave me to wear, but he examined it closely. He smiled, and showed me one that he was wearing. He did not speak Norwegian, so I just smiled back at him knowingly. They think we are their brothers in faith. It appears that Lieutenant Colonel Becker is questioning that assumption, or at least his superiors are."

"Well," said Gunnar, "thanks to Wincer Wells' Catholic codewords and perhaps these scapulars, we are still alive. Why would he tell us about his troops now having four months of provisions and ammunition?"

"He told us because he knows we would have to get that information back to London. He wants to see if we will attempt to radio it back to them somehow. Thanks to you, brother, we no longer have a wireless set. He will be greatly disappointed."

"It was you who threw it, Einar," his brother said. "You were the one who destroyed it. Besides, if he wanted to bait us with that, why tell us they were monitoring us for any transmissions?"

"He is the only one that speaks Norwegian," explained Einar. "Now he can tell his superiors that he passed on the bait, but leave out that he warned us about the fact that they will be monitoring us. He has a vested interest in us actually not being spies - think how that would harm his career if it came to light that we are, and he has been sheltering us all along."

"So, the colonel is suspicious but hopeful…" Gunnar thought aloud.

"Exactly, and it will cost Becker dearly," said Einar.

"What do you mean, brother?"

"One way or the other, Gunnar, I am going to get my hands on that Enigma device."

"And exactly how far do you think you will get hobbling along with that dead weight?" Gunnar asked.

"All the way to London, brother," Einar said. "Before you ask me how, leave that to me. One thing is for sure, we will have plenty of time to come up with an idea, won't we?"

Einar pulled one of the stale rolls from the basket and began smearing it with jam using his finger to spread it. Gunnar looked at him as Einar then drew his knife and cut loose one of the sausage links.

"You are actually going to eat that food?" Gunnar asked. "It could be laced with something…"

"They wouldn't take such a roundabout way to kill us," Einar said, "they would just shoot us. You heard the colonel."

"I can't believe you will eat that. Don't you feel guilty?"

"No, brother," Einar said, "I feel hungry. Guilt will come later, when my stomach is full."

Eleven days after the Colors and Standard were presented to the Polish Independent Podhale Rifle Brigade at Malestroit, Bogdan Bratajewski piloted General Sikorski from Paris to Brittany again. On the 21st of April, the general would engage the troops in their camp just outside their embarkation point at the port of Brest in the nearby village of St. Renan. The next day they would march to Brest and begin loading onto the French liners *Chenonceau, Colombie, and Mexique* which had been converted to function as troop transports.

But on this day in St. Renan, General Sikorski would fraternize with the enlisted men, signing autographs and telling tales of the 1920 war against the Soviets. He was invited to pin on the stars of officers earning promotions before deploying. He would dine that night with all the officers together in this small town that had come to appreciate their Polish visitors so.

A lovely letter was received from the Mayor of St. Renan expressing his regret at the troops leaving the village. That night after dinner, large bonfires were lit in its squares. Their light danced off the walls of the homes and storefronts, syncopated only by the audible crackling of the burning timbers. Fountains of embers spewed upward in arcs that spread like the wings of angels protectively over the troops. These sounds were soon accompanied by the accordionists who provided the festive atmosphere, alternating between Polish folk tunes and French improvisations. Then, en masse, the singing began, and each man opened his heart to the call of duty of their country - their brutally occupied homeland.

The chorus reached its crescendo in the singing of *"Dąbrowski's Mazurka"*. The song was written after the Partitions of Poland during the initial campaigns of Napoleon in northern Italy for the Polish Legions fighting under General *Dąbrowski.* It was adopted as the national anthem of the restored state in 1926. It echoed through the town, sung in unison by the men in their native tongue. They thunderously delivered the words *"Poland is not yet lost, while we live, while we fight (with swords) for all, that our enemies had taken from us."*

That night, while the generals dined with the officers, Bogdan had his last meal with his brother Albin. They spoke of family, the village, and of their parents in occupied Poland. Their conversation was tinged with the sorrow of those lost, as they compared their separate piecemeal knowledge of which of their village community had perished at the hands of the *SS Einsatzgruppen*. As if the invasion itself had not been horrendous enough, its murderous echo was the arrival of these killer squads throughout Poland with prepared lists of innocent civilians to be gunned down or sent to internment camps.

"The SS have murdered the schoolmaster, the mayor, priests, and many of the shop owners of our home town," said Albin, "right in the town's streets. They leave their bodies to rot there, not allowing their relatives to bury them. Killed simply because they are thought to be the cultural leaders of our area."

"Thank God Almighty that our parents are only simple peasants," said Bogdan. "Yes, I know it is a selfish thought, but still I thank the Lord, and pray they will stay safe. And our sister

Justyna, wherever in Germany she is tonight, I pray she is safe. As for us, we just have to survive this awful war."

"Save your prayers. No one is safe, brother," responded Albin, his eyes squinted with anger. "These Nazis are nothing but animals. They have no honor. They see our homeland as just a trove of treasures to plunder for themselves, no matter what misery it brings to the people who inhabit the land."

"Yes," Bogdan said, "they even have a word for it - *schadenfreude*. It means to take joy from another's pain."

"That is exactly what our countrymen are dealing with," Albin seethed. "Survival is not as important as revenge."

"Well, my brother," said Bogdan, "look around you at all these countrymen here. Tomorrow you will leave with them to fight the Nazis. Your anger will serve you well in battle. Don't waste it here."

"It comes from a well that is inexhaustible," glared Albin. "I only hope I did not make a dreadful mistake in coming to France."

"To fight for our country? Of course you made the right decision," said Bogdan. "What else would you have done?"

"I should have stayed and fought for the Resistance. It was already forming while I was there in the Tatras Mountains. It was already drawing many young men deep into the forests. They asked me to join them. But I had heard the army was re-forming in France. So now, here I sit, eating hearty meals, attending bonfires when I could be fighting the Nazis on our own homeland's soil."

Bogdan realized his brother carried a much more anguished tone than at their first meeting. That had been filled with the joy of their reunion, but this time his brother only spewed out his regrets. Bogdan knew Albin was responding to the fear of this being their last meal together. He was unburdening himself.

"If it makes you feel better," Bogdan said, "realize that as soon as you board those transport ships you will become a target for German U-boats. You are so lucky, you get to take your wrath out on those Nazi bastards. Who cares on which soil or upon which sea it takes place. Every German you kill will be a step closer to our country's regaining its independence."

"That's just it," said Albin, "who knows if I will ever even be given that chance. As you say, we could all be wiped out by U-boat torpedos. Had I stayed in the Resistance, I would have been doing something all this time. I would have been fighting, killing Nazis, not marching and training."

"Maybe that something you could have been doing was getting yourself killed," replied Bogdan. "General Sikorski shared some intelligence with me that said the Gestapo and Russia's NKVD met in Zakopane last September to strategize how to take down the Resistance networks."

"Don't you see, brother," said Albin, "that is only evidence as to how effective they already are! Both the Russians and Germans fear them."

"That I will drink to!" said Bogdan as he produced a flask. "Authentic *Zubrowka* vodka. I have been saving this for exactly this occasion. Do not ask how it came to be mine."

"Bison Grass Vodka!" exclaimed Albin. "Let us drink to Poland. To a day when her fields are no longer burning!"

"To a free Poland," said Bogdan, as he emptied their water glasses and poured the vodka into each in equal measures.

"*Na drowie*," they each said as they clinked the glasses and swallowed the potent drinks in a simple gulp.

"Now that's the taste of home," said Albin as the spirit burned within him.

"Don't ever forget that fire which burns within you, brother," said Bogdan, "not until we are reunited to savor it again. I love you, Albin. Godspeed to you."

When they separated, Bogdan thought only of how fortunate his brother was to be sent to face off in battle against the Nazis. He knew his brother would do well, and that Albin had done the right thing in joining the Brigade. He only wished his brother would stop torturing himself over his decision.

The British were indeed taking their time invading the town of Narvik because the leader of their ground forces, General Pierse "Pat" Mackesy, proved to be an overly cautious commander. He feared getting himself into an Arctic version of the Gallipoli landings, even though the naval battle in the tight *Ofotfjord* proved to be much more successful than the debacle of his Admiralty supreme commander, Winston Churchill, in the Dardanelles Strait. Mackesy had decided to wait until additional forces were received from the French and Polish Allies, much to the frustration of Churchill and the astonishment of the Germans.

These Allied forces would not arrive until late April and early May. The warships carrying the Independent Polish Highland Brigade had not left their ports in Brittany, France until the night of April 23/24. They had sailed north to the River Clyde in Scotland and transferred to a convoy of Royal Navy ships. The Brigade celebrated their National Day, the third of May, aboard the ships. Great festivities were held aboard the ships as they continued to press ever further north.

They crossed the Arctic Circle on the next day, the fourth of May. Every soldier received their "bluenose" certificate. By this time, lest the Polish soldiers think this was some sort of a pleasure cruise, the seas became suddenly very violent, reminding the Poles of the fury of the Nazis awaiting them. Just after that, their convoy was attacked by a Nazi U-boat off the Norwegian coast, but thankfully a destroyer in their escort group sank it with depth charges.

The Brigade arrived in Tromsø, north of Narvik, but not until May 5. For a brief period, it appeared the Independent Podhale Rifle Brigade would be deployed eastward to the Norwegian/Russian border area, but the Norwegians objected, believing this would only antagonize Stalin and prompt the Soviets to invade their homeland. Instead, they docked at Harstad on May 8, in order for the Poles to participate in the pending invasion of the nearby port of Narvik.

The French units had already been in place by the time the Poles arrived. Both the Poles and French alike must have been amazed by the vertical climb of these jagged, giant tooth-like peaks rising from the sea. All their experience in either the Carpathians or the Alps would be sorely tested on these massive ranges of sheer and seemingly impassible mountain chains. General Mackesy had so feared his Allied invasion forces not being able to move about in the high drifts of the snow covered landing zones, that he delayed the invasion several times.

Four days before the Polish Brigade landed in Harstad, fifty-nine of their countrymen died in the fjords of Norway when German *Luftwaffe* aircraft bombed and sank the Polish destroyer *ORP Grom*. It had been participating in the naval operations along the *Rombaksfjord*. There she would lay in wait, looking for any German troop movement along the shoreline. As soon as any were detected, the *Grom* would open fire with her massive guns upon the enemy. It was this attacking mindset that earned the *Grom* the highest priority as a target among the *Luftwaffe*.

ORP Grom's name meant *"Thunderbolt"*. After the German land forces requested the *Luftwaffe* air support with the intention of disabling the Polish warship, the *Grom* took two direct hits from a Heinkel He-111 bomber. Her internal stores exploded in what surely must have been a thundering bolt of death. The Polish destroyer *Grom* joined the four German destroyers in the depths of the *Rombaksfjord*. The arriving Polish Brigade would have another inspiration for retaliating against the Germans in these mountains and the port of Narvik.

The second day after the Polish Rifle Brigade landed at Harstad would become one of the most eventful days in all of World War II. For on May 10, 1940, the German war machine opened its assault on Belgium, Holland and France. Hitler had spearheaded a column of Panzers and infantry through the Ardennes to bypass the Maginot Line. The French underground fortress stretched south all the way to the French Alps. The Ardennes forest was previously thought to be impassible, and as such was lightly defended by the French.

The German Wehrmacht columns made their way stealthily through the Ardennes. In doing so, the *Wehrmacht* bypassed the Maginot Line, thought by the French to be impregnable. The Germans had just rendered the massive stationary fortification useless by piercing the Ardennes and then applying the full wrath of the highly mobile and extremely coordinated Blitzkrieg attack on the lands beyond it.

The world held its breath, as Germany had opened yet another battlefront in addition to the ongoing conflagrations in Scandinavia. Her resources appeared to be limitless, and her intent was apparent - to wrest control of all Europe by might.

Concurrent with this activity, King George VI invited Winston Churchill to Buckingham Palace, against his innermost desires, to form a Coalition Government to replace the Conservative Government of the disgraced Neville Chamberlain. Neville's "Peace in our time" had come back to haunt and disgrace him. Churchill was already sixty-five years old, but would soon demonstrate his inexhaustible energy and his inspiring oratory in stirring his nation to fight.

It was on the night of the 10th of May that Lieutenant Colonel Becker appeared at the door of the twins' hut, bottle in hand. The bottle turned out to be none other than Scotch Whisky, clearly bearing a Norwegian import label. Becker appeared to have already have been drinking that night, although the bottle's seal was unbroken.

At that point, Einar and Gunnar had been under the colonel's captivity for nearly a month. They assured themselves that they had passed any tests that the Germans might have laid for them to radio information back to London.

The twins had no operative radio, as the broken wireless set was still stashed in a grotto under the rails at Hundalen Station. The sight of the Scotch bottle, with a Norwegian label overlaid upon it, seemed itself like a visual parody of who the twins really were. Did the colonel know they were actually Scotsmen playing a charade of being Norwegian fishermen? The only reassuring aspect of all this was that with the Royal Navy still clearly in control of the fjords, there was no way for the colonel to get anyone out to Skrova to verify their cover.

"I have much news, *Herren*," said the slightly inebriated Colonel Becker. "Here, Einar, open this bottle for we are to celebrate. Our *Wehrmacht* has launched its attack upon the West today, and that can only mean a matter of time before the Allies pull out their forces away from Norway. Then, we can set you both free to return to your fishing village of Skrova. Here, let us drink to that, my Nordic brethren."

The colonel poured the whisky into three stacking metal cups he had brought with him. The twins only looked at each other, and without saying a word each knew this could be another trap set for them.

"I had a case of this whisky taken from Narvik, just for such a special occasion, which today is here," Becker's words were slightly slurred, and as they drank, they became more so. "We have taken good care of you both, no? Well, soon enough we will allow you to return to the fjords."

"And your armies are not concerned with those of the French?" Einar asked. "Their's is one of the largest armies in the world. What if they turn back your *Wehrmacht?*"

"Unmoglichp!" Barked the colonel. "Impossible!".

"What of the English?" asked Gunnar.

"The English, the French, cowards both," Becker said. "They have had us outnumbered for some time here, on the fjords and ashore. But they refuse to invade. They fear the fight in the heart of the German soldier. As for the Norwegians, they are good soldiers but their numbers are few. Ah, and the Poles!

Did you know there are four battalions of a Polish Brigade that recently arrived. Like the Norwegians, they are good fighters, but we will overrun them just as we had in their Slavic homeland. Drink, drink…"

Lieutenant Colonel Becker then re-filled their cups, which were only half empty.

"There can be only one thing that concerns our *Führer*. The English have replaced their leader just today. Neville Chamberlain was weak and not willing to fight. As of this hour, he is replaced with that war hawk Churchill. You know of this man?"

Both twins feigned ignorance, yet inside both were amazed at the news.

"Churchill is a threat who will not allow England to make peace with us," Becker continued, "but he is also a buffoon. He takes unnecessary risks, as he did in the Great War at Gallipoli. He threatens your country's neutrality by mining your territorial waters. The *Führer* had no choice but to send us in to protect you all. Well, my friends, we have a great surprise in store for *Herr* Churchill. This, he will very soon discover."

Neither twin took the bait, but both continued to drink along with the colonel. He rambled from topic to topic, often proudly about the rebirth of Germany, and then a melancholy diatribe on the death of Austria's independence. The twins drank slowly, allowing Becker to heavily outpace them.

About forty minutes later, as Becker droned on about how pretty the Norwegian girls were, Einar decided to circle back.

"You said you had a surprise in store for the new English Prime Minister…"

"*Herr* Churchill," Becker slurred his speech heavily, "Yes, he has quite the mishap ahead of him."

Einar could not resist the bait. "Mishap? In what sense?"

"Like you, Einar," the colonel said, "*Herr* Churchill has an Achille's Heel. He likes to travel too much. Thinks himself too important not to fly to the continent again and again to confer with the French. He thinks that if he takes a large enough escort of their new Spitfire fighters, he can go anywhere. He'll see, he'll see…"

Both twins were frightened by the dark prospects that this news could mean.

"How will he see?" Einar asked.

The colonel eyed the near empty bottle. Only a small portion of Scotch remained. He poured the last of the bottle into his own cup. Becker did not ask either of the twins if they wanted more. He only wanted the last remaining drops for himself.

"You are following his movements and have a *Luftwaffe* squadron ready to shoot him down?" Einar was bold enough to ask.

"I can't tell you, but it is even better," slurred the colonel. "Like the Ardennes, it is something that no one will ever expect. They will only see its aftermath."

"Which will be what?" prodded Einar once more.

"Of what interest is this to you?" replied Lieutenant Colonel Becker defiantly. In his drunken state, his pride had transformed to anger. Fearing they had shown too much interest in the Colonel's threats, Gunnar quickly changed topics.

"Colonel Becker, how is it you have come to have such a command of our language?" Gunnar asked, hoping to sidetrack Becker's rising suspicions.

Becker drained the last of the Scotch from his cup, and let a long heavy breath escape his lungs. It was reminiscent of a man recovering from a malady, almost as if the man bore his scars not externally, but deeply inside himself.

"When I was a *hauptmann*…" Becker began.

"What is this word *hauptmann*?" asked Gunnar.

"A captain," the colonel said, then started anew, "when I was a captain, I was assigned to the military attache in Oslo."

"This was after the Nazis came to power?" asked Einar.

"Nein, Nein," Becker protested. "It was when Austria was a proud, independent alpine country. I was a captain in the Austrian Army then. We were not yet part of the Reich."

"So, you came to Oslo," said Gunnar, "and you learned the language while here."

"I learned for her…" Becker mumbled, "I learned for her…"

"Surely, you had to learn for your posting no?" Gunnar egged him on.

"*Nein, Nein.* It was only a two year posting," Becker said, becoming angry as his memories seemed to be stirred within him. "I loved it here in your country, but I could have managed without learning the language. We had interpreters, local women, mostly who knew German fluently."

"So you learned the language for a woman?" Gunnar prodded him on.

"Astrid," the colonel said as a wave of melancholy seemed to overcome him, "her name was Astrid. She was beautiful. I told her I wanted to see the mountains and fjords of her country, your country. I was single then, as was she. We started with day trips away from Oslo. Then, one Saturday, I surprised her. I took her to the most beautiful mountain in all of Norway, the *Gausta.* Surely you both know it?"

Einar panicked at the question. Neither he nor Gunnar had ever heard of it. He knew not what to say when his brother smoothly answered, "Yes, of course we know of it, but it is a far distance from here, so we have not been there."

Einar thought Gunnar a genius. Certainly, if it was a day trip from Oslo it had to be far from the Arctic. He thought Gunnar was so fast and so smooth.

"Of course, of course," Becker slurred. "It is a thousand kilometers from here at least. Astrid and I left Oslo and took the first train and got to the Rjukan Valley early in the afternoon. I asked her if she wanted to climb it, and she looked at me as if I was crazy. What she did not know was that the hydro-power company, Norse-Hydro, had put a funicular railway inside the mountain as a gift to the people in the valley. You see the mountains are so steep there that in the winter no sunlight makes it into the valley. So the locals use it to get some sunshine atop of the *Gaustatoppen.*"

"She liked it, yeah?" prodded Gunnar.

"She loved it. We rode it and kissed in the sunshine atop the mountain. We stayed just long enough until it was time to catch the last train home. But we had a lovely ferry ride across the lake just as the sun set. It was very romantic."

"So you made love to her?" asked Einar.

"Ja, I wanted to, but she made me wait," Becker recalled as if the wait had been a sweet torture.

"Wait until when?" Gunnar pulled, knowing that Becker was very much enjoying the retelling.

"Until we took the train to Bergen for a long weekend. I know it sounds silly, but that first night together we fell in love. In a small bed in a tiny hotel on the hillside between the *Bryggen* docks and the *Floibahnen* funicular. The next day, the only break we took from our lovemaking was to ride that inclined train to the *Mt. Fløyen* mountaintop overlooking the city and harbor."

"Another funicular?" Gunnar asked?

"*Ja, ja.* That was our joke," Becker laughed, "that we always needed to have a damn funicular to ride. We were spent, and ravenously ate at the outdoor cafe up atop the mountain. Afterwards, as we walked its forest trails, as beautiful as they were, we realized we were only wasting our precious time together. We hurried down the *Floibahnen* and back to our room. We made love again all that night. The next morning, we took an early boat to the seaside village of *Flåm*, and after spending the day touring, we rode the railway back through the most beautiful countryside outside of my own Austria. We again rushed to our hotel bed on that Bergen hill. That weekend was like none other I have ever had in my life. It convinced me that I must marry that woman, and only a month later I proposed to her…"

"…And then you married her and she taught you her language," Einar finished his story for him.

The colonel paused, as Einar's words transformed the blissful look that had overtaken his countenance to that of a rejected man. Becker tilted his cup, only to find nothing more drip from its side.

"She laughed out loud," Becker confessed. "She said that she liked me very much, and greatly enjoyed our time together, but she would never think of marrying a man who did not speak the Norwegian tongue. She said already her friends gave her much trouble over her liaisons with an Austrian. I told her she could teach me her language, but again she laughed. *'What and put myself out of work?'* she joked. It was all a joke to her."

"So how did you learn?" asked Gunnar.

"What? Learn the language? It became my passion," Becker spoke like a man recanting the confessions of his darkest sins. "She stopped seeing me after several more months, so I took lessons every night from another woman. She had a face like a horse, this one, but she was a good teacher. I vowed to become proficient, and I did."

"Nearly fluent, I would say," Gunnar praised him.

"As would I," added Einar, who had stayed mostly silent as Gunnar was drawing so much from the lieutenant colonel.

"After a year's lessons, I went to her apartment in Oslo, to Astrid's place," Becker's eyes had become flat, lifeless, as if they no longer looked outward, only inward upon his scars. "In her language, I told her how much I loved her, and how I could not live without her by my side forever. I will never forget being down on my knee in front of her when she began to laugh once more. She mocked me for being a little boy in my military uniform. She mocked me for my religion. She laughed at how many times the scapular from my chest had wedged itself in the swale between her breasts. Somehow, she thought that to be hysterical. '*My good little Catholic boy,*' she called me, '*forget me and go home to the Alps.*' Which I later did."

"She broke your heart," said Gunnar, as he felt his captor's pain. He could not help the story touching his own heart. Einar did not share that emotion for the colonel and looked at his brother in outright disgust.

Upon noticing Einar's reaction, a tight smile stretched across the colonel's features. It threatened to morph into a darker, more sinister snarl, but Becker retained his composure.

"So, because of Astrid, I speak your tongue today," he said to them both, in the tone of a man destined to rebury the past that the whisky had exhumed. "It is why I liked you both so, from that very first day in Hundalen Station. The scapulars you both wear. My medic told me of Einar's, and I could later see the laces of yours, Gunnar, around your neck. I thought, why would a pair of twins from a remote fishing village in the *Vestfjorden* wear such things. Are you not Lutheran, like all Scandinavians? So, why exactly is this?"

Becker's eyes turned hard on them, full of accusation.

"Not all, you will find. For us, it is because of our mother," Einar said, catching Gunnar off guard.

"Yes, our mother," Gunnar echoed, trying not to stutter. "She was a missionary."

"From what country?" demanded Becker.

"From here in Norway," said Gunnar. He was thinking fast on his feet. "Many people are not aware that Catholicism is the second largest Christian faith in Norway behind Lutheranism. Father had fallen in love with her as she attempted to spread the Catholic religion here in the north. He was relentless in his pursuit of her. He finally convinced her to marry him, but only if he converted and their children would be raised Catholic. She refused to let father raise us in any other faith."

He did not lie about the order of the faiths, but what Gunnar intentionally did not mention that was while nearly three quarters of all Norwegian Christians were Lutherans, only three percent were Catholic.

"Where did they meet? Where was she from?" Becker seemed to be quizzing them now. Gunnar thought that Becker was toying with them, perhaps to assure they were not spies. Perhaps only to protect himself from accusations of abetting the enemy.

"Mother was originally from Bergen, also," Gunnar said. "Father met her in Tromsø, and brought her back to Skrova."

Becker seemed to be lost in thought. "Yes, I do remember a beautiful Catholic church there. St. Paul's." He paused, as if he wanted to say something more, only to stand wobbly upon his feet and say, "Now, I must go."

With this he left from them. Gunnar watched from the window as he headed towards the station house. The snow slowed him, making him concentrate on his steps in his drunken state.

"I think he is on to us, Gunnar. He knows we are spies. He toys with us."

Gunnar thought through the conversation, as an old man would sift through distant memories. Only these memories were those of the words of the drunken German officer.

"Why come to us to drink?" Gunnar asked.

"Perhaps because he cannot do so with his own troops," Einar answered. "He feels as if we are kindred spirits. He said so, with his thinking us to be Catholics, I suppose."

"Why does he drink at all?" asked Gunnar.

"To celebrate the *Wehrmacht's* assault on France and the Low Countries," Einar offered.

"No, that is his excuse," explained Gunnar. "He drinks not to celebrate, but to escape. He is a vastly wounded man. Rejected by this woman Astrid whom he loved. She mocked him for his faith, which he apparently holds dear. And above all else, he is wounded for having his country overrun by the *Führer*. You can hear the sadnesses in his drunken, slurred voice."

"So, he takes solace with us, his fellow Catholics?" asked Einar. "We know nothing of Catholicism, my brother. How did you know there were even Catholics in Bergen?"

The look on Gunnar's face spoke volumes.

"I did not," he answered, "but Bergen was always a Hanseatic League city, trading with the Germans. That even predated the Reformation, so I thought there must be Catholics there, if anywhere, in Norway."

Once again, Einar was amazed at how fast his brother was thinking on his feet.

"What do we do when he wants to have a deeper discussion on the saints or the sacraments?" Einar said, but then just as quickly changed his thought process. "Why did you stop me, Gunnar when I was asking about their plans against Churchill?"

"Because it is a trap," Gunnar said. "This whole thing feels like nothing more than a trap to me. I just don't understand why they are stringing us along. Why on earth would a German colonel tease us with such ideas as an ambush on the Prime Minister."

"Relax, brother," said Einar, "if they thought us to be spies we would already be dead. I think if they have a trap for anyone, it is for Churchill himself. The colonel trusts us for some reason, perhaps because of the shared Catholic faith that he believes flows between us. We need to make the most of this, and find out what they have planned against the Prime Minister."

What Colonel Becker had not shared with the twins was that there was a noose that, by then, had slowly begun to tighten around their positions at Narvik and Bjørnfjell, and the Ofoten Railway that ran between them. After having disembarked the entire *Gebirgsjäger* 3rd Mountain Infantry Brigade from the ten *Kriegsmarine* destroyers on that first morning in Narvik, the brigade was separated into three battalions of roughly five hundred men each.

Lieutenant Colonel Becker's objective was to secure the Ofoten Railway and the Bjørnfjell Station as the main provisioning supply route for the *Kriegsmarine* seamen who were left to defend the port of Narvik. The other two battalions took to the mountain peaks to the north of the town. They had quickly captured the town of Bjerkvik at the furthest end of the *Herjangsfjord*. They overpowered a Norwegian ammunition depot nearby before taking to the northern peaks beyond. All had gone exceptionally well for the *Wehrmacht's* elite alpine troops.When Becker had secured the Ofoten Railway and opened the line to allow the provisioning train to roll in from Sweden, it appeared that everything had gone to the Nazis' benefit. The only vexing problem for the Germans was the Brit's refusal to invade.

However, Norwegian troops were amassing just beyond the arc of the two northernmost *Gebirgsjäger* battalions. On the 23rd of April, the Norwegian 6th Division under General Carl Gustav Fleischer attacked the *Gebirgsjäger* forces at Gratangen in fierce mountain fighting that lasted through the next two days. The Germans rebuffed the attack, but only by giving up ground and falling back towards Narvik. The Norwegians had casualties at least five times as high as the German forces, but they fearlessly made it known that they would fight this invading Nazi force even if it required advancing from one frozen mountain peak to the next, no matter the losses.

Three days after this battle, the first French forces arrived. They consisted of three Alpine battalions and two battalions of French Foreign Legion forces deployed under the leadership of General Antoine Béthouart. By this point, the Allied forces were gaining a significant advantage in manpower over the German forces, but the lack of coordination among the Allies was delaying the Allied re-invasion of Narvik itself. The lack of aggression by the British commander of the Allies' land forces, General Pierce Mackesy, frustrated not only Paris and London, but the Norwegian Resistance command as well.

Also frustrating the Allied Supreme Commanders was the apparent lack of coordination, if not downright rivalry, that existed between General Macksey's land forces and the naval operations under British Admiral Lord Cork. As a result, the naval forces continued to shell the port and its surroundings, which resulted in Narvik's population having taken to the safety of numerous ski huts in the mountains above the town.

The German soldiers and seamen left to defend Narvik merely hunkered down and withstood the shelling, always awaiting the invasion of Allied ground forces that never came, much to their disbelief.

It was on the ninth of May that the four battalions of the Polish Independent Podhale Rifle Brigade arrived in the Allies command port of Harstad. They were commanded by General Zygmunt Bohusz-Szyszko. The Polish forces were split, with one battalion fighting in the areas near Bjerkvik, and the three others being assigned to the Alkenes Peninsula just south of Narvik. Amongst the Poles fighting at Bjerkvik was the alpine infantryman Albin Bratajewski. He had finally rejoined the fight.

The next several days were nothing more than sheer frustration for the twins. They observed from their ski hut all that transpired at the Bjørnfjell station. Great activity was underway, and several trains were dispatched down the Ofoten Railway to take provisions to Narvik, as well as to the troops stationed along its route. All this they observed, but had no means to report anything further back to London, as their broken radio remained stashed in the grotto beneath the Hundalen Station. Nor could they learn of Britain's wrestling under the new Prime Minister Churchill as to whether the Empire would fight or sue for peace.

The twins were allowed to leave their hut only to visit the woods to take care of their personal needs, at which point they would also be allowed to forage for firewood on their return. They were supplied rations on the colonel's command, which seemed odd to them both. The brothers were neither free men nor prisoners, and they could not discern if the colonel held them as Nordic brothers, Catholic brethren, or suspected enemy spies. All they knew for certain was that Becker kept them close, and ever since the night of their drunken discussion, always under the guard of two armed soldiers outside their door.

Inside their hut, they passed the days in their separate ways. Gunnar tracked the days, and whenever possible confirmed his count in any manner that he could. Each day was like another, and it was easy to lose track. In his mind, he kept detailed records of any train movements, but nothing was ever written down for fear of their cabin being inspected. Gunnar memorized his notes instead, and hoped that they might risk the overland passage into Sweden, once his brother was capable to do so, where they could then radio London.

Einar on the other hand became obsessed with only one thing - the Enigma machine that was operating in the Bjørnfjell Station house. Einar noted the couriers that came and went, especially those that departed toward the trackside cottage named "*Solheimsbrakka*" that had been commandeered by General Dietl as his command post. Einar schemed as to how he might capture that device, sending the general and his brigade into a communications blackout. Einar could only think day and night about securing the device, and returning it to London in pristine condition.

Both Einar and Gunnar noticed two things with each passing day. The number of German forces at Bjørnfjell thinned, and the pace of activity quickened. Eventually the two guards encamped outside their door was reduced to a single soldier. There was clearly a great battle occurring to their north and west, as the Allies were slowly gaining on the Germans, pushing them back into the hills that led up to the rolling plateau upon which Bjørnfjell Station was situated. If the Allies captured Bjørnfjell, not only would they have forced the surrender of the German troops and this vital provisioning depot, but the twins would themselves be rescued.

Gunnar pressed this point repeatedly with Einar, that they just needed to wait out the arrival of the Allies. Einar, on the other hand, dreamt only of taking action. Each day his leg felt better, and he wished for them to escape while they were to have a chance.

Then, on a clear mountain day which Gunnar had marked to be the 20th of May, the mid-morning sounds of the station and camp were drowned out by the drone of aircraft engines overhead. Both brothers watched at the cabin's window as the blue sky filled with billowing plumes of white, one after another. It was as if they watched an orderly progression of jellyfish float in the waters of the Tay back home.

However, what trailed below these silken clouds was far more dangerous than any sea creature's venomous stingers, for under each cloud of silk floated a reinforcement paratroop soldier of the Third Reich.

The twins were not trained in paratrooping, but it was clear that this day's weather was not ideal for it. The winds were high, and the silk chutes were blown dangerously hard.

There were hundreds of them, and they began filling the open but snow-laden fields around the station house. Each man landed and immediately battled the strong winds for control of his chute. It dragged several of them, as the winds billowed in the chutes overpowering the jumpers. The slick snowy fields, under which were a smattering of rocks, battered the troops as they were dragged. It was clear that these had not been the ideal conditions for a drop, but the nearing approach of the Allied forces from the north had necessitated the risk of the jump.

Plane after plane soared overhead, each leaving a trail of parachutes behind. Then, the guns of the Swedish defense forces on the other side of the mountain pass could be heard firing. The

Swedish, fearing an invasion of their own country, were fighting. It was one thing for them to allow a provisioning train to pass through their country, but another altogether to allow *Luftwaffe* aircraft to penetrate their airspace.

The Swedes had hit one of the Junker-52 aircraft, sending it crashing onto the plateau on their side of the border. The plane had only been circling for another approach over Bjørnfjell when it was hit. Many of its paratroops were able to depart the plane, but most of these soldiers were captured and interred by the Swedes upon landing. This had been the second aircraft shot down that day, as one had already been hit by British aircraft fire over the skies outside of Bodø along the German planes' route from Trondheim that morning.

The twins stayed glued to the window of the hut as the sky continued to fill with silk. The guns of the Swedes soon erupted again, and suddenly another sound filled the air. It was an unusually high pitched droning sound, and as they watched the skies it became louder. Soon, the sight of smoke bellowed from an aircraft which had come over the mountain pass in a dangerously low altitude. The wounded Junker appeared to be coming directly at them, with thick, greasy black smoke belching from the tips of yellow-orange flames from its wounded engine.

It crashed into the field directly in front of the cabin. The guard who had been encamped outside their door ran into the woods, as the aircraft plowed into the ground only a few hundred feet away. The plane immediately broke into flames as it crashed hard but flat on impact, the pilot doing everything in his power to control the aircraft. But it was too late, the momentum of the grounded aircraft caused it to slide along the rocky snow covered fields before pummeling into the thin woods that lined the ravine. After the wings were sheared from the plane when it hit the treeline, the fuselage became a spiraling javelin of mass. The body of the plane disappeared into the forest, and the impact of its nose with the trees caused it to slide laterally, and like a massive rolling pin it toppled trees three or four across. The spinning fuselage ripped open just before rolling over the edge into the deep ravine, not far from where Einar and Gunnar had stashed their contraband on that first night.

Einar threw on a parka and raced as fast as he could hobble upon his injured leg out into the field. He ran toward the tree line where the body of the aircraft had carved out a flaming swath of debris.

Gunnar, having not yet even caught his breath from having witnessed the crash, yelled for his brother to come back. It was too late. Gunnar ran to the hut's rear window which faced the woods. He saw his brother disappear into the flaming timber-strewn debris of the shattered pines. The remaining upright trees were burning around the area where they had been penetrated by the rolling fuselage. Even in the cabin, Gunnar could smell the overpowering pungency of the hot pine sap commingled with the burning black smoke of one hundred octane aviation fuel. The horrid mixture overcame him, unsettled his stomach with a powerful nausea until he retched involuntarily upon the cabin's floor.

When Gunnar recovered, what he saw next turned his stomach even more than the smell of his own vomit that filled his nostrils. Gunnar looked up to see the German guard who had hidden in the woods emerge into the open swath. He screamed orders to halt as he followed Einar into the flaming debris zone of the forest. Gunnar then saw the guard raise his rifle in the direction of his brother and squeeze off a single round.

Gunnar's heart immediately sank. He screamed aloud at the window, "No, no, no. Don't shoot, don't shoot," all very reactively in English. He slammed his hand on the pane of glass so violently that he was surprised it did not shatter.

Tears filled Gunnar's eyes, until he looked up in time to see his brother hobbling out of the woods with his hands up. He did not appear to be injured. Apparently, the guard had only fired a warning shot over his head.

By this time, many more German officers and troops were approaching the crash site. Einar was marched back to the front door of the cabin. There, the guard pushed him violently forward across the threshold before screaming the word *"Verboten"* over and over again.

"My God, Einar, I thought he had shot you," said Gunnar as he rushed toward his brother. Both twins were visibly trembling, but Einar was quicker to rein in his emotions.

"I'm fine, Gunnar," his brother said bravely. "Calm yourself. I am unhurt, brother. That aircraft's wreckage, except for its wings, is lying at the bottom of that ravine. It was throwing out its cargo as it rolled. The whole path through the woods is splintered with pine and scattered with debris."

"Just so long as you are safe, Einar," Gunnar answered.

His brother looked at him with a great reticence.

"You don't understand, Gunnar," Einar then said. "They will send a detail out here to cover every inch of those woods to recover anything useful. They will form lines to walk the woods. If they should happen upon the stash of our things, including our British passports, we will be shot."

That day, on the 20th of May 1940, some two thousand paratroopers reinforced the critical German stronghold at Bjørnfjell. The forces, which had left Trondheim, nearly a thousand kilometers to the south, were a crucial need to the overall effort at Narvik and points west. With the arrival of the Poles and the French, the Allies had gained a massive numerical advantage in the area, and as a result had recaptured much of the ground that the 3rd *Gebirgsjäger* mountain infantry battalions had seized upon their arrival the month before. The Norwegians, English, French and Polish forces had pushed eastward towards the high plateau of Bjørnfjell after they had secured the lands around the *Herjangsfjord.*

The German forces still maintained the high ground, and forced the Allies to slowly fight their way up the mountain heights. The Germans had only slowed their opponents, it had not stopped them. Without the infusion of the two thousand troops dropped that day from the sky, it is likely that General Dietl would have either had to withdraw his forces into neutral Sweden, where they would be interred, or have surrendered to the Allies outright. Instead, all the forces dropped that day were immediately rushed into action to the west and north of Bjørnfjell to hold off the impending onslaught of the Allies.

Despite the ring of forces closing in on the Germans from the west and north at Bjørnfjell, the Ofoten Railway remained in the Nazis' control. It would ultimately remain so until the Allies successfully landed forces on the small peninsula and drove the Germans out of Narvik.

Figure 33: The Historic St. Ermin's Hotel, London

49 The Shifting Tides

May 20 to 27, 1940

"We shall not flag or fail. We shall go on to the end. We shall fight in France, we shall fight on the seas and oceans, we shall fight with growing confidence and growing strength in the air, we shall defend our island, whatever the cost may be, we shall fight on the beaches, we shall fight on the landing grounds, we shall fight in the fields and in the streets, we shall fight in the hills; we shall never surrender."

Winston Spencer Churchill

The next morning, Brigand MacAlvor entered London's Saint Ermin's Hotel on Caxton Street in the heart of Westminster at six in the morning. He took the steps to the offices of Section D of the British Secret Service that had been covertly established there. Brigand had ridden the trains from Dundee to Edinburgh to London all the day before. He arrived late in the day. He did not sleep that night, nor for the matter of record, had he slept for the past several days. Brigand had not dared to take shelter at the flat on the south side of the Blackfriars Bridge, lest it be occupied by another of the service's visiting contributors to the black arts. He desired nothing greater than to have the element of surprise upon the man who had coerced him into sending his beloved sons off to a what had become an embattled war zone.

Instead, Brigand walked the streets of London all night. Twice he was stopped by Bobbies, and each time he was able to flash the credentials that Wincer Wells had long ago given him for just such an occasion. He stayed out of the parks, fearing someone would think he was some sort of vagabond, or worse a poof, but walked instead along its unending miles of pavement. As the sun began to rise, he found himself on the Thames Embankment, just outside of Whitehall. He thought this fitting, for after all, Whitehall Court had been where the betrayal of his two sons, not to mention his own soul, had long ago begun.

As a thick mist had risen from the river, not quite strong enough to be considered a fog, Brigand worked his way to Saint Ermin's Hotel, where he again flashed his credentials to enter. He knew Wincer Wells would be at his desk by that time, and likely had been so for the last hour or longer. Brigand knew they would be alone and had counted on this very condition.

Brigand entered the small room that was Wells' office. Wells looked up from the papers splayed out across his desk's blotter, and Brigand noticed they had all been neatly covered with blank sheets. There was no doubt that Wincer Wells had recognized the dragging, sliding signature of his wooden foot along the corridor's highly polished tiled floors.

"I thought I told you that I would have you arrested were you to ever roam these halls uninvited, MacAlvor."

"Good morning to you, also," said Brigand. "Since you refuse to take my calls from Broughty Ferry, you force me to travel here. If you truly wish to have me arrested, please do so straightaway. But whilst we wait for the Bobbies to drag me off to the Old Bailey, let me tell you about my last few train rides."

Wells looked up at him, suspecting that something of a threat belied his off-hand comment.

"Do then tell me of your travels and travails, my old friend," said Wells calmly.

"Yesterday's ride from Dundee and Edinburgh to London was rather unremarkable," he began, "but the day before I took to the rails, after which I hired a car, mind you, for a most interesting engagement at *Drumintoul Lodge* in the Highlands."

Wells winced at the words. Not his usual involuntary facial reflex, but a full bodily admission of an inflicted wound. Brigand noticed this and knew he had found the man's singular, but fatal vulnerability. He decided to play his threat hard against the jugular of his long-time superior.

"I know what you've done, Wincer," Brigand added, "and you've been very snakey, you have, playing the skulk. By the bye, should you attempt to have me even so much as escorted from these premises, I guarantee you that the Major General will become quite aware."

Brigand was quite sure that Wells knew that he referred to Major-General Stewart Menzies, the third and current "C", Chief of MI6.

"I only did what had to be done, given the circumstances," said Wells. He leaned back in his wooden chair, raising his arms to settle upon their rests, attempting to consciously send the signal *I have nothing whatsoever to hide*.

"I don't think 'C' would appreciate your taking liberties with impersonating his predecessor, now would he?" Brigand threatened.

"So you know about even that, then?" Wells confessed. It was only then that Brigand became aware that Wincer had crossed his arms defensively upon his last comment.

"Turns out the threat of having the lodge-master exposed for fiddling the books regarding my boy, Gunnar, was enough to have him produce the letter from 'C'. He was quite proud of it, actually. Likely doesn't get much correspondence directly from the Chief. Poor bastard doesn't realize it's a forgery. Fake as a fleecer's smile."

"How did you know it wasn't legitimate?" Wells asked.

"I really didn't until you flinched when I mentioned it just now. I suspected all along, of course, that it was your doing, given how desperate you were to get my boys over to Narvik. You'll tell me where they are, or the illegitimacy of that document becomes very public. Whether or not I return home."

"I can't," said Wells.

"You mean you shan't?" replied Brigand. "Damn this secrecy ploy of yours. You're risking the lives of my boys!"

"No, I cannot! Listen to my damn words on this, MacAlvor," Wells reasserted, "I cannot has a totally different meaning than I shall not. I simply do not know where they are currently. We issued the abort code nearly three weeks ago. They never acknowledged receiving it. I assumed they simply made straight as a crow's flight out of Norway into Sweden, as had always been the plan. I assumed that they would contact me when they were in Stockholm. We have people there awaiting their arrival. They never showed."

Before hearing Wells' explanation, Brigand had felt as alone as any vessel on the open seas, but after these words were relayed to him, he felt overpowered, as if unknown raiders had cast grappling hooks onto his being. They smashed and shredded before their torturous barbs caught and twisted within his entrails. Every syllable of every word carried with it the enmity of the wrath of a thousand hostile boarders.

After the immediate reaction of his shock, Brigand felt an explosion of rage rise within him, calling for his every muscle to rebel out in action. He reached over the desk and grabbed the blotter, flinging it to one side and a quarter of the way across the room. The papers, as heavy as they were with the gravity of their MOST SECRET classifications, nonetheless fluttered harmlessly like feathers in the still morning air.

"How could you possibly have lost my twins to the Nazis, Wells?" Brigand screamed. Then he mimicked Wells aloud, "*They are safe, Brigand, old friend, just a bolt across the border and they are free.* How dare you to have been so cavalier with their lives all along? How cowardly of you to avoid me for the past several weeks."

Wells had allowed the man his outrage and sat still in his chair. His only move had been to steady his morning cup of tea, lest it too should be disturbed by Brigand's theatrics. He waited until the last document fluttered like a windblown paratrooper to the floor before offering, in response, his defense.

"I am quite sure that Einar and Gunnar are fine, Brigand," Wells said as a matter of fact. "They are well trained and resourceful young lads."

Brigand looked scathingly at this man who had long ago leveraged the younger version of himself into this fraternity. He could feel the veins in his neck pulsing with a pressure that threatened to explode in damnation upon not only Wells, but also himself, just as the Turk's guns had done so many years ago at that damn beach in Gallipoli.

"You are quite sure of NOTHING, Wincer," Brigand screamed, "that much has already been demonstrated. You wagered your faltering career on placing my twins at risk and I was fool enough to double down on your marker. My God, what have I done? What have I done!"

Brigand became crippled with guilt. He leaned over in agony, as if he had taken a forceful jab in his stomach. He doubled over, supporting himself only by reaching out his arm and placing his hand on Wells' vacant desktop for support. Wells rose from his chair, not to console his former agent, but to reprimand him.

"I demand you collect yourself, MacAlvor," Wells stated. "You are an embarrassment to this enterprise. I am quite sure that you will see them again, rest assured of that, old boy."

At the phrase "rest assured", Brigand instantly thought of his sons' fates. *Were they already at rest? What would he ever tell Tilly? How could he bear the rest of his life if any harm had come upon them?*

"*Rest assured* of only one thing, Wincer," Brigand said as he raised only his head to glare at Wells, "that if my lads do not return in one piece, my tale of that little forgery of yours goes to Menzies straightaway, whether I am alive or not!"

With this, Brigand stormed out of the offices. His mind had become his enemy, as it conjured one dreadful possibility after another for his boys. The effect of this cerebral onslaught was of Brigand's being in the jaws of a massive vise, with the tension ratcheting from the weight of the shame with which he burdened himself.

As the sun slowly rose amid the morning mist that stubbornly refused to burned away, Brigand MacAlvor walked the parks, and then on to Euston Station. He knew of nothing else to do in London, so he caught the train back to Edinburgh. On that ride, as the bucolic countryside of northern England gave way to the more rugged Scottish terrain, all he could think of was his father, and his final path of escape. A harsh voice, as if from a great distance, told him he must do everything in his power to resist, but in the depths of Brigand's melancholy, a much more seductive spirit called to him from the sea.

Only hours later after this encounter, Lieutenant Colonel Becker arrived at the Bjørnfjell ski hut along with two guards carrying sub-machine guns. These were above and beyond the overnight guard already encamped outside their door. The guards had pushed open the door with great force, indicating that this was no social visit indeed. Becker's demeanor was terse, his face rigid with authority. His eyes noticeably scanned the room.

"Colonel Becker, it is good to see…" began Gunnar, as he rose from the table where he and Einar had been seated. Becker shouted over him.

"I HAVE COME TO ASK YOU, EINAR," he said in his German-clipped but nearly perfect Norwegian, as he completely ignored Gunnar, "AS TO WHY YOU TOOK THE OPPORTUNITY TO BOLT OUT TO THE CRASH SITE YESTERDAY?"

Becker's words rode upon a heightened wave of anger, restrained only by the level of control he commanded over the two young men. Einar looked at Gunnar, who's eyes had arched upon hearing Becker's assertive tone.

"DO NOT LOOK AT HIM. IT IS I WHO AM SPEAKING WITH YOU, EINAR," Becker screamed, "WHY DID YOU RUSH OUT TO THAT CRASH SITE?"

Einar slowly, without fear, looked back at the colonel and thereafter firmly refused to break eye lock with him. He wondered whether the fire crews had found their hidden rucksack. He waited, then said calmly, "I thought I could help if there were any survivors."

"YOU LIE!" Becker screamed, as he slammed his hand down on the small table, making it and both brothers jump. "NOW TELL ME WHY YOU RUSHED OUT THERE! WHAT WAS IT THAT YOU WERE LOOKING FOR?"

Neither twin had seen Becker in this agitated a state up until that point. Something was terribly amiss. Something that Becker surely thought was rooted in Einar's action the day before.

Einar was stunned. He had that day before barely gotten into the burning swath of the splintered pine forest before he heard the warning shot fired over his head. He had stopped and froze at the precipice of the steep ravine, where he could see the wreckage of the fuselage burning some hundred meters below on the rocks. It was then that the guard slowly walked up to him, rifle raised and ready to fire, before he was force-marched back to the hut, where he rejoined Gunnar.

Despite the fumes of the fires that had burned so closeby in the adjacent woods that night, Einar and Gunnar had not been allowed to leave the cabin. Instead they watched as the German troops worked through the late evening hours to extinguish the inferno. With great effort, the flames of burning aviation fuel, as well as the woods it consumed, were brought under control.

Afterwards, the twins had watched as the Germans began an extensive search just as soon as the sun began to rise. In this most northern latitude at that time of year, it rose just before one o'clock in the morning.

"Colonel Becker," Einar said, desperately attempting to remain calm, "I looked for nothing. It was only my natural reaction to run toward the crash. I wanted to help. If you speak to your guard, he will confirm that I was alone only in the forest for perhaps only sixty seconds or less. I could not possibly have taken anything from that wreckage, most of which, even then, lay at the bottom of the ravine."

The colonel then spoke aloud in German, and the guard was brought in, he who had followed Einar into the woods, and who then had been stationed outside overnight. Becker questioned him extensively in German, and although the twins could not understand what was being said, they could tell the guard was corroborating Einar's story by watching the colonel's body language slowly soften. It was as if Lieutenant Colonel Becker had been released from a crushing responsibility he did not wish to bear. He then dismissively released the overnight guard, but retained the two other submachine gun armed soldiers as he turned to address the twins.

"Neither of you are to leave this hut for the next forty-eight hours. I will have a bucket brought in for the purpose of relieving yourselves. If either of you is found outside, your new guards, these men, are ordered to shoot to kill on sight. Do you understand what I am telling you?"

Becker's voice was still rigid with authority, but the accusatory edge, honed with the threat of instant retribution with which he had confronted Einar, was gone.

"So much for the valued trust of our shared Nordic brotherhood," muttered Einar, just loud enough to be heard.

Gunnar quickly spoke over him. "Yes, Colonel, we understand. We will not wander from this cabin. Einar was only concerned for the safety of your paratroopers who might be caught in the wreckage."

Becker cast a hard glare at his brother, as if weighing the veracity of Einar's claims all over again. He then returned his eyes upon Gunnar, before adding, "We were quite fortunate. That Junker had no troops within it, only equipment when it crashed. We lost the pilot and navigator, of course, but thankfully no fighting troops."

"How horrible for those two men!" Gunnar said, instantly aghast with grief. Becker watched clinically as tears began to form in his brother's eyes.

"They were *schwachkopfs, nincompoops,*" Becker said agitatedly, "it was their own error that cost them their lives. They were warned not to fly over the Swedes' territory. *Dumkopfs!* What was more horrible was the loss of the fighting men when the Swedes shot down the other Junker filled with paratroopers on their side of this mountain."

"And all those soldiers also died?" asked Gunnar, as his grief deepened.

"Only a few," replied Becker, "but of those who were able to jump so low, many were badly injured. Even those who were not harmed were interred by the Swedes. They are lost to us for fighting, they might as well have perished."

Gunnar found the Austrian's utilitarian approach to these men's death and suffering to be soul crushing.

"So why even bother to recognize Sweden's neutrality," Einar caustically scorned, "when your army and navy so willingly violate Norway's own?"

Becker looked at Einar with a stabbing glance. It was clear to Gunnar that the relationship he and the colonel seemed to share was not extended to his brother.

"I apologize for Einar's remark, Colonel," Gunnar said, "his mind is still fogged by all the fumes that have filled his lungs in the forest."

At this point Becker slowly walked behind and around Einar as he sat in his chair. His gaze down on the young man reminded Gunnar of a farmer deciding just what to do with a wounded or rabid dog.

"Your brother Einar resents your both being detained here in this cabin. Yes, I certainly understand this. But what he does not understand is that *Der Führer* sent his *Wehrmacht, Luftwaffe* and *Kriegsmarine* here to free Norway from the threat of an invasion by Britain and her allies. Here we fight against those who have attacked our ships in your neutral waters, and would deprive the Reich of free and unrestrained commerce with Norway. After all, we are here at the invitation of the Norwegian government under Quisling."

"Quisling is a traitor!" barked Einar. "The King and his cabinet are the real government, and they refused your troops as they invaded our country. Everyone knows this!"

This third outburst from Einar drew Becker's acidic glare, and it was enjoined by a harsh entreaty of words.

"Your King is a coward. He has fled Oslo. He hides in these northern mountains, perhaps nearby. After we deal with the troops of the actual invaders, the soldiers of Britain and her allies, we will find His Highness and bring him to justice."

"And yet," Einar replied "the Norwegian troops are fighting alongside these invaders against you. Release us, Colonel Becker, we are no threat to you."

At this outburst Gunnar walked to the spot Becker had just vacated aside Einar. He placed his hand on his brother's shoulder in an attempt to quiet him. Einar brushed it away.

"So, I should just release you both so you should take up arms with your rebel countrymen against us?" Becker asked aloud. "You Norwegians do not realize how futile this effort is. Oslo, Bergen, all the way up to Trondheim are already under our full control. So here, in this frozen north, our struggle goes on a few days more? Not for long, for the Third Reich's power is not to be contained. As we speak, the Nazi swastika flies over the Netherlands, Belgium and much of northern France."

"Just as it does over your own beloved Austria," sneered Einar.

At this comment, Becker rushed in and pushed Gunnar aside. He grabbed Einar by his collar and pulled him to his feet. Gunnar could only watch as the unexpected action brought a searing pain to his brother's face. His leg instantly throbbed anew. The colonel pulled Einar's face within inches of his own.

"If we were not so remotely located on this snow-laden mountainside, I would have long ago sent you and your brother to a camp in the south. You are lucky that the terrain between here and Trondheim is impassable. Perhaps you are luckier still that I share your Catholic faith. It is the only thing that kept me from simply shooting you both, and ending this tiresome distraction. But if either of you wander from this hut, you will only be giving my guards the excuse to do so on my behalf."

Having said this, Becker pushed Einar back into his chair before turning away to give orders to the guards who came with him. These men moved briskly to take up the post outside the cabin.

Soon Becker left the ski hut, with the relieved overnight guard following closely behind. Einar and Gunnar were left alone inside, together once more.

Gunnar moved to close the hut's door, which the guards and Becker had defiantly left wide open. It was then that Gunnar noticed the new guards stationed outside, not with single carbine rifles as before, but with each still wielding shoulder slung automatic machine guns.

"Why must you antagonize Colonel Becker so?" Gunnar asked as he returned to his brother at the table. "Are you feeling all right, brother?"

"It's this damn leg," Einar complained, "it rewards me for sitting on my ass by feeling fine, but as soon as I put any strain upon it, the pain becomes insufferable."

"Becker's medics said you need surgery," Gunnar answered, "so stay off of it. Rest. We have nothing else to do."

"Until sunset," said Einar.

"What do you mean?" asked Gunnar.

"Don't you see? They have lost something very valuable when that cargo plane crashed," Einar explained. "Did you not see Becker's concern when he entered. Whatever it is, he feared greatly for its loss, and more so that I had somehow recovered it. That thought terrorized him. What could be so important, I asked myself. Weapons? Machine guns? Grenades? Surely not. We could have a Panzer tank and it would not worry them much, as we are only two brothers against their thousands. The only answer is Enigma. They have lost another of the Enigma devices in the crash. That is what frightens Colonel Becker so. If it were to fall into our hands, Becker would be held accountable for having allowed us to even have lived for this long. Likely, for that sin, should we come upon that device, he himself would be shot. That is what the terror in his eyes told me."

Gunnar looked at him as if he was a rambling drunkard.

"You have Enigma on the brain, my brother," Gunnar said. "You think all this is some sort of a great adventure, and Enigma merely a prize for you to capture. It is silly, only a ruse that will cost you your life. That I cannot permit."

"Don't you see," Einar said to his brother, "that there is no way we can ever hope to overpower the guards in the train station and take the device we know to be in use there. But if there is a second device lost in these woods, in that ravine, we must look for it."

"They must have had fifty soldiers searching those woods ever since the crash."

"Not last night in the darkness," Einar rebutted, "They stopped then, I was watching."

"So they took a brief break. There are only two hours of darkness or so at this time of year," Gunnar replied. "Each day there is even less, as we head toward the summer solstice when there will be none."

"Exactly, brother," said Einar with a mad look in his eye. "I must slip out of this cabin in those precious hours of darkness and search that ravine. If I can find the device, even if I only find the rotors, think how this could affect the war."

"As I said brother," Gunnar responded, "You have Enigma on the brain. If you dare slip out of this hut tonight, or any other, I will give you up to the Germans myself."

Einar laughed. "Your threat is so empty, brother. You could never live without me, just as I could never do so without you. We are the mis-stamped coin, remember? Two identical faces struck from the same medal beneath."

"I had said "*mettle*", not '*medal*'," Gunnar clarified. "It was a play on words for *'metal'*, but never *'medal'*, my brother."

Gunnar laughed to himself in such a way that Einar's feelings throbbed worse than his legs. Then he snapped and released the words that captured what he often felt about his brother but would never say,

"It is always words with you, Gunnar," fumed his brother. "Action is what is needed, not words. These words might as well be all the same, just as we are. We look alike, my brother, and we are poured from the same molten stock. Our father's father was born of these lands. It is his spirit that calls us to action against these invading, hostile Huns."

Then, in a rare occurrence, Einar cleared his throat and quoted Shakespeare, *"Our doubts are traitors, And make us lose the good we oft might win, By fearing to attempt."*

Lucio in *"Measure for Measure"*, Gunnar knew, but dared not answer. He wished not to steal even a glint from the truth of his brother's moment.

That night Brigand returned to the cottage on the shores of the Tay in Broughty Ferry. He had wrestled endlessly with his guilt during the many hours upon the trains. The darkness that befell his thoughts was tied to that of the sky. As he left the train station in Dundee, that darkness completely enveloped him. Within it, demonic thoughts jeered at him and soured any of the more pleasant recollections he might have had of his boys.

Halfway home, as he passed the high lurking shadow that was Broughty Castle, he realized he could no longer conjure their faces in his memory. It was a terrorizing recognition to have not only lost the boys physically, but to also have lost them, albeit temporarily he hoped, in the recesses of his own mind.

Brigand continued until he came to the door of his beach front cottage home. Inside, Tilly awaited him. He did not know for sure what he would tell her. Before he turned the knob, Brigand looked out one last time upon the silent waters of the Tay Estuary, so beautifully backlit by the moonlight. The firth's waters reflected the golden orb on the surface of its still waters; its mirrored calm demanded that he follow through with the plan he had devised on the trains to visit her depths that night.

The door knob turned in his hand, but not by his own doing. Tilly opened the door from within, her face tensely painted with the anxiety of awaiting what news he carried.

"Oh, Brigand," she said as she pulled him inside. "I have been frightfully worried. What have you learned, my dear?"

He put on the bravest face he could conjure in that moment. "Our boys are safely in Sweden," he lied to her. "There's no fighting there. *Safe as houses*, they are. They just have to make their way down to Stockholm. Wincer has a team there awaiting their arrival."

He beamed his best smile at her, but feared she recognized the hollowness that belied it. That night they both skipped dinner. He said he had a bite in the train station, which was also a lie. She said she could not eat, as her stomach still churned from her having been in such fear all day long. He wondered if her concerns included that he might not ever return.

She fixed him a whisky, and Brigand noticed that his wife's mood softened considerably. He thought then that his acting had bought him all the time he needed. He would wait until she was asleep, and slip out quietly. He would then remove the worries he had placed upon her, as his father had done years ago. He would answer the luring song of the sea.

After he finished his second whisky, she led him to the bedroom, and once again she soothed him with her lovemaking. He hoped his affectations of desire and delight had not worn thin, and that Tilly, being his companion for these many years, had seen through the ruse. He hoped this night that she did not detect the despondency so strongly lurking within him - that to which he had been so often prone. He fought to not allow himself to be drawn ever deeper within his mood. At least not until she slept. After which, he would give it full reign over him. So much so, that he knew this night that he would return neither from the depths of the Tay nor those of his darkened spirits.

Tilly slept after their passions were expended. Except that there had never really been any passion this night. Their lovemaking had been mechanical and wrought. Even so, they both soon closed their eyes to slumber. Tilly gave into hers completely as she rested on Brigand's still powerful chest.

For Brigand it was only the lightest of rest. His mind churned constantly like the waves of the sea in a storm. There was no escaping it, other than by outlasting it. But this night he could not endure it any further. He waited until he heard the slow rhythm of Tilly's breathing in his ear and the gentle heave of her bosom on his skin. Then he most gently extracted himself from under her, carefully left the bed and made sure her own slumber was not disturbed.

Then came the most tedious of actions. He searched the darkness of the bedroom for his prosthetic, and as quietly as possible strapped on the wooden limb. He checked to see if he had made enough noise to awaken her, but he had not. He had planned that should she stir, he would simply tell her he had to use the loo.

Brigand navigated the shadows of the bedroom and opened the bureau drawer where he kept his revolver. He carefully checked its six chambers, each was full with an unexpended round. He slipped over to kiss Tilly on the cheek one last time, but even at this he had changed his mind halfway as he feared she might awaken. He then headed to the front door, and the waters of the waiting river beyond.

Her slumber was disturbed, not by Brigand, but by the anxiety that brewed in her sleeping mind. Even as Brigand had laid awake next to her, she had been resting peacefully enough. Yet, it was not long before she felt herself buffeted as if by a rapidly developing storm overtaking calm and placid waters.

She had envisioned in a dream her sons standing before her together, laughing with great delight around a bonfire. Then, the mood stiffened, as if a curse had descended upon them. The dream was simple enough, but like all too many of the most uncomplicated of thoughts in life, it was thoroughly terrifying.

First, in the flickering firelight, Gunnar's face morphed into that of her husband Brigand, before the form of his frame dissolved into the curtain of blackness behind him. Einar, then stood alone before her, inconsolably upset, and said repeatedly in his panic that he had lost Gunnar. He had searched everywhere and his brother was not to be found.

The light of the flames that licked at the distraught features of Einar's face were like the lashes of a cat o' nine tails. She spoke to console him, telling him to calm himself, that it was not his fault. Then, Einar, like his brother before him, also morphed into Brigand and was also swallowed by the darkness.

The vastness of that dreamscape, empty of everything but the demonic laughing that then arose from the bonfire's flames, petrified her, and she instantly awoke to the terrifying uncertainty of reality.

In that awakening instant the reverberations of the dream ripped through her like a blast of frigid wind. She awoke, sweating profusely while still shaking with chills. Tilly collected herself. Her pulse was racing, her breaths were shallow and labored. She reached for Brigand, but her hands did not find him next to her. She looked at the clock which read near half past three. It was then that she heard the click of the front door, as loud as thunder, although its lock had been thrown with the sinister softness of deception.

Tilly called out for Brigand. She searched for, but could not find her night gown and robe. By the time she had, she rushed to the door and flung it open to make out in the moonlight a hobbling silhouette far ahead on the sands of the beach nearing the facile surf. She recognized it immediately to be Brigand, but could not make out the small object he carried in his hand. She rushed out to the beach, leaving their cottage door ajar.

She raced to him and again called his name, but with a greater urgency bordering on hysteria. Her husband only quickened his pace until his hobbled frame skipped into the gentle lapping of the waves.

"Don't leave me, Brigand," she cried over and over in the heartbreak of realizing his intention.

He waded deeper despite her continued calls. She saw him fall as his prosthetic leg must have slid out from under him at one point. The buoyancy of the prosthetic was fighting him, she thought. He had struggled to catch himself, but couldn't.

She moved toward him, but stopped in the oozing imprint of her own last step under the wet surf when she recognized the revolver in his hand, which he held high above the water even as he slipped. She knew he wished to keep it dry and functional for only one final pull of the trigger.

"Go back into the cottage, Tilly," he said. The gun remained at the end of his right arm, pointing upright as he regained his footing in the water beneath him. His voice was coldly impassive yet determined. There was none of the tenderness he had shown her in the few hours before.

It was at that moment when something inside her stiffened. She knew this instant would not be won or lost with her characteristic tenderness. She knew that his dark intentions could only be deferred with the anger that now brewed within her. She moved her right leg forward in the river's icy water, and then followed with her left. She ignored the chill of the waters of the Tay and waded towards him.

"I will not go back," she said defiantly, "not without you, Brigand. Whatever you intend to do here, you'll do so knowing that I have had to live the rest of my life having witnessed it."

"I lied to you, Tilly," he confessed, "the twins are not in Sweden. They are lost behind the German lines in the mountains, or so it appears."

As Brigand spoke, he continued walking backwards, away from her, deeper into the river. Tilly thought that while she had never been able to follow her husband into the depths of despair in which he often withdrew, she would follow him tonight. She still wore the night gown and robe tightened over it, both of which quickly became heavy as the waters permeated their cloth. She was determined to not lose her husband. She matched her own steps to his, but dared not rush forward on him.

"Of course they are not on their way to Stockholm," Tilly said to him, "I saw through that as soon as you said it. You never could lie to me, Brigand, and, my darling, that is a good thing. You are a wonderful blessing in my life. Stay with me."

He took another step backwards, the water now licked at the lowest portion of his groin. She followed him, stopping only when he did. He waded backwards and out further until the water came up to the top of his hips, fully submerging his deformity.

"I cannot bear my thoughts a moment longer," he confessed to her. "All that I can think of is having lost the twins, and in doing so having lost your love. Even in my dreams, these thoughts haunt me."

"You have not lost my love, husband," she said as she took another step towards him in the cold water, black as it appeared under the moonlight. "But we do not even know they are lost, only separated from us for a while longer, my love."

The wind picked up, and the foam it carried in spits stung her face. Brigand began to slowly raise his arm which bore the menace that was his revolver.

"No, I know that they are gone forever, that I will never see either of them again. This thought is deep within me, married to the marrow of my bones," he said. His voice trembled with a vibrato she had never before heard. "I'm sorry, Tilly."

She took another step in the river and closed their gap. "So your answer to the possibility of their being lost is to take yourself forever from them willingly?" Tilly said harshly. "Even worse, you plan to do this here in front of me?"

"I meant for you to never find me," he said. "I meant for all my life's failures to be washed clean by these waters. Leave me here alone, wife. Go back to the cottage. I am cursed to suffer even another day of this merciless life, after having sold my and my children's futures to Wincer Wells on this very strip of land in the very wake of my own father's death."

She had never seen him like this, not even in those low moments that he suffered for months after Gallipoli. He had overcome the crippling depression that followed the loss of his leg. It was in that second that she realized it had been only the prospect of hope in raising his twin sons that had pulled him through that. The joy of teaching them the Nordic ways, its tongue, and the values of a simple life well lived. Those values, with time, proved to be a deception.

This very moment, under the cleave of despair, Brigand felt both his sons and those values to not only be temporarily lost, but even worse, forever abandoned by himself.

"Don't I mean anything to you?" Tilly asked, coming within a step of him.

He had by then crooked his arm and raised the gun to his temple.

"Am I not your Cassie? Did I not give up my own life to willingly share yours? If it meant I had to shed my own identity as Cassandra to become your Tilly, so be it! To be the mother to those wondrous twins that your wretched Tulla could never be, I was honoured to do so. You always called me your gift from God. Don't you realize that it was you who was my gift from God all along? That you saved my very life! I will not allow you to do this! I love you too much to allow you to damn yourself in eternity."

"Turn and go inside," he exploded, with his mind's bitter conflict wobbling in his voice.

"Gift from God," she repeated, "your life is my gift from God and you would take that from me? Only to waste it here in these waters just as your father had done? The woman he loved, your own mother, Brigand, was taken carelessly from him, not by God, but only by the awful chance of accident. But I have not been taken from you, have I? I stand here, only inches from you. Don't take yourself away from me."

He drew his finger and wrapped it around it around the trigger.

"So help me, Tilly," he screamed in fury, "turn away."

"No, I will not," she refused him. "And I am not Tilly, I am your Cassie. Call me Cassie, as you once so often did with so much affection. I am your Cassie, and you are my Birger."

"So be it, Cassie" he said, and his eyes went blank.

Her throat dried, denying herself a voice with which to object. Then she found it in a tone not of pity, but instead of great anger.

"Think, Birger!" the old form of his name snapped again off her tongue like the fall of a whip. "If you pull that trigger, all I will ever remember is the sting of your remains upon my skin and the echo of that shot ringing out through the night. Is that how you wish to be remembered? Is that how you chose all this time to remember your own father, in those last seconds of his struggle in the sea for his own life?"

Tilly sensed the hardness of his intention break on these last words. She noticed his arm began to quiver. His eyes had gone from being blank hollows to being full of remorse. She thought, perhaps, just perhaps, that her words had touched something within him.

Brigand paused, and his arm trembled even more noticeably. Tilly feared then that an accident might do what his depressive intent could not. She feared that his hand's muscles might twitch and erringly take his own life. She raised her left hand to his, her fingers splayed gently on the back of his gun hand. Brigand's finger relaxed but did not release the trigger. Tilly still feared his fatigue or nerves might forever steal his light from her world. She raised her right hand to his face, and her fingers stroked away the tension within his taut gritted cheek.

"I should have never traded away my future to cover my father's debts," he said. Only then did his finger finally relax off the trigger and was soon outstretched across the metallic guard that hung looped from the gun's frame.

The wind gusted and nothing was said between them. She kissed him tenderly on his quivering lips. He hesitated. Tilly searched for a reason to persuade him to lower the gun. She thought again of his father and the torment that the man's death had wreaked upon her husband for nearly all his adult life. She had to get him to lower the gun.

"Why would you do to Einar and Gunnar what your own father has done to you?" she whispered into his ear. "Why ruin their lives as your father has ruined yours? It does not matter if I or they see you do this terrible act, for you did not see your own father drown himself. The effect upon our precious twins will be the same - total devastation. Two lives forever damned. Don't do to them only what has been done to yourself."

She attempted to slowly raise his gun hand to the safety of the sky, but his hand resisted hers.

"Do you really wish that one day they should take their own lives just to escape the weight of the memory of your having taken your own?"

She then wrapped both her hands ever so gently around his holding the gun. Only then did he yield the weapon as she pulled it softly from his grip. She unloaded the cylinder of its bullets, lest it should ever be recovered by a child. She threw the revolver as far as she could in one direction out to sea. Then she slung the bullets in another direction to the depths. They rippled on the surface in a pattern not unlike the six pips of a loaded die.

Tilly felt something break within him. He slumped in both stature and sanity. She slid her shoulder under that of her husband, who had drawn even further within himself. She helped him wade back onto the shore. Leaving the depths of the Tay, the beach's sands clung to their feet like fresh sins to the newly baptized.

"We shall help each other cope," she said tenderly to him, over and over again. He said nothing. In the depths of the darkness that was that near tragic night, they together slowly headed towards the beacon of light that was the open cottage door.

In the days that followed, Tilly took every precaution to assure that her husband, Brigand, was never alone. Not that her shadowing him would mean that they were again together. For Brigand had withdrawn so deeply into himself, he denied himself to her, only to wallow among the depths of his thickening despair. He gave no recognition of Tilly's presence around him. She merely watched him sit and gaze. Her every thought was just how close his life had come to ending in the Tay.

That night in its waters, when Tilly had precluded him of his desire to take his own life, she had come to understand that she had not rescued him at all. She hoped she had done more than merely forestall the inevitable, but did not so delude herself. She could only wonder where his thoughts wandered so deeply within him. To those places where she could not follow.

Yes, she had certainly dispensed with his immediate means to accomplish this act by thrusting the gun and its bullets into the depth of the waters, but even this failure on his part only sank Brigand's spirit further beneath the surface. For two days the man sat in his favorite parlor seat facing out upon the beach, the Firth of Tay, and the North Sea beyond. He would not even acknowledge her alongside him.

Tilly could not take the icy, catatonic silence that had commandeered his spirit. His heart still beat, but where did his deepest thoughts wander? Were they still in those nearby shallow waters, regretting how he had allowed her to keep him from escaping his mind's constant agony?

Or were they focused far beyond even the open sea, in the mountains surrounding Narvik? Did he ponder over and over again the fates of his twin sons, as she herself did? In any case, Tilly only knew that her husband had been stolen away from her.

Tilly would never know to where his wounded spirit had led him, but she knew that something had broken deep within him. Brigand had always been a man of action, and this trait he had passed on to his son Einar. She was the more reflective and cautious spouse, much like her son Gunnar. The two of them always looked to the future with trepidation and concern.

After two days of her husband having not spoken to her, having not eaten, having had no interest other than listening on the radio to the latest intolerable war news, Tilly knew she must act to save him. The Nazis were pouring into northern France, and had begun encircling the troops of the British Expeditionary Force at the beach stronghold of Dunkirk. The French fought alongside them. Tilly on several occasions had turned off the broadcasts, but after she had left the room Brigand would merely turn them back on. The thought occurred to her to break that damned infernal device, but she feared what response this might draw from deep within him. Perhaps a savage fury, she feared. Or even worse, he might sink so deeply into his isolated depression that he could never be rescued.

Tilly was haunted most by thoughts, however, of being for many years to come alongside the man she loved only to find that after having saved the breaths that filled his lungs, her actions had gutted hollow his heart and soul. She feared his adventurous self would never be returned to her. The thought of this fear becoming reality tortured her very soul. She even thought at one point, as the days stretched on, that perhaps she should not have followed him into the river that night.

Brigand had sunk to into icy depths that seemed to freeze his life, not in a preserving manner, but only one of a great waste of living. Tilly knew she must take action, some action, any action to draw her husband back to the surface. The only thought that came to her was to call on Wincer Wells, which she dreaded, but so she did nonetheless. It took her another full day to hear back from him. She explained the episode in the river, and how withdrawn Brigand had been for days afterward.

"I am frightened, Wincer," she confessed. "You must do something for him. It is only because of you that he is in this condition," *He must hear the panic in my voice,* Tilly thought. *Please, please do not hang up on me, you heartless bastard.*

A long excruciating silence stretched across the miles between them.

"Wincer," she pleaded, "please talk to me, Wincer."

She realized, after the fact, that this was the first time she had ever addressed Wells by this nickname.

Wincer Wells in response asked to speak to Brigand, but Brigand refused to come to the phone, and the handset would not stretch far enough to reach to the parlor where he idly sat.

"Tilly, tell him the following. Tell him that the Allied forces are closing in on the Germans. That they have pushed them back into the hills that overlook Narvik. The Huns only hold the town itself and the railroad up to Bjørnfjell. Tell him an invasion of the port of Narvik itself is now imminent."

"I will," she said, very appreciative of his taking the risk to share this vital information.

"I am sorry, my dear," Wells said over the phone, "that I cannot get away to come to you and help draw him out. He blames himself for what has become of the lads. He blames me, surely, but he blames himself yet even more."

The phone call ended, and Tilly relayed the optimistic message to her husband. Brigand raised his eyes slowly from their stare across the sea to hers, said nothing but nodded affirmatively, and returned his gaze to the horizon.

There is nothing for him to do but wait, she thought. *He needs to DO something. His body needs to be occupied, for only in taking action can he feel the illusion of control. But there is nothing he can DO to save the lads. God help him.*

Wincer Wells was not an uncaring man. In regard to Brigand, Wells often feared, under his great strain, just which destructive actions the man might take against himself. He knew depression ran in his family line, as Captain Cumming had so long ago duly noted. He feared that Tilly had not saved her husband in that river, but had only delayed him from committing the self-sacrifice that all his hidden demons demanded.

Wells' thoughts tended to Tilly MacAlvor also. She could not possibly long endure the haunting uncertainty of both her sons' safety and her husband's invaded state of mind.

Wells' compassion did, however, have its limits. During those seconds of silence that Tilly MacAlvor had found to be so unbearable, Wells had to weigh whether or not he would share completely the information that he had gathered as to what was truly happening around Narvik. He decided to share only a filtered version of all that he knew. It was the desperation in Tilly's voice that convinced him to do so, although he knew that his doing so violated every aspect of his country's security protocol. His actions on the phone that day could easily have cost him not only his job, but even his freedom. Yet, he knew he had to offer both Tilly and Brigand a seed of hope. Wells decided to share what he had to calm Tilly, but more so for Brigand, that it might arm him with a spark of promise which he might wield like a saber against those devils that had invaded and haunted his every thought.

What Wincer Wells had decided to hold back in those same seconds of silence formed the significantly greater secret. For Wells was already aware that even as the allied forces of Britain, Norway, France and Poland prepared their final onslaught against the German forces in Norway's frozen north, a directive had just been approved by Winston Churchill's War Cabinet. *Operation Alphabet* had just been relayed to Lord Auchinleck, the new commander of the Allied invasion forces. Its directive was simple: begin planning for the total evacuation of all Allied forces from Norway.

Auchinleck had been brought in to take over command from General Mackesy, who had proved too cautious in invading the peninsula and driving the Germans from the port town of Narvik. The fate of France was rapidly deteriorating. Auchinek's orders were to balance like a child's teeter-totter the taking of Narvik against the total evacuation of all forces from Norway.

Churchill and his War Cabinet no longer knew how long her largest ally would continue to fight. Should France fall, it would leave the entire British Expeditionary Force of over three hundred thousand men trapped upon the beaches of Dunkirk.

At Dunkirk, entrapped British troops awaited the onslaught of the Panzers and the *Luftwaffe* fighters that had surprisingly been halted. Later, it would be learned that their tanks and pilots were worn out by the near continuous assault on Western Europe and desperately needed maintenance and rest, respectively.

Thus, the Allied troops then fighting in Norway were weighed as being more desperately needed in Britain should France capitulate. It was inevitable that a German invasion of the British Isles would follow the Fall of France. Given that, it no longer made any sense whatsoever to maintain a stronghold in northern Norway while their home islands lay essentially unprotected.

And so, Lord Auchinleck proceeded with two conflicting operational orders: one to land the invasion forces upon Narvik, and the other to prepare for the total evacuation of all British and Allied forces immediately following it.

Most interesting was the fact that initially this decision to evacuate Norway was ordered to be kept secret from the Norwegians. For London had come to think of the country as a nest of spies after the traitorous actions of Vidkun Quisling.

Despite Auchinleck's orders, the secret would not be kept for long, as Norway's King and his cabinet had decided to establish a Government-in-Exile in London rather than to submit to Hitler. There was just one small problem since they were all still physically located in the northern Arctic wilderness of Norway, just behind the Allied lines in Tromsø. They, like the troops of the British, French and Poles, would also need to be evacuated.

By the time of the pending invasion, the port town of Narvik was only defended with a patchwork defense of some artillery weapon crews assisted by the sailors of the *Kriegsmarine* whose ships had been sunk from under them. The smoking husk of a town was more or less deserted of civilians, most of whom had taken to the numerous ski huts scattered throughout the mountains that rose high above the fjords there. The naval bombardments over the past weeks had reduced the port town's buildings to rubble.

Narvik's docks and harbor were strewn with the skeletal remains of bombed-out piers guarded by a ghostly armada of sunken vessels. The town itself had lost any real operational value for either side, yet remained a much desired spoil of war.

The Germans occupied only the port town itself, its immediate surroundings, and the Ofoten Railroad that led to Bjørnfjell and Sweden beyond. However, each day their holdings were threatened by the impending advances of the far larger Allied forces. Even with the reinforcement of German paratroopers, the Nazi forces were still woefully outnumbered, by a factor of six-to-one overall. Only the German's superior weaponry and training, along with command of the heights overlooking the harbor, offset the great disparity in troops.

The port of Narvik sits at the tip of a peninsula formed by the fjords surrounding it. To the north is the *Rombaksfjord*, whose silent waters had already swallowed numerous German and a single Polish destroyer. To the south of Narvik lay the *Beisfjord*, separating the city from the heights of the Ankene Peninsula that overlooks the harbor itself.

Three battalions of the Polish Independent Podhale Rifle Brigade had taken over for other Allied forces that fought for a toe-hold on the south side of the Alkene Peninsula. These Polish forces soon demonstrated their valor by fighting with reckless abandon against the Germans, even in the weeks before the invasion, and began driving their enemy back toward Narvik harbor. The Poles fought with an energy and determination that amazed their Allied brothers. Each Pole was personally motivated, it seemed, by family and friends, military and civilian, lost to the harsh cruelty of the Nazi invasion of their homeland the September before.

The fourth and last Polish battalion of the Polish Brigade had been fighting alongside the French and Norwegian forces on the peninsula of land just across from Narvik. North of the *Rombaksfjord* and east of the *Herjangsfjord* lies the land that the German *Gebirgsjäger* Mountain Infantry had commanded on the first day of their arrival, April 9. All through the remaining days of April and May 1940, the Norwegians, assisted later by the French and Polish infantry, fought a campaign that resulted in the German forces slowly being driven back and upwards toward Bjørnfjell.

The aggressive Lord Auchinleck was determined to invade Narvik, and push the Germans remaining in the port also up the mountain all the way to Bjørnfjell. He did so with a vengeance. By the 27th of May, both Allied and German forces alike knew the long awaited invasion of Narvik was imminent.

General Dietl also knew because he had covertly implanted a spy, a Norwegian national sympathetic to the Nazis in the Allied headquarters in the town of Harstad. The spy had not relayed the exact details of the invasion, only that one was forthcoming.

It has been reported that General Dietl went so far as to have a train readied across the border in Riksgränsen, Sweden for the imminent evacuation of the Nazi troops out of Bjørnfjell. One thing was for certain - the nearly two months long battle for control of the port of Narvik was about to be finally decided.

"Can you hear, that, brother?" Einar said. "That is the sound of freedom nearing."

Gunnar only heard the thunderous weapon fire that for days had echoed across the Bjørnfjell plateau. It had intensified in the days following the drop of the German paratroopers. It drew closer each day, frightening Gunnar to his core.

The Allies were arrayed in the hills on the north side of Bjørnfjell, in an area known as *Kuberget*. They were slowly driving the German *Gebirgsjäger* forces up the mountain back towards Bjørnfjell. The Germans had to increasingly pull all her remaining available forces to resist this movement. The men from the provisioning post around the train station had been re-commanded to the fight. Even those soldiers who had guarded the twins' cabin, as well as those who had searched for the cargo aircraft's wreckage had been drawn to repel the Allied forces.

"Now is our time to escape," said Einar.

"Escape?" scoffed Gunnar. "You have not even found your precious Enigma machine in that wreckage in the ravine."

"It is there, I tell you," Einar answered. "I have been only able to search for the past two nights since the guards have left us. Tonight, even if I do not find it, we should head out of this hut into the mountains until we are able to find the advancing patrols of the Allies' forces."

Gunnar looked with trepidation at his brother.

"With your leg Einar? It is impossible. Each of the past two nights when you come back from that ravine, your leg only pains you all the more. You are in no condition to hike these mountains. We shall stay here and wait for the Allies to come and free us."

Einar looked upon his brother and realized he understood nothing of war. Then he reconsidered. Perhaps his brother had the right plan after all.

The Germans had still not found their stash of Wincer Wells' faux rotors or the British passports, and he felt that perhaps two more nights of searching the wreckage might yield the Enigma that he was still sure must be there somewhere.

"Gunnar, I will agree to stay here only two more nights. You think the Allies won't rain fire down upon this hut because it might be occupied by two friendly POW's? No, if the Allies' bombs don't kill us as they advance, it is quite certain that the Germans will do so before they arrive. No, we will wait no longer than two more nights. It may give the Allies time to get closer to our position. Tonight and tomorrow I will make my last inspections of the ravine. On the third night, we will depart into the woods before sunrise, it may be our last opportunity to do so."

Gunnar trusted his brother's insights, but could not bring himself to forego the shelter of this cabin for the still freezing overnight temperatures of the mountains.

"They have not treated us adversely, Einar," he said.

"That is only because they still think we are merely displaced Norwegian fishermen from Skrova." Einar replied. "How do you think they will treat us should they confirm that we really are trapped British spies? I am sure we should not wait to find out given our opportunity to escape."

"Two more nights," repeated Gunnar, "as you said, my brother, gives the Allies enough time to draw close to us."

"I warn you, Gunnar," his brother said, "I will not allow you to change my mind. Tonight is the twenty-seventh, we stay two more nights, and on the thirtieth we make our escape."

"So it shall be," Gunnar committed.

50 Invasion and Evacuations

May 27 to May 30, 1940

"I never 'worry' about action, but only about inaction."

Winston Spencer Churchill

The Allied invasion began as the night of May 27 transitioned to the early morning of May 28. Two battalions of French Foreign Legion and Norwegian Forces were ferried across the mile long width of the *Rombaksfjord* from the port of Øyjord. This was the first utilization of modern landing craft in World War II. Their objective was a rocky landing zone just below where the Ofoten Railway began its ascent into the mountains above the fjord. The British naval bombardment from two cruisers and other destroyers had started twenty minutes earlier, in order to clear that landing zone of amassed German forces. These same naval bombardments would continue throughout that morning, its targets planned in sync with the landing operations.

Immediately upon loading for their departure, the Allied landing craft came under fire from the artillery gun hidden on flatbed rails in the Ofoten Railway tunnel. One of the first landing craft was directly hit by this gun, and several French soldiers in the process of loading for embarkment were killed. This delayed the invasion, and required the departure point to be changed from Øyjord's open harbor to the more protected shore of the *Herjangsfjord* just behind it. The Allied soldiers that made these crossings were courageous indeed, and soon for the first time they crawled out onto the rocky soil of the small mountainous peninsula upon which sat the port of Narvik.

The landings were carried out during the overnight hours. By four in the morning, already well lit by the arctic daylight, the French and Norwegian forces had landed. They were to be supported by British air cover from a squadron of British Hurricane fighters that had recently become operational there. Unfortunately, heavy ground fog prevented the Hurricanes from taking off as planned. Even more disastrous for the invading forces, that ground fog did not extend far to the south, so the sky became quickly filled with *Luftwaffe* aircraft from Trondheim. Me-109 fighters and Stuka dive bombers soon appeared overhead of the invading Allied troops. The Royal Navy's ships had to take evasive action, and some were hit in the fjords.

The British anti-aircraft cruisers *HMS Cairo* and *HMS Coventry* patrolled the *Ofotfjord.* German dive bombers appeared, and with no opposing British air cover, had landed a direct hit on the operations flagship, the *HMS Cairo*. By six thirty that morning, the *Cairo* was forced to withdraw, leaving only the *HMS Coventry* and her destroyer escorts to continue the bombardments. Eventually, the local ground fog cleared, and the British Hurricanes joined the fight, engaging the *Luftwaffe* bombers and fighters throughout the rest of the day.

The initial landing of French forces under General Antoine Béthouart and the Norwegian forces under General Gustav Fleischer's command climbed the heights with the objective of gaining control and clearing the tunnels of the Ofoten Railroad of any hidden German guns. German *Gebirgsjäger* forces laid in hiding above the railway and counter attacked using mortars and grenades. They drove the French and Norwegian forces back down the mountain to re-group at the landing zone. The Allied forces soon renewed their attacks on the relatively small German units. This secured the foothold of the landing zone, which until then was very much at the mercy of the sheltered German railway gun. The French physically hauled small artillery pieces, under enemy fire, up the shoulder of the mountain. These were used with great success in clearing out the hidden railway guns of the German forces.

Once the German forces were driven up the railway, and the landing zone was secured, then the tanks and other motorized assets were brought across. However, due to their weight, most of these mechanical units became bogged down and were not only unusable, but hampered the movement of subsequent landings. Still, the Allies had obtained their first objectives - a secured landing site, knocked out the hidden guns, and gained control of the lower railway. After the *Ofotbahnen* was secured, the Allied forces would split, with the Norwegians fighting their way down its rails into Narvik as the French climbed higher and over the port.

The Norwegian forces immediately were engaged by the German resistance from within the port along the shoreline and along the railway. The Norwegians, inspired by the liberation of their own town, fought with an unmatched intensity during their descent into the port of Narvik.

The French forces had a different tactic. Under the British air cover by then provided, their plan was to climb the lower slopes of the mountain, known locally as *Taraldsvikfjell*, that overlooks the harbor and town. Their intention was to use this elevation as a method of least resistance to transverse the city and attack down its slopes from the south while the Norwegians continued to attack from the north.

Across the *Beisfjord*, on the Ankene Peninsula, three battalions of Poles fought throughout the day to gain control of the heights that also overlooked the city and harbor. It did so in time to bring fire upon escaping boats full of German defenders attempting to vacate the harbor. At least one vessel of some twenty to thirty Germans was hit and sunk.

By eleven that morning the remaining defending German forces had already begun their retreat alongside the north shore of the *Beisfjord* to the village named Beis at the fjord's head. The Germans fought vicious rearguard actions to keep this escape route open. The Poles and Germans fought literally from rock to rock along the fjord's length, until reaching the village of Beis. From there, the German troops would go on to climb the ascending *Lakselva River Valley* to eventually join their brothers at Bjørnfjell, but were still hotly pursued by the Poles behind them.

By the afternoon of the 28th, the Allies offered the Norwegian General Fleischer the honor of liberating Narvik. What few civilians were still there were tremendously pleased to see that Norwegian troops were marching through the decimated city's streets. The port was no longer operational for the transport of iron ore, nor for that matter, for much else. Some twenty wrecks had been sunk in its harbor. The piers were destroyed and unusable.

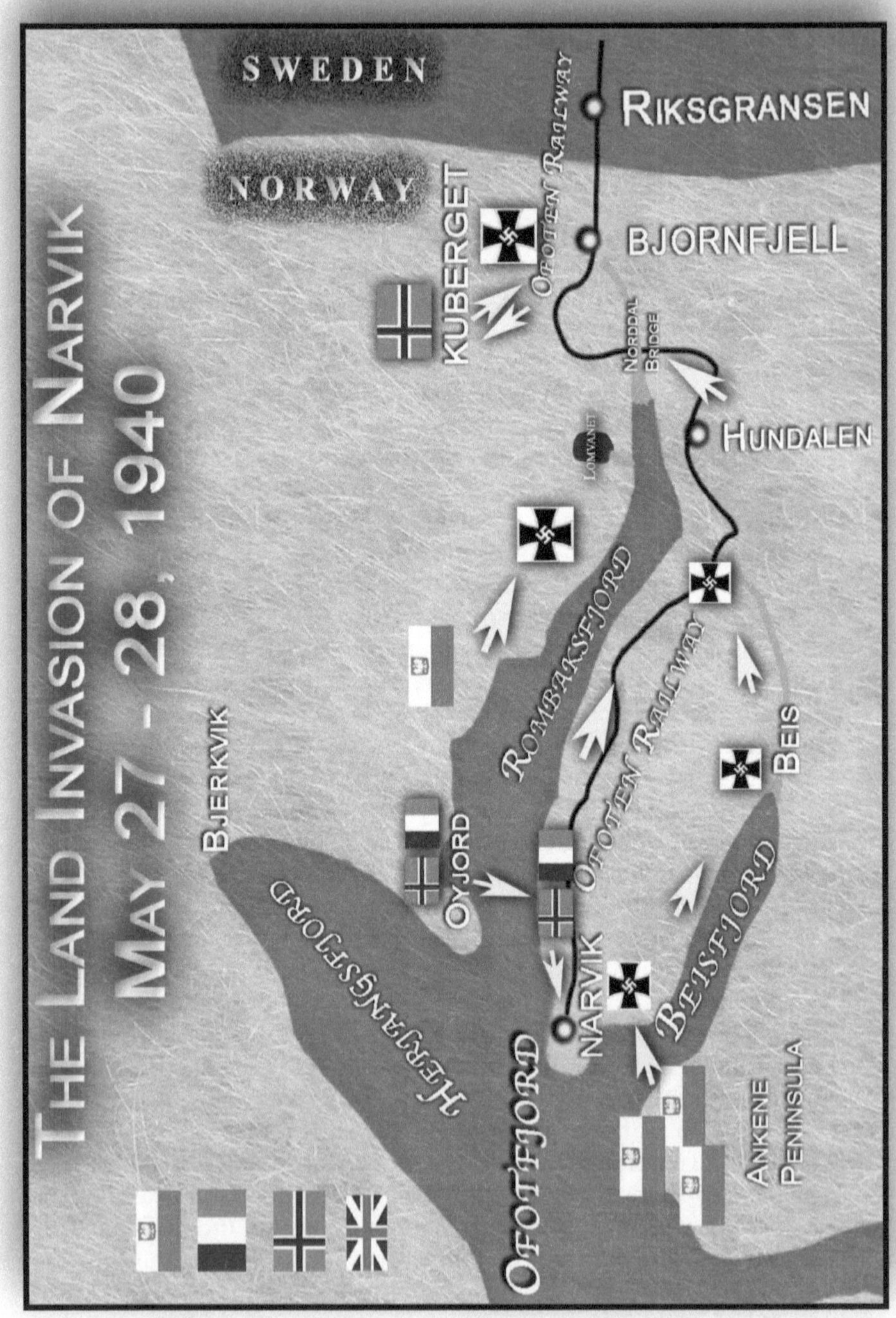

Figure 34: The Allied Land Invasion of Narvik

Nonetheless, all the damage that had torn this once sleepy port town asunder mattered not, for the Germans had been successfully driven out. Narvik had become the first captured town of World War II to be recovered from the Nazis by the Allies.

The fighting would continue for the next week and a half. The French fought their way up the Ofoten Railway in pursuit of the German forces. The *Gebirgsjäger* mountain forces tore down the electrification towers and as much of the railway as they could as they escaped upward toward Bjørnfjell.

The Poles pursued the German forces along the *Lakselva River Valley* north and east from the *Beisfjord*. Ultimately, they joined the French. These two Allied forces joined up on 2 June 1940 at Sildvik.

Across the *Rombaksfjord* from Sildvik, east of Øyjord, the Polish and French forces were driving back the German *Gebirgsjäger* mountaineers across the highly elevated and rugged mountaintops with mixed success.

Einar had convinced his brother that the time had come to escape on the overnight of May 30. They had awaited for the brief darkness to fall, as they could not be sure that they were not being watched from afar with field glasses. Neither brother wished to fall prey to a sniper's bullet.

The Arctic sunset came that night a half hour before midnight, when the twins darkened the cabin's interior, before cautiously slipping out the front and only door. It was a leap of faith, as neither young man was certain that hidden guards would not come forth from the woods to recapture them, or even worse, to fire upon them at close range. Gunnar had reminded his brother that they must act fast, as sunrise was only another hour or so off.

Einar took with him only the rappelling gear in his rucksack, a single pair of field glasses around his neck, a knife on his belt and a waterproof metal container full of self-lighting matches in his pocket. Gunnar carried what little food that they had remaining from their last German rations in the pockets of his parka.

Einar had not been able to find the elusive Enigma machine during the earlier two nights. He told Gunnar that this one remaining hour of darkness was just barely enough time for him to do one last inspection of the plane's wreckage. Then they would seek to follow the ravine as it opened into a rock laden valley. They would follow the small stream at its bottom, down below the *Norddalsbron* trestle railway bridge, and continue following it to the shores of the *Rombaksfjord*. This path they knew well from their earlier efforts scouting these areas before the German's arrival.

There were no hidden German sentries. Guarding the twins had become a low-priority function given the overall shortage of German manpower. This had precluded the guarding of their ski hut from being staffed. Instead, all of General Dietl's resources were focused on the multiple fronts against the Allies. These two Nordic fishermen, who might or might not be spies, were not worth even one soldier when compared to all else that needed to be done. The battle to the north raged against the Allies at *Kuberget*. Also, the destruction of the railway, before the Allies could utilize it, had become a top priority.

General Dietl knew that he must keep the Allies from successfully marching up along the Ofoten rail beds to advance upon his last remaining stronghold at Bjørnfjell.

Given this reality, General Dietl had pulled all remaining men not immediately engaged in fighting the advancing Allied soldiers from the north and west to be assigned to demolition teams along the Ofoten Railway. Lieutenant Colonel Becker and his team of three demolition specialists were given the crucial assignment of preparing the *Norddalsbron* trestle bridge with explosives. That was their tasking on that very overnight that the twins attempted their escape.

Einar led his brother through the darkness where the plane's fuselage had bowled down a swath in the forest, toppling trees like duckpins. Even though that had occurred a week earlier, the smell was still pungent with burned fuel soot, mixed with the solvated scent of pine sap. The brothers carefully made their way through the scattered and charred debris of forest that laid before them like a child's game of pick-up sticks. Their eyes had become accustomed to the darkness, which even then was not a deep black like the middle of night, but more so only a perpetually diffused gray as are the last glimmers of the Arctic dusk.

Einar knew his way through and over this maze of befallen woods as he had made this journey for each of the last several nights, ever since the guards had been taken away. He had on his first night of exploring the wreckage fashioned himself a walking stick, which each night he left in a location just at the edge of the woods. He could not afford it to be found in the cabin, should they have been searched. He had already retrieved it this night, and depended upon it heavily to navigate the strewn woods.

By the time the twins came to the edge of the ravine, Einar's leg was already throbbing. He ignored it and pulled the rappelling rope out of his rucksack. He fashioned it carefully around a splintered stump, and threw the coil of its length over the edge.

"I will go first, brother," he said. "I will stop at the point where our passports and Wincer's faux rotors are hidden. Thank God the Germans did not find our incriminating stash. They are still there, that I verified last night. Then, I will rappel to the bottom and after I tug the lines three times you will follow."

Gunnar's face weighed heavy with anxiety, if not outright fear, at these words. His arms began to shiver involuntarily.

"Einar, you know I cannot do that. I will panic and freeze upon the line. It is something that I cannot control. Please do not make me go out on that rappelling line, I beg of you."

"It is less than one hundred meters, brother," Einar said in an attempt to reassure his brother, as if even a fall of twenty or thirty meters was not enough to kill a climber. Einar then added, "I know you can do it."

"I cannot," Gunnar said, his eyes beginning to tear up as his stomach tightened with terror at the thought. His entire body began to shake. "Please, no, brother!"

Einar had suspected this would come to pass. He was unhappy to be correct in this suspicion, but he had planned for it.

"Calm yourself, brother. I have prepared myself for this eventuality," Einar said, as he pointed down along the ridge. "You see, each night when I would get to the bottom, with my leg being as it is, I could not climb back out. I was fortunate to find a footpath back to the top, just down along this ridge. I marked it with shreds of cloth I found in the wreckage. The rolling fuselage threw its contents everywhere, so these would not be obvious to the German search teams. Follow them down, while I search one last time for that Enigma machine, but I warn you that it may be quite steep. I will meet you at the bottom. Wait until I make the bottom and signal the three tugs. Then you can untie the rappelling line and drop it to me. We are very likely to need it again."

A great relief came over Gunnar as he realized he would not have to climb over the edge of that precipice with his life dangling on that line. He could not explain his fear, even to himself. He certainly knew the mechanics of how to rappel. He knew it was safe if done properly, as Einar had so often demonstrated. Yet, all he could think about was the fear that had risen in him physically as soon as he had dropped his body over the cliffs in the Scottish Cairngorm Mountains. He had been not only been frozen with fear, as people often would describe it, as much as he was riddled by it. His nerves would shake every time he looked down, his stomach would heave. He feared his involuntary responses would cause him to come loose from the line that singly kept him alive. Every muscle in his body rebelled in him, fearing his falling to his death.

Einar disappeared over the edge and dropped a short distance below him. He retrieved the passports and the explosively-rigged faux Enigma rotors. Then he continued his descent to the bottom. Gunnar felt the line slacken just before he felt the telltale three tugs. He unknotted the line from the splintered stump and threw it over the edge. Gunnar looked at his watch, it was just a few minutes past midnight.

Then, he made his way in the direction that his brother had pointed out. He came to the first shred of cloth marker and took the path that appeared to be nothing more than a deer run. As Einar had warned, it was steep, but was navigable without a rope. Gunnar would climb down cautiously, holding onto exposed roots or low branches to steady himself.

Gunnar searched out rocky outcroppings with his feet. Once he found one, he would release his grip, lower himself, and find new footing before grasping new roots or limbs. He was halfway down when he was shaken by the rumble of distant naval guns, soon followed by the explosion of their massive shells. It was the Royal Navy firing upon German positions down the rail line in an attempt to soften them in advance of the Allied troops working their way up the Ofoten Railway. The shells had landed several kilometers away, but the resonating echo startled Gunnar.

The twin's pulse quickened. He found himself not concentrating as he had minutes earlier near the steep footpath's top. Then a particularly loud explosion rumbled up the mountain valley, close enough that Gunnar swore he could feel it on his skin. It had come just as Gunnar had found a new piece of footing, but as he transferred his weight, the rock slid out from under his feet. He fell on his behind and began to slide. The weight of his body slipping downwards pulled his hands away from the roots he had just released. His body dropped five or so of the last ten meters down the hill before his slide was broken by something hard beneath his boots.

Gunnar caught his breath. His mind had raced as he slid, fearing he would strike a rock that would tear his limbs apart. He took measure of his health as his mind's calm was slowly restored. He had fallen, said in fact more properly, he had near vertically slid from the footpath into a wild growth of brambles below it. These had scratched harshly at his clothing, and his backside throbbed, but otherwise he was unhurt. He then wondered what in the world had broken his slide?

It was a hard surface, but even through his boot, he knew it was not another rock. For one thing, it had shifted when he struck it, but did not come free. It was too dark in the ravine to see, so Gunnar carefully lowered himself into the brambles to see what it might be.

The explosions of the naval barrage were by then nearly continuous. Gunnar feared for those beneath it, the Germans included, who were surely hunkered down, fearing for their lives. He could feel empathy for them after having spent the last several weeks on the edge of their encampment. He had come to realize that they were also only men displaced from their families and homes who had been ordered to these frozen northern lands to fight enemies they did not know.

Gunnar squatted next to the hard object. His touch told him that it was wooden, a box with only one side exposed. Halfway down its side he found hinges. It had been wedged with great force into the soft silted soil that collected at the bottom of this ravine, the soil in which these brambles grew.

What could this be? Gunnar excitedly began unearthing the box from the relatively loose soil with his fingers. The force of his falling upon it had dislodged it somewhat, so it was not tremendously difficult. After several minutes he was able to free it from its entrapment in the earth.

Then, amongst the rumble of the far-off bombardment he heard Einar's voice calling his name.

"Gunnar, where are you, brother?"

"Over here, brother," Gunnar replied.

"Where? I hear you, but do not see you. Why do you hide from me?"

"I am in the brambles." Gunnar stood straight up, revealing his head and shoulders.

In the first filtering light of sunrise, Einar saw him. He was perhaps five meters above him on the slope, in a clutter of heavily thorned bushes.

"Are you hurt, brother?" Einar asked.

"No, I am fine, but I slid off the footpath you marked."

"So, I am straining my injured leg," said Einar who was exasperated, "in searching the wreckage over there for the prize I cannot find and you are picking berries?"

"Very funny, Einar," said his twin, "but you may just be very thankful I am as awkward as I am. Come closer."

"Oh my God, brother, this just might be it," Einar exclaimed upon seeing the box. With the assistance of his walking staff, Einar climbed the hill through the brambles to help his brother down.

As he came close, Gunnar lifted the heavy wooden case. "Please tell me this is what you have been searching for."

Einar took it from him and excitedly hauled it back to the ravine's floor. He set it down on the ground, and after finding a small twig, scraped away the compacted dirt from the box's lid, revealing an oval insignia in which was written the word *"ENIGMA"*.

"It must have been thrown free from the rolling, falling Junker's fuselage," said Einar, his voice like that of a young boy's on Christmas morning.

"The search teams didn't find it because it was thrown so far from there," Gunnar said, pointing at the mangled fuselage. "It was embedded in the loose soil under these brambles, so it was unlikely to have been seen."

"This is the work of God," answered Einar, "delivering this device to our hands!"

" No, Einar, don't open it, it may be boobytrapped…"

Einar was not slowed by Gunnar's caution for one second as he freed the latches and raised its lid. But there was no blast, no charges rigged to it.

As Einar raised the lid, it might just as well have blown up in his face, for the device within was mangled. Not terribly so, but enough to make it completely unusable.

"It will still be of great use to London," Gunnar said to Einar, who had already noticed the crestfallen look across his brother's face.

"I am sure they will be excited to have it," Gunnar went on to say. "It is heavy, how will we get it off the mountain?"

"If I have to drag it down with my teeth," said Einar, "I will do so. I will not waste this great opportunity. Besides, Gunnar, you are the hero! We have to get this back to London to make the most of what you have done. Wincer Wells will come to celebrate the fact that you failed your rappelling tests, for had you not, you would never have found this device."

"There is only one problem my brother," said Gunnar. "How do we get it back to the Brits?"

The shock of reality only stopped Einar's joy for a second or two.

"In case you have not heard," he said, "those rumbles are the beginning of the final push for Bjørnfjell. We will follow the mountain valley path we already know from here down to the head of the *Rombaksfjord*, and then travel along its southern shore until we come to Narvik and the Allied forces there."

"That simple?" Gunnar scoffed, "I fear not."

"Even the most arduous of journeys are made up of only single steps. You cannot live your life in fear, Gunnar."

Gunnar cleared his throat, as he always did, before they played the Shakespeare game of quotes.

"The best safety lies in fear" he quoted.

"Macbeth," guessed Einar.

"Hamlet," answered Gunnar.

"Damn, that would have been my next guess," said Einar. "You win the game, but I suggest if we wish to get to the safety, we get moving, as the morning light has already arrived."

And with that, they followed the ravine as it opened onto a gorge before becoming a wide valley as it sloped down Bjørnfjell Mountain towards the headwaters of the *Rombaksfjord*.

It was only a few hours later when the telephone rang in the Broughty Ferry cottage of Brigand and Tilly MacAlvor. Brigand sat in his parlor chair, as he had all night, and the sun was rising over a clear and calm North Sea. Tilly dragged herself from her bed to answer it, as she knew Brigand would not.

"Who on God's green earth might be calling us at this hour, Brigand?"

Her husband said nothing, just continued to gaze out to sea. She looked in to assure he was still in the chair, and having convinced herself he was, she answered the call.

"Hello?" she said.

"Good Morning, Tilly," the tinny voice said. "This is Wincer, Wincer Wells."

"I would suspect you'd know I'd recognize your voice by now, Wincer," Tilly replied.

"Yes, of course you would," he said. "I am calling to inform you that I have dispatched three lads to your home. They are Royal Marines from the training staff at Dartmouth. They will have been riding trains north from Devon all night by the time they arrive at your door later this morning. They are coming for the *Nordlys.*"

Tilly knew that Dartmouth was the training institution of the Royal Naval College. It was located in the picturesque countryside of Devonshire in the South. Devon was adjacent to Cornwall, as both shires formed England's most westward point.

"*The Nordlys?* Brigand's ship?" Tilly was amazed, "Whatever possibly for?"

"Certainly, you've heard what is going on in France? At Dunkirk?"

"Yes, of course. I've been praying for those poor lads," she replied.

"Well, Tilly," Wells said, "it's even worse than the government has been releasing over the radio. And those poor lads don't need prayers, they need ships, especially vessels like the *Nordlys* that can get far into the shallows and get as many of our boys off those beaches as possible."

"I see," said Tilly, "well, who am I to refuse my country's call? But, tell me, Wincer, why would you send these Dartmouth marines all the way from Dover to Dundee just to gather this one single ship. There must be many, many other vessels throughout southern England, closer to the fight, that could be mustered into service."

"That's precisely what I wished to discuss with you, Tilly," Wells said. "This exercise of employing the *Nordlys* is my own operation. I am doing it not for the vessel at all, but rather for Brigand. Should you ever want your husband back, then you will allow him go with these lads. Let him help save the poor bastards trapped on those beaches. Just the tonic for what you describe as ailing him."

"It sounds terribly dangerous…" Tilly said.

"Of course it's dangerous," Wells exploded, "but it is exactly what Brigand needs. It will shed him free of that doldrum in which he's imprisoned himself."

Tilly was silent. Finally she whispered int the handset, *"It's just…."*

She hesitated. Wells became impatient with her.

"Just what, Tilly?"

"It's just," Tilly said softly as she spied in on her husband in the adjoining room, *"I am pregnant."*

"My God," exclaimed Wells. "Is it Brigand's?"

"How dare you suggest otherwise," Tilly scolded. "How dare you, indeed!"

The volley between the two had been rapid and without the providence of forethought. Wells knew he had stepped over a line with his insensitivity, and Tilly had surprised even herself with her reaction.

"I am sorry," Wells said, "I shouldn't have given tongue to that thought. Hear me now, Tilly, if you want your baby to grow up with a father who isn't an emotional hermit, then encourage Brigand to join these lads on this mission. They come strictly on my orders in the hope that this will pull Brigand out of his black dog mood, but either way, they will leave for the collection point at Dover on the *Nordlys* as soon as they arrive and the tides favor them to make way. Allow them to take Brigand along. I can personally vouch for this trio, each is a stellar sailor. Only the best draw assignments at Dartmouth, mind you. They are instructed to treat your husband as their captain. Brigand will be in the best of hands, and I pray his commanding of their respect will draw him back to reality."

"I must think on this, Wincer. When shall they arrive?"

"Should be no more than an hour or so from now, I suspect," replied Wells. "It's your call, my dear, but you know as well as I do that Brigand needs to do something to make penance for his self-imposed sins."

Tilly did not answer, but thought, *Yes, Brigand needs to* ***DO*** *something to overcome these sins. The excesses of the both of you, Wincer.*

Lieutenant Colonel Becker was perched high aloft the trestles of the bridge known by the locals as the *Norddalsbron*. His team of demolition experts were rigging the structure with explosives. Their intent was to await until the retreating German forces crossed the span, and then detonate the bridge, shearing it in two, denying the Allies its use in their upward assault on Bjørnfjell. It was especially critical should the Allies be able to press any locomotives still operative at Narvik into service.

Downhill from the bridge, German teams were sabotaging the railway as they retreated. They toppled the towers used to electrify the lines, one after another as they themselves climbed the railway in their own desperate escape to Bjørnfjell. They were at best only a few hours ahead of the French and Norwegian commandos.

As the German demolition team came upon Hundalen Station, they selected a grotto under the station house within which they would set a massive detonation charge. Inside it they were surprised to discover the broken radio handset and a British service pistol wrapped in a woven wool blanket. This information was radioed to Lieutenant Colonel Becker at the *Norddal Bridge,* who ordered them to retain the damaged equipment.

"There is one other thing, sir," said the voice over the radio. "One of our men is the son of a tailor and knows wools. He says this blanket is a British blend, likely Scottish. This stash is not from the local resistance sir."

A flame scorched along the spine of the Lieutenant Colonel.

So these Nordic fishermen had been nothing but British spies all along, he thought. He was sure that they must be responsible somehow for the missing Enigma machine from the crash site near their cabin. Both of these men had made such a fool of him. He saw, at that moment, that these twins had played upon his Roman Catholic sympathies. He thought of the woven wool blanket in which the damaged radio was found. *Scottish. It is possible that these men are not even Catholic at all?*

"Anything else, soldier?" Becker said through clenched teeth. He became impatient and wished only to return to Bjørnfjell and arrest the twins and find out where they had hidden the missing Enigma device. He had been under great pressure from General Dietl to recover it. Becker had been the one who had all along resisted shooting these two Norwegian fishermen outright, as other officers under Dietl had suggested. He knew Dietl would likely press a court martial upon him if that machine somehow would have fallen into Allied hands.

The lieutenant colonel hurried his team along. The charges were placed. The detonation wires were rolled out in length to a hillside location where they would be attached to the detonator. His crew had only then to wait for the German *Gebirgsjäger* teams skirmishing with the Allies to advance upward along the railway and cross the bridge's span before Colonel Becker's team could detonate the structure. The key was to blow the bridge in such a way that it separated the German forces from the pursuing Allies.

After about an hour of waiting, perched in the hillside above the bridge, one of the colonel's men called out, "Look there!" Becker used his field glasses to scan the floor of the gorge below, where he could see two figures traversing its rugged terrain.

The lead figure hobbled badly and used a walking stick to steady himself. He carried a heavy rucksack, which only amplified the deformity of his gait. The second figure struggled also, but only because he carried what appeared to be a heavy wooden box.

Becker instantly recognized the pair as Einar and Gunnar, and the box was just like that which contained the Enigma device. It was the very box for which his soldiers had searched. Undoubtedly, these twins had it all along, stored somewhere in the brush. An anger continued to burn in him. These spies had made a mockery of his compassion for them. They would pay a heavy price for exceeding his benevolence. They would come to understand the depth of his vengeance.

"What is the range to those traitors?" demanded Becker.

"Perhaps five hundred meters, Colonel," one of his soldiers replied. This man was the best marksman of the team. "They are heading down to the fjord away from us."

"Can you hit them from here?" inquired Becker.

"They are at the end of my range, and it is a very difficult shot, Colonel," the marksman said. "We may only give away our position and perhaps not hit the target at all."

"Take the shot," ordered Becker. "Shoot the one carrying the box first. Aim for his heart. When he falls, quickly shoot the other. I cannot afford to have either man escape."

"*Ja Vol, Oberst,*" the soldier responded. He laid himself flat on the ground of the ridge and opened the bifold stand of his sniper's rifle. He pressed its cold frozen stock up against his cheek and lined up its sights. He aimed for the nearer of the two figures that already had passed under the bridge and were now walking downhill away from their position.

"Take the shot," demanded Becker, "before they get around that bluff and out of your line of sight."

The marksman squeezed the trigger and the shot rang out across the valley. He waited a split second and watched as the figure dropped the wooden box and collapsed to the ground.

Instantly, before the marksman could get off a second shot, the other figure, unharmed, dropped onto the ground and into the heavy field grasses that sprouted there.

"You dropped him. Excellent," Becker cried out, "but you failed to take out his brother. Now take me down to them, this second."

The German marksman already had felt the sting of the colonel's rebuke and almost feared to make his next comment.

"From the manner in which he hesitated before he fell, it is likely I merely wounded him, *Oberst,*" the marksman said.

"As far as getting you down there, that will take some time from here, sir," said another of the *Gebirgsjäger* patrol. "With all the explosives and equipment we carried along for the tresses and tracks, we did not bring rappelling lines. Even so, I am sure that I can find you a way down."

"Take me down there now," repeated an agitated Colonel Becker. "Also, radio for a team to come up from the shores of the *Rombaksfjord.* If we didn't kill him, or if the second man somehow gets away, they can cut them off."

Becker told the marksman to stay with the man who would detonate the bridge. "If either of them gets back up, kill them. We will be going down there, so after thirty minutes shoot no more. I do not wish for you to make yet another mistake this day and shoot me in the process."

Colonel Becker then took one of the three *Gebirgsjäger armed* troops with him. They began to search for a pathway to the gorge's floor below them, which was not instantly obvious.

"Oh, my God, Einar, I am shot," screamed out Gunnar in terror after the being dropped by the sniper's fire.

"Stay down, brother, I am coming to you," Einar yelled. He had instinctively dropped to the ground, as he had been trained to do at the sound of any gunfire. He was covered by wild growths of stalky grasses along the stream that flowed along the gorge's floor.

"The blood, there is so much blood!" Gunnar screamed.

Einar freed himself of the heavy rucksack that contained the rappelling lines and other mountaineering equipment. He crawled as they had been trained in the Scottish Highlands, using only his elbows to pull himself. This kept his profile as flat as possible and well below the grasses in which he lay. Even given this, he clamped between his legs the walking stick which he knew he would most certainly later need.

Einar dragged himself over to Gunnar. His brother was as frightened as he had never seen him before. His hand was clamped over his upper arm and blood sieved through his fingers with a rhythmic pulsing. Gunnar's face was ashen white and riddled with fear.

"I am dying brother, leave me here and save yourself."

"How many times must I tell you that I would never leave you brother," Einar said. "Now, let me see your wound."

Gunnar was crying like a frightened child, sobbing.

"Better that one of us should live," he said between ragged breaths as his brother inspected his arm.

"Calm yourself brother," Einar said as he looked at the wound. He held a handkerchief hard over the wound's opening in the rear of his brother's parka, only to notice it continued to bleed from the front. There was no denying it bled badly, and Einar knew he must stop the bleeding.

"Good news, Gunnar," he said in an attempt to lift his brother's spirits. "The bullet has passed through your arm cleanly."

"My God does it hurt, brother, please make it stop hurting." The searing pain had already infected Gunnar's voice, and it broke Einar's heart to hear it.

"I cannot, brother," he said to Gunnar. "I would bear your pain for you if only I could, but this is not possible. I can make a bandage from my undershirt to dress the wound, but it will still hurt, First we must find out where that shot came from. I need to remove your parka, perhaps the cold will numb you somewhat."

Einar struggled to remove the parka from his brother. Each pull of it created an instant scream of pain in Gunnar, as if his brother had probed his wound with a sharpened stick. Finally, Gunnar bit his lip while Einar forcibly removed the parka from his brother, which soon created an unbearable howl of agony from Gunnar that he could almost not endure. Nonetheless, the bloody parka was freed.

Einar then told Gunnar to look in the direction of the *Norddal Bridge*. "Watch for his muzzle flash. We must make sure they are not in front of us."

Gunnar parted the winter grass just enough so with his good arm so that he could see, but without giving his position away. "Hurry brother."

Einar rolled onto his back, and then took the walking stick from between his legs, and drove it into the parka such that its end was between the shoulders. He then ripped at the stalky grass around him and stuffed it into the parka's arms. He raised the parka on the stick until it just barely was above the upper edge of the grasses. He intended it to look like the haunched figure of one of them attempting to keep low without complete success.

No sooner than he had raised the parka when a second shot rang out. It missed the parka altogether.

"I saw it, Einar!" Gunnar cried out excitedly. "On the hillside just above the bridge."

"That is very far away, brother," said Einar, "and thank God that it is, or that sniper's shot would likely have hit you in the heart or lung."

"It is bad, isn't it brother?" Gunnar asked.

"It is not good," Einar responded, "but you will live."

Einar had lowered the bloody parka and removed his own. He took off the woolen shirt beneath it and then the thermal undershirt beneath that. The cold struck the bare skin of his chest until it was like sandpaper on his goose-bumped skin. His chest rippled with a thousand screaming nerves at the extreme frigid air. Yet, he knew it should not compare his discomfort with the terrible pain his brother was feeling.

Einar pulled on the woolen shirt for some level of warmth. It then only abraded the erect buds of his frost sensitive nipples. Einar ignored this distraction as he used his knife to rip his removed thermal undershirt into strips and folded some of them into pads. He put the pads over each side of the arm's wound, then wrapped it as hard as he could with the strips. He fashioned a long ribboned strip from the shirt and tied it off as a field dressing. All the while, his brother had been bellowing in pain as he had never heard. The sound of which pierced his own heart.

"Brother, it is time for us to move. They will send someone down to this area to finish the job."

"Surely they must think me dead already," Gunnar said.

"Not with all that damn noise you are making," joked Einar. "Besides, they will send someone down to get me even if they think you dead, Gunnar."

"Please just let me rest," pleaded Gunnar. "You press on and leave me."

"I will not," said Einar. "You stay, then I stay. Either we escape together, or we stay and die together, my brother."

Gunnar looked at his brother, and knew he was serious. He knew Einar would never leave him, no matter what.

"Well, if we are going to stay together, Einar," he said with a smile, "then I would rather escape than die. But I have bad news, I can no longer carry that damn Enigma machine."

Einar laughed aloud. "You are funny when you suffer, brother. The machine and my rucksack will have to stay if we are to have any chance at all."

"At least take the rotors, brother," Gunnar had said.

"Ah, the Enigma's rotors," Einar said. "In all this commotion, I nearly forgot."

He opened the case and clawed at the inoperative machine. The cover came free from the rotors and he took the three that were installed there. He also took the two others that were included in the case but were not installed.

He dropped them into the pockets of the blood stained parka, as he had given Gunnar his own after dressing his wounds. He then pulled it on over his woolen shirt.

"Let's go," Einar said, "we need to waste no more time."

"Let us waste just a bit more, brother," Gunnar said, holding out the Wincer Wells faux rotors that his hand found in his brother's parka pocket. "Let's leave them a surprise if they should decide to try to fix this machine."

Einar was stunned that his brother could think so clearly. His extended arm still shook with the pain that surely radiated from his other arm, but somehow Gunnar had, in this critical moment, suppressed his fear, if only for an instant.

"Yes, it is perfect," said Einar, who took the explosive rotors from Gunnar and installed them in the same numbered sequence inside the Enigma. He then stored the other two in the box where the alternate rotors had been found. "Now, come brother. I know it will be in great pain for you, but we must crawl around this bluff where we will be safe from the sniper's fire."

They did. Einar crawled on his elbows for the hundred feet or so to safety, the walking stick still clamped between his legs.

Gunnar could not crawl, given his wound. Instead, he got to a squat over his crouched legs, haunched over as much as he could. He then duck-walked behind his brother. Another shot rang out as they neared the bluff, but Einar told him the sniper could only see the movement of the grasses and fired blindly into them. Neither twin was hurt.

Einar and Gunnar cleared the bluff and then the two brothers picked out another path down to the blue waters of the *Rombaksfjord* that gleamed like a mirage below them.

Brigand was assisted aboard the *Nordlys*, and the three marines from Dartmouth took the vessel underway out of Broughty Ferry harbor. As it made its way past the castle, upon the Tay River and headed to the North Sea, Tilly MacAlvor watched from the beachfront in front of their cottage. She offered a wave to her husband, but his arm did not return it.

Tilly shed silent tears as she watched the vessel ply the gentle waters of the Tay Estuary. She feared this might possibly be the last she would ever see of her husband.

Tilly had not told Brigand that they were about to have a child of their own. She meant to, but his whole personality had instantly brightened when he was told of the need for them to take the *Nordlys* to participate in the rescue of the stranded troops at Dunkirk. She dared not lay this most serious of news on him and threaten his improving mood. It filled her heart to see him excited and responsive once more, and to again have something to do that was of utmost importance.

"Don't worry, Tilly, I'll bring back those lads stranded at Dunkirk," he had said - the first words he had spoken in days. "They'll be *safe as houses* aboard the *Nordlys*, you just watch!"

Tilly noted that Brigand had used the exact same phrase which Wincer Wells had placated him with regarding his own twins being lost in Norway. Yet, what really lifted Brigand's spirits was the opportunity to actually **do** something. It was as if, in his head, he had somehow thought he was going on a mission to save the lives of his own twin sons.

The four men would sail down along Britain's eastern North Sea coast on their way to Dover. Once there, the *Nordlys* would have her ballast removed before she was fitted out with two powerful outboard motors to allow it to reach the shallowest waters of Dunkirk harbor where the entrapped soldiers could be rescued. They would arrive late to *Project Dynamo*, the cross-Channel operation made up of nearly seven hundred ships. The *Nordlys* would be one of 311 small craft that would be used to ferry the troops from the shallows to the troop transports that circled offshore in the Channel's depths.

Einar and Gunnar had walked downward along the gorge that the *Norddalsbron* spanned. As they descended, the gorge opened up into a fuller and proper valley, with granite walls from the surrounding heights rising on either side. Only by then, they dared not walk out amidst its open growth, as they had so foolishly done when they had been fired upon from that bridge. Instead, they hung close to the tree line that sprouted at the base of the granite cliffs that formed the inverted funnel to the sea. They took every advantage of the lush, stalky natural cover.

They neared halfway down that opening incline, which would end at the marshy stream bed which fed the *Rombaksfjord* with the continual waters of the snowmelt from the surrounding heights. They had believed the marshland would be free of German troops, as it was right on the fjord and subjected to bombardments from the Royal Navy. They were not aware that the Germans kept a reserve patrol unit just above the fjord for reconnaissance in case any invasion forces should attempt to land there and could ultimately threaten the German's Bjørnfjell stronghold.

They were also unaware that Colonel Becker had radioed ahead, and a team of three *Kriegsmarine* sailors, long since displaced from their ships, were headed up-valley towards them.

Einar spotted them first. The twins had stopped to take cover in the tree line, as Gunnar's wound was throbbing and he complained of being lightheaded. As his brother rested, Einar kept watch and spotted the three sailors, each with submachine guns slung from their shoulders, searching for them along the valley floor.

As this valley was the natural flow for the snowmelt of the surrounding mountains, there was much water. In summer, these raged like a small river down to the fjord. In late May, those waters were not much more than a stream. The result was that on this valley's much vegetated floor grew golden stalks of high brush that the Germans carefully searched through for them.

Einar raised his finger to his lips, telling his brother not to break the silence. He watched the Germans slowly tread through the open brush upwards towards the *Norddal Bridge*. Suddenly came a loud explosion from halfway up the mountain. The *Norddal Bridge* had just been blown, sending rocket plumes of smoking debris arching high into the sky. *This could mean only one thing,* thought Einar, *that the Germans were in full retreat back to Bjørnfjell. They must have, by now, evacuated Narvik itself. The Allies must be in control of the port. If only I could get my wounded brother there, I could surely find the medical attention Gunnar so desperately needs.*

The three searching German sailors all raised their stiffened bodies from the brush, like a population of meerkats, at the sound of the explosion. They began to call out to one another in German, which neither twin could understand, before moving at a much more rapid pace up the valley.

Both twins remained completely silent until the three *Kriegsmariners* had climbed up the valley and eventually out of their sight.

Only then did Gunnar ask his brother, "What do you reckon that was all about?"

"One does not have to speak German to understand," said Einar. "They were saying that the *Norddalsbron* had been blown. It was time to march double-time back up the mountain to the safety of Bjørnfjell."

"I am rested, brother," Gunnar said, "now that the way is clear, let us proceed down to the *Rombaksfjord*."

"No," Einar said, "if they sent three to look for us, then there must be many more yet there. It is not safe. They will likely soon all be coming up this valley to get back to Bjørnfjell."

"What do we do?" asked Gunnar.

"We will seek shelter, brother. Nightfall is soon on us. We must get out of this cold. You stay here and I will search for cover, or at least build us a lean-to from fallen limbs and brush. Rest, Gunnar, I shall be back very soon."

And so, Einar left his brother to seek shelter. First he marked in his mind Gunnar's location by aligning the downstream edge of the left valley wall with a distinctively jagged peak in the distance. This would provide him the line upon which he could find his brother. Then Einar worked his way uphill toward the base of the sheer granite wall behind them. He found no caves, but did discover an outcropping where he was able to build a lean to.

First he spanned a fallen limb across the rocks to act as a joist for the limbs he would lean upon it. He very carefully went to the stream in the valley's center and used his knife to cut as many rods of golden stalks with which to line the floor and walls of this temporary shelter. Over the top he also placed cut stalks of grasses as cover.

He returned to find his brother lying on his back, his arms splayed out. At first sight, Einar thought the worst, that his brother had ruptured his wounds and bled out. But as he neared, he was relieved to see that the other half of himself had merely given into complete exhaustion and dozed.

Einar hated to awake him, but knew he must. In the open, their body heat was wasted. In the shelter, it would be trapped, and although not enough to comfortably warm them, it should be enough to keep them from freezing to death overnight.

Einar helped his brother to the shelter, and under it they huddled together in the frigid cold. They sat upon the scattered mat of goldenrod and cattails that Einar had collected.

"How much food do we have left brother?" asked Einar.

"Three rations," answered Gunnar quickly. They had hoarded food in the days before their escape. Whenever the Germans had provided rations to them in their ski hut, they would share only one and bank the other. Now only three were left.

"You have one, Gunnar" said Einar, "I am not hungry."

"You think me an idiot, brother?" scoffed Gunnar. "We are both starving. Literally, starving. The hunger within me pains me hollow. If it is that way for my body, it is the same for your body. Are we not the same?"

"You need it more for recovery from your wound, Gunnar."

"And you for your leg, brother," Gunnar replied.

"Then we split only one ration," said Einar, "tomorrow I will hunt berries for us to feast upon."

"Yes, a feast, how my body wishes to only have one more feast!" A smile creased the face of Gunnar.

Even by that point, all Einar could think of, himself, was food, and even the pain in his leg did not assuage his mind's fixation with feeding his starving body.

Within the shelter of the lean-to, the two brothers huddled together, their faces pressed cheek-to-cheek. It felt natural to them, without any reservation whatsoever, as they had spent nine months long ago in this same insular closeness. The only thing missing was their mother's warmth, so instead each relied on that emitted by his brother.

Colonel Becker and his *Gebirgsjäger* guard companion walked down along the valley floor. The mountaineer guard, his rifle slung over the shoulder of his greatcoat, carried the heavy Enigma device they had found in its muddied wooden case. The colonel had demanded he take it with them. The guard thought to himself that as they had recovered the device, they should return it to Bjørnfjell. The colonel thought otherwise.

Lieutenant Colonel Becker ordered that they proceed down the valley and close the trap on the two British spies. They had discovered Gunnar's blood trail, but after an hour or so, it was lost. Likely the wound had been dressed and had clotted, Becker told his guard. They proceeded to descend lower into the valley.

Soon the two *Gebirgsjäger,* the colonel and his guard, came upon the three sailors working their way upwards from the fjord. Becker quizzed them, then cursed them for missing out on capturing their prey. The colonel then had his man radio ahead to set up a picket line around the approaches to the *Rombaksfjord.* Nightfall was approaching, although the darkness was still several hours off, so they made camp with a roaring fire.

In the skies overhead, the twisted, diving and climbing contrails of the battle between the *Luftwaffe* aircraft and the British Hurricane fighters faded, as the airmen of both sides wished to return to base before darkness fell. Under these contrails, the day had echoed with explosions and small arms fire that carried faintly from across the fjord. Becker already knew for three days past that the Allied invasion had been a catastrophe for his side.

Narvik had been overtaken by midday on that day of May 28. The remaining German forces that had escaped did so along the north shore of the *Beisfjord* to the village of Beis at the fjord's head. Once there, the retreating Germans had been shelled upon by the Poles from the twin heights of *Skatuva* and *Hestfjell.* Their only escape was to travel up the valley of the *Lakselva River* to the area known as Sildvik, and then follow the Ofoten Railway to the safety of Bjørnfjell Station. This all had been done, and the retreating troops that escaped capture had just crossed the *Norddalsbron*, and it had been detonated. Even given all this, those damn persistent Poles and Frenchmen were just behind his escaping countrymen in hot pursuit along the railway.

Lieutenant Colonel Becker knew that he should discontinue his pursuit of the twins and return this patchwork patrol up the valley to the blown *Norddalsbron* and follow the railway tracks back to Bjørnfjell. Yet, to do so now would risk capture or death at the hands of the advancing Allied forces. Not to mention that returning without the spies left Becker at great risk with General Dietl. No, Becker thought it imperative to return not only with the missing Enigma, but also with either the spies or some proof of their deaths.

As the five Germans sat around the fire, Becker was certain these men would most prefer returning to Bjørnfjell than what he had in mind. Becker was intent in capturing the two twins he knew by then to be spies. He would not break off his pursuit until they were captured or killed.

Then he was asked by his companion *Gebirgsjäger* guard if one of the sailors could look at the device. “He was responsible for the *Kriegsmarine* device on his ship, and thinks he might be able to fix it.”

The morning of the 31st of May came with a briskness of purpose for all parties. In Dover, the *Nordlys* was fitted out with the two large outboard motors she would use in the shallow waters of Dunkirk beginning that afternoon. Also, all her ballast was removed to decrease her draft as much as possible. The reinvigorated Brigand MacAlvor waited impatiently to set sail across the Channel to rescue those young men who were trapped on the French shore there. He wondered about his own sons, and who might come to their aid that day, should they even still be alive.

In the open valley above the *Rombaksfjord*, Colonel Becker searched the sky for anything resembling smoke from an encampment’s fire. Yet, he knew in his heart that these twins would never be so stupid as to have given in to that comfort. At least not yet. Another several days in the piercing Arctic conditions, and he knew that they would give in to risking it.

The next morning, Becker thought his patrol could not be more than an hour or two behind the twins. The picket line at the fjord was alerted to contact him should they sight the men.

Einar and Gunnar had arisen early, seeking only the warmth of motion. Einar searched for food and soon returned with a buffet of lingonberries, cloudberries and gooseberries. None of them were ripe at that time of year, but that did not prevent the brothers from grinding them in their teeth and swallowing the sour pulp to fill their starving stomachs.

After they had eaten, Einar shared the best find from his morning hunt with his brother.

"Gunnar, I have found a trail that we can access up alongside this granite beast," he said, speaking of the valley wall behind them.

"It must lead to the cliffs that tower over the north shore of the *Rombaksfjord*," Gunnar said. "They must be three hundred meters high. How shall I ever make that given my wound?"

"That is the beauty of it, brother," replied Einar. "This trail is only a switchback that we can easily ascend. We need carry nothing, except for me to clutch my walking stick."

"It will be hard upon your leg, brother," said Gunnar.

"We have no other choice," Einar responded. "There are Germans up and down this valley. We will take this trail just far enough up the valley wall to hide from them. After they give up searching for us, we will come back down and proceed to the fjord and onto Narvik."

Einar convinced his brother of his plan. On full if not slightly nauseated stomachs, and rested spirits, the twins began to climb the switchback trail up the valley wall. They did not rest until midday. Each time they reversed direction they climbed ever higher, and soon were treated to a spectacular bird's-eye view of the valley below and a portion of the fjord itself.

Here in this rocky perch they rested. It was not long before Gunnar spotted the makeshift patrol of Germans in pursuit of them below on the valley floor. He recognized the three sailors from their shoulder slung machine guns. He pointed them out to his brother.

Einar raised the field glasses to his eyes that he always kept hanging from his neck. He could make out the uniform and features of Colonel Becker, and suspected this man would not give up until they were either captured or dead. Just then the clouded sky over the mountains parted, and the sun shone brightly, centered in a patch of azure blue that seemed to be the one good eye of the Nordic god Odin himself.

On the valley floor, Becker heard the cry of one of the sailors, who said, "There, there!" The colonel raised his eyes to midway up the valley wall to see glints of reflected sunlight.

"The *dumkopf* is not aware he is catching the rays of the sun. We will follow them, they are trapped."

"Colonel, we have no climbing gear sufficient to climb that height," the *Gebirgsjäger* guard said.

Becker was irritated that any of the four others might be bold enough to question his command. He glared at the guard.

"So, you think I am not aware of that, soldier?" asked Becker, before scornfully adding, "Here is what I am also aware of - neither do they, remember? They abandoned their gear where they abandoned the Enigma. Do you not recall? Even if they did have gear, neither of them is in any condition to climb. There must be a trail, likely a switchback, along that valley wall. We will find it, just as they had."

The two twins perched upon that granite wall under one of its few scattered trees, and watched in horror as the patrol moved directly to them.

"They have seen us, Einar," screamed Gunnar, "what do we do? We are trapped!"

"Calm yourself, brother," Einar said as he tried to steady his own nerves, "we are not yet entirely trapped. We will travel in the only direction we can, upwards."

"They will be on us soon," Gunnar panicked.

"You forget, Gunnar, it took us four hours to climb to this point," Einar said, "And they are still a good hour from where we started. So even if they move faster than us, we have half a day's lead on them. So we follow this trail to wherever it leads us."

Gunnar absorbed his brother's analysis of their situation, and merely said, "Lead on, brother."

As the modified *Nordlys* sailed the Channel to Dunkirk, the sky was abuzz with a hive of hostile hornets engaged in a territorial battle with wave after wave of angry wasps. The Hornets turned out to *Luftwaffe* Me-109 fighters and Stuka dive bombers; the wasps to be either British Hurricane or Spitfire fighters. They rose and dove in the skies overhead in tightening circles of death. Below the sea churned with just about every description of floating vessel short of rowboats of Hyde Park's Serpentine.

The *Nordlys* had felt as if she had skated across the Channel, given the removal of all her ballast. As she neared Dunkirk's shore for the first approach, the first strafing run on their ship had exploded in twin rippled lines of up-splashing seawater just off their bow.

The three marines had each gone flat on the deck. Brigand remained strapped in his makeshift chair at the helm. They had been told that the man was an accomplished sailor but was having a tough go of it at present. They had treated him as if his state of mind had been as fragile as Waterford crystal. The marines all looked to their new captain for his response to the first volley of live fire.

"Bloody Boche bastards are determined to make things complicated for us, aren't they?" yelled out Brigand from his secured deck chair. He had completely ignored the near-strafing as he pointed at the smoking remains of the nearly mile long boarding pier whose deepwater use had been denied by the skillful precision of the Stuka dive bombers. "Let's do what we came for, lads, let's go get in close and pluck some of those brave soldiers out of the Channel. Time to start up those engines, mates."

The three marines from that point on were no longer concerned with Brigand's state of mind. They determined him not only to be fully engaged, but seemingly even enjoying the excitement of the moment.

Two of the marines aboard the *Nordlys* manned the rigging, dropping all sails as the third engaged the two outboards, and soon the ship was thrusting powerfully towards the clusters of helmeted soldiers in waters up to their shoulders and necks. The deep drafting transport vessels and warships could not enter these shallows, and the heavily laden soldiers could never possibly make it out to their depths. With the deepwater piers usage denied by the damage from the German bombs, thus came the criticality of the use of small craft at Dunkirk. Each small vessel would harvest the evacuated soldiers from the sea's waters as if they were its richest bounty - which, of course, they were. Then, the *Nordlys* and the other 310 small craft would ferry their catch to the larger ships, only to thus begin the cycle anew.

As for the German pilots, they quickly determined the small ships to be the target of opportunity. First they were generally unarmed, except for small arms and rifle fire, which were not a threat except for aircraft on the lowest of strafing runs. They stayed away from the larger transports because these were heavily guarded by the warship's anti-aircraft guns and patrolling British fighters alike. The *Luftwaffe* pilots quickly turned their sights on the small craft.

So, the small craft suffered most, with 170 sunk. These were the bulk of the 226 ships sunk out of the total evacuation fleet of 693 vessels.

As for Brigand MacAlvor, after completing his first trip to the transport ship, having deposited over one hundred living breathing souls plucked from the water at the base of their scrambling nets, he himself had never felt more alive. The cacophony of warfare that cycloned around him - the burnt smells of the blasts from the explosions, the whistling scream of strafing bullets, the strain of the engines of every machine man had ever built for the purpose of killing other men - all were forgotten by Brigand. As was the fear on that Turkish beach which he had so terribly remembered in every detail for every minute of the past fifteen years. All that was now forgotten.

Brigand steered the *Nordlys* back to the shallows, just as the three stout marines had cut the engines and prepared to pull more men from the Channel's waters. He sat instead of stood at the helm, but at no other point in his life had he ever stood taller or prouder than this day.

Captain Ahab had captured his long-pursued white whale, and its name was purpose. He had struggled to find it in life before this day, although he had allowed Wincer Wells to confuse it in his head with pleas of patriotism. Yet, on this day, along these foreign shores, his life's purpose was honed to a razor's edge. It was nothing else than to rescue the stranded Britons from the claws of the Huns. Nothing more, nothing less. In these shallows, purpose was found in schools of plenty.

At day's end, when darkness fell upon the waters, the *Nordlys* harvested a final hundred or so men from their deaths and bothered not to transfer them to the larger ships. Instead, she sailed them back to Dover, whose white cliffs welcomed them from afar, with many of the young men in tears. Never before had they been so ecstatic to see her shores. As for Brigand, he could not wait to return to those beaches on the morning's rising sun, to save as many more lads as it took to salve the piercing wound of having lost his own pair of twin sons.

As the *Nordlys* returned across the Channel in darkness, over a thousand miles away, an ethereal light still reigned over the Arctic mountainscape. Einar and Gunnar had crested the mountain trail they had been climbing. It delivered them onto a rocky highland dotted with mountain lakes of varying sizes. They overlooked not only all of the *Rombaksfjord*, but from their vantage point, they could see the *Ofotfjord* and even the open blue expanse of the *Vestfjorden* in the distance beyond it. In each fjord they could see the flotilla of British ships upon their waters.

They could see the still smoking ruins of Narvik, her plumes of smoke rising like burnt offerings to God to cease the madness. After all, this destruction was wrought for no other reason than to gain or deny access to a bounty of iron ore. Others would be fought for oil, others still for toe-hold strips of defended beachfront. It all was madness, nothing more.

The Ofoten Railway, across the fjord from their position, smoked in places where either battles or sabotage had flared. The railway crept upon the contours of the land like a wounded segmented snake that would deny either side its use.

The twins realized, like so many before them, that they had been drawn into this mayhem, this havoc, this maelstrom in their unsuspecting innocence. They stood for moments atop this height, not knowing if or how they would ever descend and return to Skrova, or return to Broughty Ferry, or even ever return to sanity itself.

Below them, Colonel Becker's party rested briefly at the halfway point, not far from where the twins had done so. Becker was flying blind, as messages to all commanders were being issued encrypted by Enigma to keep the enemy from knowing the locations and movements of their forces.

"Tell me, sailor, can you fix this machine that you spent so long inspecting last evening by the fire?" he asked.

"Yes, Colonel, it looks mostly intact," the *Kriegsmarine*r said. "If I can be given some time with it, I believe I can make it operational."

"When we capture these dogs," Becker then said, "you will get all the time, you need."

"Where are they leading us, Colonel?" asked the *Gebirgsjäger* guard that had been with him atop the *Norddalsbron*.

"Into dangerous territory I am afraid," Becker answered honestly. "There has been much fighting between French and Polish against our own units in these heights along the north shore of the *Rombaksfjord*. The Allies have already secured the port of Øyjord to the far west of us. It was from there that they launched their invasion of Narvik days ago. My guess is that the spies must hope to find an Allied unit on this mountain before we capture them."

"So we go one further still?" said one of the *Kriegsmariners*, so unaccustomed to the heights of these mountain surroundings. "We are chasing after mountain goats."

Becker stopped and turned to look at the sailor who dared to challenge his directions. His cold stare scoured the sailor like steel wool.

At any other time, Becker would have taken this outburst as insubordination. But unlike himself and his *Gebirgsjäger* underling, he had to remember these marines were not used to the danger in these heights, just as he himself was unaccustomed to the threats of the sea.

"But you forget," said the colonel slyly, "that you are among a pack of mountain wolves who pursue and will destroy those you call mountain goats."

Throughout that night, the twin brothers wandered atop the granite mountain searching for a path to freedom. They rested only during the two hours of darkness, during which they shared the next to last ration of food, then resumed their search in the pale light of the Arctic dawn. In the far distance, they could hear the artillery and machine gun fire from the up-mountain *Kuberget* area just north of Bjørnfjell where the battle still raged. Closer still was the sound of small arms fire from skirmishes nearby.

It appeared that throughout the entire north of Norway, the Allies had the Germans entrapped or on the run. The noose was closing. All it took was time now, the twins thought.

The still smoldering port of Narvik remained free and in the hands of the Allies, this much they could clearly see from their elevated position. The problem the twins then faced was how could they deliver themselves, along with the stolen Enigma rotors, to the Allies below.

They had only stumbled onto the switchback trail by accident. All of their earlier efforts had been focused across the fjord, along the path of the Ofoten Railway and the work-roads leading down to the water. There, they could now see swarms of Allied soldiers making their way towards the Germans. This would all be all over in a matter of days, and the Germans would either be captured or driven into Sweden. There they would be detained. Just a few days more.

A few days seemed to be beyond the bounds of the twins' destiny. Overnight Gunnar had developed a fever. Einar fed him the last ration that they had so steadfastly conserved. He himself was starving, and the pain of this had progressed out of his stomach alone into his joints, bones, and muscles. He ached and felt weak. But his sustenance was in knowing that his brother, Gunnar, was in dire need of his care, as well as his sacrifice. So, given his brother's more severe state, and perhaps this alone, the weary, emaciated Einar pressed on.

They searched the barren cliffs that seemed to dive from the granite's mountain's crest, but failed to find a route to freedom. Einar continued to lead them westward, toward Øyjord, but that town was nearly the length of the fjord away, and with much impassible terrain between them and its safety. Also, west was the direction from which the gunfire of the ongoing skirmishing continued to ring out.

Einar's leg was throbbing once more. The sinew that held his aching muscles seemed to go taut and lose their elasticity. He knew he could not go on much further, let alone expect his feverish wounded brother to do so. Einar looked back throughout the day, expecting to see the German party that trailed them. He was pleasantly surprised to not find them following across the wind-smoothed granite mountaintop. There was nearly nowhere for them to hide, for at this elevation, only scraggly growths of single bushes existed amongst the occasional tree. He hoped against all else that Colonel Becker had been recalled to the fight elsewhere. He prayed for this to be true so that he and his brother could survive the next few days and be rescued by the Allies

The day neared its end, and Einar noticed that Gunnar began to shake and sweat profusely. The winds that had whipped all day off the fjords and drove with a vengeance over this granite mount had taken their toll. What had been a mild fever in his brother was by then raging within him. We must get out of the open air, Einar thought, or neither of us will survive to celebrate the Nazis being driven out of Arctic Norway.

Late in the day they had stopped along a mountain lake atop the granite peak. Only later he would learn its name - *Lomvatnet*. Einar soaked the remnant cloths of his thermal undershirt and cleaned Gunnar's wound, which looked angry and inflamed. He re-dressed the wound and wiped clean his brother's sweat-laden, tortured forehead.

It was shortly after this that Einar decided to follow the stream bed that drained from this lake. It led to a series of smaller ponds before dropping off suddenly into a magnificent waterfall. It cascaded first down a small series of short but steeply inclined drops, before the entire stream of icy waters plunged free over the cliffs along the *Rombaksfjord's* edge.

As they could follow it no longer, Einar searched the surrounding areas. Soon he came upon a trail that lead him down to a series of ledges that descended ever lower toward the fjord. They formed what appeared to be roughly hewn steps for behemoths, what both twins thought as a staircase for the gods. He knew it was unlikely to take them to freedom, but it was likely to provide some shelter from the winds, and hide them from Colonel Becker's patrol, if indeed they were still in pursuit.

Einar climbed down the first ledge, then helped his brother from below. This they repeated another three times, until the stairs stepped only off into the air out over the fjord. They were trapped, but the ledges were between two walls of sheer granite that shielded them from the winds. However, the cold persisted. They watched as the last tip of the sun slowly disappeared over the western horizon and the darkness of the short arctic night fell hard upon them.

Gunnar continued to shake uncontrollably and complained of chills throughout his body. His wound throbbed, he said. Einar looked with pity upon his brother and felt that it was only by his own doing that this misery had befallen his twin. Einar cursed his own selfish desire to recover that missing Enigma device. His quest for adventure would surely be the death of them both.

51 The Wicked Sting of Withdrawal

June 1 to June 6, 1940

"We must be very careful not to assign to this deliverance the attributes of a victory. Wars are not won by evacuations."

Winston Spencer Churchill

The near empty *Nordlys* once again plied the waters of the English Channel as the sun had yet to rise over its waters. Brigand and the three Royal Marines were headed for a second day of fishing the shallows just off the beachhead at Dunkirk for his nation's greatest treasure - its youth. Those thought to be hopelessly trapped there.

The aircraft of neither friend nor foe yet plied the skies overhead, but Brigand knew they would again take to their tasking as soon as the sun rose. Yet, this did not deter his will in the slightest. Brigand and his three marine companions had an incredible first day. With each soldier they pulled from the sea, they lifted Brigand's despair from his deepest doldrums in which it dwelled. With each unloading of the deck of the *Nordlys'* harvest onto those transport ships, Brigand's own weight of responsibility for his sons' precarious situation was eased slightly. Slowly, the yoke of guilt he bore was lightened.

At the end of the day, when the *Nordlys* would ferry another hundred or so souls to the shadows of Dover's cliffs, after the troops had disembarked, Brigand would have the satisfaction of having ***done*** something. His reach was not nearly far enough to save his own offspring, he thought, but he could save the sons of his countrymen. His heart swelled with pride as he watched them disembark and scramble to waiting trains.

That sight alone transformed the dark gravity of his despair into the angelically light arcs of the wings of hope. Brigand prayed that God above would weigh his actions and reward him with the safe return of the twin sons with whose futures he had so recklessly gambled.

Upon the cliff ledge hundreds of feet above the *Rombaksfjord*, Gunnar slept. Einar could not tell for certain, but he hoped his fever had broken. Einar had removed his own parka, that which had once been Gunnar's and bore the massive flows of blood of his brother's wounds. Einar draped it atop his brother's already parka-clad body. He himself came to near freezing in that darkness, having given by then not only his thermal undershirt but also the parka to the cause of saving Gunnar's life. Einar wore only the heavy woolen shirt, which due to his own uncontrollable shivering on that cliff's ledge had scratched his nipples raw to the point where both bled.

Between them hung the scapula that his brother had given him. It was stained with red streaks of Einar's blood. This did not keep him from pressing it to his lips while he prayed for his brother to be spared. He cared not to whom he prayed, be it his Lutheran Christ, the Catholic Virgin Mother, or God the Father who had created the stunning cliffs on which they were then imperiled. He only prayed for his brother's life to be spared.

The sun had risen hours ago. Einar guessed it to be about four in the morning, but the sky was painted with a brightness that he had not seen for days. Its intensity of promise had not yet been dashed with the contrails of the *Luftwaffe*. The firmament remained still in its virgin state of tranquility. Death had not yet taken to the skies, nor had it yet taken his brother's life.

Einar looked below him as Gunnar rested. He could make out the Royal Navy warships in the *Ofotfjord* and even larger vessels far beyond in the *Vestfjorden*. Below him in the *Rombaksfjord* were the four scuttled German destroyers, as well as the sunk Polish destroyer *Grom*. Some, like the *Bernd von Arnim,* broke through the surface of the fjord while others, entirely submerged could be seen through her clear shallower waters. Others still were gone forever, cast to the fjord's depths.

Einar remembered his ship recognition training in Scotland, seeing in his mind's eye the black profiles on untitled white fields: flash - Battleship, flash - Cruiser, flash - Destroyer. He remembered his alphabet of descending ship's value - ABCD - Aircraft carrier, Battleship, Cruiser, Destroyer.

The machine gun fire of the skirmishes had just started again for the day, and it sounded closer to them than ever before. He could only hope that meant freedom was drawing its sweet breath nearer to them.

It was then that Gunnar first stirred. He opened his eyes to look upon his shivering brother. "Einar," he said groggily, "where is your parka?"

Einar smiled broadly at hearing the clarity of concern in his brother's angelic voice once again. "It was once your parka, Gunnar. I merely returned it to you overnight."

"Take it away from me, instantly," Gunnar demanded, "for should I heal only to lose you to this mountain's frost, I would throw myself from this ledge."

"Yes, yes, my brother," Einar said as he gladly followed his brother's direction and took the warm parka to wear once again, "you need not be so dramatic about it."

Einar took the parka from over him, but not before feeling his forehead with the back of his hand. His skin was still warm, but not the raging inferno it had been throughout the night.

"How do you feel, brother?" Einar asked.

"Exhausted," Gunnar responded. "I could not be any weaker and still draw a breath. My arm throbs still, brother."

Einar looked with compassion on his twin, and hoped that his fever had broken. Then Gunnar startled him by asking, "Your leg brother, how is your leg?"

Only Gunnar would think to ask after his brother's lesser wound. Despite his pain, despite his exhaustion, despite the fear that surely gnawed within him, he asked to his brother's health.

"I am fine brother, my leg no longer hurts me," lied Einar.

"Good," Gunnar said, although Einar knew his brother did not believe him for a second. "Why do you have me nestled so tightly in this corner of the ledge? What is that noise I hear?"

Einar did not answer at first, he only stroked the face of his brother. He took comfort in the touch of his brother's skin, with it being neither too hot nor too cold.

"Brother, I asked you a question," Gunnar reminded.

Einar seemed surprised, as if awakened from a dream.

"Oh, yes, the corner, the sound," Einar said. "My brother, our ledge is not far down from the waterfall made by the stream from the lake we followed. That is the noise you hear. The winds along the cliffs have carried some of its moisture to us. In this corner you are safe from its spray."

And so the twins started their day. They both still starved. They could only continue to bear the cold until their bodies became weakened from doing so. They remained there on that granite ledge overlooking the *Rombaksfjord*, the *Ofotfjord* and the *Vestfjorden* in the distance. It was a perch befitting a peregrine falcon, or some other raptor, but not the mirrored hopes of two lost souls.

"I am sorry, brother," said Einar, "that I have led you out onto this unforgiving ledge."

"Einar, do not be sorry," his brother called, as though the distance between them was more than mere inches. "This view from this cliff is magnificent. Can we not just stay and rest here today? I am so very weak. God has given us dominion over these lands in these daunting hours. Let us appreciate his works."

Einar feared that Gunnar was already certain that his life would end on that ledge. He thought his brother wanted nothing more than to spend his last days, perhaps only hours, looking down upon the rugged lands from which their father's father had hailed. To absorb the work of God's chisel upon the spectral grays of granite, so perfectly contrasted by His azure blues of the fjords below and sky above; to appreciate His unending palette of alpine forest greens, all dusted in the purity of snowy whites.

"No, we cannot stay here all day," replied Einar. "Are you giving up on me? We will rest a few hours more, and then we will climb out of here."

"I cannot, brother," said Gunnar. "I am too weak to do so. I cannot do it."

Einar sensed in his brother a growing susceptibility to surrender. "You are not even the slightest bit aware of what you can do, brother," Einar scolded. "Did you think you could ever scale these heights? No! Did you ever think you could find that lost Enigma device? No! Did you ever think you could survive a month as Colonel Becker's prisoner in that damn ski hut? No! That is why God attached you forever to me, to push you to your limits, not to leave you here to die on this stone crypt hewn by the ice and winds. No, we need food, brother. Rest longer here, yes, but for hours, not days. Then, we will climb out to find whatever berries, nuts or grasses we can find with which to fill our mouths and empty stomachs."

Gunnar looked at his brother in amazement. Then Einar added, "After all, he who is my own reflection has told me that if I should allow my brother to perish here, that I would then merely throw myself from this ledge!"

Gunnar laughed aloud at his brother mimicking him. "So dramatic you are, brother." He then cleared his throat for another round of their Shakespeare game.

"*The empty vessel makes the loudest noise!*" exclaimed Gunnar.

"The Merry Wives of Windsor," guessed Einar.

"Henry V," answered Gunnar smiling.

"You and your *damn Henries,* no one but you and Mother would ever even read those silly plays," said Einar.

"Yes, Mother," Gunnar repeated. "She always enjoyed reading those plays to me from as early as I can ever remember." Einar thought that a sadness came over Gunnar before it slowly morphed into a grateful smile.

Gunnar's smile then spread so widely upon his face that it could not help but to break free into laughter. It was a laughter that had abandoned him some time ago.

Einar was relieved to see this pleasure evoked from within his brother. Einar secretly rejoiced that his brother was back from his raging fever to taunt him again with this frivolous game of quotes. Yet, as well as he knew his brother, little did Einar understand that for Gunnar, reading all those plays of Shakespeare alongside his mother, time and time again, were among the most cherished memories of his life.

On the next day of *Operation Dynamo*, the *Nordlys* and its crew of four settled into a rhythm, of sorts. No one, of course, could block out the constant strafing of the *Luftwaffe* fighters on these small ships entirely. Thankfully, however, the German pilots' assaults were made more difficult by the arrival of opposing British fighters.

The battle in the skies overhead was a predecessor of an even greater battle that was to be fought in the months to follow over the Channel and the skies of England itself. Yet, even on that day over Dunkirk's shores, it was equally as much a struggle of life and death for the aerial combatants.

All Brigand could do was to put his faith in those Hurricane and Spitfire pilots to do their job. They were his overhead guardian angels, sent by God, he came to think. *Trust in them,* he told himself, *and focus upon your own work.*

In fact, Brigand was able to block out the threat and focus on recovering the wading, desperate soldiers from the waters just beyond the beach's shallows. The Royal Marines would drop sail and start the outboards as they came to Dunkirk in the morning. Brigand, strapped into his chair at the helm, would man the wheel. The rudder gave them just enough mobility to allow Brigand to keep the *Nordlys* as close to shore as possible without bottoming out the vessel. It was only Brigand's skills that kept him from doing so in these waters which should have proven too shallow for his ship.

Brigand focused on the depths as they came in under the motors' power, as measured by the soldiers immersed in the water furthest from shore, usually up to their shoulders or neck. The marines would cut off the outboards and Brigand would skillfully flare in his ship under only its running momentum. The three marines on board were impressed by his skill in doing so.

Brigand would captain the ship to within five meters of the long lines of evacuating soldiers. They would strip any gear they had not already jettisoned and swim for their lives to the *Nordlys* as it slowed to a stop just beyond them. Brigand knew if he should overshoot this distance, the ship's draft would threaten to wedge it to the bottom.

The marines would haul in these brave lads until the ship was full. Only on a few occasions did the marines need to dive in to assist those who could not swim. Never once did Brigand venture in too far on these days of rescue, nor did he ever come close to bottoming out. Yet, there was never a single soul left behind because Brigand had been too cautious, stayed too far to sea. Then, after all the soldiers were loaded aboard, be they British or French, the marines would restart the outboards and off they went to transfer their rescued catch out to the much larger transport ships awaiting in the Channel's deeper waters.

Brigand was exhilarated and focused, which kept his mind from becoming consumed with fear. This along with the athletic agility of the three marines would prove a tremendous combination, the results of which were hundreds more soldiers rescued that day. And only that evening, as his ship was again laden out with soldiers upon her decks for the return trip to Dover, did he have time to worry about the fate of his own two sons.

The day atop the granite mountain cliff on the north shore of the *Rombaksfjord* wore into the early afternoon. There was no sign of Becker's patrol. Gunnar was feeling extremely weak, but slightly better since his fever broke. However, he was too exhausted to climb up the ledges of the *staircase of the gods*.

So instead, Einar went in search of whatever food he could find, and something, anything, to burn for a fire. It was no longer a concern that its smoke might be spotted, for without it they would simply not survive.

Einar came back in a little over an hour with more unripened berries, and an armful of wood that was nothing more than small dried out kindling and a few larger fallen boughs.

He gave the berries to his brother, who demanded Einar share in the small feast. "I have already eaten while I scavenged them," he lied, "as I'd rather carry them in my belly than in my hands."

In reality, his stomach was as empty as his words. Gunnar ate, and Einar was happy to see him do so. Einar built the small fire with matches taken from the waterproof metal cylindrical container in his pocket of his woolen shirt.

"After this fire burns, my brother," Einar said, "we must climb out of here. So enjoy its warmth while you can."

Einar attended to his brother, moving him to where he could best be warmed by the flames of the small fire.

The fire burned for another forty minutes, and as Gunnar warmed himself from its last flickering flames, there was a noise at the top of the gods' stairway. Einar looked up to see five men dressed in varying German uniforms.

Lieutenant Colonel Becker stood at the center, in his mountain white tunic and ski pants. Alongside him stood another *Gebirgsjäger* soldier, dressed out in his field green uniform, but bearing the same Edelweiss insignia on his upper arm as the colonel. Both men wore the national emblem, an eagle holding the swastika in its talons, above their breasts. This guard of the colonel's carried the wooden case containing the damaged Enigma device. The sight of this made both twins' hearts drop.

The three other German men were not soldiers at all, but sailors. These were the three *Kriegsmariners* the twins had spotted below on the valley floor. They were dressed in similar blue uniforms to each other, so very different from those of the other two Germans. Each man bore the naval version of the national emblem embroidered in yellow on a blue background above their right breasts.

It was these men who most threatened Einar and his brother, as they pointed their submachine guns at them. They all looked edgy, as if they were unsure of the lieutenant colonel's intention, or where he was leading them. This made Einar, especially, very concerned.

As for the lieutenant colonel, he wore a sly smile of great satisfaction across his face. Yet, somehow, at its edges it contained a most serious threat to them. Perhaps it was the disdain for his quarry that had worn away at his satisfaction of catching them. In any case, Einar knew it did not portend well for either he or his brother.

"Well, if it isn't my *Nordic Catholic* friends," Lieutenant Colonel Becker spoke in Norwegian with heavy sarcasm. "How kind of you both to light that small fire. We had given up on finding you and had just begun to head back to Bjørnfjell when we spotted its smoke. I don't think we would have found you otherwise."

Gunnar began to speak, but stammered so terribly due to his fear that nothing intelligible came forth.

"No one stammers so in their native tongue," Becker yelled at them in Norwegian. "Fear rips away the faculty of the mind to translate. I gather your true native tongue is not Nordic at all but English."

"Leave my brother alone," Einar answered in Norwegian. "First you have him shot, then chase him down like a hare with a pack of hounds, only to corner him at this moment of his great weakness."

"And you also, his twin," Becker said, still standing over the brothers, who had only the air over the fjord at their backs. "Had you both not lied to me, nor stolen this device, I would have wasted neither a bullet nor an hour on either of you. But you have dragged me to these heavens, from which I will cast you both to hell."

He then spoke in German to the sailors, two of which then disappeared from sight. The third still kept his sub-machine gun trained on them. The *Gebirgsjäger* guard lowered the Enigma's wooden crate to the ground and drew his Luger P-08 *Parabellum* handgun.

"Actually, that was only a figurative threat," Becker then added with a smirk, "although I must admit a most satisfying one for me to envision. Tomorrow, I will drag you both back to Bjørnfjell to stand before General Dietl and there you will confess to what information exactly you have already relayed to the Allies. Your broken radio and pistol were found in the grotto beneath the Hundalen station house, so do not deny that you are spies. I suggest that in front of the General, you confess to all, and save yourselves much pain."

"We are simply Fishermen from Skrova who wish to return home…" Einar began.

"Yes, to the waters of the *Vestfjorden* where the Royal Navy's aircraft carriers and battleships patrol. Of course, you wish to go there, but that is not in your future, for either of you. After you confess, which I assure you that you will do after you are interrogated, you will either be shot or sent to Germany to be interred in a camp there. I fear the camp may be a worse option than your both taking bullets."

Einar turned to look at his brother. Gunnar's crippling fear had returned. Einar's heart crumbled for his brother, whose fever had broken only in time for him to endure the days ahead. That was, if his frail frame could even first endure this night.

"Then let us go to Bjørnfjell now," Einar demanded. He had felt no fear of what lied ahead; he felt only the responsibility for having dragged his brother into this terribly bleak situation. Then he'd demanded of Becker, "Why make us freeze another night on these icy stone ledges?"

Becker did not at first respond. He instead looked up into the sky. He measured the angle of the sun and calculated in his mind where they might be on their descent when the few hours of darkness befell them that night.

Becker then glanced at the two twins and calculated in the degree to which their injuries and maladies would slow the Germans down. Lieutenant Colonel Becker looked upon them with cynicism. He then looked across the fjord and finally back to the Enigma device the guard had carried.

"But, my friends," he said finally, " you know while it is not so late in the day, if we left now, we would be on those damn switchbacks in the dark overnight hours. Do not fool yourself that somehow you could escape from us there? No, not with your torn Achilles Tendon and your brother's gunshot wound. No, we will not leave now when you have found us such a perfect spot on these ledges. I can see the whole of the Ofoten Railway across the fjord. Also, my man is very close to fixing that device you so conveniently found for us."

Becker pointed to the wooden Enigma box.

"Tonight, while it is still light," he continued, "after that device is repaired, I can call in the positions of the French and Norwegians as they advance against our *Gebirgsjäger* elite mountain troops. I owe that much to them. They are mostly Austrians, you know, like myself. Very fierce fighters, as you can see from your Allies' slow progress. No, tonight we will build a roaring fire, as we have seen no Allies nearby over the past days atop this rock. We will warm ourselves and rest for tomorrow's descent at first light. Then we can complete the navigating of the switchbacks in good light."

A little over an hour later the two sailors returned from gathering wood and a fire was soon started on the third ledge down, the one above where the twins were held captive. The same two sailors then returned to the mountain's paths to search for even more wood. The *Gebirgsjäger* soldier who guarded them along with Becker had taken one of their MP-38 submachine guns, which he kept trained on the twins at all times. The last sailor also had his own machine gun pointed at the two spies.

The flames of the fire did not carry any higher than the granite walls on their either side. Becker warmed himself next to it and while the soldiers and sailors had enjoyed its warmth, it was soon clear that the Germans were as hungry as either twin was. Whatever rations they had carried had been consumed days ago and when the two *Kriegsmariners* returned with more firewood, the colonel was clearly distraught that they had neither found nor caught anything to eat.

When the onset of night's chill had fallen, one of the sailors asked something of the colonel. After receiving what appeared to be an affirmative reply in German, the mariner then set down his weapon and opened up the wooden case before him. He delicately handled the mangled Enigma device.

Einar and Gunnar leaned up against either corner of the ledge below them. Their faces and shoulders only cleared its height, and, as such, caught only a small portion of the radiant warmth of the raging fire the Germans had built above them. That warmth, absorbed by their shoulders, neck and head, seemed only to be instantly drained into the freezing void that was the rest of their bodies.

Einar watched intently as the sailor scraped one of the Enigma device's connector fittings across the hard granite surface of that third ledge. He seemed to be wearing away a piece of a fitting's bent metal cover that was keeping it from mating to the rest of the unit. From what Einar could see, he appeared to be near success.

The sailor had worked so strenuously that he seemed lost in his focus on his effort. He sat just far enough away from the fire to give him ample stone on which to whittle back the metal housing. It dawned on Einar that he must have been doing this for some time, during their other overnights atop this granite rock. He appeared to have repaired, as best he could without tools, all the other connections. This damaged fitting appeared to be his last hurdle to clear.

The seaman worked it hard, with all his energy, back and forth across the stone ledge, much like a child sharpening a stick on the pavement to play war. When he rested his arm, Einar noticed the patch on his uniform's sleeve. It was roughly in the same location as the yellow-on-green oval Edelweiss patch that the colonel and his guard wore identifying them as *Gebirgsjäger* mountain elite troops. The sailor's patch was instead a black circle, on which were two crossed semaphore flags in red and white with yellow staves. Einar remembered this to be the *Kriegsmarine*'s proficiency patch for the signal corps.

At that moment, Einar knew they were in peril, as this fellow was surely very knowledgeable in how to repair this machine. This was the very device into which he and Gunnar had earlier installed Wincer Wells' sabotaged faux rotors. It would now only be a matter of time until he repaired the fitting, and in doing so would make the Enigma device operational once more.

Colonel Becker from time to time interrupted the seaman's work. He seemed to be asking how much longer, and the seaman answered *"Bald. Sehr bald"* which Einar remembered from their German crash course as "Soon. Very soon."

"*Danke schoen, Herren*," said Becker to the twins, who he noticed were both watching the seamen's efforts, "for without your efforts in recovering this Enigma, I would not be able to report your comrades' positions across the fjord to Bjørnfjell tonight. I would have neither this device, nor this bird's eye view from across the fjord."

As the seaman worked on the Enigma detector, another set up the portable radio next to it that they had carried. Once the Enigma was fixed, they thought, they could listen in on the encrypted traffic over the radio, and then report the Allies' positions from their vantage point.

As the seaman focused on his scraping of the metal housing back and forth across the granite floor of the ledge, Einar watched as Colonel Becker said something to his *Gebirgsjäger* guard. They both rose and began to climb up to the second ledge, and then again to the first, and finally back out onto the trail. As they walked out of sight, Einar could see the colonel unfastening his belt. It appeared the colonel had to relieve himself and wanted the guard's protection while he did.

This left only the three *Kriegsmariners* on the ledge just above them. The one working on repairing the Enigma, another setting up the radio, and the third, who now stood menacingly on the ledge over them with the machine gun.

Einar knew there was nothing he could do. Even if he was to somehow overtake the sailor standing over them and take his weapon from him, which he deemed to be impossible, the other two sailors were close enough to their own weapons to return fire. However, by doing nothing, he could allow the signalman to complete his task of repairing the Enigma.

Einar thought this might indeed be the best course of action. He then made a hand gesture to Gunnar that the three *Kriegsmarine* guards above them could not see. He mimicked the back and forth scraping motion of the signalman. Gunnar watched intently. Einar then mimicked a motion of installing something into his other hand and the pushing of a button. He followed by rapidly opening both palms in the force of an explosion.

The signalman then stopped scraping the fitting and successfully cried out "*Ich habe es getan*" as the housing finally fell free from the connector. He excitedly moved to mate the final connection that would allow the device to be powered up.

Einar knew the operator would then be eager to test the device by depressing one or more keys to see a corresponding letter on the lampboard light up.

"Brother," Einar said in English, which he hoped none of the three sailors understood, *"Hell hath no fury like a woman scorned."*

"Nor a rotor tested" added Gunnar, indicating he knew what was to come.

The *Kriegsmarine* guard who had the machine gun on them yelled "*Nein, nein*" to stop them from talking. He came to the very edge of the third ledge. He stood just over the twins and threateningly swung the barrel of his weapon from one to the other.

Gunnar and Einar slid from their half-standing, half-leaning positions to lie flat on the ledge below him, which the guard took to be a submissive response to his towering over them.

As all this was happening, the signalman mariner attached the last connection and turned on the battery power.

The second mariner had set up the radio and by then sat astride the fire, with his machine gun at the ready.

The third continued to hover over the brothers at the edge of that third ledge, pointing his machine gun at them.

The two twins made sure their heads and shoulders were below that third ledge. They squeezed themselves hard into their respective stone corners.

Above him, Becker had returned from the mountain trail with his guard escort aside him. He stood atop the *staircase of the gods*, and took in a sequence of fire-lit actions that he did not understand. The twins were drawing themselves down below the level of the third ledge, the *Kriegsmariner* guarding them stood menacingly over them and the signalman had just powered up the Enigma device. He watched as the man moved to depress one of the center letters from among the upper most row of keys to test the machine.

A clarity of recognition befell Becker's face, making his skin go instantly tense, as hard as the granite ledges beneath him. Then it tingled in a recognition of unadulterated terror.

Becker understood in that split second that the twins were taking cover, not from their fear of the guard above them, but from what was about to occur behind him.

"*Halt! Halt!*" the lieutenant colonel screamed. He saw the marine guard towering over the twins turn to look at him. But it was too late, as the signalman was already in the motion of depressing the "Z" key. It clicked, bottoming out on its internal contact.

A tremendous blast exploded on that third ledge, just above Einar and Gunnar. They had pressed themselves hard into the shield that was formed by the granite corners of their fourth ledge, against the stone wall that rose to the ledge above. The twins felt the instantaneous force of the blast as it swept over them in a sound and fury most violent. Einar felt something deflect off his back, then both twins heard the descending scream of the marine guard who had been standing over them as he was propelled over the last ledge and fell to his death.

Einar opened his eyes. The fire was completely gone, replaced in the air only by a swirling canopy of cherry red embers that seemed to float on the moment, searching out a hard spot on which to land. Einar placed his hands over his eyes to protect them, and jumped up to the next level. The debris of the machine was scattered in small metallic shards, and marked the granite sidewalls with a scattershot pattern of impact sites. The Enigma device and the radio were both completely gone.

Both of the other two *Kriegsmariners* were dead. Their bodies were riddled with the machine's shrapnel, as well as by the disfiguring blunt force of the explosion. One guard even had a splinter of unburned wood, likely from the device's case, protruding from the pupil of his left eye.

Einar grabbed one of the machine guns, but its barrel had been deformed by the blast. He removed the magazine clip from it, which seemed intact. He tossed the weapon itself aside and reached for the last MP-38 and quickly looked it over for damage. Einar and his brother had been trained on this machine gun. This one appeared to be only scratched and scraped, but should still fire. The other machine gun had been blown from the ledges by the blast held by the sailor who had stood over them.

Einar ignored the pain in his leg and hobbled as fast as he could up the remaining ledges and onto the trail. There he found Becker and the *Gebirgsjäger* guard, still laying flat from the blast, but beginning to stir with consciousness.

Einar kicked the rifle away from the guard's grip. He pointed the machine gun at him and the lieutenant colonel and pulled back the bolt mechanism that fed a first round into the gun's breech.

"Pistols, slowly," Einar said in Norwegian. Becker relayed the message in German to his companion and they both carefully removed their pistols from their side holsters, and tossed them at Einar's feet.

"Now climb down to the very last ledge," he ordered. Becker relayed the order and both Germans did as commanded. As they dropped themselves onto the third ledge, the colonel's guard began to move toward his fallen comrades.

"No, No," screamed Einar, as he triggered a burst from the machine gun over both German's heads. The guard pulled away from the corpses instinctively. Einar knew each body still had its sidearms holstered.

"Gunnar come up to me," his brother yelled. Gunnar with great effort climbed onto the third ledge. He was exhausted. Einar then dropped himself down to the third ledge and stood next to his brother opposite the two Germans.

Einar had feared either Becker or his guard might grab his brother to attempt to use as a human shield, but they had not. Perhaps the burst he had fired over their heads sobered them, certainly removing any doubts they might have as to whether he knew how to operate the machine gun.

"Now, the two of you, get down there," Einar said as he motioned with the gun's barrel to the last ledge. As he did, the colonel and the soldier lowered themselves down onto the lowest ledge. Once they had, Einar then said to Gunnar, "Brother, remove any weapons from those dead bodies."

Gunnar had never seen a dead man up close, and the thought of touching them sent shivers through him. But he did so regardless of his fear and removed their Lugers. He returned to stand by his brother, overlooking the last ledge where the two Germans stood alone.

"Good," Einar said. "Now, hold this machine gun on Lieutenant Colonel Becker and his friend and fire a short burst over their heads so they know you know how to do so."

This Gunnar did. The small arms training they had received in Scotland had covered both the MP-38 submachine gun and the Luger pistol, so both twins were functional with these weapons.

With Gunnar covering the two *Gebirgsjäger*, Einar scampered up and retrieved the guard's P-08 Luger *Parabellum* and Colonel Becker's Walther P-38 semi-automatic pistol.

Einar then returned to the third ledge where Gunnar stood, still with the machine gun trained on the two Germans just below. Gunnar leaned heavily against the granite wall of the third ledge.

"Brother, I am exhausted," Gunnar said to him in English.

"Sit, Gunnar," Einar replied in English, "rest your back against that ledge wall. I have them covered."

"Now, Colonel Becker," Einar said standing next to his siting brother on the ledge over the Germans, "you and your guard will stand over by the edge of the cliff."

"No, don't shoot us here …" Becker began.

Einar then fired the P-38 pistol over their heads.

The lieutenant colonel heeded the command and both of the German men then moved to the edge.

"Gunnar," his brother said aloud, "point the weapon at that guard's chest. If I tell you, squeeze that trigger."

"This is not honorable warfare," exclaimed Becker.

Einar looked coldly into Becker's eyes. "What could possibly make you think that you deserve an honorable death?"

Gunnar, as well as Einar, had been trained on the MP-38 German-made submachine gun in the Highlands of Scotland. The twins knew the gun well, as they did its derivative successor, the MP-40. What they had not been taught, however, was that both guns had a single serious design flaw.

Their instructor thought it to be a marvel of engineering design and machining prowess. He explained to the twins that it had been modeled after the MP-18 that had found use late, ultimately too late for the Germans, during World War I. The MP designation was derived from the German compound word *Maschinenpistole*. The 38 designated the year it was introduced. In many ways, the MP-38 reflected the gradual design of a pistol which had evolved into a machine gun. The most telling feature of this evolution was its pistol-style grip.

The weapon had a collapsible metal shoulder stock. When used hanging from the shoulder straps, these stocks were generally stored by rotating them under the gun's housing, where they would collapse neatly into storage on the weapons underside.

The MP-38 utilized stick-design magazines holding thirty-two rounds each. The gun fired in either single action or fully automatic modes. There was no semi-automatic setting.

To use the weapon in single fire mode, there was a notch cut into the rear of the machined slot that the bolt travelled along. The bolt was slid back and jammed up into this notch to prevent repeated firing.

Herein lay the machine's only flaw, albeit a deadly serious one. The length of travel of the bolt slide, even before reaching the notch, was more than enough to complete the sequence of loading and firing the weapon manually. More simply said, even if the weapon's chamber was kept empty, as most soldiers did when not expecting combat, if the bolt was manually pulled back to just before engaging that notch and released, even if by accident, the gun would load a round into the chamber and fire it. Therefore, a soldier could be shot or killed by what he thought to be a safe weapon.

Making matters worse was that the bolt itself was shaped like the miniature horn of a steer. This was an intentional design feature to allow the soldier to find and grasp it with his finger. The problem with this design is that it tended to catch other things as well, like clothing or the recesses of a truck's door. In the field, these could, and as it turns out did, draw back the bolt, only to eventually release it, resulting in the weapon inadvertently being fired.

A growing number of wounds, and in some cases, deaths, of German soldiers caused the redesign and retrofit of the MP-40 in 1942. But very few of the MP-38s were ever retrofitted for this design flaw. None of either the MP-38 or MP-40 guns had been retrofitted by the time of the Narvik campaign.

This inadvertent firing issue had not been part of Einar's and Gunnar's Scottish Highlands training, for this particular flaw was not known at that time by the trainers and was only becoming more widely known within the *Wehrmacht* itself.

Einar wanted to keep his hands free during what he intended to be the interrogation of Lieutenant Colonel Becker. He aimed the lieutenant colonel's Walther P-38 pistol at Becker. He stood next to Gunnar, who sat with the machine gun on the ledge above the two Germans.

"If they rush us brother," Einar continued in English, "aim down on them and squeeze that thing like a young lass' teat. Make sure you kill both of these bastards."

Gunnar smiled inwardly at his brother's directions, but unlike his brother, he had never been alone with any young lasses. He suppressed his desire to laugh aloud and tried his best to look sternly down at the captors turned captives.

"Now, Colonel, you will answer my question," said Einar, changing to Norwegian. "If you do not, this man will die."

Becker said nothing. The Walther pistol in Einar's hand was trained on him. He could see Einar's thumb had already released the safety.

"Tell him that we intend to shoot him if you do not answer our questions."

Becker did so. The soldier must have understood, for he stared up at the machine gun held by Gunnar and broke out in a flop sweat.

"The night you came to our cabin, you said the Germans had a deadly surprise in store for Mr. Churchill, our new Prime Minister. What is it?"

"I was drunk and speaking nonsense," Becker said.

Einar raised the Walther and aimed it at the Colonel's forehead. He held it there, and in a last second, angled it away slightly past his ear and pulled the trigger. The shot caused both men to jump.

"No, you were drunk, but your words were quite serious," Einar said sternly, then returned his aim to between Becker's eyes, "so, what is it, this surprise?"

"There is nothing to tell," Becker said. His face was calm, as if he was prepared to die. Einar quickly glanced at the face of the other German. His forehead was roped with thick streams of beaded sweat.

"Do not let them shoot us, *Oberst*" the soldier said in German, but the twins did not understand.

"Quiet, idiot. They are not trained assassins, they will not fire on unarmed men," the colonel replied in German, "they merely are playing out a bluff."

Einar could not understand what they were saying, but decided to step up the pressure on the two Germans.

"Five!" announced Einar aloud in Norwegian. "He is your fellow Austrian, is he not? You would have him die for you?"

Gunnar kept the MP-38 machine gun trained down on the man, his arms close to his side.

The guard screamed in German, "Do not let them kill me."

"Four!" Einar counted, "Tell him to say his last prayers, Colonel Becker."

The guard did not understand, but pleaded again with the lieutenant colonel.

"Three!"

The *Gebirgsjäger soldier* knew enough Norwegian to follow the countdown. He continued to beg the colonel.

"They will not fire," repeated Becker in German.

"Two!" Einar said in Norwegian. Then, he added, for Becker to hear him say, "Ready yourself, Gunnar, my brother, to shoot that German bastard."

"*BITTE, OBERST, BITTE,*" pleaded the guard.

"One!" called out Einar.

Becker did not flinch.

"FIRE!" shouted Einar.

The *Gebirgsjäger* soldier raised his arms as if they would shield him from the spray of bullets to follow.

A swollen second lingered. It seemed Einar's bluff had been called. He knew his brother would not be able to fire upon the unarmed men. Neither twin had ever fired on a man, armed or not, before this. Einar knew that Becker had counted on this. With his gambit having failed, Einar knew not what he would do next.

The German guard, hearing no fire, feeling no spray of bullets, felt embarrassed. He slowly lowered his hands.

In reaction to this, Gunnar began to raise the MP-38 to his eye level from its waist high firing position. He thought this menacing act would be all that it would take to strike panic in the guard and that would be all it would take to convince Lieutenant Colonel Becker to talk.

The antler shaped bolt of the gun caught the lining of Gunnar's parka as it was extended. Gunnar felt the resistance as the weapon's bolt was drawn back in the slide groove.

The *Gebirgsjäger* guard who stood just below him by only a few feet noticed this and recognized exactly how dangerous the situation had become. He began to move forward, as if he could untangle the bolt from Gunnar's parka. Out of a reaction of fear, Gunnar pushed the weapon even further forward. The guard stopped his forward motion just as the retracted bolt was yanked free from Gunnar's clothing.

The MP-38 screamed out with a single explosion. It surprised no one more than Gunnar. The round caught the guard in the upper body through his lung. The German spun backward and his momentum carried him over the side of that final ledge. He screamed all the way down, ending abruptly just before the fjord's waterline as his body slammed into a massive outcropping of rock. The impact had killed him instantly.

Becker had watched in horror as his countryman fell to his death. The colonel had never thought Gunnar capable of pulling the trigger, not realizing that the twin had not, that Gunnar's finger had never even flinched, and that it was all merely an unintended accident.

Einar was shocked, but was quick to recognize the opportunity. "You were warned, Colonel" he said with the gravest voice he could affect. "Now, it's your turn. Five…" Einar once more raised Becker's own pistol and aimed at his forehead.

"You will not shoot," Becker said defiantly.

"You had my brother shot, Colonel. I assure you I can certainly pull this trigger," Einar answered. "Four…"

"Brother, what are you doing?" asked Gunnar in English, thinking it kept Becker from understanding him.

"Only what needs to be done," his brother replied. Then in Norwegian Einar counted out, "Three…"

"There is not any threat upon Churchill," Becker again said in Norwegian. "It was all nothing but brave, drunken talk."

"He lies," Einar replied to Gunnar in English, then in Norwegian counted out "Two…"

"Don't do this, brother. It is not you," Einar said, again in English. "I have unintentionally killed a man. Don't let your rage force you to do with malice that which I only did in error."

"Oh, I will shoot him, my brother," said Einar sternly.

Gunnar had been watching Becker's face intently. When he had said in English that he'd shot the guard by accident, Becker had responded by showing a flicker of surprise. It being an accident seemed to answer some question within the colonel.

Gunnar, in that instant, pieced it all together. *Becker understands my English,* he thought. *Lieutenant Colonel Becker had said he had been an aide to a military liaison in Oslo. He surely would have been selected for his language skills. Becker had already told them he learned Norwegian on assignment. So, what other languages would be of value to hold for that position. Certainly the language of their expected enemies, English and French. Becker is relieved. He doesn't think we will shoot him.*

Gunnar then decided to up the pressure on the lieutenant colonel. He cried out in a crazed, excitable stream of English words, knowing that Becker understood, "Einar, if you are going to shoot him, then just for my pleasure, aim at that German bastard's balls. The son of a bitch took great pleasure in having me shot. Shoot him in his balls! It will sear his last few seconds with an insufferable pain until he crushes his bones on those rocks below."

With this Einar yelled out *"One!"* in Norwegian to hammer home the point. At that instant, without hesitation, the lieutenant colonel yelled out as he cupped his hands over his crotch.

"Do not shoot! Do not shoot! I will tell you, I will tell you," Becker pleaded in English. "Just do not shoot me in my manhood."

"You do speak English!" cried out a stunned Einar. He glanced at his brother, as if to say, *Where did that come from?*

Einar then thrust his weapon hand forward at Becker. "So what exactly does *Der Führer* have in store for our Prime Minister Churchill?"

"*Operation Predator*," answered Becker excitedly.

"Which is what?" prodded Einar, as he waved the barrel of his gun in a "give me more" circular motion.

"There is a German airman serving undercover as a pilot in the fighter escort group of Churchill's Flamingo transport aircraft. He will, on the next opportunity, shoot that bloated bulldog bastard out of the sky."

"That's not even remotely believable, Becker. Now tell us the truth," demanded Einar, "or we will be forced to shoot you as we did your guard. What does Hitler have in store for Churchill?"

"I swear it is true," Becker said, as he rapidly glanced at Gunnar. Einar could almost feel him think that the twin looked like anything but a killer, as Gunnar continued to move nervously, his face strained with remorse. Yet, Becker would also recall how only seconds before Gunnar had shot his unarmed guard, even if it was merely an accident. Certainly, Becker would know from experience that nervous, emotional men were accident prone, and Gunnar could easily have another incident at the lieutenant colonel's expense.

The sweat that began to drip from the lieutenant colonel's forehead was certainly real. Einar thought he could actually smell the fear in the man. Of course, the colonel's claim was preposterous. How could a German agent get one of Britain's most prestigious fighter pilot assignments? England had been aflame with German spy suspicions since the turn of the century, this story could never possibly be true.

"How would you even come to acquire this knowledge?" Einar asked. "You are only a lieutenant colonel."

Becker answered excitedly. "General Dietl shared it with me the night of the *Wehrmacht's* invasion into Belgium, Holland, and France. He was always *Der Führer's* favorite general, and Hitler had entrusted him with this highly secret operation. When Churchill was named the Prime Minister later in that day, General Dietl went on about how Churchill was the only Englishman intent on fighting to the end. He alone threatened to stand between Hitler and a negotiated peace with Britain after France fell. Yet, not to worry, General Dietl had said, because Hitler had a surprise in store for the rotund, war-mongering Prime Minister. The General told only three of us of this while we toasted the invasion of France. He had a lot of liquor that night from that which our troops had taken from the port of Narvik. He shared it with his officers that night, and in fact he went on to have too much to drink, just as I did with you both afterwards. General Dietl said too much to us, again as I had also said too much to you that same night. It is all as true as I stand before you now. Should I live through this, I will eventually pay for betraying the Reich. Either way I am already a dead man."

Einar looked at his brother, "What is your take on Becker's confession, Gunnar?"

Gunnar had collapsed back against the cliff wall with weakness. He could no longer stand upright, so deep was his exhaustion. "This is some sort of a trap," said Gunnar in English. "It is misinformation he was tasked to seed in us to send to London. He gives it up too easily."

"Perhaps, so," replied Einar in the same tongue. "I admit I had the same thought, but even so, we must communicate it to London despite what we think."

"How so?" asked Gunnar. "Their radio was destroyed along with the Enigma device."

"Then, we will take Colonel Becker back with us," Einar said, "what could be more fitting? Military intelligence will know how to get the truth out of him."

"First we need to be rescued," Gunnar said, "and not by another German *Gebirgsjäger* unit."

Gunnar then slid slowly down the granite wall until he came to rest in a reclining position near his brother's feet.

At the end of the day, as darkness fell upon the Channel's waters, the *Nordlys* ferried home another hundred plus soldiers saved from the vengeful jaws of the *Wehrmacht*. Brigand MacAlvor beamed with pride as they unloaded in the safe darkness under Dover's cliffs.

"That wraps our up our duties, Captain," called out the most senior of the three mariners, the one known as Christopher. "We are ordered to return to Dartmouth upon the morning. It has been our honor serving under you aboard the *Nordlys,* sir. She is a fine craft, and you, sir, are a courageous captain."

"What?" objected a shocked Brigand. "That cannot be, lads. There are still beaches full of British soldiers across these waters. You must stay with me. I cannot navigate those shallows without each of you."

"I suppose our superiors must figure there are enough small craft present to do the job, sir."

"My God, man," Brigand shouted, "we must have seen two-thirds of the ships the size of the *Nordlys* sunk out there! Had it not been for so many of us in the area, their crew and soldiers would have all been lost. This is no time to leave a job half-done. You must stay with me at least until the operation is called off. You cannot do this to those brave lads still stuck on that sandy edge of the Continent!"

"We have our orders, Captain," said Christopher. "I am very sorry, sir, but we do not have the leeway to disobey direct orders."

"Those orders be damned!" cursed Brigand. "Think through this, Christopher, my mate. If you should abandon me now, I will only draft whatever souls I can find to act as the *Nordlys'* crew."

"That is your prerogative, Captain," Christopher said, "but we are ordered back to Dartmouth."

"You three will be responsible for whatever green recruits I am forced to take to sea tomorrow," Brigand threatened. "Should the *Nordlys* run aground and the *Luftwaffe's* bullets find her, the deaths of three inexperienced young lads will be upon your heads. I insist that you stay until I am given a chance to have your orders rescinded. Take me off this vessel."

"That we will do out of our great respect for you, sir," said the marine Christopher.

Christopher then assisted Brigand to the quayside, fearful that any trouble with his leg might send him flailing into the harbor, where he most certainly would be in great peril.

Brigand was soon able to commandeer a phone, and immediately called directly into Wincer Wells' office.

"Hello," answered the instantly recognizable voice.

"Wincer," Brigand said, "MacAlvor here. My crew of the *Nordlys* are telling me that they are ordered back to Dartmouth."

"You don't say, old man," responded Wells in a glib tone. "You certainly have had an incredible haul and should be very proud of what you have been able to accomplish. That aside, I tell you, I personally took great heat in having these three lads taken away from their officer training duties. The Admiralty was out for my head. It seems the Royal Navy is in desperate need of naval officers at the moment, so these chaps have to get back to teaching the fresh recruits the bow from the stern, or so it would appear."

Why would Wells go to such great trouble to get me on the Nordlys, only to now cut short his mission? Brigand wondered. It was at that moment that Brigand saw through Wincer's charade. He had merely used the *Nordlys'* participation as a tool to have himself removed from his Broughty Ferry home for a few days.

"Your boys didn't find it, did they, Wincer?" Brigand said into the receiver.

"I'm afraid I haven't the slightest idea as to what you are suggesting," said Wells calmly.

You know exactly my meaning, Brigand thought.

"I know you turned my cottage over these past days whilst I was on the *Nordlys*," Brigand guessed. He had only put this all together in the seconds while they talked.

"Brigand, it appears you've been out in the Channel's sun too long. You are half-baked."

"Your hooligans didn't find it, did they?" Brigand threatened. "They got Tilly out of the house, and then they went over the cottage with a fine tooth comb, didn't they? Tilly likely never even knew they what they were doing in there. But they did not find the letter, did they Wincer? That's because I have it with me, and another copy with a friend who will send it if I am detained. I am set to hand deliver it to London in the morning if I am not out with those three marines on that bloody Channel sailing for Dunkirk again."

Brigand referred to his own letter, which detailed Wells' earlier forging of the orders which released his son, Gunnar, to Norway. His letter told the tale of Wells' forgery, complete with its telltale green ink and the impersonated signature of the previous 'C', Admiral Hugh Sinclair.

"I think the Major General," Wincer referenced Stewart Menzies, the current 'C', "has much more on his plate to be concerned with than that tall tale at the moment."

"No, old boy," Brigand threatened, "I'll be heading straightaway to the black door at No. 10 Downing. Going to tell old Winston that I know of a German spy named Wells within MI6, and I'll use your forged letter as proof."

"That's preposterous," scoffed Wells. "I am as loyal as the day is long. Besides, you'll never get to see the Prime Minister. He's even more pre-occupied than 'C' at this moment. In case you haven't noticed, there is a war on, and its currently going very badly."

"I am sure you are correct on that account," said Brigand calmly. "I likely will never see Churchill himself. Yet, I am quite sure that whoever I do get to talk to about a German mole in His Majesty's Secret Intelligence Service will certainly treat the matter with great urgency. They appear to be more than a tad bit paranoid over German spies these days. You likely may have noticed. You may in the end come to be vetted and found to be nothing but a petty forger, but I am sure they will have you thrown in the hoosegow until they can find the time to investigate the matter fully. I can't imagine that whole process, cradle to grave, will be less than six months. Who knows, they might have you sit out the whole war on nothing more than suspicion. Somehow, even if you are cleared, the Major General will still not appreciate your forging his predecessor's orders, now will he? Likely to drum you out of the service, he is. Perhaps he might even forever take away your cherished cloak and dagger."

A silent chill of static whistled through the telephone line. Finally, all that Wincer Wells could muster up to ask was, "What on earth do you want, Brigand?"

"I already told you - the three marines from Dartmouth. They stay with the *Nordlys* until the operation is complete at Dunkirk. Tell me now that they stay, and don't bother having me arrested or detained, with or without my Tilly, because as I said, I have a copy of my letter in the hands of a very trusted bloke who knows to send it if I don't check-in with him periodically."

"Brigand, you are and have always been nothing but trouble to me. You have it. The Royal Marines will stay with you. I'll have their orders rescinded on the hour."

"It's the least you owe me, Wincer," Brigand said triumphantly. "You'll find that I may have saved you from an even greater peril. This operation of small craft was Churchill's idea in the first place. He might look upon you with ill favour for pulling the *Nordlys* out at this juncture."

On the mountainside cliff, in the early Arctic morning light on that lowest ledge of the *staircase of the gods*, a stalemate of sorts had settled in between the three remaining men. Gunnar, who had drawn so heavily upon his last reserve of strength during the interrogation of the Germans, was far too weak to even sit upright any longer, let alone climb up the four ledges to the open mountain trail. The night before, he had become severely winded just climbing up that one single ledge, and today he could not repeat even that feat. He slept alongside his brother, who watched over his last remaining German prisoner. All Einar could think was how would he ever get his brother off that damn cliff? How would he get him the medical attention he surely needed?

Einar forced himself to stay awake, despite his extreme weariness and hunger. He kept the captured machine gun trained on Becker, who he had allowed to climb up onto the third ledge with them. The only questions at that point were how long would it take for another patrol to find them and would that patrol be manned by Allied soldiers or German *Gebirgsjäger?*

Einar knew that Becker was only waiting for his captor's fatigue to overcome him. Should he lapse, even for a moment, he was confident the lieutenant colonel would not only disarm him, but perhaps neither he nor Gunnar would ever awaken again.

Becker, for his part, sat opposite the two twins. He had no option but to wait for an opportunity. And he felt that opportunity would soon enough present itself through the weariness of Einar.

Einar continued to feel the throbbing in his leg and his thoughts consciously drifted to Brigand. For the first time he realized he had not made the connection to his father's loss of the same limb. *How shameful that I had completely forgotten about all his own losses and tribulations that spanned forth from war over the rest of his life.* He could see his father and his distinct limping gait, ahead of him, and remembered doing so even as a small boy of only five or six.

"Your people took my father's leg, you know," he said out of nowhere to Becker, "during the Great War."

"I am sorry to hear that, my friend," Becker replied.

"I am not your friend," Einar sniped at him. "I am only keeping you alive so that our interrogators can have at you."

"Where in the war did your father's injury occur?" asked Becker.

"Gallipoli," Einar replied tersely, sorry that he had begun this conversation.

"Well, my friend, that was neither the Germans nor the Austrians. That was a matter of the Turks defending their own homeland from the British and her Allies attempting to invade, just like what we have going on here."

"Those Turks were armed and trained by the Kaiser," responded the twin. "And the only invaders here are your army."

__*Figure 35: MP-38 Machine Guns and Captured MP-38 by Polish Forces at Narvik (Sikorski Institute, London)*__

"Well," Becker replied, "the worst thing about war is that it has many unexpected, and quite tragic turns. One never really can know what to expect, or what will happen next."

Einar did not reply. Becker seemed to be sending him the message that his captivity was only temporary. Einar wanted to respond to him, but his head had become fogged with a fatigue, one so heavy he was unsure he could fight it much longer.

In fact, as the two men had been speaking, his thoughts had begun to swirl around him in a thickening vortex. Einar looked down for a second at his brother Gunnar, who slept peaceably enough by his side. Einar knew he had to resist his exhaustion, and thought the best way to do so was to force himself to continue his discourse with Becker. It took every bit of his focus to do so.

"I know that tale you spun regarding a spy within Churchill's pilots is nothing but codswallop," he said, pausing only to parse his next swirl of thoughts into an understandable sentence. "The MI6 lads will have a go at you. They'll settle out what's what. It's what they do…"

Einar had said these last words more to keep himself awake, than to share any meaning with Becker. He could feel the eyes of the German searching him, surely noticing the effect of the weariness upon his speech and thought processes. Communicating was becoming an increasingly difficult undertaking.

He then leaned his head back. He thought again of his parents, of his home, and of his brother. His thoughts drifted to when they were laying side by side in that bed in that cottage on the Tay, a warm fire in the hearth just beyond their bedroom's open door. Then, as if in a swirling pond of silt, the image changed and he was aboard the *Nordlys* with his father upon the *Vestfjorden* for the first time. They were looking up into these very snow laden mountains, and his father was telling tales of plying these same waters with his own father…

What followed next was less a series of recollections than of feelings. Warmth, safety, brotherhood, comfort, purpose, love - all swirled around him, creating a cocoon of satisfaction. Einar's mind drifted, as if it was unwillingly pulled into the solace he knew he should resist. He could feel the muscles of his body relax and, in an instant, he was with his family on a sunny morning along the beach of the Tay.

The stupor of that dream was ripped away from Einar at the moment that he felt the MP-38 being violently stripped out of his hands. His pulse quickened, and his first reaction was to squeeze the trigger, but by the time he did so, the weapon was already cleared from his hand. Einar gathered his wits to see only a blurred figure looking over him, pointing the submachine gun at his chest.

A small plane took off from an airfield outside of Paris and headed south towards the Mediterranean. It was piloted by Bogdan Bratajewski and carried within the transport the same Poles he had led to Paris only months before: Marian Rejewski, Henryk Zygalski, Jerzy Różycki and his wife, Basia, and their son. This precious cargo could no longer be risked at the chateau outside of Paris as the German armies continued to press further into France. The last man accompanying them all was the man code named *Bolek* that Bogdan had only seen briefly in the Paris train station upon their arrival there. He was Gustave Bertand, the high ranking agent of France's *Deuxieme Bureau.*

Bogdan's piloting of the transport was something of a negotiation between General Sikorski and French Intelligence. Initially, the French refused to use any pilot outside of those known to them. Sikorski had insisted that Bogdan, in whom he had the greatest trust and confidence, be allowed to ferry his countrymen to safety. Eventually, Bertrand agreed, but refused to give the final destination to either his pilot or General Sikorski. Only after the plane was aloft did Bertrand, sitting in the co-pilot's seat, instruct Bogdan to head towards the French Mediterranean city of Perpignan, close to the Spanish border.

"So General Sikorski tells me," Bertrand said in German, "that you yearn to take up the fight against these Nazis. Yes?"

German was the only language that was common between the spy and the pilot. Bogdan's French was very weak, and Bertrand's Polish was non-existent. Bogdan had told Rejewski he felt ashamed speaking the aggressor's tongue, and the Polish codebreaker just laughed.

"*Bolek* was at our conference in the Kabaty Woods," Rejewski had said, "which was done completely in German because it was the only common language we Poles shared with the French and English. Imagine, we spoke of ways to defeat their Enigma code in their own tongue. There is justice in this, no?"

After recalling his earlier conversation with the cryptographer, Bogdan responded to the French agent's question, taking time to recall the proper German phrases he wished to use.

"Do I yearn to fight the Nazis? Yes, very much so," replied Bogdan. "My younger brother attacks them in the mountains around Narvik, alongside your French forces there."

"Yes," Bertrand replied, "it goes much better there for our troops than it does for our armies here. The Germans have many of our forces and most all of the Brits pinned down at Dunkirk. Thank God the cross channel evacuation is saving so many of them. Meanwhile, the Nazi *blitzkrieg* is shredding what is left of our other fighting forces."

"So, it goes so badly we take my countrymen to a safe destination," said Bogdan.

"Yes," said Bertrand, "but one that you are never to share with any other soul. Especially not the British."

Gustave Bertrand said this last comment knowing that General Sikorski had already planned to relocate the Polish Government-in-Exile from Paris to London, along with the all Polish Armies, including those troops returning from the campaign at Narvik.

Gustave also knew that the British desperately wanted to have these Polish codebreakers join the ranks of their other cypher-sleuths at Bletchley Park. This was an accommodation that Bertrand could not make to his British counterparts. He wanted to continue to have these Polish mathematicians under his own personal control.

"I am sure that once you and the General relocate to London," Bertrand said after a brief pause, "that the British will find use for a man of your many skills. There is already a growing resistance inside of Poland that the British will certainly wish to tap into, in some form or another. You will get your chance to fight against the Nazis, but not as a conventional soldier. No, with Polish being your native language and your command of German, as well as your flying abilities, it is only a matter of time until your skills are put to use. Of this, I am sure."

"Good," said Bogdan simply.

"It makes me regret having agreed with General Sikorski to allow you this mission, Bogdan. You must remember, if you are ever sent by the British into Poland, you can never disclose the location to where we will deliver your countrymen. Do you understand?"

"Of course," he said, "I would never imperil their lives by doing so."

There followed after this conversation a long period of silence between the two men. They continued flying south to Perpignan. Soon, off to the west, the sun was beginning to set beyond the Pyrenees Mountains. They were spectacular, backlit by hues of orange and scarlet. Cast shadows lengthened from the western facades of their jagged peaks, as the entire range was only a giant sundial warning of impending night "We are getting close. I will need the coordinates for our landing zone at Perpignan, so I can plan my approach."

"How are your petrol levels?" asked Bertrand.

"We have much fuel still," replied Bogdan.

"Good," replied Bertrand, "now set a course for Algeria. We will land outside of Algiers."

"I see," said the surprised Bogdan. "Yes, we have more than enough fuel to make it across the Mediterranean Sea."

They flew over Perpignan and safely out over the sea. It would mark Bogdan's first time ever outside of Europe. Far off in the distance, well past his copilot, Bogdan could make out the silhouette of Gibraltar with the setting sun by then descending behind *the Rock*.

"These men will be safe in Africa?" asked Bogdan. "Will they not be *as well known as a colorful dog?"*

Bogdan intentionally used the German phrase which was the equivalent of sticking out like a sore thumb.

"Do not concern yourself," Bertrand replied, "we are not exactly strangers in these lands. We will take good care of your countrymen."

What Bertrand did not share with his pilot was that their time in Algiers would be short. They would soon enough be resettled to another location, where they would safely resume their codebreaking activities on behalf of the French. One that neither Bogdan nor General Sikorski would ever know.

52 Rescue and Remorse

June 4, 1940

"If one has to submit, it is wasteful not to do so with the best grace possible."

Winston Spencer Churchill

Einar had been torn from his blissful slumber by the machine gun being ripped violently from his grasp. A blurry figure loomed over him. He glanced at his brother who had not awakened from his sleep. Then he glanced at the opposite wall of the ledge and still found Becker sitting there, just as he had been before: submissive, with no attempt to move a muscle except to hold his two arms up in surrender.

Einar looked up at the figure that held the weapon, not aimed at himself as he initially thought, but instead at the lieutenant colonel. The soldier wore a uniform he was not familiar with, having elaborately embroidered collars and a strange crested metal helmet. He had seen this style of helmet before with that unusual dorsal fin running down its centerline. The French and Belgians had worn them and called them *"Adrian"* helmets in the Great War.

Then, the soldier turned his head to look upon Einar, and for the first time Einar could see centered on the front of the helmet the image of an eagle. A white eagle. *This man is a bloody Pole*, he thought, *one of our Allies. We are finally saved!*

The Pole yelled out something in his slavic tongue that Einar could not understand. He nudged his brother awake. Gunnar was slow to stir, but finally did so. Then, Einar heard what he had thought was an echo, except he came to realize it was merely a response. Gunnar pointed to the top of the staircase and Einar turned and saw four other soldiers in the same uniform.

They had been covering their companion's descent down to the third ledge. They had come upon the *staircase of the gods* and sent this soldier down to take the machine gun away from the drowsing civilian who held it on the German, before the Nazi could move to grab it himself.

"*Je m'appelle Albin, mon ami,*" said the soldier who had disarmed him. His accent was heavily Slavic and the French words sounded almost laughable. Einar struggled to remember his French schooling, but that was when the awakening Gunnar jumped in.

"*Je m'appelle Gunnar, et mon frère, Einar. Nous sommes a Angleterre.*"

"What did you tell him, brother?" asked Einar.

"Just our names and that we are British, I think," responded Gunnar. "His name is Albin."

"Bloody well fits," said Einar, "since he looks like a ghostly albino."

Gunnar looked at the man, who had just removed his helmet. He had broken into a great discourse in the language they took to be Polish with his companions. As they spoke, the remaining Poles began to settle in atop the first ledge of the "staircase of the gods."

The Polish soldier Albin's short cropped hair was indeed a snowy white, perhaps with only a dusting of blonde throughout it. His eyes were close-set slits, but they opened wide enough to evidence the purest, bluest pupils either twin had ever seen. Then, the soldier spoke again in French, "*Parlez-vous Anglais*?"

"Yes, of course we do," answered Gunnar. "Where is your unit located, Albin?"

"*Nie rozumiem,*" Albin answered.

"I don't understand," answered Einar.

"Neither do he," yelled out a second soldier. "He tell you so in Polish. Albin not speak English, but I do. He has not many French *vords*, either. But he speak German very, very well."

The second soldier was working his way down the ledges. The remaining three men took up defensive positions on the first ledge, as if expecting an imminent firefight.

"Who is the Nazi lieutenant colonel?" the second Polish soldier asked.

"His name is Becker. He is from their Austrian mountaineering unit," answered Einar.

"Yes, *Gebirgsjäger,"* said the second soldier, "*vee* can tell from uniform. *Vhy* you hold him prisoner? *Vhy* he not dead? How do we know you both English? Not German spies?"

"We are not English," interrupted Gunnar, "We are Scottish, that is British."

"You tell Albin English earlier," said the soldier, "You say you both from '*Angleterre*' in French, that is England. How you prove Scottish?"

The second soldier kept his pistol trained on the twins, while the first, Albin, pointed the machine gun at Becker."

"My brother will take from our parkas our British passports," Gunnar said, "This is to be allowed?"

"*Tak*, ah, I mean 'yes', but slowly, very slowly, *pliss*" said the soldier.

Einar removed his hands slowly, then handed over the pair of British passports.

"*Vhy* you carry his passport?" the soldier asked. "Of course you both look same, but you say you Gunnar and he Einar, but why he not carry own?"

"My brother is badly wounded, shot in the arm," explained Einar, "so I hold both. He needs care. He is very weak. Where is your medic?"

"You not hurt?" asked the soldier. "You have much blood on jacket."

"As I said, my brother is hurt," responded Einar tersely, "it is his blood. We switched parkas. Where is your bloody medic?"

"Jurek is medic," said the Pole, "he *vill* bandage your brother." He handed the passports back to the twins. "I am *'Edziu'*. *Vee* are Allies, you British. and *vee* Polish troops."

"Ed-zhoo?" repeated Gunnar.

"Yes, '*Eh-jhoo*,' E-d-z-i-u, '*Eh-jhoo*'. Like your Edward. Yes?"

"Yes, all right, I will call you Edjew," Gunnar spoke. "Is that alright?"

"Yes," Edziu said, "Call me *'Edjew'* if it is easier for your tongue."

"Thank you." Gunnar replied. "Now, where is your medic, please?"

"Edjew" then beckoned one of the three Poles on the first ledge down to him. "Jurek, Jurek," he called followed by a request in Polish.

"How did you find us?" asked Einar.

"Big boom in night. Explosion. *Vee* come when *vee* hear," said Edjew.

So the sound of the exploding Enigma had drawn them there. But how far behind were the rest of their Allied forces?

"Where are the rest of your countrymen? And the French? The Norwegians?" asked Einar.

"French and *Norvegians* there…," Edjew said as he pointed across the fjord at the area known as Sildvik. "Many more *Norvegians* there…" This time the Polish soldier pointed up toward Bjørnfjell Mountain, and the fighting ongoing at *Kuberget*.

"What about your Polish troops?" Gunnar prodded.

"Ah, *Polskiego! Tak*!" replied Edjew with a smile of pride. "Three battalion chase Germans there," again he pointed across the fjord. "One battalion behind us, *deese* side."

"Good," said Gunnar, "let's go rejoin your battalion."

"*Nie, nie*," the Pole said, shaking his head. "It is not possible."

"Why not?" asked Einar, "We have an urgent message to get to London."

"Much Germans between us and them," Edjew tried to explain. "*Vee is* scout patrol. Look for path for other *vay* around Germans. Cut off now from rest of Poles."

"Well, if that explosion drew your attention," Einar deduced, "it was just as likely to draw that of the Germans. How many of them?"

"Much Germans," Edjew repeated, "fight like devils. *Vee* sent to find *vay* around them. So our troops can attack from behind. But *vee* now, how you say, cut-off."

"Then, I must assume we will be having company soon enough," Einar stated.

"You can certainly be sure of that," Becker interrupted glibly in Norwegian.

Then Einar turned back to Edjew, and said, "The colonel speaks Norwegian and English in addition to German."

"You left out my French," Becker said. "I assure it is much better than the Pole's, but, I know none of your pagan Polish at all. Just as well, that barbarian language would only tie my tongue in knots."

At this point, the Pole known as Edjew spoke in Polish to his comrade Albin. Then Albin seemed to translate the message into German for the benefit of Colonel Becker, whose face went instantly pale.

"What exactly did you have Albin tell the colonel?" Einar asked.

"Do not call him colonel, for he is only a lieutenant colonel, and deserves no more respect than that," said Edjew. "I say to him, 'Lieutenant Colonel Becker, would you prefer to be shot before we throw you over that ledge or live long enough until you hit those icy waters below?' You see his reaction?"

"Yes," said Einar, "but at least for now we need to keep him alive. Besides, he is a prisoner of war, and deserves to be treated as such."

"My family back in Poland deserved much things," replied Edjew, "but certainly not *vhat* his Nazi brothers did to them. My father *vas* shot in the head in the town square for only the crime of being an alderman. So, let us not discuss *vhat* he deserves. He only deserves to be shot *vith* his own *veapon*."

"Spoken like one of the ignorant peasants that your people are," spat out Becker.

"*Vee* go now," said Edjew to Einar, ignoring Becker's comment. "First, *vee* kill German colonel. How you say, *Ass of Donkey?"*

"Jack ass" corrected Einar. "I will not be a party to killing Becker. Take him with us. Where will we go?"

"*Anyvhere* but here," Edjew relied. "*Avay, avay,* or Germans come. Trap us like horses in pen."

"As I said, my brother and I are both injured," Gunnar pleaded. "And we need food. Please, do you have any rations?"

"*Tak, tak,*" replied Edjew, who then spoke to the other soldiers in Polish. They shared some of their food supply with the starving twins, who ripped into them like vultures on carrion. The lieutenant colonel also begged for food, but Becker's pleas were completely ignored by the Poles.

The Polish soldier Edjew then spoke to his comrades. The one known as Jurek then advanced upon Gunnar. "Show him *vound*," said Edjew. "He is trained as medic."

The Polish medic Jurek then removed the field dressings that Einar had improvised. He then sniffed the wound, drew back his head, with a soured clench upon his face. He cleaned it out using an alcohol based solution. This drew a scream from Gunnar, which the twin tried, but failed to suppress. The medic

Jurek then applied a sulfadrug creme on clean dressings and re-bandaged the arm. He then arose and spoke in Polish to Edjew.

"He says *vound* is infected bad," Edjew whispered to Einar in a hushed voice. "Sepsis very possible."

"I was afraid of that," Einar admitted, "but I was hopeful when the fever broke."

"Fever will return," Edjew said, "*vhat* follow very bad."

"Yes, I know. He is already very, very weak."

Jurek the medic then returned to the top ledge to resume his soldiering in a defensive position among his comrades.

"*Vee* carry him to top, then he must *valk*," Edjew explained.

"You are not listening to me, Edjew. Gunnar is too weak to walk," Einar said in an exasperated voice. Then, he realized he had lost track of the days. "What is today's date, Edjew?"

"Today is fourth," he replied.

The fourth day of June, thought Einar. *If we could hold out here for just a few more days.*

On the morning of June the fourth, Brigand steered the *Nordlys* toward the beaches at Dunkirk. The operation over the past few days had been an outstanding success. By Brigand's estimate, his ship alone had rescued nearly four thousand soldiers from those shores. Today would be the last day, it had been determined earlier, for *Operation Dynamo*. Brigand was determined to see it out.

They had made eight ferries of transporting soldiers that day out to the deepwater transport ships. The *Luftwaffe* air assault was even more aggressive than in the days before. The number of small craft had dwindled. Many had been sunk by the Messerschmitt fighters, well over half. This lower density of ships had its advantages - there was more navigable space, and although their total numbers were dwindling, there were still many more soldiers to be rescued by the *Nordlys*. The downside was that there were fewer targets afloat for the *Luftwaffe* fighters. Every hour they remained upon the water, their threat of attack from overhead increased.

The other thing that Brigand had noticed on this last day was that there was a much higher percentage of French soldiers being pulled from the water. The French had provided an incredible defensive stand against the Germans, flanking and providing cover for their English comrades.

Their actions had allowed these soldiers their only chance of making their way in lines out to the small craft. The French were encircled by the Germans as much as the British had been. This day, they were finally breaking formations and making for the boats themselves.

Brigand steered the *Nordlys* in for the day's ninth run. It was late in the afternoon by then and he and the three Royal Marines knew that there might only be another one or two runs into the shallows left to them.

They came in under the power of the two outboards. Brigand held his hand up, which had been their signal. Then he dropped it sharply. The marines cut the outboards and Brigand flared the ship into the shallows, where they were swarmed by both British and French infantry. The Royal Marines hauled in as many soldiers as were near the ship, but the *Nordlys* was only three quarters full. Brigand wanted to go on desperately to fill his ship, as they had done in each run of the days past, but decided it more prudent to get these men to safety.

The outboards were started and Brigand steered the vessel out to the transport ships. A pride swelled within him, as he began to realize that fewer and fewer soldiers were left for them to extract from this shore where these men certainly faced capture, if not death itself.

"Incoming," yelled out the marine Christopher. Everyone hit the decks. The sound of the low-level Messerschmitt fighter's engine grew and grew in their ears as it was on a strafing course to bisect the path of the *Nordlys*. The chain rattle of the machine guns rang out. Twin eruptions of water exploded at a right angle to the ship, before they came alive on deck with flying shards of debris and the near instantaneous cries of the wounded. They had been hit. The plane banked to line up for another pass.

The marine Christopher rushed to tell Brigand he must take evasive actions. He must not make straight for the transport ships or they would surely be strafed again. As he stepped over the injured soldiers, he also noticed water coming up through the deck boards. He turned to look out over his shoulder to the distant transport ships. They were perhaps still another mile or so off.

He rushed to the helm only to find Brigand slumped over the binnacle. Christopher spun him around and found streams of blood radiating out of his chest and his good and only leg. "My God, Captain MacAlvor, you're hit."

"Make for the transport, Christopher," Brigand, strapped in his modified Captain's chair, said weakly. "Head straight for them. The *Nordlys* is mortally wounded. Get these men to the safety of those vessels before the sea pulls us all under."

Christopher watched as the German fighter banked over them to line up for a second pass. "Captain, we must take evasive actions. We can no longer make straight for the transport ships. We will be strafed again."

"I am telling you, mate, make for those ships," Brigand said weakly. "The *Nordlys* is going down. If we get strafed again, then some more men will get wounded, possibly drown. If we take evasive action and steer away, then all these men are likely to drown. Now take the wheel and make straight for those transports."

"Aye, Captain," said Christopher. He steered to the nearest transport as he watched the Messerschmitt draw down on them.

"Incoming," he yelled, although with the exception of the marines, everyone else was still already flat on the deck. He realized that the *Nordlys* had taken on significant water, as it became increasingly more sluggish in cutting through the sea. Christopher stayed upright at the wheel as the plane drew down on them. He stepped in front of his Captain and braced for the strafing fire from its machine guns.

It was then that the chain rattle of the machine guns burst out again. *Too soon,* thought Christopher, as the plane had not yet reached the *Nordlys*. He looked up into the sky only to see the Messerschmitt pulling up and trailing instant plumes of oily black smoke. Behind it he saw the Spitfire, close upon the German fighter as they both passed overhead. No strafing fire had come upon the *Nordlys*. Christopher watched as the pair of aircraft clocked and wheeled in near unison, until finally the wounded, smoking Messerschmitt crashed into the sea.

The men on board, those not wounded from the strafing, cheered in celebration as the *Luftwaffe* fighter broke up on impact with the water, only a mile or two off. Christopher focused on closing the gap between his sinking vessel and the transport craft. They were almost alongside. The Spitfire had no doubt been assigned to defend the craft, and had they not made straight for the transport, they likely would never had fallen under the umbrella of its protection.

The *Nordlys* was by then nearly completely swamped. It pulled alongside the transport ship. The outboards were cut by his fellow marines, and all aboard began frantically climbing up the scrambling nets to safety. Those who were wounded were provided lifejackets and awaited the winches and harnesses to bring them aboard.

Christopher turned to Brigand. He was slumped back in his chair, his eyes closed. The marine feared him dead. Nonetheless, he began unstrapping him from the chair.

It was only then, that he heard the faint, gurgled voice rise in defiance.

"No, son," Brigand said through a mouthful of spit, bile and blood. "Do not undo me. As the *Nordlys* goes down, so does her Captain."

"There are medics aboard this ship, Captain," the marine Christopher said. He had paused undoing the straps, but then returned to unfastening them.

Brigand slowly raised his blood soaked hand over that of the marine. "Stop, son," he sighed, "my body is beyond saving. But thanks to you and your mates, my soul has already been saved. Now leave me here, strapped to the *Nordlys*, as my life has always been."

"What should I tell your wife, sir," Christopher asked.

Brigand's eyes seemed to lose any muscular movement at all. They stared distantly into the sky. Christopher again thought his life had departed him, until he began to hear the rattle of his breath in his chest. He had heard of this death rattle many times before, but this was his first time to experience it first hand.

"My wife?" Brigand spoke though the rattle of breath escaping him. "Tell her…"

"Captain…"

"…tell her…" blood streamed from his mouth.

"Stay with me, Captain," said Christopher.

"…I died a noble death…", Brigand began to choke and cough, "That…I did not …"

"Captain…"

"follow my father…"

"Rest, Captain, rest," whispered the marine, Christoper.

"…thanks to her…that I love her … "

Brigand struggled to get out those last words. He fought for his last gasp of strength to say only a few more.

"…and am so sorry…for the twins."

The last word left his mouth on the last breath that escaped him. He was gone. Christopher released the strap he had been undoing.

"Rest in peace, my Captain," he said, as he choked on the emotions he tried his best to contain.

The water was up to his knees. The ship would soon sink. Christopher left Brigand, still strapped in his chair, and moved to assist the last of the wounded already floating in the water. As the last of those men were lifted aboard the transport, the marine named Christopher began to climb the scrambling net. He was halfway to the deck when he looked back upon the *Nordlys*, to see Brigand slumped in his chair, his lifeless eyes still open, pointed skyward. The marine could not help but feel that they still gazed upon himself, as if he were their last connection with his world.

The *Nordlys* faltered. The sea then swept over her, climbed to her captain's shoulders and soon washed over his head. As she sank, Christopher peered into those two lifeless but open eyes until the greenish-gray depths had swallowed forever their empty gaze.

The marine was determined to remember each of his Captain's last words for his wife to one day hear. He would deliver them himself, he vowed.

The rest of that day on the mountain ledges overhanging the *Rombaksfjord* was spent on solving a dilemma. The Poles wanted to move, but refused to abandon their two British companions. The twins said they had a highly prioritized message they needed to pass on to London, but would not transmit it over the open airwaves, as the Poles had suggested. Finally, there was Lieutenant Colonel Becker, who the Poles rightly guessed had been the source of the secret information. The British twins refused to allow any harm to come upon him.

This group of eight remained indecisive as to what to do. Gunnar was too weak to move, and his brother refused to abandon him. The Poles had donated the few blankets they carried to cover the lad. His fever, which had never quite left him, returned to a rage within him.

Einar had suggested that the five Poles move on, but their leader, Edjew, refused to consider this. They spent the rest of the day and the overnight on that series of ledges. The Poles scavenged wood and a fire was made, for without it, all feared freezing to death.

The next morning, Einar and Edjew again considered their fates. As the two men spoke in English, the Polish mountaineer Albin had lowered himself onto the roughly hewn rock floor of the last ledge. He lay flat, then inched his body out until only his head hung over the side. He peered down into the vertical abyss with a measured eye. He then spoke excitedly in Polish, as he interrupted the discussion of the other two men above.

"What is he saying?" asked Einar.

"He think *vee* can drop from here. How you say?" Edjew used his free hand to make a downward fluttering motion.

"Descend? Rappel?"

"*Tak*, rappel…" confirmed the Pole.

"That must be the better part of a thousand feet," exclaimed Einar. "You carry that much gear?"

"Five times," said Edjew. "*Vee* do five steps. Albin sees steps below. *Vee* have just much line. Five lengths. Single lines. Too far to use two lines."

"Single line?" Repeated Einar. "That's incredibly dangerous." He realized the Pole meant double lines when he had said, "two lines."

"Yes, very dangerous," agreed Edjew, "but two line no good, not long enough."

Einar then spread himself out prostrate on the ledge floor, and soon peered over and down alongside Albin.

"Where?" cried out Einar.

"Gdzie?" interpreted Edjew.

Albin worked his shoulder over the ledge and pointed. *"Jeden…"*

"One," cried out Edjew. It was a ledge hardly wide enough to allow a man to stand upon.

"I see it," cried out Einar, "good."

Albin pointed far beyond the first position. *"Dwa..."*

"Two," said Edjew.

"Yes," said Einar, again a small but negotiable landing further below. "Go on."

Albin pointed a third time, *"Trzy..."*

"Three," followed Edjew.

This appeared to be the largest so far, Einar thought. "Yes, I see."

"Cztery..." said Albin.

"Four," interpreted Edjew.

"OK," said Einar. Another small ledge, *one a goat would have trouble with*, he thought.

"Pięć," cried Albin. The Pole pointed toward the rocky outcropping just above the water of the fjord. The same outcropping upon which rested two sprawled bodies of the German dead. Then Albin rattled off something in Polish.

"Five. He *vants* to know if you climb down *deese*?" Edjew said.

Einar studied the five landings. The first two were rather tight but appeared readily negotiable, and the third was easily large enough to accommodate two climbers together. The fourth was small, a real goat's ledge. The distance from it to the large outcropping above the fjord's surface was quite considerable, greater than the rest. *Would the ropes be long enough for each descent?*

The mangled bodies of two German lay dead upon that last outcropping. Their lifeless corpses reminded him of what the consequences of attempting this climb might be.

"Yes, I am quite sure that I can do that," said Einar, although he was still concerned about the condition of his leg, "but my brother could never make this. Even if we were to fashion a rope harness or a basket of some sort, he could not make his way out onto those landings without falling to his death."

"You must do," commanded Edjew.

"Never," responded Einar, "if my brother stays here, then I stay by his side. I will not leave him here to die. I cannot and I shall not."

The Pole looked intently at Einar, almost crossing his eyes. "Then your secret is..." assessed Edjew, "... it is not so urgent. It can die here along these rocks along with your brother and yourself."

From his makeshift bedside, Gunnar had been following the conversation, but saved his breath and said nothing. He was deep in thought. Then he called Einar to his side and made a simple suggestion.

"Brother, there is another way. I know you will never leave me on this mountain's ledge alone. These Poles are mountain troops, are they not? Let Edjew take Becker's bloody secret to the Brits. He can make himself understood, within limits. You can stay with me here. The Brits at Harstad can radio it securely out to London. All is good. Maybe Edjew can tell them where we are trapped, and they can send the cavalry."

Einar looked at Edjew. He thought it could quite possibly work. All except for the cavalry, unless they were saddled on mountain goats.

Einar then put the suggestion to the Pole Edjew.

Edjew then said, "I am *villing* to try. Albin and I *vill* go together down, Albin *vill* climb back up. I *vill rad-ee-oh* for boat."

Edjew yelled out in Polish and Jurek brought the radio down from the first ledge. He transmitted instructions to a distant voice in a distant language over the airways. "Now, we *vait* for English to send boat."

"Give me some paper and a pen," said Einar.

"*Vee* have none," Edjew said.

"Check the Colonel," Einar said, and on the German was found a pen and a note pad emblazoned on its leather cover the national Emblem of an eagle with a swastika in its talons. Einar took it and the pen, flipped up the cover of the pad and wrote on the first sheet: "FOR EYES OF WINCER WELLS MI6 ONLY", then added "RADIO TRANSMISSION MUST BE ENCODED".

"You will take this to the Brits," Einar said. "They will be able to get it to London securely."

In the sheets below, Einar added the story as follows, "WARNING, INFORMATION UNCOVERED FROM SOURCE CAPTURED GERMAN WEHRMACHT LT. COL STOP COVERT OPERATIVE POSING AS CHURCHILL ESCORT PILOT STOP PLANS TO SHOOT DOWN PM ON

NEXT SORTIE STOP INFO NOT ABLE TO VERIFY BUT EXTREMELY URGENT FULL STOP."

They waited half of the day, before the radio squawked with Polish chatter.

As they did, Albin hammered pitons into crevices and secured the first length of rope in place. That afternoon the radio squawked with Polish chatter. Edjew then explained to them that the British were sending a high speed boat to recover him from the fjord below.

Einar made the Pole read the message five times and repeat it to him in English. He made sure the Pole could say the name "Wincer Wells" and "Eyes Only". It came out as "*Vincer Vells* and *Eis Oonly"* but it was close enough. It was Einar's insurance policy should the message pad somehow get separated from the Polish soldier Edjew.

"Remember, Edjew, you are only to give these notes to British Intelligence officers at Harstad. They will send to Wincer Wells when you get to England. Make him show you his bloody credentials, with his photo. You give to no one else, do you understand me?"

Then Einar thought to add, "If they don't believe you, tell them you have found *Thor's hammer*." He had given up on having Edjew pronounce the Norwegian name *Mjölnir.* "Tell them to tell Wincer Wells that you carry Thor's hammer with you. Make sure Wincer Wells knows this."

The first length of rope was in place, and the remaining four lengths were laid out in butterfly bundles along the ledge. From the last length, enough rope was extracted to fashion into rope harnesses, known as "*Swiss Seats*", around the groins of Albin and Edjew.

Albin was the first to go over the side. He wore a butterflied roll of the hemp rope over his shoulder. He made the first ledge in just under a half hour. The line was pulled up, and a second rappelling line was tied to the first and lowered. As this happened, Albin drove pitons into a small fissure in the rock ledge, and secured the second line which had been lowered. Then the third rope was passed down to him. Albin tied this to the end of the second line and then lowered both. He then awaited as Edjew was about to be lowered.

Just before Edjew was about to climb over the side to lower himself, Einar cried out "STOP! Good God, I almost forgot."

The twin reached into his pocket to produce the set of rotors taken from the Enigma. Becker's eyes became as large as saucers when he saw the five crucial elements of the device in the twin's grasp. He could not believe that it was he who had allowed these most prized of Nazi secrets to fall into the enemy's hands.

Einar slipped the Enigma rotors into the pocket of Edjew. "This is very, very important. These are '*Thor's Hammer*,' and you are only to be hand these over to Wincer Wells. Make them take you to England. Give these to Wincer Wells only. Give them to no one else. Only Wincer Wells. Make them take you to him in London. Make him show you his card with his picture. Make him tell you my father's name. It is Brigand. You understand?"

"Yes. London," said Edjew. "I go to London. *Vincer Vells*. Give *dese*. Make him take picture of your father who is a brigand." The Pole then laughed aloud. *"Vhat you think, I am stupid you repeat so much?"*

Einar's nerves were raw with the thought of releasing the rotors. He was in no mood for the Pole's humor. But this was the only way to get these precious, blood-shed secrets to Wells.

And once the rotors were secured in his pocket, Edjew went over the side and down to the first cliffside ledge. Like Albin before him, he wore the last full length of hemp rope over his shoulder. Edjew slowly rappelled downward.

Einar watched until he saw Edjew make the first ledge that his countryman Albin had just vacated. Albin had lowered himself down to the second cliffside landing. After he did so, he secured more pitons along that rocky ledge. In this way all five rope lengths were soon hanging from the side of the cliff. They fell alongside the waterfall from the *Lomvatnet*, and in this way demonstrated man's inability to replicate nature's beauty.

Einar, high above the two Poles, watched with awe. To rappel down these heights using only a single line, was an incredible feat. They had fashioned rope harnesses, so the rope was attached to the harnesses by a carabiner, and thus the rope was not sliding through their legs and shoulders, cutting into their skin with the friction of their weight, as it would using the emergency *Dülfersitz* technique. Even so, lowering oneself down from these heights was incredibly exhausting. And as only a single line was used, incredibly dangerous. If the line slipped from their grasp, if their grip faltered they would fall to their death on the rocky outcropping below.

Using a double line (a line attached at the mid-point to the piton), afforded a greater level of control in braking, and using a series of knots could be set so that the climber would merely dangle if he lost control of the ropes. But this meant that only half the vertical length could be covered. Given the height of this cliff, the use of the safer double line technique was not possible.

It was as Albin unfurled the last length of rope that their first bit of trouble arose. The final length of rope was too short to reach the fjord. It dangled some thirty feet above not only the water, but the rocky outcropping just before reaching the fjord's surface. Albin then climbed all the way up to the large second landing where he rejoined Edjew upon it.

Albin spoke in Polish to Edjew. "It appears this last length of rope is too short. You will have to go as far as you can on this line, then use your legs to push off from the cliff wall and let go. You must push as hard as you can. You must clear that last landing and allow yourself to fall into the fjord. If you fail to clear it and impact upon those rocks, you will either die instantly or live only to die slowly lying atop it. You must clear that landing."

"I will be fine, Albin," Edjew said.

"Remember," Albin said, "that I have removed the knot from the end of this last rope, so that it will not catch when you push off away to clear the rocks."

"Good," said Edjew, "I am aware and will not rappel off the end of it, I promise." Edjew then descended down to the last rope line.

Most tragedies on the mountains came when mountaineers did not tie warning knots a good foot or further before the end of the line. This alerted the rappelling soldier that he neared the end of the line. As incredible as it may sound, it was very easy to become pre-occupied while descending and rappel one's self right off the end of the line, where only unforgiving gravity awaited them.

Soon the high-speed deep-hulled wooden skiff appeared in the waters below. Edjew then lowered himself over the side to begin his final descent. He was able to get within thirty feet of the fjord's surface, and nearly twenty-five feet above the rocky outcropping just below. Much too far to drop himself onto it, as

Albin had said. He was unsure that even with all his strength that he could clear it.

Edjew then used every ounce of his energy to push himself with his legs away from the cliff wall. His muscles uncoiled like a compressed spring. He instantly arced outward and swung upward along the pendulum of the rope. Just before reaching the end of the arc, he forced himself to release his hands in what for him was the opposite movement of everything he had ever been trained. After his leg thrust, he released the line from his hand and watched as its free end whip as it slipped freely through his harnesses carabiner. He saw the line waggle as he sailed away from its end just before his body's momentum stalled and gravity's pull dominated.

He cleared the rocky outcropping by only two or three feet. He fell another ten feet to the surface of the fjord's waters.

He had straightened as much as possible to use his feet to break the water's surface, but the arc of his fall had rotated him nearly horizontal, and his body struck the fjord's surface with a resonant and full impact *thwack!*

The Polish highlander Edjew was instantly immersed in the million stinging needles of the fjord's Arctic water. He continued to sink into its depths, before he took control of his senses and began kicking and wailing his arms to get to the surface.

He could not tell if he was making his ascent, as all he could sense was the icy cold waters in which a million bubbles swirled, clouding his orientation. He could feel a pressure growing in his ears, which only drove his limbs even more furiously. Finally, as he thrashed desperately in the water's deadly grasp, he realized he had indeed broken the surface.

Edjew sucked in a gasp full of frigid air which instantly burned every inch of the lining of his lungs. He felt himself sinking again and kicked his legs to fight it. He was able to keep his head above water, just in time to see the wooden gunnels of the recovery boat come alongside him. He felt the rope thrown to him and grasped it with every bit of strength that he had. He was able to fight off the terror of realizing that he was drowning. That was behind him. Edjew was pulled alongside the boat, where several strong hands grabbed at him and hauled him over the side into the relative safety of the small vessel.

"Come on, laddie," an English accented voice joked, "get your Polack arse in here. Had a good swim, have you? Let's not loiter too longer, shall we. After all, we don't need any Jerries taking pot shots at us from the hills, now do we?"

The outboard was fired up and the deep hulled boat screamed down the length of the *Rombaksfjord* toward the *Ofotfjord* on its way back to Allied command headquarters at Harstad.

Along the way, Edjew checked his pockets for the rotors, which were still with him. But when he retrieved the sheets of notepaper, all the lettering had run from the salt water, making its message totally illegible.

"Have you noticed your army across the fjord," Colonel Becker had called out to the twins, "they are slowly evacuating. First they run from Dunkirk, and now they run from here also. And these are the Churchill's soldiers who will stop the *Wehrmacht and Luftwaffe*?"

Becker had been bound by the Polish soldiers. The Poles had also kept the fire going and Gunnar had been laid close alongside it. Einar was, of course, as always, by his brother's side. A full day had passed since he had witnessed Edjew recovered by the rescue boat.

As much as Einar wished Becker's taunts to be only that and nothing more, he had himself noted that a steady stream of Allied troops were returning down the Ofoten Railway to Narvik, away from the German stronghold of Bjørnfjell.

For the past several days, Einar had been noticing it. The ranks of the Allied troops across the fjord were slowly thinning in an orderly and disciplined manner. In the distance they could see the troops being transported out of Narvik harbor on transport vessels making their own way to Harstad.

Einar had hoped that holding out only a few days more would bring him and his brother freedom, but that hope was dashed if this was the beginning of a general withdrawal of all Allied troops.

The problem was now one of communication. The three Polish soldiers other than Albin spoke only Polish. It was clear that Becker spoke German, Norwegian and English proficiently, and also claimed to have some decent French in his repertoire.

But the only individual who could communicate with the Polish radio operator and communicate it to the twins was Albin. This even required his using his German to relay the information through their captive colonel.

Albin had, after assisting Edjew on the cliffs' landings, once more climbed the lines upward to rejoin his countrymen on the ledges above. His body was exhausted, so he lay down to sleep by the fire next to the Polish guard covering Becker. He had been sleeping for hours, and although Einar didn't wish to cut short Albin's recovery, the time had come to make use of the Pole's linguistic skills. Einar awakened the sleeping mountaineer by nudging him.

"*Bonjour, mon ami,*" Einar said in what little French he knew.

"*Qu'est-ce que c'est? Que veux-tu?*" replied Albin.

"He asked, 'What is it?, What do you want?' " interjected Becker.

"Ask him if Edjew is now safely in Harstad."

"For a ration," Becker said.

Einar had one last ration. The Poles were running out. He thought hard on Becker's offer. "All right, but only if you tell him also I want to know if his team has received an order to withdraw."

Becker said to Einar, "You swear to give me that food?"

"Yes," Einar replied, "after I get my information."

Becker relayed the first question in French, but Albin seemed not to understand. Then, recalling that the Pole had excellent German language skills, the lieutenant colonel repeated the question in that tongue.

Albin looked skeptically at the German officer. Becker said in German that it was Einar who was asking, after which the Pole looked at the twin. Einar shook his head in the affirmative, then cupped his hand around his ear as if to say, *tell me*.

Albin then spoke to Becker, which the German then interpreted for the twin. "He said that all Allied units are to begin a general withdrawal. Forces across the fjord are to report to Narvik for embarkation, our force is ordered to retreat to Øyjord. He said he was going to discuss this with you after he rested. Through me, I presume, but he did not say."

Einar was stunned. The Germans, except for a few stray units, were hemmed in at Bjørnfjell. Their backs were up against the Swedish border. Why would the Allies evacuate now?

As if reading his mind, Lieutenant Colonel Becker spoke. "Things must be going very poorly for your armies in France. The British must fear they will need all their forces to protect their home islands. But this time, unlike Napoleon, or the Spanish Armada before them, it will take more than that little Channel of water to save them. For it is nothing for the *Luftwaffe* to fly over it and destroy your cities."

The tone of his voice was insolent and cocksure, Einar thought. He was tempted to shoot the bastard, but had he done so, he would have cut off his only communication path with his Polish comrades. Beside this, Einar was still intent on delivering his prisoner to London. MI6 must interrogate him.

Albin then spoke in Polish with his countryman who manned the radio. It was a lengthy enough discussion, then the Pole began speaking in German to Becker.

A greasy smile slithered across Becker's stubbled face. "He says that you all have a very serious problem," Becker relayed, "in that there are *Gebirgsjäger* units between our current location and the evacuation point of Øyjord. You all are entirely cut off from rescue."

The response of the Poles seemed to be to check their weapons and ammunition, as if preparing for one last fight.

Becker said the last few words with a smirk that revealed just how ironic he found the situation to be. "Looks like my fellow Austrian mountaineers will not allow you to run away like the frightened rabbits you are."

"Ask him about the soldier Edjew," Einar demanded. "Did he make it to the British high command at Harstad?"

The chain of dialogue followed, and Becker once more took delight in rendering the response. "Your Polish soldier made it, but has come under suspicion by the British officers. They think he might be some sort of a German agent plant."

A look of despair befell Einar's features. "How could this all be happening?"

"Have them call to Harstad, to patch me through ," Einar said, "if they can't, have them send a boat, just as they did for Edjew. I need to confirm to them who he is."

"What about your dying brother?" Becker said.

"He is not dying," Einar snapped in response. "See, he rests, he recovers from his wounds."

"His wounds are infected," said Becker. "His fever has returned. I know that much just from watching the one they call

Jurek attend to him. I have seen many men die, but nothing is more pitiful to watch than for a man to die a slow, drawn-out and painful death. Even if he is only a lowly spy."

Einar looked down at his sleeping brother. A fury boiled within his blood. He pulled the Walther P-38 from his waistband and drew it on the colonel. His weapon hand shook in rage. "You are the cause of his wounds, you bastard."

"Feed me, Einar," Becker scowled at the threat. "I need to be healthy when my mountaineers come to my rescue and your demise. It is now only a matter of time."

Some time passed, and with it came radio chatter in Polish. The Pole, Albin, began speaking once more with Becker.

"He says that the boat will be sent tomorrow. It will be large enough to be able to carry us all. But how will your brother ever be able to climb down from these heights?"

"Tell him not to worry about that," Einar replied. "I know what my brother needs."

A short dialogue in German followed between Albin and Becker. The colonel's mood then soured. He at first refused to translate, until Einar said the following, "Come, now, Colonel Becker. You cannot be so glib when the news favors you only to refuse me my own good news, or I have no use for you, do I?"

Becker knew no harm would come to him, after all, they still wanted to turn him over to British Intelligence. Yet it was Einar's questioning his fairness that somehow prompted him to cooperate.

"The soldier Edjew has been vetted by the British and will be on the first convoy leaving tomorrow on the aircraft carrier *HMS Glorious*. He still carries the Enigma rotors you stole from the device."

"All the better," said Einar, "because that means all this misery has not been without purpose."

Einar then kept his word and fed the last ration to Becker. After which Einar watched his brother rest and although he would not admit it to Becker, he knew Gunnar was indeed slowly dying.

“My God, Diane, this story is so damn riveting,” said Jake Conley. It was nearing three in the morning. “As much as I need to hear the rest of my brothers’ tale, my weary, old, swayback hide needs some shuteye. You said you’d stay for a bit, can we pick this up again in the morning?”

Diane had been waiting for the old man to call the end to the night. She was herself exhausted.

“Certainly, Jake. I could use some sleep myself.”

Diane could feel his son, Wade, hovering in the room as his father was wheeled to his quarters. Once Jake had cleared the room, Wade walked up to her and demanded she tell him what became of Einar and Gunnar.

“All in good time,” Diane replied. “I would not be a very good investigator if I allowed anyone other than my client to first hear what I had unearthed, now would I?”

“Look, Diane,” said Wade, “you tell me here and now what became of Jake’s half-brothers and I will sweeten your fees by another ten percent, out of my own pocket.”

Diane looked at the man, who was clearly disturbed with the thought that there may be lines of his half uncle’s ancestors who might drain away some small fortune from the vast reserves of his father’s estate. The thought of his not getting everything ate at him in such a way that he was willing to waste a large sum of money just to know the answer in this moment.

“Wade, keep your money,” Diane said, “after all, you may need it once Jake starts bidding on the relics that your uncles left behind…”

Diane had intentionally used the word uncles, leaving out the “half-“ prefix that Wade had so jealously clung to all night.

53 Glorious Days of Death and Destruction

June 6 to June 8, 1940

"There is no question of subordinating the Royal Air Force to the Army or the Navy..."

Winston Spencer Churchill

The next day brought with it a continuation of both Diane's session with Jake and Wade Conley as well as Sophie's briefing with the shop owners, Henia and Mierek. While the Texas briefings were done in a luxury amidst the Conley compound that few could ever become accustomed to, the London briefing was done on a "catch as catch can" basis around the shop owners' hectic schedule. They could neither afford to pay the young investigator they called *"Zosia"*, nor could they afford a day's lost revenue from their restaurant.

"Thank you for coming in so early today, *Zosia*," Henia said to Sophie. "Mierek and I are very grateful. What you told us last night was very interesting. While we knew that my mother's Uncle Bogdan fought in the war for the Government-in-Exile, we did not realize his younger brother Albin did as well. And we certainly were not aware of Great Uncle Bogdan's connections to the three Polish mathematicians who broke the Enigma code. It is very exciting. Today, we hope you can shed more light on how mother's uncle Bogdan came to be accused in the death of General Sikorski, and how anyone could possibly consider him a spy for the Third Reich. We also hope you can prove through your significant research that he was nothing of the sort. It means so very much to us to carry forward this treasure in our hearts."

Sophie glanced at the file that was sticking out slightly of her valise. It was the very file that was delivered to her hotel room the night before by a person she had not expected to see in London. Emory Hauptmann had tracked her down and said he had some very important material from Diane for her that she needed to be aware of.

At first Sophie refused to take the file from Emory and expressed to him the need for her to complete this investigation on her own. Emory knew how to handle her. First he said he understood, and that if he were she, he would have exactly the same response.

"However, Soph," he said next, "not only is your Bogdan Bratajewski all knotted up with the Conley Case, but as it turns out, so also is his kid brother Albin. Diane had no intention of stepping on your toes, but when this info came to her from her old MI6 contacts, she knew she must share it with you. As they say over here, this makes it a *'whole different kettle of fish, altogether'*, doesn't it?"

So, Sophie reluctantly took the file from Emory, who she then apologized to for not being able to allow him in nor spend any further time with him. She had just returned from her late session with Henia and Mierek, and wished only to shower and sleep. Shower she did, but sleep she did not, as she spent most of the rest of the early hours poring through the very recently declassified MI6 file.

"Yes," she said to Henia, "today I will be able to cover all that with you. Also, I will cover what happened to your Great Uncle Albin as well. You will see it is all very much interconnected."

A large smile of satisfaction creased the faces of both Henia and Mierek. "Then let us begin. *Proszę*," said Henia.

They gathered again in the library. Jake Conley sat in his wheelchair, looking vibrant despite having gotten fewer than half his usual hours of sleep. The late night session seemed to have invigorated him instead of having sapped his energy. He was as eager as a schoolboy to begin class again this lovely morning. Wade, on the other hand looked wrought and ill-rested.

"As it was, I was lucky to catch any shuteye at all last night," Jake said. Even as tired as I thought I was, my mind just would not turn off. I can't wait to hear the rest of this saga about the twins, my brothers!"

Diane and Flake each looked over at Wade, expecting him to correct his father. He did not, but given the glances his way, he did comment on what he had heard late the night before.

"Diane, I know you've got all these great inside sources and everything, but I don't know how much of this exploding rotor crap I can buy. Sounds like an airport novel, and not a good one at that. Also, how could a pair of British spies go undetected right under the German's noses for well over a month? Is there some serious embellishment going on here? Y'all been reading between the lines?"

They expected Jake to reprimand his son for having such doubts about their veracity. What came next from Wade's father surprised Diane and Flake even more.

"Sounds like a fair enough question," he said. "Go on, Diane, set my son straight."

"Well, Wade," Diane began, "you are right, we definitely would not have this level of insight had we not had the connections within the Service, that is, MI6, that we have. That alone is only half the story's source, though, as Tilly MacAlvor's diary is extremely well documented. I guarantee you, once you read through it in detail, you will see that it paints a very vivid picture of all that I have summarized so far."

"And the exploding rotors, Diane?" Wade persisted.

"Well, Wade," Diane responded, "you'll recall from our session last night that Wincer Wells was moved to Section D of MI6 at the start of the war. *'D stood for destruction'*; that was their motto. This group you'll see today became part of the newly formed Special Operations Executive, or SOE, in July of 1940 per Churchill's direct order. They went so far as to place plastic explosives in dead rats and place them where the enemy might find them as booby traps. So the exploding rotors fits right in with their *modus operandi*."

"You tell him Diane," Jake said, as he reaffirmed his belief in her. "I have actually seen that dead rat stuff on the history channel, or one of the World War II documentaries. Now, let's get down to new business. Where did we leave off? Oh, yeah, the Pole what was his name? Edjew Palczynski. Yeah, he was heading back to the UK with the real rotors in his pocket."

"On the first ship out, which happened to be the British aircraft carrier *HMS Glorious*," said Diane, as she began her tale from there. "There is something that is quite vital to our story that must be kept in mind. At the beginning of the war, there was a lot of rivalry between the Old Royal Navy and the upstart flyers of the British. And no where did these two come into more direct competition than aboard an aircraft carrier. This was true in spades aboard the *Glorious*."

"I thought the Royal Navy prided itself on the cooperation and efficiency of operations between its sailors and aviators," Jake professed.

"It does to this day," said Diane, "but in early 1940, there was still a tremendous amount of animosity between the leaders of these two groups. In the Glorious' case, between the carrier's captain and her air wing commander."

The mountaineer Edziu Palczynski had been rescued from the *Rombaksfjord* and delivered to the Allied Headquarters at Harstad. Initially, the Pole called "Edjew" failed to pass the vetting of the British security forces in Norway after his rescue, as they suspected his story of having come across two British spies atop the mountains overlooking the fjord. This went on until Edziu demanded that the message *"I possess Thor's hammer,"* be passed onto *"Vincer Vells"* in London.

Wells was elated to receive this message, and had the Pole further questioned in Hardstad about what he knew. "Only to *Vincer Vells*," the Pole had steadfastly replied. "Tell Wincer Wells I carry a gift for him from his twin friends." After several hours, the return message came back from Wells to allow the Pole to board the first transport leaving Norway. This was to be the aircraft carrier *Glorious*.

Wells prepared to travel to *Scapa Flow* in the Orkneys to personally greet the Pole, and receive his messages firsthand, along with any hardware he might be carrying. The HMS *Glorious* had requested permission to leave a day ahead of the main convoy departing Norway so that the Captain could make it back to Scapa Flow in time to bear witness against his former flight commander who was being court-martialed.

Like all military organizations throughout the world, there exists fierce competition between the separate branches of service. In the United Kingdom, the establishment of an independent organization known as the Royal Air Force, or RAF, was initially fought furiously by both the British Army and Royal Navy alike.

It was a young Winston Churchill who fought doggedly for establishing the Royal Air Force as an equal branch of Britain's war-fighting capability. He had been the advocate for the Royal Naval Air Service (RNAS) after becoming First Lord of the Admiralty in 1911. He had seen the effectiveness of air attacks on the sinking of naval vessels during his three years in that office. Churchill would certainly have been aware of the exploits of the American General "Billy" Mitchell's sinking of the captured German WWI Battleship *Ostfriesland* by air power alone during tests conducted in the Chesapeake Bay in 1921.

Churchill would go on to champion the RAF's independence. Their prideful *esprit de corps* would later serve the Prime Minister well during World War II. With it, he would armor the skies over England, for just as armor was invented to blunt the penetrating tips of projectiles, so the RAF would blunt the efforts of the *Luftwaffe* to pierce the skies over Britain.

So, it is in the light of this ongoing rivalry that existed between the Royal Navy and her air crews, that we can understand the desire for the captain of the *HMS Glorious* to hurriedly return to Britain.

HMS Glorious was dispatched to participate in the Norwegian operations, and was a critical asset in the planned evacuation of the Allied Forces scheduled for June 8, 1940. It was the *Glorious*' Captain Guy D'Oyly-Hughes who requested permission to leave Norway a day early so that he could return to the British Naval Base at Scapa Flow in Scotland's Orkney Islands to attend the Court-Martial of his Air Commander, J. B. Heath. Commander Heath, as head of the *Glorious'* air command had earlier dared to defy an order from Captain D'Oyly-Hughes that Heath felt put the lives of his air crew at risk. Heath had been detained at Scapa Flow in order to stand trial, and did not make the trip to Norway with the aircraft carrier.

There has been much after-action attention paid over the years to the return of the *HMS Glorious* from Norway, but most parties agree that the rivalry between the ship's Naval and Air Commands contributed significantly to what would become one of World War II's most significant naval disasters. Captain D'Oyly-Hughes' overbearing and obstinate command has been, in several quarters, identified as a critical factor in causing what was to come. For on the return trip to Scapa Flow, the captain of the *Glorious* took along only an escort of two destroyers, the *HMS Acasta* and *HMS Ardent*. Incredibly, the captain refused to fly combat air control from the carrier, meaning that the small group of three vessels lacked any real visibility as to what enemy warships might await them ahead in the open Norwegian Sea.

As the *Glorious* departed the coast of Norway, the ten Hawker Hurricane fighters dispatched to Arctic operations around Narvik were flown out and landed upon the aircraft carrier's flight deck. Never before had this been done. They had been loaded and unloaded by crane earlier on the trip out, and thanks to their skilled landings, the pilots hoped only to have earned a day's early return to Britain.

At approximately four in the afternoon on June 7, the smoke from the *Glorious'* stacks was spotted by a pair of patrolling German battleships, the *Scharnhorst* and *Gneisenau*. The battleships' guns far outranged and overpowered those much smaller deck guns of the two British destroyers *Ardent* and *Acasta*. Had Captain D'Oyly-Hughes authorized a naval air patrol, it is most likely these German warships would have been spotted, their positions reported and the convoy's course replotted to avoid an encounter at sea.

Instead, the Captain, with great hubris, ordered that no planes were to be allowed aloft, nor any readied on deck to deploy on that fateful transit. It was a decision for which the captain would gamble not only his own life, but the lives of all the sailors aboard the three ships combined.

At 4:27 in the afternoon, the *Scharnhorst* opened fire with her 11 inch deck guns on the closest British escort destroyer, the *HMS Ardent,* from a range of approximately 16,000 yards, or almost eight nautical miles away. *Ardent* immediately took evasive action and began laying a heavy smoke screen in an attempt to save the *Glorious*. The British destroyer launched torpedoes and fired on the German battleship with her 4.7 inch guns, and was even able to get at least one hit from on the *Scharnhorst*, but over the next hour, *Ardent* herself, was hit multiple times from the enemy's secondary guns. At 5:25 that afternoon, less than an hour after the *Scharnhorst* had opened fire, the *Ardent* was sunk.

While battling the *Ardent* with her smaller guns, *Scharnhorst* had switched her main guns onto the *Glorious* from a distance of 26,000 yards, or nearly thirteen nautical miles away. The *Glorious* unexplainably neither increased her speed nor changed her course.

Scharnhorst's third salvo struck a direct hit upon the aircraft carrier's forward flight deck, and opened a massive hole in it. A fire ignited in the deck immediately below. Any hope of getting aircraft aloft at that point was quickly abandoned. If her planes, fitted with torpedoes, had been patrolling as her air crew had desired, there might have been a chance for the carrier. Instead, *Glorious* became merely a sitting duck for the gunfire of the two German battleships as they closed in on her.

The other British destroyer, the *Acasta* had also been laying smoke in an attempt to hide the *Glorious* from the two German warships. *Acasta* bravely waited behind her own smoke, and as the *Scharnhorst* neared the *Glorious*, *Acasta* broke through the oily veil of fumes and fired torpedos upon the *Scharnhorst*, with a direct hit registered on the battleship.

The *Acasta's* gallant efforts proved to be in vain. With the *Glorious* and the *Acasta* fighting valiantly, they each came under withering fire from the guns of both the *Scharnhorst* and the *Gneisenau*. The aircraft carrier *Glorious* was sunk at ten minutes after six that evening and the destroyer *Acasta* went under ten minutes later. Between the three sunken British warships, a total of 1,519 sailors perished. Less than fifty men survived in the water.

Wincer Wells was preparing to leave London when word came that the *Glorious* and her escort group had all been sunk. Edziu Palczynski, along with the five Enigma rotors carried in his pockets, as well as Einar's secret message regarding Churchill in his head, all treated as "eyes only" for Wincer Wells, ended up with the *Glorious* at the bottom of the Norwegian Sea.

All Wells could then do was wait for the names of the few survivors to be wired to London. He would not, of course, find Palczynski's name among them

Even in this darkest of tragedies, there was a silver lining. The tremendous fight put up by the *Ardent* and *Acasta* had inflicted enough damage on the *Gneisenau* and particularly on the *Scharnhorst* that the two ships immediately left the area of engagement.

They did not realize that the *Glorious* and her escorts were running under radio silence. The German captains assumed their positions had been radioed in and other warships would soon appear. They did not know that when *Glorious, Ardent and Acasta* needed to break that silence, they encountered communication issues with the rest of the Allied fleet. Had the German battleships known this, they may have lingered in these waters, picking up survivors. Instead, thinking that the *Glorious* had called for assistance, the two German battleships made haste to occupied Norwegian ports for repairs. Had they instead lingered, these battleships would most likely have encountered and surely sank the *HMS Devonshire.* That ship in only a few hours would soon be within fifty nautical miles of these waters.

However, the German warships did not linger; they did not engage the *Devonshire*; and the manifest of the *Devonshire* was delivered safely to London. For on that day, the *Devonshire* carried as her cargo King Haakon VII of Norway, the rest of the Royal Family and the country's escaped cabinet. Those leaders would become Norway's Government-in-Exile for the remainder of World War II. Over 1,500 British sailors had died valiantly, and in doing so, an entire nation was spared.

The sinking of the *Glorious* and her escorts was not reported to the British Naval Authorities. In fact, as the small convoy was traveling under radio silence, they were not expected to be heard from. The Admiralty did not become aware of their loss at sea until they heard it reported on German radio traffic. Most of those few men who survived in the water were later picked up by Norwegian fishing vessels en route to the Faroe Islands. At least one of these ships was boarded by the

Kriegsmarine and the rescued men were taken to German POW camps for the rest of the war.

The traffic of fishing vessels from Norway continued during the war to the Shetland, Orkney and Faroe Islands. This went on despite the great dangers involved, both from the Nazi enemy as well as the wrath of the sea itself. In fact, throughout the war, there existed a covert route of contraband supply to Norway through these ships. This route became known very simply within the British Intelligence Service as the “Shetland Shuttle”. The “Shuttle” would be used extensively by the Special Operations Executive (SOE).

The remainder of the evacuation of Allied troops from Norway was scheduled for the morning after the *Glorious* was sunk. On June the 8th, all remaining British, French and Polish forces were evacuated by sea. It was this drawdown that had been first noticed by Einar from their camp atop the rocky mountain ledges. Incredible as it seemed, on the verge of total encirclement of the German forces at Bjørnfjell, the Allies were pulling out all of their soldiers, sailors and airmen.

On those ledges remained the twin brothers, Colonel Becker, Albin Bratajewski and three other Polish Highland Brigade mountaineers. Their own extraction was planned to take place in only a few more hours. It would be no difficulty for either the Poles or even Colonel Becker to descend the series of rappelling lines that Albin had secured for their escape. It clearly would be a great difficulty for Einar given his leg wound.. There was no chance whatsoever for Gunnar, even when healthy, making that descent.

Lieutenant Colonel Becker had a long dialog ongoing with Albin in German. Einar who had been watching over his sleeping brother asked the colonel what they were discussing.

“He asked me what I thought you will do with your brother,” Becker said, with no attempt to soften the translation.

“And what did you tell him?” asked Einar.

“I told him you would take the only course of action available to you,” Becker said.

“And exactly what do you think that to be?” Einar inquired.

“Your brother cannot possibly rappel down to the boat,” the German said. “If he stays here, he will die an agonizing death alone. I told the Pole that you will do the respectable thing. You will watch us all climb down, and after you are alone, when our eyes cannot see, you will shoot your brother, saving him from his misery, and then follow us down to the boat."

Einar was ashamed that he had thought out exactly that scenario. It was perhaps the only way to deliver Colonel Becker to MI6. Of course, the Pole "Edjew" was already steaming back to the Britain. He would convey the message personally to Wincer Wells, along with the five stolen Enigma rotors, but how much more rich the treasure would be if Becker were delivered also to the interrogators.

"You are almost correct, Colonel Becker," Einar said slowly. "I will let these Poles take you down the lines before me. I will be last. However, I have always promised my brother that I would never leave him, and I won't. I will stay up here on this ledge with my brother until God calls home his soul."

"You mean to tell me," Becker said, "that you will risk capture by my fellow *Gebirgsjäger* just so you can bury your brother? You will turn me over to these pagan Poles? You surely cannot be serious."

"I am completely serious, Colonel," Einar replied. "I will stay alongside my brother until he draws his final breath."

"You are weak," Becker responded, "I think you a fool."

Einar could not suppress the quote from Shakespeare, and said aloud, *"The fool doth think he is wise, but the wise man knows himself to be a fool."*

Becker looked at him with a befuddled look.

"What does that even mean?" Becker asked. "Does it mean that you have endured so much, that only now, as a path of rescue has availed itself to you, that you would throw it away only to attend to the last moments of your brother's life? He will endure his moments of pain and uncertainty whether you are by his side or not."

"It means nothing more than that I love my brother," Einar answered.

"More than you love life yourself?" Becker probed.

Einar glanced down at his sleeping, feverish brother.

"There is no life without him," Einar said, having had progressed through exactly this logic as he stared into the fire.

At that point, the radio squawked. Albin was frozen by its message and after regaining his composure, murmured its translation to his fellow Poles. They in unison turned slowly, coldly to stare at Becker, all with eyes whose evident shock quickly exploded into rage. Albin began barking at the lieutenant colonel in German, his words unknown to Einar, but his voice was strung taut with emotion.

"What is it? What is it?" Einar yelled.

Becker slowly turned his head from Albin to Einar and said with all the glibness of the devil himself, "German radio reports the *Kriegsmarine* has sunk the carrier *HMS Glorious* and her escorts. There appears to be few, if any, survivors. It is likely that the delivery of your message to British Intelligence has been interrupted somewhat."

Einar thought of the Pole "Edjew" and envisioned him struggling for his life in the open waters of the sea. A sea whose surface was likely broken white with foam as hundreds of flailing sailors fought to survive. Even if Edjew had been lucky enough to have been one of the few saved, he surely was a prisoner of the *Kriegsmarine*. A rage boiled within him, one that Einar could no longer control.

"You bastard!" Einar snapped. He muscles reacted independent of his thoughts, and instinctively drew the pistol from his waistband. In his haste, his finger had found the trigger, and as it twitched had accidentally fired off a shot into the air.

"It looks for certain that you must come with us," Becker said wryly. "If not, one of these Poles will surely push me to my death from a ledge on the way down. Then your British Secret Service would have nothing at all, would they?"

Becker said all this with a smile that teasingly laid upon his lips after his words had been delivered.

"You bastard," Einar repeated, "you deserve nothing more than to be shot with your own pistol!"

The errant shot Einar had fired into the cold Arctic air had stirred Gunnar from his fevered rest. He looked groggily up at his brother, the Walther P-38 pistol in his hand, pointed at its owner, Colonel Becker.

"Brother, what is happening?" Gunnar asked, still unsure if what he was seeing was even real. Gunnar seemed to have had emerged from a deep sleep, perhaps one that he had not expected to return from.

"Gunnar," his brother replied, "a boat is on its way for us. But the ship on which our Polish friend Edjew was sent to Britain has been sunk by the Germans. We must presume that he drowned. We must take Becker back alive. It is our only hope."

"Brother," Gunnar said weakly, "you must take him. As for myself, there is no hope. I have seen my death, it is to take place here where I now lie. You must take Becker back and leave me here. There is nothing else you can do for me."

The words of his brother penetrated Einar. He knew them to be true. Still, he was hollowed empty by the stun of reality.

"No, Gunnar," Einar said, "I will never leave you. I will have the Poles radio back the secret of *Operation Predator*."

His brother's face was sweating, his skin pallid. "I am not thinking clearly, brother," said Gunnar, "but even in this state I can see that it would only be picked up by the Germans, who would then know to tell their agent to stand down until a later date. You must go back with Becker."

"No," shouted Einar at his brother, "then I will write out the message, as I did for Edjew, and have Albin carry it back with the colonel."

"Only so this crafty German can distort it without your being present? No, Einar, you must go. Leave me here."

Having said this, Gunnar rustled under the blankets that had been laid over him. He seemed to be searching for something. After a few seconds, his left hand produced the front side of the scapular which hung from his neck. Gunnar seemed to be praying silently with it in his grasp.

"I will never leave you here, my brother," Einar repeated. "I was by your side as we entered this world, I shall be by your side if…"

Einar could not bring himself to finish the sentence in his own words. Then, in a divine intercession to his lips came those words of Shakespeare,

"We came into the world like brother and brother, And now let's go hand in hand, not one before another."

Gunnar appeared to have finished his silent prayer. "I feared that you would quote that passage from *'A Comedy of Errors.'* No title could be more befitting this life's ending. At least humor me, my brother." Gunnar then cleared his throat.

'What ugly sights of death within mine eyes!' Gunnar then said painfully.

Einar wept. His brother's suffering, interwoven with his own remorse and lined with Gunnar's sweet anticipation of life's release, swept over him. "*Richard III*" was all he could bring forth from the cruelly tortured features of his face. His tongue was thick with regret. It choked out all other utterances.

Gunnar stirred beneath the blankets. He said nothing, only nodded to Einar that his response was indeed correct. Gunnar was saving himself, his energy, as if for one last gesture.

Einar's heart broke as he looked down upon his dying brother. He could see tears running from the corners of Gunnar's eyes. Why was he squirming about so oddly beneath the blankets?

Gunnar's left hand still clasp his scapular. He clutched it between his fingers as a man clings to his last memory, to his last decision made.

"I will tell you up front that these next words are from *The Tempest.*" Gunnar turned his head to tenderly kiss the Sacred Heart of Jesus image imprinted upon the scapular. He then looked into the eyes of his brother to offer his final quote:

"Farewell brother! We split, we split, we split!"

As he said these words, Gunnar removed his right hand from under the blankets to reveal the Luger his brother had much earlier given him. Still laying upon his back, he jammed its barrel end up into the soft stubbled fold of loose flesh hanging from his jaw, just above the Adam's Apple.

"No! Gunnar, No!" screamed Einar. He dropped to his knees and leaned over his brother as he tried to grab at the gun. Gunnar had it shoved in place, but had not yet slipped his finger upon the trigger. To prevent him from doing so, Einar was able to force the tip of his own finger inside the trigger guard.

"Allow me to do this, brother," Gunnar whispered. "Allow me to set you free!"

"I would not be free without you, Gunnar, only lost, forever lost." Einar's voice cracked with torment.

"And yet, one way or another it comes," answered Gunnar. "I have made my peace with God. I do this not to end my suffering, only to lighten yours, brother."

"I so regret ever pulling you into all this," Einar said, tears by them flowing thickly down his own face before dropping as a cascade of pregnant sorrows onto Gunnar's cheek.

"I have no such regrets, my brother," whispered Gunnar. "For these last months you have allowed me to live a life of adventure. Not from words in books, but from actions fueled by courage. For that, I am most grateful. It has been my great gift, to live life as you have always lived it, with vigor and abandon. Now, one way or the other, I will die upon the rocky crypt of this ledge, so please release me to do so of my own choosing."

It was then that Einar realized that his brother had all along planned this drastic action to sever the coil between their mortal lives. Gunnar knew that the weight of his untimely death would become the anchor dragging his brother to his own demise. He only wished to hasten its arrival and save Einar.

Einar thought through the situation, and came to the conclusion that there was only one viable action to be taken.

"I cannot allow you to take your own life, brother," Einar whispered into his brother's ear. He then kissed his brother on the soft vulnerable skin of his temple. He drew his face back so he was once again looking into his brother's eyes.

"Goodbye, my loving brother," said Gunnar, his tears draining profusely from him like the last breaths of life itself.

"Goodbye to you, my always loyal brother," answered Einar, whose own face also was stained red with emotion. "I will always love you." *More than I love myself,* he thought.

Einar then tightened his own finger around the trigger until a loud shot echoed over the fjord. Einar could feel the sting of his brother's flesh and blood as it splattered upon the tender skin of his own face. He did nothing to wipe it away.

From deep within him welled forth these words from a Shakespearean sonnet that had been a favorite of his mother's:

"Like as the waves make towards the pebbled shore,
So do our minutes hasten to their end;
Each changing place with that which goes before,
In sequent toil all forwards do contend."

Strangely enough, Einar would not before his brother's passing have thought to be able to remember these words at all. Yet, the crack of the Luger's shot had drawn them forth from him with a clarity he had never before felt. A clarity of thought carried coarsely over a torrent of emotions released.

Einar, upon his knees, hovered over his brother's lifeless body. He placed the gun on the ground next to it. He drew back the blankets, and folded his brothers hands, those that had held the scapula and fought for control of the Luger, in a prayerful pose upon his chest. Then, he took the knife that he always carried and cut free the scapula from his brother's neck. It was smeared with blood and other human debris, which Einar made no attempt to wipe clean. Instead, he knotted the cut ends of the cords and slipped it over his own head. From that moment forward, he wore not one scapular but two.

Einar felt a hand on his still heaving shoulder. It was the hand of Albin. The Pole pointed to his watch, indicating it was time to descend the ropes to the boat that would rescue them in the *Rombaksfjord* below.

Einar knew there was no time to deal with his brother's remains. It was impossible to take his lifeless body down the series of rappelling lines to the fjord. Yet, he could not stand the thought of leaving his corpse exposed upon this ledge. A heavy feeling of remorse, tinged with the inadequacy of not knowing quite just what to do, rained down upon him. Then, as if this thick despondency was but a wedge that opened the doorway to his heart, he was instantly filled with a flood of memories of himself alongside his brother. He began to shake as he gave into his sentiments. Einar's nostalgia then morphed into a full blown veil of guilt. Not for pulling the trigger, but instead for pulling his brother into this operation in the first place. He knew Gunnar had always looked up to him, and Einar wanted this assignment desperately. He had killed his own brother with his selfishness.

It was then that a crackle of machine gun fire came from outside the camp. Einar looked up to the top of the *staircase of the gods* just in time to see one of the three Poles stationed there fall. The other two returned fire. They were under attack.

Sophie began her day with Henia and Mierek by explaining what had happened to Henia's great-uncle Albin Bratajewski. She began tentatively, not knowing how they might react to the news of the fate of the man.

"Your Great Uncle Albin had been deployed to the area north of Narvik in Norway's Arctic Circle. He was leading a forward scouting patrol when they came across two Norwegian soldiers holding a German lieutenant colonel captive. The files later showed these two twin brothers, who posed as Norwegian fisherman, were in reality British spies. They were soon surrounded by an advanced unit of elite German soldiers. They were trapped high upon that mountain, the only way out was to rappel down the cliff face."

"One of the twin spies was killed during the attack by the Germans." She reported, having read that from the MI6 file. "Your Great Uncle Albin then grabbed the other and lead him to the rappelling lines."

Sophie did not have the access to the diary of Tilly MacAlvor, only the MI6 records of the event. Therefore her version of the events differed somewhat from what Diane described to the Conleys. Sophie did not have the knowledge that Gunnar died not at the hands of the attacking Germans, but rather at the hand of his own twin brother.

The attack of the German patrol had long been expected, but even so, the opening rounds caught the three Poles atop the ledges by surprise. The first was hit and fell, leaving only Jurek, the medic, and another Pole to defend the position. Jurek could not even attend to his wounded comrade, as it was essential to them all that he continued to return the German patrol's fire.

Albin by this point had grabbed the twin Einar as he had stood in a daze over the corpse of his brother. Albin spun him around by the shoulders, before the Pole dropped to his knees. In his hand was the *"Swiss Seat"*, the rope harness that had been fashioned for Einar.

Albin worked the harness up the legs of the still stunned Einar, who was compliant in lifting his feet as might a small child being readied with boots for an outing in the snow. Having completed his task, Albin grabbed the carabiner centered in the *Swiss Seat* and led Einar to the first rappelling line. As he clipped the twin onto the line, Albin made hand gestures to Einar indicating he would send down Colonel Becker next, and then the Poles would follow.

It was then that the automatic fire on the top ledge of the staircase of the gods became much more intense. Some of the Germans had moved to a higher position and were by then firing down on the Poles. The second Pole was dropped, leaving only Jurek to return fire.

"It is over, now," screamed Becker in Norwegian over the automatic fire. "Run, you coward English spy. We will hunt you like a dog. Right after we piss on your brother's cold body."

Albin felt Einar tense stiffly with rage at the lieutenant colonel's words, those which the Pole could not understand. Albin then boldly embraced Einar, before putting his hands on his shoulders and slowly pressing them back toward the cliff's edge, as if to say, *Don't let him taunt you, go, begin your descent.*

Einar took the rope and ran it through his guide hand, his right, and around his back before taking it in his brake hand, his left. Albin watched as the twin leaned back on the edge's lip and steadied himself. Then Einar slowly, mechanically began to descend and disappeared over the edge. The taut line was the only evidence he had ever been there.

Albin then returned to the next higher ledge, the third in the staircase, to retrieve the German colonel. As he did, he saw that Jurek was pinned down. The weapon's fire upon that highest ledge had by then become nearly non-stop from the advancing Nazis. Albin knew it meant that the German patrol's heavy fire was to cover their advancing troops. It was clear that it would not be long now.

Albin moved to the lieutenant colonel, and drawing a knife from its sheath on his belt, cut loose the bindings on his hands. The Pole had already drawn his pistol and had it shoved it in the small of the back of the German officer. He waved the colonel towards the rappelling line with the blade of his knife, but Becker simply folded his arms in defiance.

"*Nein*," Becker screamed in his native tongue. "Shoot me if you will, I will not be taken by the British."

Albin, who spoke the tongue of the Hun effortlessly, then said as he raised his pistol, "I will gladly kill you, you Nazi bastard, for all your people have done to mine."

Albin pushed with the gun's barrel. As they crossed past where Gunnar's body lay, Becker spat upon the corpse.

This drew an instant rage in Albin, who without thinking ,spun the German round and buried the tip of his knife blade inches deep into the thigh of the German colonel. A fount of blood gushed forth. Becker screamed as he collapsed in a heap alongside the corpse of Gunnar. Using his boot, Albin flipped him on his back as he aimed his pistol to the chest of the Nazi. He knelt beside him only to twist the knife with great force inside Becker's leg. Becker's screams wailed like a siren.

"You have no respect for life," Albin said in German, as the lieutenant colonel howled in pain, "and I need not respect yours a second longer. But first I wished you to feel great pain."

With a tremendous strength Albin then pulled the blade from the German's leg. Blood sprayed up instantly. Becker yowled in distress. It was a shriek that was sharp with the panic and uncertainty of survival overlaid atop the unbearable pain.

Albin then realized the automatic fire above them had ceased. That moment of pounding silence was broken by Jurek's voice as it frantically yelled out the word *"Grenade!"* in Polish.

The explosion ripped through the uppermost ledge, and Albin, who had crouched, protected himself below on that third ledge. He realized that Jurek, the last of his unit's resistance was now gone. It would only be seconds before the Germans bounded onto the *staircase of the gods*.

Albin immediately broke for the last ledge and the rappelling line. As he did, Becker began screaming in German, "I am here. Get them, get them all. Kill them all."

Albin grabbed the rappelling line, and could feel no resistance in it. This meant Einar had cleared the first line and was likely working his way down the second by then.

Albin pulled up a length of the line and ran it through his leg, under his buttock and over his opposing shoulder in the emergency *Dülfersitz* technique. As he leaned back on the cliff's edge to lower himself, on the ledge above him he saw the image of Colonel Becker writhing in pain next to Gunnar.

Albin was frozen as he looked above the colonel to see the frenzied movement of the German patrol swarming onto the uppermost ledge. In that second, he lost focus on Becker and knew he must rapidly descend the line.

Albin dropped the full weight of his body upon the rappelling line and instantly felt the burning friction of the rope running under his ass cheek, across his back, and over his opposing shoulder as he dropped. He knew it would be only seconds until Becker or his rescuers would be leaning over the cliff and firing down upon him. Or worse still, cutting loose the line upon which his life dangled.

Albin eased the grip of his hands that controlled the speed of his descent. The rope responded by not only burning his skin, but by burrowing into it, causing a pain unlike any he had ever felt. Yet, Albin knew he must endure this pain, or lose his life altogether in the moments that would follow.

He dropped from that final ledge of the *staircase of the gods* supported only by the slithering snake of rope making its burning mark as if its scales were gouging at his tender skin.

Soon he felt the frozen sting of the waterfall that ran just upwind from his position. Albin focused on the rate of his drop, but thought only of the threat that he knew would come from above.

The rappelling line had become slick with the frozen breath of the waterfall which was both a curse and a blessing. A curse because the ropes icy surface made it harder for Albin to grip the line and control his speed. A blessing because the iced runs of rope seemed to numb the burning scars of its burrowed friction on his body.

Although Albin had earlier made this run with his fellow Pole Edziu, this time was very different. He did not have the benefit of the *Swiss Seat* harness as he did then, and as Einar did below him. The other harness had been worn by Edziu when he had been recovered by the Brits, and was no longer available.

It was then that Albin felt a twinge pulse through the line. He wondered if the Germans above had taken a knife to it, but refused to look up. Instead he concentrated on the rope running through his hands. It was then that he felt the warning knot and immediately stopped his descent. He hovered over the first landing, the one that secured the second rope.

A shot was fired from above him. *Must be a Luger,* Albin thought, *as firing a carbine straight down over that ledge was surely impossible.*

Albin dropped onto the landing. After he had done so and as he released the first line, he felt another twinge pulse through it. He looked up to see what he feared most, another *Gebirgsjäger* mountaineer beginning his descent down that line.

Albin reached for the second line and ran it into the same *Dülfersitz* configuration and dropped off the second ledge. He could not stand the anticipation of the line running again through the tracks of his burning wounds, but he knew the only chance he had was to keep far ahead of the rappelling German. His only solace was knowing that the German mountaineer pursuing him also did not have a harness and would be subjected to the same biting of the slithering snake that was the rope.

Albin dropped himself as fast as he could stand. He had attempted to offset the rope an inch or so from the burning scars of his initial descent on the first rope, but as soon as he began lowering himself, the sliding rope found itself into the grooves of his wounds, and re-enflamed their nearly unbearable pain.

For the first time Albin looked below as he dropped along that second line. He could see Einar on the next rope below him. Beyond him, he could see the same deep hulled rescue boat just coming into position in the fjord below.

It was then that Albin felt his weight shift, and for an instant, a terror sprinted through him that he would fall from the line. He slowed his descent and was able to recover his balance. From that point on, he refused to look either up or down, just to concentrate on his technique. But as much as he did, he could not ignore the burning pain caused by the rope as he slid down along its length.

The shooting from above had stopped. The Germans on the ledge would no longer risk hitting their own mountaineer. Besides this, Albin was out of their range as even a bullet shot straight down would eventually slow into nothing more that a tumbling non-ballistic fragment. But Albin knew that the German on the line above him was certainly armed.

Albin again felt the warning knot and slowed himself to hover over the second landing. He carefully lowered himself onto it. He looked up to see the *Gebirgsjäger* approaching the first landing. Below him he could see Einar just leaving the final landing, the rescue boat waiting below its length.

Albin knew he had to move quickly onto the third rope. Yet his wounds screamed at him in protest. If he stayed there, he knew he was dead. Yet even given this he could not stand to once again bear his weight upon that line. The *Dülfersitz* technique was something they had trained for emergencies over short distances only. It produced a pain that Albin could no longer tolerate. Albin then reached a compromise between what he knew to be safe and what he knew to be necessary.

Albin pulled the third line up and wound it around his body in a reverse *Dülfersitz* configuration, under his virgin, unscarred buttock, across his back in the other direction and over a fresh shoulder. His lead hand became his brake hand and vice versa, as all he was familiar with became opposite and unknown.

Albin would attempt this third drop in this unnatural-feeling, reverse configuration, one that he had never before attempted. He knew his rope-burned flesh would not allow him to continue as he had, and that above all else, he must continue!

It was the shot that barely missed him that overcame his last hesitation to proceed. The *Gebirgsjäger* above him had stopped his descent and was firing from the rope down at him.

Albin dropped his weight upon the rope and lowered himself from the second landing. His legs were spread wide to stabilize himself against the granite cliff as he rappelled. His rate of descent was significantly slower in this reverse configuration, as its mirrored movements were foreign to his muscles. Yet, he persisted and slowly adapted to it.

Albin was perhaps three quarters of the way down the length of that third rope when his weight shifted. The rope that had been burning anew under his ass cheek had slid over the crest of its rump and then bore directly and instantly upon the tender recesses of his crotch. The pain was severe, unlike any he had felt up until this moment. The sliding rope bore against his testicle and the pain from it was immediate and disabling. He had to stop his descent and figure out how to redistribute his weight along the rope to alleviate this pain. As he did so, he dangled along the line and was subjected to the pelting wind spray of the waterfall. He knew with the *Gebirgsjäger* closing down on him, he did not have the benefit of taking much time.

Albin seemed to feel it before he even heard it. An instant burning spear of fire pierced his gut as the bullet penetrated him. His body went into a frenzy that he could not control. His legs became entangled in the rope line as his frame twitched spastically. He looked up to see the *Gebirgsjäger* on the landing above squeeze off another pistol shot, this one which missed altogether. The mountaineer then holstered his weapon and returned to his descent.

The grip of Albin's left hand, which had become his lead hand, slowly weakened as the blood spread from his gut wound. The pain was insufferable. His instinct was to move his hand to cover his wound, which he gave into and before it could reach his stomach, he fell back and away from the rope.

Yet, as he began to fall, Albin felt a countering force as the rope that had ensnarled his legs tightened around them. He hung upside down along the rope line, saved by nothing other than the rope wrapped around his legs and arrested by the grip of his right hand on it.

He swayed upside down on that rope knowing that he would die. The blood had drained down and dropped in thick ribbons upon his face. It smelled vile to his nose and he knew it was his own bile that sickened him so. Despite his devastating pain, he felt the telltale surge of the *Gebirgsjäger's* weight being added to the line above.

Albin looked beyond his inverted forehead to see Einar on the last rope. Despite his rope harness, he was progressing much slower than Albin would have hoped. He then remembered the wound of the man's Achilles Tendon.

It was then, as he was so helplessly suspended upon this third rope, like an insect entrapped in a web, that Albin realized the spider descending down upon him was more intent on devouring not him, but the escaping British spy below.

Albin looked down at Einar as the life drained slowly from him. The pain became less intense, as if through a dusty haze. Albin thought of his own brother, Bogdan, and this brought a warmth into his soul. He loved his brother so. He knew Bogdan would do anything to protect his own brother. Albin next thought of Einar, who had just lost not only his own brother, but his twin. It was in those last seconds of life that Albin realized what he must do.

The Pole's right hand grasped strongly on the rope. If he would let go, even for an instant, the snake would uncoil from around his legs and he would fall free of the line. With every ounce of concentration, he used his left hand to draw the knife from its sheath along his waist. It, like he, had been inverted, but soon the knife was in his left hand. He reached with it over his head, which was the lowest point of his dangling mass, and began to cut at the rope hanging below him. In this way he would keep the *Gebirgsjäger* from pursuing Einar.

There was a problem that he had not expected. The rope below his right hand was flaccid; it hung free with no weight on it. There was no resistance to his blade, and as such, no slicing of the line occurred. His only recourse was to cut above his brake hand, where it was taut with weight. But to do so, to slice through it, would have the same effect as letting go of his brake hand. He would fall to his death. Except, it would have the additional benefit of denying the *Gebirgsjäger* any additional descent.

Albin knew he was already dead. He could feel his life draining away. He took the knife to the stiffened, strained rope above his brake hand. The blade, still reddened with Becker's blood, smeared and slid along the line, refusing to bite. Albin knew it was due to his ebbing strength.

Concentrate, Albin, he heard his brother Bogdan's voice say. He could not tell if the sound of his voice was real or not, from the present or the past, from this world or the next. But he heeded its message.

The knife slowly edged into the rope. Albin had to focus on every thrust of his knife. Soon he was a quarter through its width.

Good, my brother. You are doing well.

Albin's concentration became harder and harder to focus. His vision blurred. His strength ebbed from him. He began to drift in attention and spirit. He made one last thrust of the blade.

His energy had all but left him. The knife fell from his grip. He focused what strength remained on holding onto the rope in his break. Albin looked at the partially cut rope. He had gotten just beyond halfway across its width.

You have done well, my brother. Time has come to rest.

Albin obeyed his brother's gentle, calming voice. He released the last of his life's force, resulting in his right hand's opening. As if in slow motion, the rope unfurled along his leg and his body fell. Strangely, Albin watched all of this happen from a close distance. He could even see the waterfall that raced his discarded body downward. He did not see nor feel his body smashing onto the rocky landing a hundred feet below.

Einar Alvorsen had been resting his throbbing leg along that last length of rappelling line when he heard the third pistol shot from the descending *Gebirgsjäger* mountaineer. He could not see the German clearly, but he knew it was not Becker, for he had been wearing the white snow tunic. This *German* did not wear white and was continuing to descend at a rapid rate after having squeezed off the rounds.

Einar returned to his own descent. It was the clatter of the knife as it struck the landing above that next caught his attention. He looked up in time to see the knife above him bounce off that landing and continue to fall past him. He watched as it dropped below him and came to rest onto the rocky outcropping that was his own barrier to escape in the fjord. The knife lay there beneath him, a weapon as useless as the jagged rock it laid upon.

Then Einar looked back up at the Polish Highland Brigade member as he dangled above. Albin was clearly in trouble, hanging by his entangled legs from the rope. Then Einar was stunned to see his body drop from the line, accelerating as it fell more than a hundred feet. It crashed onto the landing that Einar had just left, and while the twin could not see the impact, he heard the defining thud it produced. There was no chance that Albin had survived that fall.

Einar now focused once more on descending to the rope's end. He remembered Albin had said that there was no knot in the rope's end, and to be very cautious on that last line. Einar was by then at the point near the rope's end, still some twenty feet above the massive outcropping upon which the knife had come to rest.

He knew that he would have to push off with his legs, release the last line and pray it was with enough thrust to clear the outcropping. Einar had watched from above as Edjew had done so, and he appeared to have barely cleared the rock.

The problem was that Einar's leg was throbbing as it had not done at any point since the original injury. He had thought that the rappelling action down the lines would not bother it much, as the rope was bearing his weight, not his legs. They would be used only to stabilize him, like a tripod including the rope. Yet, the slamming into the granite mountain wall and the pushing off away from it, produced a terrible pain in his heel.

Below him the rescue boat circled idly in the waters of the *Rombaksfjord*. The two men aboard waved their arms in rapid swirling motions as if to say, *Come on, already!*

A fourth shot rang out. It came from the *Gebirgsjäger* on the line above. He had stopped in about the location from which Albin had fallen to his death. He seemed reluctant to go beyond that point. He raised his pistol and fired off another round, the fifth by Einar's count. Both shots had missed Einar widely. He was some two hundred feet below the German at that point and only blind luck would strike him fatally from that range, even if it were all downhill.

The *Gebirgsjäger* must have decided the same, as he cautiously began to lower himself further, past the point where Albin had fallen. As soon as he did so, he began descending in great leaps. He pushed off with massive thrusts against the granite wall and would allow himself to drop dramatically as he swung out and back in again like a clock's pendulum. He was nearing the ledge upon which Albin had fallen, perhaps only twenty feet above it when he pushed off one last time.

The *Gebirgsjäger* swung out to allow him to release his grip and allow the line to run through his hands. But the thrust of his legs created a tension in the line, like those of each thrust before. Only this one completed the rupture of the line above where Albin had partially severed it using the knife in an attempt to cut the rope line.

The snap of the line was audible like a that of a rifle shot. The *Gebirgsjäger* instantly fell the last twenty feet onto the ledge where Albin's body lay. Like Albin, Einar could not see the impact. Unlike Albin, the fall did not prove fatal. After the impact, the German rolled under his own momentum off the landing and fell another two hundred feet. Einar knew he was still alive, because the *Gebirgsjäger* screamed out in terror for the entire distance until he came to a collision upon the final rocky outcropping.

The terrified scream stopped suddenly, as if swallowed whole into the deafening thud of the impact. Einar only then realized that he had heard no scream from Albin as he fell. Only the same thud that seemed to vacuously consume all other sound around it. As all sound disappeared around him, Einar came to the conclusion in the last few seconds of life, Albin Bratajewski had taken the very actions that saved his own.

"Will you bloody jump already!" came the call from the boatsman below. Einar was perhaps only thirty feet above the fjord's surface, but it was as treacherous a distance as any along those cliffs, for he still had to clear the massive rocky outcropping.

Einar haunched on his legs, rocking on them as he prepared to release their springs. He then thrust as hard as he could to push himself away from the granite cliff. As he did so, he felt something snap in his injured leg and the pain was both immediate and unbearable. He let go of the rope before he had climbed the full arc of his swing. He lost outward momentum.

He felt himself falling. He fought the instinct to grab at the rupture of whatever it was within his foot, and in doing so might have saved his life. For after the rope had slid free from his hands, Einar arched over like a diver coming off the board backwards. And if he had another ten or twenty feet, he most likely would have been fine. Instead, just as he was about to clear the outcropping, his legs smashed hard upon it. The unforgiving overhang tipped him into a sprawling fall, smacking hard flat upon the fjord's surface before penetrating its depths.

“Bloody ‘ell” screamed the first boatman, as he kicked off his boots, removed his anorak, grabbed the end of a rescue line and dove in after Einar. The second boatsman cut the engine, so as to make sure neither man in the drink should wander up into its prop. He waited for endless seconds until he felt a tug at the line. He immediately began pulling up on it with great effort. As he did so, the first boatman surfaced, and after gasping for air yelled out, “I bloody well ‘ope I wasn’t too late.”

The second boatsman pulled the line until Einar’s body broke the surface. It seemed limp and lifeless, like dead weight, until Einar began coughing up water from deep within him. Then, after he had caught his breath, Einar began howling in pain from his wounded legs.

“It would appear this bloke is quite alive,” said the seaman inside the boat.

“I just ‘ope he was the one they were making such a bloody fuss over!” the second seaman said.

Einar was hauled into the runabout, followed by the second seaman. The engine was restarted and Einar was taken through the interconnected fjords to Harstad, howling from pain the entire way. On their arrival he was taken into the infirmary. Even a cursory examination identified the rumpled tendon knotted under the skin of his calf, indicating that his Achilles tendon had been ruptured completely in two.

Einar was taken aboard the aircraft carrier *HMS Ark Royal* and immediately into surgery. His torn Achilles was surgically repaired, and his other wounds were tended to, but no further surgery was required. As the Chief Surgeon came out of the operating room, he was greeted by the ship’s captain.

“SIS in London wants to talk to that chap at the earliest possibility,” said the captain. “Seems he’s one of their own.”

“Where are you taking us, Captain? Scapa Flow?” asked the surgeon. “Best have them question him there.”

“Is there not the slightest possibility of their questioning him before we get underway in the morning?”

“With the trauma I just treated to his legs,” said the surgeon, “he will be heavily sedated for the next several days. Even if I could bring him around sooner, are you seriously willing to break radio silence after what just happened to the *Glorious*?”

“I’ll tell them to meet us at Scapa,” answered the captain. “Bloody spooks will just have to cool their heels.”

54 A Day of Closure

June 10, 1940

"There is in the act of preparing, the moment you start caring."

Winston Spencer Churchill

General Władysław Sikorski sent for his pilot, Bogdan Bratajewski, immediately upon the latter's return from flying the Polish codebreakers to Algiers. There were more pressing issues, as France was on the precipice of falling completely into the control of the Nazi invaders. The Panzer Tanks of the *Wehrmacht* were drawing close to Paris, so much so that the French Government had abandoned the capital and withdrew to Tours.

"Thank you, Pilot Bratajewski, for your service in delivering these men from harm," said the general. "You have performed a dangerous and tremendous service for our nation. Now, we must prepare for the next evacuation, that of all Polish forces from France, particularly the Podhale Rifle Brigade."

"I am honored to do so, General," answered Bogdan, "but are they not still in the Arctic near Narvik?"

"No, my friend," General Sikorski through hand gestures invited Bogdan to be at ease, "they boarded their transport ships yesterday and are enroute back to Brest. Tomorrow, Prime Minister Churchill is expected to arrive at Tours for final discussions with Premiere Reynauld and his staff."

"If I may, my General," interrupted Bogdan, "that is only if the Polish transports reach Brest before the German *Luftwaffe* does. As for Prime Minister Churchill flying into France again, this is becoming more and more dangerous every day. My own flight back was not uneventful in that manner. I had to keep a keen eye out for the Messerschmitts when the winds required that as I approached Paris from the east."

Sikorski paced back and forth behind his desk. His angular face only highlighted the grievous concerns he had been harboring for many days now.

"Yes, you certainly would know, Bogdan, but Churchill flies in his transport aircraft, which for some odd reason he calls his Flamingo…"

"It is the aircraft designation, my General," interrupted Bogdan. "The de Havilland DH-95 Flamingo is a dual engined monoplane. It carries up to eighteen passengers. Very new. Just put into service in 1938."

"Yes, well, as it is," resumed Sikorski, "this meeting is very crucial, so I am told he flies with an escort group of a dozen RAF Spitfires. I would think that was sufficient to drive off any *Luftwaffe* fighters that might stray upon them. It is urgent that Churchill's plane not be kept away. One of the topics for discussion is the evacuation of our Polish troops and the Government-in-Exile itself to Britain. Therefore, assuming these discussions go as I suspect they should, I will need you to be prepared to escort myself and my daughter, and any members of our cabinet that we can accommodate to London on a moment's notice."

"Of course, my General," snapped Bogdan in response. Then he softened his tone and asked, "If I may be so bold as to enquire, why are our Polish troops evacuating Norway when they appeared to be doing so well against the Nazis?"

"It was the decision of the British to evacuate all Allied forces, given the imminent fall of France. England needs her Royal Navy to guard the Channel and other shores now more than ever. Without those ships, the French and our troops cannot go on."

"But they were so close to driving the Germans out of Norway…" Bogdan said, "… at least in the Arctic." He was used to conversing informally with Sikorski when they were alone, and Sikorski encouraged it. In public, or even when anyone else was present, even if only Sikorski's daughter Zofia, the tone would be much more regimented with respect to the general's authority.

"Yes, yes," said Sikorski, "our troops had Dietl's *Gebirgsjäger* pressed up against the border. This is true. Of course along with the French and Norwegians as well, let us not forget. But the Germans had already started bringing reinforcements overland up from the south at Trondheim. The

Allies would have had a hard time holding onto the frozen north, and certainly would not do so without presence of the Royal Navy. So, it is done, and as our soldiers sail home, they race against time, as you have pointed out so astutely. But there is much fight left in them, I assure you. For now they have proven that the Hun is not invincible in retaking Narvik."

"Only to give it back through evacuation," said Bogdan.

"Yes, unfortunately so," added General Sikorski.

"And what becomes of our Norwegian comrades?" Bogdan dared to ask.

"The King and his Cabinet are safely on their way to London," said Sikorski. "It appears we will not be the only Government-in-Exile residing there. As for their troops, they will surrender to the Nazis soon."

"They fought very gallantly, did they not, my General?"

"They did indeed. As did the French, and our Highland Brigade."

"I cannot wait to congratulate my brother, Albin, for so fiercely engaging the Nazis. I wish I could only have fought by his side."

The words stopped Sikorski pacing in his tracks. He slowly spun on his heels to look directly into the eyes of his pilot.

"Bogdan, as a courtesy to you, I had an aide search the manifest of all the boarded Polish troops. I am very sorry to tell you that your brother was not among them. It appears that his forward patrol unit may have been ambushed by the Nazis."

"You mean they were captured?" Bogdan said in shock. "Or were they …" He could not finish the sentence.

"That I am afraid we do not know," answered the general.

Bogdan stood quickly at attention, and saluted Sikorski as he said in an earnest, formal voice, "Sir, I request to be deployed to Narvik at the earliest possible opportunity to search for my brother."

"I know you are upset, Bogdan," said General Sikorski, "and understandably so, but it is impossible for you to leave me now. I need you your skills more than ever, and your country needs you here with me. But still, I promise you as I did when I said I would release you to fight the Nazis, that I will give you a chance to go to the hills around Narvik, if nothing else, than to pay your respects to your brother's sacrifice."

"Thank you, sir," Bogdan said in a crisp, but defeated tone, "but my brother's sacrifice is made only for the Germans to retake the port he fought so hard to free from their hands."

"The Germans will retake Narvik," Sikorski tried to put in perspective, "this is true, but they will march back into a shelled out town which will likely be unusable as an ore port for the rest of the war. Your brother and his comrades have done what was asked of them. They have denied the Germans this port to ship the Swedish ore."

That same day in the Broughty Ferry neighborhood of Dundee, Scotland, Tilly MacAlvor buried her husband in the graveyard of the nearby church she attended. It would be more accurate to say that she entombed a coffin shaped box filled with his remembrances: photos, a few pieces of clothing and even an old sextant that his father had once given to him. Of course, the remains of Brigand, or as she would forever remember him, Birger, was at the bottom of the English Channel near Dunkirk, still strapped into the Captain's chair of the beloved Nordlys.

And that was the problem. As the *"Pall Bearers"*, which consisted of Wincer Wells and the three Dartmouth marines, lowered the near empty coffin into the freshly dug grave, all Tilly could see in her mind's eye was his bloated corpse, and its fine locks of his uncut hair flowing with the current, as if to wave, morosely enough, goodbye.

It was when the service was concluded that the lead marine named Christopher came to her, and repeated, word for word, what his captain had asked him to transmit to her.

She took it all in a sort of stunned, surreal stride. She did not cry, nor shake, nor flail. She felt only a great and overpowering heaviness. One which threatened to pull her down into the open earth herself. One which she only resisted because of the new life that grew within her.

"Thank you, Seaman Christopher," she said tenderly. "Not for your generous presence here today, but for your days at Dunkirk with him. He deserved a death with dignity, and thanks to you all, he has received that. Through you he saved innumerable lives before going down with the *Nordlys*."

What Tilly did not say was that he was responsible for another life as well, that within her. Wincer paid his respects to her, then handed her the proceeds from Brigand's insurance policy covered by the "Club". It was one that the insurer balked at paying, as technically Brigand died during an act of war. Yet, when the weight of the British Government bore down upon that insurer, and consequently offered to fund half the pay-out, monies for the claim were found.

"I can't begin to share with you the condolences from C's office on down," Wincer lied to her, for he had no such message to forward to her. "And I regret to bring this up at this hour, but procedures require me to do a detailed search of your home for any materials that may be covered by the Official Secret's Act that Brigand may have left behind. I am sure you understand."

She could not believe he had the bollocks to even begin this discussion. Somehow she mustered the startling response, "Wincer, I know fully well what you hope to find, and I can fully assure you that it has been moved to a safe location."

"I am quite sure I do not know of what you refer," he said, lowering his tone.

"The letter, Wincer," she went on, "the one detailing the fact that you forged the document allowing my son Gunnar to go to the bloody Arctic with his brother Einar. You are quite aware that forgery of government documents, especially those covered by the Act, is itself a very serious offense. For you see, Wincer, Brigand's last words to me were not 'I love you' or even 'I'll be back', but I am ashamed to say were 'beware of that snake in the grass Wincer Wells. So you best be off to London straightaway, for you will not search my home."

Wells looked shocked, momentarily, before he replied, "I am afraid that's all water over the dam, Tilly. You see, I am off not south to London but north to Scapa Flow where I will await the arrival of both your sons. Out of sheer respect for you and your monstrous grief, I will forgo the search procedure today, but save it for my return with Einar and Gunnar in hand."

Wincer Wells knew that only Einar was listed on any of the manifests of the evacuation ships. He did not, at that time, know of Gunnar's death, but likely would have guessed so given his not being listed. But this was a detail he was unwilling to share with Tilly. As was the fact that Einar was in a medically induced state to assist in his recovering from his surgeries.

"Well, that certainly is unexpected good news," said Tilly, changing her tone to Wells entirely. "You say you'll bring the lads by?"

"As soon as they are released from the ships," he lied more. "So please have that letter ready to be turned over then."

Shortly after, all four men headed to the train station, with three Royal Marines bound south for Dartmouth and one headed north for the ferry to the Orkney Islands. Tilly lingered over Brigand's *"grave"*, before then proceeding on to the Parish offices. There, from the proceeds of Brigand's insurance payout, she paid in full for the four burial lots she had ordered: One for Brigand, one for herself, and one each for the twins she had just been told to expect home soon. She had truly thought they would only come home in government coffins.

Well, they won't be a total waste, will they, she reasoned to herself, *for one day these lads will need these plots, won't they?* She had no reason to know that they never would. Neither of them.

Aboard the *HMS Ark Royal,* Einar MacAlvor awakened from his unconsciousness in a process that can only be compared to a man thought to be dead clawing his way out his grave. Every element of his bruised being cried out for rest, although even collectively these were no match for what drove him. Once the slurry of medications was sloughed off, Einar recalled that which he had hoped could only be a dream. Yet somewhere within him, he knew the death of his brother, as well as the self sacrifice of the Pole, Albin, were both all too real.

What Einar could not do was to allow both of these lives to have been given up in vain. It drove him. He had been told by the attending nurse to calm down, that he was safe on a Royal Navy aircraft carrier *Ark Royal. This only caused Einar to* think of the other Pole, "Edjew" Palczynski, who he himself had sent to his death aboard the *HMS Glorious*. No, he told the attendant, he needed to see the captain immediately. Einar knew what he must do, and demanded to do so before fate rose to again steal away the opportunity.

The Surgeon-Lieutenant on duty was called for. He initially thought the patient to be having a manic reaction to the drugs administered for pain. He had not performed the surgery, that was done by the Chief Surgeon, who was currently needed upon one of the escort destroyers. Einar wore away at the junior medical officer's patience, until he eventually made the Surgeon-Lieutenant understand that he was an operative for the secret service and the life of the Prime Minister hung in the balance. He must make radio contact with London.

The Surgeon-Lieutenant was prepared to administer another dose of sedative to the lad who he thought was becoming exceptionally excited.

"Just two words, please," screamed out Einar. "Just have the captain send two words to the Admiralty. Churchill's life depends on it. Just have them send the words *'Thor's Hammer,'* and I guarantee you that a response will be forthcoming."

The Surgeon-Lieutenant held the hypodermic over him, preparing it for injection. "Relax, my good man, this will settle you out."

"So help me God," screamed Einar, "if you inject me with that I'll see to it that you are court-martialed, if not drawn and quartered."

The Surgeon-Lieutenant laughed at the idle threat, in case anyone witnessed his delusional insubordination. He then moved forward to inject the troubled lad when an orderly touched him gently on the shoulder to gain his attention.

"Surgeon-Lieutenant, sir, before you administer that dosage, may I have the courtesy of your ear?"

"Yes, Seaman," said the surgeon, "but be quick about it. This man is nearly hysterical."

"Sir, I was on medical duty a few days ago at HQ in Harstad when a Polish fellow uttered those same two words, *'Thor's Hammer'*, and all hell broke loose. He went from being totally ignored to being flown out to the *Glorious* in less than an hour. As I understand it, Lord Cork himself was consulted and signed off on the order."

"Thank you, Seaman, that is a most interesting tale," said the Surgeon-Lieutenant, who halted in his administering the dosage. Instead, sensing the potential for reprimand, he instead pushed the needle to the orderly. "This man needs this sedative. I am ordering you to administer it to him."

"I *would not* do that, sir," said the orderly.

"Seaman, that was not a request," barked the Surgeon-Lieutenant, "it was an order from an officer. Now, would you like to alter your response?"

"Yes, sir," answered the orderly. "My response now is I *will not* do that."

"Thank you, seaman," said the Surgeon-Lieutenant, "I will have you reprimanded for your refusal to follow my order!" Then the Surgeon-Lieutenant callously proceeded with the injection. Within a minute, despite Einar's every effort to fight the drug's effect, he was once again unconscious.

Only after the Surgeon-Lieutenant administered the sedative, did the orderly add, "Within the hours after we were aware of the *Glorious* sinking, we received frantic radio traffic wanting to know if there was any chance whatsoever that the bloody Polock never made it to the carrier. When they found out that he had, they quizzed every one of us who had spoken to him about every accented word that we remembered he had said. Those intelligence types were swarming like a hive of hornets. If you read this man's charts, you might have seen the annotation to notify the captain as soon as he came to."

The Surgeon-Lieutenant suddenly turned a little green in the gills in having heard this last line. He instantly regretted having been so rash.

"Thank you, Seaman. Since you have been so traumatized by your experience at HQ, I will not bother to summon the sergeant-at-arms for you insubordination. I will personally bring this to the captain's awareness."

Within the hour, the Surgeon-Lieutenant made his way to the bridge.

"Captain, might I have a moment of your time?" asked the surgeon. "It is possibly quite urgent."

"So is our encounter with the *Scharnhorst.* She's been spotted in for repairs at Trondheim. Can't you take whatever this is to the Chief Surgeon?"

"No sir, the chart on patient MacAlvor said to contact you personally, immediately, sir."

"The spooks' agent? Make it quick, Doctor."

The Surgeon-Lieutenant told the captain the story of both Einar's words and his orderly's witnessed response to them at Harstad. He left out the fact that he had administered a dosage of sedative rendering MacAlvor useless for the next dozen hours.

After hearing the Lieutenant-Surgeon's summary, as incomplete as it was, the captain thought through the situation.

"We are running radio silent, but if this somehow really does potentially pertain to a threat to the PM, I am willing to send a two word message, encrypted of course, to the Admiralty."

The captain had the message encrypted and transmitted. Then they waited, the captain busied himself over charts of Trondheim, weather reports, and aerial photos of the target *Scharnhorst*, while the doctor waited impatiently. The minutes for the junior officer dragged like hours, but within the actual half hour the radio traffic incoming was astonishing. The captain then returned to the Surgeon-Lieutenant.

"The bloody spooks want to talk to whomever spoke these words immediately. When I passed on that it was MacAlvor, they asked which one. Do you have another?"

"No, sir," said the surgeon. "Only Einar. Is there another?"

"Apparently he was deployed with a brother, said the captain. "Well, in any case, they want your Einar fellow on the wireless immediately. Is he healthy enough to get up to the W/T?"

The W/T was ship slang for the radio room, or Wireless Transmission station.

"Sir, if I might be so bold as to ask, what happened to radio silence?" The Surgeon-Lieutenant hoped to avoid the discussion that was sure to follow.

"Your Einar MacAlvor happened to it. No sooner than a quarter hour after we sent his *'Thor's Hammer'* message, we received an order from the Admiralty to break radio silence. Then the damn spooks lit the wireless up. So, good Doctor, can you get MacAlvor up to the W/T or not?"

"I am afraid I had to sedate him," said the surgeon.

"Well, give him something to offset it. Get him to the bloody W/T straightaway…"

"I can't, Captain, sir. What I gave him will keep him out for another twelve hours at least. He needed the rest. In any case, he is in no condition to be moved."

"Damn it, Doctor, you come to me with a story of impending doom for the PM and have me light up the spooks and the Admiralty, only then to tell me your patient is out of commission for twelve bloody hours. This is likely to push back our air assault on the *Scharnhorst*. Damn it all to hell, man! You get your arse back down to his bedside and do whatever is necessary to bring him around as soon as possible. And make bloody well sure he is coherent when you do! I don't need this carrier group full of men returning home to be re-routed across the North Sea because your man's memory is playing tricks on him. Understood, Lieutenant-Surgeon?"

"Yes, sir, of course, sir," replied the Surgeon-Lieutenant with a salute.

The captain returned the salute in a halting slice of his hand that echoed his frustration. "Doctor, do not allow me to drop in on the infirmary and not find you nearby this MacAlvor's bedside. Am I clear?"

"Most thoroughly, sir," said the doctor, then taking full advantage of the opportunity to leave the bridge.

"And get the damn *sparkies* to set something up for him in the infirmary by his bed," the captain growled, becoming all the more agitated. He referred to the radio technicians as they were called in the ship's vernacular. "After all, they have half a bloody day to do so thanks to your incompetence!"

Wincer Wells had taken the train from Dundee north to the northern coastal town of Thurso, Scotland. He could have taken a much shorter train ride to Aberdeen and caught the ferry to Kirkwall, but he preferred the shorter ferry ride.

Upon his arrival, Wells was made aware by the driver who met him at the station that the ferry to the Orkneys was out due to rough seas. It was then that he was sure to have made the right decision. In the morning, he would have the much shorter ferry trip and arrive at Scapa Flow earlier. The driver then took him to a local hostel where they both slept the night through.

The next morning, on the 11th of June, the seas had calmed and the driver took the car around the bay to the town of Scrabster to catch the ferry to Stromness on the Orkneys. From there it was a short trip to the Scapa Flow Base Intelligence Headquarters.

Scapa Flow is a deepwater naval port to the British Royal Navy much as Pearl Harbor is to the American Pacific

Fleet. Like Pearl Harbor, the name is of the sheltered body of water. "Scapa Flow" comes from the old Norse word *Skalpaflói* meaning "bay of the long isthmus." The naval base there had been the Royal Navy's primary base during World War I. In fact, Wells had been alongside Mansfield Cumming's, the old "C", on the day of 21 June 1919 when the German Admiral von Reuter decided to scuttle the seventy-four ships of its navy interred at Scapa Flow since the end of the Great War's hostilities in order to prevent their being inducted into the British Navy.

As a naval base, Scapa Flow had deteriorated badly in the interwar period due to Britains decision to voluntarily disarm itself. Yet, when the Second World War broke out, the far northern base was desperately needed, as it was generally out of range of the *Luftwaffe*'s bombers. Even then, in October 1939, just one month after the war had started, the German submarine U-47 managed to slip past the eroded defenses and enter Scapa Flow's harbor. It sunk the battleship *HMS Royal Oak,* killing 833 of the 1400 sailors aboard. Since that debacle, security on base, as well as on the seas surrounding it had been airtight.

Wincer Wells arrived on base expecting the imminent arrival of the carrier *HMS Ark Royal* and its prized patient, Einar MacAlvor. He was quickly brought up to speed on the ship's delay for the impending aerial attack on the *Scharnhorst*, one of the two German Pocket Battleships that had only days ago sunk the *HMS Glorious.*

Wells was then told of the signal they had received from Ark Royal of *"Thor's Hammer"* the night before. Based on the twelve hour dosage, Einar MacAlvor was beyond the hour he was expected to regained his senses.

"Get the *Ark Royal* on the wireless immediately," Wells demanded. "And use the encryption codes, I don't want the bloody Huns intercepting this string!"

Wells was excited to potentially have a second shot at gaining an Enigma. He realized at that juncture that the same codewords had been given by the Pole, "Edjew" Palczynski, who went down with the *Glorious.* Wells did not then realize that only Palczynski carried the rotors stolen from the Nazis.

Thor's hammer, thought Wells, e*ven Einar won't use that bloody codeword Mjölnir.*

Figure 36: Churchill's beloved de Havilland Flamingo

55 A Flamingo Dances with Death

June 11-14, 1940

"... how dense and baffling is the veil of the unknown."

Winston Spencer Churchill

At that time it was already the late afternoon of the eleventh. Within minutes of Wells having ordered contact with the carrier and before this order was acted upon, reports from the *HMS Ark Royal* began pouring in over the wireless. A squadron of twelve RAF aircraft had been launched against the *Scharnhorst*. Only two of the aircraft squadron's payload of 250-pound bombs were reported by pilots to have found their target, but subsequent battle damage assessment determined that the raid had overall been a complete failure.

There was much follow-up encrypted wireless traffic that suggested another raid by *Ark Royal* aircraft was imminent in coming days. This meant further delay of the carrier's arrival, as well as that of Einar MacAlvor.

"Get them on an emergency encrypted frequency," demanded Wells. "They are going to continue to screw around with *Scharnhorst* until they lose *Ark Royal* like they lost the *Glorious*. That damn carrier should have been here in Scapa Flow by now."

"Personally, Wincer, I hope they get the bugger," said one of his peers in the Intelligence HQ. "That damn ship along with the *Gneisenau* cost us near fifteen hundred souls. You believe me, they will take every shot they have at it."

"What I have potentially on that ship will save the lives of that tally hundreds, if not thousands, of times over," replied Wells coldly.

"We have your line established sir," interrupted the wireless operator. "Ready for message to be deployed."

"FOR PATIENT EYES ONLY STOP IDENTIFY SELF AND PROVIDE NAME OF BASE OF OPERATIONS AND FAMILY NAME OF RELATIVES THERE FULL STOP"

A few moments passed while the query was encoded and sent. A slight delay before the return transmission and a few moments more to decode it:

EINAR BROTHER OF GUNNAR MACALVOR STOP SON OF BRIGAND AND TILLY STOP SKROVA STOP ALVORSEN FULL STOP

"Send this," replied Wells. "DO YOU POSSESS THOR'S HAMMER FULL STOP"

Another delay ensued. The reply read:

NEGATIVE STOP GUNNAR GAVE HIS LIFE TO POSSESS IT STOP SENT WITH MESSENGER POLE PALCZYNSKI ON GLORIOUS STOP FATE OF PALCZYNSKI UNKNOWN FULL STOP

"So Gunnar is indeed deceased," Wells said in a mutter, although he felt no real remorse for the fact. His only desolation was for the loss of the Enigma rotors. *Einar's way of castigating me for not asking, I suppose,* thought Wells.

"Operator, send this response: PALCZYNSKI LOST AT SEA PRESUMED DEAD STOP WILL AWAIT YOUR ARRIVAL IN SCAPA FLOW FOR COMPLETE DEBRIEF FULL STOP END OF TRANSMISSION FULL STOP"

The massage was encoded and sent. As the operator awaited the EOT recognition, a response soon came back which read:

NEGATIVE STOP DO NOT TERMINATE TRANSMISSION STOP VITAL INFORMATION FOLLOWS STOP GAW EYES ONLY VIA OTP FULL STOP

Wells knew the GAW were his initials, and OTP meant One-Time Pad. This meant the next message to be transmitted was only for Wells to read, and would be encoded per their earlier agreed upon One-Time Pad.

Wells then had the three word message sent: *PROCEED FULL STOP*

A One Time Pad was a nearly unbreakable technique, assuming both parties had the matching pre-printed pads. Using an OTP, a message is sent where each letter corresponds to the letters of a longer document (the One-Time Pad) that both sender and receiver shared. If they do not share a pre-printed one-time pad, then an agreed upon standard length of printed material could be substituted.

What was that OTP text? thought Wells. *Damn it, what was it?* Then he remembered. The first mention of twins in the Bible - Genesis Chapter 25, Verse 19 - the story of Jacob and Essau.

In this case, using Genesis 25:19 as a OTP could be called a Bible code, but that would give the source of the key away. It was likely that Einar had encrypted the message in advance, given the speed with which the response was sent. The message came in the form of an unintelligible stream of alphabet characters. Wells went to the reference shelf, where materials commonly used for this purpose were stored. He reached for the King James Version of the Bible. He began the painfully slow process of hand decrypting the message. When eventually finished, it read:

SOURCE GERMAN LTCOL STOP OPERATION PREDATOR STOP GERMAN PILOT INFILTRATED INTO PM FLAMINGO ESCORT FIGHTER PILOTS STOP OBJECTIVE DEATH OF FLAMINGO FULL STOP

Wells could not believe his eyes. He encoded a one word message which read "Disinformation?" and had the operator send it. While he awaited a response, he picked up a secure line to SIS HQ in London.

"Put me through to Penny Quidling. Urgent. Thank you."

"Hello?" her voice answered on the third ring.

"Penny, this is Wincer…"

"Oh, Hello, Graham…" she started.

Wells ignored her pleasantry. "Penny, this is urgent, where is 'C'?"

"Not available, I'm afraid," her voice sounded bruised by his own tone.

"Where is the PM today," he asked urgently, "I know 'C' has you track that daily."

"You couldn't possibly expect me to share that with you, Wells," she said tersely.

"Listen to me, Penny, and take heed of what I say. The PM's life may be in danger. Is he in the air today? Yes or No?"

There was a terrible reluctance at the other side of the line, then quietly, almost inaudibly she said, "He's in the Flamingo at present."

"To where? Damn it, Penny! Where is Winston going? This could mean the man's life, as well as anyone who is with him. Understand?"

The heavy silence was then even more pervasive. Wells thought he heard a click. *Good God! Had she hung up on me?* he thought.

Then she finally said, "Supreme War Council. Tours. And I shan't tell you an *iota* further, Wells."

"Get in touch with 'C' immediately. Tell him it is desperately urgent I speak with him. I am at SIS Office Scapa Flow. Here is the extension. I won't move away from this phone. Say as little as you have to over any open lines, but get him in touch with me."

Wells hung up as the radioman began receiving another stream of gibberish. He passed it on to Wells who decoded the response to his inquiry. It read:

DISINFO POSSIBLE STOP LT COL SOURCE ATTRIBUTED MESSAGE FROM GENERAL DIETL STOP MAY 10 CELEBRATION STOP COL SOURCE APPEARED DRUNK STOP UNABLE TO SEND WARNING SOONER FULL STOP

It all seemed to play out quite nicely, Wells thought. He knew May 10 was the day that Germany had invaded Belgium and France with tremendous advantage. *Caught us and the French napping, didn't they? Same day Churchill was made Prime Minister? General Dietl, being at the height of his strength in the mountains around Narvik blows off some steam and celebrates. Perchance a little too much? But how would the lads come to learn of it?*

"Operator, send this message," he handed the encrypted stream of nonsense letters to the radioman. Although only Wells knew it, the message read, "Provide Name of Lt Col source."

As the operator sent the stream, the phone rang. Wells answered it only as "Hullo?", which was standard practice.

"What the hell is all this about?" said Stewart Menzies, the third Chief of SIS. "You've pulled me from an urgent meeting. I have to tell you, I find your coming directly to me highly irregular."

"This line is secure, sir?" Wells asked.

"Yes. Damn it," said C, "I am on the HQ secure trunk line. So speak freely and get on with it already."

"Sir, I have just received information from a field operative that Prime Minister Churchill's life may be endangered. Imminently."

"Exactly how so, Wells?"

"Well, sir," Wincer replied, "it appears the Germans claim to have embedded one of their own, or someone loyal to them, in the PM's Flamingo fighter escort group with the intention of downing his transport. *Operation Predator*, they are calling it, sir. What better way to take out a sizable chunk of our government? I understand the PM rarely flies alone."

"Sounds extraordinary, Wells," said Menzies. "Has your man been drinking? Heavily?"

"No sir," Wells replied, and opted not to include that Einar had been medically sedated. "Source of the material was General Dietl himself. Hitler's favorite general, no less."

"Yes, I am rather aware of General Dietl, Wells," scolded Menzies. "How did your man speak directly to Dietl?"

As the question was asked, the operator handed another random text string to Wells, who attempted to decode it while he spoke to C.

"No sir, it was through another German officer. A lieutenant colonel."

"Are you sure it wasn't from their bloody cook?" "C" laughed, "A lieutenant colonel? Really, Wells!"

Wincer went on to explain the May 10 connection, as well as his man being held captive by the Hun at the time. Then "C" asked for this German Lieutenant Colonel's name. Luckily, Wells had just decoded it.

"Alois Becker, sir."

"I have never come across this name in all my life," "C" replied, "but if the potential threat is to the PM, then I need to treat it as such." He then spoke to an aide, but Wells could hear the order, "Harris, get me everything we have on a Boche Lieutenant Colonel Alois Becker. Top Priority. Wells, still there?"

"Yes, sir," replied Wells, "I am here."

"Wells, you had better be right about this," Menzies then said. "Sounds like an elegant disinformation campaign to me. As it is, I have to tell the RAF leadership that one of their most select pilots just might be a Boche spy. Not the best way to gain their confidence if its all nothing more than a red herring, is it?"

"No sir," said Wells, before adding, "I understand the PM's in the Flamingo as we speak sir?"

"Interesting, and just how might you know that, Wells?"

"Just a source, sir," he answered.

"Well," Menzies said, "tell your *source* that Mr. Churchill just landed in Tours at an airfield. Safe and sound as the pound on the ground. Now I have to get busy and vet his escort group before they fly back tomorrow. Stay put at Scapa Flow, Wells, or if you must leave, be sure to let your '*source*' know where she can you reach you."

The last statement was Menzies way of telling Wells that he knew Wincer had pressured his secretary, Miss Penny Quidling, into revealing information she should not have. The tone of "C's" words told him he found this approach to be most distasteful.

Earlier that day, the 11th of June, Churchill had made his fourth trip to France since the war had begun. They had departed London at approximately 2 PM for the roughly two hour flight. Escorting the Prime Minister's de Havilland Flamingo transport aircraft were a dozen RAF Spitfires. Traveling with Churchill were the Secretary of State for War, Anthony Eden, also Churchill's Chief Military Assistant, General Hastings "Pug" Ismay, and the Chief of Imperial General Staff (CIGS), General John Dill. Due to the incursion of the *Wehrmacht* deep into France and more specifically the air threat posed by the *Luftwaffe*, the Flamingo that carried this group had to swing far westward out over the Atlantic.

Paris was no longer a viable meeting site, as the Panzers were already well on the road to the capital. The French Government had relocated southwestwardly towards Tours. The

Flamingo and her escort fighters landed at a small airfield identified to Churchill only that morning in his call from the French Premiere. The British party were then driven to a nearby chateau where the conference was held. The French were represented by Premiere Reynaud, Marshal Philippe Pétain, General Maxime Weygand and a very young and upcoming General named Charles de Gaulle.

The French had advocated for more air squadrons from England to be diverted to fight the *Luftwaffe* in the skies over France. Churchill and the other Britons told the French that this was not possible, that they would be needed to stave off the upcoming air assault on England expected in advance of invasion. The French then replied that they had not much else with which to resist the devastating Nazi Blitzkrieg tactics. Despite Churchill's pleas for them to continue on, the French were ready to surrender in order to prevent the destruction of the remaining provinces and cities of her homeland, most especially the jewel of Paris.

Further discussions ensued, including very late in the day the topic of moving the Polish Army upon their return from Narvik, to a new location in the Scottish Highlands. The Polish fighter pilots in France, who had finally been released to fight against the *Luftwaffe*, would relocate to London and be incorporated into the RAF. Sikorski was not present, but Reynaud represented his interests faithfully. Finally, Churchill gave his assurances that the Polish Government-in-Exile would be relocated to London, along with its fighter pilots, as soon as was possible. The Polish Rifle Brigade returning from Narvik might be desperately needed in France, but immediately afterwards they would be transported by ship to Scotland.

It was shortly after this discussion that the MI6 "C" Stewart Menzies made contact with the group to raise the suspected threat. Menzies and his trusted staff members had been pouring over the backgrounds of the fighters that had flown protecting Churchill. At least half of these men had distant, and in some cases not-so-distant relations to German, Austrian, Czech or even Alsatian family groups. Others had travelled extensively abroad in Germany prior to the war. In the end, Menzies and his team could not fully assure that any one of the twelve was "pristine" in regard to potential German collusion. At least, not yet. "C" requested another twenty-four hours to continue the vetting, or fly in pilots trusted by the intelligence service. Someone quipped in response that given another twenty-four hours their current position would likely be surrounded.

The British leadership retired that evening agreeing to make the final decision the next morning. Overnight, Churchill had come to the conclusion that it was absolutely essential that he be back in London on the evening of the twelfth, and that if necessary he would fly home without any escort at all. He offered that any of his companions that found this approach overly risky could stay behind and arrange alternate accommodations, but the Flamingo would, given the intelligence forewarning, return home solo.

There was great discussion that morning. Many felt that this was surely a German disinformation campaign, designed to do exactly what Churchill planned to do, that is, to drop his escort group entirely. Despite this, Churchill stood his ground.

The military aides amongst them asked what excuse they would give the dozen fighter pilots. It was agreed to tell them that there was a severe lack of petrol to fuel the fighters.

"They will ask the obvious question," someone argued, "in all of France enough petrol could not be found for even one or two Hurricanes to make the flight back with the Flamingo?"

"Then let them wonder," said Churchill. "Tell them the bloody weather will not support their fighters. After all, as I am told, there is to be heavy cloud cover all the way along our route back to London."

As it was, the French Premiere Reynaud was on the phone that morning with General Sikorski updating him on the outcome of the previous night's discussions, when he mentioned that the Prime Minister's Flamingo would be flying home unescorted. Instantly, Sikorski volunteered his pilot, Bogdan Bratajewski, who had been trained as a fighter pilot, to accompany the Flamingo. This offer was extended to the British entourage, but instantly rejected.

"Ok, Diane," said Wade, "I gotta throw the bullshit flag on all of this. You expect us to believe that Daddy's *half-brother* Einar got wind of this plan to shoot down Winston Churchill and that the old bulldog actually gave up his fighter based on some second-hand intel squeezed out of a drunk German colonel?"

"Lieutenant colonel," corrected Flake Ferris, drawing a scorching look from Diane that said, *I don't need any help.*

Diane had listened to Wade's outburst and turned next to look at Jake Conley. Mistakenly thinking that she wanted his support, Jake looked at her and simply said, "Diane, I was thinking along those same lines myself."

"Jake," Diane said as she shook her head no, "I wasn't going to ask you to bail me out. I wanted to ask if you would mind my reading from your copy of Churchill's *The Second World War*".

"Be my guest," laughed Jake, "I knew there must be a good reason we were doing this here in the library."

Diane walked over to the shelf where she had spotted the beautifully bound six volume collection. She passed over the first volume entitled *"The Gathering Storm"* and picked up the second, *"The Grand Alliance"*. From her pocket she pulled a small pad, much like that of a reporter's, and flicked through the notes on it until she found the page number she needed. She then walked over to stand directly in front of Wade, who had voiced the objection.

"Wade," she said softly, "I want to read this passage of Churchill's own word verbatim to you."

"The morning was cloudy, thus making it impossible for the twelve Hurricanes to escort us. We had to choose between waiting till it cleared up or taking a chance in the Flamingo. We were assured it would be cloudy all the way. It was urgently necessary to get back home. Accordingly, we started for home alone, calling for an escort to join us over the Channel. As we approached the coast the skies cleared and presently became boundless. Eight thousand feet below us on our right hand was Havre, burning. The smoke drifted away to the eastward. No new escort was to be seen. Presently I noticed some consultations going on with the captain, and immediately after we dived to a hundred feet or so above the calm sea, where airplanes are often invisible. What had happened? I learned later that they had seen two German aircraft below us firing at fishing-boats. We were lucky that their pilots did not look upwards. The new escort met us as we approached the English shore, and the faithful Flamingo alighted safely at Herndon."

Then, a dead silence befell the room. Diane interrupted that uneasy quiet by adding, "This is a beautifully signed first edition, naturally, as you, Jake, would have nothing less in your library. And Wade, you don't have to take my word that in the Revised Edition of 1950, Churchill actually updated that passage to say that the reason was due to "Lack of suitable petrol made it impossible…" for the twelve fighters to escort the Flamingo. I have a photocopy of that passage in my papers. Churchill also updated those fighters to Spitfires, not Hurricanes. So, why the difference in wording? Who knows? The point is that Churchill indeed flew back to England that morning without an escort. That is a fact. And his transport nearly got engaged by the *Luftwaffe*. That is also a fact. As to the notes in the MI6 files regarding *Operation Predator,* it very clearly could have been a cleverly thought out deception. Or there could have been a real threat, but once the Germans observed that Churchill flew home unescorted, they must have realized their plan had become known to the British Secret Service."

"I see," said Wade, as he rubbed his chin, "that you have certainly done your homework."

"Well, here is another tidbit my team uncovered. In the weeks that followed this incident, all twelve pilots were rotated off the Flamingo escort detail. All but one were eventually returned to it."

"And, I assume the one who did not," said Wade, "came to a mysterious end?"

"Nothing mysterious about it," said Diane. "He was on routine air patrol over the Channel the next week when he was engaged by a Messerschmitt. Chased the German pilot back over the Belgium coast, where he abruptly reported a mechanical malfunction and landed. He was never heard from again. His family never recovered his body or came to know of where he was buried."

"I would say this little lady couldn't have burned you more, Wade, if you were soaked in creosote!" Jake interjected with a hearty slap of his thigh. "Now, c'mon, Diane. Let's get back to the story. I want to hear what happened to Einar."

Einar recovered amongst the other patients in the sick bay of the carrier *HMS Ark Royal* which was still delayed in the Norwegian Sea. They had launched another aerial assault on the *Scharnhorst* in Trondheim, this time in the early hours of the thirteenth. The attack was yet another disaster, as eight of the fifteen dive bombers sortied against the German pocket-battleship were shot down. Of the remaining seven, only one bomb hit its target, and even that failed to detonate. In addition to all this futility, two of the carrier's escort destroyers collided in the heavy sea fog during the launching of the ill-fated raid.

Einar by then had satisfied himself that he had honored his brother's sacrifice. Prime Minister Churchill had returned safely home to London, this much had been reported back to him. Whether *Operation Predator* was real, or only a disinformation deception, Churchill was safe. That was what weighed so heavily on Gunnar's mind in his final seconds.

As for the state of Einar's mind, it was conflicted still. Of course, he bore the crushing weight of mourning for the loss of his twin brother, but within this deep trough of despair raged another conflict in his mind. He understood that his brother, Gunnar, already dying of his infected gunshot wound, prepared to commit suicide for no other reason than to free Einar from his pledge to stay by his side to his last breath. Yet, Einar could not allow his brother to take his own life and be eternally damned. So, Einar instead carried the guilt of knowing that he had pulled the trigger that had ended his own twin brother's life. He would live the rest of his life wrestling with that decision, made under fire in that dark instant. He had killed his brother, damning himself, but in doing so had saved his brother from Hell's eternal flames.

The carrier *Ark Royal* finally made her destination of Scapa Flow late in the day on the 14th of June. Awaiting Einar was Wincer Wells, who had the wheelchair-bound lad brought over to the Intelligence HQ offices for a full debriefing.

"How long did the doctor tell you you'd be off your feet?" Wells asked.

"Six to eight weeks for the Achilles to heal," Einar answered. "By then the rest of the bruising will have taken care of itself."

"Terribly sorry about Gunnar," Wells said, almost casually.

"He should have never been there," Einar answered.

"You mustn't blame yourself, Einar, " Wells said.

"Yet, I do," answered the twin, "but still I blame you even more. Why couldn't you have just left us alone?"

Einar's anger emboldened the twin. Wells had treated Gunnar's death almost as something that must be gotten out of the way before the business at hand could be started.

"If that helps you deal with this tragedy," Wells responded coldly, "then rest it upon my shoulders. It can balance out against the other weight you'll be sure to bear upon me."

"That being what, exactly?" asked Einar.

"I didn't wish to burden you with this news whilst you were aboard *Ark Royal*," Wells said, "but I regret to inform you that your father perished on the last day of *Operation Dynamo*, rescuing our lads from the beaches at Dunkirk."

"Oh, my God, my poor mother," responded Einar, as his already reeling sanity took another heavy blow, like that of a fallen boxer unsuspecting another looming impact as soon as he staggered again to his feet. "What was he doing out there, given the condition of his leg?"

"I did everything I possibly could to get him off the *Nordlys,"* Wells said, prideful of it being true, "but your father demanded to carry on to the end. Got strafed by the *Luftwaffe* on what was likely to be his last run of the operation. It just may comfort you to know that by the count of our marines sent to assist him, the *Nordlys* under your father's command saved the lives of several thousand of those desperate boys."

"The *Nordlys* was lost as well?" asked Einar.

"I'm afraid so," said Wells, "your father went down with her. Look, should you need an hour or so to digest all this, I would certainly understand and accommodate you."

"No!" barked Einar. "Let's get on with this so I can get back to my mother at Broughty Ferry."

"Certainly," said a pleased Wincer Wells, and the debriefing commenced. It took place over the next six hours, with Wells extracting every possible remnant of memory from his agent. He scribed exhausting notes, those that some nearly eighty years later would be declassified and provided by Malcolm Devereaux to Diane Sterling.

Finally, at the end of the session, Wells briefed Einar on the events that surrounded the Prime Minister's return to London in the Flamingo unescorted.

"So, we may never truly know," Einar said, "if a Nazi agent had penetrated Churchill's escort detail as a pilot?"

"Likely, we will not," Wells replied, "but that is how this business plays out. One does his best to disrupt the enemy's plans, and in doing so may never know exactly how impactful their devious intentions could have been. I am sure of one thing though, had we lost Churchill, the rest of the buggers in the government would never have had the will to carry on the fight."

"So, Gunnar's sacrifice meant something," Einar said.

"The both of your sacrifices may just have saved England," Wells reinforced. Einar felt guilty, because even in the depth of their debrief he could not bring himself to tell Wells that it was he who had pulled the trigger that ended Gunnar's life.

"I assume this will enhance your standing within SIS?"

"To the contrary, I'm afraid," said Wells. "My superiors were incensed that I went directly to 'C' with this. I have become somewhat of a pariah amongst my own peers, it seems."

"I would have thought this information might have brought 'C' into Churchill's good light," Einar speculated.

"Entirely the opposite, I'm afraid," explained Wells. "The PM was miffed about being forced to fly back unescorted, and 'C' was held responsible for that."

"At least Churchill doesn't have to worry again about traveling to wartime France," Einar stated.

"Again, just the opposite, lad. That tenacious Bulldog went back to Tours yesterday morning, with an entirely new slate of escort pilots, mind you," said Wells. "Just couldn't stay away. They reported that the airfield they had just departed from the day before had been bombed overnight, and the Flamingo and the fighters had to avoid the craters upon landing. Met with the French Premiere one last time."

"Why on Earth would he think it necessary to return there?" Einar asked.

"Trying desperately to keep them in the fight, I suppose," answered Wells. "They don't exactly clear all this with me, mind you. They flew back last evening, full escort, plenty of petrol, clear skies, totally uneventful. But who knows when or where old Winston will be off to next. He is drawn to the excitement, like a gadfly to the flame."

"What bothers me," explained Einar, as if he were asked, "is that if the Germans had an agent amongst the escort pilots, why hadn't they blown the PM out of the sky earlier?"

"I have given some thought to that," stated Wells, "and there appears to be two plausible answers. First, and most likely, they were waiting until they could pull off downing Churchill without their agent doing the actual firing. You don't spend that much effort getting someone so well placed to give him up so easily. He could have been passing info to the enemy in-flight that somehow tracked where he, and thus Churchill, was."

"What, like a homing pigeon following the Flamingo?" asked Einar.

"Does it not seem odd to you that the very airfield Churchill departed from on the twelfth was bombed before he could return on the thirteenth?"

"Yes, very much so," admitted Einar. "So what is your second reasoning?"

"The most obvious, dear boy," laughed Wells, "that there never was an imbedded German pilot, and this was all merely a ploy to get the PM to drop his escort, lower his guard, so to speak."

"To what end," asked Einar, "hopeful that by luck the *Luftwaffe* might stumble upon the unescorted Flamingo?"

"Oddly enough," Wells said, as if this had been something of a thorn in his side, "The Polish General Sikorski immediately offered his pilot to fly as a lone fighter escort for the PM back to England on the twelfth. Thank God that Churchill never went for it. Let's suppose that Sikorski's pilot, this man called Bogdan Bratajewski, was the real German agent the whole time. If so, these devious Boche bastards nearly succeeded."

"You really think this could be so?" Einar asked.

"I don't know," Wells answered, "but I have begun digging into this Bratajewski's past. Let's see just what we can uncover."

"Do you think the French will keep fighting, Wells?"

"Unfortunately," Wincer responded, "today, being the 14th of June 1940, will be entered into history as the day the *Wehrmacht* entered Paris. Even given this, the French carry on the fight in western France and in her southern mountains along the Rhine. But ask yourself, how much longer can the arms of a nation fight on when her beating heart has already been cut out?"

56 Last Gasps On the Continent

June 15-18, 1940

"We repeated now on a considerable scale, though with larger vessels, the Dunkirk evacuation."

Winston Spencer Churchill

The French did fight on, but only for four days after Paris fell. Even then the French did not fight alone. True as it was that the French continued to fight by themselves along the lower Rhine in the Vosgues Mountains, having by then already lost the towns of Colmar and Strasbourg, in the north of France the story was entirely different. The remaining British forces in France after the Dunkirk evacuation still numbered some 136,000 men, who fought on the northernmost Cherbourg Peninsula, as well as the western most peninsula of France, near the port city of Brest in the province known as Brittany.

The Polish Podhale Rifle Brigade had returned from Norway to that same French port by the 15th of June and immediately rushed forth to engage the Germans in the area to the south of St. Malo. Here in Brittany, the British and Polish forces fought alongside the French Tenth Army in what was becoming an increasingly fragmented defense.

On the 17th, the French Government, by then under the leadership of Marshal Pétain, agreed to a ceasefire of all French troops against the *Wehrmacht* in exchange for their agreement to establish a "free" French zone in the South to be ruled by Pétain's Government from the city of Vichy.

Figure 37: Churchill and de Gaulle in France June 1940

A day earlier, Premiere Paul Reynaud had tendered his resignation in disagreement with this path forward. Like Reynaud, there was another French leader who disagreed with this armistice. On the day of the eighteenth, General Charles de Gaulle, in defiance to his superiors, escaped his beloved country from an airfield in Bordeaux. He would carry forth, from abroad, the fight for France's independence.

With the signing of the armistice on the 18th of June, the French troops laid down their arms. The Poles and British continued to fight, but now only so that they could get back to their evacuation vessels at the ports of Cherbourg, St. Nazaire, St. Malo and Brest. From these ports, the last of the British troops would be removed from Continental Europe, but they would not depart alone.

The Polish Independent Podhale Rifle Brigade fought the Germans as late as the eighteenth. That day, at eleven o'clock in the morning, three armored Panzer columns came down upon them near St. Malo. The Poles, refusing to surrender, managed to fight their way back to Brest, and late in the day, boarded the British vessels that would allow them to continue their fight against Nazi Germany from the United Kingdom.

Earlier that day, Bogdan Bratajewski flew General Sikorski, his daughter Zofia and the highest ranking members of the Polish Government-in-Exile to London. There, they would continue to represent the nation that the Nazi war machine had first brutalized, and vowed to never stop fighting until Hitler and his third Reich were defeated.

A third element of the Polish emigrated war effort departed France in any manner they could. The Polish Air Force, consisting of some 8,000 men, commandeered French planes wherever possible. Those that could not fly directly to England made their way south to Algeria. Those that could not get a plane made their way to the closest ports to board ships. All in all, just as they had done some six months earlier, the Polish Air Force began to slowly arrive in yet another foreign country. This time it would be England, and the British would not know what to do with these pilots, as so very few of them spoke any English whatsoever.

It would take some time, but the British would ultimately find out exactly how valuable these pilots would become. In the immediate months ahead, the British would build aircraft faster then they could train pilots to fight the *Luftwaffe*.

On that awful dreary day, the 18th of June, Einar MacAlvor returned to Broughty Ferry to stay with his mother, Tilly. She was overcome with joy to see her son, but this was soon tempered when she saw the crushing weight that young Einar carried. It was not the gravity of recovering from his wounds, as he so nimbly offset these with the crutches as he hobbled off the train. It was something far darker, far more penitent. Something Tilly detected in her young Einar that he could not prevail over.

Tilly had not expected Einar to have been accompanied by his brother Gunnar. Days before Wells had had sent a telegram expressing his condolences for the loss of her other son. *The bastard knew all along that Gunnar had perished,* she had said to herself. *That is why he did not have the common courtesy to share this news earlier. Wincer had misled me just to escape off to Scapa Flow. This is the coward that Wincer Wells is.*

Tilly embraced Einar on the platform. The crutches made an awkward, stiff event. While she hugged him, she said, "Darling, I am so sorry to have heard about what happened to your broth…"

Einar pulled away from her, as much as was possible given the crutches, and cut a staring glance that ripped through her. It stabbed at her all the while her son visibly trembled in her eyes. That look seemed to say, *I will discuss anything with you, but not Gunnar's death. Not today. Only when I am strong and ready to do so.*

She had been forewarned by friends and neighbors to expect strange reactions from those returning from war. That their emotions could range from extreme volatile peaks to iced valleys of indifference in an instant. But this look was at once both vacuously emotionless and filled with an unspoken but raging terror. It was unlike any stare she had ever encountered in her life. Even her husband Brigand, on his darkest of days, had never produced any thing like it. Then it struck her why it terrorized her so. The look had produced in her the fear that Einar would go on to take himself from her, leaving her all alone with only her expectant child. This was a reality she could not bring herself to embrace.

"Come Einar," she said as the porter removed his duffel sack from the train, "we will catch a taxi home and get you all set up in the parlor."

She thought to herself, how appropriate that she should establish him there after it was the last refuge of his father. From one hobbled MacAlvor man to another, but at least this one's leg would heal. She could only hope that time would heal his soul as well.

Tilly paid a boy on the platform some change to carry the duffel sack to the cab. The ride home was short, and under any other condition, even the foulest of weather, she would have walked it. But given Einar's temporary disability, they rode home in the luxury of a cab.

Einar entered the cottage home upon the River Tay beachfront. He had negotiated the door and stood in the entryway leaning forward on his crutches. He looked upon the rooms where he and his brother had been raised.

Tilly had been forcing the taxi driver to accept payment, as the hack said he could not expect wounded veterans returning home to pay a fare. After failing with all other arguments, she countered that "technically" her son was not a veteran at all. Whatever that meant, he was unsure, but the cabbie's position then crumbled, and he accepted her payment. He carried the duffel sack to the door for her, but could no further with her son blocking the entryway.

It was then, from behind, that she noticed her Einar quietly sobbing, his shoulders gently heaving. The taxi driver must have also, for he dropped the duffel sack and returned to his motoring car with great uneasiness.

Tilly laid her right hand upon Einar's shoulder from behind. She could feel it tremble. She said simply, "Welcome home." The tremor then amplified to a full blown quake. She slid around him and flowed smoothly like an advancing morning mist engulfing a tree in the forest. From in front of him, she pried her arms under his, wedging out the wooden crutches that fell to the floor with a pair of discordant clacks.

Einar embraced the only woman he had ever known to be his mother. She felt him sob in a way that she had never remembered him having done so as a child. Gunnar, certainly, but never the strong and independent Einar. He had never in any way given in to fear or remorse that she could remember. Not to say he had never failed, only that he had no fear of failing.

She remembered that whenever Einar felt he had any failing, be it on the football or rugby pitch, or even sailing upon the sea with his father, he would always respond with an attitude of *I know I can do better*. And he always did. He would always return to the sport or task if only to prove to himself that he could indeed master it.

Tilly began to tremble with emotion herself. She wept along with Einar, and in doing so discovered this had a steadying effect upon him. Finally, when Einar had composed himself, she whispered to him, "Promise me that when you are ready, you will tell me everything."

He remained quiet for a second before saying, "I promise, Mother. Just give me the time I need to do so."

"Well, dear," she answered, "we appear to have all the time in the world, don't we, now?" She did not realize the full story just might take every bit of that span to be told.

At that Einar said exactly what was expected by Tilly.

"I was so sorry to hear about father," he said, "and I am embarrassed that I was not here to help you face that loss."

She wept anew in his arms. "Your father died saving soldiers' lives. Right up til the last hour. I had been told he was on one of the last runs along that beach. He would not quit so long as a single soldier needed to board the *Nordlys*."

Then, Einar asked the question of Tilly that she completely did not anticipate."Did he know?"

"What, of your brother's death? Of your situation? How possibly could he?"

Einar said nothing further, instead he gently placed the open palm of his hand on the small swell along her waist.

His mother's tears ran harder. Her lip quivered. Her eyes expressed her solemn surprise, followed by a sorrow of what could never be.

"Wincer told you," she said, "that bastard. I wanted to break the news to you that you were about to have a sister, or perhaps another brother."

"Did Father know?" Einar repeated, still holding his hand on her belly.

She lowered her head and simply answered, "No." She collected herself, before adding, "Your father was in a lowly state not knowing about you and your brother until the Dunkirk Operation came about. It lifted his spirits. I did not wish to interrupt that revival of spirit."

"So, at the time of his death, he did not know that he had lost one son," Einar said, "or that he potentially might have a replacement in the offing."

"Please don't hate me, Einar," Tilly said. "Your father's last message to me, from beyond the grave, as it were, was that he died an honorable death serving his country."

"Yes, he did," said Einar. "Dunkirk was a miracle."

"This child is a miracle," She replied. "I was told I could never have children again."

"After Gunnar and I were born?" Einar asked.

She would not lie to him. Yet, neither would she offer the truth. She merely smiled sadly and again lowered her head as if to cry.

"You must name the child after Father," Einar said, breaking the moment.

"I wished to, but he made me promise if we ever were to have a child, it was to be named after me. Matilda, or Matthew should it be a boy. I will honor his request."

"I will ask no further," Einar said. "I will stay with you long after my leg heals, until the birth and well beyond until you are on your feet again, Mother. After that, I will be off, on my own. Do you understand?"

Tilly could only nod in the affirmative. She could not bear to think of his being away from her again, but knew his personality would demand it. He had to conquer that at which he had failed. She then thought that she would focus on enjoying the upcoming months that they would be together, and she determined that she would make the most of each day.

With this, she led Einar to the parlor. The wooden crutches remained on the floor, and she instead became his human crutch. As they entered, he could see that she had outfitted it with a canvas cot upon which he would sleep.

"I thought there would be no sense in forcing you to climb the bloody stairs until you are ready to do so," she explained.

"Thank you," he answered, "this will be perfect until my leg heals. I had forgotten how lovely that view was."

He stared out across the Firth of Tay and onto the North Sea just beyond. She thought him lost in that gaze, not so much in distance as in time. Just as his father had so recently been. The only difference was she knew Einar would come back to her.

"I tell you what," she said, by then fully in command of her emotions once more, "you get settled in and I'll put the kettle on."

"A spot of tea would be grand," he said, still gazing out upon the sea. "In fact, Mother, I would like to propose a deal with you."

"A deal?" echoed Tilly from the kitchen only a few steps away. "Well, that depends on what my end of the bargain might be, doesn't it?"

"I will tell you the entire story of my and Gunnar's time in Norway if you allow me to do so over breakfast tea each morning."

"You think it will take more than one kettle?"

"I will tell you everything," Einar answered, "every action we took, every word we said to each other, every fear we shared, as honestly as my memory allows. So yes, it will take quite a few kettles of tea. I only ask that you allow me to tell it from the beginning, straight on through to the end. At my own pace."

"I most certainly can do that," Tilly said, "but I do have one proviso. You allow me to take notes such that I can complete an entry into my diary each night."

"Done," he said triumphantly.

"Not quite, dear," answered Tilly. "After all, what is my side of the bargain?"

"Ah yes," Einar said, "you will spend each afternoon with me reading Shakespeare, just as you used to do with my brother."

Tilly thought it a very unusual request for Einar, but quickly came to understand he thought it would be therapeutic to his dealing with Gunnar's death.

"You'll tire of that quickly, I'm sure" she snickered softly, "but, I agree. Tomorrow we'll begin with Macbeth. Only appropriate."

"Wonderful," he said, "but I rather we begin with those Henry's. *Henry IV. Part I* specifically."

It was then that the kitchen's kettle screamed with steam. It was a sound that Einar had terribly missed.

The next day was the 19th of June. In London, General Władysław Sikorski had a meeting with Winston Churchill where he committed all Polish forces, be they the Army, the Navy, or the Air Force, would fight on alongside the British forces for the duration of the war. Churchill welcomed this commitment gracefully, but must have been somewhat remiss about the limited size of these committed combatants. For the Polish Army extracted from Brest, in total, numbered only about twenty-thousand men. Later in the war, this number would swell to about a quarter of a million after the Soviet Union released the Polish Army prisoners held in Siberia to the command of Polish General Władysław Anders. In fact, General Anders' II Corps Army would go on to fight in Syria, North Africa, and Monte Casino, Italy with extreme valor.

The Polish Navy had been the first of the country's forces to come to Britain under *Operation Peking*. This force was very small, numbering only the 3 destroyers, and 2 submarines. These ships sailed from their Polish ports just days before the war started and arrived at the British Naval Station along the Leith Docks in Edinburgh on September 1 at about five in the evening. Of the three destroyers, by the time of Sikorski's meeting with Churchill, the Polish destroyer *Grom* had already been sunk in service at Narvik during the preceding month.

The next most immediate contribution would come from the Polish Airmen. Some eight thousand pilots and ground crew arrived in the United Kingdom only a month before the Battle of Britain was to commence. It would prove to be a battle in which these Polish pilots would play a considerable role.

As Sikorski pledged the allegiance of the troops under his command to Churchill, an ominous group was consolidating in Germany. For ten months earlier, on the very first day of the war, September 1, 1939, a group of German scientists formed what was known as the *Uranverein*. Their responsibility was to determine the feasibility of weaponizing the newly discovered science of the theoretical fission of uranium.

The head of this quest for a Nazi nuclear bomb was a world renowned research physicist by the name of Werner

Heisenberg. Heisenberg had done ground breaking research in subatomic physics, and in 1932, when he was only thirty years old, was awarded a Nobel Prize "for the creation of quantum mechanics."

Werner Heisenberg would go on to become the leading nuclear physicist driving the effort to produce weapons and energy from uranium. There were two approaches that appeared feasible. The first was the approach that the United States would undertake with its *Manhattan Project*: to enrich uranium into its pure state known as the isotope U235. But of all the natural uranium mined throughout the world, less than one percent is U235. The remaining is the non-fissile isotope U238. Therefore tremendous quantities of natural uranium needed to be separated by large industrial centrifuges, (as would later secretly be built in 1942 at Oak Ridge, Tennessee) in order to render the amount of U235 needed to build a weapon.

In Germany, Heisenberg did not have access to this level of separation technology, and thus he experimented with the concept of a natural uranium reactor. In theory, it used layered quantities of natural uranium and a material known as a moderator. The function of the moderator was to slow down the neutrons freed during fission of each uranium atom to a slow enough speed so that it could collide with another uranium atom and keep the chain reaction process going. If the neutrons moved too quickly, the chain reaction could not be maintained. Without the chain reaction, there could be no energy generated,, and no atomic bomb. Natural uranium was readily available. Heisenberg viewed the moderator as the material most critical to his efforts.

The material Heisenberg so desperately needed to moderate the process was called *"Heavy Water"*. It was a relatively newly discovered compound, and required extreme amounts of electricity to create. It had been found almost by accident. During the Second World War, it was only produced in a single facility in the entire world. That facility, known as the Vemork Hydroelectric Plant was run by the Norwegian company Norsk Hydro in the Rjukan Valley in southern Norway. The Rjukan Valley opens as it runs east, until its stream flows into one of the deepest lakes in Europe, the *Tinnsjå*, or Lake Tinn

The Vemork facility was located at the bottom of a very steep cliff, and had been established to harness the nearly uninterrupted flow of water descending from the high plateau above. This continuous waterfall was soon harnessed as uninterruptible hydroelectric power once this plant was constructed. That hydro-power was used to create nitrogen and ammonia based fertilizer products.

Soon it was discovered another product of the electrolysis process used to make these products was heavy water, or water produced with one or both hydrogen items replaced by their higher weight isotope of deuterium. The deuterium oxide, or D_20, was the heavy water needed so critically for Werner Heisenberg's research.

The mass of this heavy water proved to be perfect for moderating, or slowing, the speeds of neutrons such that an atomic chain reaction could be sustained.

The French and British scientists took note of this rather specialized commodity. The French attempted to buy up all of Vemork's stock of heavy water at the onset of the war, just to keep it out of Heisenberg's reach. However, once Germany invaded Norway, this facility came rapidly under Nazi control.

When the war ministry of Great Britain noticed the level of security the Nazis were applying to the Vemork facility, it did not take them long to understand why the Reich was so interested in controlling this unique production process.

Churchill knew exactly what was at risk. In his famous *"Finest Hour"* speech, rallying the British people to stand firm against Hitler, Churchill included the following passage:

But if we fail, then the whole world, including the United States, including all that we have known and cared for, will sink into the abyss of a new dark age made more sinister, and perhaps more protracted, by the lights of perverted science.

The Norsk Hydro company's Vemork facility in the *Rjukan Valley* of southern Norway near Lake Tinn was certainly one of those "lights of perverted science." It would become the most prominent target of the soon-to-be-formed Special Operations Executive.

Figure 38: Fighting Soldiers of the Polish Independent Rifle (Highland) Brigade Deployed at Narvik (top), and (bottom) General Sikorski Presentation of the Virtuti Militari to that Operational Unit (July 21, 1940)

57 New Beginnings

June - December 1940

"...the Battle of France is over. The Battle of Britain is about to begin, upon this battle depends the survival of Christian civilization, upon it depends our own British life and the long continuity of our institution and our Empire."

Winston Spencer Churchill

Churchill immortalized these words just hours after the last of the last British forces were evacuated from France on June 18, 1940, some two weeks *after* Dunkirk. The speech was given on an auspicious British historical date - the 125th anniversary of the Battle of Waterloo. Like the English legendary Iron Duke, Wellington, defeating Napoleon Bonaparte, Churchill called on his countrymen to stand up to another egotist usurper of unimaginable power in Hitler:

*Let us therefore brace ourselves to our duties, and so bear ourselves, that if the British Empire and its Commonwealth last for a thousand years, men will still say, "**This was their finest hour.**"*

Churchill knew that Hitler would next attack England. He used this speech to prepare his countrymen for the invasion of their home islands. Churchill was certainly savvy enough to realize that before any invasion vessels could be launched across the Channel, the *Luftwaffe* would first have to clear the skies overhead.

In any case, with the exception of General de Gaulle and the French Resistance, France would fight on no longer. England would essentially stand alone. Yet not truly alone, for within her numbers she counted the forces of the entire Polish Army, Navy and Air Force as well as the Norwegian Governments-in-Exile. These two relatively small Allied forces would soon prove themselves invaluable on two separate occasions, both of which would have a most immediate impact on the war.

It was in July of 1940 that two events of considerable importance took place. First, on the tenth of that month, the Battle of Britain began as the *Luftwaffe* attacked southern England. Second, twelve days later Winston Churchill established the Special Operation Executive (SOE) as a commando organization, aligned to, but independent of, British Intelligence and all branches of the Royal military. It was chartered to conduct sabotage and resistance efforts on the Continent. Or as Churchill more colorfully described it, "*To set Europe ablaze!*"

The SOE was carved out from portions of other existing military and intelligence organizations. From MI6, the logical contribution was Section D, as in "*D for Destruction*", that in which Wincer Wells was employed. From July 22, 1940, on, Wincer Wells was no longer a member of MI6. The SOE was officially independent of MI6 and as such became somewhat of a natural competitor. Wells had by that time gone from being in "C's" inner circle to being a mid-level agent in a rival organization. And one of the SOE's first projects was to cripple the heavy water production facilities at the Vemork plant in Norway.

This should prove beneficial for me, thought Wells. After all, he had been running agents in Norway prior to joining the SOE. He soon found out, however, that his new chain of superiors thought themselves to be just that - *superior* - to the efforts of MI6 in Norway during the Narvik battles.

In fact, the SOE set-up their own training facility in the Scottish Highlands for the training of Norwegian commandos who would participate in the heavy water operations. The SOE took over the STS26 Scottish Highlands Training Facility where the twins had prepared for Narvik. *Damn my luck*, Wells thought, *I need to stay as far from Drumintoul Lodge as possible. Damn those forged MI6 orders regarding Gunnar's deployment.*

Wells got his wish, but was in for something of a shock, as he was merely given responsibility for running the interpreters and was assigned as the lead for the London based communication team that would be in contact with any agents to be later deployed to Norway. To his dismay, he would take no significant role in the planning, training or execution of the Norwegian plant raids themselves.

The same month that Churchill ordered the SOE to be established came the beginning of the Battle of Britain. Hermann Göring had been humiliated when his *Luftwaffe* had been neutralized by the RAF in the skies over Dunkirk. He had subsequently boasted to Hitler that he would wipe the RAF from the skies over the Channel altogether. Gaining air superiority was a critical precursor to the invasion of England, code named by the Germans as "*Operation Sea Lion*".

The formal beginning of the Battle of Britain started on 10 July 1940. That battle has been been officially recognized to have lasted for just under four months, ending on 31 October 1940. Not that all *Luftwaffe* raids ceased after this day, for the bombing of London would go on through May 11 of the following year.

During these three months and three weeks of extreme aerial combat, over fourteen thousand civilians were killed and another twenty thousand wounded. In addition to this, the "British" forces lost nearly fifteen hundred airmen and over seventeen hundred aircraft. As daunting as these numbers were, the *Luftwaffe* lost nearly twenty-six hundred pilots, as well another seven hundred wounded and over nine hundred captured. All told, this represented a staggering forty-one hundred pilots lost to the *Luftwaffe* for the purposes of waging war. Additionally, the German air force lost nearly two thousand aircraft.

With this level of attrition, it was clear that skilled pilots were the most precious resource. Aircraft could be, and were replaced with increasing capabilites in England's factories. However, a pilot's skills took time to develop. Time was a commodity that the British could ill-afford.

Ultimately, victory was achieved by the "British" forces. As it turned out, nearly one quarter of all pilots employed in the defense of England during this battle were not British at all. Some were New Zealanders, Canadians, Australians, as might be expected. Even nine Americans were recognized as having flown at least one sortie during this battle, but the largest non-English speaking flyers were the Poles and Czechs. But before the RAF would even allow them to fly, things had to become very dour indeed.

Initially, The German *Luftwaffe* concentrated on attacking aircraft and airfields, as well as aircraft manufacturing factories in the south of England. Their pilots could not understand why whenever they flew across the channel they seemed to be instantly engaged by the RAF. How did they know where to find them in the skies?

The answer was two fold. First, the British Universities had only recently been investigating the 1935 discovery by Scottish scientist Robert Watson-Watt of using reflected radio waves to identify and track the location of aircraft. The RAF under Commander-in-Chief Air Marshal Hugh Dowding was quick to recognize the potential of this newly emerging technology of RAdio Detection And Ranging, or RADAR. Towers were set up along the coast of the south of England and proved immediately capable of sensing enemy squadrons forming up over the shores of France, Belgium and the Netherlands.

The second innovation introduced by Air Marshal Dowding was to have all radar, on-ground spotters and squadron status called into a west London facility in Uxbridge (just north of today's Heathrow Airport) where the information was "displayed" on a table-top map of the United Kingdom and surrounding locales. Markers bearing the information of enemy and friendly squadrons were pushed about that map by women with long curved sticks not unlike that of a casino's craps stickman. Thus, Dowding had achieved a primitive level of "data fusion", a term used in modern jet fighters.

The result that even as the *Luftwaffe* attack aircraft were forming up over the continent, the RAF could scramble their fighters and in real time direct them to intercept the German aircraft. Typically the RAF fighters would climb high and drop down on the *Luftwaffe* aircraft from seemingly out of nowhere.

Without the rapid advent of radar, it is easy to understand that the RAF would never have stood a sporting chance.

Even given this advantage, the early going in the Battle of Britain was admittedly going in Germany's favor. While the aircrews were mostly already airborne by the time the *Luftwaffe* arrived over southern England, much damage was done to air squadron installations on the ground. Also, aircraft factories were heavily targeted. But the greatest disadvantage was in sheer numbers, as the RAF was considerably outnumbered in the number of fighter aircraft and trained fighter pilots.

Bogdan had spent a grueling summer of 1940 as the personal pilot of General Sikorski, constantly transporting him throughout England and Scotland for this or that ceremonial review of troops, ships, or to meet local politicians in provinces housing Polish troops.

On the 20th of July that year, Bogdan had flown the general to the Scotland Highlands, where on the next day Sikorski presented the highest honor of the Polish military - the *Virtuti Militari* - to the Polish Independent Highland Brigade, as the Rifle Brigade would then be known. It was earned in recognition of their heroic service at Narvik. A young Polish corpsman knelt in the Scottish grass and lowered the regiment's Standard, as General Sikorski stepped forward solemnly to attach the award in the form of a black and blue ribboned sash to hang proudly from its flagstaff.

Next, General Sikorski awarded the same decoration, this time in the form of the traditional ribboned medal to the two commanding officers of the Narvik campaign. First to the Norwegian General Fleisher, and then to the Polish General Bohusz-Szyszko who had commanded the Brigade. For the Polish general, it was the second *Virtuti Militari* medal he had earned for service to the homeland in battling fascism.

Then, the *Virtuti Militari* medals were pinned on to those who had served with distinction in Norway. This group stood at attention in their long flowing capes and donning their crested campaign helmets. It included one soldier on crutches, an eighteen year old Polish soldier who had lost his leg in those mountains. Also awarded were two female Red Cross nurses who served in the field throughout the campaign.

Then the general approached Bogdan himself, and presented him the *Virtuti Militari* medal posthumously awarded to his brother, Albin. Next to him stood another man on crutches, the man who his brother, Albin, had saved by giving up his own life. The Scotsman named Einar MacAlvor, who had been invited to attend the ceremony.

Bogdan had been told in advance the general would be presenting Albin's medal to him, and he prepared himself to receive it. Yet, as the man his brother had given his life to save stood next to him, still recovering from his wounds, Bogdan could barely combat the emotions within him threatening to spring forth. In the end, his feelings of pride for his brother overwhelmed him, far beyond any level he had anticipated.

After the ceremony, Bogdan watched as the man's mother - at least he presumed it to be his mother - came from the crowd and stood beside her son. Bogdan walked up to her, knelt and kissed her hand. A light gust of Highlands wind blew through his thick brown hair. In what little English he had mastered for the occasion, the Pole said, "I understand, Madame, that you have lost another son. For this I am most profoundly sorry."

The woman looked on him with a great and sincere pity. "Thanks only to the bravery and sacrifice of your brother," Tilly MacAlvor said, "I still have a son to comfort me. My family owes your family a life. It is a debt I'll never be able to repay."

The general's interpreter, for even Sikorski's English was limited, stepped forward and translated her comments to Bogdan. At this moment, the pilot could no longer contain his feelings and a small trickle of tears ran from his eyes. Still kneeling in front of her, Bogdan lowered his head so that they would not be seen.

Tilly bent forward and gently grasped Bogdan's strong jawline. She lifted his head until his eyes met hers. She then leaned forward and kissed the tears escaping his eyes, first from the right, then turning his head, from the left. The interpreter then translated her next comment.

"There is nothing more sacred than the sadness of one brother mourning another. God bless you for all the pain you bear this day. May it fade away quickly and be forever replaced by the pride for your brother that I know swells within you."

With that she turned and escorted her son Einar from the ceremony grounds.

A month later, the Polish pilot found himself ordered by General Sikorski to take two days off to regenerate his energy. On the Saturday afternoon of August 20, Bogdan could think of no better way to enjoy a day of rest than to be with other Polish pilots. He had recently learned that the 303 Squadron of Polish airmen had recently been relocated from Blackpool to Northolt Air Base, only a stone's throw from the Uxbridge RAF Operations Centre on the Northwest side of London.

Bogdan was dropped by Sikorski's driver at the base. He had been granted a pass to stay the night with his fellow pilots at their quarters with the general's blessings. Bogdan dropped his overnight duffel in the squadron's common room, then walked out onto the field to find his old mates. These were the men he had trained with at Dęblin in Poland before the war, and with who he had visited regularly in France.

Bogdan was shocked to find these highly trained combat pilots outside in a training exercise on bicycles. Their instructor was attempting to teach them British flying formations before they would ever be allowed to take the Hurricane fighters slotted to their squadrons to the skies.

Bogdan waited until the pilots were released, at which they quickly came over to see him.

"Well, well," said a pilot named Zygmunt, "if it isn't our comrade Bogdan the bus driver? What brings you to Northolt?"

Bogdan had always enjoyed the spirited camaraderie of these men, and never took their derision of his having failed out of fighter training as anything but playful banter.

"General Sikorski ordered me to take two days off," replied Bogdan, "and I thought I would put them to good use to learn how to ride bicycles."

"Aren't you afraid you'll fail out and be given a tricycle?" replied Zygmunt after Bogdan's own riposte.

"Behave yourself, Ziggy," said another pilot named Jan. "*Witamy*, Bogdan, it is good to hear your voice and to see you standing here with us. We heard you were coming. Tonight we will drink vodka in the officer's club like old times. Come, let me show you to your bunk for tonight."

At this, the scramble siren wailed, and the squadron of British fighters colocated with the 303 soon came running excitedly to their aircraft.

"They are all so young," said Zygmunt as he jealously watched them take to their aircraft to intercept the *Luftwaffe*.

"They are no younger than you were when you began training at Dęblin," replied Bogdan.

"But they are so inexperienced," clarified Jan, "many are not coming back from their first missions against the Germans. It is a sin, while the British have so many experienced fighter pilots in us and the Czechs who they will not allow to take flight."

A third pilot named Zdzislaw then added, "they have us relegated to bicycles to learn British formations, or classrooms to learn English. All the while they have these wonderful Hurricanes, so much better designed aircraft than the old PZL's we were fighting the Germans in over Poland. They have gear that retract up into the aircraft. The speed is incredible."

"Yes, that is part of the problem," admitted Jan. He said nothing further, but Bogdan understood.

General Sikorski had been fighting with the British RAF leaders to get these men in the air, to join the fight. The Battle of Britain had been raging by then for six weeks, and had not been going well for the British. They had barely been able to hold on. The pilots they were forced to put in the air included many who had come out of initial combat training. All the while these battle experienced Polish pilots remained grounded. Part of the issue was that during the first training sorties they were allowed, the Polish pilots on more than one occasion failed to lower the gear before landing. They were not used to aircraft with retractable gear and had simply forgotten that the gear were retracted. The resulting belly landings on the grass fields did terrible damage to the Hurricane fighters, although both pilots and aircraft survived. However, these cases were brought up time and time again to General Sikorski as evidence that these men were not ready to engage the *Luftwaffe*.

"I know from my position that General Sikorski is fighting hard for you all to get back up in the air again," said Bogdan. "After all, when the French got desperate enough they allowed you to fly, didn't they?"

"Yes, they finally did," admitted Zygmunt.

"So who is the ace among you all?" asked Bogdan.

"That would be Josef František," said Jan. "He is credited with 11 *Adolfs* in his fighting over Poland and France."

"František, the Czech pilot?" exclaimed Bogdan. The thought of a Czech taking away a position that he, a Pole, so desired, gnawed at him.

"He is one of us, now," said Jan. "He refuses to fly with the Czech squadrons. He says he trained with us in Poland at Dęblin, and will only fly alongside Polish airmen."

"And what is this *Adolfs* business," asked Bogdan.

"It is what we have taken to calling kills of *Luftwaffe* aircraft," replied Zdzyslaw, "and we are eager to get more, many more, my friend."

"I am certain you will get your chance soon enough," said Bogdan, "as General Sikorski continues to fight for you. Just be sure that his efforts are well rewarded by your performance once you all get your wings."

"Don't worry, bus driving Bogdan," said Zygmunt. "We have weeded out those who could fly but not fight long ago." Despite Zygmunt's ribbing Bogdan enjoyed his two days with the squadron, which he learned had taken the historic name of the Kościuszko Squadron from the Polish Soviet War of 1920. They adopted an updated version of that unit's insignia, which was painted on each of the unit's Hawker Hurricane aircraft.

"That is a very significant name to take on," said Bogdan that night over vodka.

"Don't worry my friend," said Jan, "with what they have done to our country and our families still there, we will have no problem living up to it."

And they did not. For after Bogdan departed from them, on the 30th of August 1940 the squadron would officially record its first kill during the Battle of Britain. On a training sortie that day, pilot Ludwik Paszkiewicz noticed another squadron engaging the *Luftwaffe* and broke away to shoot down a Messerschmitt Bf-110 fighter. The squadron was declared operational the very next day, which happened to be the one year anniversary of the eve of World War II.

The Polish airmen did indeed fight with distinction. Whether it had been due to their having trained on inferior aircraft in Poland, or just plain guts, the Poles would bear in much closer than other pilots on the *Luftwaffe* aircraft. They would close to within a hundred yards before triggering their guns. The result of this fearless tactic was staggering. Despite having started two months late, the 303 Kościuszko Squadron would go on to register more kills than any other squadron in the entire RAF during the Battle of Britain.

During the Battle of Britain, there was one day, September 15, 1940, on which Goering was committed to finally wipe out the RAF. He sent two of the largest formations of enemy aircraft that England had ever seen. That Sunday morning, Prime Minister Churchill and his wife Clementine happened to be visiting the Air Operations Centre at Uxbridge when hundreds of *Luftwaffe* aircraft were picked up by radar amassing over the continental coast. That morning the British skies were knotted in turbulent contrails as the RAF scrambled everything they had to defend their island. Included in this was the 303 Kościuszko squadron. No sooner had the skies cleared, after the dogfights and bombing ceased, an even larger mass of *Luftwaffe* aircraft were detected forming for an afternoon raid. As over four hundred enemy aircraft crossed the channel, the 303 and every other squadron in Britain were again scrambled. That day alone the 303 Squadron were credited with shooting down 15 *Luftwaffe* aircraft. September 15 is known to this day as Battle of Britain Day. Goering and his *Luftwaffe* failed in this all out gamble. Two days later Hitler called off plans for Operation Sea Lion - the Invasion of Britain.

The 303 Squadron blazed the path for other Polish fighter squadrons to get into the fray. In total, there would be sixteen Polish squadrons for a total of 145 Polish pilots. Thirty died in combat during the war. This ultimately included both the 303 Squadron pilots František and Paszkiewicz. The former pilot, Josef František, had by the time of his death, recorded 17 kills, and is acknowledged to this day as the overall "Ace of the Battle of Britain". The latter pilot, Ludwik Paszkiewicz, had a different sort of record, a diary written in its country's native language. After Paszkiewicz' death, that diary was continued by the squadron, eventually coming to number seven volumes.

The 303 Kościuszko squadron recorded 126 *Adolfs* by the end of the Battle of Britain, more than twice the number of the next highest performing of the other 66 RAF squadrons. By the end of the war, that number of kills had grown to 178.

Polish airmen were celebrated by Britons throughout the country for their heroics. At least one ball was thrown in their honor at the swanky Dorchester Hotel in London. The young

English girls were mesmerized by their Continental customs, including kissing a girl's hand upon greeting them. So adored were these Polish pilots that the shoulder patch "POLAND" began disappearing from their uniforms, as some non-Polish airmen were pilfering them just to impress and steal the affections of the girls and women of London.

Perhaps the Polish pilots' greatest recognition of all came after the war when Commander-in-Chief Air Marshal Sir Hugh Dowding captured the sentiment best in writing,

> *"Had it not been for the magnificent material contributed by the Polish squadrons and their unsurpassed gallantry, I hesitate to say that the outcome of the Battle (of Britain) would have been the same."*

In the late autumn of that year, Winston Churchill came north to Scotland at General Sikorski's invitation to review the Polish troops stationed there. The Polish I Corps, or First Armored Division had been given the responsibility for guarding some 200 kilometers of the eastern coast of Scotland from potential German invasion from Norway. They were stationed around along the coast from below the Firth of Forth, throughout the Edinburgh area to above Dundee on the Tay. These troops were under the command of Polish General Stanislaw Maczek.

General Maczek had fought the *Wehrmacht* during the invasion of Poland until September 20, 1939, when he was ordered to take his 10th Armored Division into Hungary. He and his troops then made their way to France, where they fought the much superior German Panzers before being ordered to evacuate to the UK. Their most recent assignment was to protect the Scottish eastern coast.

Churchill arrived on an unpleasant Scottish morning full of driving rain and howling winds. The Prime Minister was accompanied by his wife Clementine. General Sikorski in his capacity as Prime Minister-in-Exile accompanied them both as the Polish troops demonstrated their readiness for the fight.

Einar was made aware by Wincer Wells that the Prime Minister would be visiting the fortifications at St. Andrews that day as well. When told of this by her son, Tilly MacAlvor was extremely excited and begged that they attempt to see the Prime Minister. She had never seen Churchill in person, but she actually was more interested in seeing Lady Clementine.

Einar requested a pass, and thanks to Wells, was able to obtain seating under a covered review stand for his very pregnant mother. They saw both the Prime Minister and Lady Clementine up close, and left the town of St. Andrews thoroughly chilled but extremely satisfied. Wincer Wells was happy to do favors for the MacAlvors, not for what they had done in the past, but more so for what Einar could do for him one day in the future.

Einar stayed with his mother through the birth of his infant brother, Matthew, in late December. After the birth, he told his mother that he would stay with her through the end of May, after which he would be relocating to London to take up a position as a Norwegian communication specialist offered by Wincer Wells.

Tilly had expected it all along. She knew Einar always had been a child that should he fail at any undertaking would immediately get back into the game until he succeeded. She made him promise that he would never go back to Norway itself. Although Einar agreed, Tilly knew he would eventually return there. The call of his brother would be too powerful to resist.

Einar and Tilly had spent a perfectly lovely six months together, and she could look forward to another four until April. Her son had concluded telling her the entire story of his and Gunnar's time together in Norway. She had recorded all the details religiously in her diary. It was somehow therapeutic for her to record as it was for him in the telling. But what she did not know was that her son had decided to modify the ending. Instead of telling her the awful truth - that he, Einar, had pulled the trigger that killed Gunnar, if only to keep his brother from doing so himself - Einar instead told her that Gunnar had been killed by a bullet from the attacking *Gebirgsjäger* patrol.

Einar's justification for this was not to upset his pregnant mother with the truth. He told himself that he would correct it after the birth, but over the five months that followed he could not bring himself to do this. Just as Tilly could never bring herself to tell Einar she was, in fact, not his mother at all. Or that, by extension, the infant Matthew was only his half-brother.

58 A Year of Survival

1941

"Never in the field of human conflict was so much owed by so many to so few."

Winston Spencer Churchill

The RAF having won the Battle of Britain in the autumn of 1940 did little to end the *Luftwaffe* bombing of London. The *Luftwaffe* switched tactics to mostly nighttime bombing raids over London. The "Blitz", having started the first week of September 1940 would go on well into 1941. However, the failure during the Battle of the Blitz to have Britain capitulate solely to aerial attacks forced Hitler to realize he could not take England strictly with the *Luftwaffe*. Nor did he have the fleet required for a naval invasion after having lost so many destroyers at Narvik earlier that year. Having neither control of the skies nor a large enough naval armada, Hitler called off Operation Sea Lion on September 17, 1940.

Even after this point, the bombings continued. However, slowly they lost the fullness of their veracity. By January and February of 1941, the weather adversely affected *Luftwaffe* bombing capabilities, much to the delight of Britons across the Isles. On the morning of May 11, 1941, the last bombs of the Blitz which had reigned down in the overnight hours burned brightly in the British capital. The House of Commons in Parliament suffered a direct hit, although her chambers were empty. Nearly all railway operations into the capital were disrupted, as were the East End docks.

The Blitz had cost a terrible loss of civilian life. Over forty-three thousand civilians had been killed, and another fifty-thousand injured. Despite this tragic loss, Britain had persevered.

As May 11, 1941 marked the end of the Blitz, it was also notable for the incursion of another single *Luftwaffe* aircraft over the airspace of Scotland. On this Sunday, while taking in the diversion of a Marx Brothers film at a friend's country estate, Winston Churchill was made aware of the fact that a lone pilot had bailed out of a Messerschmitt Bf-110 fighter over Scotland, south of Glasgow at about 10:30 pm the night before. Upon capture he had given his name as *Hauptmann (Captain)* Alfred Horn, and said he carried an important message for the Duke of Hamilton. It was later determined that this pilot was none other than Rudolf Hess, the Deputy Führer of Nazi Germany.

Hess' plane had been detected and pursued. Nearly out of fuel on a clearly one-way mission, he climbed to several thousand feet and bailed out. Hess had injured his foot during the parachute landing. He had intended to reach Lord Hamilton's estate at Dungavel House. Hess' fighter crashed within a dozen miles of the property. He was found by a farmer in his field.

Lord Hamilton, who Hess had met at the 1936 Olympics in Berlin, had been on military duty at Edinburgh. Hamilton was notified and later that night interviewed Hess. Lord Hamilton, then in turn, notified his friend Winston Churchill on that same night of the 11th. Supposedly, Churchill was quoted as responding, *"Hess or no Hess, I'm going to watch the Marx Brothers."*

Rudolf Hess was treated for injuries in Glasgow. He was eventually transported to the Tower of London under heavy guard, before he eventually was granted more comfortable confinement.

Hess' mission was a fanatical one. Churchill defined a fanatic as *"...one who can't change his mind but won't change the subject."* A truer description could not be applied to Hess' message. He said his mission was of his own doing and was designed to convey a message to Lord Hamilton (who he mistakenly thought was a leader in an English anti-war movement). The message was that Hitler did not wish war with the British and only punished them so because of their leaders, meaning foremost Churchill himself, who would not agree to peace with Germany. Hitler would leave their Empire alone in exchange for their giving the Nazis a free hand in Europe and Russia, including all Asian Russian holdings. He denied that the Führer had any knowledge of his journey, nor that the Führer had any upcoming intent of invading Soviet Russia.

Hess claimed he only wished to see the unnecessary killing of women and children to stop when the English people came to their senses. Hess argued he had sacrificed spending the rest of the war without his own wife and children to bring this most urgent message to Lord Hamilton.

Hitler vehemently denounced Hess as a "deluded, deranged" individual. Perhaps Hitler needed to keep Russia and Italy from thinking he was trying to secure a separate peace with England. Yet, the timing of Hess' mission just as the last bombs of the Blitz were falling is intriguing, especially given Hess' comments relative to civilian casualties. Also interesting is that after this, the bulk of the *Luftwaffe* aircraft would be moved eastward, away from the Channel coast.

The questions posed to Hess about a planned German invasion of Russia were well informed based on information received via the Polish underground. It confirmed the arrival of numerous squadrons of *Luftwaffe* aircraft following the Blitz near the new border with Russia. The underground also noted throughout May and June of '41 a large number of *Wehrmacht* forces and equipment amassing along the Nazi-Soviet border. Prior to the 1939 invasion, Germany had no border with Russia until both powers attacked and divided Poland, once more erasing the country from Europe's map.

This information was relayed through secret channels to General Sikorski and the Government-in-Exile in London, who passed it on to Churchill's intelligence services. There is little doubt that the information was leaked to Stalin by the network of double agents he had embedded in the British Secret Service during the early 1930s. In fact, Kim Philby had himself warned the Soviets of the British Intelligence Service's knowledge of Hitler's preparations for an upcoming invasion, codenamed *"Operation Barbarossa"*.

Kim Philby, by this time, had already secured himself a position in MI6's Section D and was known well by Wincer Wells. Together, they had been absorbed into the SOE upon its creation. By then Philby had already established a substantial network of agents within MI6. During his time with the SOE, Kim Philby and his fellow Soviet spy, Guy Burgess, would teach raw recruits the methods of sabotage.

But Kim Philby was not the only source of warning to Stalin. The Soviet generals on the front had also warned Stalin of the Nazis' amassing of troops along their new shared border.

Despite the warnings, Stalin adamantly refused to believe that Hitler had turned his sights away from Britain and onto the Soviet's territory. He told his subordinates that *Der Führer* would never violate the non-aggression pact between the two countries. To do so would mean Germany would have to fight a war on two fronts, an extremely risky gamble. Also, Stalin insisted that Hitler was his staunchest ally, despite his professed hatred of the Bolsheviks and Communists in his published manifesto *"Mein Kampf"*.

Of course, Hitler unleashed his army on June 22, 1941, to invade Russia. With the onslaught of the *Wehrmacht's* attack, Stalin suffered a breakdown. He became a recluse inside his dacha near Moscow, cutting himself off from all military decision making. His generals, already extremely cautious from Stalin's purges of their ranks during the 1930s, were reticent to take decisive action on their own.

The results of Operation Barbarossa were nothing less than spectacular for *Der Führer* and his generals. The Russian forces along the border were routed, and the end of the year saw German forces advancing on the city of Leningrad (the Soviet name for Saint Petersburg) and just beyond Moscow's outer perimeter.

The year 1941 was a remarkable one for Władysław Sikorski as well. In the closing days of 1940, he had been promoted to *Generał Broni*, the rank of a three star general. The new year found him deploying Polish forces in Scotland. In March, Sikorski visited the United States. In April, he moved the Independent Carpathian Rifle Brigade, who like the Podhale Rifle Brigade had evacuated Poland, from the British Protectorate of Palestine to North Africa. There, they would support Britain's engagement of Rommel in the desert.

Then, with the surprise of having the Soviet Union as a newly made ally to Great Britain, Sikorski began negotiations with the Soviet Ambassador in London, Ivan Maisky. They together produced a pact that would allow joint cooperation between the Polish and Red Armies. One critical element of the pact was for the Soviets to release all Polish POW's and political prisoners. The Sikorski-Maisky Pact was signed in London on July 30, 1941.

Sikorski capped off his year with a visit to Moscow on December 5, 1941, just two days before the Japanese attack on Pearl Harbor and with the Battle for Moscow against the

Germans raging just outside the capital. Soviet Foreign Minister Vyacheslav Molotov awaited Sikorski's arrival at a frozen, snow-laden Moscow airfield. After receiving a military welcome, Sikorski was taken to the Kremlin where he held an audience with none other than Joseph Stalin.

A major discussion point between the two leaders regarded the deployment of Polish Army personnel who had been held in Russian captivity since 1939. One of those detained had been General Władysław Anders who had ben released from Moscow's notorious Lubyanka Prison as a result of the pact between the two nations. General Anders had been held there in isolation and was subjected to interrogations and torture.

Since the invasion of Poland beginning September 17, 1939, Polish Army personnel, including leadership, had been sent to camps scattered throughout Russia, mostly in Siberia. The question at hand was how could these newly freed men be congealed into one force and where would they be deployed.

General Sikorski wanted the Polish Army to fight alongside the Soviet Red Army on the Eastern front with Germany. General Anders, who had refused to agree to join the Red Army during his imprisonment at Lubyanka disagreed vehemently, opting to fight alongside the British in the Mediterranean. The Army was ultimately released to do so, and became known as the Polish II Corps, although Anders and his fellow emaciated former Soviet prisoners had to make their own way out of the USSR and through Iran to join British forces in Iraq.

To appease Stalin and Sikorski, a small division of Polish soldiers would fight alongside the Red Army and would be known as the Polish First Army.

As Bogdan flew General Sikorski back to London after the visit, the general joined him for a portion of the long flight in the cockpit where he shared with his friend and pilot his concerns.

"General Anders has no trust for the Soviets," the general said. "If I had been imprisoned in solitary confinement and mistreated as he has been, I would feel the same way. I am not worried. General Anders will lead these men back to the war and they will fight against the Nazi scourge. Of that I am most sure."

"If you will forgive my saying so, my General," Bogdan replied, "something clearly bothers you still. May I ask what it is?"

"You are very observant my friend," said General Sikorski. "My concern is this, after reviewing all the lists of the released army personnel, there are still tens of thousands of men unaccounted for. Stalin makes no attempt to answer my concerns, saying only they must be prisoners of the Germans. Yet our intelligence of the German prisoners of war is good. We could never account for every single soldier, mind you, but to have some thirty-thousand missing is impossible. This gnaws at me, my young airman."

One other event of 1941 deserves mentioning here. On February 25, the *Kriegsmarine* commissioned its newest and most powerful battleship, the *Tirpitz*. It was the sister ship of the *Bismarck*, and both were thought to be impenetrable to standard naval shells because of its superior armor over 20" thick. After the ceremony, the *Tirpitz* would begin sea trials in the Baltic.

Churchill had feared both *Tirpitz* and *Bismarck.* So much so that *Tirpitz* was bombed by the British while she was being constructed, but to no avail. Churchill's greatest concern was that either or both of the ships would make the open Atlantic and wreak havoc with the convoys bringing supplies from the United States. This was exactly Hitler's desire. However, this would prove to be an ill-advised usage of these behemoth warships, and this was demonstrated not long after *Tirpitz* had been entered into service.

In June of 1941, the *Bismarck,* along with the German destroyer *Prinz Eugen,* were sailed through the North Sea, along the coast of Norway, across the Norwegian Sea and then around Iceland to gain entry to the North Atlantic. She had been spotted by British reconnaissance aircraft and the *HMS Hood* and *HMS Prince of Wales* were sent to engage her. In the resulting sea battle, *Bismarck* quickly sank the *Hood*, which had been the most feared battleship of the British Navy for the past twenty years. However, due to damage from that battle, the *Bismarck* began to leak oil. She made a speed run heading back to Brest in occupied France. The British ships could not match her 30+ knots and

Bismarck was soon out of the range of their guns. She appeared to have escaped pursuit.

But because the *Prinz Eugen* kept sending *Bismarck* radio communication, English radio stations were able to triangulate and pinpoint both ships locations.

Bletchley Park Enigma intercepts had alerted the Admiralty that *Bismarck* was headed back to Brest. Knowing where she was and where she was heading, torpedo planes were sent to sink her. While they did not, they scored a direct hit disabling her rudders, which left her vulnerable, making circles in the open Atlantic. The trailing British flotilla caught up to her, and after a massive barrage, the *Bismarck* was sunk.

This left only her sister ship, *Tirpitz*, which Churchill had nicknamed "*the Beast*". In the autumn, *Tirpitz* was ordered to the fjords of Norway, where she would be readied to attack the new Arctic convoys transporting Allied supplies to Russia.

Having sunk the *Bismarck*, *"the Beast"* became Churchill's primary obsession.

Figure 39: Polish Pilots Pose (above) with Tailskin from the 178th German Plane Shot Down and (below) the Same Tailskin on Display at the Polish Institute and Sikorski Museum (London)

59 The Turning Tide

1942

"Do not let us speak of darker days; let us speak rather of sterner days. These are not dark days: these are great days – the greatest days our country has ever lived."

Winston Spencer Churchill

December of 1941 had seen Japan perpetrate the sneak attack on Pearl Harbor. As a result, the United States declared war on Japan. Fortunately for Winston Churchill, Adolf Hitler reciprocated by declaring war on America. A greater mistake could not have been made. Both Germany and Britain were limited in their war efforts by availability of resources. America, on the other hand, had a seemingly unlimited abundance of all necessary resources: natural resources in food, fuel and minerals; production resources in factories which could quickly be converted from consumer goods to supplying the weapons needed by the war; and human resources in soldiers that only needed to be trained to fight.

The year 1941 had demonstrated the devastation of the *Kriegsmarine* U-boats and surface ships in sinking incredible tonnages of supplies headed to Britain. But with the addition of American naval destroyer escorts added to Atlantic convoys, as well as submarine-hunting aircraft deployed from the coasts, along with decrypted information coming out of Bletchley Park under the program code-named *"Ultra"*, the tide began to shift. *Kriegsmariners* using the Enigma devices still thought their radio transmissions to be unbreakable, but each transmission gave away U-boat and surface ship positions. The truth was that the head start given the Bletchley Park team by the Poles resulted in the war turning in the Allies' favor as early as 1942.

Despite the success of the operations at Bletchley Park, the year began with a truly tragic event concerning the Polish cryptographers still working with French Intelligence. Gustave Bertrand, the French Intelligence officer known to the Poles as *"Bolek"* had established two secure sites for the Polish cryptographers. Several were located safely in French Algeria, but in order to more closely interact with the three primaries, Bertrand had Marian Rejewski, Jerzy Różycki and Henryk Zygalski moved to a country house in southern France near the town of Uzès, just west of Avignon. The location's code name was "*Cadix*". It was in Vichy France and interference from the Nazis was minimal. The three Polish code breakers lived there in relative safety under assumed names and false identities, all the while breaking Nazi codes for French Intelligence.

On the 9th of January, returning from a conference with his peers in Algiers, Jerzy Różycki boarded the passenger ship *Lamoricière* to cross the Mediterranean Sea to Marseilles. The weather turned bad and the seas heavy. The *Lamoricière* began to take on water, and off the coast of Spain's Balearic Islands, she sank. Jerzy Różycki, only 32, drowned and left behind his young wife of three years, *Basia,* and their two-year-old son, *Janusz*.

Einar MacAlvor spent the first half of the year 1942 as he had the last half of 1941. He had left his mother Tilly at Broughty Ferry in June '41. He returned to London as a communication officer for the team of Norwegian and British SOE agents preparing to be sent into southern Norway. Their target was the Vemork heavy water facilities in the Rjukan Valley. Einar would become their lifeline, the man on the other end of their radio communication link in London.

Einar found the work monotonous and unexciting. He had thought joining this operation in any capacity would have taken away the void in his life since losing his brother. While he understood the critical urgency to deny Germany's scientists this novel material, heavy water, Einar was not allowed to know exactly what its end use would potentially be. Even if he had been told, no one at that point knew what an atomic bomb was, or if it would ever come to even exist.

Einar had pleaded with Wincer Wells to allow him to train to be one of the British commandos who would raid the plant. Wells steadfastly denied him this role. Einar could not determine if Wells' denial was due either to the debacle of he and his brother's earlier deployment to Narvik, or was it due to Wells' internal guilt at having lost Gunnar. In either case, Einar would continue to volunteer for any opening in Norway, be it either in the Arctic or much further south, just so one day he might be closer to the final resting place of his brother.

Wincer Wells had denied Einar's request for strictly one reason. He wanted never to disturb the forgotten file on the earlier deployment, that which contained Gunnar's forged deployment order. Wells knew should this document come to light, it would mean the end of his career.

The year 1942, like the war itself, progressed slowly. The summer in London was peaceful, although the city was still on a war footing. The bombings of the Blitz were a thing of the past, but the threat of recurrence hung over the city's head.

In August, there had been the catastrophe in the attempted Channel amphibious landing at Dieppe in Northern France. The Germans made short work of the forces attempting to land and open a second front. Their objective was to attempt to draw Nazi resources away from the Russian front. An intelligence officer observing the ill-fated operation on one of the English ships in the Channel was none other than Ian Fleming.

The real fighting was once again a long way off. Montgomery and Rommel fought a back and forth battle along the desert and shores of eastern North Africa. In early November, *Operation Torch* would land the first American Armies in the war at the other end of North Africa in Morocco, including those who would fight under General George S. Patton.

On the same day as Operation Torch commenced, November 9, 1942, the Polish cryptographers were rapidly evacuated from the chateau codenamed *Cadix* outside of Uzès near Avignon. Marian Rejewski and Henryk Zygalski escaped just in time, as the Gestapo had been closing in on them. By the 12th of November, the Gestapo had stormed *Cadix*. By then, Rejewski and Zygalski were in Nice. The only escape route open to them was to head west along the Mediterranean coast. They proceeded to Marseilles, then the beach town of Narbonne, and onto the coastal city of Perpignan. They were trapped in the South of France, as the Gestapo searched for them both.

In the preceding month of October, the time had come for the SOE to finally execute the first element of its Heavy Water Operations. Four Norwegian locals from the Rjukan Valley area had been trained as a reconnaissance team in advance of the planned deployment of a British Commando assault team. On October 18, after several aborted attempts due to bad weather, the *Grouse* team of four Norwegian agents, trained secretly in the Scottish Highlands were dropped back into southern Norway. Unfortunately, they had been released far from the intended drop zone. It took these four rugged outdoorsmen fifteen days to hike back to the intended drop location.

Having not heard from the team for two weeks after the parachute drop on the 18th, it was assumed that they had either died or been captured by the Germans. Einar spent day after day monitoring the frequencies to be used by the team, but no attempt was made by the *Grouse* team to contact London. Finally, on day 16, the radio frequency came alive with the call signal and the appropriate pass codes. Einar called out for Wincer Wells to come to his station as he began to communicate with the team via encrypted morse code.

Wells came rushing to Einar's side

"What have they reported so far, MacAlvor?" he asked.

"Only that they were dropped far off course due to foul weather, sir. Took them a fortnight to make it back to their intended landing zone. The pilot's report confirmed that the weather was rather nasty during that drop, sir."

"This could be a bloody trap," Wells said, "if the *Operation Grouse* team had been rounded up by the Gestapo or SS, they would have had ample time to interrogate them and prepare a counter-op against us. These men could be held at gunpoint, forced to contact us."

"You'll remember, sir, that we have built in a contingency just for such an event," said Einar. He then transmitted a coded message across the frequency. When the team at the other end decoded the message, it read, "What did you see on the early morning of September 24th?"

Einar waited patiently for their response. The coded message began coming across the headset, and Einar recorded it letter by letter. Then he decoded it by hand. A broad smile creased his face.

"It's them, sir," Einar said. "No doubt about it, it's definitely them."

Wells looked down at the pad on which Einar had decoded the message. It read, *"Three Pink Elephants"*.

"Smashing! Spot on!" exclaimed Wells. "Now we can get on with planning *Operation Freshman*."

Grouse had always been planned as a reconnaissance mission only. *Freshman* was the follow-up operation to drop in the British sabotage team that would penetrate the Vemork facility and destroy the heavy water production facilities in its basement.

The SOE would not entrust this critical raid to be carried out by the Norwegians, although the locals begged to do just that. No, this was strictly the work for trained SOE commandos.

On November 19, two Halifax Bombers, each towing a Horsa glider full of SOE commandos, took off from Britain. Once airborne, the tandem were told to expect heavy clouds over the four hundred mile journey, but also to anticipate clear skies over the drop zone. This was the first practical use of gliders against the Nazis during the war. The Brits were about to find out exactly what could go wrong.

The Halifax bombers being used as tugs approached the Norwegian coast to find clear skies as predicted. However, the bombers began to experience severe turbulence and icing of both tug and gliders and the cables connecting them. One can only imagine the ride the commandos in the gliders were enduring. The Halifax bomber's instruments used to pick up the navigational beacons set on the ground by the *Grouse* team failed to work. On a second pass to locate the landing zone, the iced cable snapped forcing the iced Horsa glider to crash land on the Norwegian mainland. Three of its seventeen commandos died on impact, and many of those that survived were heavily injured. The Bomber reported the incident and called for search and rescue but there were no British assets in the vicinity to conduct such a mission.

The second bomber, having also encountered severe turbulence decided to seek a lower altitude, and in doing so flew directly into the side of a mountain. That glider broke free and sailed on to a more survivable landing, not far from the first, although their fate was not immediately known to SOE personnel in London. All Einar knew was that once again, he could not make contact with the deployed team over the radio.

Then on the 21st of November, his colleague monitoring the German wireless transmissions picked up the following message: *"On the night of November 19-20th two British bombers, each towing one glider, penetrated Southern Norway. One bomber and both gliders were forced to land. The sabotage troops in the gliders were engaged and killed to the last man."*

Later, it would be discovered that the surviving British commandos had not been engaged in battle, but had been rounded up by the Gestapo. They were tortured and interrogated, and summarily executed per Hitler's order on dealing with all commando raids. Including those on the crashed Halifax bomber, 41 British lives perished in attempting this raid. It was assumed that the Germans were by then very well aware of Churchill's and the SOE's interest in rendering the Vemork heavy water facility inoperable.

The SOE remained undaunted. At the urging of the Norwegians, it was agreed that the next attempt would be made by Norwegian commandos again being trained in the Scottish Highlands. Through the network of sources in Norway, the SOE was able to determine that the surviving *Operation Freshman* commandos had come into contact with a local farmer, but as they could not speak Norwegian and he had no English, any opportunity for subterfuge had been lost. Norwegian commando's would have been able to converse with the locals, would be more familiar with the terrain, and most certainly more adaptable to the climate.

The decision was made, the Norwegian team prepared in the Scottish Cairngorm Mountains.

"At least allow me to train with them," Einar pleaded of Wells. "Even if I don't deploy with them, I can be an asset in aiding their preparations. I promise you that my Norwegian is still very good. I swear to you that I won't let you down. Just let me get back to the Scottish Highlands and train with them. I can't stand to sit behind a radio mic for another mission."

"MacAlvor, lad, the die is cast," replied Wells. "This will be an all Norwegian team. I'm told the trainers are very impressed with their mountaineering skills. Like a pack of bloody mountain stags, I'm told. They have picked up the explosives handling rather quickly. Now, all we have to do is drop them and their equipment into their country, somewhere close to the blooming target. Then, we'll have a bookmaker's odds of pulling this op off."

Einar was dejected, but resolved himself to continue to be the communication link for the team, sitting in front of his warm, gently buzzing wireless set on the highest floor of a nondescript London office building. In addition to being the away team's comm link, he also serviced regular transmissions from agents within Norway. In the north, near the Lofoten Island chain, there was one agent, who like the others reported in encrypted signals to avoid detection. Einar's responsibilities included receiving the encrypted transmission, and then to decode it after the agent went off the air. The agent's codename was *Grieg*, like the Norwegian composer.

It was the contents of *Grieg*'s transmissions that gave away his location. Each of this agent's transmissions was like a dagger to the heart of Einar. He could not read of Nazi troop movements or new radar site construction in the Arctic and not think of his brother, Gunnar. *Where was Gunnar's body? Did it lie in an Allied cemetery there, or had it been left to decompose in the elements? Even worse, was it pitched by the Gebirgsjäger into the waters of the Rombaksfjord?*

Einar had never been able to get these haunting thoughts out of his mind. Nor did he really wish to. His greatest fear in life, or what he internally referred to as his *half-life* since Gunnar was gone, was that the memory of his brother would fade and eventually be forgotten. Instinctively, he knew that process would accelerate the longer he stayed away from the Lofoten Islands, from Narvik, from Norway. That is why he pressed so hard to get deployed there once more.

Einar had first pinpointed *Grieg's* location when in March of that year (1942) the agent had reported confirmed visual sighting of the German Battleship *Tirpitz* in the *Vestfjorden*. Decoding that message immediately took him back atop the Hogskrova on Skrova's main isle, together with Gunnar scanning the massive fjord for activity of any enemy ships. He could remember the summer's wind blowing in from the sea, and the smell of the sweet summer grasses intermixed with ocean salt. How Einar longed to be alongside his brother once more. It was impossible, but Einar knew that should he return to the Lofoten, the illusion of being closer to his brother would lessen the heartache he continually felt since leaving him there. It etched like a hollowing acid within him, consuming more and more of his being with each passing day. Einar knew that one way or another, he had to get back to Norway

The message regarding *Tirpitz* had been handed off to Military Intelligence and a few days later a squadron of Halifax bombers had been dispatched, but with little effect. The *Tirpitz* had truly proven itself worthy of the name *"the Beast"* as Churchill had christened it. It appeared to be indestructible.

From that point on, the field agent *Grieg* seemed committed to finding the *Tirpitz*. The battleship had been moved north to the fjords around the northern Arctic town of Alta. It had been placed there to position it to interrupt the convoys of war supplies being transported from Britain to Russia via the Arctic passage. *Grieg* reported regularly as to the many northern fjords that had been searched but with no sighting of "*the Beast*".

Then, just after the *Operation Freshman* debacle, after Wells had told Einar he could not join the next operation with the Norwegians, *Grieg* went silent. December passed without a transmission. Nor did they resume in January. Finally, during the first week of February, Wincer Wells came to see Einar.

"We have now confirmed that agent *Grieg* has perished."

"I am shattered to hear that," said Einar, and meaning it sincerely, as in his mind *Grieg* held a special connection to his departed twin brother. "He was found out by the Gestapo?"

"Nothing so dramatic," Wells replied. "*Grieg* was hiking the ridges of the mountains around Alta, spying down into the fjords. He climbed out on a ledge for visual access down into a fjord when the ledge gave way and he fell to his death."

"My God," stammered Einar. "This is confirmed?"

"Took his wife with him," said Wells. "Always did. Made for perfect cover. Family alpine hiking outing."

"My God, she watched him die?" asked Einar.

"Watched him, heard his screams, I'm afraid," Wells said coldly. "She's quite rattled by it, but she is a professional, she'll recover and carry on her mission."

"She's one of us?" Einar asked.

"A dues-paid member of our little *club*," Wells responded. "Grieg and she trained in Scotland, same site as where you and your brother took your instruction."

Dues-paid? Einar could not believe how hard-hearted Wincer Wells could be in situations such as this. Describing his agents as commodities, with no real comprehension of the human cost of dealing with the loss of someone deeply loved.

"As tragic as all this is," Wells pressed on, "it creates a great opportunity for yourself. We need to keep pressing against the *Tirpitz*. Churchill is absolutely consumed with sinking that behemoth. The Huns, dirty buggers that they are, have begun to construct a radar station on Andøya Island. We need to be prepared to disable it."

Einar was familiar with this site. It was just on the other side of the Lofoten Islands. Andøya was the outermost island near the fjord town of Harstad which had been home to the headquarters of the Allies back in 1940. Andøya faced out to the open Norwegian Sea, a perfect location for detecting squadrons of British bombers on their approach to attack the *Tirpitz*.

"We need to be prepared to take out that radar installation once it becomes operational. We can send you back to the Highland for some updated training on explosives and sabotage techniques. After that we shall deploy you to Lofoten, where you can take over his wireless set. His wife has agreed to allow you to stay with her there."

"Why on earth would she do that?" Einar asked. "She's just lost her husband…"

"Two months ago," corrected Wells. "The proper answer to your question is that she, like her late husband, hates the Nazis more than we do. Invaded their country. They were the reason her husband fell to his death. Probably imprisoned their friends, and so on. No love wasted on their behalf. The old girl is one hundred percent committed to keeping her husband's operations going. Says she owes it to *Grieg* to carry on the fight. She just didn't have the explosives training that he did. That's where you'll come in, lad. The question is whether you're up for the test, brother."

In all the time that he had known Wells, Wincer had never referred to him as "brother". It was a common enough term among the British, especially when one man spoke to another, but Wells had never used it with him. Did he intentionally use the term to motivate him, to remind Einar of Gunnar? To use his brother's death as a lure to action?

Despite this reaction, Einar said simply, "I'm in."

"It's settled then, as soon as the next operation goes off later this month, we will get you dropped into Lofoten again."

"What is the next operation?" asked Einar.

"*Operation Gunnerside*," Wells said, "and I'm prepared to brief you on it this morning, if you can muster the time."

Rjukanfossen

Town of Rjukan

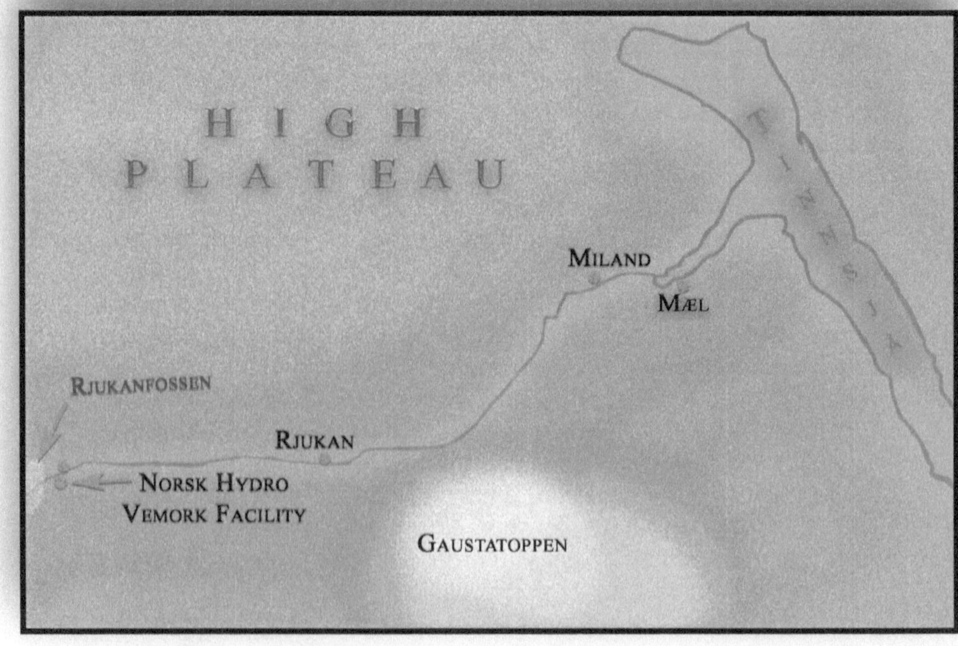

Figure 40: The Rjukan Valley: Home of Heavy Water

60 Operation Gunnerside

February 1943

"Success is the ability to go from one failure to another with no loss of enthusiasm."

Winston Spencer Churchill

In January 1943, the two Polish cryptographers Marian Rejewski and Henryk Zygalski were still on the run in southwest France. They moved constantly. They spent time in Toulouse before eventually making their way to try and escape from Vichy France across the Pyrenees Mountains. They were to depart from the small French border town of Ax-les-Thermes. The town was renowned for its hot mineral springs and was a favorite with the winter skiers. They waited there to make contact with a border crossing guide, who was to take them under the cover of darkness using his knowledge of both the terrain and the Spanish, French and German border patrols.

The night came for their crossing and the guide led them up the mountainside from Ax-les-Thermes. After they had crossed beyond the border at the peak's crest into Spain, the guard said they would rest and allow the Spanish patrol expected shortly to pass.

The man then pulled a pistol on the two mathematicians and took from them all their money and any jewelry they possessed. He then slipped back across the border into France, knowing they would not follow him there. Rejewski and Zygalski then wandered down the mountainside into a small Spanish border town where they were arrested and ultimately imprisoned. There, in that Spanish prison, they would stay for the next six months.

Operation Grouse, launched in mid-October 1942, had nearly been tragic, but in the end had succeeded in putting a four man reconnaissance team into southern Norway near the Vemork facility. *Operation Freshman* deployed a month later and with the loss of 41 commandos had become one of the SOE's greatest failures. By February 1943, the SOE was ready to try again, this time with an all-Norwegian commando team trained in Scotland.

At this time six commandos and their equipment would be dropped into the Norwegian countryside by parachute. The aircraft were deployed on the 16th of February. Once more due to poor weather, they were released a great distance from their intended drop zone. The *Gunnerside* commandos then took their provisions from their parachuted airborne containers, which included cross country skis. It took another two days for the skiing commandos to make it back to the *Grouse* team.

The four man Grouse team had been sequestered away in a high plateau ski hut since their drop in October. They had run out of provisions, and had been living off the land eating linchen, moss and berries until they were able to track and kill a reindeer for meat. They were delighted to finally link up with the *Gunnerside* commandos, which brought their total number to ten. The combined team then began to plan the final assault on the Norsk Hydro facility at Vemork.

The Rjukan Valley begins as the waters of the *Måna River*, flowing from west to east, drop some 300 feet creating the Rjukan Falls, or in the local vernacular, the *Rjukanfossen*. This waterfall had once been a remarkable natural feature, its waters churning as they fell and resulted in a veil of white, translucent mist.

In 1905, Norsk Hydro diverted much of those waters, robbing the falls of some of their natural grandeur. The waters were piped down an adjacent hill to the newly built Vemork hydroelectric facility. A local village was situated just after the falls on the north side of the *Måna River;* the Norsk Hydro plant along the south side. Between the two lie the river in the 300 foot ravine created by the *Rjukanfossen*. Only a suspension bridge of some 75 feet in length connected the village to the plant. A train line ran from the plant for ten miles as the ravine opened to a steep valley and led to the town of Mæl on Lake Tinn.

The Norsk Hydro power station produced enough electricity for the valley's usage, as well as its needs to produce ammonia and nitrogen based fertilizers. It also produced electricity for the railroad running through the valley to take these products to the company's ferries on Lake Tinn, or the Tinnsja, Once the freight cars were loaded onto the ferries, they were carried its length to the destination town of Tinnoset. There the railcars were unloaded onto the rail line that would carry them to Oslo.

Norsk Hydro had always been a community-minded company in the valley. In addition to the jobs they produced for the local workers, they also allowed the valley's townspeople passenger usage of both the railroad and the ferry systems. Norsk Hydro even built the inclined railway to carry locals to the top of the nearby Gausta Mountain, or *Gaustatoppen*. The field behind and above the power plant had been heavily mined after the *Operation Freshman* debacle.

Of course, it was the discovery of the material called Heavy Water that had caught the world's attention. Producing it required enormous electrical power, which Norsk Hydro had no problem supplying. When the material was tied to the emerging science of quantum mechanics, and as its criticality became understood for potentially producing atomic weapons, the facility became a priority for the Nazis as they invaded in 1940.

The Germans immediately assigned security details to protect the facility. Having the river's 300 foot deep ravine which isolated the plant with only a single bridge spanning across it, the Nazis decided they only needed to patrol the single suspension bridge crossing it. However, after the debacle of *Operation Freshman*, ending with the execution of the captured British commandos, the Germans decided to increase the facility's security by mining the grounds behind the plant that rose up the mountainside.

This led the combined *Grouse-Gunnerside* team no other option than to rappel down the ravine in front of the plant, wade across the river in its center, and then climb up the other side. Which is exactly what these courageous Norwegian commandos did under the cover of darkness.

The Germans had considered the ravine to be impassible, other than via the suspension bridge towering over it. Yet these men, who had climbed these local mountain faces their entire life, only took the ravine as a challenge. Nothing more.

On the night of February 16, 1943, *Operation Gunnerside* commenced. Einar worked the communication desk in London as all ten commando's deployed to Vemork. Nine of

Figure 41: The Vemork Norsk Hydro Plant in the Rjukan Valley and Heavy Water Cells in Basement

the commando's rappelled down the ravine from the north side of the river. One commando stayed behind to guard the team's method of escape - their long-distance skis.

After crossing the turbulent river and then scaling the south ravine wall, the group of nine Norwegian commandos followed the train tracks leading to the plant. They cut through the perimeter fence unnoticed.

The team had an insider at the facility who had been passing along the interior layout information. The set of nine heavy water columns which were in the facility's basement had been expanded by the Nazis to 18 columns. The commandos were to gain access to the facility, place plastic explosives across the columns and detonate the entire heavy water capability. They were to access the basement through a door which was to be left unlocked.

However, after cutting through the perimeter fence, the commandos located the door only to find it locked. Two of the commandos then found an overhead access way through which they could crawl and drop into the basement. When they did, they surprised a night operator of the facility. He was sympathetic to what they were about to do, and watched intently as they began to wire the explosives to the eighteen columns. Then, he was told to go up to the first floor, lay flat upon it and keep his mouth wide open so as not to rupture his eardrums when the blast occurred.

It was then that a window was smashed in the basement and the two commandos thought themselves caught. However, it turned out just to be their mates joining them inside. When the wiring was completed, the team decided to shorten the fuses from two minutes to thirty seconds. The nine member team escaped the facility undetected.

The explosive blasts were surgical, and did not produce an overwhelming demolition force. It was enough that all the columns were destroyed in their totality. The raid was a complete success. Even the finishing touch of leaving behind a British Thompson submachine gun convinced the Germans that the raid was conducted by the British commandos. Given their earlier attempts during *Operation Freshman*, it appeared only logical that the Brits, and not the local resistance, was responsible.

As the alarms blared, the nine commandos then egressed the facility, rappelled back down into the ravine, recrossed the *Måna* river and climbed up the ravine again on the other side.

The commandos donned their skis and escaped into the snowy hillside, without so much as any shots coming near them. The team later split up, with the six *Gunnerside* commandos cross-country skiing some 250 miles to the safety of neutral Sweden. The four *Grouse* reconnaissance commandos returned to their ski hut, and to the best of anyone's knowledge were never tied to the raid by the Gestapo.

Einar manned the radio in London. The first confirmations came from the 4 man Grouse team. A few days later, a message was passed from the informant inside the facility. The entire raid had been a smashing success. The production of any new heavy water within the Vemork facility had been totally disrupted. But unknown to the raiders, unknown to the informant inside the plant, and thus unknown to Einar himself, a significant supply of heavy water produced prior to the raid still existed in secret storage at the plant.

61 The Lonely Red Rorbu

April 1943

"We have a lot of anxieties, and one cancels out another."

Winston Spencer Churchill

With the Vemork facility's heavy water operations having been destroyed, Wells sent Einar MacAlvor to the Scottish Highlands for refresher explosive sabotage training before his deployment back into Norway. He spent a month there, and passed all tests with top marks. In early April, he was to deploy out of the Royal Navy's Rosyth Dockyard on the River Forth near Edinburgh. Einar took the opportunity to make one last overnight trip to Broughty Ferry to see Tilly, the woman he had always known to be his mother. She was expecting him and was overjoyed as he walked in through the door.

"I'm off to be deployed, mother," he said to her after their greetings had been made. "I'm afraid I am not at liberty to tell you where."

"Where else?" Tilly scoffed. "Wincer has been training you for one mission since before you were ever even a man. Had his eyes on you ever since he heard you speak Norwegian. Now that he's discarded your brother, there was nothing to stop him from deploying you back to Lofoten. I knew I could never ask you to stay away from there. So, we have one night together, let's make the most of it."

Einar hesitated, not knowing if he should put up false protestations or lie to her. Then, he remembered that this woman had already lost a husband and a son at the altar of Wincer Wells.

Clearly Tilly assumed this would be her last night with her son Einar. He would not insult her with a web of fiction. Her insights were too sharp not to cut through the deceit. It was enough that he had not told her the truth, but he could not keep her from knowing it.

"Where's my brother," Einar then said.

"Matthew," she replied, is down for a nap just now."

"How has he been?"

"Wonderful," she said, "for a boy who will never remember his father or his brothers."

"Surely he remembers me, Mother," Einar pleaded.

"He'll surely will recognize you when he awakens," Tilly said, "but Matthew is not yet two and half years old. By the time he is eight he'll no more remember you than his own father."

Tilly turned away from him and cried. She could no longer harbor the swell of tears brought on by this moment. All her resolve washed away with each teardrop shed.

"I swear to you I am coming back, Mother," Einar said as he moved forward and wrapped his arms around her.

"I don't believe that will be the case, my son. Your heart lies in a distant land, alongside your twin brother. There is nothing I can do to bring you back to me. If I learned one thing from your father, it is that having you here, staring out to sea, is no less agonizing than never knowing what became of you."

As she said these words, her shoulders heaved and a torrent of emotion was released from deep within her. It was only at this moment that Einar fully realized the depths of his mother's sacrifice for her country.

"There is one thing I must show you, Einar," Tilly said as she produced a letter in addressed to Chief - Her Majesty's Secret Intelligence Service, 5400 Broadway, Westminster, London.

"After your father died, a good friend of his, a seaman from the Leith Docks, returned this letter to me. He said he had held it at Brigand's request, and with his death at Dunkirk did not know what to do with it. I took it from him, and was shocked by what I read. You must read this, as it pertains to your and Gunnar's deploying to Norway. It pertains to what type of a man this Wincer Wells is that you will be dealing with. Read it and leave it with me, a bit of insurance never hurts in your line of business."

Einar deployed the next day from the Rosyth Dockyard aboard a British destroyer. Off the Shetland Islands, he was transferred to a Polish submarine, the *ORP Wilk*, which he had been told meant "Wolf". The Poles would reinsert him into Norway, fittingly, as they were responsible for his extraction.

It was the *Wilk's* mission to deliver him to the landing zone just south of the village of Nyksund along the coastline of the Vesterålen Archipelago under the cover of darkness. Like the wolf she was named after, the *Wilk* was accustomed to operating in the stealthy world of the night.

The *Wilk* surfaced during the few hours of darkness that April held in the Arctic. A rubber dinghy was inflated on her deck, and Einar and two Polish seamen, all dressed in black commando attire set out for shore. Einar carried two watertight duffel bags, one of which was full of nothing but plastic explosives.

Einar was put ashore along the rocky coastline. The dinghy then slowly faded away into the blue sea mist to return to the submarine *"Wilk"* which Einar could no longer even see. The landing had gone off without a hitch, and had taken less than thirty minutes. Within another thirty minutes, he heard a soft voice call out to him.

The agreed codeword had been *"an dàrna cothrom,"* the Scottish Gaelic term for "second chance". It had been thought it would be unintelligible to native Norwegians, if overheard, while to German speakers it would most likely be indecipherable from the Norwegian tongue.

Einar turned slowly to face her, haunched down behind a small boulder along the coast. He wondered if she had been there watching him for the entire time.

"*Spiorad ag èirigh*" He replied, meaning "Spirits rising" in the same Gaelic tongue.

"Einar?"

"Kari?"

She came out from behind the stone. She was dressed in dark, but not black clothing. She moved with purpose, grabbed one of the duffel sacks, and drew a mild rebuke from Einar.

"You had best let me handle that duffel," he said.

She turned and looked at him. They were only a foot apart. She could clearly see his eyes in the blue Arctic haze into which the darkness had already devolved.

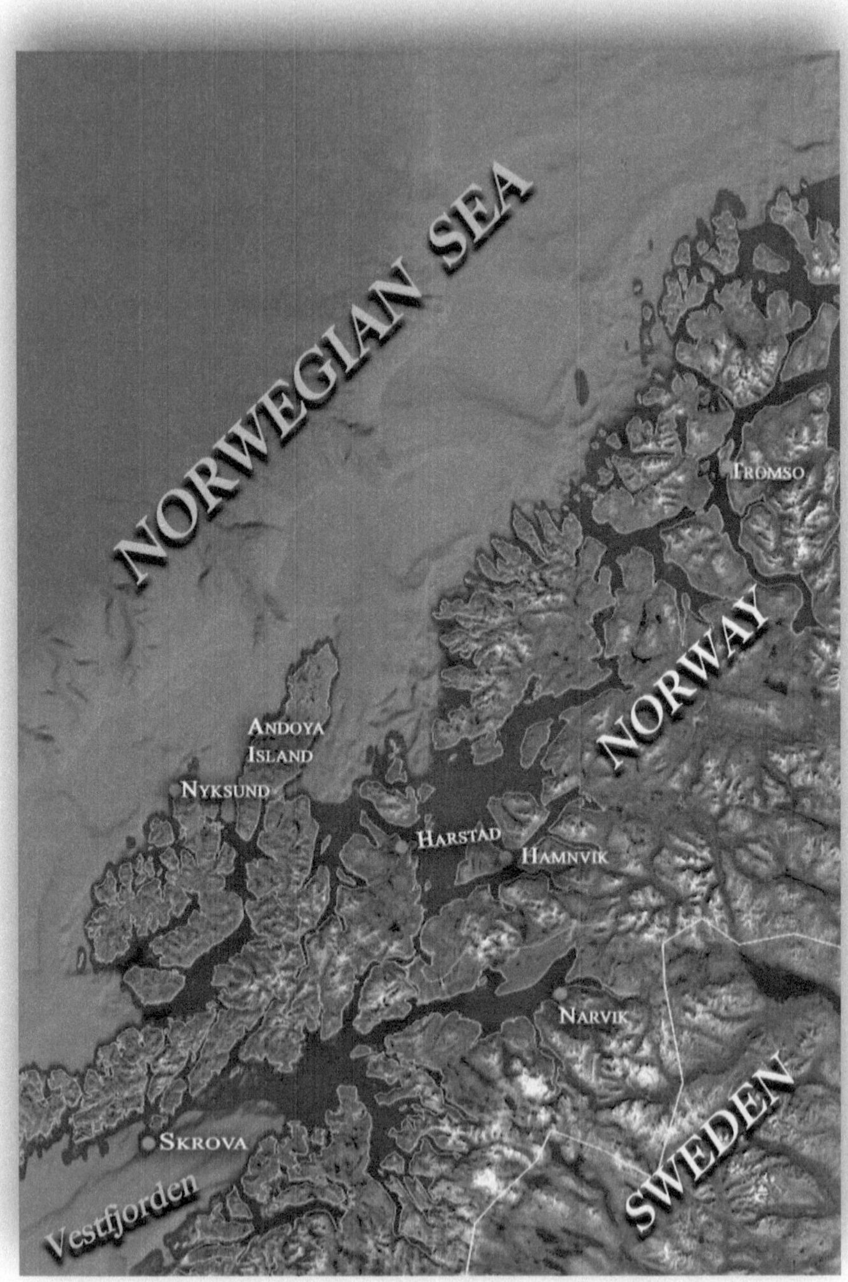

Figure 42: Nyksund, location of Einar's Reinsertion Into Coastal Norway

"What difference does it make?" Kari whispered. "If you are to see to follow me, you'll have to stay close. If that *plastique* goes off, I guarantee you it will take us both out. But if you want to carry it, its not a problem for me."

They spoke in Norwegian. Einar had enjoyed listening to her speak it, and had to laugh to himself at her reasoning. She was absolutely correct. They traded duffels and he followed her along the coast. It was not far until she came to a lonely red *rorbu* hut built on the bed of rocks with two stilts dropping from its seaward side into the water.

"Watch your footing on these steps," she said, "they are pretty roughly laid, and can become very slippery."

Einar followed her up the rocks to the door on the side of the *rorbu.* Once inside, she made her way to the windows and drew close the blackout curtains. She then lit a small lamp. It was his first good look at her. He thought her small, well-featured and very young. Her face was serious, but not overly so.

"Tomorrow, in the daylight, I will show you where to stash the explosives," she said. "It is not far. After I show you, tomorrow night when it is again dark we will move them. So for tonight, we will just have to be very careful."

The light was shining off her now. It seemed to flicker before curling in silhouette around her form. She smiled warmly at him, and her brown hair framed the portrait of her face.

"Why don't we just move it now?" Einar asked. He thought she would appreciate his desire to act in the here and now, not to defer anything to the uncertain future.

"I thought they said you had been here before," she laughed. "In another thirty minutes it will be light enough that you would wish you had never started."

"So when do we go to Nyksund?"

"This is home, Einar," she said. "Too many eyes up at Nyksund. Besides it's just a few minutes walk up the coastline. You'll see when the sun comes up."

"How many eyes is too many?"

"Right now," Kari said, "there are perhaps some thirty people in town. Takes a pretty hearty soul to live out a winter here along the coast. Only about half of them are married, though. Not many of us women about. Do not be surprised to see them here approaching the *rorbu.* They think I am ripe for the taking since my husband died. By middle of summer, it will explode with another thirty or forty fishermen. Almost all of them men. Like I said, too many eyes. I'm glad you're here, they'll think you're my new man and leave me alone."

The flame had taken a strong hold of the lamp's wick and as Kari spoke, Einar took in the small hut. It was a traditional r*orbu.* The word r*orbu* was derived from the Norwegian words to row *(ror)* and a little house *(bu).* The idea of having these huts right over the fishing waters where a fisherman could row to for a night's rest after fishing all day went back to the 12th century.

Most *rorbus* were only two rooms. The smaller room was usually secured for storing fishing equipment. The larger room would serve a combined function as bedroom, living quarters and kitchen. Cooking was usually done on the same stove that heated the hut. They were always well insulated, with the entire interior being tightly packed planking of firs or other woods. In Kari's *rorbu,* there was a bed wedged in the corner furthest from the stove, a table and two chairs.

The bed was covered with what must have been the skins of twenty reindeer. Generally, these were incredibly warm furs, covered in shades of overlapping white, grey and warm brown tones. Most were small, but soft as a baby's first breath. Beneath the scattered skins was a warm woolen blanket.

With the exception of the bed, the *rorbu* reminded Einar of the ski hut he and Gunnar had spent a month in at Bjørnfjell in 1940. Instead of a bed, that hut had two wooden benches mounted into the wall and were anything but comfortable, no matter what was laid upon them.

"Do you have extra blankets?" Einar asked. "So that I can sleep on the floor."

"You'll sleep next to me in the bed, Einar," Kari responded, "it is more than large enough."

"I don't want to impose on you," he said.

"I have been sleeping alone for several months now," Kari said, "and frankly I don't care for it. Don't worry, I won't bite. At least not on the first night."

Kari then took off the jacket and sweater that she had worn to brave the freezing April Arctic night. She then sat at the table where the lamp burned to remove her boots.

"I am so sorry to be here to replace your husband," Einar said, "I didn't expect to take over his spot."

"Einar, let's get one thing straight up front. You can never replace my Jorun. What happened to him was truly tragic.

I will never get it out of my head, but in a strange way, I do not wish to. Over time, I will no longer hear his scream as he fell but only his voice when he spoke so lovingly to me. Whether you sleep in the bed or on the floor will not hasten that."

As she said these words, the lamp's light glistened off her shoulder length hair, its color was the exact shade of brown running through the reindeer pelts. Neither chestnut nor auburn, exactly, but very attractive fusion of the two shown in the flickering light. Her face was alluringly featured, her eyes lovely but commanding, and her jawline was strong, although sculpted in a graceful manner that it could never be considered masculine. All together, her looks were totally consistent with the *"this is how we are going to do this"* attitude she conveyed.

"All right, Kari," he said. "I will sleep alongside you."

She turned out the lamp and Einar could only hear the seductive swoosh of her removing more of her clothing. Then she spoke as she slid under the woolen blanket.

"Einar, your Norwegian is very good," she said, "but I don't care for how you are pronouncing my name. You are saying, *'Care-ree'* when the correct pronunciation is *'Kah - ree'*. It is a very common name here, so you must learn to say it correctly. Please correct that and I am happy. Now come to bed. I need to sleep in the warmth after hiding behind the frozen boulders on the beach tonight."

Einar stripped down to his undershirt and shorts and crawled under the woolen blanket. Kari was already in the spot up against the wall. He could smell her scent, which excited him.

She rolled over and onto him. She said into his ear, "This bed is not so large that we will not be bumping into each other, so I suggest you get used to it quickly. It feels good to have a man with me again, but don't worry, I won't take advantage of you, Einar. Take off this shirt, please. I want to feel the warmth of your skin on mine. I have missed this so terribly over the past few months."

She laughed delightfully. Einar had thought she would resent him, but in reality the only thing she resented was being alone with only her sorrows. He sat up and removed the undershirt, but left his shorts in place.

While he did this, Kari sat up and reached for the reindeer skins. She piled them high around them. As they laid back in the darkness, the edge of one fell upon Einar's chest. Its thick blanket of fur caressed his skin. Her arm snaked under it and probed the muscles of his chest. Her bare breast pressed up against him.

"Kari," Einar said, pronouncing her name as she requested, "I wish for you to take me very soon for a hike to the north cliffs along the *Rombaksfjord* near *Lomvatnet*. There is a formation of ledges there …"

"No," she said sharply, and then craned her neck up to kiss his cheek, as if to take the sting out of her words. "I have been given orders to never take you to where your brother died."

"You know?" he said incredulously.

"Of course I know," she said rolling onto him, "directly from the old man Wincer Wells himself. '*Never take him to Skrova, and never take him back to where his brother died,' he said.* Besides, there is nothing there to see."

Einar was stunned that his past had already been revealed to her, but then thought on Wells and knew he should have expected it.

"You've been there," Einar asked, "when?"

"About a month after the evacuation, Jorun and I went together. We were sent to search for remains. We found the ledges, saw the embedded debris in the stone from the explosion, but saw no remains at all. None from Gunnar, none from the Germans, and none from the Poles. Just lots of blood stains and bullet casings."

"That son of a bitch Wells had you both checking out my story," said Einar. "How dare he!"

"Relax, Einar," Kari said, "it's just business. Every story gets checked out. Hey, what are these?"

Her fingers had found the strings of the scapulars he wore around his neck.

"Scapulars," he said. "One is mine, the other Gunnar's."

Kari instinctively pulled her hand away.

"It's OK, Kari," Einar grabbed her hand and pulled it back onto his chest. "He wasn't just my brother, he was my twin. He was the other half of me. This is all I have left of him."

Her fingers returned to strum his chest. "I understand. I have also lost the other half of me. Your trinkets are more than I have left from Jorun."

—•—

"I am relieving you of your service to me, Bogdan."

The eyes were stern, peering into the young man that was Bogdan Bratajewski.

"What have I done to displease you, my General?"

"You have done no such thing," General Sikorski said plainly. "Your service to me has been exemplary."

"I wish only to serve you, sir. To serve my country."

"Bogdan, you have served me well over these past three years," Sikorski said, "now it is time to serve your country."

"I do not understand, sir."

"I told you I would find the right time and allow you to fight the Nazis, did I not?"

"Yes, General, you certainly did."

"Then that is what you shall do," Sikorski replied. "You shall leave me and go to Scotland and train with Churchill's SOE. After which, you will be dropped into Poland to serve with the *Armia Krajowa*."

"The Home Army! My God. It is too good to be true," Bogdan gushed. "Send me now. What will the British teach me that I do not already know?"

A gentle smile creased Sikorski's face, tenting the thin bars of his mustache. "You know the proverb from our country, *'if only a beard was needed, even a goat could preach!'* You think because you are trained as a soldier you can be a saboteur? You think you can move like a vapor in the night, and not be detected by the enemy? You think you can kill without a sound?"

"You mean the SOE will train me to be a *Cichociemni?*" Bogdan said.

"*The Silent Unseen.* Yes, of course. I have been asked to make recommendations to them. From what I have seen, you appear to have the aptitude. I will let the SOE determine whether or not you have the proper spirit."

"I am honored, my General," said Bogdan as he lowered his head.

"You will honor me by doing what is asked of you. I have a particular mission in mind for you."

"Tell me, sir," Bogdan said with the enthusiasm of a schoolboy.

"Only when you are ready to deploy," Sikorski said, "for the world can change many times between now and then. Now, I have already arranged for a new pilot. You will stay with him for a week, and then off to the Highlands with you, Bogdan."

Shortly after this conversation, after Bogdan took up his Highland's training, General Władysław Sikorski found himself embroiled in a tremendous controversy. Surprisingly, it had come from the propaganda of the Nazis, not a forum in which he had ever placed much faith for factual reporting. But this was one time within the war when Sikorski found himself believing Joseph Goebbels' apparatus.

The Nazis had pushed well into Russia and even though the tide was already reversing, the Nazis still held much Russian territory. They announced on the 13th of April, 1943 that they had uncovered in the woods outside the city of Smolensk mass graves of what would eventually be estimated at some twenty-two thousand Polish officers. Each man died with a single bullet through the back of their head. Each man's hands had been bound behind their back. Among their midst was a single female officer, a pilot named Janina Lewandowska.

This killing ground was forever to be known by the single word name of these woods - Katyń.

The Nazis were using the gravesite to demonstrate to the world the ruthless cruelty of Joseph Stalin. He had been painted in both England and America as a patriarchal "Uncle Joe", although both Winston Churchill and Franklin Roosevelt knew exactly what type of man they were dealing with. *The enemy of my enemy was their ally,* or so the reasoning of the war went.

General Władysław Sikorski would not delude himself in this manner. He knew these to be the bulk of the tens of thousands of his army's officers that had been unaccounted for after Stalin had released General Anders' troops in late 1941.

For their part, the Soviets blamed the massacre on the Nazis and attempted to date it as having took place in 1941, after Hitler's invasion of Russia. Sikorski knew better. He knew exactly what Stalin was capable of.

When the Nazis invited a commission led by the International Red Cross to Katyń to investigate, Sikorski's government agreed to participate. This immediately caused Stalin to declare a break in relations with the Polish Government-in-Exile. General Anders II Corps was already well clear of Russia's borders by then. Stalin used the cleaving of Polish/Russian relations to drive a wedge between the exiled government and its allies in the United States and England.

All information from the commission's investigation pointed to the atrocity as having been committed at the hands of the Soviets, which likely had occurred in May/June 1940. Stalin's government simply responded to Katyń as being a Nazi propaganda activity, and continued to blame the Germans for having committed the murders in late 1941, after they had pushed through the area in *Operation Barbarossa*. It was not until near the fall of communism at the end of the century when Russia would admit to having committed this catastrophe of epic proportion.

Einar and Kari bonded together quickly. They proved an effective team, as they scoured the fjords of Arctic Norway searching for the location of the *Tirpitz*. Also, they monitored the progress made by the Nazis in erecting the radar installation at Andøya. They knew the *Tirpitz* must be nearby, as the only logical function of that radar would be to protect *"the Beast"*.

Einar and Kari bonded in more human ways as well. Each had endured a personal tragedy. Sharing such devastating albeit separate griefs drew them closer. They knew each other's suffering. Ever so partially, they filled each other's voids.

Their sleeping together under the reindeer skins soon turned to lovemaking atop them. It had been initiated by her, on a morning when the pair found themselves trapped in the little red *rorbu* at the mercy of a fierce coastal storm. That morning the lightning cracked the sky, the rain pelted their roof borne amidst a ferociously howling wind that rattled its walls. The sea crashed against the *rorbu's* pilings in unrelenting waves, each stronger than that before it, until its very foundation quivered.

Within the shack, Kari had drawn Einar onto her, where she could feel the warmth of his being, and the strength of his brawn. It was neither love nor infatuation for her, only amusement. She needed the physical emptiness in her to be fed.

Loneliness is an invasive beast. It is never expected. It pounces like a predatory cat when least expected. Yet, even when initially fought off, the wounds of the conflict bear an aching inflammation that soon burrows deeper and more insidiously within one's being. After too long, all that is left is a desire for the remnants of what was once had. A look in the eye, a smile, a little conversation, a touch, an embrace, and perhaps an intimacy. The most devastating effect of loneliness is the realization that even when all these are achieved, the result is temporary. The replacement could never equal the replaced. They do not fill the void within the lonely, they merely line its exposed surfaces with a temporary balm. But the heartache always returns.

The winds hurled viciously around them and the sea pounded unrelentingly beneath them. Then, just as the storm's crescendo was peaked, silver beams of illuminated light penetrated the grayish black clouds overhead. All that had been threatening to destroy them eased, and the Arctic winds caught their exhausted breaths. Both Kari and Einar knew the new reality: this would not the last time they enjoyed each other in this way, and this was anything but not love.

Physical intimacy is often mistaken for emotional closeness, but neither Einar nor Kari had been fooled themselves in this way. For Kari still pined for her lost Jorun, and Einar for someone that haunted him still. Einar still chased the other half of himself. He felt it there in that lonely *rorbu* more than anywhere. Einar took his fill of the companionship and sensual pleasure of Kari, but he never let himself forget that he still grieved, deeply and fervently for his brother Gunnar.

"What are you thinking, Einar?" Kari said to him as she lay on her back atop the skins. Her body glistened with the intermingled sweat she shared with him.

"Only of how wonderful that was," he said unconvincingly.

"It was wonderful," she admitted, "but that is not what is in your head at this moment. You think of another. It is understandable. I will admit that I do. I think of Jorun, and how I have missed doing exactly that with him. So, as I have been brutally honest with you, be so with me."

She reached over and took his hand. She raised it to his face, her fingers interlocked with his. He had not shaved since he had arrived, and a thickening beard had emerged along his jaw. She moved the back of his hand against it. She watched as the bristles of his beard flexed against the strength of his hand. "This is a good look on you, Einar. Promise me you'll grow it out."

"Did your Jorun have a beard?" he asked.

"Yes, very red," she replied, "and I loved it. He did not need it to remind me that he was a man. But the beard is what I have missed most in my loneliest moments. The brush of it against my skin. The way it shadowed his face with seriousness, or would stretch wide to divulge his smiles and laughter. Who is it that you are lonely for, Einar? I can feel it within you, you know."

"I was just thinking…" he had said before hesitating.

"Yes, tell me," she pleaded.

"…thinking that my brother Gunnar had never had the touch of a woman in the way that I just have."

"But I am not the first woman you have ever touched," Kari said, "that I can surely tell. A woman knows this."

"No," Einar laughed lightly, "you may well be the best, but not the first, Kari."

"You have had many women in Edinburgh, haven't you?"

"In Edinburgh, in Dundee, and even in London," he admitted. "I have had my share, and even his, I am afraid."

"And yet you never arranged this pleasure for your brother?" she asked.

"I tried," Einar admitted, "and yet he would not partake. He said one day the experience would find him, he would not go off chasing after it."

"Poor fellow," Kari said as she pulled his hand away from his face and to her naked breast. "But let us put your brother and my husband aside for now. Let us enjoy this time together. For if there is one thing that both Gunnar and Jorun would scream out to us, it is that one never knows the number of our days."

He then rolled over atop her and together they endured another storm, one which only existed within them both.

Late June of 1943 came and Bogdan Bratajewski's training in the Scottish Highlands came to an end. As he was preparing to leave, he received a telegram from General Sikorski. It read:

I HAVE RECEIVED WORD OF YOUR SUCCESS STOP YOU ARE TO FLY TO GIBRALTAR FOR A MEETING WITH ME ON YOUR ASSIGNMENT STOP MEET ME ON AFTERNOON OF 4 JULY STOP PREPARE TO FLY TWO PASSENGERS BACK TO LONDON WITH YOU ON RETURN FLIGHT STOP PLAN ACCORDINGLY FULL STOP

Einar and Kari effected their mission in two parts. First, they monitored and reported on the construction of the radar installation at Andøya Island. They prepared to sabotage the installation once it became operational, which meant they had to be fully cognizant of its layout and structural or operational weaknesses.

The second part of their assignment was to locate *"the Beast"*. The *Tirpitz* had, in effect, been in hiding ever since the sinking of the *Bismarck*, her sister ship. Where does one hide a battleship that displaces nearly 43,000 tons? One logical answer was in the fjords of Norway, of which there are seemingly an endless number. Kari and Einar were tasked to find a very massive needle in an enormously rugged haystack.

It was well known that the *Tirpitz* had been sent north to disrupt the Arctic convoys transporting war supplies from the United Kingdom to Russia. She was known to be in these far north waters after having been sighted the previous year in the *Ofotfjord.* But the last attack by the British on her had been in October 1942, with no significant damage.

Why were the fjords so effective in hiding such a large vessel? Of the several reasons, foremost was that these fjords constituted a maze-like network of seawater flowing between mountain ranges. Aerial reconnaissance would have to fly directly overhead to spot the warship, for any less angle and the ship would be obscured by the mountains themselves.

The other major reason was weather. Very often these fjords were socked in with dense sea-level fog or heavy clouds that hovered along these mountain ridges. Aircraft overhead would have zero visibility under these conditions. That was where a team of ground spotters came into play. By cresting a peak, they could spy into fjords even when the cloud ceiling was low.

Kari and Einar would depart from their base just below Nyksund and head north on journeys that would have them camping weeks at a time. Einar enjoyed these summer excursions, as he found them relaxing. They reminded him of the time he and Gunnar had spent surveying the Ofoten Railway before the arrival of the Germans.

They would take a tent along with them on these excursions, although Kari was aware of nearly every mountain hut available in these Nørdlands. On the few nights they actually had to sleep in the tents, they would build a large fire. With their cover as a typical Norwegian couple enjoying the outdoors, it would be expected. But these mountains were wild and undeveloped, save the occasional mountain survival hut, and Kari and Einar nearly never came into contact with others. This played to their benefit, for the fewer who knew their whereabouts, the less chance it would be leaked to the Nazis.

There was one exception, as in early August of '43 they were high in the mountains surrounding the town of Alta, most of the way to the North Cape border with Russia. There was a light snowpack still high on the mountainside. The summer melt was on, but in these mountains the winter snow had been heavy. It clung on despite the summer highs in the low forties Fahrenheit. The melt was never complete here in these parts, the snow only thinned before winter returned.

Kari and Einar's wanderings had been fruitless to this point. Even so, they were enjoying the splendor of the mountain scenery and the kiss of the breath of the gods on the Arctic breezes. They had also been enjoying each other. Kari had proven herself to be insatiable for sex, and Einar had tried his best to accommodate her needs. The nights they slept in the tent were those when she was most in need of him. He thought it was something to do with the crackle of the fire and the shadowy ripple of its light upon the canvas that drove the desire in her. They would make loveless sex and then collapse into a deep sleep in the freshness of the alpine surroundings.

One of the mornings after they had enjoyed each other in the tent the night before, they were awakened by a growing ruckus of sound coming up the mountain. Two teams of dogsledders - each team with eight dogs - approached. They were Norwegians who were running the huskies for sport, when they had spotted the tent and the smoldering fire of Kari and Einar.

The two sledders brought their dogs into the small camp to make sure everyone was safe. It was an expected courtesy in these parts. The two young men brought their sleds into the clearing where the tent was pitched just as Einar and Kari emerged from it. Kari was delighted by the visitors, more the huskies than the two men.

"Good morning," the first sledder said, "I am Torbjørn, and this is my brother Einar. Do you mind our stopping here to talk with you?" It soon became apparent that Torbjørn would do all the talking for the brothers, almost as if the visiting Einar wished not for his voice to be heard.

"Good morning, my countrymen," Kari welcomed them. "I am Kari, and this is my brother, also an Einar. Can I offer you both a cup of our coffee?" Kari swept her hand to the pot hanging over the open fire.

"*Takk*, that would be delightful," Torbjørn replied. "We were just passing with our sleds and wished to make sure you were not lost this high up on the mountain. We are forced to bring our dogs up to this elevation to find any good snow for summer sledding. It is very unusual to find anyone here."

"No, no," answered Kari, "We are just out enjoying the pleasant weather. Your dogs are so wonderful. Can I pet them?"

"They love that, just beware the others will get jealous."

The dogs, no sooner than they had stopped pulling their sleds had begun clamoring to run once again. The noise of the dozen and a quarter mixed-breed Huskies was a cacophony over which they spoke. It broke into a festival of sound once Kari began running her thumbs over the ears of the dog closest to her. Others nearby turned their rumps to her, inviting her pet them just above their tails. She did so and moved amongst them.

"Ignore these dogs," said Torbjørn to Einar. "They will take all the attention one can cast on them. They are bred for only one purpose, to pull a sled, and when they are not running they become very agitated. Where are you both from?"

"Just outside Tromsø," Kari forcibly interjected before Einar could answer truthfully.

"What brings you this far north?" asked Torbjørn.

"My brother and I are on a mission," she said, surprising Einar. "I told him I would take him to see the best display of the *Nordlys* he has ever seen."

"You are in the right place," Torbjørn said. "Although this is widely known to be a very poor month for doing so. Too much light. Of course it all depends on the activity of the sun, doesn't it. It was very beautiful last night, wasn't it? Just not for very long at all, given the night is so short."

"Beautiful indeed," Einar MacAlvor said, "but I have seen the lights around Bjørnfjell many times which were just as inspirational."

"He doesn't know what he is talking about," Kari said, teasing him as a one sibling might another. "He moved to be with me in Tromsø when the war drove him from Bjørnfjell."

"But that was three years ago," said Torbjørn cautiously, "be careful if you return there as I hear the Germans are still in force there protecting the railway to Narvik."

"Thank you," replied Einar, "but I have no desire to return there so long as the Nazi invaders are amassed there. I only pray they will soon be driven from these lands."

Kari looked at Einar with great shock, as she had striven to stay out of the subject of the occupation. One never knew if these countrymen might be sympathizers of Quisling's regime and its Nazi aligned government.

"My sentiments exactly," said the second sledder, the other Einar, who spoke for the first time.

"Well, as the occupiers are still with us," said Torbjørn, as he cut off his brother's voice, "and as a matter of general caution, best that you stay away from the *Kåfjorden* and the mountains around it. There have been many Germans spotted there as well."

"Thank you," Kari said. "The last thing we wish to do is run into those bastards."

"Thank you for your hospitality," said Torbjørn, as he handed the empty metal cup that the two brothers had shared. "Stay well and happy hunting…"

A look of shock flashed across Kari's face. Did these men know they were searching for the *Tirpitz*?

"… For the *Nordlys*, no?" continued Torbjørn, having read her momentary terror. "Now, we must run these dogs before they get too used to your attentions, Kari."

The two sledders departed, in a single file, gliding through the tracks their teams had made on the way in. The dogs, who had been so vocal during their rest, pulled fervently in a controlled symphony of muscles and energy. Soon they had disappeared behind the sculpted hills of the snowy mountain terrain.

"Do you think they knew we are not brother and sister?" Kari asked.

"If they heard you moaning this morning," Einar replied. "Then they surely knew we are not." A wide grin stretched across his face."Perhaps they heard and thought it only was the sound of an injured reindeer?"

"You are very funny, my Einar," she replied, smacking his arm. "Why can't you be as quiet as that other Einar. He was like the air of a mountain during a snowfall."

"Yes, that was quite odd, was it not?" Einar stated. "At first I thought he did not wish us to know the sound of his voice, until he chimed in about driving the Nazis from Norway."

"Do you think they might have been Quisling's agents?" Kari asked. "They seemed to be pumping us for information - who we were, where we were from, what we were doing…"

"They certainly did not buy that you were taking me to see the *Nordlys*!" Einar smirked. "Really? In mid-July? And with me as your brother who lived all his life in Norway, it makes no sense. Had they been Quisling's people we would be in chains already."

"That is true," Kari concluded. "But I did not accept their story of bringing their dogs this high on the mountain just to find snow to sled in. Something about these two rings untrue."

"That is for certain," Einar said, "come now let us break camp before anyone else comes looking for us."

"Yes, we need to get to the *Kåfjorden,"* she said, "for where there are Germans, there are things the Germans wish protected, like the *Tirpitz."*

As Kari and Einar broke camp, they did not realize that they had just met the brothers Torbjørn and Einar Johansen, key members of the Norwegian Resistance unknown at that time to them. They were on their return from the *Kåfjorden,* where they had visually confirmed the presence of the battleship *Tirpitz* and the smaller but still very lethal pocket battleship *Scharnhorst.*

Wincer Wells sat at his desk in London. He was tired, feeling every bit of his years. He had been a young man of thirty-five when Mansfield Cumming had initially set up shop in 1909. By the start of the war in 1939, he was 65, old enough to consider retirement. But since the Prime Minister, Winston Churchill, was also near that same age, Wells had no real grounds on which to close out his career. After all, Britain needed every able body it could muster to get it through the war. And Wells wanted only to serve his country until the war's end, and then collect his pension and take up a quiet fireside chair and immerse himself in his reading.

The war was very much on, and that luxury would have to wait. His station in the intelligence world had steadily eroded over the years, but his health was still excellent. Yet, on mornings such as this, his felt drained of all energy. Everything he undertook required a strenuous mustering of his strength.

Wells received the deciphered messages that had come in overnight, with one marked urgent from agent *"Lark"*, Einar and Kari's joint codename.

The message read, WE HAVE LAID EYES ON THE BEAST IN KÅFJORDEN NEAR ALTA STOP VISUALLY CONFIRMED STOP SCHARNHORST ALSO ANCHORED THERE STOP RETURNING TO HOME BASE FULL STOP.

Wells felt the spark rise within him. He strolled out of his office and down the hall to his superior's. His little operation was paying dividends, just as he had planned.

In the old days he would have had the reward of relaying such vital news directly to "C" himself. Now, he was not only out of the Chief's inner circle, he was entirely cut free from that orbit as the SOE openly competed with MI6 for fame and glory.

Wells relayed the message and his much younger supervisor was well pleased with the news. "Appears your chap has struck a find, Wincer, a true find at that."

"*Lark* is a tandem operation, sir," Wells replied, "if you'll recall the wife of the agent that fell to his death."

"Ah, yes," the superior said, nose to the air, "I forgot about the young widow. I can only imagine that she was useful in showing *Lark* the lay of the land there."

"Sir," Wells interrupted, "she was *Lark* for several months. Operated alone. She's quite steady, I assure you. Now *Lark* is the pair combined."

"Yes, yes, of course they are, entirely capable" the superior said as if wishing to break off the discussion. "I need to run this up the chain-of-command straightaway, Wells. Good work, old boy."

With being dismissed so stiffly, Wells indeed felt once more like the old boy that he was. Even when he did succeed, even in a large way as this morning, he received nothing more than a pat on the back from his mid-level superior. Gone were the days when he felt so vibrantly a part of the mechanism of the intelligence apparatus. After all, he had been instrumental in creating it.

Wells wandered back to his office, to go through the rest of his morning messages. Amongst them was a message received in his absence from an old colleague in MI6. It read, *Up for a walk through the park this noon? Bit of a chat? Meet me at Horseguards parade grounds. - Harry.*

Wincer knew that *Harry* was none other than Harold Allan Maycock, one of the MI6 staff that was known to be in league with Kim Philby. Philby had been in Section D and had made the jump to the SOE along with Wells. Wells had become close with him while the two worked together, for, if nothing else, Philby had always included Wells in the sharing of closely held intelligence. Wells had always reciprocated with some lowly intel of his own, chicken scratch mostly, but that was how the game was played. Wincer decided he would indeed meet Philby's alternate, Harry Maycock, at noon.

When the hour came, the two men greeted each other warmly and strolled along the Pall Mall towards the palace in their gray suits, black wingtips and umbrellas, totally unnecessary this fine day. They spoke only in general terms and minor niceties until they had crossed over the Kensington Road and into the more open expanses of Hyde Park.

"By the bye, Wells, Brother Kim says warm greetings are to be passed on to you," Maycock said. "He's back at MI6 with us again, you know."

"So one hears," said Wells, his face contorting at the reference to Philby's name. "I understand he is running things on the Rock these days."

"I'm not so sure anyone in Intelligence runs anything at Gibraltar, do they?" Harry said. "Far too many military types there. Hard to get anyone to listen to you if you're without stripes and stars on your jacket. Eisenhower ran the *Operation Torch* landing of the Americans in North Africa from the tunnels of the Rock, I understand. Nonetheless, Brother Kim seems to be anchored very soundly there."

"So glad to hear it, Harry," said Wells to Maycock, "as I always had a fondness for Kim. A real up and comer, he is. I must respect anyone who was sly enough to get himself extracted from the ranks of those filthy sodders." Wells last comment was in reference to his own outfit, the SOE itself.

"That's the reason for the walk, Wincer," Maycock said, "Brother Kim feels like your being ploughed under over there. They have no recognition of your abilities. He said he has something to pass on to you, in case it should help you climb up to the surface again where you rightfully belong. *'No one has done more for British Intelligence over the years than old Wincer Wells, not even the Old Man himself,'* says Kim."

"God, I miss old Mansfield, I truly do," admitted Wells. "He was a cock-on leader. A little quirky, perhaps, but a man's man, through and through. Not like all these bleeding politicos running things today. Cumming even had the grace to die with dignity, suddenly and unexpectedly. Instead of whiling away to nothing like I am doing in my old age. He and I couldn't be more *chalk and cheese* in that regard, could we?"

"Well, Wincer, Kim wanted to pass on a message to you," Maycock said. "Regarding that Pole being trained up at the Highlands. He said it's common knowledge that your sodders intend to drop him back into Poland. Kim feels we are playing right into the Gestapo's hands. We are merely allowing their man, who has been spying on us throughout the entire war, to extract himself and at our expense, no less. The SOE is making a terrible mistake, and you, my friend, can help us rectify it."

"You mean that this Bratajewski chap is a Nazi *dopple*?" Wells asked, using the German term for double agent. "Not that business again. I passed along the information you relayed to me about his being tied to Goering through the Schenning farm. I told them about your data that said Schenning's brother-in-law was a colonel on his staff. C's staff determined it to be too thin. *Rightly can't go along accusing General Sikorski's personal pilot of being a plant for the Nazis just because he picked vegetables for a few summers from the wrong German family* they reasoned."

Harry Maycock appeared ready to rebut the logic, perhaps even before Wells espoused it. "So now they train him to be part of the resistance?" he asked. "What better way to weaken the Polish Home Army than from within? You watch, no sooner than a month after he drops into country, the Gestapo will start rolling up all the networks of the Polish Home Army in country."

"Harry," answered Wells, "I am with you and Brother Kim a hundred percent on this Bogdan Bratajewski. I believe him to be rotten to the core. I think you and Kim have made your case. However, there are several layers of stiffly starched white shirts above me who aren't buying it. Not even with Sikorski causing this unnecessary row with Stalin over that dreadful Katyń business. What do you expect me to do?"

"You can stop him, Wincer. That's what you can do. See to it he comes to an unfortunate accident before he gets dropped back into Poland. It's the right thing to do, and deep within yourself, you know that it has to be done."

"You wish for me to take out one of our own agents?" Wells was stunned.

"Brother Kim says there is much more information that Sikorski may be holding back on this man." Maycock replied. "You wait and see, it will come all come out. Perhaps Sikorski has been compromised by this Bogdan fellow in some way. Why else would he be forcing the Katyń issue and alienating Stalin and the Russkies when England most needs them?"

"No, Harry," Wells replied, "it couldn't possibly have anything to do with 22,000 Russian bullets found in the skulls of Sikorski's missing officers, now could it?"

"Now you're buying into this nonsense, too?" Maycock scoffed. "I, for one, believe Katyń was the work of the Nazis. Go ahead, let this man make it to back to Poland. Let the Resistance get rolled up. There will be a day of reckoning that comes. I only pray, Wincer, that when the scales are weighed, you are not judged on what you failed to do."

62 The Sacrifice at Gibraltar

July 1943

"Death and sorrow will be the companions of our journey; hardship our garment; constancy and valor our only shield."

Winston Spencer Churchill

Gibraltar is a mere three mile long strip of British possession at the tip of the Iberian Peninsula along the Mediterranean Sea where it transitions to the namesake strait leading out to the Atlantic Ocean. It is separated from Spain by a crook-necked international border, the length of which can readily be measured in yards in lieu of miles. In front of this British territory lies the Mediterranean Sea itself, while behind it lies the Bay of Algeciras.

Perhaps the singular most known vestige of Gibraltar's territory is the Rock. Its jagged ridges rise some 1400 feet into the sky at the peak, offering a breathtaking view of the eight or so miles of the strait separating it from the Spanish autonomous city of Ceuta on the tip of North Africa bordering Morocco. It was the fortifications along these peaks that allowed the Allies to control all Mediterranean shipping ingressing from and egressing to the Atlantic during World War II.

Below these heights at sea level lies the singular runway of its airport. The runway is adjacent to the border with Spain, although it is, by necessity, straight and not crook-necked.

Figure 43: The Rock of Gibraltar (airport shown beyond) and General Sikorski Inspecting the Rock's Fortifications

The airstrip had only been built in 1941 for the RAF, although by two years later nearly as many American planes taxied its length. Royal Engineers were forced to extend it out into the bay of Algeciras due to the lack of available flat land.

The sun was setting in the west over the ocean on the night of July 3rd, 1943 as Bogdan Bratajewski brought his empty transport aircraft in for a landing from over the Mediterranean. He landed without any difficulty, and was signaled to a reserved spot upon the tarmac. He looked for Sikorski's aircraft, the B-24 Liberator II that he himself had once so meticulously maintained and piloted. The plane was nowhere to be found. He later was to learn that it was expected to arrive from the Middle East in advance of their meeting at noon the next day. Bogdan looked forward to seeing the general and his daughter Zofia once more.

Bogdan slept that night in the quarters kept for visiting airmen. These were at the airfield barracks adjacent to the tarmac. That night he tossed and turned as a peaceful sleep had eluded him. He thought all night as to whom the pair of passengers might be that he was to fly back to London at General Sikorski's behest.

He ran through the timing in his head, calculating just how long the flight to London would take to determine at which hour he needed to depart Gibraltar. He would of course leave himself a buffer for any unexpected weather, or if he might need to fly clear of any reported enemy aircraft.

The morning came and Bogdan was pleased to see General Sikorski's B-24 on the tarmac next to his own aircraft. He then walked over to the pool of jeeps used to transport the military officers to the meeting rooms carved out along the tunnels that burrowed into the Rock itself.

"Take me to General Sikorski," he said to the sergeant running the pool.

"Name?"

"Airman Bogdan Bratajewski"

"You are sure as sod going to have to spell that mouthful, mate."

Bogdan did, and soon after a call confirmed that he was expected, the jeep whisked off. Instead of carrying upward to the rock, however, it snaked its way along the beach lying beneath it just down for the airfield.

"Your general is reviewing some Polish troops this morning that are currently passing through our little outpost," said the driver. There was no traffic other than military. The territory's 30,000 residents in peacetime had all been evacuated at the war's beginning to Madeira, Morocco and even Jamaica.

“First time here, mate?” The driver asked. As Bogdan nodded his head, the man unexpectedly broke into his best impression of a tour guide. “Gibraltar, from the Arabic *Jabal Ṭāriq or Mount of Ṭāriq,* after the Berber son-of-a-bitch who landed here in the year of our Lord 711. Of course, Spain finally got around to kicking them out in 1492, before they even knew that Columbus’ expedition had found the New World. Then we took it from them in the War of the Spanish Succession in 1704. Lord Nelson knew this place well in Napoleon’s day. In peacetime, they say half of the world’s shipping comes through this strait. Africa is less than nine miles across it.”

They were driving along the road that ran at the base of the Rock along the strait. Bogdan listened as the driver rambled on and wondered if every new arrival here got the same canned discourse. Not wishing to insult the man, Bogdan listened patiently, although his mind was surely elsewhere.

Soon they arrived and just as had been explained, General Sikorski was greeting each soldier with a salute, followed by a handshake and words of thanks for their service to the country that soon would have been completely overrun by the Germans for three years.

This seemed to be a service of which the general never tired. In fact, it energized him. Whether he was meeting with Polish Army Battalions in Cairo, as he had been doing just the day before, or Polish sailors along the Leith Docks of Edinburgh, or escorting King George VI as he congratulated the Polish Airmen for their courageous fighting over England and the Channel, General Sikorski never failed to come from these events more refreshed than going into them.

General Sikorski engaged the men while his staff looked on. This included his daughter Zofia Leśniowska, who had always been so kind to Bogdan as he transitioned into his role as the general’s pilot. She was beautiful, and despite traveling everywhere by her father’s side, she showed no signs of weariness from the road.

After the ceremony ended, Zofia walked over to Bogdan with a radiant smile.

“C*zęść, Pan* Bratajewski,” she called out. “If it is not my father’s favorite pilot here in Gibraltar.”

“C*zęść, Pani* Leśniowska,” replied Bogdan, “how is your husband Lieutenant Stanislaus? Does he fare well in this war?”

"You know that my husband is an engineer, Bogdan. He sleeps like a log anywhere he is allowed to, so long as he fixes anything that is broken. How can he not be faring well? After all, there are many broken things to fix and much sleep to be caught up on. I very much look forward to seeing him soon."

"Tomorrow in London, perhaps?" Bogdan asked.

"Sadly no, " Zofia replied, "but at least I will be able to get in some excellent riding there. Between my horse and my husband, it is a close call which I miss more." She laughed loudly.

Bogdan laughed before asking, "Who travels with your father on this trip?"

"Many people it seems," Zofia said, "all eager to get back to London in the overnight hours. We are eleven, not counting the crew."

"I was told to expect to transport two passengers back to London when I leave here. Is it two of your party?"

"No, and I will tell you that there is a delay to the arrival of the two Polish cryptographers my father had wished to give you the honor of transporting back to London. Unfortunately, *Pan* Rejewski and *Pan* Zygalski have been detained in Portugal and are not here as expected. Father wanted you to carry these men to safety, they have been through so much."

"I am amazed," said Bogdan, "the last I heard they were in a Spanish prison."

"Yes, they had been for six months after their border guide robbed them. Then they were released and made their way from Madrid to Lisbon. But their ship to Gibraltar was held for U-boats in the area. So alas, they are not here as expected."

"That is very unfortunate, for it would indeed have been an honor to pilot them to freedom. So it seems I made this journey for no other reason than the joy to see you again, Zofia."

"Do you see that man there?" Zofia pointed to a very sharp looking uniformed officer who was at that moment approaching her father.

"Yes."

"He is Major General Tadeusz Klimecki, the Chief of the General Staff for the Polish Army. You and father will be meeting with him and that other man."

Zofia pointed to a sharply dressed man in a civilian suit and tie.

"And who might he be?"

"He is *Pan* Jan Gralewski," she answered, "one of the top couriers between my father and the *Armia Krajowa*. He is a most interesting man to have a conversation with. Well-trained at the University of Warsaw in Philosophy. Before the war, he published papers on philosophy and literary theory. Once the war started he became a significant member of the resistance, as did his wife. I believe the three of you - father, General Klimecki, and he - are to discuss your upcoming assignment. What you are about to do is very brave, Bogdan. I respect you so much for putting your life on the line for our country."

Bogdan raised his hand in protest. "It is nothing any other Polish patriot would not do. To serve within our country alongside the Polish Home Army, it is exactly what I have been waiting for. It is exactly what the SOE has trained me for."

"Many would *like* to do this, it is true," said Zofia, "but you, *Pan* Bogdan Bratajewski, will be the one actually doing it. And in doing so, you have my greatest respect and admiration."

She leaned over and kissed him gently on his cheek. Bogdan replied with nothing more than a meager, "*Dziękuję*".

The three men had walked through a long linear length of tunnel known locally as one of the *Galleries,* short for *the Great Siege Tunnels*. General Sikorski explained that some of these dated back to 1797 and the Great Siege of Gibraltar by the French and Spaniards. These tunnels were all hewn in the Rock's stone, made up of shale and limestone. The Galleries had been greatly extended over the years, and especially during the beginning of this war. They were improved only with metal conduits connecting a series of low hanging explosion-proof lights. The cage around each bulb reminded Bogdan that in these tunnels, there was always a fear of gas leaking, and great lengths were taken to assure nothing could ignite if gas were present. Of course, even if not ignited, gas could asphyxiate those inside, although this had not been a major issue since the installation.

"First, Airman Bratajewski," General Sikorski began, "all of us want to recognize your courage and dedication in training for the *Cichociemni.* Not many are worthy of joining *the Silent Unseen.*"

The *Cichociemni* were the elite element of the Polish Resistance, trained by the SOE, but working nearly autonomously behind enemy lines. Anyone joining their ranks committed to put his life on the line in order to free Poland. The other men pounded their open stretched palms on the wooden surface of the table in a show of their respect. Bogdan merely dropped his head in recognition and strained not to blush at their praise.

"I have asked you to travel here for two reasons. The lesser I understand my *Zosia* has already shared with you. I hoped to bestow the honor on you of flying our two surviving Enigma code breakers back to freedom, but I am sorry to say that they are still in Lisbon. So then, let us proceed on to the main reason for your coming so far."

General Sikorski then waved his hand as if it signaled an invitation for *Pan* Jan Gralewski to speak. Instead of doing so, he opened a leather briefcase and extracted a photograph.

"Airman Bratajewski, are you familiar with the *Man in the Red Circle?"*

"Yes, *Pan* Gralewski," Bogdan replied, "but only after I came to pilot General Sikorski after escaping the invasion. *The Man in the Red Circle* was first noted in some chatter picked up by our listeners on the German Radio frequencies back as 1936. The Nazis thought he might be leading a resistance movement and were looking frantically for him."

"This is that man," said *Pan* Gralewski, sliding a photograph face up onto the tabletop. Bogdan inspected it. "His name is *Herr* Otto Landverstokt, a worker in the Bloom and Voss Shipyard. Do you notice anything about it."

The photo was black and white, and it showed a crowd of several hundred people giving the *Heil Hitler* salute. In it a gray circle was drawn around one man, who not only refused to raise his right arm, but actually had both arms crossed in protest.

"*Proszę*, allow me to guess, in the original photo this superimposed circle was red?" Bogdan joked. "Even in black and white it is a very significant act of defiance."

"More so than you might think," added General Klimecki, "for visiting the shipyard that day was *Der Führer* himself. It was amazing that *Herr* Landverstokt was not pulled from the crowd and shot on the spot. Perhaps because it was not noticed until later, when the photo was developed and enlarged? We can not be sure. But as you said, it lit up the Nazi airwaves searching for *Herr* Landverstokt."

"I have another photo of *Herr* Landverstokt for you to look at, I am afraid," said *Pan* Gralewski. "It is more recent, taken only a few months ago in Breslau. I hope it is not too disturbing for you. What do you notice about it?"

The courier slid the second photo face up onto the table alongside the first. In it, a crowd surrounded a raised platform. The German civilian mob taunted a man and woman who were tied back to back at wooden stakes. The man was clearly *Herr* Landverstokt, older and aged beyond the five years that spanned the two photos. The woman was dressed in torn and tattered peasant garb. Her head was shaved. On her right breast was pinned a diamond shaped insignia bearing a single letter "P". The photo was also in black and white, although Bogdan knew the insignia letter was in black on a yellow background. It was the insignia all Poles were required to wear in public.

"It is clearly a public shaming," said Bogdan. "This *Herr* Landverstokt was caught in a shameful act with this Polish laboress. She is likely a farm worker, or perhaps a factory worker. If he was caught defiling her, the Germans are extremely unforgiving of these mixed relations, of any kind, between *racially pure* Germans with the *Untermensch*."

Bogdan noticed that General Sikorski was watching his face intently. General Klimecki then leaned over to the Prime Minister and whispered, "He does not see it…"

"Airman Bratajewski," Sikorski addressed Bogdan, "your mission will be to enter Germany through Poland, find this man, and extract him. He is to be brought to London or a place of our choosing to be interrogated. We need to understand the resistance against Hitler that may be organized within Germany."

"Yes, my General, I can certainly do this," Bogdan said.

"Don't be so quick to answer, my former pilot," said Sikorski, "and take another look at the second photo. Look at the face of the woman shamed along with *Herr* Landverstokt."

Bogdan looked once more at the photo. The two images on the stand in the town square were small and grainy. The woman's face was at an oblique angle to the camera. The image was shot almost over her shoulder.

"I cannot make out who this woman may be," he said.

"The sources within our Home Army Intelligence Group believe this woman to be your sister," declared *Pan* Gralewski.

"Justyna?" Bogdan reached for the photo, and took it in both hands holding it close to his face as if that would increase his recognition.

"It appears your sister has had a relationship with *Herr* Landverstokt," said *Pan* Gralewski, "although most likely against her will. Our agents in Breslau say that she has been released, and that she is pregnant. We wish you to use your sister to find Herr Landverstokt."

"Justyna! What has become of you?" Bogdan said mournfully. "What have those bastards done to you?"

"Bogdan," Sikorski said, in a rare display of using his first name in a public setting, "we know that what we ask of you is an extreme burden. You would likely rather kill this man than bring him back to us. I certainly understand that, but we have decided to use you not only because your sister is a connection to this man and therefore can get you close to him, but also for your piloting skills. You will readily be able to fly him out of Poland from one of our bases there. If this task is too much for you to bear, just let me know and we will find another to carry forward with it."

"No, my General," Bogdan said excitedly, almost cutting him off, "I must do this. I must see my little sister once more. This is how God intended for me to use the skills He has given to me. I am prepared to carry on with this mission."

"*Dobrze bardzo*, Bogdan. I hoped you would respond so," said Sikorski. "Now I will leave you with these men who will go over the details of your mission. Do you have any last requests of me before I leave you?"

"Yes, General," Bogdan answered, "I have two, in fact."

"What are they, my friend?"

"I assume that I will be dropped into Poland from an airfield in southern Sweden. My request is that as I travel to Sweden, I will be allowed to stop in Norway to see the site where my brother, Albin, gave his life to save a British agent."

"Done," Sikorski said, although the faces of *Pan* Gralewski and General Klimecki expressed dismay. "What is your second request?"

"That I be allowed to inspect your plane before I leave tonight for Edinburgh. Knowing that your aircraft is in excellent condition will comfort me greatly. Also, I have grown somewhat sentimental about my old friend, and would like to say goodbye to her."

"Of course," said General Sikorski. "I cannot deny you that. I will send word to allow you access to the Liberator. You will fly back to London this evening?"

"I thought as I have no passengers to ferry, I might fly on directly to Edinburgh instead. I was told that was where I would deploy from, is that correct?" Bogdan looked on to Gralewski and Klimecki, who nodded in agreement.

"I had a thought about your taking Zofia along for a ride to accompany you on your flight home," Sikorski said, "but as you are not going to London now, she can wait a few additional hours and fly with us tonight. No, Airman Bratajewski, fly directly to Scotland. May our Lord watch over you as you do."

All stood as General Sikorski rose. Bogdan saluted him, and the general returned his salute with his trademark precision. After he had left the room, the three men sat once again.

"This should take no more than a few hours," said *Pan* Gralewski, "but first let me see your right hand."

Bogdan looked surprised by this request.

"Your scar, Agent Bratajewski," said Gralewski, "show me your scar."

Bogdan held out his arm and unfurled the fingers of his right hand. His palm was exposed upright, and in its center was the scar, long ago healed, of his burn received in the Siedlce railroad station during the bombing there. It was shaped like the cross of our Lord, although somewhat irregular around its edges.

"Yes, this is excellent," said Gralewski. "It will be an unmistakeable recognition trait for those who are to covertly meet you. We will photograph it later in the sunlight outside, so it can be forwarded to our agents in Poland and Germany."

It neared 1900 hours, or seven in the evening when Bogdan Bratajewski descended the Rock back to the RAF airfield hiding in its shadow. As he prepared for the return flight to Edinburgh, he was still troubled by the weight of the information that the three men had burdened him with. *So, they expect me to save the life of a man who appears to have taken my own young sister's innocence by force. Can I do that? Can I resist the temptation to kill the German bastard when I have the chance? How much more can I bear in this war, having already sacrificed Albin in Norway, and now Justyna's innocence. How can I be expected to carry on without taking my own vengeance?*

As he walked up to General Sikorski's B-24 Liberator II transport aircraft, he noticed another transport nearby with Soviet markings. It was odd that there was no one guarding the aircraft. Bogdan inspected Sikorski's Liberator, easily accessing its interior and cockpit with no resistance or interruption. He went so far as to check the controls in the cockpit. All seemed normal. He articulated the control surfaces, and they moved freely and with no unexpected delay or binding of any kind. He inspected the cabin and then walked the exterior of the aircraft. Everything seemed intact. It was good to see his old partner one last time, and feel her respond to the touch of his hands, even if he could not take her once more into the heavens.

Bogdan walked into the duty office to file his flight plan to Edinburgh. He asked the duty officer about the Russian transport, and was told it belonged to the Soviet Ambassador Ivan Maisky who was visiting that day as well. Bogdan then commented that he saw no guards posted at any of the three aircraft and was given a lame excuse.

"Sorry, mate, guard details are not in my purview, now are they?" he said. "Remember not to roll until we have the barriers down and all cross traffic is bottled up."

He spoke about the fact that this airstrip, nestled so tightly in this territory's only flat patch at sea level, was crossed by the main road coming in from the border with Spain. Every time a plane landed, or in this case took off, barrier arms were first deployed to stop the flow of all vehicular traffic crossing the runway. It was a very unusual arrangement necessitated by the lack of level land which, thanks to the extensions made by the Royal Engineers, barely accommodated the runway's length.

Bogdan returned to his aircraft. He completed his pre-flight checks and walked its exterior. Everything was as it should be. He taxied out for take off at precisely 1940 hours, or twenty to eight in the evening. The sun was only then beginning to set in the west. There would be another two hours until sunset. Bogdan watched the barriers deploy, and smiled to himself as the traffic backed up in each direction as he prepared to release his roll. A voice in English commanded him to do so, and before long he felt the freedom of his wheels lifting from the ground. He flew out over the Mediterranean before banking to his starboard side. He had a magnificent view of the Rock, as the long rays of the sun struck upon it, casting shadows to the east. Bogdan thought of his own upcoming journey eastward, beginning at Albin's grave.

Bogdan soon was out over the Atlantic Ocean and wide awake as the threat of enemy planes flying south or west from Nazi occupied France were to be expected. Yet his flight was not eventful, even the weather was accommodating him that night.

There is much to this day that is still not known about General Sikorski's flight later that night. What is known is that his aircraft took off at 2307 hours and ended only 16 seconds later. The plane had climbed before suddenly pitching down as it crashed into the Mediterranean Sea. All eleven passengers perished, including General Sikorski, his Chief of Staff General Klimecki, the Home Army Courier *Pan* Gralewski and eight others. Among those was General Sikorski's Secretary and daughter, Zofia Lewandowska, although her body was never recovered. There was only a single survivor of the crash, the Czech pilot Eduard Prchal, who was significantly injured. He claimed that the controls of the aircraft had jammed and became unresponsive. Later, an inquiry board found that this *could* have occurred due to shifting of cargo within the aircraft upon takeoff.

Immediately several conspiracy theories were advanced claiming this not to have been an accident at all, but a well planned assassination of General Sikorski. It had not even been two full months since relations between Poland and Russia had broken down over the Katyń Commission. Sikorski's demand for Stalin's Russia to be held responsible was seen as having driven a wedge between the otherwise cohesive group of nations allied against Hitler and Nazi Germany. Many claimed that Stalin was behind Sikorski's removal, while others even suggested Churchill himself. Much later, after he defected to Moscow in 1963, others would point to the fact that Kim Philby, the Soviet Spy and head of the Cambridge Five ring, was stationed at the Rock at that time.

A subsequent review board had ruled that the aircraft crashed due to an unidentified mechanical failure, but ruled out sabotage as a cause, which only led theorists to ask, *How can they know it was not sabotage if they cannot identify the cause of the "mechanical failure"?* One thing is certain: Poland never again had so respected a leader as it had in Władysław Sikorski.

"I am afraid at this point I must stop," said Sophie to Henia and Marcin. The woman looked at *Zosia* with disbelief, as her husband wrapped his arm around his wife to console her.

Henia then asked abruptly, "You have not yet answered the most pressing question - did Great-Uncle Bogdan have anything to do with General Sikorski's accident?"

Sophie looked meekly at her. The best response she could muster was, "It appears not. But, I will tell you that there were some within the British Intelligence community who were advancing that very rumor, if only to cover their own tracks. Your Great-Uncle Bogdan had been trained to become a resistance fighter who was to be sent into occupied Poland. This was done on General Sikorski's recommendation. It makes no sense that he would have had any part in the general's death."

"So this is all you found, *Zosia*?" asked Henia.

"*Pani* Henia," Sophie began, "this is where the trail of your great-uncle appears to end. Tomorrow I return to Poland, and I will soon take the train to Warsaw to further investigate the files of the Home Army and the Resistance. If his name appears there, we will confirm that Bogdan Bratajewski was inserted successfully, and was in no way connected with General Sikorski's death."

"And should you find no record of his name in those archives?" Henia asked.

"That could mean several things," replied Sophie tactfully. "It could mean he never made it there, was killed in transit, for it was wartime. Or it could mean the British Secret Service had him executed for the general's death. Lastly, I am afraid it could mean he was simply a Nazi spy all along who disappeared back into Germany. But I assure you of this - I will investigate this with all my abilities until the truth is known."

Figure 44: Four Man WWII X-Craft Mini-Submarine

63 A Decision of Destiny

July 1943

"Honours should go where death and danger go."

Winston Spencer Churchill

Einar MacAlvor watched the fjord's calm surface in the brief overnight stillness from a wooded section overlooking the shoreline. To his left lay the small fjord-side hamlet of Hilleshamn, Norway. He was alone, and was so by his own doing. Einar had demanded that Kari was safest alone back at the coastal *rorbu*. Einar demanded that Wincer Wells instruct her that this mission was strictly a solo run for himself. Coming from Wells, Kari reluctantly agreed.

Einar waited in this nexus point of intersecting fjords. He was much further in from the coast, his position was at the mouth of the *Gratangenfjord.* His was the extremely risky mission to meet the man put ashore by the Royal Navy and guide him overland to the assigned location before accompanying him to the neutral Swedish border.

What made this mission so very dangerous was that it occurred only a few weeks after the Summer Solstice, June 22, the longest day of the year, which in this part of the Arctic meant the Midnight Sun. On this particular night, the 8th of July, there was still too little true darkness to surface a submarine off the coast near Nyksund, as when Einar had been so stealthily inserted. A submarine was too large, and too likely to be spotted against the steel gray haze that only charaded as darkness. And this Arctic summer night, that haze would only last for about forty minutes after sunset at 12:30 am. It was determined that surfacing a Royal Navy submarine was far too dangerous. So instead, Einar waited and watched the stillness of the fjord.

Einar looked at the semi-luminous face of his wristwatch. He had his night eyes adjusted to the darkness. Three minutes past midnight. Another twenty minutes before he could expect any company. He was nestled between two trees adjoined at their trunk, making a wooden "V" which afforded good cover.

Einar thought on how odd were the communications for this mission coming from Wells. It came through their back-up frequency, even though other messages were still transmitted through the primary frequency. Wells' messages were encoded via the one-time pads that only he and Wells held. It was as if that old bastard was trying to slip in instructions around the formal channels. When Einar translated the message Wells sent, he thought he could see why. The SOE needed plausible deniability, after all, if he were to execute these orders faithfully.

Einar was instructed to make this rendezvous, and then by a predetermined overland path, he was to take this agent to the very site where his brother had died, before getting him on to the safety of Sweden. There was just one major problem, the location where the agent's brother had died turned out to be the same location where Einar's own brother, Gunnar, had died. The "*staircase of the gods*" - that single spot on all of the earth that tortured Einar in his dreams. Also, that meant the agent's brother was one of the Poles who had come to their rescue only to die there.

Einar had been the only one to escape those cliff's ledges. Well, there had been the Pole "Edjew" also, but his rescue had been short-lived when he had a damn aircraft carrier sink from underneath him and drowned.

Fifteen minutes passed, the placid waters rippled, before they silently parted and exposed the black metal upper surface of the X-craft. These new four man miniature submarines were only 51 feet long, but what Einar saw exposed in the fjord was significantly less length. The vessel made virtually no noise whatsoever in surfacing.

Einar's heart raced as he raised his field glasses to his eyes. He watched as a small hatch opened and the shoulders and head of a gray figure emerged. He then climbed out and lowered himself alongside the craft into the water. Another gray figure emerged from the vessel and handed a parcel to the first, who very gently and quietly laid it upon the fjord's surface. A quick motion made by the submerged figure caused the parcel to inflate, making no noise other than a flop as it unfurled.

The second gray figure then assisted a third man down into the inflatable dinghy, as the first man in the water pulled himself up and into it as well.

Einar continued to watch as this silent ballet continued. Every step rehearsed, choreographed to meet an unforgiving timeline. And soon the rubber dinghy, under the power of a silent electric outboard motor, crawled toward them.

Einar scurried down to the shoreline to receive his visitor. As the dinghy approached, he and the motoring seaman exchanged near whispered passwords.

"In ya' go," said the man, covered in the flat matte of his frogman's skin. He hopped effortlessly out of the dinghy, and assisted Einar in. "She's got just enough power to make the end of this fjord. When you get close to shore, jettison the motor and battery into the fjord and use the oars the rest of the way in. Deflate the dinghy and hide the carcass and oars. I understand the rest of the way she'll be no use to ya'?"

"Not at all," said Einar, "it's all overland and uphill from there. Do you want us to run you back to your vessel?"

"What? And spoil my moonlight swim? Don't you fancy a good swim in near freezing water every chance ya' get? Be off lad. Godspeed to you."

"And Godspeed to you," Einar replied.

The frogman began his short swim to the X-Craft, and Einar manned the motor. As he pulled away from the shore to head up the *Gratangenfjord*, Einar said to his passenger, "Show it to me."

"What?" asked the man in broken, Slavic accented English.

Einar extended his palm, face up.

The man looked and nodded his head to acknowledge he understood. He held out his right palm, and exposed the scar of the cross so long ago burned into it.

Einar relaxed as he guided the dinghy inland along this dead-headed fjord. He looked behind just as the first of the morning's light was trapped in the filter of the sky, but could see nothing but nature's own beauty. The X-craft had submerged and was by then surely headed back to the coast where it would once again tether itself to its assigned full size Royal Navy submarine. The rendezvous location had been selected because the labyrinth of fjords interconnecting there that would allow the mini-submarine multiple underwater paths to the open sea.

Einar steadied the dinghy and switched off the electric motor. As instructed, he dumped it and the nearly drained battery into the fjord, and watched them sink rapidly to its depths. Then, he took the oars and made for landfall.

As he labored, he thought on the orders he had received regarding this other man in the dinghy. What made no sense to Einar was that the directive he had received from Wells was marked *"Eyes Only"* to Einar, which meant under no circumstances was this to be shared with Kari. He and Kari had become ever so close over their months together. She knew Einar was decoding a message she was not cleared to read, but it still hurt her when he refused to share its contents with her.

What could she have possibly thought? *Who would ever know other than Einar and I? Why won't he say, "Orders be damned," and let her in on the secret? Did he not trust her to keep it? Did Wells not trust her to know it?*

The truth was that Einar did not wish her to see this message. In fact, he wished he had never seen it. He read over the words, again and again, and each time a flash of chill ran through him. It read:

TAKE AGENT TO PREDETERMINED LOCATION STOP AS HE REFLECTS ON HIS BROTHER'S DEATH, DISPOSE OF HIM STOP BULLET TO THE BACK OF THE HEAD STOP DUMP REMAINS IN FJORD STOP ACKNOWLEDGE RECEIPT OF THIS ORDER FULL STOP

Einar did not acknowledge. He hesitated. He rolled the words on the transcription sheet around in his head. They clashed noisily into other words, something his father, Brigand, was prone to say, *There is no shame in asking a question to which you do not know the answer. The only sin is in living with the question unasked.* So, taking his dead father's advice, Einar waited thirty minutes to send the single word response.

WHY FULL STOP

Within five minutes came the response. *That was fast! Did Wells have it already worked out on the one-time pad in advance of his asking?*

The message was received and decoded by Einar. It read, *AGENT HAS BEEN FOUND GUILTY OF SABOTAGING AIRCRAFT OF GENERAL SIKORSKI AT GIBRALTAR STOP EXECUTION ORDER OF THIS AGENT ORIGINATES FROM POLISH GOVERNMENT-IN-EXILE STOP ACKNOWLEDGE ORDER FULL STOP*

Einar read the message over again and again. Each time with more questions than answers. *Since when would the service, either MI6 or the SOE, take orders from the Polish Government-in-Exile? Even if they did, why would the Polish Government not want to question this man who was at that time confined in the hull of a British submarine? Why would they not want him returned to London?* Most taxing to Einar was, *Why would the British government risk doing an X-Craft landing in a fjord under near Midnight Sun conditions only so that man put ashore could be summarily executed? Why risk the mini-sub and the lives of the sailors aboard? Why not surface in the North Sea and throw the bastard overboard with some ballast tied around his neck?*

Einar knew he would never get the answers to these or any other questions he might have. He knew he had but a single decision to make. Would he accept the order, or refuse it and risk being pulled out of Norway. Away from his Kari. Away from the resting place of Gunnar. This mission to that sacred ground that he was otherwise denied would be scrubbed. Einar waited another half hour before sending a two word message.

ORDER ACKNOWLEDGED FULL STOP.

Einar looked at the face ahead of him in the dinghy, It was the expectant face of a dead man. And yet, there was something familiar about it.

Einar landed the vessel. He and the agent deflated it, and hid it in the brush along with he oars. They walked a bit along the shore until Einar found the rucksack he had pre-positioned there. It was heavily laden with food, as Einar did not wish to have another hungry moment upon those damn ledges. Tied to it were two bedrolls with enough warmth to get them through the Arctic summer nights. And in its side pocket was the Walther P-38 Automatic that Einar had taken from that bastard Becker upon that cliff.

It had all begun in the immediate aftermath of the plane crash during the last hour of July 4, 1943. The next morning, as the aircraft debris and bodily remains were being fished from the

Mediterranean Sea, Kim Philby's representative in London, Harry Maycock, made an urgent beeline to Wells' office.

"Damn it man," he began with Wells, "we've been feeding you information all along that this Bratajewski was a German plant, and you have done nothing with it. The result of which is now that he has murdered General Sikorski. Kim is stationed at Gibraltar. Bratajewski was seen fiddling about that Liberator only a few hours before the crash. And this Bratajewski chap is a man fresh off of sabotage training, no less. Knows the aircraft inside and out, literally. Mucked up the controls, for sure. Then, just before all hell breaks loose, Bratajewski takes off and flies to Scotland and puts out to sea on a submarine just this morning, before he can even be interrogated by the Intel Unit there. All just too convenient given the circumstances. He must not be allowed to drop back into Germany, Wells, and you are the last man in place to stop him."

The truth was that Philby, via Maycock, had long ago shared with Wells their concerns of Bratajewski. Wells had accepted their position that the entire ruse with Churchill's Flamingo flying home solo from France in 1940 was nothing more than an attempt to have the German agent Bratajewski fly fighter cover for the Prime Minister. Thank God Churchill had dismissed Sikorski's offer immediately out of hand. Wincer Wells was convinced by Philby and Maycock that Bratajewski would have shot down the Flamingo and then headed directly for German occupied portions of northern France.

Thanks only to Churchill's insistence that he and his ministers fly home without fighter support, that well thought-out ruse had failed, these men insisted. However, now it appeared Bratajewski has caused the death of another Prime Minister, in General Sikorski. This caused Wells a myriad of other questions. *General Sikorski had been Bratajewski's cover, so why execute the man? Had General Sikorski somehow developed information that Bratajewski was a German double agent in their midsts? Was that why the Polish agent had been called to The Rock so suddenly in the first place? All who had attended that meeting in the Galleries, save Bratajewski, had died in this crash. But if that were true, that the reason for this secret meeting was his being a spy, why was Bratajewski ever allowed to depart Gibraltar at all? Why wasn't he detained by force?*

On the other hand, why would the Germans want Sikorski executed? They had, after all, used the Katyń situation to drive a wedge between the Polish general and Stalin. Did it not make more sense that Stalin would have taken action directly against Sikorski after their falling out?

Wells then became aware that Harry Maycock claimed to have in his possession information that thoroughly exonerated the Soviet Union in this Katyń business. That material was very classified indeed, and according to Maycock, had been presented to Sikorski that very day on The Rock. It was the reason that Soviet Ambassador, Ivan Maisky, was even there that afternoon. According to Maycock, General Sikorski was about to go public with it, blame Katyń on the Nazis and resume relations once more with Stalin and the Soviet Union.

The theory that was presented to Wells was that the German high command had caught wind of all this and activated their sleeper agent, Bratajewski. He sabotaged Sikorski's aircraft and then had a convenient deployment planned to drop him back into German controlled Polish territories. Once there, Bratajewski would be picked up by the Gestapo, taken to the Berlin Reich's Chancellory, and receive accolades for a job well done, along with a pat on the back.

The news of Sikorski's death had come as a shock to the world and to Wells personally that morning. Philby and Maycock had been pointing to the Pole as a security risk all along. Now, the worst had come to pass.

"But what do you expect me to do?" Wells asked Maycock. "Am I to just gun down this man in the field?"

"Don't you see, Wincer," Harry answered, "you are in the catbird's seat. Sikorsky had before his death given orders to have Bratajewski deployed through Norway. Have your man MacAlvor take Bratajewski to see where his brother died. Then have your man give him a shove over the side and we all report up the chain that it was a most unfortunate accident. MI6 will stand behind you all the way. We might even *'intercept'* a message from the *Wilhelmstrasse* a few weeks down the line *'confirming'* the loss of their double agent. But time is of the essence, Wells, you must signal your man in Norway to take immediate action."

Wells wondered how Kim Philby and Harry Maycock had become knowledgeable so quickly of Bratajewski's drop into Norway. Then he reasoned that Philby might have had reason to have a follow-up discussion on The Rock with either General Sikorski or his Polish Home Army liaison, Jan Gralewski, to that effect. In any case, Jan Gralewski was on Sikorski's plane and both were dead. The only person who knew the truth for certain was likely Philby himself.

All of this was nothing more than a swirl of arguments, counter-arguments, conspiracies and literal dead ends. Based on it all, Maycock wanted Bratajewski dead. Not returned for questioning, but silenced forever. Why?

Wells wrestled with the decision throughout the day. He finally convinced himself that Bratajewski could not be allowed to drop back into Germany, or any part of the former Polish territories under its control. He signaled the *Eyes Only* message to Einar himself, and destroyed all traces of its content immediately thereafter. It was all set. Kari would stay behind while Einar led Bratajewski to the site where both their brothers had died. Once there, Einar would dispose of Bratajewski, and make sure his body ended up in the fjord below.

Einar led the agent under his command that day through the valley that led from the head of the *Gratangenfjord* down to the town of Bjerkvik, at the head of the *Herangsfjord*. They rested at the line of lakes approximately half way there. Before they reached Bjerkvik itself, they detoured to their left and ascended the heights that would eventually lead them to *Lomvatnet*, the high mountain lake that would mark their proximity to the *staircase of the gods*. Exhausted, the two men made camp in the hills overlooking Bjerkvik, about a quarter of the way to *Lomvatnet.*

Despite their time together, the two men conversed little. They both spoke English, although Bogdan had only done so for a few years and his vocabulary was often strained for the words to convey what he tried to say.

Einar thought even if Bogdan had the full command of the language, he would not have much to say. Bogdan was quiet by nature, he thought, but he also seemed to be preoccupied with heavy burdens, be they from his past or in his future.

That night they shared a fire, food from Einar's rucksack, and a few friendly smiles. Bogdan prayed in his native tongue, and the two men rested in the warmth of the bedrolls.

The next day in Norway was a strenuous hike for the two agents. Einar led Bogdan to the top of the granite mountain that made up the north side of the *Rombaksfjord*. By mid-afternoon, they had found the beauty of the mountain lake, *Lomvatnet*. There they rested knowing they were close.

At the *Lomvatnet*, both men were nervously quiet. Einar did not know how he would react to going back to what had become in his mind his brother's grave. A tension ticked through him, like the seconds of a timer wired to high explosive charge. Einar knew what to expect with the ratcheting sound of each tick, except the very last - when the full fury of emotions exploded within him and his capacity to reason was as wasted as scattered debris of the aftermath.

The time came to do it. To go there. Einar and Bogdan left this lush pool of Eden that was the *Lomvatnet* to seek out the barren lonely steps of the frigid hell that had consumed each of their brothers. The trail was much overgrown from what Einar remembered, almost to the point that he doubted he had even found the right path. Then it opened up to that series of rough ledges hewn into both the mountain's side and Einar's memory. This was what he and Gunnar had called *the staircase of the gods.*

An instant heaviness befell Einar. It was a feeling unlike any other he had ever felt. Equal parts *déjà vu* and penitent reverence. He thought of all the killing that had gone on here, and he was expected to add one more soul to the devilish tally.

"Is this where it occurred?" asked Bogdan. Einar answered only with a look that left no question of the answer. Einar then led Bogdan carefully down the ledges until they came to the fourth ledge overlooking the *Rombaksfjord.* Einar removed the rucksack from his shoulder and laid it in the corner of the last ledge. As Bogdan looked out across the fjord, Einar slipped the Walther P-38 automatic from its pocket on the rucksack's side into that of his jacket.

"It is absolutely beautiful," said Bogdan, "I would not have expected it to be so."

Einar rejoined him and pointed to Hundalen Station along the rail line across the fjord. Its red walls and white trim stood out against the tawny summer colors of the mountain. Even the greens of the trees seemed so muted and drained. Einar then told Bogdan the story of how, from there, he and his brother had watched the crews of the four German destroyers scuttle their ships to prevent them falling into the hands of the Allies.

Bogdan said stoically, "Often, life demands sacrifices."

What a damn odd thing for a man who lost his brother here to say, Einar thought. *Is he validating the Nazis scuttling of their own ships? Perhaps he indeed is the double agent the club thinks him to be...*

"This is where it all happened," Einar then said. "My brother died of his wounds, there, on that third ledge. Wounds from a *Gebirgsjäger* colonel named Becker. Your brother, I believe, would have been up there on this first ledge providing for our defense when the Germans attacked. Thanks to them, I survived. I was the only one who did."

"I am afraid this is not true," Bogdan said in his broken English. "There was that Nazi, Becker, yes, that is correct. He was stabbed in his leg very badly, but that lieutenant colonel lived. The Polish Resistance relayed the story of his recovery from the hospital in Breslau. The bastard lived but he lost his leg. I am told he is back in Norway in some non-combat capacity."

"My God," replied Einar, "I assumed Becker was dead all this time. I had thought the Pole Albin shot him after I started down on the ropes." Einar felt the emotions of the site reverberate through him. The Walther P-38 that had been Becker's felt hot and heavy in his grip. *Why on earth do they wish me to kill this man?*

Bogdan looked up at the first ledge with a confused stare. Einar then caught a glance of the face of this man in the sunlight looking upward just as the wind swept up from the fjord blew back his dark brown hair. In that moment Einar's vague remembrance of having seen before this man's face flashed in front of his eyes, but so quickly it was like the after-image of a lightening bolt. Something in the wind's gust had triggered it.

Despite this Einar still could not place exactly what made this Bogdan's features so familiar to him.

"No, no, my friend," Bogdan said, after pondering the ledges, "you must be confused. My brother was on the ropes, I have ben told. The report could only have come from your words. It said that Albin died on the lines."

Albin. Of course! Albin the fair haired one, thought Einar. *He who was such a natural on the rappelling lines. He who threw himself between the Gebirgsjäger and myself on the lines. The Pole, Albin, he who died to save me.*

The name Albin had stung Einar's ears. For reasons he could not explain, he had assumed that Bogdan's brother was one of the remaining Polish defenders. Einar had failed to make the connection to Albin. They did not look similar in appearance, as Albin's hair was blond and Bogdan's own was a dark brown. Yet, beyond this, Einar could only at that second see that the faces matched.

Another breeze rifled through Bogdan's hair. Then the lightning of his memory struck twice. *Scotland. The presentation of the medals to the Poles.* His mother had demanded they go. This man, Bogdan, who had received the medal on behalf of his brother, knelt before his mother, took Tilley's hand and kissed it.

A whiff of a Highland summer gust had blown through Bogdan's hair. Then the words filled Einar's ears. Bogdan had said to Tilly, *"I understand you have lost another son, Madame. For this I am most profoundly sorry."* And Tilly thanked him for his brother's sacrifice, for it had given her back a son.

Indeed, Albin had saved a British agent's life on the ropes - his own. It was then that the full weight of his guilt descended upon him. He was to kill the brother of the man who had given his own life to save Einar's.

"My apologies, Bogdan," he said. "I failed to realize that your brother was the man I knew only was Albin. I had also forgotten we had met at the medal ceremony in Scotland."

"Not just a medal, the *Virtuti Militari*. The recognition of all honor and sacrifice. Do not let your forgetfulness embarrass you. Those were very troubled times for us both. Please, show me where these ropes were."

Had Bogdan even remembered me? Does it matter? I must do what is asked of me...

"Come to the edge and I will show you the cliffs your brother so effortlessly scaled. Look, these were the pitons he drove in by his hand. This is where the rope lines began."

"You mean the line of ropes upon which he died," Bogdan said.

"Yes," Einar said.

But his response was incomplete. Bogdan's eyes searched his face for the remainder of the words.

What does he expect me to say? Why does he play upon my guilt?

"Yes," Einar repeated, before he added, "the ropes upon which he died so that he could save my life."

Bogdan's face creased with satisfaction, but well short of a smirk or smile. Just a glimmer of pride.

Yes, he saved my life, Einar thought, *only that I could live to one day take yours. Why? Because you are traitor to your own people, to all of us. That is enough of a reason. Although, I suppose that makes me a traitor to the sacrifice that Albin made for me...*

Einar's hand sweated as he grasped the automatic in his pocket. The feel of the grip became slimy and loose.

Einar then offered to show Bogdan the progression of landings along the cliff that his brother had found and later deployed the lines to. Einar laid flat on that last edge of the *staircase of the gods*, and Bogdan followed. Both men laid with only their shoulders and heads extended beyond the cliff's edge. It was the same position that Einar had been in with the Pole's brother in 1940, only on this day it was Einar who pointed out the landings as Albin had done back then.

"Where exactly did my brother die?" asked Bogdan.

"There, on that fourth landing just above the fjord's surface."

"He fell to his death?" asked Bogdan. "I would never have imagined that."

"Albin was being pursued on the ropes by a *Gebirgsjäger* above him. I believe he had been shot, and was already dying. Wait, I have something to show you that might help you understand, Bogdan."

As Bogdan laid and took in the arrangement of the cliff landings below him, and imagined the fall of each rope, Einar pushed himself up and stood over the Pole.

Now is the time to do what I must do, Einar thought. *He is vulnerable and unsuspecting. Just as Gunnar was when he was shot by Becker's marksman. As this man is also an agent for the Germans, I am right in executing him.*

He reached in his pocket and pulled out the P-38 automatic that had once belonged to Lieutenant Colonel Becker. He pointed it at the Pole, whose attention was still focused on the cliffs below. Einar aligned the gun in the direction of the Pole's head but could not yet bring himself to pull the trigger and execute the man stretched out at his feet.

It was then that Bogdan, still looking down at the cliffs, began to ask another question. He rolled onto his side, and asked,

"Einar, why do you believe Albin was shot? He was above you on the lines, no? Why did they not shoot you, also?"

Just shoot him. Let this be over. Don't let his curiosity drag you back to that moment. He only lost a brother. But then again, is that not all that I also lost? No, I lost a half of my own being, half of my life in Gunnar's passing...

"He was above me on the lines, yes," Einar offered, feeling he owed the man a last minute or two to explain how his brother had died. Einar would want only the same consideration. "I heard the shots. I looked up to see Albin hanging, entangled in the line. He hung upside down, bleeding, but he then cut partially through his own line before he fell. He made no sound when he hit the landing, so I thought he must have already been dead."

Still looking down, Bogdan asked, "But why would he cut his own line." As he said this, Bogdan rolled over and saw Einar standing over him with the automatic drawn.

The question pierced Einar. He froze for a long pause, then stammered out the answer. "Only so that the *Gebirgsjäger* could no longer pursue me."

"So my brother saved you only so that you could later murder me?" Bogdan asked, as he focused on the gun. "Why?"

The Pole's voice was taut, but with surprise more so than fear.

"It is my order," said Einar matter of factly.

"But to what end?"

"To the end of justice, for what you have done to General Sikorski."

"You have convinced yourself that his accident was somehow my doing?" Bogdan asked.

"Yes."

"Well, you are right in one regard, for it was no accident. I checked the General's plane before I left Gibraltar. The control surfaces were working as they should. The cargo pallets were secure. Yes, I agree, the General was assassinated. Only not by me, for I loved the man. Why would I kill him? Or it is better said that others have convinced you of this nonsense?"

"You are a German plant," Einar answered him, not sure he truly believed it himself. "A *'dopple'*. A double agent."

At this point, Bogdan Bratajewski began to laugh. Loud. Hard. Einar felt mocked by his laughter.

"I am sorry, Einar." Bogdan then said. "If I am to die here today at your hand, then so be it. I cannot stop you from doing so, lying here at your feet. But before you kill me, please answer me three simple questions. I think that is only fair."

Einar felt as if he was being lured into a trap, something to take away his focus. *Just pull the trigger and kill this man as you have been ordered to do! Do it now!*

"Three questions?" Einar repeated instead. "Yes, I will answer your three questions. But if you try anything, I will kill you immediately."

"I am quite sure of that," said Bogdan, who seemed to have no fear within him. "My first question, please. You said your own brother died upon these ledges. Does being here help you deal with tremendous void of his loss within yourself?"

His words reverberated through Einar as echoes do from canyon walls. This man could never know how sacred this place had become to him. For it was Einar alone who had led his brother here. Einar alone who had gotten Gunnar wounded by gunshot. Einar alone who had dragged his twin, the other half of himself, along on this dangerous adventure. Einar alone who pulled the trigger to end his life.

"Of course," replied Einar, "in ways perhaps you can never imagine."

Why would a man waste one of his last few breaths on earth on such a meaningless question? Yet, the question was as meaningful as any I could imagine myself asking...

"You see, I can very much imagine, Einar, as my own brother perished here along with yours," Bogdan replied as he still lay on his side.

"What is your second question?" queried Einar as if he wanted to escape the thoughts provoked by the first.

"What can you tell me of my brother, Albin, from what you saw go on here?" Bogdan then asked.

"I could not speak to him," replied Einar, "he spoke only Polish."

"I repeat my question." Said Bogdan. "What can you tell me of my brother Albin from what you *saw* go on here?"

He stressed the word *saw,* like a weapon, as if it somehow ripped through Einar's lame excuse

Einar thought for a second. He imagined himself asking the question of Bogdan about his brother Gunnar, were their roles reversed. Einar knew the question deserved an answer. He knew why Bogdan asked it. *What did my brother's actions mean to you?*

"Bogdan, your brother, Albin, was incredibly dedicated to the cause of your country, enough to give up his own life so that others could carry on the fight against these Nazi invaders."

Having said this, deep feelings stirred once more within Einar. He would have wanted to know as much about his own brother's life also, especially the last moments of it, had Einar not lived them out alongside Gunnar, etching a torture of memories within him. Einar would never escape feeling accountable for his brother's death, no matter how long he lived. And not just for pulling the trigger that robbed him of his life.

"Good, Einar. Thank you for those words" Bogdan said. "Now, my final question. Do you remember your mother's own words to me after that ceremony celebrating Albin's sacrifice in Scotland?"

The progression of questions hit Einar like a rockslide. Einar thought of Tilly, and then, as if totally out of place, he thought of Kari. The image of Kari lingered.

"You ask these questions as if I have the gun aimed at myself," Einar answered.

"Perhaps you do," said Bogdan. "Killing me here today will not ease your guilt, only increase it. I know what you wrestle with every second of every day. You blame yourself, it is obvious to me, if not others. As for me, I blame myself also for my brother's death, as well as General Sikorski, his daughter Zofia, and every other soul on that plane. I wish to live only to rescue my younger sister from the hands of those Nazi beasts. If you kill me, I am not sure it changes anything, except perhaps for Justyna. The rest I leave in God's hands. But when you kill me, it will be just another dark spirit that will haunt the rest of your days. Now, you have not answered me as you said you would. Do you remember your own mother's words?"

Einar looked down on Bogdan, He could see no quiver of fear, no tears flooded his eyes, just a quiet, passive resolve. Instead, Einar could feel the Pole's eyes measure him, wondering what he would decide to do. Then, he thought of that ceremony in the Scottish fields.

"I do remember," Einar admitted reluctantly, "You knelt before her with tears in your eyes. She raised your head as a breeze blew. She kissed away your tears so tenderly, and said, *'My family owes your family a life. It is a debt I will never be able to repay'*. You wish me to repay that debt here?"

"No, Einar," said Bogdan, "I do not expect you to repay *her* debt. And those are not the words I wished to hear. Only the ones she said just after those."

Einar was stunned. *"Her" debt? This man is refusing to allow me to repay "her" debt?* He thought on his mother's other words from that day. He spoke them aloud, slowly:

"There is nothing more sacred than the sadness of one brother mourning another. God bless you for all the pain you bear this day. May it fade away quickly and be forever replaced by the pride for your brother that I know swells within you."

Bogdan let his words resonate before he added, "These words of your mother apply to you as much as they ever did to me, Einar. Heed them. Allow your pain to fade. Don't let it consume you. As for me, I would like only to die with honor as my brother Albin did. For there is nothing greater in life than to die with purpose. I wish to die just as my brother had."

These words, *"to die with honor as my brother Albin did"* reminded Einar of two memories. The first was Gunnar, on these very cliffs, only moments before he died, saying that he was thankful for the adventure. For having lived life, if only for a month, just as his brother Einar did.

Second, Einar thought of the months he spent afterwards with his mother reading Shakespeare. He did so not because the words would ever bring Gunnar back, but just because he wanted to live his brother's life in return, if only for that short while.

"Rise to your feet," said Einar, as he backed away but still trained the Walther P-38 automatic on the Pole. Bogdan slowly rolled onto his knees and then stood before him. Einar was ready to shoot should the man rush him, but somehow knew Bogdan would not.

"Stand by the ledge," Einar instructed him. He raised the weapon and took aim at his shoulder. He knew at this range he could not miss. The shot would not kill Bogdan, but instead carry the Pole over the side, and at this height there was no possibility that Bogdan would survive the fall. He would die exactly as his brother had - shot, fallen to his death.

"I am ready," said Bogdan. His face was at total peace. A shallow pool of tears clung to his eyes. Einar knew they were for his brother, not at all for himself.

Einar extended his arm to its furthest reach, as if this somehow brought him closer to concluding this awful task. He was unsure if he could fire that shot. *Am I to execute a man whose only sin before me was to love his brother as I did? As I still do? My Father in heaven, show me a sign. What must I do?*

It was during Einar's hesitation that Bogdan then slowly raised his right hand. It was not in any way threatening, but in a peaceful motion. He slowly made the sign of the cross while he spoke aloud these words, "Father in heaven, give this man the strength to do what he knows in his heart to be right. Give him the strength to honor the memory of his brother, of his family, of his country."

When his hand had finished this blessing, his arm still extended, he opened his palm as if to shower a blessing upon Einar.

Einar watched as his hand slowly opened like a flower unfurling in the sunlight. In his palm Einar once again saw the burned scar of the cross. He thought of Gunnar, and both scapulars he had since his brother's death worn around his neck. Something surged through him, weakening him, but also bringing him a deep and meaningful peace.

"You have other brothers?" Einar asked calmly.

"No," replied Bogdan. "Only my sister, Justyna, is left."

"And your parents?"

"I do not know if they are alive or have perished at the hands of the Gestapo," he said honestly.

"And no one else?"

"Only my sister," Bogdan repeated. "I believe Justyna still to be alive."

"You would go into Germany to save her?"

"I go into Poland," he corrected Einar, "to fight for my country. Yes, I will save Justyna, I will certainly do so."

In that instance, Einar knew exactly what to do, and lowered his weapon. He was tired of living half-truths and half a life. He knew his own existence could not go on much longer. He could no longer exist without his being's other half. Not without Gunnar. He knew by then that Bogdan, although not a twin, shared a similar fate with his brother, Albin.

"Go," Einar said as he removed the magazine of bullets from the gun and dropped it to the ground. He then racked the slide of the weapon, ejecting the last bullet from the chamber. He knew that Bogdan would realize the weapon no longer posed a threat to him. "Go on, leave me here. Take this map. It will show you the route to the border."

Einar reached into the rucksack and produced the map.

Bogdan walked over to Einar and laid his hand on his shoulder. "I know every feeling with which you wrestle for your brother, Einar. I have had them all in my own heart for these many, many months. I assure you I am no German spy. The Bible says, *The people walking in darkness have seen a great light; on those living in the land of deep darkness a light has dawned.* My countrymen live in a plague of darkness. I return there for no other reason than to help lift it. Both our brothers now live in the Light of Our Lord, as someday so we both hope we may do ourselves."

Einar handed the map to him, and said almost as if only to himself, "Have peace in knowing this, for light always drives out the darkness before it." The words had come instantly to him, as if passed on from another realm. *Had these once been the words of my brother? Was Gunnar speaking to me now?*

Bogdan embraced Einar, who could not help but think of his last embrace of his brother, Gunnar, just before he pulled the trigger that ended his life.

Bogdan pulled away, and said, "I will find my own way to the border. May God bring you peace. The peace that Albin and Gunnar now find themselves in. They are forever connected, and so always shall we be. Remember, Einar, you have done God's will today. It was His hand that lowered your own. May God bless you, my friend."

Bogdan left Einar on that lowest ledge, and climbed back up to the trail where only hours of hiking separated him from the safety of Sweden. He disappeared from Einar's sight.

Einar then sat himself on the lowest ledge of the *staircase of the gods.* His feet dangled over the cliffside. He inserted the ejected round back into the P-38's magazine clip, before reinserting the clip back into the gun. He gazed out over the fjord, whose waters appeared placid and serene. A breeze whispered past him, causing him an instant chill. It prompted Einar to recall surviving the overnight frost on these ledges as Gunnar slowly died.

Having allowed the Pole Bogdan to live did not erase his guilt, but he knew it had been the right thing to have done. At this point, given all his recent experiences, Einar put brotherhood ahead of national patriotism. If this Bogdan had fooled him and really was a spy, let someone else hold him accountable. Einar had known he could not.

He wondered where his brother's body rested. He already had Kari check all the cemeteries known to have Allied troops buried within them, but with no luck. It was most likely, he supposed, that the Germans just threw his brother's body into the *Rombaksfjord* below.

Einar looked at the weapon in his hand. He caught himself repeatedly ejecting the magazine on the Walther P-38, only to then reinsert it again. Click/Snap. Click/Snap. Click/ Snap. Einar looked studiously at the weapon and thought about rejoining Gunnar. He thought of how empty his life had been since losing his brother. He felt incomplete, like a shadow unattached to the man who cast it. With a mere movement of his finger, all this could end.

Einar took the Walther P-38 pistol and raised it under the soft fold beneath his chin, just as Gunnar had. The barrel was cold and unforgiving, and for this reason Einar kept his finger off the trigger, but outstretched along the gun's frame. He knew if he triggered it, he was damned to eternity. There would be no one to come and pull the trigger to save him this fate. Yet, then again, as he had shown his brother this mercy, was he not already damned?

As he played with this fatal logic in his mind, movement from across the fjord caught his eye. A Nazi supply train was making a downward run on the Ofoten Railway towards Narvik. Einar oddly thought only of the months he and Gunnar had spent together reconnoitering that rail line. These had been the happy, even joyous months that he and Gunnar had shared before the German invasion. Einar thought these had been the most fulfilling days he had ever shared with his twin. The thought lifted his spirit. Einar understood the railway car and the memories it stirred were a signal from his twin. *Go on with your life, brother, I am fine.*

As Einar lowered the Walther, he thought of Kari, once more all by herself in that lonely red *rorbu* on the coast. No, he decided he would not use Becker's gun to take his life. To do so would have allowed Becker to have won.

Einar thumbed the safety on and slipped the P-38 into his jacket pocket. He carefully rose to his feet, retrieved the rucksack and began the long trek back to rejoin Kari in the *rorbu* on the sea.

Figure 45: A Traditional Red Rorbu in Norway

64 The Solitude of Duty

Late 1943

"Solitary trees, if they grow at all, grow strong."

Winston Spencer Churchill

Einar MacAlvor returned to Kari and then reported back to Wincer Wells that the Pole Bogdan Bratajewski had escaped him and had slipped off towards the Swedish border. Wells was outraged, and expressed it through back channel messages using the One Time Pad. Einar awaited the notice of his recall from the field, but that never came. Only an unbearable silence followed. He sent the following message to Wells encoded from the OTP.

DURING MY LAST TIME SPENT WITH TILLY I WAS MADE AWARE OF YOUR METHODS TO OBTAIN GUNNARS RELEASE TO NORWAY STOP FATHER HAD LETTER PREPARED READY TO SEND TO AUTHORITIES STOP PULL ME FROM NORWAY AND THAT LETTER TO BE SENT BEFORE I RETURN FULL STOP

No message of recall was ever sent to Einar, but he knew by the threat of doing so he had crossed a line with Wincer Wells. Potentially a very deadly line.

In the aftermath of his not being able to perform the execution order from Wells, coupled with his inability to take his own life and leave Kari alone in the little red *rorbu*, Einar began to question what was truly important in his life. Kari was delighted to have him back again, and this brought him solace. As summer gave way to autumn, Einar began to grow out his beard for her, just as she had once asked of him. He told her it would keep his face warm in winter, but he suspected she knew he did it to please her.

He had never in his life felt more alive than during the seven months that followed Bogdan Bratajewski's visit to

Norway. He grew in his emotional bond with Kari, but still wondered if he could ever truly love her. She had been a warm, caring distraction in what had been the emptiness of his existence. She had become a sharing partner, one in whose companionship he felt a growing depth of attraction. But how could he allow himself to love her with so much death all around them. Slowly, he came to realize that his loving her was not something he could control. His love was something that she would slowly steal from him.

After Kari's and his sighting of the *Tirpitz* in the *Kåfjorden* near the northern town of Alta, the next few months proved truly remarkable. In actuality, the presence of the battleships *Tirpitz* and *Scharnhorst* had first been reported by another team within Norwegian Resistance, that of the Johansen brothers, Torbjørn and Einar. Yet, having a second independent team confirm this observation was a Godsend for Wincer Wells back in London. This made the intelligence actionable, although the leadership questioned whether these two teams were truly independent.

"Might you have had the first team lead the second team to the *Kåfjorden?"* Wells was asked by a review panel of his superiors.

"I assure the gentlemen empaneled before me that is not the case," Wells responded to the inquiry. "These two teams operating in-country have no knowledge of each other's existence, and so that shall stay to protect them both should either team be penetrated by Quisling's agents."

"Commander Wells," the senior SOE official there began, "the strength of your response is curious. Are you suggesting that these two teams have *never* come in contact with each other? That this precept is not even remotely possible?"

Wells thought about the back-channel network he kept with the Johansen brothers, just as he did with Einar, although not Kari. Each had their own one-time pads for communicating directly to Wells. He thought of his having decoded and read the message from the Johansens and having tossed all physical traces of it later that night into the flames of the fireplace of his home drawing room.

CONTACT MADE STOP SWALLOW AND SHADOW ENGAGED STOP SUBTLE DIRECTIONS GIVEN STOP EXPECT THEM TO CONFIRM OUR EARLIER PRODUCT FULL STOP

"Swallow" and "Shadow" had been the codenames assigned by Wells to Kari and Einar. Wincer Wells was sure that there was no traceable way for anyone to prove that his first team had "steered" the second team to the *Kåfjorden.* His face contorted at that moment, which he could not control, but despised lest it be misread as a twitch betraying a nervousness within him.

"No sir, that is not even remotely possible, as either one or the other teams would have reported it to me."

"Even if neither knew the other were SOE agents, Commander Wells?"

"Both teams are trained to report *anyone* who might be an agent for *either side* back to me. Therefore, gentlemen, I am quite convinced these are indeed two independent sightings of the *Tirpitz* and *Scharnhorst.*"

After the panel deliberated further, it was finally decided to report the sighting of the vessels to the Military Intelligence community as *"confirmed and actionable".* Wells was relieved, but dismayed that his methods had even been questioned at all.

Upon the material reaching Military Intelligence, a British Mosquito reconnaissance aircraft was dispatched to photograph the *Kåfjorden* to verify the finding, which it did. Having done so, *Operation Source* was quickly planned using the latest naval weapon, the X-craft midget submarines. These were the same X-craft as the one that had rendezvoused with Einar in the *Gratangenfjord.*

The X-craft Midget Submarines were a very new class of weapon. Only 20 were built during the war. Three of the X-craft (midget subs X-5, X-6 and X-7) were assigned to plant mines under the *Tirpitz*. Two others (X-9 and X-10) were instructed to do the same to the *Scharnhorst*, and the final X-craft (X-8) was to mine the heavy cruiser *Lützow* stationed in a nearby fjord. Each vessel was equipped with a pair of 2-ton explosive mines. The X-crafts were towed into place by conventional submarines and released from their tow cables. The Midget submarines only had a limited range under their own power, but more than enough for this mission. The subs were all equipped with devices to cut through the torpedo nets in the water that shielded the warships.

Then, slowly, *Operation Source* became diluted of X-craft resources. It seemed that fate was once again interfering on behalf of the *Tirpitz.*

During the deployment, but before the attack, X-9 was separated from its tow cable and immediately dove un-commanded to the sea bottom. She was lost along with her crew of four. X-8 suffered leakage and was ultimately scuttled at sea.

On the night of September 22, 1943, the remaining four submerged X-craft successfully navigated past the submarine netting at the fjord's entrance. Each X-craft was approximately 51 feet long and carried a crew of four extremely courageous seamen. X-craft midget sub X-10 suffered mechanical problems and aborted the mission. With X-8, X-9, and X-10 no longer available, the attacks on *Scharnhorst* and *Lützow* were called off. This left the remaining three X-craft to attack the *Tirpitz*.

X-5 was last heard from as she deployed from her tethered tow submarine that evening. Her fate is unknown but she is presumed to have been sunk. There is no evidence that she ever laid mines on the *Tirpitz*.

X-6 and X-7 did, however, mine *"the Beast"* that night. They placed three of their four 2-ton mines under the keel of the massive battleship before becoming detected, when they came under extensive fire. Vessels X-6 and X-7 were then sunk. Their crews were captured (all except two seamen who drowned along with their sunken mini-subs). The six surviving seamen were taken aboard the *Tirpitz.*

The explosions that ripped through the massive battleship were enormous. Even though the *Tirpitz* displaced 43,000 tons, the blasts produced crippling structural damage. The three mines lifted the massive battleship from the water enough that it its own massive weight racked the structural backbone of the warship. The blast derailed the D-turret from its tracks. This was the last of its four main gun turrets, each housing two massive 15-inch guns.

The charges set below the screws and rudders disabled the battleship altogether. Another charge set forward did tremendous damage, causing the battleship to suffer extensive hull structural failure and caused partial flooding of *"the Beast"*. Although only one German sailor was known to have been killed, the damage by this attack caused the *Tirpitz* to remain out of action for the next six months.

Operation Source had been a resounding success, despite the loss of nearly all X-craft mini-subs and several of their crew. The *Tirpitz* lay crippled in the *Kåfjorden* and now was subject to bombing operations by both the British and Russians. *Tirpitz* would not threaten Arctic supply convoys for the rest of the war.

The attack on the *Tirpitz* lifted the spirits of Einar and Kari. Its success was based upon their reconnaissance and had given them purpose. It was an injection of energy for them both.

Kari was perceptive in an intuitive way as most women are, but more so perhaps due to her clandestine posting. Yet it did not take extensive operational training to detect that with each passing month, Einar was becoming more attached to her. Not only had there lovemaking become more tender, it had regained a passion that it had once contained, and gone were the mechanical interludes between them. They began to speak more to each other of what they would do after the war was over, although that still appeared a long way off. They even began to discussed the possibility of spending their post war years together, which while in no way was a promise, still delighted Kari to no end.

It was in late October 1943 that Wincer Wells had sent encrypted directions for Kari and Einar to tie into a radio network of Norwegian Resistance members operating in the areas of the Lofoten Island Archipelago, and just above it the Vesterålen Archipelago including the Andøya Island radar installation, and points north. The network was code named Venus, and it soon became Kari's fixation.

The Venus Network became an operational thorn in the side of the Nazi invaders. The Germans had by then developed the procedures for triangulating on radio transmittal sources. But Venus consisted of ten operational radios, of which only a few ever were transmitting at any one time. This game of cat and mouse became effective in precluding the Germans from shutting down the network. One of the sites was used to monitor and report on the status of the German's repair efforts on the *Tirpitz* within the *Kåfjorden* near Alta.

As Kari became more active with the Venus Network, Einar attempted to release himself from his mourning of Gunnar. He took several trips back to *the staircase of the gods,* each time demanding to do so alone. On each occasion of his leaving, Kari wondered if he would ever return. If the German patrols didn't stumble upon him, she thought his own depressive moods would. She envisioned the silhouette of his sitting on the cliff ledge and raising that damn Walther P-38 pistol to his temple.

But this was not the case. Each time he travelled there, the sullen morose memories of his brother's demise were offset and eventually overpowered by those of the visit of the Pole Bogdan. Each time Einar revisited there, he could hear anew on the whisper of the winds of Bogdan's final blessing:

May God bring you peace. The peace that Albin and Gunnar now find themselves in. They are forever connected, and so always shall we be. Remember, Einar, you have done God's will today. It was His hand that lowered your own. May God bless you, my friend.

In recalling these words, Einar would always see the palm of Bogdan open and that cross burned within it held up to his sight. It told Einar he had done the right thing, that this man Bogdan was not a German spy, and would deploy to his native Poland to do God's work. This could only mean the work against the Nazis, and the slow, painful recovery of peace.

As autumn's days had slowly ceded to winter, Einar's thoughts focused on his one bit of unfinished business. He had never admitted to Tilly, his mother, that it was by his hand that Gunnar had died. He told Kari that he had something to tell his mother that he did not know how he ever could. She suggested that he begin writing her letters, something he had never before considered. There was no way to get them to her as long as the war raged, but just putting the words to pen would assist him. He did find the process helpful, although each letter was burned shortly after his writing them.

Kari by then knew Einar struggled with a great secret, but would not pry for him to reveal it to her, as he would take this to be a very serious transgression of his privacy.

The depths of winter descended upon the little red *rorbu.* Einar's gift to her was his beard, which had grown in thickly, and gave him a most rugged appearance. It was a shade lighter than the hair of his head, and even had a lightly reddish hue to it.

Kari's gift to Einar was her unabated love for him. She had never said the words directly, for fear of driving him away, but Kari knew she loved him. She would do anything for him. All he need do was ask. Yet, he never did ask so much as a favor.

One evening a few nights after Christmas 1943, Einar and Kari lingered after a thoroughly exhausting bit of lovemaking. Kari lay on Einar's chest, as she traced the edges of his beard. She would pull softly at the little tufts that curled outward in places. She was content. She was secure.

Kari then did what she least wanted to do at that moment. She broke the spell of intimacy to tie into the expected broadcast from the Venus network.

She said, "Einar, I am sorry but I need to get on the frequency in a few minutes to pick up the network." She tuned in the receiver while Einar lay naked in the bed, covered only by sheets and a woolen blanket.

Kari tuned in the receiver on the night's assigned frequency, and instantly they heard two voices speaking in Norwegian. This was unusual, as messages were always encoded in morse. Only rarely were voice transmissions sent out over the air. This night, it appeared the two voices did not realize they were transmitting at all. They appeared to be unaware that the microphone was "hot".

"It is wonderful news tonight, is it not brother?" said a very familiar voice. "The *Scharnhorst* being sunk off North Cape near the Russian border. What better Christmas present could we Norwegians ask for?"

"Yes, brother," said the second voice in an eerily familiar timbre that struck Einar in bed like the lash of a dog sledder's whip. "I whole heartedly agree."

"That's the other Einar," MacAlvor said from the bed. "The other voice is his brother, Torbjørn. The dogsledders we met up near Alta. They do not realize that they are transmitting. Kari, you need to get them off this network immediately. The Gestapo will triangulate the source and roll-up this entire network if they find these brothers."

The two men continued to jabber over the air unaware.

Kari reached for the radio transmitter power dial, and ramped her dial setting to as high as it could in an attempt to break through the brothers' transmission. Just before she reached for the microphone, it was grasped by the naked Einar who by then was standing at her side.

"Let this be a man's voice," he said, "as your female voice will stand out more than a Scotsman's kilt would on the hips of a fishermen up here."

Kari laughed out loud. "Do it," she said.

Einar flicked the transmit switch and said in as deep a voice as he could draw, "OPERATIONAL ERROR. UNINTENDED TRANSMISSION. ABORT, ABORT, ABORT."

Within a few seconds, the entire network shut down. Kari shut down her wireless set.

"Well, that was fortunate that we even got through, at all. Certainly they were not on long enough for the Gestapo to triangulate their location," Einar said.

"What could have happened?" asked Kari.

"Could be they just left the microphone switch set on transmit last time they powered down," Einar reasoned. "Or perhaps a failure in the switch itself. Either way, I don't think there was any harm done unless someone recognized there voices as we did."

"That explains why the brother Einar was attempting to say nothing that day," Kari realized aloud.

"Perhaps," said Einar. "But we obtained two good pieces of information tonight."

"The first being the *Scharnhorst* being sunk," said Kari. "Do you believe that?"

"Well," Einar said, "we can listen in on the German open radio frequencies tonight. Neither of us speak German, but if we hear the name *Scharnhorst* mentioned repeatedly, then it is likely true."

"So, Einar," Kari said, "what's the other good news?"

"Should anything ever happen to me," he told her, "then you always have the Johansen brothers to fall back on."

The words crushed Kari. She feared his comment was nothing more than a sharpened edge with which he would cleave through the bindings connecting her to him.

65 A Mission in the South

February 1944

"Without courage all virtues lose their meaning."

Winston Spencer Churchill

A few days into the new year of 1944, two things came to pass. First, as expected, the sinking of the *Scharnhorst* was confirmed. The repairs to the *Tirpitz* continued, closely monitored by the Norwegian Resistance, but best estimates were that the massive battleship would not again be seaworthy until the springtime.

The second interesting occurrence of the new year was the communication from Wincer Wells directing Einar to take twenty kilograms of plastic explosive to the resistance cell in the Rjukan Valley near the Vemork facility. The instructions were encoded as "Most Urgent and Most Secret."

This time, the instructions included directions for Kari. She was ordered to be on the assigned radio frequency each day at noon and again at 2100 hours, in case of immediate need for assistance. It made no sense, as Einar would be traveling near a thousand miles on this assignment. What good would she be in case of an emergency or change in plans. Clearly these orders were nothing more than an excuse to keep her tied to her transmitter, assuring she did not ignore Wincer Wells' directions to stay behind. The message from Wells was unmistakeable. She must allow Einar to complete this mission alone.

Einar took on the mission with relish. The agents at the destination he would be meeting were some of the same men he had been in contact with during the successful Vemork heavy water raid a year earlier. He had been in London at the time, as their Norwegian language communication specialist.

This time, however, he would see the Vemork facility, along with its once thought impenetrable ravine that ran beneath it like a moat. He would see the town and the mountains surrounding it with his own eyes. These were the targets that they had spent so much time discussing in preparation for the Gunnerside raid. But the heavy water production facilities in those targets had been destroyed. Einar could not understand why the local team would need the explosives unless those production facilities had been rebuilt by the Nazis.

Einar prepared himself for his journey. He took cash, enough to buy him passage to southern Norway and back. He took small quantities of dried foods, enough to keep him alive for four or five days, if needed, in the wilderness.

He prepared his rucksack, saving space for the *Plastique* and its detonators. The amount was not a tremendous load, but along with his other materials it would make for a sixty pound rucksack. The explosives were very stable.

He left the *rorbu*, and climbed the rocks high behind it. Near the top of the rock hill, set inside an enclosure of a high rim of grayish rocks was the operational stash of explosives. This site had been selected for its ability to withstand a massive blast without collapsing down onto the *rorbu* below. Einar had been there for six months, and the explosives stored there had never been a problem. They were stored in a heavy Bakelite chest, over-wrapped with thick rubber sheets to prevent rain or snow from penetrating into it.

Einar had remembered his training. Before beginning to access the explosives, he had to ground himself to discharge any static electricity. This was most important in winter, he remembered. He removed his glove and grasped the metal rod that had been driven into the ground close by for exactly this purpose. He then unwrapped the plastic explosives, removed his twenty kilograms and packed it into his rucksack carefully. There was more than enough explosive left behind for any future assault on the radar facility on Andøya Island that, by then, neared completion.

Einar left his rucksack in the rim of boulders. He removed the edible dried foods and returned to the *rorbu*, where Kari awaited him. Grieg's *"From Holberg's Time Opus 40"* was playing in the background on the phonograph. The strings mourned with a sadness befitting the occasion.

"Einar," Kari said, "just tell me and I will go with you. Wincer Wells be damned. I can take the remote wireless set with me."

"No, Kari," said Einar. "This is the way it must be."

"But why?" A stream of tears began to track down her cheek.

"Better to lose one agent instead of two," Einar said, "should something go wrong."

"You don't intend to come back to me, do you?" The tears were flowing abundantly now.

Einar shook his head. "If God wills it, I will come back to you, I promise that to you."

She reached for him, unaware of her own intentions. Her arms needed him to steady her. She felt as though her world was collapsing around her. As if she stood on only a sliver of soil that next would erode away and take her along with it. Only then did it occur to her how much her feelings had been transferred from her husband's death to this strong brooding man she by then shared her life with.

Einar wrapped his strong arms around her as the strings of Grieg's work enclosed on them, much like a tightening cage in which two animals are trapped. "Take me," she cried into his ear.

"I cannot," he said, "you must stay here."

"No. Take me one more time, my Einar." She had stopped her tears, but her cheeks were still stained with their sorrow. She kissed him tenderly. He responded. She nibbled his lower lip hungrily. He kissed the remaining tears from the corners of her eyes. They collapsed onto the bed of reindeer skins that she had laid out. His lips probed her neck, just as she had always liked, as he had quickly found out not long after his arrival. She sighed and arched her back. His mouth found her cleavage, and he kissed the swale between her breasts. There was something quite sad about it, about her, that night. It was then that he realized he could smell gentle wafts of a stale fear of being alone. Not desperation, only isolation. An isolation she was just beginning to remember her disdain for.

They made love. Slow, unhurried and full of emotion. In its throes they wrapped themselves in a tenderness shared between them. One that had long since replaced the greed of desire that had initiated their couplings. The pair were stitched together by a silken ribbon of intimate embrace. A closeness as they had never experienced had pervaded them both.

When Einar was deep within her, Kari flashed open her eyes as if something was amiss. She said nothing, she only kept her deep breathing in time with his. Their joint passion had lingered for what seemed hours, before it had given way to moments of a joyously blended apex. Two bodies, encircling each other, as the universe slipped by. Two faces speaking without words as they had never before conversed. Heart queried heart, each searched for what had until this point eluded them. Yet this night, the illusive bounty was found.

In a sweet second shared between them, their carnal lust was expended and fell away, creating a vacuum in which a delicate bliss was shared. Both feared to breathe should they be the one to disturb it. On its own, the bliss crested into something even lighter, more fragile than either of their own pleasures, because this was shared between them.

At this time, *"Aase's Death"* from the Peter Gynt Suite played. Its strings as delicate as a confection, as sweetly mournful as their moment. They collapsed together in a heap atop the skins and furs.

"That is a moment I will spend a lifetime chasing to enjoy again," Kari said with a satisfied grin. It was not born of a sated sexual desire as much as it was having unlocked the emotion in the man in whose arms she then rested.

Einar looked into her eyes as he had never before dared to do. His face was serious but gentle. He kissed her lips and then softly, almost too quietly, whispered to her, "This is the very first time that I have allowed anyone in my life to flow so deeply into the depths of my heart."

Then Einar lowered his head upon her bosom and cried tender tears. She could feel him tremble softly. The teardrops collected in the hollow swale between her breasts and as she was flat on her back, slowly drained upwards toward her neck.

"Why did you open your eyes just before we finished?" Einar asked.

She paused before answering. Had he noticed that? Had he been watching her face in ecstasy, only to see her eyes open unexpectedly? It was so unlike him to be this caring, this tender, this attentive.

"I just became aware of their not being there…"

"*What* not being *where*?" he asked.

"Your scapulars, your own and your brother's."

"And this bothered you?"

"No," she admitted, "it was pleasant to not have them hanging down on me, as they usually do. No slapping of Gunnar's, nor your own, scapulars on my skin. Their laces did not hang down and coil upon my cheek or chin. I felt, for once, as if there was nothing between us. I felt free. Unconstrained. No religion, no cultural differences, no shadows from our pasts to separate us."

"No shadows of Jorun?"

"No, no shadows of Jorun, Einar" Kari said in an exasperated tone. "Haven't you noticed I no longer speak of Jorun? I loved him deeply, yes, that will always be true, but now he is gone and I have made peace with that. If only you could release your thoughts of Gunnar as I have done so with Jorun."

"There is a difference, Kari. Gunnar was a part of me, as much as my arm or my leg. Even more so, for we always made up a half of each others' souls. Can't you understand that?"

She looked at him so tenderly in response. "I understand this. You have never been in love, for it is no different than what you describe. That is what makes this conversation so frightening, Einar. I have fallen in love with you. I wish you could see that without being told. I know that you are not yet ready to commit your love to me, but promise me that you'll release Gunnar's ghost to make room for my heart."

He looked at her as tears began to form in her eyes.

"You ask me to make promises I cannot keep, Kari."

"That is fair, Einar. So, here is a promise you can most certainly keep. Promise me that you'll come back. Come back to this *rorbu* of ours. Come back to this heart. Come back to discover the depths of the love that rages within it for you."

"I will come back," he promised. "We are not done."

"You don't know how pleased I am to hear you say these words." Kari could feel a swell of joy inside her. A triumph had been achieved.

"I have a promise to ask of you also," he said.

"Anything," she agreed. Her tears of angst had turned to those of happiness and flowed freely across her smiling face.

"If anything happens and I do not return, not of my own doing, but of that of fate, then make sure my mother gets that package of letters I have left on the table. It is most urgent."

"Of course," she answered. "I promise."

Einar left her the next morning and walked with his rucksack to the Nyksund docks and took a small skiff with an outboard motor. In these lands it would not be considered a theft, only the emergency need by a neighbor. Einar knew the owner would be assured it would be returned in due time.

Einar navigated his way through the maze of fjords on his way to the open waters of the *Vestfjorden*. His left hand shook with the vibration of the outboard. His nostrils filled with the fumes of the burnt gas-oil mixture upon which it was fueled. The waters were still blue-gray with haze among the inner fjord passages, with great walls of granite looming over him. It was when he exited out onto the open waters of the *Vestfjorden* that he began to feel the small wooden boat roll with the swells. It became so pronounced as he neared Skrova, he feared the skiff might overturn. It came precariously close to doing so, but Einar was able to preclude its doing so by his deft skills.

He arrived and tied up to the docks at Skrova. He sought out his father's cousins, Hakron and Erik. He arrived at Erik's *rorbu*, and was greeted by an old man whose wrinkled face was overgrown with ragged, unkept gray hair and snow white beard.

"I am sorry," said Einar, "I was looking for Erik Larsen."

"Einar," the man said shallowly, "it is me, your Uncle Erik. How good to see you."

Einar was shocked. He had not seen this man for only four years, yet he seemed to have had aged twenty more. He knew the man to truly be his father's cousin, but made the mental adjustment to address him as "uncle".

"Uncle Erik," he said, "I have great need to get to the area of Lake Tinn in the south, and with great haste."

"Come in boy," Erik wrapped an arm around him, pulling him inside, "Outside is not the proper place to speak of such things."

Einar left his rucksack and its deadly contents outside.

"You can bring that in with you, Nephew," Erik said.

"You do not wish for me to do that," Einar replied, a stern look in his eyes.

His uncle returned a knowing gaze, and said, "So be it."

They entered and the frigidly windblown Einar was greeted by the welcoming warmth inside of Erik's *rorbu*. His uncle moved with the slow trepidation of a beaten man as he prepared a warm tea for them both. Einar was thinking that was a figurative beating administered by time, only to soon find that it was all too literal.

Coffee would have been preferred to tea, but it had been unavailable since shortly after the start of the war. Einar took the mug in his hand. His arm still shook with memories from the vibrations of the outboard, even though the motor had long ceased. He brought the tea to his lips. It was steaming hot. He instantly recognized its weak taste as that made from a local root flavored with mashed berries.

"I am afraid this is all I have to offer," said Erik. "Tea is a drink for women and children, I know. But this is all that can be made so long as the war rages around us. Whatever coffee or real tea makes it to Norway is quickly absconded by the Nazis. I hope it warms you at least."

"It is wonderful, Uncle" Einar exaggerated.

"What are you doing here again, boy?" His uncle's use of the term "boy" rang hollow in his ear as he was by then upcoming on his thirty-first birthday. He did not understand an old man's eyes always filtered through the protective lens of his own youth, and as such Erik still saw Einar as a boy. "We were so delighted when we heard you had made it back to your mother in Scotland. As much as we were saddened to learn of Gunnar's death."

"I have been in Norway for six months, Uncle," Einar said, "but until today I was forbidden to return to Skrova. I was hoping that you and Uncle Hakron could take me in your boat to Lake Tinn."

The words flickered across Erik's face like flames of a great fire, too hot to be comfortably near. "You do not know about your Uncle Hakron? About us?"

"No," said Einar, his jaw dropping low in surprise, "Tell me, Uncle. Tell me please."

"Your Uncle Hakron is dead. Soon to be a year since his passing."

"What happened?"

"We were on the open waters of the *Vestfjorden* when a *Kriegsmarine* patrol ran us down. They discovered the supplies for the Resistance we were running. Explosives mostly. Some small arms. They took our haul of contraband and forced us aboard their craft. We had always believed that had we ever been caught, they might take us to a camp, but Hitler had demanded that his issued order that all commandos captured were to be killed instantly was to be followed in all theaters of operation. First they demanded we kneel before them. When we both did, the beatings started. Rifle butts to our ribs. Punching from one crewman after another. Then, when we had dropped to the deck, the kicking from their jackboots ensued. I will never know why they did not just shoot us each in the head. Instead, the crew seemed to enjoy assaulting us, taking out their rage on those of us brave enough to smuggle arms to be used against them. When they thought we were finished, they dropped our bodies back onto our boat and set us adrift. It was a message intended for the other fishermen in this area. What they would encounter should they pick up our missions."

"But you lived, God be praised, my Uncle," Einar exclaimed.

"By only the thinnest strand of Thor's golden locks. My brother was by no means as lucky. He succumbed to his wounds, and was dead when the drifting boat was recovered. I wished I had gone to rest with him, but it was not meant to be. It took me months to recover. I am not the man I once was. I am a broken smuggler who has grown old before my years, I am afraid."

Einar listened to the tale, which rang remarkably similar to his own experience with his brother Gunnar.

"Then, I suppose any hope to get to Lake Tinn is ill placed," Einar said dejectedly.

"Perhaps, not," said Erik, "but Tinn is an inland lake. It is a long way south. There is no path through the Leads alone. It will require you to brave the open sea for a stretch, which can be a very dangerous undertaking this time of year, even without the German patrols. Given all that, you will still have a perilous journey just to get to the Rjukan Valley and the *Tinnsjå.* I did not see any overland skis that you carried."

"No, uncle," Einar confessed, "I hoped to get those here as well."

"You are not very well prepared to risk your life again, then are you?"

"No, I am afraid not," Einar said.

"Than this must be most urgent," his uncle reasoned. "Tell me why this is so pressing."

"I cannot," Einar said.

"Well, nephew, neither can I take you," Erik said, "for as I said, I am a broken man. But I know of others here who might take this mission on just to defy the Nazi oppressors. You rest while I walk down to their *rorbu* to speak to them."

"Do not say too much to them," Einar pleaded, "only that you know of someone who needs to get south urgently."

"I know nothing else," Erik responded.

His uncle left the *rorbu* and Einar relaxed. After a brief respite, a fear overtook him that he was not safe. That perhaps his own uncle would betray him. It was just then that the *rorbu's* door opened and his uncle crept once more inside. Einar half expected to have uniformed Nazi guards follow him in.

"You are back so quickly, uncle?"

"I went nowhere, Einar. I only inspected the contents of your rucksack outside. That is quite a load of *plastique* you carry."

Einar suddenly felt very vulnerable. He began to think of how easily he could overtake the old man that his uncle had become. Erik took off his parka and rejoined him at the table.

"I know some men here that will help you, but will expect to be paid for their efforts," he confided. "I am in no condition to join you, but you can take my skis for your overland journey. I certainly will no longer need them."

"Thank you, my uncle," Einar said, as he relaxed.

"Well, it is too late, my nephew, for you all to leave today. I will contact these men and see if they can be ready when the sunrise comes."

The next six days produced a journey unlike any Einar had ever before endured. Three days in a powerboat commanded by two young fishermen named Knute and Torp weaved along the coastal waters through a maze of fjords, and when necessary, out upon the open sea. They breezed through the glassy smooth waters of the fjords, but on the open sea faced hammer blows of rolling, shearing waves. Einar felt once more as he had in the outboard skiff, as if the vessel would be violently overturned. When he admitted this to the two fisherman, it merely precipitated laughs followed by a litany of tales of much more severe waters. Einar thought the men nearly as nervous as he was, and this was their defense mechanism.

"Relax," Torp said, "this ship was made for these waters. And it is very fast."

On the second day they were pursued by a Norwegian coastal patrol boat. They could only assume it was staffed by the government, who under Quisling's rule would not be friendly to them. So they ducked into a fjord and opened up the throttle to outrun the larger vessel. They skimmed along the fjords surface, all the while Einar feared their hitting a submerged rock or a sandbar. There was no way they could possibly know the waters of all these fjords. Einar thought he had transformed into his cautious twin Gunnar, and then smiled at the thought of how terrified his brother would be on this mission. Soon the trailing coastal vessel disengaged.

Finally, they came to Bergen which they bypassed. They proceeded further south to enter the network of capillary fjords leading to the much larger *Hardangerfjord*. After the third day was completed, they anchored in a sheltered cove to sleep, as they had the previous two nights along the extensive journey. When the sun rose, Knut took the helm and travelled along the shore of the *Eidfjord,* that body of water into which the *Hardangerfjord* led.

Einar was struck by the near vertical climb of the mountains around this fjord. He knew Knut searched for a landing spot on which to deposit their human cargo. If they were discovered within this dead ending fjord, there would be no escape. Einar wondered, *How will I ever get out of this valley to the high plateau above?*

A flash of reflected sunlight twinkled along the shoreline. Then another.

"There!" yelled out Torp, pointing with his arm, hand and finger. Knut headed toward the spot with an urgency that could not be denied.

They came along the fjord's heavily wooded shoreline. A man came out to greet them on the rocks at the water's edge. Torp threw him a lead line from the craft.

"Who is this?" asked a surprised Einar.

"Nils, your guide for the overland journey," Torp replied.

"I did not ask for a guide," said Einar.

"We were not about to risk our lives getting you here just to have you die on the overland route to *Tinnsjå*," Torp said. "You wish to lead yourself into another dead end as you did above the *Rombaksfjord*?"

The shock on Einar's face surely showed through, before he responded, "We were being chased by *Gebirgsjäger*."

"And you think the Nazis won't pursue you here? You won't have any Poles to save you here, my friend!" Each word cut at him sharply, which must have been apparent because Torp then lowered his voice and said more softly. "Yes, of course we know what you and your brother endured. You are heroes in Skrova, the entire place celebrates you and mourns your brother. Now, you wish to get to *Tinnsjå*? Nils is how you get there!"

Einar was then put ashore. The vessel was pulled close to the rock and Einar reached out his hand to take the guide's arm. Nils was young, perhaps three or four years younger than Einar, and in excellent shape. He pulled Einar onto the rock, and then Nils retrieved first Einar's ski equipment, then his heavy rucksack. When the weight of the rucksack was more than Nils expected, the man nearly lost his balance and pitched into the fjord. He quickly recovered and did not.

Without so much as a wave, Torp and Knut sped away from the shoreline, their mission completed. Nils looked over Einar, from head to toe and back again.

"Nils, I am Einar," he said.

"I know who you are, and so also would anyone within earshot, had I not assured the area was clear. No names. Not here, or anywhere. Not amongst others, and not when we are alone."

"What am I to call you?"

"Nothing," Nils said, "just yell, I'll hear you. You look fit, I hope for your sake you are."

"I am in excellent shape," boasted Einar.

"We will see," said Nils, "for before we ever get to skiing the high plateau we must climb out of this valley. Lucky for you I have only a moderately difficult trail mapped out. My things are waiting for me there in the forest atop our climb. Now let's grab your things and then we begin. I will get you as far as the town of Rjukan, not far from Vemork. Once there, others will await to take you the rest of the way."

"Where have all these helpers come from?" Einar asked.

"Perhaps you are not as bright as we have been told," said Nils. "Your mission is known to the Resistance. These are the men, Torp and Knut included, who make up its backbone."

"So why must I travel along on this journey?" EInar asked. "Why could you not have passed the material along without me?"

"Express and direct orders from London," Nils replied. "You, whose name I shall not speak aloud, must deliver the explosives. On this, there can be no exception."

What for Nils had been a moderately difficult climb had been for Einar extremely strenuous. But he was able to keep pace with the young guide. After many hours, they reached the beginning of the high plateau and took a well deserved rest, although not as long as Einar would have liked.

Nils then pulled from his rucksack two thin white snowsuits for each man to pull over their outerwear. They provided no warmth, only camouflage against the plateau's white fields or among its snow laden forests. *These jumpsuits must have been specifically constructed for this purpose*, Einar thought, *because they were constructed such to even accommodate the rucksack beneath them.* Einar and Nils then donned the snowsuits, before fitting and adjusting their boots and ski equipment. They then were prepared for the long distance ski route across the plateau.

The pace of the overland skiing was brisk, and once again Einar had difficulty matching the cadence and stride of the younger, more athletic Nils. They trekked along trails weaving through forests of old growth, still heavily dusted white with recent snowfalls. Nils carted a pack weighing half as much as Einar's, and often was forced to stop to wait for Einar to first catch up to him. Einar was out of breath, but Nils was unrelenting in pushing him. Only periodically would he allow a rest for Einar to recover.

The trail Nils meticulously followed through the forests opened up to a broad field. Nils stopped at the forest's edge and allowed Einar to catch his breath once again.

"We cross this field, fellow, you understand?" Nils commented.

"Yes," Einar replied.

"Fields are most dangerous, you understand? Even with the white camouflage, a sniper's eye will detect movement. We must move with purpose."

"Yes." Einar thought of he and Gunnar, and how his brother had been shot from a great distance because due to his thoughtlessness they had failed to maintain cover. That gunshot eventually took Gunnar's life. *My carelessness took my brother's life,* he thought.

"If there is an airplane, or if you hear any gunshot, even from far away, you are to fall to the ground and stay as still as possible. You understand, fellow?"

"Yes, I fully understand," said Einar.

"Stay behind me. There is a trail, but the snow has blown and the drifts may have obscured it. Never go around me, understand?"

"Yes," Einar said one more time.

"Keep up," said Nils before he thrust himself from the canopy of the forest out onto the open white field. Einar followed, and immediately felt like a mouse out in the open waiting for a hawk to pounce, but this day there were no airplanes overhead, no gunshots in the distance. They worked their way as rapidly across the expansive white field as the accumulated snows would allow.

At the end of the first day, Nils led Einar to a ski hut for their overnight stay. They would sleep only long enough to refresh, but not satisfy, them both. They began the second day in darkness, and would end it as well without light. The second overnight cabin was somewhat larger, its beds a little more comfortable. But again they stayed only long enough to refresh their bodies, but not give in to the desires of their aching muscles.

On the final day, they rested briefly at the edge of another forest route and looked out upon what Nils said would be their last open field to cross. Nils confessed to Einar that they had done well, and should make the town of Rjukan late that night.

Einar looked beyond the open field to the safety of the evergreen forest beyond. Looming over the distant forest was a massive white slope.

"What is that mountain?" He asked Nils.

"That my friend is the *Gaustatoppen*," he said, "which is a most welcome sight. You see it lies to the south and west of our destination. It is nearly two-thousand meters high, and without war is a favorite of the recreational climbers here. Instead, the Germans have placed 88 millimeter guns atop her."

Einar had heard that peak's name somewhere before, but could not place it. Yet the syllables lurked in his mind like a dark, blurry omen.

"Come," Nils said, "our last dash across an open field. Follow me. If anything happens to me, head directly towards the *Gausta.*"

They bolted one last time across the snow laden field. As they reached the center of it, a shot rang out in the distance. Nils fell to the snow. Einar laid himself flat before a second shot followed. His heart pounded. Both men lay flat in the snow.

"Are you all right, Nils?" Einar called out.

"No names, fellow," came the response. "Yes, I am fine."

Then three more shots fired, further in the distance, their echoes trailing them in close succession now.

"I don't think they were aiming for us, fellow," said Nils, "let us get back to our skis and finish this. You are all right?"

"I am fine," said Einar, "and I like your idea. Let's finish this, my friend."

Both men struggled to their skis and finished the dash to the treeline. There, they collected themselves before following the trail in the new forest. Soon, Nils led them to a commanding view of the Rjukan Valley and beyond it, the imperious *Gaustatoppen*.

They had skied to the edge of the high plateau that hovered over the town of Rjukan, and there, within the woods they rested. It was late in the afternoon. Nightfall would be upon them soon. Einar thought the length of day was noticeably longer than in the Arctic, nearly a thousand miles north.

Nils had guided them far to the east of Vemork, the Norsk Hydro facility, which was heavily guarded. The grounds around it were known by the Norwegian Resistance to be strewn extensively with land mines.

Einar and Nils removed and carefully hid the skis, and both men then removed the white snowsuits. Nils repacked them into his rucksack, which he then stored carefully alongside the well hidden skis. Then the two men laid down their aching frames, their muscles depleted from the exhausting cross-country excursion. Einar rested while Nils kept guard for any possible German or Norwegian patrols. None were found that day, and Einar's rest was uninterrupted. His muscles ached in ways that he had never imagined after the three day journey.

Once darkness began to fall, Nils awakened Einar and they carefully climbed down to the level of the valley below. The hillsides were steep, but generally the trail they followed necessitated only a careful hiking descent. There were some stretches that were very steep where the two men were assisted by a series of ropes prearranged almost like handrails, but no spots where any rappelling gear might be needed.

Einar assumed this trail was maintained by the Resistance, and the ropes likely had been tied off in days, if not hours before they arrived. He further assumed within hours of their using it, some brave and hardy soul would climb up and remove the ropes, along with any trace of bootprints left behind by them.

As dusk deepened into night, Nils and Einar cautiously emerged on the village outskirts, where a man approached them. He carried two small reindeer hides over his left arm.

"It's OK, fellow," Nils said. "Wait here." Nils walked forward and engaged the man in conversation. The hides had been a recognition symbol. He had been carrying them high in the crook of his elbow, but immediately after Nils approached him, the man dropped the arm and the hides dangled more naturally. After a few minutes, Nils waved over Einar.

"This man is our friend, you understand, fellow?"

"Yes," Einar said to Nils, before looking over to the stranger with the dangly hides. "Hello, friend."

The man responded by tossing the hides at Einar. He was surprised by this, but focused and caught the skins. Then he turned to ask Nils what came next. The young overland guide was gone, disappeared into the night.

"You are with me now," the friend said, before turning away to walk. Einar followed with the skins.

This man in front of him was a broad fellow. It was then that in the opposite direction two German officers walked towards them. The broad friend steered wide of their path, a showing of mock respect, and greeted them with a nod. Einar followed his lead and did the same. The two officers walked past them, as if it were just another night amongst the locals.

Einar waited for them to range out of earshot, before he asked, "Friend, why did they not stop us?"

This drew a strong rebuke from the broad fellow. He put his arm around Einar almost as one close friend would another. Close to Einar's ear he barked. "Never ask such a question. You are lucky they did not hear it. It is a normal Friday evening. They are merely out seeking refreshment tonight. Why should they want to stop a couple of locals? They would rather get to the *bier* and the girls, now wouldn't they?"

The man released his arm from Einar's shoulder, and as it slid off, he again turned his back on the younger man. Einar could not help but think of a quote he had once heard the Prime Minister say, *"If you stop to throw stones at every barking dog, you'll never get to where you re going..."*

The man led Einar to Rjukan station, where they waited for a train. It arrived and they boarded. It carried them eastward, in the opposite direction away from the Vemork facility to the waterfront village of Mæl. There were no other Nazi uniformed soldiers or officers on the train. They soon passed the town of Miland and arrived at Mæl. Einar noticed the rail lines extended to the water's edge. It was part of an intricate series of rail and ferry connections crucial to this valley and the transport of the Ammonia and Nitrogen based fertilizer products from the Vemork facility.

Mæl is a transitional location for a town. It stands where the Rjukan Valley's flow meets and drains into the *Tinnsjå*, or Lake Tinn. This is the deepest lake in Norway, a wonder of nature over the millennia collecting the waters of the snowmelt between deeply diving mountain walls.

Einar and the broad man disembarked from the train in Mæl. Einar was led by the man to a small house where he was quickly hustled inside. "Relax, Einar, you have made your destination. Welcome to Mæl. Now, give me what you carry. That which will turn the waters of the *Tinnsjå* into a maelstrom."

The man laughed at his own joke, and as he did so extended his arms to take possession of the rucksack. Einar passed it to him, and the man placed it on a small table. He unpacked the rucksack carefully, and soon removed the twenty kilograms of plastic explosives. The man set it on the table and simply stared at it. Einar watched him carefully.

"We thought you would not make it in time," a strong voice said from behind him. Einar spun to look upon a lean fellow, middle aged, with a great mustache. As he spun, Einar became aware again of the Reindeer hides he still carried, that had flared out like a dancer's skirt. "Just throw those damn skins anywhere, Einar. And for God's sake relax, you are among friends now. Even better, you are among co-conspirators. We will look after you well, if only to save our own necks."

Einar looked at the man and dared not ask his name. All this secrecy had been drilled into him since leaving the boat in the fjord to meet Nils. "What am I to call you gentlemen?"

The mustache was soon dangling over a broad smile, "How about our names. You have risked your life getting this *plastique* to us, so we will risk ourselves just a little. I am Alf and this man you followed over here is Rolf. Now, my brave friend, What took you so long, Einar? You almost missed the boat."

Einar assumed he spoke figuratively, but would soon discover otherwise. "But I am here, am I not?"

"Ah," the mustachioed Alf replied, "but the Hydro was scheduled to depart tomorrow morning. It is too late tonight to rig the explosives on that ferry. Thankfully, we have people inside the Vemork facility who were able to delay the shipment by one day. We feared you might not make it in time even for the ferry sailing on Sunday morning."

Einar was shaken by the string of sentences. "You are going to sink the ferry as it crosses the lake? Won't there will be passengers on board?"

Just then, Rolf, the broad shouldered escort, cried out, "What have we here? The *plastique* - it is our old friend Nobel 808, no? Green like pistachio, but yet I can smell the almonds. And 20 kilograms just as was ordered." Rolf removed the explosive from its wrapping and held it up to his nose. "Yes, this will do nicely."

He then pulled a pistol that Einar had packed in the side pocket of rucksack. He gave an inquisitive look to Einar.

"That," Einar said as he twisted toward Rolf, "is my pistol. It is a Walther P-38. A very good sidearm."

"These are great weapons," said Rolf, "the German officers all carry them instead of those old damn Lugers that they issue to the privates. But you were very foolish, my friend, packing this anywhere near the explosives. Had any spark from it, even static electricity, reached that plastique, you would have been blown to bits, as would our entire operation."

Einar was becoming exasperated. "Look, I got the explosives here safely, did I not? Now will someone tell me what I risked my life for? Why did we not head for Vemork as I expected, but instead I am brought here, at the other end of the Rjukan Valley? And why are you men so willing to blow-up innocent civilians on a Sunday morning ferry crossing of the lake. Don't you have any decency?"

"Tomorrow," replied Alf, "after you have rested we will explain it all. Rolf take that *plastique* down to the rest of our team."

As Rolf began to reach for the explosive, Einar erupted. "NO, NOT TOMORROW, NOW," he screamed. "YOU WILL TELL ME NOW OR ELSE…"

The friendly faces of Alf and Rolf froze instantly in stone. The room had become tense and hostile. It was as if the two men were measuring up their courier, as to just how volatile he might be.

"Be very careful with your threats, Einar," said Alf. "We know you are one of us, but don't threaten us. We would hate to have to send you down to the bottom of the *Tinnsjå* along with the Ferry Hydro. Rolf, don't be silly. Please put down that gun. The muzzle flash will be enough to ignite the plastique and kill us all. It would be a pity to waste young Einar's efforts."

Einar turned to see the broad shouldered Rolf pointing his own pistol at him. The man slowly lowered it before laying it flat on the table.

"Gentlemen, I no longer have anything to make me unwilling to die," Einar said bravely, but instantly thought of Kari and knew it was a lie. "I have no reason to threaten anyone. I only wish to not lay awake all night wondering what your mission is. Why you are willing to cause innocent civilians to perish to achieve it."

"Rolf, take the *plastique* to the men waiting for it," Alf said. "I will brief Einar."

With that Rolf wrapped the green doughy plastique in brown butcher paper and carried the package out of the house like some meat he was taking to a home along the lake.

"That's it," Einar said, just after Rolf left. "Nothing more than butcher's paper for the material I risked my life to get here?"

"That's how we do it here. The Germans rarely stop anyone here. At least any locals. The key is to appear unconcerned. Sit, Einar, I have some food for you, you must be famished."

Alf produced a plate of Brunost cheese and Lefseroll. Einar did not realize how hungry his body was for nourishment until he saw the plate.

"Go ahead, Einar. Sit. Eat your fill and I will explain everything while you do so."

Einar reached for the tasty brown cheese. He sensed his mouth watering as he did so.

"I know that you were working the other side of last year's Vemork raid from London. Yes, don't look so surprised. I had been briefed on it. The Nazis all thought that it was a British commando raid. Very successful. When that was coupled with the Americans bombing the valley, with no real effect I might add, it convinced the Germans that the Allies would not stop their assaults here in this valley. And they were right, weren't they. They decided to remove what is left of the heavy water equipment to the relative safety of the Fatherland."

"I was briefed that the raid on Vemork had been a complete success. That the equipment to make the heavy water had been destroyed. How can this be of such consequence that you are willing to kill innocents over it?"

Alf looked down at him. Einar had stopped eating. Alf made a gesture with his hand that said continue.

"We thought it was such a success that nothing further needed be done," replied Alf. "We have people, faithful to our cause, inside Vemork. They uncovered a secret stash of the heavy water that had been made before the raid. In fact, there are drums of the stuff. Enough to bridge the German physicists until their engineers can inspect the damaged processing equipment and build their own. It will not take them long."

"They have drum after drum of the heavy water?" Einar was stunned. He remembered then that Wincer Wells had once briefed him that this material was critical to building a super weapon. A single bomb that could destroy an entire city. No wonder these Resistance plotters were willing to sacrifice the lives of their countrymen to keep this heavy water out of Hitler's reach.

Alf continued, "Perhaps, most importantly, are these many drums full of heavy water. Tomorrow, they will load what's left of the drums, as well as the remaining equipment onto rail cars which will come through the ferry terminus here in Mæl. The rail cars will be rolled onto the ferry, just as all shipments of fertilizer coming from Vemork must be. It is the only way out of the valley. The explosives you risked your life for, which you claim not to care about, those explosives which you carried for almost a thousand miles to get to us, will be used to sink that ferry. The heavy water will drop to the bottom of the *Tinnsjå*, one of the deepest lakes in all of Europe."

"My God," gasped Einar, "those poor unsuspecting people. Will there be women and children aboard?"

Alf walked behind Einar and placed his hand on his shoulder. "That is up to God, my friend. If we lose some civilians, we will grieve with their families, certainly, but the world will be a much safer place for their sacrifice."

"I am so sick of that damned word sacrifice," muttered Einar. "Anything is excusable so long as it is deemed a *sacrifice!* And worse even is the phrase *heroic sacrifice*, which seems reserved for the grossest of atrocities."

"Einar, no one likes the loss of even a single life, be it civilian or military. But our intelligence network is aware that the Germans are already testing flying bombs, the V-1 and V-2," Alf said, "imagine if they could put Heisenberg's super-bombs on those rockets. They would control the war. No country on earth would be safe, not one."

Alf referred to Werner Heisenberg, Germany's pre-eminent physicist.

"That is why we can't allow that heavy water to reach the Reich, and the Ferry Hydro will sink Sunday in the deepest part of the lake. Those materials, the drums of heavy water will sink with it. It is crucial that we deny Germany any chance of developing more advanced weapons. If that means some innocents die, I am greatly saddened, but nonetheless, stay ever more committed to our cause."

"Can't you get the word out to your people to stay away from the ferry on Sunday?" Einar asked.

"And tip our hand? Scare off the Nazis? Have them inspect the ferry and find your explosives?" Alf made a face that this was not possible. "No. We have a perfect opportunity. The Nazis do not have their own guards on the ferry at night. Only company guards. Our people know them. They will gain access tomorrow night and rig the boat. It will sink on Sunday morning.

You will be our guest until then. After that, you will be released to make your way back to your home in the Arctic. I understand you have a girl there waiting for your return."

"Her name is Kari," Einar said, "and yes, I have grown fond of her. But if I could somehow give my life to save any of those who will perish, I assure you I would."

"Yes," said Alf, "we know all about Kari. She is quite brave. You will sleep tonight, and tomorrow you will begin your trek home to her."

"How can I possibly sleep?" Einar replied. "How can I rest knowing what will come from my efforts?"

"This will help," Alf said as he passed a small vial to him. "Only use a few drops, or your sleep will be much deeper than you wish."

Einar took the vial, wondering if he should trust the man. "What is this?" he asked.

"Just the sedative chloral hydrate," said Alf. "It will calm you and help you sleep. Now, Einar, I must join my comrades. I hate to do this to you, but I must lock you in the bedroom. Take the food with you. You can finish it before you fall asleep, which I think you desperately need. The locks are only to protect you, to simply keep you from wandering the docks and getting picked up, my boy. You have a lot to think about. So come with me."

Alf led Einar to the second story bedroom. The window was boarded up.

"I apologize for the view," Alf said, "but it will not help to tell you that were the boards removed, you'd have a great view of the *Tinnsjå*. So I won't."

Alf laughed. Einar did not. He simply laid himself on the bed, a prisoner of his own efforts.

"Einar," Alf said just before closing the door. "You really have done a remarkable job in getting us that *plastique*. The Germans have clamped down on our supplies. We were air dropping it, but they figured this out and began shooting anyone we sent out to collect the stuff. Anyone they even suspected of doing so. And they would shoot them in the public squares, in front of the townspeople. Our volunteers dried up quickly. Thank you for doing what you have done. We will see that you get back to your Kari in good shape. Do not fear us. We are honorable men."

The door closed and Einar heard the key twist in the lock. He was too exhausted to get up and try the door. He simply accepted it was locked. He put aside the food, and looked at the vial. They no longer needed him, this could be poison of some form. His mind raced thinking about the ferry. Einar put the vial to his lips and imbibed as little as he could. He laid his head flat on the pillow and closed his eyes. In his head he heard Alf's last words, "We are honorable men."

Yes, he thought, *honorable men who are willing to kill innocent families aboard a ferry on a day unlike any other Sunday's lake crossing. What has the world come to?*

Figure 46: Norsk Hydro Ferry at Mæl on Lake Tinn

66 The Furies of Fate Await

February 1944

"Sure I am this day we are masters of our fate, that the task which has been set before us is not above our strength; that its pangs and toils are not beyond our endurance."

Winston Spencer Churchill

Einar slept throughout Friday night and through most of Saturday, well into the night, in fact. His rest was itself a dichotomy. It was a deep slumber and restorative physically, as his muscles and bones begged for the renewal of their strength. However, as he came out from under the influence of the sedative, his mind raced and turned over upon itself as if seeking a resolve from the sins against innocents that would be carried out with the explosives he had so strenuously labored to deliver.

He rose from the bed and for some reason wandered over to the boarded window. He attempted to peer through the cracks between slats, but all he saw was darkness. Einar traced his fingers over the boards, running his fingers over the thin slits between them. He could feel the cold air penetrate even these remote gaps. The tactile feeling of the edges of the boards for some reason made him all the more aware of the fragility of life.

It was then that he heard a key sliding into the lock, and the resultant click as the knob turned. The door behind him opened. In its frame stood Alf.

"Well, how is our guest? It appears the sleeping prince has arisen."

"Your guest?" Einår replied. "More like your prisoner."

"I am so sorry my friend. Your mind was so fatigued last night, we feared it might cause you to do something foolish."

"Like kill women and children? That foolish, Alf"?

"Come downstairs and eat," Alf replied. "We will answer all your questions as you are now well rested."

Alf departed from the doorway, but left the door ajar. Einar soon heard him descending the wooden steps, which creaked and groaned under his weight.

Einar washed from a pitcher and basin that had been placed in the room. He cleansed his bearded face with the cool water. He looked into the mirror and examined the cleansed but unclean face that stared back. He thought of the ferry. *Who am I to allow these innocent people to plunge to their deaths?*

Einar descended the creaky wooden stairs to find a number of men gathered around the table in the kitchen area. There was Alf, of course, and his friend Rolf from last night. Also, two other men joined them. They all turned toward Einar as he approached.

"This man, my friends," said Alf, "is who we have to thank for our success tonight."

Einar searched their eyes. What success? Should he ask who the other men were? Would they truthfully even tell him?

"Einar, these men are some friends of ours. They share the same name, Knut." Alf had volunteered their names freely. But were they even their real names. For that matter were Alf and Rolf's names truly their own?

"You have done well, my friend," the Knut closest to him said, reaching out to shake his hand. Einar responded with a trepidation that was apparent. "Without you, our night tonight would have not been successful."

"You mean it is done?" Einar asked.

"Our kilos of *plastique* sleep tonight in the hull of the Hydro, instead of myself," Knut teased.

"I do not understand," Einar replied.

"Knut makes a joke, that is all," Alf explained. "The Hydro was very lightly guarded by two company guards, men from the valley. We cut the fence and got onto the vessel when one of them stumbled upon Knut. They knew each other. Knut lied and said he worked on the ship and wished only to sleep aboard until morning when he was due to work. He was allowed to do so. It is common courtesy here to accommodate others who need to escape the cold, as one can lose his life in it in these conditions."

"These are not very good guards," Einar assessed. "Where are all the Nazis?"

"These guards are perfect for our needs," said Alf.

"The German colonel in charge of this move has called all uniformed Nazi troops back to Vemork to guard the shipment as they are loaded on to the train cars and along the way," the other Knut chirped in. "They will travel with the train in the morning."

"Who could be so foolish?" Einar was stunned. "Who is this colonel?"

"Colonel Alois Becker," the second Knut responded. "He is in charge of protecting this shipment from Vemork to Germany."

"My God," mumbled Einar.

"You know this German?" asked Alf. "The former *Gebirgsjäger*?"

"Yes, I ran across him at Bjørnfjell, in the mountains above Narvik. Why on earth would the Germans take one of their best leaders away from the mountains?"

"I suppose he was no good there when he lost his leg," Alf said. "The story we have heard is that some Pole drove a blade deep into his thigh up on the mountainside. The Pole was killed making his escape on rappelling lines, but by the time the colonel was brought off the mountainside, his leg was gangrenous and had to be removed. So now he walks with a prosthetic and a heavy limp."

"Albin," Einar again mumbled, "the Pole's name was Albin". *It was Albin, just as Bogdan had said it was all along. I was right to allow his brother to live. This proves it.*

"Now, gentlemen, eat up," Alf said to them all, "for in a few hours, we all need to be gone. We will watch the ferry Hydro sink from a safe spot above the lighthouse bend, after which we will scatter like the last rays of the sun."

"Not me," Einar announced. "I need to see this man. I need to watch him walk to his fate upon that ferry. I need to be on that loading dock as he does so."

"You cannot interfere with those who board," warned Rolf.

"Einar here is very concerned about the innocent souls aboard the Ferry Hydro who may be lost tomorrow." Alf said. "I had told him we delayed the shipment one day, from Saturday morning to Sunday, when there are the fewest passengers aboard, just to minimize the civilian losses. And we have the explosives rigged to go off in the deepest part of the lake, but also when the ferry is closest to the shore, rounding a point. There anyone in the water will have a fighting chance of swimming ashore."

"Yes, mothers with their young will have no problem making that swim in the frigid waters," Einar scoffed. *But if Becker will be aboard, somehow that makes this all the more permissible? Perhaps my soul has grown as dark as the colonel's. Am I now willing to sacrifice the innocent just to avenge Gunnar's life?*

No one slept that during the remainder of that night. The morning came and the men all departed the safe house. At first, they insisted Einar come into the mountain with them, but he resisted, telling them all he must watch Colonel Alois Becker hobble onto that ferry. He told them all of the story of his brother losing his life on the *staircase of the gods*. They allowed him to go free on two conditions. First, that he not interfere in any way with the mission. Second, that he leave the Rjukan Valley as soon as the ship sank to the bottom of Lake Tinn. Einar agreed, although he was unsure if he could do either.

Einar braved the February cold to go down to the ferry loading platform. He watched as the train arrived. Two boxcars were carefully rolled aboard the ferry, which had tracks to accommodate shipments from the Norsk Hydro company. Most times, this was mere agricultural grade ammonia or nitrogen fertilizers, produced at the Vemork Plant. This morning, it was the highly prized heavy water. The heavy water was stored in drums within the boxcars nestled so neatly on the ferry's deck, just below the passenger lounge. Once it was loaded aboard, a figure in a gray German greatcoat came out of the warmth of the railway locomotive and, surrounded by two columns of his Nazi guards, hobbled onto the ferry. Only once the Germans were aboard would the passengers be allowed to come onto the ferry.

Einar stood within the clutch of civilians waiting to board and watched the procession of Nazis slowly parade by. Einar first noticed the limb of their commander, so much like that of his own father. As Colonel Becker hobbled by, Einar examined his face. Stern, unsmiling, looking off into the distance. Then, the colonel turned to scan the crowd. His gaze swept over them all. The locals knew to look away, but Einar would not. The colonel's gaze swept past his, stopped and then doubled back.

Did he recognize me? After all these years? I did not have such a full beard then, only heavy stubble, a few days growth, as I had shaved during our time in the cabin.

The colonel returned his gaze forward and limped onto the Ferry Hydro. He gave directions to his aides, who then picked up a radio to relay them to someone else.

Seeing the colonel commit himself to his fate, Einar fought the intense impulse to board and watch as Becker thrashed about in the water. He longed to watch the bastard die in return for shooting his brother. Then he thought of Kari, alone in the *rorbu*, and his vengeance was sated. Einar knew he could walk away just in knowing that Becker would be on that ferry when the explosives went off.

Then, the direction was given to allow the waiting civilians to board. Einar stood still as families surrounding him slowly shuffled onto the Ferry Hydro. There were about forty civilians or so that drained away from around him, leaving him exposed like a sandbar at low tide. He turned to walk away, only to see two Nazi guards behind him, both with Lugers drawn.

"Auf der Fahre," they screamed at him, *"schnell, schnell."* Einar objected. *You are mistaken* he remembered in German and said, but not the words for *I am not getting on the ferry.* It did not matter.

One of the guard holstered his weapon, moved forward and spun Einar by his shoulders before pushing him hard toward the ferry. Einar recovered his balance just before he would have fallen, only to feel another shove. The other guard followed, carrying the rucksack that Einar had at his feet.

As he approached the ferry's boarding gate, the German soldier shoved Einar as hard as he could. Einar tumbled onto the vessel, and looking up saw that Colonel Becker watched over him from the outdoor deck that wrapped around the overhead passenger lounge. He made hand a gesture that seemed to say bring him to me.

Einar began to rise to his feet, only to be struck across his face hard by the back hand of a guard. He stumbled to his knee, just in time to receive a vicious kick from another soldier to his ribs. He rolled over onto his side and another kick landed. Then he heard something yelled out in German from above. The beating stopped. Einar was assisted to his feet. It was only then that he noted the ferry had departed the dock and was heading across the lake.

The guards pulled Einar roughly along the deck and up the flight of the Hydro's metal steps.

As he was being pulled, Einar was glad to see that the ferry had picked up considerable speed and had pulled far away from the shoreline. He could see the point that the vessel had to round in the distance, and thought it would be mere minutes before the explosive charges went off. He looked through the metal slats of the stairs to see the two boxcars side-by-side and laughed to himself. Then he was on the decking above the boxcars and saw through the windows the civilian families in the lounge. All laughing within him withered away, as he was reminded of their fate.

Einar was dragged to Becker and handcuffed to the railing, his arms held wide apart exposing his chest. Becker slowly walked over to him. He looked upon Einar's face, which was heavily bearded and his hair long, even ragged. Einar was amazed that the colonel had recognized him.

"So, Einar," Colonel Becker began in Norwegian, "you look like such an overgrown troll. I would have never identified you, except like all those around you, you failed to look away from my gaze. Had you done so, you would not now be going back to the Fatherland with me. But you never would look away from my gaze. Not in Bjørnfjell, not on that damn cliff, and not this morning. It has cost you your life."

Einar searched Becker's eyes. "Just as you took my brother's life?"

Colonel Becker laughed sharply. "As I recall, I merely wounded poor Gunnar, it was you who pulled the trigger that killed him."

Einar look at the colonel and then past him to the point of land and its lighthouse which the ferry was approaching. Then, a Nazi guard pressed through the surrounding gaggle of soldiers and presented the colonel with the Walther P-38 pistol along with the rucksack it had been hidden in. He said something in German to Becker. Einar assumed it was the equivalent of "He carried this weapon."

"Ah," Becker exclaimed, "so you carry a pistol. You came to kill me? This is a very nice pistol. Wait, is this my Walther that you took from me on that damn mountain ledge?"

"It is your gun, Colonel Becker," Einar said, his voice harsh and accusing. "I have kept it through these years since you murdered my brother. I hoped one day to kill you with it. That would be the only fitting use for it."

Again, Colonel Becker laughed. "Oh yes, you once bragged that you would shoot me with my own pistol. To take revenge for your brother. I am happy to tell you that today will not be that day. Nor will any other."

Einar stared harshly at him for a second before correcting him, "What I said was that you deserved to be killed by a bullet from your own pistol."

The defiance in Einar's voice clearly angered Becker. He raised the gun to Einar's forehead and pressed its barrel against his tight skin. Einar sweated, but was ready to lay down his life.

He heard the click of the trigger. He clearly heard the hammer strike. But there was no boom, there was no pain, only an infinity of time in which Einar saw his father drowning, his mother crying, his brother's face, and Kari standing alone on the rocky shoreline.

"So, Einar carries my gun with no round in the chamber." Becker then racked the slide, and raised the gun once more. He raised the pistol slowly. Yet, this time instead of raising the pistol to his head, he took aim upon his shoulder.

"As I recall," Becker said slowly, "Gunnar's wound was just about here." He pulled the trigger, and the gunshot rang out. Einar could feel the round rip through his upper arm, searing hot, as if he had been pierced with the sharpened end of a red hot fireplace poker. He fell to his knees, and the metallic cuffs around his wrists bit hard against his bones as the weight of his body pulled him down.

"It is a pity your brother had to die," Becker mocked him, "but he was a traitor to the Nazi cause, so it was appropriate. But you, his cocksure mirror image, you are not only deserving of death, but it will be my pleasure to kill you and have you thrown over the side. Like your brother, your body will slowly rot alone at the bottom of a Norwegian fjord. Get him up."

Einar was sweating heavily. As the guards grabbed and raised him, the pain in his shoulder ripped through him like shards of shattered glass pressed hard into the wound. The blood cascaded down his arm and chest. He could feel its warm, sticky flow against his skin. He had to breathe deeply to collect his thoughts. He knew there was no surviving this encounter.

"You are wrong on two counts, my Colonel," he found the strength to say, "for this is an alpine lake, not a fjord, and unlike my brother, Gunnar, I will not be alone."

Einar turned his head to look at the point of land the vessel navigated past. He looked back at Becker to see a flash of recognition in the colonel's eyes. Becker then frantically opened the rucksack and searched it. He found nothing incriminating, but as he neared its opening to his face he detected a faint scent. He then held the canvas bag to his face, driving his nose as deeply into it as he could. The scent grew stronger.

Einar watched as he was sure the colonel recognized the aroma of almonds, the telltale signature of the plastic explosive.

"Search the ferry," yelled out Becker, first in Norwegian, for the crew, and then again in German for the guards. "Head to the shore there, immediately." he added in both languages, "and prepare at once to offload the drums of heavy water. Go, all of you, now, and search the ship, I have this man under control."

Einar recalled the surprise in the colonel's voice, just as when Becker had realized that the Enigma machine on the *staircase of the gods* had been booby-trapped. He hoped that the colonel's recognition had once again come too late.

It was just the two of them along the deck's handrail. Becker spat at Einar, "I will empty every round of this pistol into you, Einar, and delight in watching you die."

"Tell me, Colonel, was it hard for a once-great *Gebirgsjäger* like yourself to live in the shadows of these mountains, knowing all along that you would never again climb with that stump of a leg we left you."

Becker's face turned to stone with these words, just before a smirk of superiority chiseled its way upon his countenance.

"My recollection is you had nothing to do with that," Becker replied, "just the Pole who died on the ropes within a few minutes."

"Yes, the Pole Albin, who gave his life to save mine," Einar said, "only that I might live long enough to kill you, my Colonel."

Becker began to say, "It hardly appears you are in any position to …" The blast that interrupted him was felt as though it was contained, and was almost completely muffled.

The Ferry had just begun its turn toward the shoreline when the explosion ripped through the underside of the bow. A large section of the structure was obliterated. The ferry shuddered, and the resultant pitch of its bow down into the lake due to the intrusion of water caused Becker to stumble forward on his wooden leg. His weight shifted and he fell against the wounded Einar, who was still handcuffed to the rails.

The pistol remained in Becker's grip, but Einar was able to get his right hand on it. With his wound, he could not wrestle it free from the colonel, but he was able to feel for the magazine release button and depressed it. The clip, which originally held eight rounds but now only six, fell free. One round had gone through Einar's shoulder, and one remained in the firing chamber of the gun. Einar was able to kick the clip of six remaining bullets over the side into the lake.

The ferry was by then listing heavily. Beneath them, passengers and crew were already throwing themselves into the lake's icy water. No guards came back to aid the colonel, who called for their help. Instead they had already begun to take off their heavy gear for the swim to shore.

Einar was sweating harder and harder. His stomach had become filled with bile. All he could think of was his brother Gunnar, and how he had dragged his poor soul up the side of a mountain in this condition. He had led his brother to a dead end there, just as his own actions had led himself similarly this day.

The stern of the ship had risen out of the water, making it impossible for the captain to navigate the vessel to shore. The ferry by then listed heavily as the rail cars shifted, and again threw Becker hard against Einar.

Einar was still contained by the handcuffs to the rails. His arms were of no use to him. Becker struggled to raise the gun to Einar's head. Einar wrapped his unconstrained legs around the colonel's, keeping Becker from freeing himself.

"You only have that single round left, Colonel," Einar said, fueled by spite. "It may be your only alternative to drowning."

Einar recalled his father's prosthetic. He raised one foot which he planted on the colonel's lower abdomen near the crotch. He pulled with his other leg still wrapped against the false leg of the German. With both legs off the deck the handcuffs bit their metal edges hard into his wrists. Einar focused only on what he must do. He applied all his strength and smoothly shifted weight as the colonel screamed. The prosthetic leg did not come free, but rather angled away from the German, rendering him immobile. Einar recognized fear in Becker's eyes as he began screaming for help in German. None came.

Then Einar himself screamed as the leverage of his own weight snapped the bones in his right wrist. He focused on not releasing the colonel from his legs, for he feared even on one leg Becker could hobble along the handrails.

Soon the water was rising on them both. Becker continued to squeal with terror as he realized he was trapped. Einar suppressed his own pain and began laughing. He could not control himself, and it came from somewhere deep within him that he was not aware even existed. Then he said to the colonel, "Come, Alois, drown with me. We will meet the devil together."

The water was soon up to their chest, and then their chin. Becker held the pistol out of the water, before pointing it at Einar's head. At this point, each man knew the other would die, and gave up any expectation that they might be miraculously spared.

Finally, Becker spat in his face and said, "Damn you Einar, you can drown alone this day."

Becker raised the pistol to his own temple and pulled the trigger. The sound of the weapon's firing reverberated off the rising water just below it. Einar could feel it upon the tender skin of his own cheeks. It was as if Einar could feel the life being violently ripped from the German's body.

Einar's own body screamed with the pain from his shoulder wound and broken wrist, but even these seemed to diminish somewhat as Becker's corpse began to float in the water aside him. The weight of the body upon Einar slowly lifted, and all force of struggle had immediately ceased. Seconds later, the ship rolled just as both Einar and the colonel's corpse were drawn downward below the surface of the lake. Einar was still handcuffed to the ferry, which drew him unrelentingly into its the ever-deepening waters. As the icy waters enveloped him, they somewhat numbed but did not relieve his pain.

Einar's fellow saboteurs, Alf, Rolf and the two Knuts had watched this deadly struggle through their field glasses from the shore. Each man would include it in detail in the after-action reports they sent back to London. In that way, Diane would some seventy-six years later know of the final deadly grapple between Einar and Becker on that ferry's upper deck. She would know that Becker had ultimately taken his own life, yet the report would be incomplete because it did not include that fact that the colonel had died from a bullet fired from what had long ago been his own gun.

What happened next would be lost forever to time. Even Diane's skilled investigators and all their connections within the Intelligence Services could never reconstruct what occurred under the waters of Lake Tinn that day.

Einar's legs still intertwined with and clung to the dead German. He could see streaming from the dead man's head a red ribbon of blood wafting in the lake's clear water. Einar had one last thought of Becker as the vessel pulled them faster down to the bottom and the pressure built in his ears. *You deserved to die from a bullet of your own gun,* he thought

As he fought to hold on to the last gasp of air in his lungs, Einar watched as a stream of rising bubbles of air seemed to coalesce into a dark image in the increasingly murky water resembling his father's face. Then more of the air soon followed, collecting into the image of his brother Gunnar's face alongside.

Einar's last breath burned like a lit fuse within him. When he could no longer stand its scalding fire, Einar released it. Its tortuous flame transformed within him into an all-encompassing blinding shroud of light. All pain from the bullet wound and fractured wrist immediately disappeared. He felt his soul slip free its mortal coil in an invigorating burst of mixed energy and serenity. His spirit began to ascend through the lake's turbid waters. His father's and brother's spirits now glowed brightly in the brilliance that his own liberated spirit projected. Their souls fused with his and led him upward from the sea into the heavens in a feeling of total peace. Yet, as he looked below, no matter how high he ascended, Einar could clearly see the two still entangled corpses of himself and Alois Becker being dragged down by the sinking ship away to the lake's bottom.

Then all was peaceful. Before long, Einar could feel the waves of sorrow that emanated forth from the lonely red *rorbu.* Slowly they faded, eventually giving way to Einar's spirit being comforted by Kari's fond remembrances of him and their wondrous times together.

Figure 47: Sir Winston Churchill

67 *Epilogue*

"Now this is not the end. It is not even the beginning of the end. But it is, perhaps, the end of the beginning."

Winston Spencer Churchill

Diane was exhausted. The telling of this story had taken three days under Texas skies and some twenty hours in total to relay.

"My God, Diane," Jake Conley said, "you sure do know how to deliver results for a man's fee. So, you cobbled all this from the MI6 and SOE notes, along with the information from the diaries, and it appears you have unraveled quite a saga. After all this I learn that my mother was actually Norwegian, and that I did have two older half-brothers, both who died tragically, but not together, in World War II. Thank God that the real Cassandra, that is Mrs. Tilly MacAlvor, got pregnant just before that Brigand character went off to Dunkirk. Had she not had a late son, and had he not given her a granddaughter, those diaries would likely never have survived. Amazing!"

Wade waved his hand as if shooing away an unforeseen horsefly. His face was anxious. It was apparent to all he was biting his tongue.

"Looks like my son is just dying to make a fool of himself again," Jake said. "Go ahead, Wade, don't let us stop you from securing your place as the jackass of our family."

Wade stood from his chair, as if needing to stretch. Then he slowly began his objections.

"Well, Diane, Mr. Ferris, thank you both for taking the time this week to walk us through this *tale*." He stressed the word tale as if he meant it as a work of fiction. "I can only wonder where the facts left off and the embellishments began."

"Such as which embellishments, exactly, Wade?" Diane asked.

"Well, let's start with the dialogue relayed between brothers in Norway…"

"All in the notes Tilly took from Einar after his return," Diane answered briskly. "I took the effort to cross reference them and can pull them up should any one have need for to do so."

"Ok, Diane," Wade said, "I am sure you can. What about the dialogue and events that occurred between Einar and Kari? Now where could that have come from?"

Diane looked stunned that the man could so openly antagonize her in this way.

"Wade, you are certainly very observant," she confessed, "that I had not yet revealed, my source for that. You see, after Einar drowned and was pulled to the bottom of Lake Tinn, Kari joined up with the Venus Network in Arctic Norway. Remember the brothers who had set this up, they looked after her. She eventually penetrated the radar installation at Andøya Island, and played a key role in the sinking of the *Tirpitz*. You see late in the war, after it had been repaired and returned to service, that mammoth target of a battleship was taken to Håkøya Island near Tromsø. The British sent wave after wave of bombers after it. Even created a special 12,000 pound bomb to penetrate its armor. The Tallboy Bomb they called it. The Germans had a fighter wing at the nearby airbase at Bardufoss. On November 12, 1944, only nine months after Einar had left for the Rjukan Valley, a squadron of heavily modified Lancaster bombers, with extended range thanks to added makeshift internal fuel tanks, attacked the still *Tirpitz* for the last time. Two Tallboys hit directly amidship and at least three others were near misses, but those three may have done more damage than the direct hits, causing the ship's hull plates to buckle and allow in the fjord's water. The ship listed radically and eventually capsized with some 1200 *Kriegsmarine* sailors lost. The *Tirpitz* had only ever once fired her guns in anger. Churchill's *'Beast'* had been slain."

"Nice change of topic, Diane," accused Wade, "still you did not answer my question. How do you know the discussions that took place between Einar and Kari?"

"You see, Wade, even though the German radar on Andøya Island detected those Lancasters on their run, the message to the fighter base at Bardufoss wasn't sent for another ten minutes. By the time the fighters got off the ground, they were too late. The *Luftwaffe* pilots never laid eyes on the Lancasters, only on the inconceivable damage they and their Tallboy bombs did. Do you know why this fits so critically into our story Wade?"

"You are going to tell me, Diane, that Kari held the message for those crucial ten minutes?"

"No," Diane admitted, "but a team of communication operators she developed, sympathetic to the cause, did on her behalf. You see, Wade, Kari was back at her coastal *rorbu* giving birth to a son. She named him Einar. Imagine that! Your father has another branch on the family tree to flesh out, because like his father before him, her Einar went off to his death not knowing that his wife was pregnant."

The news hit Wade like a ton of bricks. It was his worst fear. He recovered to continue his assault on the veracity of Diane's findings.

"You still haven't told me how we know all this!" Wade was becoming agitated that Diane was stringing him along, and each time she revealed more and more news that he wished not to hear. His only defense now was to have it all proven as having been conjured up by Diane to embellish her story.

"Wade," Diane continued, "after the fighting ended in Europe six months after the *Tirpitz* was sunk, Kari travelled to the town of Mæl on Lake Tinn to speak to the survivors of the ferry *Hydro's* sinking. There were actually a fair number of them. Twenty-nine to be exact. Only eighteen people died that morning, and that number included four German soldiers. Why the Norwegian rescuers ever bothered to pull out those remaining Nazi soldiers from that lake I can never understand. But the passengers that survived recounted to Kari exactly what happened, even the dialogue as best they had heard it."

"And let me guess, Diane, Kari just conveniently left a diary as well?"

"No, Wade, she did not," Diane said angrily, growing tired of Wade's tone. "Kari did something even better, you see. She went in late 1945 to see Tilly at Broughty Ferry. She felt it necessary to share everything with the grandmother of her son, Einar, and to tell Tilly of the heroics that Einar had displayed upon the *Hydro*. And to hand deliver the stack of letters he had left with her for his mother. Of course, Tilly captured all this in her diaries as well. So, Wade, that is exactly how all the info I relayed became known to us. Not embellishments, just cold hard facts."

"I told you he'd make an ass out of himself, Diane," added Jake Conley. "My own flesh and blood, go figure. I do have one very simple question for you that has been nagging at me. I am 100% confident of everything that you have told us over these past few days. But, best to my knowledge I have no recollection of my mother ever traveling back to Norway. How did she become aware of all this? How did she know?"

Diane looked at Jake slyly.

"Well, Jake, thank you. I was going to get around to that and something else, as well. You see, in March 1963, Tilly MacAlvor met with one Cassandra Conley in Paris. Joining them was Kari and her eighteen year old son, Einar. They met over three days. According to Tilly's diary, your mother had paid for it all. Cassandra even arranged on the last day for a special after hours mass in the Cathedral of Notre Dame for them all to pray together for the souls of her sons, Einar and Gunnar. It was all very touching for all parties involved. It was there in Paris, that your mother was offered something very special in return. Tilly generously offered Cassandra the blood-stained scapulars of the two brothers. The ones Kari had hand-carried back with the packet of letters from Einar. Tilly offered the scapulars at no cost, she just figured a caring mother would wish to have them."

"My God," Jake said, "that Tilly woman sounded like the kindest soul on earth."

"And she was, Jake," Diane confirmed.

"Do you think we ended up throwing them away with all her other stuff after my mother died?" Jake asked of Wade.

"No," answered. Diane, cutting Wade off. "Cassandra never took them. Said she didn't need them. So Tilly kept them, and passed them down to Mattie who retains them to this day, along with the original diaries and all the letters."

Jake's eyes became as large as dinner plates. "You said they were blood-stained? Flake, any chance that the twins' DNA could be extracted from those things."

Flake, caught off guard, having sat quietly for so long, replied. "It's a long shot, Mr. Conley. Those things have been doused in the fjord's water. Been subjected to extreme cold, let alone what high end temperatures they may have seen in storage over seventy-five years. But I do know some labs who specialize in that exactly that sort of antique DNA recovery. They're as good as anyone on earth in testing this sort of thing, but it will be very expensive and with no guarantee of success."

"Good," said Jake, "you contact them and I want you, Diane, to begin researching the lineage of Kari's son, Einar. Did he have kids, did they have children? Are there relatives alive today that trace back to Einar and Kari?"

"Jake," Diane interrupted, "these are all good, no great, and noble things to be understood, to be researched. However, this is where I have to get off this train. I believe I have answered all your original questions, but I have other clients waiting. I have discussed this with Mr. Ferris, and he has agreed to carry on, separately from my firm, if you so desire his services, but I must move on to other cases."

"Are they going to pay you as handsomely as I am already doing, Diane?" Jake asked.

"Not even close, Jake, but sometimes money isn't everything…"

Jake Conley looked strangely at her. "You know what, Diane, as recently as five years ago I would have come back with *'that's only what people who don't have any money say…'* or some such nonsense. But just the fact that I'm sinking a small fortune into this quest proves your point. Thank you, Diane for all you have done so far for me. Don't forget the NDA that you and your firm signed. I'll have my business manager wire you the rest of that renumeration package we settled on for your efforts. You can stay with us here if you like, but I need to get some things started with your man Flake here."

"Officially, no longer my man at all," Diane answered. "Mr. Ferris is a free agent at this point. Thank you Jake, and Wade, for hosting me. Your generosity has been outstanding."

"Sure thing, Diane," Jake said. He then excitedly turned to Flake Ferris and said, "So Flake, in addition to determining if the testing of them scapulars is feasible and documenting Kari and Einar's blood lines, I want you to work with my lawyers to secure the purchase of all of Miss Tilly's diaries from that Mattie MacAlvor…"

Diane was escorted from the library and went upstairs to pack her things for the return trip. *They never even asked the important questions,* she thought. *Jake was so eager to get on with the chase with Flake, and Wade was so enveloped in his thoughts as to how he would defend his inheritance from erosion, they did not ask the most important questions.They never asked if*

Einar had ever disclosed to Tilly that he had pulled the trigger on Gunnar. Or if Tilly had ever disclosed to him that she was not his natural mother. The answers are there in her diary, and if only they had asked I could have directed them to the 1963 entry directly after returning from the three day visit with Kari and Jake's Mom. "

Diane, alone in her room by this point, flipped through her papers and found the brief entry. She assumed it had been made on the Calais-Dover Ferry. She read it to herself as she thought how sad that no one asked these questions.

> March 25, 1963 - I am exhausted, not so much physically as emotionally. As I look out on the choppy grey waters that carry me home, I regret having spent three days with the woman I was forced to call by my own birth name. It was humiliating and unbearable. She never once commented on the fact that today would have been the week of their 50th birthdays, had they survived the wars. Could she possibly have forgotten that?
>
> Kari and her son Einar are on their way back to Norway. She is such a blessing, I would never have survived this trip had it not been for her company. In preparation for coming to Paris, I finally got the chance to tell her what I have never confessed to another soul since the war - that I was not Einar's natural mother. I confessed it all to that splendid young woman, that the vile woman we were to spend three days with had birthed Einar and Gunnar, only to have subsequently abandoned them to my care so that she could chase her own hedonistic lifestyle.
>
> Kari said that she could not believe it, but then neither could she believe it when Cassandra expected us all to go out each night to enjoy the city's nightlife. When we deferred, using young Einar as a reason, she protested that he was eighteen years old and we should bring him along. She said, *"the child has to grow up sometime! Where better than Paris? By the time I was his age, I'd been taken in three different countries."* When we still refused to join her, she simply had gone out on the town alone.

It was our last night in Paris, as Cassandra took to chasing the city's many nocturnal pleasures, that I unburdened my suppressed emotions from the trip to Kari.

I broke down emotionally. I prattled on about how callous Cassandra's heart had become. She would not even spend the nights in moments of reflection for her own sons. I thought about them both dying in that Nordic land. I suddenly began to cry uncontrollably, as I sat on the bed of my room. Kari rushed from the chair to sit next to me, and wrapped me in her warm embrace.

I told her I was so ashamed to have kept this secret untold for so long. I told her how sorrowful and remorseful I was that I had never told either her Einar or his brother, Gunnar. I still have not told my son, Matthew, even though he is from my womb. I do not wish to implant in him the seed of suspicion - that he might somehow not be my own birth child and that I am somehow keeping it from him.

Kari said not to let it trouble me so, that Einar and Gunnar were better off in knowing me only as their mother. Kari surprised me with what she said next. *Some secrets are best left untold, and that perhaps Einar had kept his own secret from me.* I told her that it was impossible, that between the time we shared during his recuperation after Narvik and his letters that Kari herself had hand carried to me, that I was convinced that Einar had told me everything.

Kari replied that she had never read Einar's packet of letters. She said she could have easily steamed them open and done so after his death, but she felt she needed to respect the sanctity of his request to deliver them to me unopened. Then, she asked what I first thought to be a very intrusive question, and had it not come from her, I would not have given it an honest response.

Kari asked if Einar had ever told me how his brother had died. The question brought a surge of emotions through me. When I finally answered, I told her that, of course he had told me. Einar had explained that Gunnar died at the hands of a German weapon during the assault on the cliff.

I watched Kari's face as I uttered this response. It was as if a great wave of disappointment, not totally unexpected, broke over her. It was a disappointment not with me, but with the man she had loved.

Kari's eyes immediately filled with tears. She choked on them as she told me that Einar carried within him a terrible secret of his own. That Gunnar had tried to shoot himself on that ledge because he knew was already dying. That Einar could not allow him to do that, so he pulled the trigger that ended his brother's suffering.

I was shocked. I could not believe that Einar had shared this with her and not myself. I coarsely accused her of selfishly holding this back from me for the past eighteen years. She owed it to me to tell me everything that Einar had shared with her, I said, chastising her.

She told me Einar had never told her this, and that she had assumed he had included it in his letters to me. Then I asked her just how she came by this scurrilous knowledge. I hoped that I might be able to discredit it in some way and perhaps prove it was untrue.

She said it had been she who had convinced Einar to put his thoughts of what he wanted to tell me down in letter form. For the longest time he did so only to burn them afterward, one after the other. One summer day after he had burned a draft letter to me, he became distracted and forgot to crush the ashes in the stove, which was cold at that time. When he left the *rorbu* to check the explosives stashed high above us, Kari said she lit matches and by their light was able to read the ashen but otherwise undisturbed letter. She said she had been long ago taught this technique in her training. It was in reading that ashen letter she learned of Einar's great burden. That secret he carried to his watery grave was seemingly too heavy for him to ever confess. Kari said it haunted her to this day that she had never discussed this with Einar. Kari then broke down in tears herself, and it was my turn to comfort her.

Now, only a few hours later, I still wrestle with this sad news. But at least I carry with me the whole truth back to the cottage on the shore of the Tay. There I will digest it, make peace with it. At least, now, I know the full depth of it.

Diane closed the entry gently, reverently in her mind, as if she held the physical diary itself in her hands, not mere reproductions. She threw her travel bag on the bed and began to pack her clothes. Her own exhausting three days had taught her that which *Zosia* had always stressed, that the accumulation of wealth and the worries that accompanied it were nothing more than a distraction from those things that are important in life.

As she packed, she thought of her friend Sophie, and hoped that her friend's debrief to her Polish clients had gone as well as Diane's own had. She worried that her *Zosia* would never reconnect with her again, but somewhere deep in her heart she knew this would not be the case.

Six weeks later in his Berlin office of Sterling Investigations International, Emory Hauptmann received a package from MacNaughtan's Bookstore in Edinburgh. He unpacked it to reveal a set of *The Works of Dickens* in beautiful red Morocco leather binding. Along with it was a computer printed note, undoubtedly sent to the bookshop from the purchaser. It read:

Emory, I hope you have not already procured a set of Dickens to impress your home's Fraulein visitors. Had it not been for your love of this author, I would never have wandered into the best paying appointment of my professional career. I will always consider you my very special dinner companion. Enjoy.

Your friend,

Flake W. Ferris

THE END OF "THE TWINS OF NARVIK"

Author's End Notes

Very often I am asked where do my ideas for a story line originate. Sometimes that is a very complicated question to answer, but in this case it is quite easy.

I was reading Winston Churchill's history of the Second World War when I came across the passage which I have included in the beginning of this volume. I was struck at how odd it was that the Prime Minister of the only country soon to be still standing free against the tidal wave of fascism sweeping across Europe would consider flying over a war zone with no escort whatsoever. Lack of petrol was a terrible excuse, I thought. Weather was an even worse excuse. *Could not enough fuel be pulled together for only one or two Spitfires to have escorted him back?*

That led to my imagination coming up with the only viable answer - *there must have been fear of a German agent embedded among the pilots, but exactly which one was unknown.*

And the story grew from that seed. I set out to tell this story with twins, but unlike every writer who has seemingly ever written a twin story, I did not want them changing identities. And yet, I could not resist introducing a swap of identities to the storyline after all, could I?

So what is real and what is complete fiction? Well, to start, while the waterfall from the *Lomvatnet* is real enough, although there is no *"staircase of the gods"* hanging high above the *Rombaksfjord*. That fiction was inspired by the stairs of the Temple of Apollo, as they bear that name. And as Apollo and Cassandra share a myth together, I thought it only fitting.

I intend this book to be the first of a trilogy of lesser known World War II stories and engagements. This first was intended to focus on the Polish Army being reconstituted in France, but as I researched their fighting in the mountains around Narvik, I fell in love with Norway, and the way the Norwegians fought so valiantly against the Nazis. I had been to that country before, mostly in and around the capital of Oslo. But it was the Arctic, and particularly the *Vestfjorden* that grabbed my interest so. After researching the battles of Narvik, I had to go there, and it had to be in winter.

Luckily, my travel to the Arctic took place in January of 2020, just before the worldwide wrath of the coronavirus was truly felt. My lovely wife, Marie, and I did so on a cruise ship out of London, so in addition to experiencing the spectacular vistas of the fjords interlaced between near vertical volcanically formed mountain ridges, we experienced the severity of the winter lashings of the North and Norwegian Seas.

Marie and I were able to explore Narvik, the highlight of which was our ride on the Ofoten Railway. We departed the train at Bjørnfjell in about four feet of snow. The stop, to this day, is not much more than the station houses and a handful of winter ski huts in which the locals take their cherished rest in nature. During our time there, one gentleman came by on his cross country skis, as well as a family on skis pulling their toddler through the snow on a small sled.

Militarily, I became enamored with not only the Battles of Narvik, but with the entire Norwegian Resistance movement. I could not believe the heroics at Vemork in the *Grouse, Freshman and Gunnerside Operations*, the sinking of the Ferry *Hydro* on the *Tinnsjå* (Lake Tinn), or the dedication of the Venus Network in locating the *Tirpitz* so that Churchill's *"Beast"* could finally be slain. That was ultimately concluded on the thirty-fourth Allied attempt by those brave British Lancaster crews with their Tallboy bombs. As I was writing this story one of those "Earthquake" bombs was found and detonated in the Polish harbor at Gdynia. But, to me, the most daring operation occurred on November 12, 1944, when Britain's fearless Lancaster bomber pilots and crew, totally unescorted and unprotected, as their guns had been removed to increase their range, sortied across the North Sea for the final attack near Tromsø. With the *Luftwaffe* fighter base nearby at Bardufoss, it was amazing that not a single Lancaster was shot down. There is evidence that indeed the Norwegian Resistance infiltrated the radar installation at Andøya Island, and although the bombers were detected there, the message was relayed late or perhaps never to the fighter base. In fact, it may not have been until the on-board radar of the *Tirpitz* detected the incoming aircraft that the general alarm was sounded at Bardufoss.

So what else in *The Twins of Narvik* is not fictional? We can start with Alan Turing meeting with the three Polish cryptographers outside Paris. That is quite true, even down to his bringing along metallized Zygalski sheets, but his getting there on General Sikorski's plane is quite fictional. The pilot Bogdan Bratajewski is a totally fictional character, as is his family. Also, the twins, Einar and Gunnar and their families are fictional. Wincer Wells is entirely fictional, but I must admit I came up with the character's name after reading about another British intelligence officer named "Blinker" Hall, who also earned his nickname via his facial attributes. The source of the nickname is the only similarity, I am happy to report.

In fact, I have fictionalized several historical figures, most notably General Władysław Sikorski, Captain Mansfield Cumming, and to a much lesser degree, Dilly Knox. Mansfield Cumming's eccentricities of embellishing stories and driving letter openers into his false leg are not only real, but well documented. He really was the character both Ian Fleming and John le Carré are reported to have had in mind for their leaders of the Secret Services, *"M"* and *Control* respectively.

The histories of the Secret Intelligence Service (MI6), the Special Operations Executive (SOE) and the Ofoten Railway are all highly researched and accurate to the best of my knowledge. I could not resist working some of the characteristics of the first three *"C"'s* of the SIS, whether it be Mansfield Cumming's eccentric nature, Hugh "Quex" Sinclair's stern but visionary leadership, or Stewart Menzies deft establishment of Bletchley Park and his leadership throughout World War II.

As I mentioned previously, in preparation for writing this novel, my wife Marie and I rode the Ofoten Railway and departed at Bjørnfjell in about four feet of snow. It was interesting to research the railway, as significant changes took place after the war to rename several stations. For Instance, you won't find Hundalen Station today, because it was renamed to Katterat Station in the 1950s.

Even a newer set of tunnels and bridges were added after the war. Today, not one but two *Nordall Bridges* span gorges, but the second was not present during the war. I have tried my best to keep all the geography as faithful to the conditions during the war as possible, but must admit I took liberties with the switchback trail the twins took to ascend to the heights on the north shore high above the *Rombaksfjord.*

The misfiring of the MP-38 submachine gun described herein is indeed very accurate, as are the depictions of the Walther P-38 pistol, the X-craft midget subs, and even the description of the texture and odor of the Nobel 808 plastic explosive, right down to its telltale almond scent. Most of all, I heavily researched the operation and construction of the Enigma machine itself in my visits to Bletchley Park and other war museums, and I believe it to be highly accurate.

The exploding Enigma *"faux rotors"* were, of course fictional, but were based on the reality of the SOE stuffing plastic explosives into almost anything, including dead rats, to make some of the world's first Improvised Explosive Devices or IED's. While on the Enigma subject, the history of the Poles cracking the Enigma code as early as 1932 is very real indeed, although there is no evidence of any rotors lost in the very real 1940 sinking of the Aircraft Carrier *Glorious*. Jerzy Różycki unfortunately did drown crossing the Mediterranean on a ferry that sunk. His wife Basia may have never left occupied Poland with him, it is unclear, but she did attempt to do so with a baby son named Janusz. Janusz Różycki grew up to become an Olympic swordsman, taking home a Silver medal in Fencing in Tokyo during the 1964 Summer Games.

Kari is a character I fashioned after one I had read in a 1970s naval thriller called *"Storm Force to Narvik"* by the British seaman-turned author Alexander Fullerton. A Christmas gift from my lovely wife, unyielding editor and chief book hunter, Marie. It was a great read. Another book she found for me *(Marie is amazing at finding rare out of print books!)* was a mid-war Polish Government-in-Exile publication called *"Polish Troops in Norway"*. It its a photo-album of images taken by the troops themselves in France, Norway and Scotland. It was invaluable in my research for and visualization of this novel.

Finally, I left the story of Jerzy Różycki's compatriots unfinished. We left them as having been robbed by their guide crossing the Pyrenees. They made it into Spain where they were promptly arrested and imprisoned for six months. Then, via Portugal, they made their way to Gibraltar, arriving in early August 1943, about a month after General Sikorski so tragically died there. The two surviving code breakers of the big three, Marian Rejewski and Henryk Zygalski, were finally flown from *The Rock* to London, arriving on the 3rd of August 1943. However, these two Poles never made it to Bletchley Park. By the time they arrived, the top secret ULTRA program was running full stride. These men who had initially cracked the Enigma code were enlisted as privates in the Polish Air Force and rode out the war in North London, working on breaking far lesser codes.

After the war ended, Rejewski returned to his wife and family in Poland, his secret was safe, and he was unharmed and not harassed (to my knowledge) by the postwar Communist government. Other returning war heroes were not nearly so lucky, as anything aside from fighting with the Red Army was viewed as unpatriotic in Stalin's time.

Henryk Zygalski decided to stay in England and lived out his life as a respected academician, teaching statistics at the University of Surrey. Both men were precluded from ever speaking of their exploits in breaking the Enigma code before and during the war. Zygalski was restricted by Britains Official Secrets Act, and Rejewski for fear that such knowledge would somehow offend his Communist overlords and earn him a one-way trip to Siberia, the fate that befell so many other Poles who had been war heroes upon returning home.

If there was one element of this novel I would have liked to have dived further into, it would be the 303 Kościuszko Squadron's performance during the Battle of Britain. Poles made up the largest number of non-Commonwealth fighter pilots in the RAF, closely followed by the Czech pilots. Both groups gained instant notoriety for their fearlessness in attacking the *Luftwaffe* fighters and bombers. Each Polish pilot likely had tasted the bitterness of having family, friends or other loved ones killed, imprisoned or otherwise severely assaulted during the invasion of their homeland. The Polish Airmen became the toast of London during the Battle of Britain and The Blitz. Legend has it that the arm patches of the their uniforms which bore the word POLAND were often stolen, because these airmen were so popular with the ladies.

By the end of the war, the Polish soldiers and airmen who had been such heroes fighting alongside the British became competitors for jobs in the crippled postwar economy. They were expected by the Brits to return home, even though that home was a country surrendered by the Allies to a puppet Communist regime subservient to Joseph Stalin. Churchill was viewed as a traitor by many Poles, who saw him as the man who gave in to Stalin at the Yalta and Potsdam Conferences. In reality, without the backing of the United States, it is not clear his objections would have mattered much.

I would like to close these notes by focusing on the beautiful land of Scotland. Having traveled several years ago to Edinburgh, I was amazed at all I saw. I met a fellow author named Allan Foster who provided a remarkable literary tour of the capital. With his permission, I used his guidebook *"Book Lover's Edinburgh"* to refresh my memory on the sights and history of that city. I recommend his book highly, and understand he has a sequel upcoming called *"Book Lover's Paris"* which I look forward to obtaining and poring over.

McNaughtan's Book Shop was kind enough to allow me to use their edifice as a setting in the story, and I am thankful. Being a great lover of bookshops, their's is a magnificent one. My apologies for putting an American's corruption of the Scottish "burr" in the tongues of the bookseller in that scene.

The restaurant The Witchery at Castle Gate is real, and my thanks for their allowing me to reference their establishment in my novel. The restaurant is perhaps the most beautiful at which I have ever dined the world over, and the food exquisite.

I was pleasantly surprised to learn that Scotland's largest immigrant community is indeed the Poles. The country welcomed them during the war, and it appears still do to this day. They never turned their back on those who protected their shores from Nazi invasion. Polish armor was routinely seen in the streets of coastal towns such as Dundee and its suburb of Broughty Ferry during the war. There was much good natured fraternization between the Poles and the Scots during this time. So much so, it felt only natural for Tilly MacAlvor and her beloved granddaughter Mattie might have knowledge of the Piast line of Polish Kings.

Allow me to journey back to London one last time and thank my friends at the Polish Institute and Sikorski Museum. If you are enamored by Polish history as much as I am, this is a true treasure trove of artifacts and remembrances from the proud history of the country. I could think of no better place to have my fictional *Zosia* go to research the history of General Sikorski. I was lucky to visit there, only weeks before the coronavirus temporarily shut down the Institute.

Finally, I would also like to comment on the recurring themes in this novel. Many ancient languages did not have punctuation like exclamation points to show the importance of a word, sentence or concept. Instead they did this through repetition, with the most important elements being repeated three times. This is seen throughout the Bible, most notably with Peter denying Jesus three times on Good Friday. Orthodox Christian wedding rituals to this day repeat the most sacred elements three times before declaring a couple man and wife.

In this saga I wanted to impress the importance of several themes through their thrice recurring repetition. First, the theme of a pregnant mother surviving a departed partner. This occurs when Tulla becomes pregnant with the twins after Birger departs (although he returns for her), Tilly becoming pregnant with Matthew after Brigand goes off to rescue the soldiers at Dunkirk, and in Kari becoming pregnant with Einar's son after he departs to take explosives to the *Tinnsjå* saboteurs.

The second theme employing this characteristic is that of suicide. Throughout the book it is attempted by three characters: Birger's father (with success), Birger himself (as Brigand), and at least contemplated by Einar. The last two attempts were thwarted by the women the men loved, Tilly and Kari. I wanted to show the power of love in overcoming severe desperation.

If you wonder why I did not include Gunnar's attempt on the ledge in my accounting, it was only because his was more an act of self-sacrifice than of desperation. Gunnar only wished to save his brother by freeing Einar from the obligation to stay behind with his already dying self.

The last thrice recurring theme is that of characters being physically incomplete which is personified by the loss of their legs in "C", Brigand, and Colonel Becker. Each man is missing a limb due to war, and in this tale it is shown through their all eventually having prosthetic limbs. Symbolically, I wanted this to show that war, no matter how justified, becomes an assault on mankind itself. If you are wondering if Mansfield Cumming really did lose his leg, the answer is yes. The story told of he and his son's car crash near the front lines of WWI in France is factual, and was what gave me the idea of employing this particular literary device.

Also, I have used the terms *colonel* and *lieutenant colonel* nearly interchangeably. I do this with no disrespect for all the *full-bird* colonels out there, as the distinction is hard earned. Rather I do this because in my professional career before becoming a novelist, I worked with many lieutenant colonels of the United States Air Force. Nearly to a man, they preferred being addressed simply as "colonel", ostensibly as a convenient short-hand for the longer "lieutenant colonel". Yet, on the occasions that I did address them by the full title, I thought I could have sworn they felt slightly wounded. Unless of course there was a higher ranking officer in their presence.

And while cleaning up some things, allow me to say that I realize that the diminutive Polish form of the name Ed is *"Edziu"*. However, as an homage to a lifelong friend, who from childhood I knew only as Edjew, I have included that form of his name in this novel. I hope my purist Polish readers will forgive me this indulgence.

Thank you for working your way through this very long, expansive work. I enjoyed researching and writing it, although at its finish I feel very much as Winston Churchill did himself in completing his own works. Being able to describe the process no better myself, I will end with his quote:

"Writing a book is an adventure. To begin with it is a toy and an amusement. Then it becomes a mistress, then it becomes a master, then it becomes a tyrant. The last phase is that just as you are about to be reconciled to your servitude, you kill the monster and fling him to the public."

Until the next adventure,

David Trawinski

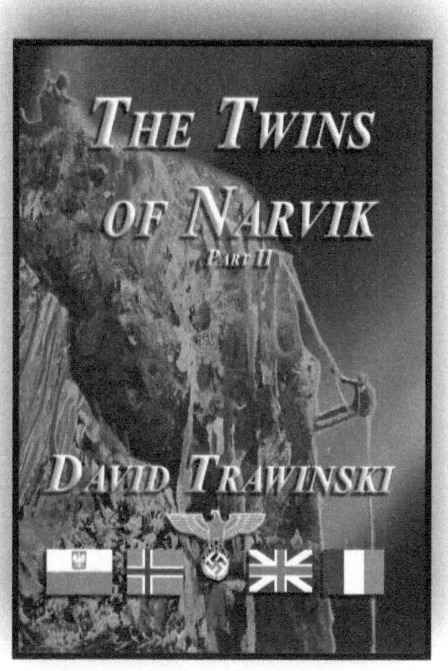

The Twins of Narvik

Is Proudly

Published by

Figure and Image Attributions

Front Cover Images

Rock Climber Artwork Image - Original creation Kellen Churchill
Copyright 2020

Background Photos - Original Photographs Mountains and Fjords
Copyright 2020 Elizabeth Marie Trawinski

Interior Images

Figure 22 Winter Mountain Landscape in Narvik, Norway by Per
Licensed Adobe Stock Image # 222647074

Figure 23 Map of Poland 1939 Prepared by David Trawinski
Using Wikimedia Blank Map Image

Figure 24 Bombed Town of Wieluń Photo, Public Domain Image

Figure 25 Narvik circa 1928, Public Domain Image

Figure 26 Trans-Scandinavian Railroad Image,
Creative Commons license
Attribution: Jniemenmaa

Figure 27 First Narvik Sea Battle Map Prepared by David Trawinski

Figure 28 2nd Narvik Sea Battle Map Prepared by David Trawinski

Figure 29 Hundalen Station Photo
Copyright 2020 Elizabeth Marie Trawinski
Rombaksfjord Photo
Copyright 2020 Elizabeth Marie Trawinski

Figure 30 Bjørnfjell Photo
Copyright 2020 Elizabeth Marie Trawinski

Figure 31 Bjørnfjell Station Photo
Copyright 2020 Elizabeth Marie Trawinski
Nazis at Bjørnfjell, Pinterest
Creative Commons 2.0, posted by Øystein Mikelborg

Interior Images (Continud)

Figure 32 Sámi Herdsman, Pinterest
Creative Commons 2.0, posted by Russavia

Lávvu Tent Encampment, Public Domain Image

Figure 33 St. Ermin's Hotel Photo, Wikimedia
Creative Commons Share Alike 3.0 Unported License
Attribution: Tim Fordham-Moss/Own Work

Figure 34 Map, Allied Land Invasion of Narvik
Prepared by David Trawinski

Figure 35 MP-38 German Machine Guns, Composite of
Licensed Adobe Stock Image # 366845806
Licensed Adobe Stock Image # 237894162
Captured MP-38 Photo
Copyright 2020 Elizabeth Marie Trawinski
Used by Agreement of Polish Institute
and Sikorski Museum (London)

Figure 36 de Havilland Flamingo Transport, Public Domain Image

Figure 37 Churchill and de Gaulle Photo, Wikimedia
Original Source: Imperial War Museum
Public Domain Image

Figure 38 Polish Rifle Brigade Photos, both,
Public Domain
Taken from "Polish Troops in Norway"
Book Form Publication by the
Polish Ministry of Information
Polish Government-in-Exile
London, 1943

Figure 39 Polish Pilots with Tail-skin Image, Wikimedia Commons
Public Domain Image
Tail-skin Alone Photo
Copyright 2020 Elizabeth Marie Trawinski
Under Agreement of Polish Institute
and Sikorski Museum (London)

Interior Images (Continued)

Figure 40 Photos, both, Wikimedia Commons
Rjukanfosse Photo
Creative Commons Share Alike 3.0 Unported License
Attribution: Hau-maggus/Own Work
Town of Rjukan Photo
Creative Commons Attribution 3.0 Unported License
Attribution: G. Lanting/Own Work
Rjukan Valley Map by David Trawinski

Figure 41 Norsk Hydro Facility at Vemork Photo
Wikimedia Commons Public Domain Image
Heavy Water Cells Photo
Norsk Industriarbeidmuseum

Figure 42 Arctic Norway Map Prepared by David Trawinski

Figure 43 Rock of Gibraltar Photo
Licensed Adobe Stock Image #188989705
Attribution: Lea Digszammal
Sikorski at Gibraltar Image, Wikimedia
Creative Commons, Public Domain Image

Figure 44 X-Craft Midget Sub Photo, Wikimedia
Creative Commons, Public Domain Image

Figure 45 Red Rorbu Photo
Copyright 2020 Elizabeth Marie Trawinski

Figure 46 Norsk Hydro Ferry on Lake Tinn Photo, Wikimedia,
Public Domain Image

Figure 47 Sir Winston Churchill, Public Domain Image

Author's End Note Photo at Bjørnfjell
Copyright 2020 by David Trawinski

Author's End Notes

Front Cover Images

Front Cover Montage
Original Artwork by Kellen Churchill
Background Photographs
Copyright 2020 Elizabeth Marie Trawinski

Rear Cover Images

Rear Cover Montage
Licensed Adobe Stock Image # 0384194656
Attribution: Larauhryn
Licensed Adobe Stock Image #0182706942
Attribution: Jaroslav Moravcik

Author Photo Copyright 2020 Elizabeth Marie Trawinski

www.ingramcontent.com/pod-product-compliance
Lightning Source LLC
Chambersburg PA
CBHW020603310726
48979CB00008B/1319/J

* 9 7 8 1 7 3 6 8 4 7 0 3 9 *